HOWLING
DARK

Also by Christopher Ruocchio from Gollancz:

THE SUN EATER

Empire of Silence
Howling Dark

HOWLING DARK

THE SUN EATER: BOOK TWO

CHRISTOPHER RUOCCHIO

GOLLANCZ

LONDON

First published in Great Britain in 2019 by Gollancz
an imprint of The Orion Publishing Group Ltd
Carmelite House, 50 Victoria Embankment
London EC4Y 0DZ

An Hachette UK Company

1 3 5 7 9 10 8 6 4 2

Copyright © Christopher Ruocchio 2019

The moral right of Christopher Rucchio to be identified as
the author of this work has been asserted in accordance
with the Copyright, Designs and Patents Act of 1988.

All rights reserved. No part of this publication may be
reproduced, stored in a retrieval system, or transmitted
in any form or by any means, electronic, mechanical,
photocopying, recording, or otherwise, without the
prior permission of both the copyright owner and the
above publisher of this book.

All the characters in this book are fictitious, and any resemblance
to actual persons, living or dead, is purely coincidental.

A CIP catalogue record for this book is
available from the British Library.

ISBN (Hardback Special Edition) 978 1 473 22948 8
ISBN (Trade Paperback) 978 1 473 21829 1
ISBN (eBook) 978 1 473 21831 4

Printed and bound in Great Britain by
Clays Ltd, Elcograf S.p.A

www.orionbooks.co.uk

To my parents,
Paul and Penny.
For always being there.
I'm going to be all right.

ACKNOWLEDGMENTS

What a first year this has been! Since its release in the summer of 2018, *Empire of Silence* has found its way into the hands of several thousand readers, people to whom I will be forever grateful. If the last set of acknowledgments was for the people who saw me to publication—my family, my friends, my agents, the good people at DAW Books and my coworkers at Baen, to my teachers and the rest—this page is for you and yours, Reader. Without all of you the first book would be rotting away on a shelf or in some warehouses and I would be forced to take up some honest trade. Let me thank several of you who didn't make it into book one in particular, but in no particular order.

Firstly, to the booksellers! To the folks at Quail Ridge Books in Raleigh—especially Rene and Tim—and the good people at Anderida Books in the UK, for their kindness and support. To Glennis of The Missing Volume and Alexi of Bard's Tower, for their friendship and for helping me navigate the labyrinth of conventions.

To the reviewers! To Petros, Tracy, Emily Grace, Nils, the folks at Unseen Library, and more. I am touched that you all enjoyed the book and hope that this one is all you were hoping for. It has been nice getting to know the lot of you.

To the readers! Many of you have reached out to me online and off, and though I cannot possibly list you all, I am grateful to each and every one of you. To David K, TJ, Lena, Alex, and MaryAnn, to Luca in Italy, and Emil in Sweden, and Nathan down in Australia. And of course to my online friends. I couldn't do this without you all.

To the new friends I have made (if I may so claim). To Gerald Brandt, Ed Willett, EC Ambrose, Joshua Palmatier, and Julie Czerneda, for making this new kid feel welcome at the DAW family get-togethers. To Dan Stout and Cass Morris—for being the new kids along with me. To my Baen family: the Webers, the Drakes, the Correias (thanks for helping me hit my single biggest day of sales, Larry!), Kacey Ezell, Jody Lynn Nye, Mike Massa, Griffin Barber . . . and everyone. To RR Virdi and LJ Hachmeister, for being the coolest. And of course to DJ Butler, one of the finest and most generous people in the entire industry.

And lastly, to Jenna, who in the last year and a half has gone from my friend to my fiancée. I will always be grateful to Jenna. For everything. I love you, dear lady.

CHAPTER 1

THE RED COMPANY

DARKNESS.

Green eyes watched from the darkness like statues in a fog. I felt them like fishhooks in me, dragging me upward. I felt wrong. Cold. The image of Bordelon's face on the holograph—moments before I wiped it from existence—seemed to float on the air. His was not alone. Gilliam's was there, lips twisted as he was, a sneer made flesh. And Uvanari. A confusion of sound filled my universe: the screams of dying men, the cheering of the Colosso crowd, my own blood pounding in my ear.

I knew then, knew that I had been dead, and that all this sensory *weight* was the cost and burden of consciousness returning. Of being alive. I was alive. Again.

"Lord Commandant?" A familiar voice, strangely accented, hinting at a language I could not remember—if indeed I knew it at all. "Lord Commandant?"

I was hiding in a basement on Pharos, that was it. There was a woman with me, a woman I loved, her hair blacker than the shadows. We were hiding from Bordelon and the Normans after they sold us to Admiral Whent. No. No, that was a long time ago, and a long time since Emesh, but my confused brain drank the scent of her and of burning wood, recalling the warmth of her and the taste of the ration bars we had shared alone in the darkness.

"Lord Commandant?"

The fog was clearing, retreating into the depths of history and of time as yet uncounted. I could still hear shouts, sobs, and I knew they were my own, conducted through bone and time to make me feel and see the horrors of my past because to know them was to be alive. Hard fingers tore my clothes that night in Borosevo, Cat's body sank into the canals . . . At once sharp as new experience, my memories retreated from me like votive lanterns to the skies. I grasped at them, and found my arms like trunks of lead, unmoving. Warmth was rising in me, chasing out that pelagic cold, bleeding in from both my arms.

Bleeding.

I was in a bed. Or else in something very like a bed, and someone was standing over me. I beheld old Tor Gibson, his gray eyes green in my delirium—green as his robes—his leonine mane and whiskers bristling in the wind off Meidua's waters.

"Dead?" I croaked, unsure if I meant himself or me.

The old scholiast smiled. "Not yet. We might avoid that yet."

"Lord Commandant, lie still please." That strange voice. Familiar. It came from Gibson's mouth, or so I thought. "You're still fugue-blind."

"No," I said, looking at the scholiast. "I can . . . can see Gibson."

"There's no one here but us!" The voice had moved, was opposite Gibson now, but the scholiast had not changed.

When Gibson spoke, his lips did not move. *The actor knows he is on stage. The character knows there is no stage.* It sounded like one of his scholi-ast's aphorisms, but I could not remember it.

I was going mad. I was in a basement on Pharos—or was that years ago? She had been there with me, with Admiral Whent's thugs out after us, and we had come out alive. And Gibson was dead. And I'd been dead—or nearly so. Frozen.

"Do you know where you are?"

A question, a question that spoke to the oldest exploratory and orient-ing circuits in the ancientmost corners of my brain. *Do you know where you are?*

As if the curtains on a stage were pulled back and the holography of the set pieces generated, the fog cleared and the real world took form. I was in medica. White walls, white floor, white ceiling. Too clean. I lay in the opened husk of a portable fugue crèche that someone had floated in here and bolted to the slab for revival. Turning, I saw that Gibson was gone. A hallucination? A vision brought on doubtless by the fact that there was still a part of me that thought in Gibson's voice.

Twelve years since Emesh.

It came back to me. "We're on the *Pharaoh.*" We had acquired the ship on Pharos, had taken it after that business with the Normans and Admiral Whent, after Bordelon betrayed us. We had been hired—alongside Bor-delon's company—to run weapons to freedom fighters attempting to overthrow the planetary dictator Marius Whent, all part of our efforts to build our credibility as a mercenary outfit as we hunted for Vorgossos. But Bordelon had betrayed us, and we had been forced to fight our way out. Marius Whent had been forced to surrender. Emil Bordelon had been killed, betrayed in his turn by his own soldiers—because I'd made them an offer they could not refuse.

The woman at my bedside, an ink-skinned Norman with hair like curling steel, nodded a judicious little nod. "Yes. And do you know who I am?" She wore a set of burgundy fatigues, form-fitting. A uniform. My uniform, I had designed it, with the flapped pockets and piped sleeves.

"Doctor Okoyo," I said, an address and not an answer, "I don't think there was any cryoburn." I tried to sit up, at once aware as Adam of my nakedness.

"Don't move, Lord Marlowe." She pushed me down, gentle but firm, and said, "I've not got all the TX9 out of you."

Turning, I saw the blood bags hanging from their staff beside me. AB Positive. Opposite was a drip pan emptying the anti-freezing agent from my veins. It shone cerulean in the too-white light; almost black. After a moment, I said, "You could have left me for a medtech, doctor."

Okoyo snorted. "Commodore Lin would skin me if I did that, and you Imperial types actually skin people."

"You have a point," I conceded, "but you've nothing to fear from us, surely." We sat in silence a moment, the doctor busying herself with a diagnostic terminal while I pretended I was not naked and aware of it. I tried to sort the visions I had seen. Waking from fugue was never easy. The men who had abandoned me on Emesh had shoved just enough blood in me that they could not be accused of murder, and I had been unconscious for that ordeal, but on each occasion since, I had passed through a warren of memory and noise to the quiet of the world. The brain hyperacted, so they said, on returning to consciousness. It was like dying, I thought, for in fugue the processes of my life were suspended as in formaldehyde, and that was as good as being dead. I was little different than a corpse, or a side of meat in a freezer.

I was wrong, of course. It is nothing like dying. Nothing at all.

"What's the standard date?"

"Sixteen two-nineteen point one-one." She did not turn her head.

"November," I mused. Of the Year of our Empire 16219. Forty-eight years since Emesh, though I had lived but twelve of them. Forty-eight years pretending to be mercenaries. Forty-eight years free of Count Mataro and his designs on me for his daughter. Forty-eight years a special conscript of the Legions of the Sun.

Forty-eight more years of war. Of the abortive, genocidal crusade against the Cielcin, the xenobites who drank of human worlds and preyed upon our people like wolves among sheep. Forty-eight years hunting for Vorgossos, carrying Cielcin prisoners and the hope of parley. Of peace.

"Is there some news?" I asked, sitting up now that the doctor could not stop me. My head swam, and I braced myself against the hard edges of my crèche. After a moment I stabilized, and tore a folded robe from the slab beside me. "Did we get a lead on that arms dealer the pirates gave us back on Sanora?" The doctor turned at the sound of my movement and hurried to my side. Her voice strained, she tried to lay me back down, but I held up a hand. "I'm just trying to cover myself."

Okoyo glowered. "You're just trying to make yourself pass out, Lord Marlowe."

"It's all right," I murmured, voice suddenly faint. "It's all right."

She kept an arm around my shoulders, and it was all I could do to puddle the robe in my lap—but that was enough. My own breathing consumed my attention, thick and wet. Rolling, I bent over the drip pan and coughed up a glob of the violet suspension fluid that yet settled in my lungs. "You're not all right," Okoyo said. "You've been an ice cube for the last six years."

"Six years?" I asked, surprised. I had not done the math. "Where are we?"

The doctor shook her head. "Best leave that to the Commodore, Lord."

Bassander Lin looked older than I remembered, and I wondered just how much of the intervening travel time the prickly captain had spent awake. I say captain, of course, because that was what he was. His role as Commodore was a mask, a persona, as much as was my position of Lord Commandant. The change in him was a subtle thing: no creasing about the eyes or mouth, no gray at the temples. But then, Lin was patrician, a bronze-skinned Mandari from an old family, his blood nearly so elevated as mine. The only real change lay within those black eyes of his. Something had hardened in them, the slow venom of our long association transmuted to amber; crystallized. His quarters aboard the *Pharaoh* had belonged to the Norman Commodore Emil Bordelon, and Bassander Lin had made some effort to remove all signs of the rooms' previous occupant.

The pornographic artwork was all gone, the ornate frames discarded, the carpets removed. I could still see the fixtures in the floor where the Commodore's too-large bed had been, replaced by a simple soldier's cot. There were no blankets.

"Sleep well?" he asked, surveying me from behind his desk. "Okoyo gave you a clean bill of health." He had an annoying habit of answering his own questions. So I didn't speak, but slumped low in my chair, uncomfortable in my crimson uniform. Bassander was dressed identically, but on him the high collar and tokens of rank seemed to rest easy. I at least had no badges to wear, save the sigil I had made, picked out in gold thread on the left bicep. Bassander toyed with a heavy mug on his desk, not looking at me. "That woman Corvo thinks she's found our man."

I sat upright, leaning over the edge of the desk. Lin's flinty gaze tripped over my face, and he took a drink. "The Painted Man?" That was what the Sanoran pirates had called him.

The captain shook his head and stood, turning his back. "Some bastard called Samir. He works for The Painted Man, or so Corvo tells it." He was built like a rapier, rail-thin and slim-shouldered, and stood framed against a holograph plate depicting a collage of security feeds from inside the *Pharaoh*. "She sent one of her lieutenants down to the planet. He made contact."

"We have Vorgossos, then?" I asked.

Bassander did not move, save to toggle the feeds on his holograph plate, displaying other parts of his ship. "No." He put his hands on his hips, and I noticed the highmatter sword clipped there. It had belonged to Admiral Marius Whent, who had nearly cost us our lives during the Pharos affair. "Corvo's man says Samir's a local, just someone who covers for the Extrasolarian."

"We need to set up a meeting . . ."

"It seems that way." The captain shrugged, running hands through his wood-smoke hair. "Wouldn't be a problem if we had the 437th with us, but . . . with a band of misfits like ours . . . it's a joke." We could not have called for reinforcements in any case. They were thousands of light-years and decades of real time away.

"Just because we're a front, Bassander," I said, biting off his name, "does not mean we're a joke."

Bassander Lin made a small dismissive noise in his throat and looked back at his screens. "We're outnumbered six to one by those Normans you picked up, as if your Colosso rats weren't bad enough."

It took a long, steady breath to keep me from hurling his mug at him. I crossed my arms instead. "We needed reinforcements."

"We needed soldiers."

"They *are* soldiers."

"They're foederati!" Bassander turned around at last. "They're loyal so long as we pay them. They'd turn on us in a moment if they saw a better offer."

"Then we don't let them get a better offer." It was my turn then to snort derisively. "We're paying them half again as much as Bordelon was."

"That's not to say a higher bidder won't come along. I don't trust them. I don't trust Corvo. It's only working because the money is steady."

"Won't it stay that way?" I asked, putting my face in my hands. My head was pounding; I'd left medica far too soon. "The Empire. The Legions are backing us. Corvo knows that. The Meidua Red Company—"

"The Meidua Red Company," Bassander sneered, shaking his head as he slung back into Commodore Bordelon's old chair. "Do you know what it is? For me?"

I pressed my fingers against my eyes, tried to clear my head. "The tribune gave us a mission, to find the Cielcin, to try and—"

"It's a punishment post. She's saddled me with you and your misfits, Earth only knows why."

My eyes narrowed. "How long have you been awake?" He spoke like a man too long on his own, like he'd rehearsed this conversation with himself a thousand times in the naked corridors of the *Pharaoh* while the rest of us slept. Bassander seemed to take my point without answering it. He glowered, allowing me the opening to ask, "So you want me to head down to the surface? Find Samir? Find this Painted Man?"

The Commodore who was truly a captain frowned. "I just want you holding Corvo's leash. Like I said: I don't trust her."

"She's been with us now for seventeen standard years," I said. "I gave her command of the *Mistral*." At another look from Bassander I raised my hands, temporized, "We gave her command of the *Mistral*. She's good at her job." Before that, Otavia Corvo had been Emil Bordelon's third officer on the *Pharaoh*, and if the way she turned on her previous master was any indication, the man left much to be desired where commanding officers were concerned. Still, I couldn't say that I did *not* understand Bassander's trepidation. Unbidden, my eyes went to the front of the desk, where tangled relief carvings of nymphs and satyrs writhed in unprofessional ecstasy.

Bassander took a long drink from his mug. "I just . . . want you around for it."

I felt myself smile, knowing it did not reach my eyes. "That's very kind of you to say."

Lin grunted. "I don't want you leading another bloody away team, though. Not after Pharos. We nearly lost you and Captain Azhar. And the last thing I need is the Jaddians upset I lost their representative."

"Someone important to the Company has to make contact with this Extrasolarian, The Painted Man. We can't send Corvo and I won't send Jinan." When Bassander looked to be on the verge of interrupting, I said, "Neither represents the Empire, Bassander. That rules out Corvo and Jinan, that rules out Valka. That leaves you and me, and we can't send you. It has to be me." The quiet tossed between us like a fish upon the strand. "But we don't know anything yet . . . Corvo's man's setting something up, right?"

"He's made it known we're after atomics . . . antimatter weapons, that sort of thing."

"Daimons?" I said, unable to help myself.

"What?" Bassander's eyes went suddenly wide. "God and Emperor, no!"

I understood his antipathy. I was a son of the Imperium myself, raised in the long shadow of the Mericanii, whose inhuman congress with artificial intelligence had nearly consumed mankind in the days before the Empire. I half-expected the fastidious Bassander Lin to reprimand me and accuse me of heresy, but he only ground his teeth, affording me the chance to shrug and say, "I'm only saying that if we're going to the Extrasolarians, we shouldn't just ask for a crate of plasma burners."

"Where in the word 'atomics' did you hear 'plasma burners'?" He looked up at the ceiling as he spoke, as if looking for some god to give him patience.

I dismissed this with a gesture. "Do you want me on the away team or not?"

"No, I do not." Bassander leaned back in the huge chair. "But it's been nearly fifty years since we left Emesh, Marlowe. Fifty years. Do you know how many colonies the Cielcin have razed since we started off on this ridiculous adventure of yours?"

"Knight-Tribune Smythe agrees that—"

"Thirteen." Bassander cut me off. "Thirteen, Marlowe." He rattled off the names: Bannatia, Lycia, Idun . . . "I go into fugue, and each time I wake up there's another one on the list. Millions dead. Each time. And I haven't done a thing to stop it." His voice had risen with each passing word until he was almost shouting.

I had to struggle not to stand. "What do you think we're doing?"

"Wasting time!" he spat. "I have another transmittal compiling from the telegraph right now, for Earth's sake! Another attack, Marlowe—I don't know how bad."

"If we can secure a peace with even one Cielcin clan, we'll have changed the face of this war more than any battle has." I did stand then, tugging at the hem of my short jacket to straighten it. "Whether you like it or not, I have to be on that away team."

Bassander only bobbed his head in agreement, rubbing the spot between his eyes. "You're probably right. Earth forgive me."

"I'll need a shuttle over to the *Balmung*," I said, turning distractedly away. "Is there time?"

The captain in Commodore's clothes massaged his jaw, but did not look at me. How small he looked, in Bordelon's oversized chair, behind that vasty desk, bent by the weight of the years we had in common and those he'd spent alone. "We're still waiting on Corvo's man. There's time." As I turned to go he said, "Marlowe."

I stopped. "Yes, Lin?" I switched back to his last name. He never seemed to notice a difference, as if such shaded distinctions were meaningless to him.

"Joke or not, we're a military operation. Not a chauffeur service for your harem."

Rage flickered through me like an electrical current, made me twitch. Fists clenched, shoulders tightened. I let it go, said, "One woman is hardly a harem, captain." I did not look back, but I felt a disturbance in the air. The *captain* had stung our Commodore.

"Are you all right?" A familiar voice asked when I stepped from Bassander's quarters into the gunmetal hall. Turning, I found my lictor standing at his post just beside the door. His crimson company uniform looked rumpled, as if he'd been leaning against the arched bulkhead. "You look like someone's been using you for combat practice."

"I feel like it, Switch," I said, rubbing my eyes. "And Lin's been his charming self all afternoon."

"That bad? And it's morning, actually," Switch said, falling into step beside me as we went down the hall, bootheels clacking on the decking.

"Is it really?" I said dumbly. "Dark take me . . ."

We passed a pair of junior technicians—some of our Normans—and I returned their salutes and their "Lord Marlowes!" with a smile and a wave, the effort of which made my head ache.

Switch thumbed the controls to summon a lift and we stood by the doors a moment. He'd gained some years on me in fugue. There were crow's feet about the muddy green eyes, and straw and silver fretted in his reddish hair. The face I saw in my own mirror had not slipped or aged a day since Emesh, while Switch's had *leathered* just a bit. But then, I was born in a castle, grown by design and to order while my parents waited, my every gene surgically exact and more than human. Switch had been born the son of a clerk, sold to settle a debt and abused up and down the spaceways until his childhood ended. His blood was low as it came, and yet Fate or Chance had danced and there we stood together as comrades.

"Shuttle's waiting in the hold," Switch said, adjusting his hair and his uniform in the faint reflection of the lift door. It hissed open, and he grinned sheepishly at the legionnaire inside. The man shouldered out, bowing—not saluting—to me as he sped up the corridor. "Captain Azhar had me sent over the minute she got word Lin was decanting you."

I stood a little straighter at the mention of Jinan Azhar. "Excellent, I can't stay on this ship another minute." Bassander had moved to the *Pharaoh* after we'd taken it during the Pharos affair, declaring it the flagship of our newly expanded fleet. The Norman, Corvo, he'd shunted over to the *Mistral*, a small Uhran interceptor we'd taken when we took the *Pharaoh*. Our original ship, the ancient, refitted Imperial destroyer *Balmung*, he'd left in command of our Jaddian emissary, Captain Jinan Azhar. Bassander trusted her and her copper-skinned soldiers from the Principalities. They were professionals, after all, true soldiers honor-bound and sworn to the service of His Highness, the High Prince Aldia di Otranto, First-Among-Equals of the Princes of Jadd. She was like Lin—and very unlike Lin—and so we'd filled out the command structures of our three ships. One Imperial captain, one Jaddian, one Norman mercenary, with the lower-ranking officers of each group distributed between the three ships so that everyone watched everyone else, and Bassander watched them all.

That was why I needed off the *Pharaoh*. It was bad enough there were Imperial officers reporting to Bassander every time I left my room, but on the *Balmung* he could not watch me through his camera feeds. And there were . . . other reasons. Our Cielcin prisoners were on the *Balmung*, for one. The massive fugue crèches we kept them in—the sort used to transport livestock between the suns—couldn't be moved between one ship and the other, and so Bassander had left them in Jinan's care when he gave her command of the old flagship. Valka Onderra was there, unwilling to move her many papers and data crystals from the study she had made for herself in the *Balmung*'s hydroponics department. Many other of my friends were there: Switch, for a start. And Ghen and old Pallino, a few of the other myrmidons from my days in the fighting pits of the Borosevo Colosso. The rest were distributed between the *Pharaoh* and *Mistral*. And there was Jinan herself, who was as much an improvement over stolid Bassander as a flower is over sand.

"You been up long?" I asked, massaging my temples.

Switch shoved his hands in his pockets. "About three weeks. Jinan woke me when Corvo sent Crim down to the surface."

"Crim, eh?" I asked, thinking of the young Norman lieutenant, Karim Garone. "Good, I was worried Lin might have sent Soisson or Dulia."

I could hear Switch grin. "Only if he wanted to start another fire."

We laughed then, and the lift hissed along. The *Pharaoh* was a proper Uhran-made capital ship. Two miles long, with a profile like a knife blade: wider than it was tall, pointed on the front end, with the bridge far in aft atop a conning spire like a fin two hundred and fifty meters high. Bassander's quarters were in that spire, near the bridge, but we plunged out of it before the lift entered a horizontal shaft that carried us along a good hundred meters of tube before dropping us down and further aft. Toward her stern, the *Pharaoh* flared wider to accommodate her engine cluster— enclosed in the ring of her warp drive—as well as the docking bays for her various shuttles and the two dozen Sparrowhawk lighter craft she could field for inter-ship combat. I watched us descend on the lift's terminal screen, a little red node moving against the blue wire frame.

Leaning my forehead against the wall above the screen, I said, "How's Etienne?" Meaning the Norman soldier who was the latest in Switch's string of lovers.

Switch didn't answer for a moment, then said, "Done, but he's over here and I'm on the *Balmung* so that's all right."

"I'm sorry to hear it," I said.

"I'm not," he replied. "He had it coming. What about you and the woman?"

Thinking of Bassander's comment about my harem, I looked down at my feet. "Good. It's good." Whether out of respect for my migraine or because he had nothing more to say, that was all Switch said, and so we exited into another hallway, larger but identical in design to the one we had just left: square, rounded corners, with ribbed supports arching every ten meters or so. Diode lamps built into the ceiling or ensconced high in the walls shone unflickeringly as I followed Switch out, past three legionnaires in their burgundy fatigues. If they saluted me, I did not see.

The shuttles hung in open bays beneath the *Pharaoh* like remoras beneath a great shark, accessed by an umbilical gangway. Switch went first, per protocol, and cleared the shuttle for me. There was no one aboard except the pilot officer, a young Norman man with olive skin and blond hair. Switch took the seat behind him—facing me—and I sunk into the bench in the rear. I returned the pilot officer's greeting as best I could and settled back. For the first time since my revival I could look *outside,* through the alumglass windows.

"Canceling suppression field," the pilot officer said, and a moment later the artificial gravity was gone, leaving me floating against my restraints. Addled as I was and fugue-sick, it was not a pleasant feeling. Switch was studying his hands. A loud metallic sound reverberated through the hull around us. "That's umbilical separation."

The rest of the pilot officer's technical patter fell away as we did, dropping out of the *Pharaoh*'s hold and into darkness. As we cleared the dark mass of metal and came out into open space, I beheld the cloud-streaked umber disk of the planet Rustam. It had been an Imperial colony not long ago. Now it was nothing at all. Through the window I could just make out the black scar on the face of one continent—very near the terminator—where the Cielcin had gouged a city out of the native rock.

I swallowed, and for a moment forgot my aching head. Seldom had I seen a thing so horrible, and seldom since. I knew Switch was watching me, and I looked down at my lap.

"Wiped out the palatine house completely," he said, "the whole government, about ten years back. The new city's on the far side, can't see it here."

"How many?"

"Dead?" Switch asked. "Not sure. Lin reckons about two million. There's twice as many down there that lived, though."

I had to look away. The black ruin was like a slitted eye peering at me. Through me. "Maybe Lin's right. We're taking too long."

"You couldn't have stopped this."

"No," I said, "but we might stop it happening ever again." A lie. We both knew it. As we spoke, in some corner of the Norman Expanse the Cielcin were burning another world.

I shut my eyes against the Dark, and found only another darkness, deeper still.

CHAPTER 2

SUSPENDED AND UNDEAD

COLD. THE CUBICULUM WAS always cold. Frost rimed the floor and filigreed the utilitarian shapes of the crèches where slept our bottled demons. Wind off the ventilation systems thickened the air like whispers, and even with my uniform jacket on I shivered. I had spent a great deal of time in that chamber, especially before the Pharos affair. The place reminded me of our necropolis beneath Devil's Rest where my ancestors' eyes and brains and hearts languished in canopic jars. Perhaps it was for this morbid reason that I enjoyed the place. Or perhaps it was the cold. After what had felt an eternity on tropical Emesh, I had reveled in the bone-chilling cold of that place, and the quiet. No sound but the whirring of machines and the patter of my own breathing and the crunch of ice beneath my bootheels.

Within those chilly sepulchers the Cielcin slept, suspended between binary heartbeats like wights awaiting the blood moon to rise again and walk and drink the blood of men. The only survivors of the ship that had crashed on Emesh. Eleven of them. I crossed my arms for warmth and moved along the row of containers, advancing further into the cubiculum, breath frosting the air. I had written their names on each: Etanitari, Oanatoro, Svatarom, Tanaran. I lingered beside Tanaran's crèche, fingertips melting points on its frosty surface. It was their leader. Some sort of priest, or so I'd gathered, or else some manner of nobile. It had agreed to my plan, to this treatment.

"We're nearly there," I said, and imagined it could hear me. I turned round, wondering where the captain was. Switch had gone to tell her I'd returned. The indicator lights on the crèches glowed a pleasant blue. All was well. "You're going home."

"You still think so, do you?"

I started. Turning, I beheld the woman, but not the one I'd been expecting. Valka Onderra Vhad Edda stood in the door to the hall. I still felt a pang on seeing her, despite all that had happened to us since Emesh . . . and indeed because of it. She was like a glass image of a woman: hard-eyed, thin, pale. Do not mistake me. I do not mean that she was fragile. Rather that one could not encounter her without being cut. Thus it was for me. She was Tavrosi, of the blood of the old Travatskr people who fled the Norde colonies on Ganymede.

The bonecutters who had shaped her genetic makeup had fashioned a creature remote as Pallas. Tall she was, and beautiful, and severe. Her hair was black almost as my own, so black it was almost red, with highlights like deep fire that contrasted with the frost of her pale skin. She smiled, though her golden eyes did not, and said, "I'm not so sure."

I chafed my arms to warm them, took a couple mincing steps toward her. "Not you too . . ."

She raised those winged eyebrows. "I'm sorry?"

"I just had this talk with Lin. He still thinks we're wasting our time."

"Ah." Valka seemed not to feel the cold, dressed as she was only in trousers and a long shirt printed with a pattern of skulls and Tavrosi writing I could not read. She pushed a curtain of dark hair back behind one ear and said, "I'm not so sure he's wrong, Hadrian." I compressed my lips and moved past her, back into the hall. The *Balmung* was darker in design than the *Pharaoh*, all black gloss and brass and polished angles. The Imperial style. It had been a Legion destroyer once upon a time—in a sense it still was. It was by far the oldest of the three vessels the Red Company claimed as its own. Valka followed me, still speaking. "I have my own research to think of, you know? Lin won't even let me decant one of the Cielcin to speak with."

"I know," I said. "I'm sorry."

"Not one shred of new information, not in years, I—"

"I know, Valka." Why was she bringing this up now? Right after I'd awakened from fugue? I pressed my palms to my eyes, turning to keep my back toward her. "I just woke up. Can we . . . can we talk about this later?"

Her eyes were like guiding lasers on the back of my head. I thought I felt my hair crisping. "Later? 'Tis been years."

"I know that, too." I turned to face her. They had been good years, for the most part. Valka had spent fewer of them conscious than I had, had spent longer periods in fugue. We'd made a respectable mercenary outfit.

But the road toward Vorgossos was long, and we did not then know for certain if the place even existed. I cannot now blame Valka for doubting, or for her frustration. I could not blame her then. I took her aside, into an alcove off the hall containing softly glowing monitor equipment. "We have something." She was about to object, but I overrode her. "Bassander woke me himself. He says Otavia sent Crim down to the planet, that he found someone who can take us to the Extrasolarians."

Valka's face changed almost at once, the faintest smile pulling those lips. "You're serious?"

"Why else would I be awake? Lin wants me on the away team." She made a face. "Well, Lin knows he needs me."

"That sounds closer to the truth." She did smile then. Properly. That was something. I was back on solid ground. Negotiating the waters around Valka was never an easy task, made harder by the affection I still held for her, coiled snake-like about my innards. "Did you sleep well?"

We were back on surer footing. "It's not the being frozen that's hard." I knew what she meant, though, and shook my head. "More nightmares. Waking up." It was normal, Doctor Okoyo had said, for people to experience visions when they came out of fugue. Something about the way the brain's sub-cortical structures came back before the heavy apparatus of consciousness. Amygdala. Hypothalamus. The machinery of memory and motivation. Of fear. "I saw Bordelon again. Dying again. Gilliam. Uvanari." Those last two had died by my own hands: Gilliam in a bone-grass field in Borosevo, Uvanari in a dark cell of the Chantry's bastille. Bordelon was different. I'd had control of the *Pharaoh* then. I'd burned his ship from the skies. The way the holograph feed went white, then dead . . . there were weeks when I couldn't stop seeing it.

Valka cocked her head, lips pursed in . . . pity? She put a hand on my upper arm, squeezed. Concern. It was concern, not pity. "The thawing process dredges up old memories. Junk data. 'Twill pass."

"You too?"

"My memories are not in my brain, *anaryan,*" she said, tapping her temple knowingly.

I swallowed. Valka was not of the Imperium. She did not have the same terror and disgust of machines I had. She was—in the eyes of the Holy Terran Chantry—a demoniac. She had permitted machines to cloud her flesh and her mind. In Tavros, whence she came, such was commonplace. Here—to me—it made her a sorceress like those in the operas my mother used to write. Still, I did not fear Valka. Her penchant for forbidden machines and technical expertise had proved invaluable in the past: on Emesh first, and later at Ardistama and Pharos. It would prove so again.

"I'll be all right," I said, eager to change the subject from the things I'd done. Valka was Tavrosi, and the Tavrosi did not approve of violence. They'd evolved another sort of warfare where she came from: detente. An old form of war, and an insane one. The Tavrosi clans each held an arsenal capable of destroying the others, so that any act of violence might destroy their entire confederacy. And it was we who were the mad ones . . . "Look, if Crim's lead turns out, I'll talk to Lin again. I'll try and get him to let me thaw out one of the Pale."

"The leader," Valka said, prodding me in the chest.

"I'll try."

She smiled at me, but I could feel the strain in it. She was tired. Gods in hell, we were all tired. Even in fugue, forty-eight years was a long time, and I'd spent twelve of those awake. When I'd left Sir Olorin Milta on the strand at the Borosevo starport, I'd imagined my mission accomplished in conscious months. How little I'd known of the nature of space travel. "It's been a long journey, Hadrian." She stepped back, leaned against the far wall. "I'm an academic, not a . . . soldier. This is soldier's work." She smiled sadly.

"It won't always be that way," I said. "When we find the Cielcin, you and I will have plenty to do." I had taught Valka much of the xenobites' alien tongue when we started out from Emesh. She had proved a too-adept student, acquiring tenses and declensions and the language's complex gender-voice system with a speed that astonished and confounded me. I supposed it was the fault of that machine daimon wired to the base of her skull.

She dismissed this with a wave. "I know, Hadrian."

I tried to lighten the mood. "Look, you'll be speaking to them better than I can before long. I haven't had practice in years."

That worked, for she flashed her white teeth and chuckled softly, teasing. "I'm already better than you. But perhaps 'twould be good if *we* put some time in before long."

I allowed that that was so and we peeled out of the alcove, proceeding down the shimmering dark of the hall. Distorted reflections of ourselves shone in walls and floor, cast by the stark white lighting overhead.

"Switch brought you over, didn't he?" Valka asked as we exited the hall into a low-ceilinged gallery that followed the *Balmung*'s arrowhead design. Slit windows barely as wide as my chest punctuated the outer wall, heavy alumglass looking out onto Dark. In the distance, some miles hence, I could make out the dark shape of the *Pharaoh* like a knife with a too-large handle, the bridge and conning spire an angled knuckle-guard. "I passed him in the hall."

I stopped, looking across the blackness to the other ship. "Yes, he did." Almost I pressed my face to the glass, looking back and forth. "Where's the *Mistral*?"

"Low orbit," Valka said. "I knew Corvo had sent a team down to Arslan, but 'twas the last anyone said to me." She looked sharply up at me, cocking one eyebrow. "I'm not so sure Jinan trusts me." Arslan, I later learned, was the new city the surviving colonists had built on the planet below in the wake of the Cielcin invasion.

"What makes you say that?" I asked, turning fully from the window. I knew full well that Jinan didn't trust Valka. Jinan was Jaddian, as dubious of machines as any pious citizen of the Empire. But I suspected it was something more than that. Something deeper, older. They were both women, after all.

"Nothing in particular," Valka said with an ineloquent shrug. "It's just that—"

"There he is!" a heavy, masculine voice cried out. "Didn't get any freezer-burn, did you, Your Radiance?" Two men had appeared round the corner, each dressed in the deep burgundy of the Red Company uniform, each with the triple stripes in gold on the left arms of their tunics to mark them as centurions. Of the two, Pallino was the elder: a grizzled, forty-year veteran of the Imperial military service with a scuffed leather patch over one eye. Ghen was younger, taller, built like a heavy armored drop-shuttle, dark-skinned with jug ears and a permanent subcutaneous beard. It was he who'd spoken, his voice like the smashing of mighty stones.

Valka broke off speaking abruptly, turning as I did. I moved forward and embraced the big ox of a man. "If I did, I'd still be a damn sight prettier than you, Ghen."

Ghen grinned and affected an expression of false fury. "If you didn't think you were Emperor of the known universe, I'd thrash you for that one."

"You'd try!"

Everyone laughed, even Valka. "Thought Switch would be with you," I said. "I sent him on to Jinan when I stopped in to check on our . . . our cargo."

When Ghen finally moved out of the way, Pallino grasped my hand, keeping that one blue eye fixed on me. "Captain wanted you in the ventral observatory; the ox here and I thought we'd come get you." He seemed to notice Valka for the first time—she'd been standing on his blind side—and he bobbed his head, "Doctor, ma'am." She returned his greeting and his nod. "Didn't see you there." He turned his attention back to me. "How's that Mandari son of a bitch?"

"Lin?" I made a dismissive gesture. "The same. Says we ought to turn round and rejoin the fleet. Figures this whole thing's pointless."

Pallino chewed on his tongue for a moment, said, "I know his type. Man puts his principles before duty. Ain't the worst thing in the world, but it'll get folk killed."

"Not today, though," Ghen interjected. "No one's making planetfall til we get word from Crim."

Valka blinked, folded her arms. "You knew about it?"

Ghen shrugged. "I was on the bridge when Corvo called, didn't think it was a big secret. That's why we're here, ain't it?"

I waved both of my hands for quiet. "You said the captain was in the ventral observatory?"

Ghen looked a bit affronted to have been cut off, but he spread his hands, palm up. "Yes sir. Going over some reports."

"I'll head down that way at once," I said, and started toward the hall.

"We'll come with you!" Ghen said. Without Switch around, I supposed I needed a guard, but the *Balmung*—the Meidua Red Company— was home. I was home.

Laughing, I turned back and said to the three of them, "No, thank you. I know the way."

The ventral observatory was a small room built far to the rear of the *Balmung* and against the outer hull, amid a series of armored panels that, when opened, allowed its occupants to peer through a glass bubble that looked out onto the deep, bright Dark of space. It was meant for conferences, but for the moment it was nearly empty. Captain Jinan Azhar of the Red Company, Lieutenant Jinan Azhar of the armies of Jadd—and my captain most of all—sat alone at the round conference table with her back to me.

Below, through the glass geodesic beneath the observatory platform, I could see the umber eye of the planet. Rustam was in full daylight below: fields of ochre, brown mountains touched with ice, yellow seas with here and there a patch of green. Not the most beautiful of worlds, but beautiful in the way that only planets can be. Immortal, changeless, uncaring—the nearest thing to a material god. Only that wasn't quite right, was it? There again was the scar, the half-a-hundred-mile-long rent in the face of the planet, as if someone had dragged a branding iron across the planet. Briefly I imagined the forces required to leave such a wound: the plasma cannons, the rods. All the unholy force and fire of Destruction.

I took a step forward. Jinan twitched. "You are thinking of sneaking up on me?" Her slim shoulders looked tense beneath her epaulets.

I had been thinking just that. How she had heard me I could not guess. "Of course not!" I lied. I pressed a hurt hand to my chest in mock-offense. "I would never." I would. And had. She fiddled with a stack of crystal paper reports, pushed a holograph projector back and away before she stood. "You know," I said, "ship's captain shouldn't be sitting with her back to a door like . . ."

She turned around, and her smile stole what little wit and few words remained to me. My migraine seemed to lessen almost at once, and an idiot smile possessed me.

She hadn't changed while I slept. Not an angstrom. Jinan was taller than I—testament to her high breeding—with the copper skin and dark coloring endemic to the higher castes of Jaddian society. If I were a poet, I might say that she was built like a dancer, slim and compact. But that would be a lie, as is all poetry, in part. Slim she was, with scant curves and a soft, oval face, but those large black eyes and the azure ribbon braided through her shadowy hair gave the lie to her truth.

Jinan was a soldier, and had been one for more than thirty years. She was the commanding officer of all the Jaddian soldiers who had been loaned to us for this expedition by the Satrap Governor Kalima di Sayy-iph. She deferred to Bassander as commodore of our little fleet, but the two were equals in any formal sense. But she was more than that to me.

There were scars in places none but we two ever saw: an old knife-wound on her ribs, a thin sheet of plasma burn on her left side, an old bullet wound high—very high—on the inside of one thigh. "What is wrong?"

I realized I'd not spoken for perhaps ten seconds. I couldn't, and so took her in my arms instead. It was like embracing a steel sculpture wrapped in velvet. We stood there a long moment, neither speaking. I might have ceased even to breathe, were it not for the scent of jasmine wafting gentle from her hair.

"I missed you, *mia qal*."

"And I you, dear captain." I held her at arm's length a moment, peering up at her. "How long have you been out of the cold?"

Jinan looked off to the side, biting her lip. "Two months, I think? Alessandro woke me when we came out of warp." She wrapped a hand around the back of my neck and pressed her forehead to mine. Her voice came soft and breathy, almost husky to my ears, "I had wanted to wake you sooner, but Lin was not hearing of it."

"I'm here now."

She'd noticed that, as it happened, and stifled my words. She kissed me for an unprofessional length, fingers tight in my hair. My own hands wandered by long acquaintance, and so I held her close in turn, and we two banished the unquiet Dark and the grim reality of our mission and of the wounded world beneath us—if only for that limitless instant. You have heard that the Jaddian God is a God of Fire? It is true, and a spark of that secret flame was in her, as it is in all the women of that strange country. I loved her for it, whatever else is said of her in your stories . . . whatever else became of us.

The Mandari have a saying: *One lover is many who is seldom seen.* I forget which of their poets it was as wrote it, but like all poetry, it was a little bit true.

After a while—I cannot tell you how long it was—Jinan and I broke apart. She'd been leaning against the rail at the edge of the platform, the planet Rustam behind and beneath her. I was unspeakably glad not to be on the *Pharaoh*. I shudder to think what Bassander might have said to see us.

"You have been practicing!" Jinan said, accusing, playing with the tassels at the end of the blue ribbon in her braid. "Udhreha! Who is she?" But she smiled, eyes darting away from mine.

"You wouldn't know her," I said teasingly, settling myself down in the chair beside the one she'd been in when I arrived. "She's foreign."

Jinan snorted and sat next to me, pulling her chair close. She rested her head on my shoulder. I leaned into her, and we sat in silence for a long moment. My fugue-sick migraine—momentarily forgotten—surged back with a sick vengeance. I shut my eyes. "I think Okoyo was right, I needed to spend a little more time on the slab. My head's killing me."

My captain reached up and scratched me behind the ears. It helped.

"You are always dashing off too quickly. The Cielcin are not going any-where." She spoke the standard well, but after a slightly stilted fashion that served her heavy accent well.

"That's the truth." My eyes wandered over the table, taking in the as-trogation chart of the Rustam system gently rotating from the projector, the local reports detailing the Cielcin invasion—extracted from the local datasphere. "Is this our man?" I pulled a dossier out from where it lay hid beneath a map of the city of Arslan. It showed a round-faced, utterly hair-less little man with gimlet eyes and a wet smile. The image was blurry, badly lighted, as if taken from a distance. I wondered if our man, Crim, had been behind the camera, or if we'd pulled the data from what was left of local law enforcement databases.

Jinan craned her neck. "That is Samir, yes. He looks like a homun-culus."

"Might be," I said, frowning. "We're far out in the Veil now, Jinan. I'm not sure it's so easy to tell which is which out here." I shook my head, re-gretted it instantly. "Ugly bastard, though. Crim's sure he's who we want?"

"Karim," she said, using Crim's right name, "is fairly confident that Samir knows where we can find our Extrasolarian. He has met with him a few times now. The bastard is—how is it you say? Afraid but . . . like a mouse?"

"Timid? Er . . . skittish?" I pushed the dossier away. "He's a criminal, I suppose skittishness is to be expected."

"Indeed." She pulled away from me and reshuffled everything on the table. "Crim will pull through."

Without Jinan holding me up, I slumped onto the tabletop, pressing my forehead to the cool, black glass. Jinan stood and moved about the table, dragging files and storage chits that had slipped further away than arm's reach. I stayed there a good while, not moving while Jinan shuffled about with her work. At long last I said, "Bassander and Valka both think this whole misadventure is a waste of time."

"So do you," she said, standing over me, "if you are calling it a misad-venture." Her eyes were heavy on the back of my head.

Inhaling sharply I sat up, rubbing my face. "Are they wrong, Jinan?"

The Jaddian did not answer me at once, and my gaze tracked from her face to the gaunt reflection of my own in the smudged glass of the table. Despite the exhaustion and the fact that I could barely have been consid-ered alive mere hours before, I could have looked worse. The reedy youth from Delos was gone, burned out by the ragged piece of gutter trash I had become, by the myrmidon I had made of myself, the courtier-prisoner, the Cielcin translator, and the Lord Commandant of the Meidua Red Company. What once had been a hawkish sharpness of feature had transformed into a profile regal and aquiline, with thick black hair falling in short waves halfway to my chin. It wanted cutting.

"Tell me they're wrong." I watched my mouth form the words, and it seemed they came from some other part of me, not the Commandant of the Red Company or the Lord of Devil's Rest, but from the part of me that wore those masks. My soul, Hadrian himself. Chin resting on one hand, I looked up.

Jinan leaned her stack of files against one pointed hip, lips slightly downturned. She looked like someone preparing to tell a very sick relative that none of the news from the doctor was good. She set down her stack instead and resumed her seat. Her hand found mine. Another, unnamed piece of me felt healed almost at once, but the rest lamented as she said, "I understand where it is they are coming from."

I shut my eyes and half-turned my face away. "I see."

She squeezed my hand. "Do not you worry about Lin and the Tavrosi." I might have laughed at that if I'd felt up to it. Jinan never called Valka by her name. My captain was no fool—and I had been honest with her—regarding my past and complex feelings for Valka Onderra. "We have come a long way out into the Dark. It is not easy, what we are doing, and no end in sight." She smiled, and flipped her short braid back over her shoulder. "Besides, I am not ready to give up, *mia qal.*"

Few words in all the galaxy had more power to heal me at that point in my life. It was an innocent time, a period of happiness between two oceans of storm, and the skies were getting darker. She leaned in and kissed me again, this time on the cheek. Standing, she dragged me by the hand, and unwilling to be parted from her I rose and permitted myself to be led out of the observatory to her cabin and bed.

CHAPTER 3

THE SUNKEN CITY

THE BLACK OF SPACE gave way to a sky the color of old cream as our drop-shuttle roared around us with the force and friction of reentry. Our decade of peltasts—their gray armor hidden beneath dusty cloaks—stood in the central compartment, grasping handholds in the ceiling. I glanced sidelong at Switch, who was similarly garbed, but with a body shield strapped to his waist. He fidgeted with his plasma burner, checking its air-scoop for when the reservoirs ran dry.

"Corvo's man is meeting us at the landing site?" asked Bassander's executive officer, Prisca Greenlaw, her pale eyes narrow with her customary dislike. Greenlaw had come over from the *Pharaoh* just as we were preparing to depart. She was one of the officers Raine Smythe had sent along with us from Emesh. Less precise than Bassander, less fastidious, but with as little love for me.

"Nah!" Ghen said from where he stood at the head of the decade, bucking as the shuttle slalomed around an aerobraking curve on our rapid descent. Not speaking, I kept my eyes focused out the small window, watching the rocky landscape arcing nearer. "Crim's a little further into town. Don't look far, though." Turning to me, he asked, "You still want us hanging back?"

Looking up, I nodded. "We'll look too military if we all go in at once. Let's stick to the plan. I'll go in with Switch, Greenlaw, and Ilex. Once we find Samir and get a location on The Painted Man—if he's here—you follow on. If this lot catches a whiff of the Legions on us we'll be in for a real bad time."

Ghen leaned toward Greenlaw where she sat strapped in opposite me and said, in a stage whisper, "He means you, lieutenant." He grinned, his teeth crooked but very white against his dark face, which only made the smile more infectious, despite the slit in his nose from his time on Emesh. Soon his troops were grinning too, a motley collection of Imperial legionnaires and Jaddian *aljanhi*. Greenlaw said nothing.

"I'll put us down on the edge of the city, Lord Commandant," said Ilex, who had shuttled over from the *Mistral* last minute to accompany us. The Norman homunculus sat in the pilot's chair, green arms darting across the controls. She was a dryad, one of an ancient people made before the rise of the Imperium and the Writ of the Chantry. Her skin glowed thick with chlorophyll, so that she was green as Midsummer in the forests of Luin. She ate little, save what she drank of the sunlight, and could always be found in her place aboard the *Mistral*, busy with some machine beneath the light of heat lamps.

Abruptly we came out of our steep bank and leveled off on our approach to the city. Safety lights clicked on, allowing that those standing could step out of their clamps and unstrap themselves, and that we in the few crash benches might stand. I did, and retrieved a travel-worn greatcoat from one of the overhead lockers. Pressing toward the cockpit, I was conscious of the rattle of the metal grating beneath me and of the sway of the deck as the shuttle gently circled down toward the city in gradual spirals. Ilex was an excellent pilot, had grown up in space, amid the stations that cluttered the orbit of her homeworld—before she'd been captured and sold to bonecutters who wanted her for her hide.

Shrugging into the heavy black coat, I held onto straps in the ceiling just behind Ilex. I could hear Ghen moving behind me, and so was not surprised when he said, "The fuck's gone on with this city?"

I had known and so was not surprised. "It's not really a city, you know."

"It wasn't even here before the invasion," Ilex said, her voice light but measured.

Beneath us stretched a flowering ruin, a tangle of crooked domes and leaning towers hanging together like old bones, some held up by taut cables misty in the orange light of morning, others pressed against one another like the shapes of men spent by long exhaustion. Greenery sprouted on rusty terraces beneath, where the bodies of what once had been massive starships lay sunken and cracked upon the surface, falling into the hills.

"Captain said that after the Cielcin attack, the interim governor ordered what ships were left grounded to build this camp," Switch said, hanging back by the doorway. "I'd seen a couple of scans, but Earth take me . . ." He broke off, made a sign of the sun disc to ward off evil times.

We dove lower, and I could see where bridges and the cords of cable cars had been built up between the grounded ships, turning what had been a collection of cargo carriers and mining ships into a confusion of old metal sagging under its own weight. The camp city of Arslan was built on the edge of a vast plain, sheltered on one side by the ice-capped face of a nameless mountain, huddled there as its people huddled within its walls.

"How can something so new look so ancient?" I asked. Ten years. No time at all for us. And an eternity for those who had lived through it. It was like looking at the bottom of the sea. This new city had been built to no plan save necessity, its component ships pressed together as closely as possible. One might have thought it a graveyard, such as the mythic elephants made of their bones, were it not for the circumfusion of meaner structures built upon the backs of those massive vessels. New growth had sprouted about the ruined ships like mushrooms after a heavy rain, clinging to them as to rotten logs. I could make out the passage of fliers and of shuttlecraft—of more than I had seen in Meidua or in Borosevo or in anywhere since.

Ilex pressed her headset against her ear, said, "Understood, Arslan control. We will comply." She glanced briefly up at me, then took us lower, circling down below the level of the highest towers, past plumes of steam venting from the reactors along the back of what once had been a mining rig.

"These boats ain't flying again," Ghen said, pointing. "See all them stress fractures?"

"They weren't ever meant to carry their own weight," Ilex said, voice trilling in that strange way she had. "Any flight down-well for something that large is a one-way trip." She was right, those vast ships were far too massive to ever climb back to space again. Their own weight would tear them apart as they ascended, if one could even find an engine mighty enough to lift so great a load.

Switch spoke up. "Anyone tried raising Crim?"

"Said he'd meet us at the *Murakami*," Ilex said, pointing toward an ugly, cuboid supercarrier nearly a mile high and several times as long. It dwarfed one side of the city, despite its cracked and crumbling edifice and the rust stains that ate through the steel fixtures of its hull. "That Nipponese ship, there."

"That don't exactly narrow shit down, green," Ghen pointed out. The look Ilex flashed Ghen would have withered him, were he half as like a plant as she, or if Ghen were capable of shame. The dryad took a dim view of people pointing out her difference, and no wonder. It was no easy thing to ignore, between the color of her skin, her orange-yellow eyes, and the woody growth that passed for hair—or a crown—upon her head. Switch reached up and flicked Ghen in the side of the head. He yelped, "What in the Dark was that for?"

I was first down the ramp when we landed, and turned my collar up against the damp and the chill. The air felt oily against my face, and tasted faintly acrid, like aluminum. It made me want to spit. There was no one to greet us at the gate from the landing field, and the street beyond was only sparsely populated, with here and there a bent figure hurrying along, an umbrella over their head. Vents and great stacks studded the street and the faces of the ships-turned-buildings, belching steam and worse vapors into the cloudy day. The orange sunlight I'd spied on descent was gone entirely, turned to an umber gloom made weighty by the great steams of that place and the knowledge that the very city hummed to the pulse of several dozen nuclear stardrives.

"Earth and Emperor," Ghen said, pulling his hood up over his bald scalp to shadow his disfigured nose. "What a shit hole."

Clothes hung from lines across the streets, high above the ground, and higher up still a massive cable car swayed on a carbon cable, carrying the sort of people too well off and dignified to walk upon the ground.

"I don't like it either," said Lieutenant Greenlaw. "Visibility's low."

I couldn't decide whether I agreed or not. The place was a warren, to be sure, but as we stood there I watched a pack of children chase a lighted hoop down a side alley, dodging beneath the landing peds of a small freighter. Up above, beneath the dripping clotheslines, hydroponic planters bulged with new growth—green and gentle black—with here and there a flowering plant thick with blossoms. Humanity was trying, as it always did, to make the desert bloom. Still, I was glad to be only visiting.

Turning to Ghen, I said, "Wait til you hear from us about the meeting place, then you and the others follow on. We'll have specifics, and we'll need cover. None of us has any idea what we're getting into, so stay sharp." I clapped the big man on the shoulder, staggering a bit in the new gravity. Rustam only pulled point-eight gees, far less than the Emeshi one-point-

three I had made standard on the Red Company ships. I felt strong but . . .
clumsy. It would take some getting used to.

"Don't seem right you lot all going in," he said darkly, and patted his
plasma howitzer where it hung beneath his rain cloak. "Without the heavy
artillery and all."

"We've got plenty of kit, Ghen," Ilex said from inside her own hood.
Homunculi such as she were not uncommon sights on the border worlds,
but she never did like the staring.

Switch shrugged his own coat tighter. "He means him. Not the guns."

"I am the guns," Ghen said with a wry smile that drew matching
smiles from Switch and myself. It was a tired joke, but comfortable as only
old jokes between friends can be.

"All right," I said, checking the drape of my highmatter sword against
my hip, "let's move out. Ilex, Switch, Greenlaw: shall we?"

"Watch yourself out there, Your Radiance," Ghen said with a half-
hearted salute, tapping his fist against his chest. "Try not to have too
much fun without me."

"And you just stay with the shuttle until we find Lieutenant Garone,"
Greenlaw said, not looking at the big centurion. She moved off then toward the neon lighting at the gate, Ilex trailing after.

When she had gone, Ghen leaned toward me, voice hushed. "You best
watch yourself there, Had. You got competition for the 'Your Radiance'
thing if she keeps on like that."

We must have walked for an hour as the streets grew increasingly thick
with foot traffic. The vast hulk of the starship *Murakami* filled the sky
ahead, casting the world beneath it into deep gloom. It wasn't long before
I began to wish for a cable car, a flier, some mode of conveyance. I found
I had difficulty getting my bearings. Meidua had been arranged along
city blocks, and though the streets had wandered with the hills they still
had a precise logic to them: streets and avenues ran perpendicular to one
another—at least in a less-than-Euclidean sense. Borosevo, too, had had a
logic to it, with the White District divided into neat blocks and the canals
of the lower districts cut radially and in great circles. But no two cities are
the same, and this one had been less planned than accrued all at once in a
desperate need for shelter. If the *Murakami* had not dwarfed most of the

other vessels piled together beneath its shadow, we might never have found our way through.

Stranger still was the way the protocols of the Imperium had relaxed. Great holographic advertisements moved like ghosts through the streets, or else towered like the buildings. A school of jewel-bright fish larger than my head followed us for a hundred meters down a street, projected from a lensing suite above the door to a supermarket, and further on the colossal image of a fashion model in a fluorescent dress turned this way and that. She must have been fifty feet high.

Switch seemed to know where he was going, and I followed him as he pushed through a line of people waiting for a noodle cart operated by a huge, hairless man in grimy whites. Further on, I saw a man with the silk robes and twin swords that marked him as a Nipponese knight, and a group in the drab purples and blacks of the Durantine Republic, merchants I did not doubt. Two women in red latex stood upon a corner and lifted their skirts as we passed. I could sense Switch's disquiet, and we hurried on. There was something in their painted faces—white and blue—that struck me with a sense of unreality.

Beyond, a monorail line rattled uneasily past us, winding upward toward the summit of the ship-buildings where distant trees flowered above the gloom and vapors of the lower streets. Somewhere—over loud-speakers, perhaps—the prayer call of a Chantry sanctum rang out.

Attend! You Children of the Earth!
The Sun and hour is now!
Through sacrifice, there is rebirth,
through prayer! And disavow
the evils of your heart and age!
And by your faith renew
what Mother Earth and Emperor
themselves made green for you!

We had to stop for more than a minute as a throng of suppliants passed, making their way along the street and up an arcing stair toward the clear and chanting voice, which even then was chanting still: "Attend, O Child of Dust! And come on bended knee!" Switch made the sign of the sun disc, as he always did when he heard the call to prayer. I turned away, thinking of the torture chamber in the basement of the Chantry bastille on Emesh, of the cross they'd tied Uvanari to, and of the mutilated people

I had seen . . . on sanctum steps or in the streets. Victims of the Chantry's forgiveness, their mercy.

This, then, was Arslan, the sunken city. Her ships would never fly again, and in later days perhaps, when the grime and chaos of her birth was washed away and her streets ordered, she might be something strange and wonderful.

Something like a plaza had been left open near the center of the vast ship *Murakami*, where a jointed structure of sheet metal and new plastic had opened up into some sort of mall, sprouting from the side of the Nipponese cruiser. The crowd here had grown to a thick press, and all manner of men and women moved past. None speaking to one another, unless it was at a shop booth or between friends. Elsewise they hurried about their business as if the rest of the humanity about them was no different than the holographs that flickered, little better than ghosts, about the stalls and storefronts.

"William!" A voice called out as we passed a vendor selling imitation handbags from the back of a groundcar. Karim Garone emerged from the crowd, dressed in a flowing red kaftan covered in white paisleys. He looked every part the Jaddian merchant, with a gold medallion at his throat and a diamond stud in one ear. He grinned and embraced Switch. "It is exceedingly good to see you again, my friends! Hadrian!" He embraced me in turn, long enough to whisper, "I did not expect for you to be here, boss." I liked the young lieutenant. He was one of the finest swordsmen I ever knew, with the easy humor of a dockworker. The son of Jaddian immigrants to the Norman Freeholds, he was a man of two worlds, with one foot firmly planted on the ground of each.

He pulled back, grinning at us like an enthusiastic uncle might on greeting his family at the starport. He *was* pretending, of course. At least he was pretending that I was not someone of importance. I clapped him on the shoulder. "Didn't expect to be coming, Crim." I looked round at the crowd around us, and so leaned in to ask, "Where is he?"

"Samir?" he asked, rubbing the back of his head, his black eyes darting across our faces in turn. He smiled when he saw Ilex under her hood, then said, "There's a jubala den in the *Murakami*, not far. He said he'd meet us in about three hours." He checked his wrist-terminal. "Make that about two and a half."

Greenlaw pressed forward. "What do you know about our man?"

Crim looked around startled, as if just noticing Greenlaw for the first time. Then he smiled toothily at her and said, "Samir? He's a local, survived the sack of Suren. God only knows how it is he fell in with the . . ." He glanced at me. "Should we perhaps . . . go somewhere more private?"

I nodded, and frowned at the back of Greenlaw's pale head. Crim turned and led us aside, past the main avenue of shop stalls and out from under the metal canopy onto an emptier front street that paralleled the bulk of the *Murakami*. The great grounded ship loomed over us like a mountain, balconies rough-welded to its surface rising, rank upon rank, into the foggy day above us. A single cable car bobbed directly above us, descending toward a platform five stories above our heads. I watched it go, noting the graffiti that covered its surface, the letters too stylized to read.

"I've not been able to work out the relationship between Samir and this Painted Man of his. How they met," Crim said, seating himself on a retaining wall that surrounded one of the huge spars that held the *Murakami* level, like the ribs that supported a sailing ship while under construction. He rummaged in his pocket, produced a white paper bag. "Those Sanoran pirates we met made it sound like The Painted Man's been here a good long while. How long I don't care to guess. Samir's plebeian as they come, and he sure talks like The Painted Man's been here forever . . . but I'm inclined to think he's only *really* surfaced since the Cielcin burned Suren ten years back."

Ilex sat beside Crim, green hands folded in her lap. "Makes sense. With the Empire gone from here there's got to be all kinds of opportunities for an arms dealer that wouldn't exist under the Imperium's thumb." Her amber cat's eyes gleamed from the shadow of her hood, watching Greenlaw as she spoke.

"Reckon he's has some good years," Switch said soberly.

My hands deep in my pockets, I looked up at the confusion of bent shapes that passed for buildings in this mad parody of a city, at the rust and the defaced surfaces and the dirty balconies. "There are some places that just feel you're standing at the edge of the world," I said. "Like any second they'll crumble over the edge and . . ." I waved an inarticulate hand. "Chaos."

"What the fuck is that supposed to mean?" Greenlaw hissed, and I could feel her eyes on me.

"You want to try that again?" Switch asked, rounding on her.

I raised a hand, and looked the rigid Imperial lieutenant in the face. She was plebeian herself—pure-blooded human, no tinkering, with a square face and heavy cheekbones. The flesh had already begun to hang heavy from them, though she was not yet forty standard. "It's all right,

Switch," I said with a smile, then to Greenlaw, "You don't read very much, do you?"

Greenlaw turned away with a huff, ushering in an uncomfortable, if agreeable, silence. Crim proffered the white bag to Ilex, who took one of his candies without a word. Smiling, he held it up to Switch, who declined. "Would you like a gel, boss? They're rose flavored."

I took one of the gels, a little lump of sugar with the consistency of wet clay. Crim was always carrying them. He made them, I think, on the *Mistral*. "This one's cherry, actually."

"You're kidding!" Crim said, aghast. "I thought I'd eaten all of those!"

Jubala smells like coffee tastes: bitter, dark, and unpleasant. The drug house into which Crim led us was thick with the smoke of it, lit by holographic flames that danced ghost-like through the air to the wailing of rebec and sitar. Worse drugs there were to be tasted on the air: denwa, hilatar, and ancient opium. Men and women lay about on pillows—in varying states of undress—or at tables with wine cups and tankards near at hand. It was not the first such place I had been, nor would it be the last. I longed for a kerchief such as the nobiles of the court might use to mask an unpleasant stench, but that put me in mind of the intus Gilliam, and I overcame my desire out of shame and loathing.

As Crim had said, the plagiarius Samir sat in a booth in the back, bent over a cup of some liquor cartoonishly small in his round hands. He smiled when he saw us. The expression of a rodent imitating a snake. He was taller than I expected, and larger than Jinan's phototypes could show. Grossly obese and hairless, he looked like a caricature of the Mandari plutocrats, such as one sees in Eudoran masque comedies, grown fat from his excesses. Crim and I settled down opposite him with Lieutenant Greenlaw while Switch and Ilex settled into the adjacent table—all the better to keep an eye out for trouble.

Samir licked his lips, as if tasting something there. His eyes darted from my face to Greenlaw's like a frightened bird—I was struck by how close together those eyes were, as if he had some cyclops in him a few generations back. "Which one?" He addressed his words to Crim, and jerked his chin at Greenlaw and myself.

"This is Hadrian Marlowe, Samir," Crim said in a conspiratorial tone, leaning in over the table. "Commandant-Owner of the Red Company."

The plagiarius looked sidelong into the crowd, touched his cheek with damp fingertips. He hesitated a moment, as if struggling with some thought. "You're brave to come yourself. Arslan is a dangerous place. A very danger-ous place."

"The price you pay for your freedoms, I assume," I said, smiling not unkindly. "A failed state like the Rustam Barony offers men like you and me a set of rare opportunities." I felt Greenlaw stiffen next to me, un-comfortable with my small treason. "Karim here has made you aware of our . . . interests?"

Samir's eyes were so close and squinting that they seemed little more than ink spots in his face, like buttons sewn onto an overstuffed doll. He had no eyebrows, making his expression very difficult to read. At last he bobbled his great head, said, "Yes. Yes indeed. You want to meet *him*." The way he said that word—him—made it seem as if it were made of crystal, delicate and precious, posing danger to any as spoke it, should they drop it. "Guns Samir could procure for you, yes, but *atomics*?" His voice went soft, and he lifted his tiny cordial glass to his lips. "These the Empire would burn us for. The black priests . . . they watch even still, though the Baroness is dead. They keep their ways, and keep from us." His pinprick eyes widened, sable as the night between the suns.

"Only the houses palatine may keep them legally within Imperial bor-ders," I agreed in hushed tones, my words lost beneath the wailing of the rebec.

Crim put a hand on the table, rapping his knuckles for attention. "We'd want to arrange a pickup out-system, in the heliopause."

"That is for *him* to decide," Samir said.

"The Painted Man?" Greenlaw put in.

Samir whistled and made a sharp gesture with his hand. "Don't say *his* name again." He looked round, as if expecting some sinister prefect to emerge from the crowd of drug addicts. "The priests' eyes are every-where, even where the cameras cannot be."

I looked briefly down in my lap, shook my head to clear it. The drug smoke was getting to me, making me lightheaded and just the smallest bit numb. My palatine metabolism would break it down soon enough—I wondered what it was like for Greenlaw and Crim. "The Chantry have taken control then?" I asked.

"And the urban prefects, everyone who escaped Suren. A man called Zhivay set himself up as interim Consul, but it is said the Chantry keeps him. What is left of them, at any rate." He looked like he wanted to spit, but smiled instead, revealing too-small teeth. "But their grasp is not yet so tight as it might be."

Greenlaw hissed through her teeth, "Which is it? Have they got eyes everywhere or not?"

"Caution, girl," the plagiarius said, leaning back affronted, his brows pulled down, "is never a mistake. You want to see *him,* we must be careful. They do not know where he is. That is . . . better. But they know of him . . . people come asking. Asking Samir. People who are not what they claim." He eyed me the way a snake might, contemplating the rodent, which I found entirely unsettling at the time, despite the hand I kept firmly around the hilt of the sword Sir Olorin had given me. After a brief hesitation, he said, "You have a palatine look about you, M. Marlowe. Like you were whelped in a castle somewhere, from one of those cold replicators. No one's got skin like that." He held up a finger, as if he meant to stroke my face. "Not even lifelong spacers are so pale." I seized his wrist before he could touch me and held his gaze. He smiled his wet smile, but took no obvious offense. Slowly, I forced his hand down. When I released him he asked, "You're Empire, aren't you?"

"I was born there," I said, wiping my hand on the leg of my breeches—his flesh had been moist to the touch. I felt instantly unclean.

Greenlaw's tension was palpable, but Crim only laughed, an easy, bored sound. "Where'd you think the money came from, Samir?" He flashed his toothy smile at the plagiarius and at myself, clapping a big hand on my shoulder.

"My father owned a mining contract with the Vicereine of Delos," I said, and that part was true. "Uranium, mostly. A monopoly on all in-system trade with the Mandari. I've a line of credit but no other inheritance." Reflexively, I touched the hoop of burn scar around my left thumb. Once, I had worn a silver ring there, square and with a carnelian bezel inscribed with the sigil of my house: a prancing devil with a trident in its hands. I'd lost it years ago, had thrown it away on Emesh after it had gotten me into trouble—into my mad duel with Gilliam over Valka.

Samir's piggish eyes widened. "A monopoly? The Solar Throne does not hand those out lightly. Why would a scion of such a house turn pirate? Samir wonders."

It was my turn then to smile, showing my teeth in a very Cielcin display. "Samir will keep on wondering. I came for business. I want to meet your man."

The plagiarius matched my smile, ran a hand back over his scalp. In his rasping, nasal voice, he said, "I don't like you much, high-born. I don't like nobiles, even black ones with no family. You think as you've not been shoved out of some woman that you're better than we are." He glanced at Crim, as if for support. "But there's a demon in you, like in all the rest of you. It'll make someone want to *put you down*."

My smile didn't falter. "Does this mean you and yours won't take my money?"

"Oh, no," Samir said. "Money spends, and it's not in *his* interest or mine to turn away so . . . exalted a customer. I'll take you to *him*."

I had seen wolves broadside one another in my grandmother's menagerie, displaying their size and fangs. I knew what this was, what Samir was. A predator trying to cow me. His softness did much to disguise it, but it was there. I did not back down, for one cannot back down in the face of such a challenge and yet remain a man. Like Dante, I was thirty-five—the midpoint of life to primordial man. Like Dante, I stood upon the edge of a dark forest, where the true path was lost . . . and here was the wolf, slavering, on the hunt, and ready to drive me into darkness. Where the leopard and the lion were then I did not know.

I did not doubt they were out there, and that they were hungry.

CHAPTER 4

THE PAINTED MAN

A CHILDHOOD FILLED WITH Mother's operas had led me to expect that The Painted Man would have entrenched himself in some grimy brothel, in a dance club or winesink. I was prepared for carbines and chunky plasma burners and tattooed faces, for women naked and abused. I expected the angry music of revolution, the synthetic noise I'd so often heard in such places in the Norman Expanse throughout the past twelve waking years.

I was not expecting the stately tea house at all.

I have never much cared for tea. It seems almost unpatriotic for a palatine nobile of the Imperium to confess such, but it is so. The tea house had been built recently, on the back of a great starliner that stretched for nearly a mile in the shadow of the vast *Murakami*. Indeed, several such structures flowered there, like limpets on a rock at low tide. Artificial terraces had been added, transforming the leeward side of the old starship into a stepped hill that rose—level upon level—to a neighborhood of fine brick houses and whited roofs cracked already by the constant damp.

The tea house itself was an imitation wood structure built in the Nipponese fashion: slope-roofed with heavy beams, clean-lined and open. It perched upon the very edge of the grounded vessel upon which it sat, on a platform overhanging the level and the street far below, supported by heavy steel struts tied into the superstructure beneath.

We were ushered in by two willowy women in black uniforms, their hair—one black, the other golden—tied back and secured with long wooden pins. Samir led the way inside, his huge bulk seeming to bend the walls closer to him like a planet warping space. I followed with Greenlaw, expecting at any moment that the big guards I imagined would appear and search us for weapons—or for comms devices such as the sub-vocal transmitter Ilex wore under her cloak and behind her elongated ears.

None came.

Samir said nothing as he led us through a crowded central chamber, past chatting patrons and laughing men and around a large brazier where staff were boiling coffee in sand after the Jaddian fashion. "Just this way," he said, mounting a wooden stair that arced up the back wall and onto an open portico under the sky of early afternoon.

The fitful vapors of the morning were gone, and though columns of steam yet rose from Arslan all around, the orange sun was bright and clear, and fretted only a little with the fitful clouds. The portico, too, was crowded, with small tables and small conversations, some hushed and private, others expansive. Paper screens painted with the images of birds and of women blocked one corner from view, and beyond the railing I could see the whole of the city rolled out like a man new-woken from fugue.

For someone supposedly hiding from the Imperium, the place Samir and The Painted Man had chosen for their meeting seemed terribly exposed. One could easily imagine a Chantry remote camera flying overhead, driven by some poor anagnost in an office somewhere in town. Yet there was no real sense of secrecy about the place. With the crowd so near to hand, it was almost public.

Two men emerged from behind the screens, and I was almost relieved to see their thick muscles and black suits. They did not take our weapons, but stepped aside with a nod and opened the screens wider for Samir to pass. The fat plagiarius blocked my view, and so the first thing that struck me about the Extrasolarian arms dealer was his voice. High, cold, drawling and nasal. "Here you are. Brought the mercenaries, have you?"

A shadow of the menace that so frightened Samir moved in me, and I stopped moving forward at once. Switch nearly banged into me and had to steady himself. Hearing its voice, I froze: sick, cruel, imbued with a poisonous quality, as if one might expect fangs in the mouth that spoke with it instead of teeth. Not even the Cielcin were so disturbing, for this voice used the tongues of men. Samir bowed his head, shoulders hunched. "Yes, master."

"Well, stand aside then, my dear. It's them I'm here to speak to, not you."

Neither of The Painted Man's two minions were looking at us, or looking anywhere. It was like they'd gone away inside. I stood looking at one of their faces for a good few seconds, confused by that deep emptiness. What sort of man engendered that kind of fear and self-control? Not even my father's guards had been such, and he was the hardest man I'd known. Not even Emil Bordelon—for all his depravity—had shut down his own people so.

Samir stepped aside, and I saw The Painted Man's face, and it was like no man I had ever seen.

Inmane. Inhuman.

It was a homunculus, like Ilex and yet as far removed from Ilex as a man is removed from a shark. Red-haired it was, with skin like time-eaten porcelain: translucent, veined with blue. But the worst part was the eyes. All-dark they were, putting me in mind of the Cielcin. But where those xenobites' eyes were black and empty as caverns, this was something far worse. They were pupil-black—as if its whole eye were dilated in the throes of some deep arousal. Its was the face of ancient terror, of the predator in love with the hunt. And worse yet, it knew what it was, for it had painted itself to heighten the terror it engendered. Neither woman nor man it seemed to me, but some monster fashioned in man's image. The lips were red, like a clown's parody of a Jaddian cortigiano, and when it smiled it revealed far, far too many teeth. What black magus had grown and designed such a being and why I did not care to guess. For some sadist's pleasure house on some planet whose name I did not dare imagine, I daresay.

But here it was . . . in the open air under the sun. In a tea house. How it had walked in past all those *ordinary* people and not driven them off with the sight of it I could not say. Indeed, how it could be present and not sensed by those same ordinary people the way we know there is a snake in the grass I cannot begin to guess. I wanted to scream, to turn in terror. To draw my sword.

My hand flitted toward the hilt in its leather holster strapped to my thigh. Seeing this, The Painted Man smiled, and in that drawling voice said, "You must be the one, then?" It bit its lip. "What a looker you are, boy." The smile widened past anything any human face could achieve, revealing every one of the Extrasolarian's teeth—there must have been a hundred of them crowded behind those carmine lips. "Marlowe, was it?"

It offered a pale hand, long-fingered, with pointed nails red as its painted lips. Finding my voice, I looked it in the face and said, "And you're The Painted Man, I assume?" I moved to take the frightful white hand, noting the tattooed eyes peering out from its wide sleeve.

It snatched its hand away, holding it above its head, bracelets rattling as it wagged its finger at me. "I am no one, boy. Remember it." It leered at me, settling back in its chair. "Samir, darling. Fetch us tea." It waved that hand in dismissal, and the fat plagiarius went back out past the screens. All was quiet for a moment, the five of us alone with the demon. Over its shoulder, I could see the strange and sprawling city unrolled beneath us. A towering rocket stood not far off, blinking with holographic advertisements and the ever-present scaffolding that endeavored to turn the peculiar architecture of Arslan into something enduring.

"Messer," I said, taking the careful point against using the homunculi's name, "I am Hadrian Marlowe, Lord Commandant of the Meidua Red Company. I assume Samir has spoken to you of our needs?"

The Painted Man rubbed its arms under the sleeves, the images of lidless eyes and leering mouths painted on its skin blinking from beneath the violet silks. "There's only one thing people, uh, come to me for." Its nails snicked on the tabletop, and it turned its head from each of us to the other. I could not track its eyes—there were no whites in them—and it seemed to look everywhere at once. I read once that our ancestors had evolved whites in their eyes for precisely that reason: that the rest of us might know where the other looked. It was no wonder those humanish creatures with the lying eyes had been stamped out. I could not trust it. "Sit, sit, sit!" It waved me to the opposite chair, then, realizing there was only the one, shrugged and said, "Your little . . . friends here. They will have to stand, I'm afraid."

As I seated myself, I could feel Switch move closer behind me, taking up a position at my shoulder. I knew it was him without having to turn. I took in a deep breath, trying to quiet my grated nerves from the shock of seeing The Painted Man's face. I had a plan, and I meant to stick to it. I had to shock the creature—no small task—and hoped the brain behind that horrid face was still human enough to understand. "I'm here for information."

A muscle spasmed in the homunculi's cheek, and its brows contracted. Hit. "Information, you say?" It stroked the hollow of one cheek. "Samir said you were in the market for atomics?" It almost pouted with those bloody lips, the painted shadows around its eyes stretching down the *inmane*'s face. Tugging on the silver hoop in one ear it said, "Do not test my patience, little boy."

I told myself I had faced worse creatures than this, whatever its monstrous appearance. I had faced truly inhuman monsters before, I had faced an Ichakta-captain of the Cielcin and lived to speak of it. I had burned Emil Bordelon out of the sky. I had fought in Colosso and sat at table with my own father, the Butcher of Linon, more times than I could count. I had nearly been killed in the streets of Meidua, and faced the other boys that dark night in Borosevo. What was this—what was it—next to all that? The poets say that one's fears grow less with trial, that we become men without fear if tried enough. I have not found it to be so. Rather, on each occasion we are tested, we become stronger than our fears. It is all we can do. Must do. Lest we perish for our failings.

And so I spoke. "You are an Extrasolarian. I wish to deal with the Extrasolarians. With your masters, whoever they may be. I want a way to contact them."

"My . . ." The creature mulled over the words. ". . . masters." It looked at me—or so I thought—with those eyes like drops of ink. It smiled again, smiled with its whole face. "You don't know what we are, do you? You ask after masters, but we are not the bloody, fucking *Empire*. There are no masters. You deal with me."

"I meant no offense." I splayed one hand on the tabletop, narrowed my eyes. "Weapons are the smallest part of what I want," I said, playing the mercenary captain. "Things that can't be had under the Imperial Sun. Do you follow me?"

The homunculi's demeanor changed at once. It sat back, and the too-wide smile—momentarily banished—returned with astonishing speed. It laughed, a high, grating sound like air escaping an old instrument. "Is that how it is, then?" It leaned forward, black eyes turning blacker as it grinned, attention flitting from one of us to the next. "Oh, but this is amusing." It pointed squarely at me. "Civilization's on the wane, you know? They say the Imperial Sun is red because it's grown supergiant. And supergiants burn out. The xenobites burn cities, take millions . . . and here's a nobleman of the blood of old King William himself, asking after daimons. What a time to be alive."

Samir chose that moment to return with a metal tea service, which he placed on the table between us. I took a moment to compose myself, rattled by The Painted Man's remark about old King William. It meant the Emperor, of course, the first Emperor. How had the homunculus known that I was a part of the Peerage? Of the blood Imperial itself? Or did it only mean that I was palatine?

"You misunderstand me," I said, taking the tea service before the creature across from me could. Bassander's discomfort with the idea of even pretending to have truck with daimons floated up in my mind. But I'd had a better idea. One closer to the truth. "I'd been given to understand the Extrasolarians were the very best to go to for . . . unnatural requests." Emboldened, I added, "You're living proof that must be true."

Reclining against the back of its seat, The Painted Man smiled. "You don't know the half of it, little boy." Then it smiled, and the red paint about its lips stretched, flowing as if from under its skin until the points of its smile stretched horribly from ear to ear. "You still don't seem to understand, though. There are no *Extrasolarians*. Not the way there's an Empire. We don't organize. That's why I don't have any masters. No gods or emperors. No hierarchy."

I snorted, glancing at Samir where he cowered as invisibly as an obese man could. "No hierachy, eh?" With difficulty, I pulled my attention back to the pallid face with its horrid too-wide smile. "The fact you don't pay taxes doesn't mean you're free, or that there's not someone out there who can squash you."

"Why would they? I'm a businessman. I provide a service, and for a modest price," The Painted Man said, combing its too-red hair back from its too-white face.

"What service is that, exactly?"

"If you didn't know that, you beautiful idiot, you would not be here." It turned its head to Samir. "My lovely friend explained, did he not?" He had. The Painted Man salvaged nuclear ordnance from abandoned Imperial and Norman bases throughout the Veil, or else raided house stores on the borders. It did other things: trafficked in smaller arms and less caustic technologies. Things like starships, terraforming hardware, even the dreaded daimons of artificial intelligence. "So what is it you're really after, if not the atomics?" The red pigment twisted into evil spirals across its cheeks. They vanished almost as fast, leaving me contemplating the nightmare before me.

"I *do* want the atomics," I said, taking only the smallest sip of the tea. I had to suppress a grimace. "But not only." The situation called for delicacy. I did not know what it was I needed to ask for. I could hardly say that I wanted Vorgossos because I was an Imperial agent, could I? "The Chantry forbids the trade of xenobitic artifacts between worlds within the Imperium."

The Painted Man put down its teacup suddenly and held a hand to its mouth, as if in surprise. One of its tattoos floated up its wrist and filled the back of its hand. A grinning mouth, twin to the one on its face. It widened, revealing a tongue red as its lips. Then it was gone, and The Painted Man asked, "Xenobites? The Cielcin, do you mean?"

"I'm a collector, you see," I said, spreading my hands. "And I had word from a Durantine trader on Pharos that there was a place where the Extrasolarians—where people, I should say—where they traded with the Cielcin." It was all a lie, of course. There had been no Durantine merchanter at Pharos.

I realized only then that The Painted Man's stunt with the tattooed mouth had been a distraction, meant to hide its genuine response. I had surprised it, for it said, "I have heard . . . stories."

"Vorgossos," I said, preferring again to speak shortly and sharp. "I had always believed it was a myth, but . . . this merchanter . . . he said he'd been there." Had it been my imagination, or had the homunculi's inhuman eyes darkened at the name *Vorgossos*? Samir had flinched as he had in the drug den when I spoke of The Painted Man. Switch had caught on as well, for his fingers tightened on the top of my chair, just behind my shoulder.

"Vorgossos? Now that is interesting," The Painted Man said with another of its frightful bouts of laughter. "It must have something to do with the way they *breed* you nobiles. You're all so baroque." It glanced up at the others behind me and spoke in a stage whisper. "Is it sexual, your interest? Because there is trade in that, you know? You wouldn't even have to go to the Undying. March Station would be far enough. The Exalted would be all too happy to drug one of the Pale long enough for you to get your play—I hear you don't want them awake—they bite more than I do." At this it gnashed its teeth and chortled. "Aah, humans are so *interesting*. But then, you're as human as I am."

A series of emotions flashed through me: disgust, contempt, anger, disgust again. I slammed my eyes shut, trying to gather my scattered thoughts. Deciding not to rise to the bait, I said, "What's the Undying?"

The homunculus threw an arm across its face in exasperation and turned away. The eyes tattooed on its pale flesh shut themselves and vanished entirely. "You ask for Vorgossos but do not know its lord?"

"I thought you said there was no hierarchy among the Extras?"

It laughed again, then without warning slammed both its hands flat against the table, half-standing. Switch and Ilex each took a half-step forward behind me, but the homunculus rocked back in its seat, laughing. "The look on your face!" It pointed again, its red smile spreading across its face without the lips moving at all. Scowling through its grin, it said, "Shall we stop dancing, Lord Marlowe? I thought you'd be more amusing than this . . . with your reputation. What you did to dear sweet Admiral

Whent's men . . ." It sucked in a breath, as if about to cry. "Hilarious." It grinned, and the red pigment in its lips faded away.

Glancing up at Switch and Greenlaw to my right, I said, "Very well. I want the location of Vorgossos in addition to the supply of atomics my man discussed with yours." At this I jerked my head in Crim's direction. "If this is agreeable to you, I—"

The Painted Man raised a hand. Its long red nails snicked against one another. "I can't give you Vorgossos. It can only be *found* by those its master allows to find it."

"And why is that exactly?" I asked. I was running out of patience. I had traveled too far and for too long to give up so easily. I hoped Ghen was close with his troops. Ilex would still be in communication with them, ready to move on my signal.

"Because it is a planet without a sun, and those are not easy to find. Enough of this." It drank again, and turning to its toady said, "Samir, dear. You promised me a mercenary company, not a nobleman on holiday."

The fat man bowed so rapidly I thought he'd fallen. "Forgive me, master. They seemed serious."

I stood then. That was a grave mistake. "I am serious."

The Painted Man raised a hand, and at once the two thugs on the other side of the screens came through. How they had known when their master signaled I couldn't guess.

Switch spoke up for the first time. "Hadrian, we should go." He put a hand on my arm.

I brushed him off angrily, only to find the hands of the two thugs on me. "I came to trade, homunculus."

"No, you didn't!" the homunculus said, stepping lightly up onto the table, robe flapping in a sudden wind from over the railing. "This whole thing is a joke, Lord Marlowe. And while you are very funny, I've had enough. I know exactly what you are." It looked straight down at me and grinned, its impossible smile widening beyond all human imitation. With a jerk of its chin, it dismissed the two thugs, who hauled me backward, despite Switch's politic objections. No one went for their weapons, for which I was privately grateful—my shield wasn't on. We passed out onto the crowded portico.

No one looked at us. The conversation didn't even stumble. On the street in Borosevo we used to say someone could beat you down in the street and no one would stop to help. Many times I'd watch another urchin like me turned to pulp by the prefects or less legitimate thugs in full view of other people. Rousseau was wrong.

"I need to get to Vorgossos!" I shouted. Still no one looked our way. My four compatriots stood, assessing—Ilex, I hoped, was signaling Ghen. We'd have to move fast to take The Painted Man. I prayed the big myrmidon was in place.

"I may be a great many things, boy," The Painted Man said, and it jumped down off the table, pressing past Crim with as little regard as you or I might give a cockroach, "but I don't trade with Imperial spies."

I had nothing to say to that. It had me right. It smiled entirely too close to my face—its tattoos were flushing up its neck like a fever. A cloud of little black eyes opening. At that precise moment a shot rang out. Not the cough and roar of plasma fire, nor the simple pop of a laser as it flash-boiled its living target. This was the concussive blast of a simple firearm. A sniper. One of the thugs holding me *fell away* and a fine spray of blood washed over my face, my coat. I thought I spied the flash of a targeting laser from the scaffolding about the rocket that was becoming a tower opposite us. At that precise moment a half dozen soldiers in heavy gray cloaks sprang over the railing at the edge of the porch, led by Ghen.

It was the strangest thing, not because the ordinary world—a tea house—had plunged off a cliff into the ocean of chaos that roils beneath all things, but because it hadn't. The diners kept eating. Drinking. Talking. They kept laughing. They hadn't missed a beat. I couldn't afford to, either; couldn't afford to dwell on it. I drew Olorin's sword with my free hand and whirling planted the mouth of the hilt against the fellow's chest and squeezed the activator. The blade sprang into being. She gleamed in my hand, faintly phosphorescent highmatter glowing blue-white as moonlight. I tugged up and away, slipping a finger through the finger-loop to shore up my grip even as I opened the man from sternum to clavicle. He fell away and turning I faced The Painted Man, blade held en garde. She sang naked and bloodless in my grasp, the exotic metal in her blade rippling like seawater over itself. "I didn't want to have to do it this way. You're outnumbered. Come quietly."

Without smiling, the red pigment in The Painted Man's inhuman face spread in cruel mockery of a smile, rising almost to its equally scarlet hairline. *Something* hit me in the back, and I staggered, my sword slicing through one of the paper screens and a part of the metal railing as if it weren't there. The Painted Man moved quickly, leaping into the crowd—which as a unit found its feet. Each and every man, woman, and child in the group—who moments before had been laughing and dining and living their lives—went silent as the tomb. Only the wind spoke, and Ghen, who swore.

"I told you," the homunculus said, tapping its head with one red-tipped finger. "You don't know what we are."

CHAPTER 5

EYES LIKE STARS

HAVE YOU EVER SEEN a corpse? You'd be surprised how many people have not. I remember the first I saw: my grandmother, the Lady Fuchsia Bellgrove-Marlowe, when I was just a boy. Something happens to their eyes . . . It's indescribable. It's as if some fluid pressure slackens—whether in the eyelids or in the orbs themselves I cannot rightly say—and they cease to be eyes at all. I say this because the light in each eye of every living child of Earth tells us something of the mind behind it. It's a subtle thing, hard to quantify or even to describe. I met a strojeva once, a Durantine android serving as quartermaster on one of their ships. She had eyes that looked human—and indeed might have been grown from human stock. But I knew, knew with the metaphysical certainty of the devoutest priest, that her eyes were dead, and had always been. There was no light in them.

The eyes of that crowd on that porch above the tea house were like the eyes of that strojeva. Hollow. Glassy. Dead. And yet the faces . . . they were the faces of men. Women. Life and care had etched lines on their faces, weathered their skin. There were even a couple of children mixed among them to sell to me the lie that they were still living human beings. What they were in truth I did not then know.

I thumbed the trigger on my shield-belt and pivoted as the energy curtain collapsed around me. Olorin's sword thrummed in my hand, the strange matter rippling as it moved, the blade's cutting edge shifting with its direction of motion. Switch fell in behind me, and Ilex; each activated their own shields. "What are they?" I asked The Painted Man, who stood smiling—truly smiling now—amidst his thralls. "Your puppets? What have you done to them?"

The creature didn't answer. Another shot rang out, making me flinch.

One of the diners fell smoking with a fist-sized hole in its chest, and everything changed at once. Still utterly silent, the mob threw itself at us. There must have been fifty of them. Throwing her hood back, Ilex stepped past, drawing a heavy phase disruptor. She fired, the hiss of lightning fuzzing the air.

"Stop that ugly one!" Ghen's voice was raised above the crowd. "Oh-two, three! With me!" I saw his huge mass gesturing over the heads of the crowd, saw the violet shout of plasma, felt the heat of it even through my shield.

Then I had other problems, as two men hurled themselves at me. I lashed out, retreating into a lunge that caught one in the chest. The high-matter sword met no resistance, its edge as fine as hydrogen. Without slowing, I tugged the weapon sideways, cleaving effortlessly through the ribs and right arm in an arc that severed the head of the man beside it.

Neither of them bled. I slid forward, mindful of Switch at my back and the too-deadly weapon in my hand. I risked a look down.

"Holy Mother Earth protect us," I heard Switch swear. The first thing I realized—absurdly—was that I'd seen wrong. There was blood, but not nearly so much as there should have been. It dribbled out upon the wood planking, flowed out past . . . "It's a daimon," Switch said. I had to move, sidestepping another of the diners as she lurched toward me. But I had seen the metal in the flesh, the severed wires, the tubing. Something white spilled upon the floor, mingled with the blood like milk. They were machines now, and had not always been.

"Ghen!" I shouted, waving my sword. "The stairs!"

"On it, Radiance!"

Shots rained from above, brought down from the tower opposite. Ghen's snipers. Four of the daimons went down sparking, their flat eyes flashing in the light like the eyes of some night predator. Crim howled past, a high-energy laser in one hand, a long ceramic knife in the other. His kaftan fluttered in the wind, white and crimson. We were outnumbered at least five to one, more if you didn't count the three or four snipers Ghen had kept on the tower opposite. But we were armed, and the diners had nothing.

"Where's the homunculus?" Greenlaw shouted, ejecting a spent plasma cartridge from her burner.

I looked round. There was no sign of The Painted Man anywhere. Howling in frustration I cleaved forward through another of the daimons, slicing it clean through from shoulder to hip. It fell with a heavy thud, but the legs stumbled on a moment, trying to find the body. The arm still

attached to the head and torso reached out, as if guiding the legs. Switch
kicked the legs over and shot them. I reached down and drew my phase
disruptor with my free hand, checked the settings. Stun. Good enough. I
hadn't the time to sort it properly. I fired, catching one in the throat as it
lunged for Ilex. At once it seized up and slumped, black lines burning its
skin from within where wires seared into flesh. I must have scored a lucky
hit, for the next two stunner bolts seemed to have no effect on the machine daimons.

Switch seemed to hunch over his plasma burner, his posture as folded
in as his broad frame would allow. I felt for him, for the terror of the
moment.

"Machines," I swore. The reality would not process. How many times
had I heard stories of the Extrasolarians? How many times had I heard they
packed their artifice into the bodies of the men and women they took as
slaves to turn them into something less than human? I had not believed it
possible, and so had walked directly into a trap. Had The Painted Man
known what we were the entire time? Had Samir?

Samir.

Where had the plagiarius gone? I cast about. He was still cowering by
the table where I'd sat but moments before. Frowning, I shot him with my
stunner. If The Painted Man had escaped, Samir was better than nothing.

Ghen stood at the top of the stairs now with two of his legionnaires at
his back. The big centurion's rictus—part focus and part delight—was
visible even at a distance. They fought as Pallino had taught us, the way
true Imperial soldiers did: back-to-back-to-back in groups of three.

I saw a dense knot of the diners clustered about a prone figure on the
ground beside an overturned table. I holstered my stunner, deactivated
Olorin's sword a moment. The blade melted into smoke as the highmatter
decayed from liquid crystal to gas, vanishing into the air. I tugged my
heavy coat from me and tossed it aside.

"What the hell are you doing?" Switch asked, drawing Ilex's attention.
The homunculus cocked her head at me, cat's eyes wide.

I reactivated the sword. It glowed pale, like moonlight on naked steel.
"Just stay back."

"He's dead, Had!" Switch said, putting the dots together.

He wasn't. I knew he wasn't. "I said stay back!" I checked my shield
and bounded forward. In the weaker gravity, my every step carried me up
and forward faster than I could believe. For so long I had lived in the high
gravity of Emesh. Muscle had grown heavy on me, and I had grown

strong as old tree roots. I could see the body of my downed peltast lying prone beneath the swarming machine-puppets, could see the blood there. Seldom had I felt so righteous.

There are few things in the universe that highmatter cannot cut. Adamant, or the long-chain molecules of nanocarbon, or the energy curtains of high-class static fields. Or highmatter itself. Anywhere the atom-fine edge could find a chink—a gap between molecules—it could cut. Not stone, nor steel, nor ablative ceramic could slow a knight's highmatter sword. It never dulled or broke or wanted oiling. It could take any shape its maker asked of it, and built itself of the very air by some alchemical process I did not understand, transmuting the nuclei of common elements to something strange. Once, I'd cut the wing off a Tanager-class lighter as it took flight, severing carbon fiber and the metal endoskeleton all at a stroke.

Flesh was no object, nor whatever foul praxis the Extras had contrived. They fell like blades of grass, scattered like leaves. Five of them rose at my approach. Five of them fell in pieces. I went to one knee beside the body of our man, went to check his pulse. The flesh there had been *torn* as if by some wild thing . . . Switch was right. Our man was dead. He'd been Jaddian, one of Jinan's boys. Artur, I think. Or Arturo. I hadn't really known him.

A hand hard and cold as iron seized my leg, squeezing with superhuman strength. I gasped, struggled for my feet. Another hand seized me, dragged me back down. Twisting, I looked down, found a headless man dragging me down with the help of a woman's torso. She leered soullessly at me, like a statue. There was blood around her mouth and on her teeth. Looking at the dead soldier and the torn flesh there, I did not have to guess. Blood and the strange white fluid soaked my boots. The whole pile of dismembered people churned about my feet, slipping in the blood and fluid, clawing toward me. The woman's eyes were on me, fixed like stars, unblinking. I put out those eyes with a slash. Switch hurried over, firing his plasma burner. Violet flame turned to orange as the bodies caught, still moving toward me.

I managed to shake myself free and stumbled sideways into a table. My sword fell *through* it, notching the surface. It broke as I staggered into it, knocking me from my feet. I fell, and at once the headless man fell upon me, clawing, crawling its way up the length of me. I'd lost my sword in the confusion, buried in the debris of the table. A sudden, horrible memory swelled up in me of a night on distant Meidua, when the other boys had dragged me from the dinted box I called home in the loading depot behind the old desalination plant. Almost I could hear their laughter, their jeering, could feel their hands on me.

My own hands scrabbled through smashed china and splintered bits of table, blindly seeking the touch of silver and Jaddian leather. The headless man bore down on me, and turning I could see blue light flickering in the holes of its throat, and the flapping of tissue in the damaged trachea where the lungs still pumped. The sound it made was awful, a wet rattle like some damned thing. Sparks flared from the ends of wiring planted in parallel to vein and tendon, and blood dribbled down its front to soak what had been a white business shirt.

Was that silver I felt? Leather? The sword? I could not get a grip on it, could not close my fingers round the weapon. I brought a knee up hard between the machine man's legs, but found there was nothing there to bruise. Its hands found my throat and squeezed. Bassander was right. I wasn't a soldier at all. This mercenary game we'd played was just that. I would never see Valka again, or my Jinan. My vision blurred, and in the dimming of it I saw my father's face hovering where the headless man's should be, his eyes turned red from their true violet, his face white as the funerary masks of my forebears hanging about the palace door.

I didn't find my sword in time.

Light smashed over me, blooming back. The hands that crushed my voice vanished as the light returned, and I coughed and spat upon the ground, rolling out from under the headless body where it smoked from plasma fire.

"On your feet, Your Radiance!"

Ghen of Emesh stood over me, grinning a strained grin, his gray cloak spattered red and white and charred in places. He offered me a hand, and I stood, sagging against him. Switch and Ilex covered him—where was Crim? Bleary, I looked round, spotted the Jaddian hewing down one of the machines. Where was The Painted Man? Had it gone over the side of the rail? Breathing hard, I gasped, "You almost shot me." The plasma burner had chewed fist-sized holes halfway through the back of the headless man. Bits of metal and ceramic glistened in the wounds, melted and warped and dead.

"And don't you forget it!" Ghen said, clapping me on the back.

Ilex stooped and handed me my sword with a quiet nod. There was a wound high on her temple, just beneath the woody crown of her hairline. Her blood flowed thick as amber and just as slow, black as black. "Are you all right?" I asked, nodding at the wound.

She smiled, "No one's strangled me."

"Cute," I said, "I deserved that."

"I'll say," Switch hissed, eyes wide with concern. "The fuck were you thinking?"

"Not now!" I shouted, and pushed him aside. "Ilex, wave the shuttle. We need a pickup like . . . ten minutes ago. I have Samir by the table."

If she answered, I missed it. I drew my stunner fast as was possible and fired as one of the machines rose up behind Switch. There was still enough human tissue in the thing that it staggered under the impact, and rocked back. Ilex was fastest, training her phase disruptor and firing with an electric spat. The weapon was designed to fry the human nervous system, but it melted copper and fiber optic just as well. The daimon fell smoking, and I asked the question that had plagued me moments ago. "Where's the homunculus?"

Ilex twitched at the word, but I had no time for apologies. Ghen turned. "Stairs?"

"Shit."

We ran, cutting our way through a few more of the daimons. There seemed no end of them. There had not seemed so many when they were seated at the table. We passed another of our soldiers dead upon a table, his guts torn out beside him. I ground my teeth and made for the top of the stairs, where Crim and Greenlaw held our remaining peltasts together. A disruptor burst flew just past my shoulder, and turning I found that one of the machine-men had taken up our dead soldier's sidearm. Being shielded, I turned back and charged the machine. Ghen, Switch, the rest had shields, but the peltasts did not, and I would not lose another soldier. Sniper fire from Ghen's men rained down—it was hard to imagine that the local authorities had missed the struggle, but if what Samir had said was true, there were barely any authorities to speak of.

Another burst from the disruptor caught me in the hip and coruscated through my shield, turning the energy field radiant about me. That didn't slow me down, nor did the next shot, which would have fried my chest and shoulder. My sword sprang out, silver blue in the mist and vapor of the fight. I struck the arm, disarming it, carrying the arc through to cut the right leg from beneath it and to the ground in pieces. Another slash clove the head and torso and finished it. I turned back, and found myself face to face with a slack-jawed woman, a knife raised to take me in the back. Only the sniper had stopped her, had saved me. The first shot had stunned her, wrecking the shoulder whose arm held the short blade. The knife would have passed through my shield as if it weren't there—my attacker moved slow enough. It would have killed me and there would have been nothing I could do. The second shot knocked her down and away, and I hurried back to the stairs. There was great tumult in the room below, as of scrambling feet. People escaping the chaos, I imagined. More than two dozen of the machine-men yet stood upon the rooftop.

"Where's that shuttle?" I asked Ilex.

The frown in the dryad's voice was evident, though I saw only the back of her head and her long ears. "On its way, Marlowe."

"Ain't that fat son of a bitch over there?" Ghen asked, pointing.

I swore. I'd been so preoccupied guarding the stairs I'd lost track of the fact that when I'd moved us to regroup I'd put two dozen daimon-augmented human slaves between us and our consolation prize of a plagiarius. I wanted to scream. "I'll think of something," I said. "Just hold for the shuttle, that'll change things."

"You fucked this up," Greenlaw spat. "You really fucked this up."

I ignored her as Ghen's snipers peeled off another of our enemies. It crumpled jagged to the ground, crumpling as no human crumpled. Pieces of our fallen opponents yet crawled among the upturned tables and shattered china, undead.

"Down the stairs, Ghen," I said, "take two and check our escape. We may need to leave that way."

The big man clapped me on the shoulder. "Will do, Had." He waved his gun at two of our peltasts. "You lads, with me. Down the stairs now, double quick. You heard His Radiance."

They left in a rustling of gray cloaks, boots slamming against the treads.

He'd called me *Had*. I have not forgotten that. He almost never used my name. I didn't quite notice at the time, but later . . . looking back, it stood out clear and sharp in my memory as the edge of my own sword. I'd no time to dwell on it then, for the shooting began anew. Sniper fire rained down, shattering tea sets and splintering furniture.

"They're on their way!" Ilex called, meaning the shuttle, I assumed. That was something.

Beside her, Crim fired his laser, burning a thumb-sized hole in the chest of one of the machines—a woman little more than a girl. He swore darkly, and I imagined him shutting his eyes as he fired again. I held my ground then, waiting for the others to come close. Much as I hated to admit it, Greenlaw wasn't wrong. I'd gotten us into this situation. I was in command. The fault—for our failure to get the intelligence we needed and for the deaths of our two men—was mine.

"We need to secure Samir," Greenlaw said.

Switch glared at her. "Are you enlisting?" he shouted, firing again. His burner whirred in his hands, indicating he was out of plasma in his reservoir. His gun was sucking air, slowing his rate of fire.

Something changed without warning. It was as if whatever malevolence animated the daimons before us changed its mind and plan, for the score or so of hollow men before us froze, their glassy eyes watching, flickering as if with a blue light.

"I do not like this, boss," Crim said, voice strained. Was he injured? I'd not noticed in all the commotion. He swore in his strange Norman pidgin. "Where is Ghen?"

He shouldn't have opened his mouth, for the next instant all twenty of the machines—or so it seemed—sprinted straight at us. They crashed like a wave under the dominion of a mighty moon. We could not fire fast enough to stop them all. I stepped forward, sweeping one of them in half with Olorin's sword. The liquid metal hummed in my hand, delicate filaments of blue-white highmatter dripping and trailing to and from the blade, following micro-lines of force the way solar flares arc to and from their mother stars. I took the arm from another and retreated, backing down the stairs. One of the peltasts came with me, but none of the others. Four of the machine puppets pressed us back.

"With me!" I cried, voice lifted as high as all my speech training would allow. "Red Company, with me!" I do not know if they heard. Greenlaw was shouting about Samir, and the sound of gunfire and scuffle rose like the chaos of a concert and drowned out all order. My sword cut through wall and railing, leaving dark, cold gouges in wood and plaster and steel, littering the steps with pieces of our foes.

"We have to go back up, Lord!" the peltast said, quite rightly. "The others!"

I tripped over something behind me. Not a stair, I'd taken those carefully, retreating as I was. Something soft and uneven. Keeping my wits about me, I immediately deactivated the Jaddian sword I held so as not to maim myself in the fall. I did not yell, but tumbled over the thing there to land on the bamboo mat at the base of the stairs. That clumsiness cost the peltast her life. The remaining machines leaped at her without me to aid, and before I could regain my feet she lost hers, borne down by the weight of the two grown men. As I staggered up one sunk his teeth into her neck, tearing as they had the other on the portico above. To her credit, she unloaded her sidearm into the daimon's chest, but the simple bullets in her weapon were not enough to crack whatever metal or ceramic it was protected the daimon's internal organs. She fell beside the *body* that had tripped me on the stairs. One of the other peltasts I had sent with Ghen.

Ghen.

I threw myself at the two machines, sword flashing back to life in my fist. The legs came out from under one of them with little effort, my blow cleaving the balustrade in twain. I caught the bloody machine that had killed—I did not know her name—by the throat with my free hand. In Rustam's weak gravity, I lifted the man bodily from the floor with one hand. It pulled back a fist to clock me, and I dragged the atom-sharp sword through its chest, tossing the head and shoulders away.

The blood beaded on my hydrophobic clothing, ran off toward the floor. Chest heaving, I cast about madly, trying to remember what it was I was looking for, what I had just been thinking of. I couldn't see past all the *red,* but remembered after a few short breaths.

"Ghen!" I called. "Ghen, we need you!"

I found him then, sprawled in the tea house foyer. The two women who had escorted us up the stairs to meet The Painted Man lay broken around him, white blood and red pooling on the Tavrosi carpet. They'd been machines, too. Some titanic force had pulled their arms from their sockets and staved in their breasts. On Emesh, Ghen had been strong as an auroch; in Rustam's gravity, he must have been like Herakles.

Must have been . . .

A gaping hole smoked in his back, put there by a plasma burner. But whose? None of the machines had carried weapons, except those they took from us. Had someone taken Ghen's? And where was the other peltast? I had sent two with him.

The taste of copper filled my mouth, dry and thick and fuzzy. I sagged to my knees, and a chilly laugh echoed in that close and candle-lit space. I had heard it only minutes before, on the portico.

"Put up quite the fight, that one," The Painted Man said. "Ooh, the balls on him, tearing those poor girls to pieces, can you imagine?"

Stunned, I thought, falling onto my side. The creature must have come up behind me, gotten its stunner inside my shield curtain. I was lucky my own sword didn't fall on top of me—what an end that would have been.

I could still move my eyes, could just turn my head. Footsteps sounded on the floor behind me, and looking up I saw . . . I saw the second peltast I'd sent with Ghen looking down at me, a Jaddian woman with copper skin and short, dark hair. She looked not a little like Jinan. All at once I wasn't sure of the ground on which I stood. Or lay, as the case was. I had fallen out of the ordinary worlds and into some space other and mysterious. Why was the peltast just standing there? Why was she holding the stunner?

She made a hushing sound. "Don't try to move, you'll hurt yourself." When she smiled, I saw the glint of far, far too many teeth. I was hallucinating. I must be. The stunner had damaged my perceptions, perhaps. "Good of you to come down here after the big oaf. Makes my life just that much easier." The smile widened. The gray cloak and the combat armor beneath it vanished as if switched off. Holograph? Beneath it there was only a skintight suit, darker than black and studded with little silver lenses. The Jaddian bronze leeched out of her skin, and as I watched, astonished and unable to speak, the curve of hip and breast and slope of shoulder narrowed, slimming to something lean and less than human, a trim and sexless silhouette. The black hair grew at an alarming rate, turning steadily to crimson, and the whites of the eyes went dark as coals.

The Painted Man grinned at me, its lips blossoming to scarlet. "You're mine, lordship."

The second stunner blast—when it came—felt like nothing at all.

CHAPTER 6

THE ROAD TO VORGOSSOS

I SWAYED IN A soft dream, buffeted as by wind, floating on Lethe's gentle forgetting out of a province deeper than sleep. The current rocked me, and I dozed, limbs sluggish as they had been when I awakened from fugue aboard the *Pharaoh*. The light ahead dimmed, as if we'd passed under an overhang or into the mouth of some cave. Mouth. Remembered terror jolted me to wakefulness, and I lurched for my feet. I couldn't find them. My legs gave out and I fell back into the deep bowl of the seat.

"Why don't you get comfortable, Lord Marlowe? Since you can't walk," the drawling voice said, punctuating the deep quiet. "We've a ways to go yet."

What sounded like a tram rattled overhead, shaking the office—if office it was—in which I was undoubtedly a prisoner. A pair of couches stood in the corner opposite, along with a rack of shelves glittering with bottles and crystal storage chips neatly ordered. The walls hung thick with Eudoran theater masks, brightly painted and wildly emoting. The Painted Man itself reclined on the couch opposite, perhaps five yards away. It held a strange device in its too-long hands, an oblate silver disc bristling with buttons and switches. A cable ran from it in a tangle to a spot behind the homunculi's ear. As I watched, it pulled the wire free of its head with a mechanical clicking sound.

Saying nothing, I focused on my injuries instead. I felt fairly certain that I was only stunned. That meant functionality would return before feeling. I tried to lift one leg, to cross it over the other. I thought I felt a brief twitch, then . . . nothing. My arms moved, though—that was something. When at last I was sitting straight, I asked the obvious question. "What are you going to do with me?"

"With you?" The homunculus grinned evilly, setting its silver device—some sort of terminal, I didn't doubt—aside. "Nothing at all, dear boy. If by *with you* you mean *to you,* that is. You're no good to me dead." It reached into a bowl on the table beside its seat and produced a set of silver and bone-white rings, which it began fixing about its fingers. It eyed me over its long red nails, licked its teeth. "We might do something together."

Teeth clenched, I said, "I beg your pardon?"

The creature rolled its eyes, painted smile vanishing a moment. "My my, you Imperial palatines aren't all so serious, are you?" It swung lightly to its feet, pressing its hand against the wall for balance as it crossed the distance between us, passing a heavy metal trunk of the sort used to carry small-grade firearms straight from the manufactory. "You're very valuable, don't you know?" It reached down and ruffled my hair. "I'm sure the rest of that mercenary outfit of yours will pay to have you back . . . the way you were just throwing money around."

"Ransom, then?" I asked, massaging my legs. "That's your plan?"

It shrugged, turned away, its spindly arms akimbo. "For my trouble." It sank back into its seat. "You destroyed nearly all my SOMs. They're not cheap, you know."

"Your what?"

"My little helpers." It waggled its fingers. Reaching back with one hand, it rummaged in the folds of its couch before drawing something out. My sword. Olorin's sword. The homunculus poked a hole through the finger-loop in the rain guard and twirled it about its finger. "Now this is a pretty thing." The Painted Man tightened its fist around the grip, and silently the exotic matter of the blade sprang forth with its faint iridescence, reflecting moonlight that was not there. The homunculus reached up with one finger and gently pressed it against her single gleaming edge. The silver-blue metal rippled, shimmering, recoiling as if burned by the *inmane* creature's touch. The Painted Man's huge black eyes widened, and it drew its finger back. Briefly I saw the blood incarnadine against skin like aged china. "Where did you get a thing like this?"

I saw no reason to lie. "It was a gift, from one of the Maeskoloi of Jadd." What Sir Olorin Milta might say about a blood-born homunculus touching so sacred an object to his order as a sword I did not like to think. Nothing good.

The Painted Man spat and—turning off the weapon—cast it aside. It landed on the other couch. Watching it, I leaned forward in my seat. Beside my chair a small table stood, displaying an assortment of what I took at first to be art: blobs of metal or of stone pitted and melted. Meteors. I kept trying to move my legs. The numbness had transitioned from no feeling to a red tingling.

"What happened to my friends?"

The Painted Man propped its head on one fist. It didn't speak at once, but the red shape of its mouth grew, spreading across its face, lips turning white in a tattooed imitation of teeth. "Dead."

I sat a little straighter, tried to stand. I felt my legs spasm, but they didn't move. "You're lying." It was all I could do not to hurl one of the meteors at the beast.

The homunculi's red smile retreated from its face entirely. It shrugged. "I've no idea. You did abandon them in not the best of circumstances."

"I didn't abandon them!" Again I tried to stand.

"And yet here you are!" The creature laughed full in my face. "Some friend you turned out to be." It leaned back against its couch and with a languid motion drew its stunner from some fold of the loose robe it wore. The Painted Man admired its weapon a moment. It was of a design strange to me: black and geometric and slim, with a looping handle more like unto the iron knuckles of lowlife thugs than the mythic praxis of the Extrasolarians, those technocrats of the Dark. It set the thing aside with a deliberate gesture, its threat clear.

"They're not dead," I said.

"Keep telling yourself that," it replied, "but that big bastard certainly is." It tilted its head back as if basking in the glow of some music only it could hear. To my horror, the crimson hair retreated into the creature's scalp, the shoulders broadened, arms thickened, the bones of cheek and jaw grew more robust. How it did such a thing I could not guess, but even before the ink flooded its pale skin and turned Emeshi brown I knew what it was doing.

I wanted to scream. To break something.

Ghen's face stared at me from where The Painted Man had sat. It wasn't quite right: the constant stubble was missing, and the notch in the old myrmidon's nose. But the damned grin was the same, rueful and rude at once, coarse as the man himself. "Too bad you weren't faster, eh boss?"

The voice wasn't quite right, but it lodged in my heart and tore. I ground my teeth. "One more word, *mutant*, and you'll wish your masters never pulled you out of whatever *tube* you crawled out of."

Ghen's laugh—and not Ghen's laugh at all—filled the office. I had to close my eyes not to see my friend's laughing face, but when I did I saw his dead one instead, and the smoking hole in his back. Still in Ghen's voice, the monster said, "I'd love to see you try it." An involuntary smile pulled across my face, and I snorted. My knee twitched. The legs began to ache. I tightened my hands into fists until they went numb as my legs. When I didn't speak, the homunculus grinned, and Ghen's face shrank and melted away back into the likeness of The Painted Man, pale as a Cielcin, as Death herself. "That's what I thought."

"What sort of name is The Painted Man?" I asked, slashing across the beast's amused superiority.

The creature hissed loudly, baring its too many teeth. "Not a name, little man." It ran hands back again through its shaggy red mane.

"But what are you?"

"Homunculus," it said, pronouncing each syllable like a word. "The same as you."

I bit off the smallest smile I could manage. "We're not the same."

"Aren't we?" The total black of its eyes resolved, whites blossoming, the iris emerging as if from a deep gloom. My eyes. "Tell me, little man, which tube did you crawl out of, eh?" As it spoke its voice shifted to a pitch-perfect mockery of my own, the Delian nobile's accent—like the villain in so many bad Eudoran operas—dripping with every dram of my disdain.

We were not the same. Whatever my genetic augmentations, they were within the limits prescribed by the Chantry and Imperial law. None of the gene complexes that elevated me above common humanity were imported from other species. I was not part tree like Ilex, nor the product of anything so clearly artificial as this *creature*. I could not change my face, could not breathe underwater as the undines of Mare Aeternus could. Nor had I received any medical enhancements after my birth. Some homunculi did not even have free will, were born instead with crippled minds and bred to service. Whose hand had wrought The Painted Man or to what purpose I cannot say, but they had not meant to make a traditional human being. That was the heart of the difference between us. The magi who crafted my embryo for the tanks so long ago meant to create an exemplar of the human form.

The Painted Man was a mockery. A monster.

I waited for its face to change, but it never did. It only watched me with my own eyes.

"You're from Vorgossos, aren't you?" I cannot say how I knew it, but knew as the words escaped me that I was right. It blinked, posture hardening to alertness, and when its eyes opened they were black again. Blink. Violet. Blink. Black. I sat a little straighter, knee shifting a little of its own volition. "No . . . you *escaped* from there, didn't you?"

It was quiet for a moment, nothing but the rattling of the tramway above us and the shifting of light through the curtained windows. "You don't know a damned thing."

"True," I said, rocking back, curling my toes within the security of my boots. "But that's not something you'd say if I weren't right. What were you? Someone's pet?" The Painted Man took up its stunner and brandished it at me, grunting low in his throat and deeper than that thin chest should allow. It stood. I shielded my face. "I was serious, you know. I mean to find Vorgossos."

The Painted Man did not lower its stunner. But it did not speak or mock me.

"When you've sold me to my people, sell them the road to Vorgossos."

"Were you not listening?" the creature said. "I do not know where it is."

"You must know something," I said coldly. "Put us on the path. We'll *pay* for it." It was all I could do not to choke on the words. I could still hear Ghen's laughter echoing in that low-ceilinged space, and if Switch and the others were dead . . . My eyes flickered to the displayed meteors, to the theater masks on the walls, the neat display of bottles and storage chips in one corner. "Please."

At that small courtesy, the homunculi's mouth widened to its full and impossible extent, revealing easily one hundred little teeth in its head. It sat back down, hand going to the silver tablet it had wired into its skull not long before. "Put you on the path," it repeated, and laughed. "You're one of *them,* aren't you? The pilgrims?"

"I'm sorry?" I said, shutting my eyes. I felt suddenly motion sick, like someone not at ease on the water. "Pilgrims?"

"You Imperial palatines were the worst. You came seeking immortality. Youth. To change your sex. Whatever your Imperium would not allow, the Undying would give you. For a price. The bonecutters would make *anything* for you. Anyone. Soldiers. Slaves. Sex objects." Its tongue flitted obscenely past its thicket of white fangs.

"Which were you?" I demanded, flippant. I had to keep it talking. I could feel my legs returning to me, my palatine's overclocked nervous system restoring itself faster than a normal man's. And I'd noticed something about the office—perhaps you've noticed it, too? Noticed it was no office at all.

The Painted Man's obscene smile faltered a moment—all its art and artifice fell away, leaving a shrunken, subhuman *thing* in fine robes before me. "I am as you see me. An idea. Any idea."

"That thing you do," I said, gesturing at the creature. I flexed my calves. "Your . . . changing. Is it holography? Some daimon?"

"I am a Painted Man," it said. "I am whatever I need to be."

A skin-changer.

"There are more of you, then?" I asked.

The homunculus did not answer. It drifted to the window beside its couch, and peered out around the curtain. I could see nothing. Whatever the answer was, yes or no, it did not matter. Wordless, The Painted Man unspooled the cable from its terminal and clicked the jack back into its skull behind one ear.

Here was a creature of the most unfortunate kind. Unlike Ilex, who was a homunculus as well but as free of will as any palatine, this Painted Man had been tailored body and soul, its mind shaped by its makers to serve their purposes. What that use was—as assassin or plaything, spy or idle fancy—I dared not guess. It had rebelled, but I sensed it was still acting out the patterns other men had put in it, still living out a life of criminality and deceit.

Surely it had been sequenced by some vile magus in the very pits of Vorgossos, wearing the faces of others because its own was abhorrent. Almost I could pity it, but for the fact it had escaped and made for itself a mean, vile heaven of the hell of its life. Master though it was of its own destiny, the world had turned it cruel, or perhaps cruelty had been its nature. Evolution would not have shaped a beast with such teeth for kindness, and Evolution is blind. Men are not. Those teeth then and the vileness of its shape were either a cruel confirmation of purpose or a maleficent jape, like poisoning the thorns on a rose.

"What a farce," I said to no one in particular, shifting my heels up against the base of my chair. I could still not quite feel them, but the mind commanded the body now, and instantly it obeyed. Thank the High College and whoever sequenced my superior nervous system when I was but an embryo. I recovered fast. "You remind me of the monster in Shelley's *Frankenstein*," I said, referring to a novel in the Classical English Gibson had suggested to me long ago. "A reminder that mankind's reach exceeds her grasp."

The homunculus jerked its attention onto me. "What?"

"It's a story about a scholiast who creates a homunculus. This was before there were homunculi in truth. I think it was before we understood genetics, before Apollo gave us the Moon." I reached out a hand and grabbed one of the larger meteors and tested it. It might have massed thirty-five kilos, so dense it was. The *inmane* told me to put it down, so I only turned it to give myself a better look. "The scholiast makes his homunculus from the bodies of the dead, sewing their parts together. He imagines—as all artists must—that his work will be a masterpiece, more beautiful than nature. Quite like a palatine, I suppose." I smiled, allowed myself a moment to let the insult sink in. "Only it isn't. His skill was not up to the task. He made a monster. The scholiast spurned his creation out of loathing and fled, and the monster fled itself. And here you are."

"You're projecting, palatine," The Painted Man said, fiddling with the wired connection behind its ear. The tramway rattled above our head, and I felt the sensation of seasickness again. "Like I said, you're only as human as I am, and we are both very far from home."

It was my turn at last to grin. "You have me there. We are both uncommon." Hesitantly, I rolled my ankles inside my boots. I would have only one shot at this. Only one. "But there is a difference between us two, I think." The creature only cocked red eyebrows at me and for once did not speak. I quoted, changing a couple of the words, "Satan had his companions, fellow *devils*, to admire and encourage him, but *you* are solitary and abhorred."

"Are you always like this?" The Painted Man sneered.

"Melodramatic? Oh yes," I said with my customary lopsided grin. "Ask anyone who knows me." At this I seized the meteor on the table beside me, sinking fingers into the bubbled holes on its iridium surface. On Emesh, my strength would not have availed me, but here on Rustam, it weighed less than two-thirds what it might, and the massy stone lifted easily. Rocking to my feet, unsteady, I threw the weighty thing straight at The Painted Man's face before it could stun me. The creature yelped and fell back onto the couch, its fingers prisoned in the loops of the stunner handle, its body wrapped in its terminal cord.

Lurching to my feet, I became suddenly aware of the way the office *rocked*. It moved, slewing slightly as on a short chain. The homunculus made a choking sound, and I said, "Stupid of you not to keep me stunned, really. But I suppose you wanted a gloat." I picked up the munitions chest that stood on the floor between us; it wouldn't open. "I can understand that, but you weren't very careful. I might have been content to sit out my rescue if I didn't know where I was, but when I woke you said 'we've a ways to go yet,' meaning we're in transit to whatever miserable little hole it is you call home. This is a private cable car." I nodded at the curtained windows.

Hefting the heavy chest as the executioner does his sword, I had a brief impression of the homunculus. It had fallen to the floor, its face a bloody mess, one long hand clamped over the ruin of its mouth. I might then have truly pitied it, but for the back of that hand. A tattoo had formed there, the image of a grinning mouth. Its face bubbled and pitted, flowing through a series of impressions. It did not speak, perhaps it could not. It raised its stunner to shoot me. I stomped on its hand as a man would a snake. "You shouldn't have taken Ghen's face," I said, and slammed the crate down on the homunculi's own face with all the force I could muster.

There was ink in the blood as it soaked the fine carpet, so many colors joined together they were only black. I kept the box atop the body—I did not want to see what remained of the face. Hurriedly, glad to be alone for now but certain that this office pod was traveling somewhere I did not want to be, I retrieved Olorin's sword and found my shield-belt on the corner shelves. Unwilling to leave empty-handed, I returned to the body. Regret is stronger than fury, and is comparably immortal. I bit my lip as I knelt by the homunculi's corpse and fished the wire out of its head. I tucked the silver terminal disc into a sabretache on the back of my belt and—lacking a stunner—took its for my own. Then I turned and went to the door.

It would not open, and so I took up my sword and cut my way out. The door tumbled onto a crowded street thirty feet below. Air rushed in and sound. I heard people gasp and shout, but no one screamed. At least I had not crushed anyone. After the gloom of The Painted Man's mobile office, the orange daylight was striking. We passed by at the level of advertisements: great billboards—painted and electronic—depicting groundcar and alcohol sales. A smiling woman, red-haired, naked but for a sarong about her generous hips, hawked genetic enhancements for as low as ten thousand marks. In the lesser gravity, I might be strong enough to leap the three or so meters to the scaffolding about the base of that massive image. I stood in the mouth of the doorway for a long moment, one hand on either side of the frame. "Come on, Marlowe," I whispered. "Come on." Then I leaped out of that dismal office pod and into the free and vaporous air.

CHAPTER 7

THINGS UNSEEN, THINGS REMEMBERED

WITHOUT A TERMINAL, I had no way of contacting my fleet. I had no way to home in on my shuttle. I had no map of this impossible labyrinth they called a city. Where had I lost my terminal?

"It was in your coat, Marlowe, you damn fool," I muttered, shoving my hands in my pockets and hunching against the inconstant wind. "And now your coat's on a balcony uptown surrounded by Earth only knows how many dead daimons." I was not having my best day. The adrenaline high of my brief battle with The Painted Man had worn off and—as I say—regret is immortal. At least I had some money. I could find a holography booth and wave the fleet above.

I must have cut a strange figure, dressed in a black tunic-jacket of semi-military cut, with high boots and a high collar and the shield-belt with its sabretache and the Jaddian sword hilt bouncing against my thigh with every odd step. Despite having been so long removed from Delos and my home, I never had quite shaken my penchant for black clothing.

"And how well did that work out?" said the part of me that spoke in my father's voice.

My knee twinged from where I'd banged it against the scaffolding jumping out of The Painted Man's mobile office pod, and with the stunner numbness fading it ached as I walked. People kept looking at me, eyes wide before they averted their gazes. After a mother moved her children across the street to get away from me, I turned up a side alley and tried to get a look at myself in the dark reflections of a low shuttle that served as the foundation for a large, prefabricated structure made of interlocked storage units like a tesselated pile of old crates. I couldn't see a thing, just a dark blur.

There was a rain barrel open not far on, filling where a gutter dripped down from on high. Standing over it I saw the blood on my face, turned black by the orange light of afternoon. It wasn't mine. I cannot say how long I stood there, hunched over the water. Hardly did I recognize the young man peering out at me. When did I get so tired? Time had not yet traced her delicate channels on my face, nor frosted my hair, but something lurked behind my eyes: something aged and thin as old parchment. As if a painting of Hadrian Marlowe watched me out of the rain barrel, and not the man himself.

"Pull yourself together, man," I breathed, cupping water in my hands. I splashed my face and neck and waited. When the water quieted, it was still a pale shadow of myself that loomed out of the darkness, not the image of myself I held in my mind, young and wryly smiling. "You're alive. You're alive." My hair defied my attempts to fix it, even damp. I wished I wouldn't look at myself like that. With Gilliam's eyes peering out from behind my own. And Uvanari's, and Bordelon's, and The Painted Man's. Other eyes there were, staring out of mine—back at mine.

Grief is deep water. Gibson's words sounded in my head, and almost it felt he was at my shoulder. The scholiasts' aphorism was an injunction, a reminder that the extremes of emotion were destructive by their nature.

I can swim, I thought, flippant.

No one can swim, Gibson said. Had said. *The rightly tuned mind does not deny its emotions, but floats with them. It accepts what it feels and so incorporates that feeling to itself. Thus the mind is not subject, but rules itself.*

I had been perhaps eight when he told me that.

It was after my grandmother had died. Against my father's orders my brother Crispin and I had stolen into the porphyry chamber where her body lay for its customary three days after the surgeons had removed her brain and heart and eyes, before the flesh was taken to the crematorium. Sir Roban had been on vigil, and tried to shoo us out, but I had stayed. A tenebrous cloth—blacker than space—lay across her eyes, those same eyes I would carry in their canopic jar for the funeral procession. I had wanted to *see,* to know that my grandmother was gone.

Gibson had found us. Crispin was too young truly to be much affected or to remember, but the leonine old scholiast had taken me aside. "It's all right to be sad," he said in that serious way of his; all eyebrows. "It's all right to be angry or sick or scared, or whatever it is you're feeling. But you can't let it crush you, all right?" I'd nodded then, and rubbed the tears from my eyes. "Sad is like a big ocean, and you can't breathe deep down. You can float on it, you can swim a little, but be careful. Grief is drowning. Grief is deep water. Say it." The way he'd said *say it* told me it was a lesson, another of his incantations for trying times and hard thoughts.

I knew I was *not* going to be a useless child wailing in the corner, smashed to pieces by his first brush with death. Funny thing about lessons: the idiot student thinks when he is given a little fact that he owns it—that two and two is always four no matter the circumstance. Just as it was not true for Orwell, it is not true for anyone. True lessons require not only knowing, but that the student practices his knowledge again and again. Thus knowledge becomes us, and we become more than the animal and the machine. That is why the best teachers are students always, and the best students are never fully educated.

I had forgotten Gibson's lesson for a moment, but stood a little straighter, shouldering as a pack my grief, my regret and self-loathing. I carry Gibson with me even still, and often it is with his eyes that I see myself, and through them that I have come to know who and what I am.

"And the others?" I asked. "They all made it back?"

Comms latency with high orbit was less than a second, and Jinan's voice crackled over the line almost instantly. "Yes, they are all right. Switch, Crim, Ilex, the soldiers . . . even Greenlaw."

"Shame about that last one, eh?" I tried to laugh, but the sound wouldn't come. The relief was almost too much. Jinan laughed, and to my shame I crushed that sound, asking, "Did you get Ghen's body?"

"No," she said, and I could see her shake her head in my mind's eye. Far better it was than the grimy view through the glass of the telecomms booth. I picked at a peeling sticker with the number for the Free Traders Union's quantum telegraph service printed on it, available to anyone with a membership number.

It took me a moment to respond, to compose myself. "We'll have to do . . . something. He's a long way from home." I didn't know if he had any family. He'd never spoken of them, and I'd not thought to ask.

Jinan's words came slow, heavy with their own weight. "I'm just glad you're all right. When they came back without you . . ."

"I'm all right, my captain," I said soothingly, hunching against the wall of the booth. "I'm a little banged up but it's nothing Okoyo or one of the junior medics can't patch up." It was all I could do to force a laugh into my voice. "I got the one that got Ghen, though. The Painted Man."

"I'm heading down now, you just stay put now, *mia qal*." I'd told her where I was already.

A weary nod was all I could manage for a moment, then realizing it wasn't helpful with no video link I added, "Will do," and closed the line. I stood in the booth in silence for a moment, until an angry man in a leather coat made a rude gesture and motioned for me to clear out. After the day I'd had, I considered stunning him, but settled for a glare instead.

A little cafe crouched beneath the landing peds of an old freighter, built to fill the gap between earth and hull. Like much of the ground-level building in Arslan, it looked slapped together, pressed up into that gap like insulation foam, expanding into every joint beneath the ship.

No one looked at me as I entered and seated myself by the windows in the storefront. I must have sufficiently fixed my appearance. I sank into the plastic armchair without a word, hoping to go on unnoticed until Jinan found me.

Jinan.

This was not the first time she'd had to pull me out of a bad place—even if it was the last, though I did not then know it. She had come for me on Pharos, after I'd let Marius Whent get the best of me. She'd pulled me out of Whent's compound alone and through the capital city with the warlord's reavers on our tail. We'd each saved the other's life a dozen times by the end of that awful month. No plan, no backup, no weapons but my sword, which I'd taken off Whent's desk as we made our escape. We'd been hired to kill the admiral, to help the rebels who supported Imperial annexation. The campaign had taken another three months, culminating in Bordelon's death and Whent's surrender. Its success had marked the high point of the Red Company's short career. Bassander had resented it. It took away from our central quest, though we had strengthened the Empire's hold on the Veil of Marinus and better prepared our position against the Cielcin.

And Jinan . . .

She hadn't said anything that first time, alone in the sweating dark after our victory on Pharos, after Whent's surrender. Only held me. Hands. Mouths. The iron scent of her skin thick in the close air. I do not know if it was love for her at first, as it was not for me. Relief, yes, and the animal joy of life having laughed in the face of Death and her many-fingered hands. The hunger of that life for life and the cellular ecstasy of that oldest of biological imperatives: Create. Create. Create. And through that the acute awareness of the self not as spirit, but as an embodied thing, complete not in itself—as no man is—but by its sharing in the spirit and body of another.

"Messer, if you are going to sit there, you must order."

"I'm sorry?" I looked up into the face of a smiling young woman in a tidy uniform. "Oh! I'm sorry!" Promptly I ordered a bowl of noodles—the first thing I saw on the menu printed beneath the glass of the tabletop—and the woman went away.

Satan had his companions, fellow devils . . . I had told The Painted Man. My hand went to the shiny wheal of scar about my left thumb where my old signet ring had burned in cryonic fugue. Fellow devils, indeed. I'd paid homage to the Marlowe devil in the logo of my Meidua Red Company: the devil's trident piercing a five-pointed star. My devils.

The noodles swam in some light and salty broth with bits of some fishy protein and green onions. Simple. Clean. I ate quietly, fishing mouthfuls from the clay bowl with a flat-bottomed spoon. No thoughts came to me, who thought too much and too often. I could not escape the image of the machine-woman—the SOM, or so The Painted Man had called it—who had nearly stabbed me in the back during the fight at the tea house. She would have stabbed me just where Ghen was shot. Between the shoulders, just right of center. There is a reason that Many-Fingered Death is depicted in stygian robes. She is our shadow, ever at our back, ever at our feet.

She is never far.

Food helps.

Fish.

I had eaten a great deal of fish in Borosevo, on Emesh. In the streets. I had stolen fish from guild warehouses with Cat and off the back of float palettes and freezer carts. Cat was dead, too. Dead not because of my efforts, like so many others, but despite them. Sometimes, it is only nature who is cruel, not mankind.

The dinner hour came and went, and patrons filtered in and out and past me. The waitress, too, came and went and was increasingly frustrated that I did not leave. She bore it well, as so many of that unloved profession must, and kept my water cup filled. Once, I would have had wine and in great amounts after a day such as mine, but I had not the money for it; had only a couple dozen kaspums left in a pouch of my belt by mistake. I had not thought to need money for the meeting with The Painted Man.

"You look awful, love."

I shook myself awake—when had I dozed off? And why had the waitress not come to yell at me? Jinan was smiling at me from across the table, dressed in her Red Company uniform and wearing . . . "Is that my coat?" I asked, massaging my temple.

"And a good evening to you, too," she huffed, but her smile did not waver. "Switch brought it back from that disaster at the tea house."

"I'm sorry," I said. Then thinking of the tea house, I added, "Did they get Samir?"

Jinan propped herself up on one fist, eyes never leaving my face. "The plagiarius? No. They had to leave in a hurry." I could sense that she wanted to say more, about the machines—the SOMs—that had attacked us. About Ghen. She didn't. I can only assume there was something on my face that stopped her, some shadow of exhaustion or pain. Or of both. "Are you all right?"

A weak laugh ran out my nose, and I rocked forward in the little seat, cradling my head a moment in my hands. I worked stiff fingers through my tangled hair and, inhaling sharply, said, "I will be." I could feel the frayed gaps in my smile, though.

"How did you escape?" she asked. "Switch said you were taken." She pawed at the blue ribbon in her heavy braid, hard fingers straightening the bright silk against the dark strands.

"I was," I said. "I did. I . . . I killed him. It. Whatever it was. The Painted Man, I mean. The homunculus meant to ransom me to the fleet, or so it claimed."

Jinan took my hand where I'd left it on the table. Warmth bled into me from her. She smiled, warm and constant as a main sequence sun. *"Nómiza ut ió uqadat ti,"* she said in her native tongue. *"Avrae trasformato hadih poli hawala an eprepe."* She'd meant it as a joke, but the thought of Jinan taking the city apart to find me was not amusing at all, it was . . . precious. Indescribably so.

"I know," I said in Jaddian. "I would have done the same."

She ran her thumb along the back of my hand, tightening her grip before she broke away, reaching across to hold that hand to my cheek. The rest, the obvious, did not need saying, but she said it. *"Ti ahba."*

"I love you, too," I replied, then, "Can I have my coat back, please?"

Jinan's black eyes widened. "What? You were not letting me keep it? Some gallant knight of the Empire you are!"

Standing, I left a five-kaspum note on the table—it was far more than the noodles were worth—and said, "I'm not a knight, dear captain."

"Clearly not!" she said, pretending outrage.

I let her keep the coat.

The growing night was cold, and the days short on Rustam, as days so often are. And I was of Delos, and used to colder climes than she, who hailed from hot and arid Ubar worlds and worlds away. See us as we go, arm in arm, she walking tight beside me, my arm about her slender waist. We might have been two lovers returning from the opera—were it not that we were armed. You might think nothing of us at all. Arslan was, after all, a place for hard people in harder times. Two drunks perhaps, or two sailors recently out of freeze. Yet when I look back upon that moment, I can point to but few moments that are as shining and simple as that warm and gentle quiet we shared . . . or the small pressure of her hand on my arm, or the way I nestled against her shoulder in the back of our shuttle and for a moment forgot that my friend was dead.

But the ugliness of the world does not fade, and fear and grief are not made less by time. We are only made stronger. We can only float together on their tides, as otters do, hand in hand.

Before it ends.

Before it has to end.

CHAPTER 8

THE COUNCIL OF CAPTAINS

"AND WE'VE NOTHING TO show for it!" Bassander practically screamed, leaning over the head of the long conference table. "Nothing! Unless you count four dead men." The captain-who-would-be-king alone was on his feet. The others—the collected captains and their first officers of our little fleet and the survivors of the Rustam mission—sat about the long ellipse of the *Pharaoh*'s conference table. Eleven in all.

The table itself was an artifact of Emil Bordelon's that even Bassander— for all his spartan tendencies—could not bear to have removed. The surface was a two-inch slab of Mandari-printed marble, sable but for the veins that like white smoke suffused it, inlaid with a holography suite done in hair-fine wire. It must have weighed a ton. It certainly cost a fortune, when one accounted for the dragon-clawed mahogany legs. The old commodore's tastes had tended to the gaudy, but here at least he had struck true.

"So we are worse off than when we arrived?" asked Alessandro Hanas, Jinan's swart, bearded second-in-command. "This is a disaster."

Bassander waved a hand at the lieutenant, underscoring what the Jaddian had said. His jaw worked as he swept his attention over Crim, over Ilex, Switch, and myself. I sat directly opposite him, at the far end of the ellipse, not speaking. "If you'd all managed to come away with the fat man at least we might have had something!" He directed these words at Switch, of all people.

"You weren't there," my friend and lictor said. "All due respect, Captain Lin, but you'd have gotten out of there as fast as you could, too. Those things . . . they weren't human."

"Not anymore," Ilex said. "They'd been hollowed out. The Painted Man was controlling them. We walked into a trap. He knew we were working for your Legions, or guessed at any rate. The whole place was filled with those machines." The dryad's long face turned inward at that, and she looked down at the table, green skin flushing black.

"SOMs," Valka said, speaking for the first time in half an hour's bickering. Her Tavrosi accent had a way of cutting across other speech. All eyes turned to her except mine. I had heard the term from The Painted Man, and at any rate was not surprised that Valka knew it, who knew so much about everything. "Surrogate Operating Medium. Media. They are human, or they were."

"Were?" Bassander asked.

Valka's bright-edged voice cut the air like fruit. "He would not ask that question, he who saw the things."

Switch shuddered. "You've seen them, doctor?"

"I've been round," she said, baring white teeth. "And, speaking as scientific advisor, 'twas wise of you to retreat when you did." Valka looked down, those sun-bright eyes hidden behind her short fall of dark hair. "Nasty things, SOMs."

"They didn't die when we shot them, Bassander," Greenlaw said, clenching her jaw.

"Well, the damage is done," said Bassander Lin, sagging into his seat like the chief of a pride of lions after a starving night. "We've no choice, people." His eyes narrowed as he took in the others gathered round the table. "We have our orders: we return to the 437th, regroup with the fleet and the war effort."

Jinan stopped fiddling with her braid, brows contracting. "We never left the war effort, Lin. What is this?"

"First Strategos Hauptmann is mustering his forces at Coritani. We received a general order to return."

"What?" I said, unable to stop myself.

"I did not sign up with this company to fight in pitched battle," said Otavia Corvo, the third and last of our three captains, who had been uncharacteristically quiet until then. "The *Mistral* is not equipped for it, and I am not risking my men."

I think it was Otavia of whom the ancient Herodotus spoke when he wrote of the Amazons. Whether by design or by incident of nature, she stood nearly seven feet high. High as a palatine. Even sitting, she radiated the threat of the coiled serpent, arms crossed, broad shoulders hunched, betraying the corded muscle that hid beneath the crimson uniform. She was less dark than her ebon-skinned second-in-command, with long golden hair that tangled and defied the ship's gravity and played about her face like mane. She alone of our captains was the true-blooded mercenary, and knew no oath to Jadd or to the Solar Throne. She was free and fierce, and her word was final.

Bassander felt it, too, for he changed tactics, saying, "We found nothing on Rustam. We have nothing. And how long before the provincial government links these . . . SOMs to us?"

"A hundred years at least," Crim said, chewing another of his gels. He extended the bag to Ilex, who sat beside him. "This system's a damn mess. Machines or no machines, Commodore, the Imperial Chantry doesn't have the resources here for an Inquisition. They'll be too busy on damage control to be worrying about who it was the beasts were fighting."

Jinan's first officer, the square-faced, bearded Lieutenant Hanas held up a finger. "The city must be surveilled."

"It is," said reedy Bastien Durand, Otavia's second. He had the same juddering, strange accent as our Doctor Okoyo—they shared a homeworld—and a scholarly affect. He was the sort one could easily imagine as scholiast back in the old Imperium. In truth, he reminded me in no small part of Tor Alcuin, my father's principal advisor back home. "But you Imperial types give the review of that footage over to human beings, and human beings are not so good at sifting through thousands of cameras and tens of thousands of hours of footage to find a pattern."

"Besides," Valka put in, glancing briefly at me, "we've no way of knowing if The Painted Man hadn't altered the cameras near to himself. He must have . . . have had the technology."

An image of the homunculus seated on its couch with the terminal wired into its head swam up behind my eyes. I shifted my sabretache in my lap, feeling the weight of the strange device.

I was about to pull it out when Bassander plowed ahead. "Then we should be able to leave the system unmolested. This discussion is academic."

"Leave the system?" Otavia said. "Just like that? You're . . . running home?"

Bassander leaned forward and tapped the tabletop, triggering the holography suite. "I'm not running anywhere," he said, looking directly at me. "I have a duty as a soldier of the Empire to return to the front, to my commander."

"Then you go alone," Otavia said, too sharply, too proudly, thrusting out her chin.

"Not alone!" Jinan said, for she too was a soldier.

The Norman Amazon shook her head. "My people will not go with you."

Bassander stood so quickly I thought he might knock his chair over, hands planted flat on the tabletop. "You have a contract."

"Which does not extend to the sacrifice of my ship and all my people in your fool crusade!" Not to be outdone, Otavia stood as well, and for her the effect was far greater. Bassander was only patrician, and next to Otavia's freak height he seemed small indeed. I almost pitied Lieutenant Greenlaw, who sat between them, staring fixedly down at her hands.

"Fool crusade?" Bassander echoed. "Fool crusade! What exactly is it that you think we've been up to since your lot signed on?"

"Fighting to end the damned war! Here. In Norma," Otavia Corvo replied, shaking her head so that the knot of flyaway golden hair at the back of her head drifted as in freefall. "It's our worlds that are burning, captain, not yours. That's what Hadrian sold me. Peace!" I shut my eyes a long moment. I'd been starting to wonder when my name would be dragged into this.

"*Hadrian,*" Bassander said, emphasizing the use of my first name, "does not run this company. I do." There it was, the crux of Bassander's complex. I said nothing, hand on the terminal in my sabretache.

This is not your moment, the part of me that thought in Gibson's voice admonished.

"You want to talk of peace, Corvo?" Bassander asked. "Peace? We finished compiling the data from the last telegraph transmittal we received from my fleet along with Strategos Hauptmann's orders. Do you know what it said?" The Commodore's eyes fixed sharp and bright as lasers on Captain Corvo's face, and a murmur went through the room as Lin paused for breath. I sat a little straighter, glanced sidelong to Jinan—who did not see me—and to Valka, who shook her head. I knew we'd received another entangled burst shortly after arriving in Rustam system, and guessed the news could not be good. "We engaged the Cielcin at Tyras. Let me share with you the details," he said, and counted on his fingers. "It wasn't like it was *here*. We lost the planet completely. House Jurnau. The primary cities. The orbital factories. Seven million people, captain. Seven million. Now, say of me what you will, but I tend not to sleep well at night knowing that it happened, and that it's happened *again* while we're dancing about the ass end of the universe chasing fairy stories because my commander saw fit to countenance the outlandish notions of this palatine lunatic!"

"Lunatic?" Sensing that things would only get worse, Jinan stood, coming to my defense. "I'm thinking that is quite enough," she said, and her dark eyes were hard as glass. It was easy, sometimes, to forget that Jinan was nearly twice my living age—her breeding was such that she looked no more than thirty—but it appeared from time to time: the reminder that she had been a soldier before I was born. "We can discuss what will become of our Norman friends when we return to the fleet—" Otavia showed signs of interrupting, but Jinan finished anyway, "—*if* returning to the fleet is what we are doing."

The air felt almost like it did before a thunderstorm in the desert: every molecule thick with static charge. My father's council meetings were often such. He would let his attendants, his logothetes, his scholiasts, and the representatives of the Chantry dicker and wheedle and wring their hands and rattle their sabers until all their energies were spent and their sympathies laid bare. Whatever else he was, my father was a patient man, and a more effective administrator I had never seen. It was just such a moment as I'd wanted, just such a moment as I'd been waiting for.

Without a word, I drew The Painted Man's terminal from my sabretache and set it before me. Only Switch and Valka took notice, who sat to my either side. So I raised a hand and struck the table as hard as I could. The bang attracted the three captains' attentions and the attentions of those as watched them. Ten sets of eyes focused on me, shocked by the violent interruption where before I had been an inert feature of the environment.

In a voice barely more than a whisper, I said, "I can't listen to this. I can't." My quietness drew them in, as I had seen from my father with his councilors on more occasions than I could count. I had a brief window of shock in which to speak, and no time for the logical appeal. "We're not chasing a fairy story, Lin. Just today, we met a . . . man, who could change his face. He commanded an army of dead men and he *claimed* to come from Vorgossos. Besides"—I rocked back in my chair, raising my eyebrows— "on Emesh, the Cielcin *knew* of the place. I've said it before, and I will keep saying it until it penetrates: How would a xenobite, an alien, know of a human world that even the Empire cannot locate unless it exists? Do you imagine those creatures we have frozen in our hold are chatting with the prisoners they carted off from Tyras? From Rustam?"

I made a disgusted sound and looked down at the terminal sitting on the edge of the table before me. Almost I could feel the tattooed eyes and grinning mouths of the homunculus hovering at my shoulder. Despite them, I persevered. "You call me a lunatic. If it is lunacy to want to end this war as quickly as possible, then you can call me whatever you wish. I

don't care, because whether you *accept* it or not, Bassander—or whether
any of the rest of you accepts it—I know we need this." Here I paused,
patting the Extrasolarian terminal with one hand, my eyes never leaving
Bassander's face. Any who saw us then must have seen the struggle between us: like a line of smoldering fire drawn eye to eye.

"What is this?" Greenlaw asked, meaning the terminal.

I ignored her. "And you would have us what? Go back?" And here I
raised my voice. "For what? To fight and die among the others? To add
your name to the list of names? Please . . ." I looked away, shook my head.
"We're not dancing at the edge of the galaxy. This is center stage." Judging the moment right, I stood, that I might align myself as equal and opposite to Bassander in that instant. "Emesh bled to give us this chance.
Tyras burned. And Lycia. And Bannatia. Millions of people. Maybe
more." Bassander was marshaling, I could see. Otavia and her Lieutenant
Durand were nodding. Jinan's lips were pressed together, her face a paper
mask I could not read. The rest I did not see. I did not need to see. "This
is our best chance to do the most good. Here. Now." I rapped my fist
against the table. "Now."

"Hadrian," Jinan said, a frown folding that loved and familiar face, "is
that . . . ?"

"It's The Painted Man's personal terminal," I said, resuming my seat
with a crooked smile. Leaning over the device, I cupped my hand in my
chin. "I don't know what's on it or how to use it, but there must be something on here relating to The Painted Man's business operations. That
means ledgers, that means locations. Ilex?" I shoved the heavy device across
the table to the dryad before Bassander could gainsay me.

She caught it with one green-fingered hand, turned it over, a deep
furrow forming between hairless brows. "I haven't seen anything quite
like it," she mused, scratching behind one ear. "Reminds me of some
Tavrosi models I've seen. I'll take a look."

"Thank you."

"Why didn't you mention it sooner?" Bassander scowled at me across
the table. The laser line between us redrew itself. "Were you waiting for
an invitation?"

Ignoring him, I spoke to Ilex. "The Painted Man mentioned a
place . . ." I struggled to remember the strange name. "March Station, I
think it was."

"What's that?" asked Lieutenant Hanas in his thick Jaddian accent.

"A trading post," said Otavia Corvo, surprising us all. She had not resumed her seat, but stood—arms crossed—surveying the rest. "You hear tell of it, time to time, but I've never been there."

"Do you know where it is?" I asked, turning to her.

Otavia shook her floating hair back from her face. "No. You know how it is with these Extrasolarian black sites."

"It's supposed to be somewhere in the Veil," Durand said, glancing nervously at Bassander Lin. "Between the stars . . . but without coordinates . . ." He shrugged. I took his meaning. Without coordinates, we could spend a million years combing the Dark without finding so much as an asteroid.

"Enough!" Bassander said. "We have chased this fantasy for long enough. Whatever intelligence is on that terminal you recovered, I say we deliver it to the fleet. Let Hauptmann and Knight-Tribune Smythe decide what to do."

My teeth groaned as I clamped my jaw. It took all my strength not to say, "You can't be serious!" Gibson's voice rose up instead, deep and quiet, and murmured—as it so often did—*Rage is blindness*. I shut my eyes a moment, opened them. "That wasn't the mission."

"The mission has changed, Marlowe," Bassander said. "We've been gone too long."

"But we're this close," I said, gesturing with thumb and forefinger an inch apart, "this close!" I looked round the table, seeking support. From Valka. From Switch. From Otavia and Lieutenant Durand. From Jinan.

Jinan.

My dear captain would not look at me for a long moment—had looked away, down at her hands clasped against the black marble. Her braided hair hung between us, hiding her face. All was quiet for less than a second. It might have been eons. She shook her head, twitched the braid back over her shoulder. "And then what, Hadrian?" Her lips pressed together, and she glanced to Captain-Commodore Lin. "Another clue? Another step? We can't keep chasing after ghosts."

"Ghosts?" The word came out, but it sounded lost, as if it and I had stumbled into the wrong conversation, unformed and rudderless. "What?"

"Maybe . . . maybe Captain Lin is right. Maybe we should turn back." There must have been something in my face, for she faltered and—looking away—said, "Perhaps if we were to telegraph the data and await orders before returning."

I'd fallen out an airlock. That was it. That was why I couldn't breathe. That was why I couldn't hear Otavia Corvo shout at Jinan, though her face darkened with rage. Bassander was nodding. And Greenlaw and

Alessandro Hanas. Even Switch looked relieved. Somewhere along the way I had lost something. Control maybe or . . . vision? The thin ice beneath my feet had cracked and given way to admit me into the ocean of chaos that dwelt forever beneath the world.

Jinan, who had been solid as the Earth herself and always, always there . . . Jinan had shifted. I looked at her, at the arched brows, the full lips, the azure ribbon threaded through her braided hair. I saw a stranger, a soldier of the Prince of Jadd. I felt as though a mask had fallen away—though whether it fell from her face or my eyes I cannot say.

I shoved my chair back from the table, straightened my short jacket roughly. Everyone stopped for just a moment, even Otavia, who had a finger in Bassander's face. The words would not come. Jinan had taken them with her . . . leaving me drowning in the cold. My mouth opened but what was left of my rationality shut it again, shutting out and down the reptilian urge to bite and scream.

"You're turning your backs on everything we've done so far," I said, and it sounded like another man's voice, as if I were watching some recording or an opera about some other Hadrian, some poor fellow against whom all had turned. "Forty-eight years, Bassander. Jinan. Forty-eight years. If we go back now, what was it all for?"

Bassander stood with a fluid grace that infuriated. How dare he be so calm? So at ease? That laser-bright line that connected our eyes had transferred his earlier chaos and fury to myself, and so he had grown strong, and I diminished. "Giving up?" he asked in a voice flat and dispassionate as glass. "Like you said, Marlowe: it's been forty-eight years since we left Emesh. That's long enough! We should regroup with the fleet, come up with a new plan of attack."

"At least wave Smythe on the telegraph first!" I said, glancing at Jinan, who had suggested it. "We should hold position here until we have orders. We shouldn't incur the time debt of another journey until we're sure."

Jinan—my Jinan—was nodding, and I found myself wondering if she and Bassander had been discussing this before this meeting, before even she'd come to retrieve me from the planet. "We ought to," she said in dry tones. "Bassander. It may be that your tribune has ideas of her own."

"I say again," Otavia put forth, "if you set sail for a rendezvous with the Imperial fleet, you do so without my ship or my people."

"Your ship?" Bassander repeated, pursing his lips. "The *Mistral* is the property of the Meidua Red Company—that makes it the Empire's property, mercenary. You retain your captaincy so long as we retain your services. If you wish to part company, I will see to it that you and your people are shuttled to Rustam and given severance."

The muscles flexing in the Norman woman's jaw might have been the pistons of some great locomotive. I had my private doubts about Bassander's ability to deliver on that threat, but held my peace. I was still standing at my end of the table, still trying to find my way out of the dark I'd fallen into. Jinan had been a source of light, and for that moment that light was veiled. I had needed her, needed support, and she had supported Bassander.

Captain Corvo was diplomatic enough not to respond, but the look she gave Bassander could have stripped paint from steel. Jinan spoke again, and her lilting Jaddian accent fell foreign as a stranger's on my ears. "We have much to consider. Perhaps it is best we wait, and hold our position until we can get a response from Smythe and the Legion. I should like to get word to my lady as well." She meant Kalima di Sayyiph, the Satrap Governor of Ubar whom she served, who had loaned her to the Legions and the Company after the Emesh affair. Her black eyes turned themselves on me. Once, they had seemed the color of ink illuminated by candlelight. Now I saw only Bassander Lin's cold professionalism reflected in those black pools. "Are we agreed?"

She found me when it was over. I had not gone far. I had wandered the gray corridors of the *Pharaoh* in a grayer fog, as if I had never seen the place before . . . as if I had not lived in them for twelve and forty-eight years. How fast familiar ground becomes unknown territory when our world breaks down.

"Hadrian!"

Her voice—trying for warmth—burned instead. I ground to a halt, shoulders pinched together. It was only with a great effort that I straightened myself and, turning, said, "Jinan."

The Jaddian lieutenant hurried toward me, high boots pounding the deck plates. In spite of myself, I felt an autonomic smile pull my lips, but banished it. She caught me by the wrist as I stepped back. "What is the matter with you?"

"Really?" I asked, ducking my head and glancing up at her from under heavy brows. "You have to ask?"

"I didn't propose anything that was not reasonable!" she insisted, fingers tightening on my arm.

"Unreasonable?" I echoed, taking a step closer. "You enabled Lin. He's been trying to drag us back since we left Emesh. He doesn't want to be here."

"Enabled Lin? Hadrian, he has orders. We have orders."

Tugging free, I jabbed my finger at the ground. "We have the best chance of winning this war, Jinan. The best chance. We have a Cielcin nobile frozen on the *Balmung.* It's willing to work with us to make peace."

She tried to take my hand again, but I clasped my hands behind my back and squared my shoulders to her. "I know . . . I know, Hadrian."

"Isn't that the whole point of fighting?" I asked, conscious at once of the cameras in the *Pharaoh* and certain that Bassander would hear. "To make peace? Or is it to fight until there's no one left? Because so far as I can tell, that's all that will happen if we go back now. And I understand that Bassander's developed some sort of survivor's guilt because he's here and not on the front, but that's a personal problem and not something that should be directing our actions. We have a solid lead, Jinan. If Ilex can crack The Painted Man's terminal, then . . . then maybe Ghen won't have died for nothing."

There it was. Spoken and made real. I had not even known why I was so upset until I spoke the words. Ghen of Emesh and I had not met as friends. Convicted of a series of violent crimes, the Chantry and the County had sentenced him to a term of combat as a fodder pool myrmidon in the Borosevo coliseum. Destitute as I was and desperate, I had signed up for the same treatment. Switch and I had met there, and Pallino and Siran, Elara and the rest. Ghen had been a terror, the loudest voice in the smallest room. He'd counted on his tremendous size and strength to win his battles, and bullied the others—save Siran, who knew him best. Siran. I would need to speak to Siran. Did she even know? Was she still in fugue aboard the *Mistral*?

"*Dolá Deu di Fotí!*" Jinan swore. "*Mia qal,* I am so sorry. I did not think." She touched my cheek and this time I did not flinch away. I did not move either, but permitted her to pull close, to press her forehead to mine and wrap her arms round me. The embrace lasted five seconds, or perhaps it was five years, but when it was over the gray fog had cleared a little, and I saw that it was behind my eyes and not before them.

"It's fine," I said. It wasn't. "I just . . . it wore his *face,* Jinan. The Painted Man."

"What?"

"After it killed him, it *changed.*" I heard the words—my words, my voice—but I felt I witnessed them more than spoke them, as if the whole scene were playing out on a holograph plate, or on a stage such as the Eudorans still use for their masques. "It could make itself look like anyone it wanted. Change its size. Its voice. It put on his face, Jinan. Ghen's face. That's why I killed it." I spoke into her hair, finally embracing her in return. She smelled like jasmine and old metal at the same time—like that first night on Pharos, drunk on Admiral Whent's wine and our victory.

She said nothing—and what could she say? She was of Jadd, the daughter of a wealthy spicer and a retired military officer. We were both creatures of the known world, but we were beyond knowing now, touching the very edge of the infinite space where lurk those things the lights of Empire and of Jadd destroyed. All my life before the Red Company—even on Emesh—I was a denizen in a walled garden. For all the hierarchy of the Imperium: its imposition of caste and class, the surveillance, the Chantry, the violence and violent suppression of dissent . . . it would never allow The Painted Man to menace its heart, or to let its people be taken, hollowed out and made into SOMs. It shames me none, Reader, to say that I was afraid. Not just of what monsters I dreamed might lie in wait— machine or man or blood-drinking Cielcin—but of the thought that I was and would ever be unequal to the task of facing them, so deep was that Dark before me.

At last I pushed her away. "I need to sleep, Jinan."

The Jaddian lieutenant rubbed at her eyes. "Yes, of course. I've got a shuttle ready to take us back." Her hand slipped down, caught my wrist, and half she turned away, started to move.

I didn't. Stalling, she turned back and leaned in to kiss me. I turned my head down and said, "I'm going to stay here tonight. In my room."

"I'll come with you, then."

The words took a moment to come, had to shake my head to loosen them. "No, I . . . I need to be alone."

The way her lovely face collapsed broke a piece of me, but there was another piece yet too angry with her to be ashamed. The broken part squeezed her hand and smiled its sad and crooked smile, and the rest of me turned to go.

CHAPTER 9

ABSENT FRIENDS

ONE ENCOUNTER WITH BASSANDER the next day drove me from the *Pharaoh* again—this time in possession of the black leather pencil kit and folio I'd left in my room, along with a few others of my possessions. I shuttled over to the *Balmung*, intended to spend the rest of my time there before the jump to warp and my inevitable return to fugue. It was easy to pretend—as the days went by—that Jinan's siding with Bassander had not rattled me. I knew she was only doing her duty, and I was grateful we were holding position instead of returning to the Imperial fleet.

Superluminal communication takes time. Only a single pair of slaved particles is shared between our telegraph and the other; data dripped across the uncounted light-years one bit at a time. Short messages, text, were quick enough. But images, video, complex files . . . these took time to compile, and longer for the fleet to reply to. If our little meeting had been a nightmare, it was nothing next to whatever Raine Smythe and the high officers endured. Secure as we were in our position, we might hold out for days.

And we did.

"I don't know how you deal with it," Elara said, setting the serving board on the center of a glass dining table. "That Lin gives me the creeps, him always watching those security feeds."

I glanced at Jinan and smiled despite myself. "Well, mostly I try not to sleep there." Jinan squeezed my knee under the table. "I like it here better. It's all his people over on the *Pharaoh*."

Pallino came through the arched bulkhead from the small kitchen that serviced the *Balmung*'s executive dining room. With his paramour and Switch in tow he finished setting the table. I was grateful for Elara's statement; it had broken the tense silence with Jinan and myself and whatever it was between Jinan and Valka.

"Well, we're all much better looking," Switch said, taking the seat opposite me with a huge serving bowl filled with a pasta tossed with onion, pepper, and mushroom pulled from the hydroponics section. "But that's mostly me." Valka snorted, and Elara hit him in the back of the head with a spoon. Switch yelped.

"Lin's a right peacock. Parents were Legion, probably their parents were Legion and that's how he got his commission. Got his baton shoved up his ass more than in his hand, you take my meaning," Pallino said, settling in between Switch and Elara at the round table. Over their shoulders, a holograph plate projected a vision of the *Pharaoh* and the smaller *Mistral* ahead of us in orbit above weeping, umber Rustam. "You get his like all the time. Competent, but he lets his . . . his principles run him into bad decisions. The sort of officer who thinks using his dead mates for sandbags is glorious."

At my left hand, Valka took the water pitcher from Switch and poured for herself. "'Tis nothing glorious in that."

"In using your mates for sandbags? Nah," Pallino said, working a finger under the strap of his eyepatch and adjusting it against his stiff white hair. "The glory's in being the sandbag, in saving your brother's life."

"We've hit a dead end. Don't be too hard on him," Jinan said in her Captain Azhar voice, a little more stiffly than the woman I knew. "Bassander is acting on the intelligence he has."

Valka passed me the water pitcher, saying, "Indeed, but therein lies your problem, captain." She held her hands like the pans of a scale. "Military intelligence can make up for the other kind, and vice versa, but Lin's short on both."

"That is not true," Jinan said. "He's overworked. You know he spent the whole flight from Sanora awake, yes? Coordinating with the fleet? He's exhausted. Anyone would be."

"Then he should put himself in fugue for a while," I suggested. "It's not an excuse for running back with his tail between his legs."

My Jaddian captain did not look at me as she said, "We still have no idea what intelligence is on The Painted Man's terminal. Once we know that, we can make an informed decision."

I bit back the retort that came to mind, stared down at my empty plate. Thinking better of saying anything further, I busied myself serving Jinan and then myself. Ordinarily, my captain would have slapped my hand away and served herself. That she did no such thing struck me as a bad sign.

"You made all this yourself?" Valka asked Switch, lifting the serving dish to spoon the short noodles from their golden ceramic bowl and onto her plate.

The lictor grinned ruefully. "No, it was mostly Pallino. I was just the fetch and carry."

"The kid doesn't give himself enough credit!" said one-eyed Pallino. "He did the roast this time, and the sauce for the pasta. I mostly glared at him and chopped things." Valka grinned, passed the bowl to Jinan with a polite smile, and shook her head. Seeing this, Pallino asked, "What?"

"You never cease to astonish, you *saichdattr*," she said, meaning those of us who came from the coliseum. "'Tis not a chef one envisions when one pictures an Imperial fighting man." She raised her glass in salute.

"Meaning no disrespect, doctor, you're not what one pictures when he thinks of a Tavrosi sorcerer." Pallino mirrored the salute. "Besides, grow up with a grandmother like mine and see how far you get without learning to cook. Woman would die of shame if any *nipote* of hers couldn't make a proper meal."

"Nipote?" Jinan repeated. "Was she Jaddian, you grandmother?"

Pallino frowned, taking the serving bowl from Jinan. "No, I don't think so. My family lived on Trieste, well . . . since the beginning. I was the first of my village to go to the Legions in over five hundred years. They knew they would never see me again, but my old nona was so proud. Her boy out there fighting for the Emperor. She were right pious, that one."

"It is a Jaddian word," Jinan said. "Perhaps we are cousins somewhere far back."

The one-eyed old soldier shrugged, ladling the pasta to his plate without ceremony. "Might do, aye. Might be there was something of what went on to be your people as settled on Trieste on their way out from the old-old Empire. Might do . . . might do." He set the serving bowl on the table. "Ask His Radiance, here. Had's got the head for this sort of thing."

I flinched and almost dropped my fork. The *His Radiance* hit me too close to where I lived. Ghen had called me that, and it was catching. It seemed almost a sacrilege that it could still be said, now that Ghen was gone. I did set my fork down with great care. "It's possible. It's not easy to track migration patterns anymore, and I don't know so much about your homeworld, Pallino, but . . . sure." I looked at my plate the entire time, at the dripping slice of imitation beef beside the pasta in its red sauce. Becoming aware of this, I inhaled sharply and sat a little straighter. "Sorry. I . . ." I took up my cup—water, not wine—turned it in my hands. "I wanted to say something." All eyes turned to me as they had in council, though here the effect was of warmth, not coldness.

My friends, such as I had found and had found me. Switch, transformed from boy to man, victim to victor. Pallino, who had been like a father to us both, or at least a gruff old uncle. Elara was there beside him, younger and quieter than Pallino and with an easy smile and a laugh the years have not obscured from me. And there were Jinan and Valka, who mattered to me and would matter more than all the gold in Avalon— though I paid more dearly than any Emperor. My friends. My family. Made and not begotten. Only Siran was missing, who was stationed on the *Mistral* and had not joined us.

And Ghen, who was dead.

"I wasn't sure what to say," I began, voice tripping over itself in a way that sounded very much not like the Hadrian Marlowe I knew. "And to be honest I still have no idea. But we've an empty chair at our table, and we'll always have that empty chair." At once I found I could not look the others in the eye, and focused instead on my reflection in the gleaming dark of the wall between Switch and Pallino's shoulders. "He died brave as he lived. Pulled two of those monsters apart with his bare hands, I think. But I sent him down those stairs to try and find us a way out. He didn't question me—and Earth knows the bastard had questions in him. But he went." I was lying. Trickery had killed Ghen. Trickery and cowardice. He'd been shot in the back by The Painted Man while the vile creature wore the face of a friend and Ghen had grappled with those SOM demons. And so I turned my lie into blame. "I should have been faster . . . If I'd gone with him."

"Now hold on, Had," Switch said, who alone of the company had shared the last horrible adventure with me, "That wasn't your fault. That homunculus would have killed Ghen anyway when it took you. There wasn't anything you could do."

That drew a sad smile from me, but I suppressed the urge to say that yes, it was my fault. Instead, I shook my head and said, "Ghen was a good man. Hard to learn to like but easy to keep liking." His face flickered before me, laughing in the coliseum, then again in the dark of The Painted Man's office. My knuckles whitened on the cup. "He gave his life for us, same as the others, but was our friend. He was my friend." I found the strength to look at Pallino, at Elara. Switch. The cup, when I raised it, weighed some amount I could not gauge. Too heavy, as if it held all the blood in a man's body and not the little water there was in truth. "Ghen. We will never see his like again."

"Ghen!" all said.

It is hard, Reader, to find words for the dead when one has no religion. One cannot say the deceased is in a better place, or that they are better off—though perhaps it is so that not to exist is better sometimes than to suffer in the world. One cannot offer prayers, though one may light the votive lamps and send them drifting to the sky. It would be a long while before I lit a proper lamp for Ghen, as it would be a long while before I found myself in a shrine, and when that time came his was but one of several lamps released unto the sky. I think it was Orodes who said the first act of civilization—the moment culture was born—was when those ancient pygmies, our forefathers, held the first funeral. *The bright line,* he writes, *between man and what was before man is drawn by that dignity with which we honor the dead. Man does not leave her dead to rot, but burns or buries or builds, protecting the body and the memory of the fallen. There is civilization: its cornerstone a grave.*

"Don't seem right," Switch said, having drained his own cup. A rueful smile pulled across his chiseled face. "If it were one of us, that big bastard'd be running down the whole list of dumb shit we did. He wouldn't have gone all solemn." He rubbed his sleeve over his eyes; a weak and soundless laugh escaped him. Pallino and I joined in. "If you told me he'd be the one to go first . . . before me . . ." He shook his head, and Pallino clapped him on the shoulder.

"You can't let that get to you," Elara said. "It's just like fighting in the pits, lad. There ain't no reason he died instead of you or Had or that Greenlaw woman. Like you just said to Had, it ain't your fault."

Switch nodded, shut his eyes. When they opened they no longer shimmered with unfallen tears. "No, I . . . I know."

Of all people, it was Valka who cut in. "He's still a part of us." Her strange Tavrosi accent gave a weight to her words. "Every memory we have is still here. I did not know him well as you, but I think you're right: he would not want us all solemn. Come!" And she told a story about how Ghen had gotten into a fight with one of Jinan's *aljanhi* commanders after Ghen made fun of the man's hat. The man had sent Ghen a matching hat, hoping to shame the Emeshi myrmidon. But Ghen had no shame, and had worn the thing in a heartbeat, and the Jaddian commander had backed down at once. "'Twas the ugliest thing I'd ever seen," Valka said. "It had these green feathers all over. Where the *aljanhi* got another I've no idea. But Ghen wore the bloody thing for a week."

"I missed that!" Elara proclaimed, laughing.

So it went on for the better part of an hour, each of us swapping stories about Ghen. Switch recounted a story of how Ghen had kept leaving him fake love notes back in the coliseum at Emesh. "I knew it was him at once. Bastard could hardly spell, but I let on I thought it was this chappie up from Tolbaran I'd had eyes for—this was before you'd come along, Had. He kept it up for weeks."

"And you just let him?"

Switch grinned. "Yeah! I think he was mocking me for . . . well, you know what he was like, but I kept letting on how much I liked them. He didn't know what to do with that!"

Pallino had another story, about how Ghen had stepped in at a bar on Ardistama, not so long after we'd left Emesh. "To teach these local boys some manners, he said. To impress the girls, I said. Ghen tossed those blighters round like they were sacks of flour. I ain't never seen grown men run so fast."

By the end we were all laughing, and what tears fell were not all of grief. Even I, who among those gathered was perhaps the most somber—having shouldered the blame for Ghen's death—even I was moved more to laughter than to sorrow or shame. We have little control over our ends, and none over what passes beyond them. But if we live well and truly, those who follow on may remember us for our lives and not our deaths.

Perhaps it was for that reason I blurred the circumstances of Ghen's death. It was not that I lied, but that I valorized those final moments because the truth is so much larger than those material facts of the world. Better to recall his rough laugh than imagine whatever horrid sounds he'd made with damaged lungs in those final moments in the tea house.

Better the reassuring fable than the clinical truth. Fables are more real than reality. Such are your stories about me—many of which I began, knowing the power of stories as I do. I could not have made peace at the Battle of Aptucca years later if my legend were not more true than myself. By this fact of human nature and belief, we are made larger than ourselves: some better, some worse, some only more complicated. Thus two and two is made five, and so we grow beyond ourselves.

CHAPTER 10

JINAN

OVER THE LONG YEARS since Pharos, when we had acquired the two Norman ships, Jinan's quarters in the captain's suite of the *Balmung* had grown more comfortable one item at a time. The ceramic basin was hers—used for the ritual cleansing of face and hands every morning—and the incense tapers, so often unused and forgotten about in their bronze holder. The various drawers and cabinets in one wall hid behind a red silk curtain she'd found in a Pharos bazaar after Whent's surrender. It showed a heroic figure fighting a smoke-belching dragon outside the gates of a walking city, the figures all done in cloth-of-gold. She'd liked the dragon, she said.

It is strange how we humans make our homes. We arrive in a place and—finding that place foreign and uncomfortable—place objects just as foreign in it until it becomes lived in and all strangeness is gone.

"Jinan," I began, unbuttoning my uniform jacket and peeling it away, "we should talk about—" The Jaddians, they say, are men of words only when all actions are exhausted. It is so. She was on me mid-sentence, stooping slightly to press her lips to mine. I banged my head against a cabinet door as she pinned me, and winced. She made a deeper, older sound, and I felt myself responding to some Bacchanalian impulse more ancient than the human capacity for thought. My hands found her trim waist and the slim curve of hips; squeezed. It took all my self-control and my least favorite of the scholiasts' stoic aphorisms—*Love consumes*—to stop myself and say, "Can we talk about this?"

Small teeth pressed themselves against the fullness of that bottom lip, and she drew back, keeping one arm planted on the wall behind me as she looked down her nose at me. "About what?"

"About Bassander," I said, not letting go of her waist, either, "about the council meeting and . . . and going home."

A breath rushed out of her—I could smell the little wine we had shared at the end of the meal, and she broke away, claiming a seat by her small desk, long fingers tugging at her braid, beginning to unwind it. "You are unbelievable. Can you not let it go for a day? Two? We do not know what was on that terminal you recovered. I've said a hundred times." She pulled her azure ribbon free and shook out her hair; it was like a falling of summer shade beneath some flowering tree. "You are always like this."

Always. That was a bad sign. I could not afford to make this discussion about *always*. It needed to remain about *now*—and about the hurt I felt like a knife in the ribs . . . like a plasma shot in the back.

I found suddenly that I could not look at her—it was like looking at the sun. "It isn't that," I said, pacing to cover that shame. "You took his side." Those words said, I found the strength in me and turning faced her and repeated, "You took his side." She was unbuttoning her jacket—I wanted to seize her fidgeting hands. I settled for slow breathing instead. *Fear is death to reason.* And it was fear I felt, not anger. Fear that she would not understand—or would at least fail to see my point of view, which was at any rate so valid as her own. Fear that we would fight, as we had already. Fear that I was losing her to the work. To the mission.

Fear.

That oldest and most animal of demons, older than trees, old perhaps as the trilobites who shuddered at the approach of the predator when Earth was young. Its fingers were on me, cold as she was not. "He's always hated me, Jinan. Even before we met, you and I." I gestured past the black metal walls, as if Bassander were some omnipresent force. "That's all this is about. It's not about going back to fight or Bassander's outsized sense of duty. He's doing this because he doesn't like *me*."

Jinan paused in her removal of her jacket, eyes downcast in thought. At length she skinned out of it and tossed it onto the foot of the bed in its recess in the wall. Massaging her eyes with one hand, she said, "You are being dramatic."

Must everything you say sound like it's straight out of a Eudoran melodrama?

I shook my head to clear it. "I'm not. He's tried to keep me from helping since the Cielcin crashed at Emesh."

"You are no soldier, love."

"I am now!" I said, and pointed at myself. "I've been fighting for twelve years, Jinan. Twelve years. All across the Veil. Three more if you count *every bloody day* in Borosevo. I'm as much a soldier as any of you. He just doesn't . . . believe."

Jinan's brows arched, supporting a cathedral of skepticism. "Believe? In what, *mia qal?* In Vorgossos?"

"In peace!" I almost shouted. "In an end to all this. It's like I told Olorin: soldiers don't end wars, not usually. Wars end after the fighting's done, not during."

She rolled her eyes. "It is not that simple."

"Of course it's not that simple!" I sagged onto the footlocker against the far wall that held all I'd shuttled over from the *Pharaoh*, hands open before me. "What part of this is simple, Jinan? We are fighting a war of extinction with the Cielcin. Where do you think that will end? How many more worlds do we have to let them burn before all is said and done? How many of their ships will we destroy? How many billion dead? On both sides?"

Jinan was silent a long time, as if she were lost deep beneath the surface of those dark eyes. In a voice like dry leaves, she asked, "Why does this matter so much to you, Hadrian? Making peace?"

"Why?" I almost laughed, lurched uneasily to my feet. "Why?" I searched the gloss ceiling for an answer, for the words to an answer so plain to me it had needed no words until that moment. I had wanted to help, hadn't I? On Emesh, when the crisis came, when the Cielcin ship had crashed. Everyone at the Calagah dig site had been running away from the noise and fire. I had run toward it, had begged that Veisi centurion to let me go with the relief force. It had been the only thing to do. And then . . . "You weren't there, Jinan. In the bastille in Borosevo. You didn't see what the Chantry . . . did."

I could smell it. The copper smell of blood, the stench of filth and sweat and rotting meat. Burning lead, shattered teeth, the torment and torture and the endless questions.

Why have you come to Emesh?
When does the next invasion fleet arrive?
Why have you come to Emesh?
Why have you come to Emesh?
Why have you come to Emesh?

Man's inhumanity. What could be more human?

"You saw the scar on the planet?" I asked. "The old city? Suren?" She had. "I saw scars, too. I saw what the Chantry did to that Cielcin captain, Jinan. I'm not blind. I know the evil that *we* do. I was part of it. I'm still part of it." Pacing about the room, I remembered the Umandh slaves in Borosevo, the coloni xenobites scarred and abused, their stony hides chiseled when they disobeyed. And then there were the human serfs, the ragged poor as I had been—choked and dying in the streets, wracked by plague and unhelped by the palatines in their castle. "They're good people, Jinan."

"Who?"

"Our people," I said, encompassing the fleet with a hand-wave. "Switch, Pallino, Otavia, Ilex, everyone. They should not have to live like this. No one should have to live like this."

A sad smile stole over my captain's face, and sharply was I reminded that she had been a soldier for far longer than I. "Why do you think we do what we do? What do you think an army is for? So that the rest of the people can go on living, Hadrian."

"It's intolerable," I said, "It's intolerable that good people should spend their lives fighting."

Jinan pushed back in her chair, crossing her arms in a way that emphasized the strength of her shoulders beneath the white shirt. "Better good men do what we do than bad ones."

"It would be better if no one had to do it at all."

"Then you will wait until the stars are embers and all men are dead," Jinan said. "The need for soldiers will not go away when this war is done." She shook her head, blew air out past her teeth. "You take a lot on yourself."

"That's not what I mean," I said, and fretted over resuming my seat. Deciding against it, I pressed on. "That's why I'm here. Because better me than . . . than someone like my brother." Jinan knew a little of Crispin, and I saw her face flicker. Was that doubt? I couldn't sit down. "I know I can't stop *war,* Jinan. But if I can make *this* war just a little bit better, than maybe—maybe—a few good men can stay at home, and maybe we can go home when it's done. You and I."

Only I had no home. I would not return to Emesh whence I came, where lay an arranged marriage to trap me in the arms of Anaïs Mataro, who by now was twice my age, a woman grown. I could not return to Delos, to the house of my father, whence I fled in terror of him and his plans for me. To Jadd, then? To Ubar? To retire and run Jinan's family spice business while she finished her service to her prince? I imagined myself living out my days in peace, a silly old country squire with a passion for museums and alien artifacts—a passel of children underfoot. In

Jadd, it was said, the genetic keys that held the palatines in thrall to the Imperium were held by the nobiles themselves, by the *eali al'aqran* of the Principalities. There perhaps whatever proprietary code there was in my blood might be undone, and Jinan and I might start a family.

I went to her and knelt like a knight receiving the sword at his investiture, took her hands in mine. "Bassander's way is just more fighting. We've had almost four hundred years of fighting now. It's not enough. If I could make peace with one Cielcin clan, that clan could help make peace with the others. Our prisoners can unlock the end of the war, and we can go home." My hand squeezed hers, and she returned the gesture, smiling but sadly. "We could be together, Jinan. You and I. In Jadd or back on Ubar or wherever you want."

"Ubar?" She smiled, and a piece of me broke. "Hadrian, please. I do not know what to say to you." We'd spoken of this before. So often when she spoke of home it seemed there was some piece left unspoken, as if it were a hand lurking just below the surface of some deep water waiting to drag me down. Her fingers squeezed mine, but the smile slackened, as though it remained on her face only by the half-attention of her muscles— and not at all by her heart. "We do not know if we have *anything,* and even if we did, there is no guarantee we could find this . . . Vorgossos place."

My hands slipped out of hers and I slumped until I sat at her feet. "So you keep saying."

"What are we supposed to do?" she asked, shifting her legs apart and stooping over me. "You heard Bassander. Another planet destroyed. That is more than a dozen since we left Emesh. Do you expect him to do nothing? He has orders from his commander."

I ground my teeth. "I had hoped he'd see sense."

"Sense?" she asked. "And do what? Disobey orders? We are talking about *Bassander Lin,* are we not?" She had a point, but she wasn't finished. "*Mia qal,* he has given decades to this venture. We all have. We have been chasing ghosts now for so long, and I am not convinced we are any closer to an ending here than we were when we started. We lost people at Pharos. We lost people here. You have to see it from his point of view: we've been fighting battles that have nothing to do with the crusade. Everyone we have lost should have been back fighting the real battle."

"I have to see it from his point of view?" I turned my face away from her where it rested on her thigh. "Jinan . . . what if . . . what if Ilex comes back with a lead? The coordinates to this . . . Extra trading post? Would you go with me if Bassander refused?" *Refused.* The thought lodged itself in me like shrapnel in an innocent chest. I could refuse. I was glad Jinan could not see my face to see the way those words lit something in my violet eyes. It was a thought.

The muscles tightened in her legs beneath me, as if she'd been stunned. "What?"

Turning, I looked up at her and—catching her hand—kissed it and did not let go. "Hauptmann is not your commander," I said. "We go on to Vorgossos, you and I."

"You should not be joking about these things."

"I know," I said, but the damage had been done. Ideas are like sparks and my mind was dry with exhaustion and the need for new invention. I blazed, but shuttered my eyes, burying my face in her lap. I was tired also, and pressed thin as a sample under glass. "Jinan, if we go back . . . I'll never see you again." She would return to her people, and they to their own mission.

Already tense, she stiffened. "I know."

"I don't . . . don't want . . . I want us to stay together." I broke off and looked up again at her oval face, at the canny arch of brow above the wide, deep eyes; the faint scar white on her golden cheek; those lips and the sharp tongue behind them and the knowledge they would as soon smile at me as that tongue might cut. "I love you, Jinan."

There was that smile, and the throaty voice saying, "Well, you're not wrong." She tossed her hair. I pushed her chidingly in the shoulder, and she laughed, leaning toward me. "I love you, too, you strange man."

I snorted, but she kissed me all the same.

I could taste the fire there, the desperation, but cannot say if it was on her tongue or mine. Critics of the oldest stories used to say that men believe women to be goals, prizes to be won or bought. They did not understand. No man could think such a thing and remain a man, for to love is in part the attempt to become a creature worthy of love. That Jinan was worthy was self-evident as the stars. It was my own worthiness I questioned. Like the prince in every storybook legend, like Cid Arthur and Tristan and Ram, I knew I might become worthy only through my deeds and present myself to her as a knight before the throne of some mighty queen. So love is not merely an emotion, but a vow made one to another. A vow renewed in each moment, until it hardly needs making at all.

Or until it is not made, and death or deed does them part.

Pulling me to my feet, she stood, her hands tugging my shirt from my trousers. Cold air plucked at me, pulling hairs tight. She led me toward the bed, and there was something in the sway of her walk that held my attentions. Kissing me, Jinan pushed me onto the mattress. The gold accents on the tapestry glinted in the steady light of the room. A word from Jinan dimmed those lights but for a few safety lamps low and red, marking the exit and the way to the washroom. "Do you really think I would let them take you from me?" she husked, and threw aside her own shirt. There was nothing underneath. Her high breasts rose with her breathing, and she lowered herself atop me.

They won't give you a choice, I wanted to say, but her tongue was in my mouth, and it didn't seem so important all of a sudden. There were hands in my hair, down my sides. My own hands found her smooth length of muscled thigh. I undid the clasp of her trousers, and she almost snarled, squeezed me through my pants. A breath vibrated from me, and I took her face in my hands. She pinned me back when I tried to roll on top of her, and for a moment I could see the familiar contours of her face, the high cheekbones, the mocking eyes beneath that mass of curling hair dark even as my own. "Don't you dare." She bit her lip. The hand she wasn't pinning rested on her flank. She kissed me. My mouth, my jaw, my throat. Released the hand she'd pressed to the mattress—it was like sparring, really. Her hair trailed against my skin. Tickled. Itched.

I wasn't cold anymore.

They say the ancients believed that one day the universe would contract. That time would run backward and all the world would shrink again to its native form and angels dance on the head of that pin. For a moment, I say it did, for all the worlds beyond our bed and that little room were banished, and all Creation made to house just her. And me. The rest of it: the Cielcin, The Painted Man, the Empire and Jadd, Bassander and Otavia . . . and Ghen. All vanished, obscured by Jinan as relic radiation obscures the very beginning of time. For the fever and flame of that moment and the strength of her arms I would have given all of myself. I was in love, and we were in love, and that love built the whole of our world—if only for that private moment. A paradise for us two. A walled garden sheltered from the world.

But every garden has its snake, and every light its shadow.

It did not last, nor did I.

It could not last.

But nothing is beautiful because it lasts.

She tasted like a soldier, like iron and sweat, and every cord of her was lean as the bronze statues of the Icon of Fury on the Chantry altars. And when it was ended, we did not speak, but faced one another. Those un-spoken facts lingered between us: that a return to the fleet would very well be the end of us, of these nights.

There were faint lines at the corners of Jinan's mouth. Lines her laugh-ter eased in waking life. So too was the crease between her black brows, a perfect line folded as if by some logothete in confirmation of her burden. She had only put that burden down for a few short hours, but she knew it was there. I shuddered to think what I must have looked like. I do not shudder now. Reader, I have woken often in the night of my exile here soaked and shivering and alone. There are burdens one cannot put down, even in sleep.

For what I have done, there is no respite. Even in Death, you would pile scorn upon my grave.

CHAPTER 11

YOUR RADIANCE

I PUT OFF MY visit to the *Mistral* for a day and a half after word reached me from Otavia's medtechs that they'd taken Siran out of fugue. I told myself I was still grieving, still lost inside memories of the horrible, flat eyes of the SOMs and the way they moved even cut to pieces. The truth was that facing Ghen's closest friend was something I did not think I had in me. The big ox and Siran had been myrmidons together, prisoners together, criminals together—and both had left Emesh and followed me together, and that at least had cost Ghen his life.

They would have followed anyone out of bondage, said the part of me that sounded like Tor Gibson. *You cannot blame yourself for offering the road, no matter where it ends.*

Grief is deep water, I told myself, and the voice of the telling was mine. *Grief is deep water.*

We shuttled over—Switch and I—through the static field and out of the *Balmung*'s hangar bay toward the smallest of our three ships. Three and a half hundred meters from end to end and shaped like a spearhead, the *Mistral* gleamed like a shard of silver by firelight. Like the *Pharaoh*, she was of Uhran manufacture, and her incept plates bore a date harking back to when there were still kings on that distant world. By far the fastest of our three ships, she was rated for 0.8 Kc. Eight hundred times the speed of light. The *Pharaoh* could barely manage 0.6.

"You want me to go with you?" Switch asked.

We were alone in the rear compartment, sealed off from the pilot officer in her ventral blister. The hum of the drives only complementing the oppressive quiet.

I shook my head for the better part of five seconds before I realized I hadn't said a word. "No. You don't have to."

"That wasn't what I asked, Had," Switch said, pressing his lips together.

Plowing past that, I said, "Does she know? Did Corvo tell her?" The fact that Ghen was dead was becoming an existential fact to me, and so— as in the parable of the fish who do not see that they are in water—I had not thought to ask again.

"I'm not sure," said my closest friend, leaning forward to get a better look at me.

". . . should have died hereafter," I said, slipping into the Classical English.

Switch's face twisted into a melange of confused frustration and amusement. "What?"

He hadn't understood. In Galstani I said, "Sorry. Being ridiculous."

The older-looking, younger man smiled and clapped me on the arm. The light of that smile did not touch his eyes, but froze on the lower half of his face, stiff as the joke: "Well, what else is new?"

"I'm losing Jinan."

The words came as if from some spinal reflex. I hadn't thought them, or known they were so coldly in me until I'd spoken. It was as if I'd held some peculiar sculpture in my hands and, rotating it until its facets aligned and revealed its secret image, I had not known what it was.

"What?"

I chewed my lip, eyes torn from Switch's narrow face to the sliver of planet I could see through the triangular window. "If we go back to the fleet, she'll return to her people. Smythe won't let me go."

"You don't know that."

I didn't feel like arguing.

"Maybe she will," Switch said.

"She's made me her immunis," I said, using the formal word for a kind of special attaché. "Jinan will sail off to regroup with her satrap's forces and we'll be folded into the 437th, mark my words."

My lictor frowned. "You might be right."

"I am right," I said with the certainty of a scholiast's mental arithmetic— though I had perhaps little right to that certainty. "I don't want that to happen."

"Empire will take what it wants," Switch said. "I'm no patriot, but I'd rather work for them than end up one of those . . . drones." It was his turn to break eye contact and stare out onto space.

"They won't thank us," I said, "particularly if we go back failures the way Lin's setting us up to do, William." I hadn't meant to use his right name, but I had conveyed the depth of seriousness that moved me.

"What are you saying?"

"I don't know," I said, though the thought had occurred to me: I would not be the first palatine lord to turn renegade in the name of some higher cause. *Would you go with me if Bassander refused?* Did I dare ask Switch, as I had asked Jinan? I almost held my breath as I tried—really tried—to articulate my vision. The desire was there—but not the plan—and he who desires without a plan is like the man who leaps from a high place, though his hands are bound. It was as if I stood again in that dark forest, with no sign of the path. Dante was lucky. He had Virgil.

But I could not say anything. It was not that I did not trust my friend, but there *was* a pilot officer on the other side of that bulkhead, and he would report anything he heard—or would hand Bassander any in-flight recordings there may be. Though we were in the depths of space, in Norman territory, we were in the Empire still, and the Empire was always watching.

So I shook my head. "Nothing. Never mind." I glanced at the sealed gray of the bulkhead, indicating the pilot. "Have you spoken to Siran?"

"No," Switch said, pressing back into his seat. "I hope they told her."

"So do I," I said, and my voice was the voice of a man very much older than my thirty-five years.

"So let me ask again." Switch's voice turned down, growing weighty and without any pretense at mirth. He was a man speaking honestly to another, without mockery or pretense, with concern and the love borne of old friendship. "Do you want me to come with you?"

Inside, the *Mistral* had the same industrial design as the *Pharaoh*, bare metal and rounded halls and door, all white-padded and with handles to facilitate movement in the event the suppression fields failed or were turned off. Unlike on the *Balmung*, we entered through a docking umbilical and climbed up through a port in the ventral hull. Switch went first, nominally to secure the room above, though there was no danger aboard our own ships. I followed soon after, smoothing my tunic front once I regained my feet.

Commander Bastien Durand, the ship's First Officer, was waiting by the door to the ship proper. The small Norman bowed when I approached.

"Welcome aboard, Lord Marlowe." He wore a pair of antique wire spectacles whose exact function was a mystery. He could not possibly need them.

I inclined my head. "Commander." I did not much feel like talking.

"The Captain would have been up to meet you herself, but she is closeted with Lieutenant Ilex going over the data from The Painted Man's terminal."

That had my attention. "Is there news?"

Durand adjusted his spectacles. "No, lordship. The dryad tells me the device is encrypted. They've had Doctor Onderra in for a look, too, but she's made no headway, either."

We exchanged small pleasantries, then, and Durand led us out of the vestibule and along a low hall barely higher than my head. Faces peered out of side passages, pale and bronze and Norman dark. I returned salutes casually, with a smile stapled to my face. My family. Otavia's lot were the strangest of the bunch. Only a few of Bassander's soldiers and Jinan's had been shuffled over to the *Mistral*, leaving the interceptor in the hands of Whent's defectors. The Red Company uniforms seemed ill to fit them—I saw one woman who had torn the sleeves off her jacket to bare arms covered in bright, Nipponese-style tattoos. Jackets were not buttoned to the throat, or not worn, or other garments were worn instead. The ship was more relaxed in itself, even with the climate of concern flashing in the odd face.

"Are we for the freeze again, Lord?" one man asked. "We just come out!"

"Is it true the Mandari has us turning back?" called a woman—one of the Jaddian *aljanhi* by her accent.

It stung to say nothing, but say nothing I did.

We passed out along a catwalk overlooking the main hold; a high, open space that ran nearly a third the length of the ship. The ceiling arched gracefully, humming with the gentle thunder of the fusion reactors above. On the bulkhead to our left hung more than a dozen battle standards, each the emblem of some other company or Norman freehold—and one Imperial house—the ship had toppled in its long service. Admiral Whent's gold standard hung amongst them, the black, eight-winged angel there still defiant, though its master was gone. The large door in its center led along the main access shaft to the bridge at the far end of the ship.

Siran was waiting in the starboard gallery, a relatively large space that was part recreation space, part mess. She was not alone. Some dozen others of Otavia's mercenaries lounged on the couches and at the game station, perhaps wondering why it was they'd been brought out of fugue only to be shoved back in again.

"Eat it, you bastard!" One laughed, punching her companion in the arm over some sim game. "Eat it!"

"Hey, stuff it! The Commandant!"

The laughter collapsed to murmuring as I entered, the others suddenly feeling they intruded on something not meant for them. From the corner of my eye I saw two duck out into the hall, and another scarper through the door to the mess.

Siran of Emesh sat by one of the holograph plates that imitated a window against the outer wall of the ship, silhouetted against the orange eye of the planet. The black scar of the city of Suren could just be seen, kissing the terminator as our orbit carried us round into night. She smiled when she saw me, set aside her clay drinking cup. If there had been tears, there were none now. She'd shaved off all her hair—she'd always worn it short, but her scalp gleamed nut-brown in the steady fluorescence.

I didn't say a word, but went to her and—stooping—threw my arms around her. No one spoke, and for a time there was no sound but the distant shuffle of feet, the awkward sounds of men and women witnessing something too private or too uncomfortable for them. Siran stood when I released her and held me at arm's length. After a pause she said, "Are you all right?"

"Am I all right?" I almost laughed. "Are you all right?" Her clipped nostril reminded me of Ghen's, and I had to look away.

"Otavia said you were there," she said, one hand still on my shoulder. "I was an ice cube."

After biting my lip, I replied, "Yes, but he was your . . ." Her what? Had they been lovers? I'd never thought to ask, never known. On Emesh, the two of them had been squirreled away to the prisoners' block and did not stay with the rest of us, save in combat or training. After Emesh, well, they'd been mostly on different ships.

She didn't answer, but held herself a long time. "Was it bad?"

How was a man to answer that? My boots were at once very interesting, and I said, "He fought bravely."

"That isn't what I asked." Brown eyes flashed at me, and I was sharply reminded that she was still the elder of us two. She bore the intervening years better than Switch had done, without the graying or leathering. I wondered if she had patrician blood in her, so remote did she seem—as a queen of men.

I clenched my jaw, seeing the smoking plasma wound and The Painted Man's mocking theft of Ghen's face. "There were daimons, machines wearing men's bodies, Ghen . . ."

"Don't bullshit me, Marlowe!" she said, drawing murmurs from the crowd. "That isn't what I asked."

"Siran," Switch said, stepping forward, hand raised to grasp her shoulder.

"Don't *Siran* me!" she snapped, stepping back.

"What do you want me to say?" I asked.

She glared at me, not speaking.

So I told her everything. About the battle and my ordering Ghen downstairs. About the SOMs, about The Painted Man and its horrible tricks. About how I had avenged Ghen's death.

Switch had not heard it all, and listened just as intently. When I finished there was a knot of people gathered as close as they dared about the four of us—Switch, Siran, Durand, and I. They shrank back the moment I ended, pretending never to have been listening at all.

Siran was nodding. "Thank you."

"For what?"

"For smashing that bastard's head in," she said, baring her teeth.

Switch shrugged with his mouth and ran hands through his graying hair. "We should have brought some wine over from the *Balmung*. I wasn't thinking."

The other myrmidon lifted her cup. "This is just fine."

"Tea?" I made a face.

She snorted. "Vodka."

"But it's not even noon!" Switch exclaimed, blinking. "The hell did you get it, anyhow?"

The woman made a rude hand gesture, then grinned. The cloud that had hung over us since I'd entered dispersed a little, and we all smiled, well and truly. "Crim sent a case up while he was doing his intel work, apparently. While I was still frozen . . . Speaking of," and here she narrowed her eyes, retaking her seat by the window plate. "Is it true Lin's putting us all back in the ice, that we're to rendezvous with the Imperial fleet off Coritani?"

"That seems to be his plan, unless Ilex can turn up something really good."

"And Jinan?"

I glanced sidelong at Switch before answering. "She's playing like she doesn't have a say. Word is Legion brass has ordered all ships to Coritani, like you say. I keep trying to tell Jinan she's not Empire, we could split off, take the Jaddians and make for Vorgossos without Imperial support, but . . . she won't gainsay Bassander."

Siran hissed and crossed her legs. "Sounds to me like she's made up her mind and doesn't want to say."

"Maybe not," Switch put in, looking to Durand for support. The First Officer kept his silence. "I'm sure Jinan is just being careful, Had. She is stuck between you and Bassander, you know. That's not exactly a fun place to be."

A faint smile stamped Siran's lips, and she said, "It is a bit of a cop-out, though. She's a captain, too." It was at about this point that a call came for Commander Durand over his wrist-terminal, and the First Officer begged leave to answer it, hurrying from the room. After he was gone—when it was just we three veterans of the Borosevo Colosso remaining—Siran asked, "How's Pallino taking it?"

"Same as ever, really," Switch said. "Stoic son of a bitch. Nothing makes him blink."

"Well," I said dryly, "he only has one eye. He can't blink."

Switch's eyes flashed daggers, but he restrained the impulse to hit me, and said, "That wasn't funny."

I snorted. "Yes it was."

"Go to hell!" he muttered, mindful of the other soldiers in the room. It would not do for the Commandant's lictor to strike the Lord Commandant.

Siran was grinning, and that—at least—was good. "Have you spoken to that Smythe woman about all this? Just go over Lin's head and your girl's?"

I had been so intent upon solving the problem myself that I had not stopped to think there were other powers in play. Powers that—while not so great as the First Strategos—were greater than Bassander Lin.

Raine Smythe.

Knight-Tribune Raine Smythe.

"No," I said. "No, I hadn't." I felt the grin spreading across my face.

"I know that look," Switch said with dour humor. "Stop it."

I composed myself, rubbing my face with my hands. I could have kissed Siran, then. There was a way forward after all. *Always forward, always down, and never left or right.* We were in the labyrinth again—or else had never left it—beneath the shadows of those dark trees in my mind.

"Don't listen to him, Your Radiance," Siran said, peering up at me from where she sat. "I like it when you get this way." She smiled, threw back what was left of her vodka. "You boys want a drink? To send Ghen off proper?"

   She'd already begun to move, for which I was grateful. She missed the tears. Switch grabbed my wrist, and startled I looked round at him—at the concern deep-carved in the lines of his face. I shook him off and dried my eyes, muttering, "Your Radiance."

CHAPTER 12

A JOURNEY'S END

"AS YOU CAN SEE," Bassander said, speaking through the constellation of holographs from his place behind Emil Bordelon's obscene desk, "the star charts the dryad recovered from The Painted Man's terminal contain no reference to Vorgossos."

The volume map glimmered like frost on spiderwebs in a cylinder projected by hardware in the ceiling. Beside it, an index of names and coordinates scrolled on permanent loop. Holographed stars hung like gems in that gleaming web, motes large only as my thumbnail. They were too large for how close they were together, connected by the major trade routes in glittering white. But all my attentions were given to what hung between them in venomous, fructant red.

Drawing attention to them, I asked, "These are the dark worlds?"

"Dark worlds?" Greenlaw sneered from Bassander's side. "This isn't an opera."

I sniffed, turning instead to Ilex where she stood beside Captain Corvo. She'd forgone the heavy uniform jacket, wore a white vest tucked into red fatigues and high boots. Presently she uncrossed her green arms and answered me, saying, "It's a list of Extrasolarian outposts in the Veil and the Expanse. I'm sure it's not comprehensive."

My eyes skipped from the dryad's face to Jinan's, and I said, "Well, it doesn't have to be." My captain's eyes fell, interested suddenly in something near her shoe. "Thank you, Ilex. You've done a fine job." The dryad stood a little straighter, beaming, and I said, "Is there any sign of a March Station?"

"It's not the nearest of the outposts," Ilex said, crossing from Otavia's side to stand beside me. Her finger jabbed at a red cube some few hundred light-years distant. "We could make it there in about about eighteen months, normal cruising speed. There are closer sites, here and here"—she pointed—"but I don't know what made the arms dealer reference March Station in particular."

"Kremnoi and Tanais," Jinan said, reading the names. "They sound like planets . . ."

"Enough!" Bassander said coolly. "You promised me Vorgossos, Marlowe. This is not Vorgossos." Muscles worked in his jaw and temples, drawing attention to the fact that he'd newly shaved the sides of his head again almost to his crown.

I ignored him. "Captain Corvo, do you have any idea why The Painted Man might have named March Station over these others?"

Improbably tall Otavia Corvo brushed back a strand of her flyaway blond hair and shrugged. "It could be a larger outpost, or else allied with Vorgossos in a way the others are not. It's hard to understand the allegiances of these backspacers."

"Even as we stand," Bassander said, crossing his arms, "it will take some fifteen years to reach the fleet. This mission is a failure."

"No, it's not!" I said, voice going high. I pointed at the holograph projected before us. "We have a list now. A list of—" I counted. "Seventeen backspace sites."

"And you propose to search them all?" Bassander asked.

"If that's what it takes," I said.

The Commodore snorted, dropping into his chair behind the huge desk. He reached out and took the leather-wrapped hilt of his sword—Admiral Whent's sword—from where it lay like a paperweight. He waved the hilt like a baton, shaking it in my general direction. "We don't have the time. Our colonies do not have the time."

"Then go back, captain," I said, sidling past Jinan to face Bassander across the desk. The use of his proper rank stung him—and in front of the Normans, no less. It was a mistake, I knew, but I had decided not to care. "Give me the *Balmung* and the prisoners. I'll find Vorgossos myself if need be." I glanced at Jinan, but my captain stood silent. I did not want to do this alone.

"Find it yourself?" he sneered. "As if you could fly so much as a rusted tub without my officers to assist you."

This stung as much as my calling him *captain* had. I could, as it happened, fly one of the Sparrowhawk-class lighters we kept in the *Balmung*'s bays perfectly well, thank you. But I didn't mention that. Instead I said,

"You are throwing away everything we've done since Emesh. Everything we've built."

"Everything we've done?" Bassander raised his eyebrows, tightening his grip on the sword-hilt he held. "What? Toppled a Norman dictatorship and scrambled a few pirates? You may not know this, being a perfumed palatine, but those deeds hardly account by the standards of the Empire."

"Then give me the *Balmung*," I said again, not retreating. The others . . . Jinan, Otavia, Ilex, Greenlaw . . . vanished as if in a gray mist. Bassander and I stood at the center of a dim universe, neither bending.

Presently he reversed his grip on the weapon and slammed it emitter-down into the surface of the table. "I am not giving you the destroyer or any of my officers."

"Then I will go," Otavia said, stepping forward to place a hand on my shoulder. "You lose nothing but the coin you were already paying me and a ship you did not have when you parted with your fleet." By her words, I stood a little straighter, knowing I had such support. Whatever else I'd done, winning the Norman mercenaries was my accomplishment. It was I who had rid Otavia of Whent—and of Bordelon. *Bordelon*. That she'd been willing to enter this room at all after what that creature had been and done . . . It spoke of a strength of will and a force unlike any I knew in myself.

The universe has no shortage of mad dogs, Corvo had said when I told her the vile Commodore was dead. She had not wept, only nodded her approval.

Bassander stood, an entirely undramatic gesture given that he barely rose to the level of Otavia's breast. He narrowed those eyes like coals. Before he could speak, I stepped forward, freeing myself from Otavia's hand. "Bassander, listen. Please. Give me the prisoners, if not the *Balmung*. We can shuttle them to the *Mistral*, then. She's faster anyway. I can find them. The Cielcin. I know I can."

"Give you the prisoners?" he repeated, incredulous. "We have a Cielcin nobile on ice—or have you forgotten? We should never have come out here. We should be holding him hostage and waiting for the Pale to attack."

"That's a lovely plan," I said, unable to suppress a sneer all my own, "but if the colonies are not attacked by *its* fleet then Tanaran is good as useless, and the others more so. You'd do as well trying to negotiate with Jadd for a peace with the Commonwealth."

I could see Bassander's grip tighten on the sword he held, and old fencing instinct had me take a step back from his desk. "And what," Bassander asked in a voice small and deadly as spiders, "makes you think the Extras on Vorgossos can contact his fleet in particular?"

"Its," I said, unable to help myself. "Its fleet." He'd used the wrong pronoun; the xenobites had no sexes as we understood them. Before he could brush this aside as meaningless, I pressed on. "Because the captain I killed at Emesh named Vorgossos itself. If it has been there, then the Vorgossene must have some knowledge of how to find them. You know this. We have discussed this a hundred times."

Unwilling to admit his error, Bassander said, "I cannot give you the prisoners. Look—" He raised a hand. "I understand. You do not wish to be returned to Emesh. To Count Mataro and his daughter."

I blinked. "What?" I looked round at the faces of the others around me, at Ilex and Corvo, who looked confused, and at Jinan, who alone understood what the captain meant. "That has nothing to do with this."

"The fleet is massing at Coritani. That's more than two kilolights from Emesh. You have my word I'll do all in my power to keep you from the Lady Anaïs's amorous intentions." The smirk that took over his face was like the first cracks in a pane of glass. I suppressed the urge to smash it.

Anaïs Mataro. The girl—woman now, she was almost certainly decades my elder—had all the makings of the classic palatine lady: beautiful, clever, ambitious. Her fathers had sheltered me when I washed up on their doorstep from the Borosevo streets, had agreed to keep me from my own family. But it had been a trap, a gilded cage. Like the princess in some antique fairy tale, I was kept for political reasons. For my blood. For distantly through my mother's line I was cousin to the Throne itself, to the Emperor William XXIII and the House Avent, and a member of the Peerage. My forced marriage to the Lady Anaïs would have brought his out-land house into that most high and ancient constellation, and so elevated the blood of the children his house would sire through me. I would have been little more than an old racehorse, prized for one part of me and set aside to live my life as Count-Consort of that miserable swamp of the planet where I had met with so much misery.

"Your charity is overwhelming, captain," I said coldly, "but that wasn't my primary concern. Like I said, we can change the nature of this war. Peace with one of the Cielcin fleets could open doors to peace with the others. We can understand them. Trade with them. We don't have to fight."

"You would have me forgive the slaughter at Tyras? Bannatia? Idun? Lycia? Here at Rustam?" Bassander growled. "You would have peace with creatures that *eat* us, Marlowe? That butcher children as you might a pig? Holy Mother Earth! We hardly butcher animals at all anymore. We're not dealing with people, Hadrian. They're monsters."

I smiled a smile to scratch the glass of that smirking face. "And how many times has that been said across human history? About how many peoples?" In my mind I beheld the long roll of time; the oppressors' wrong. At once I recalled the pit-slave I had seen that day in the Meidua coliseum, his face smashed by the gladiator's boot until all semblance of humanity was crushed out of it. *Homo hominis lupus.* How many men had died thus? How many genocides had our ancestors committed? How many cities burned? Gods defaced?

Xenophobia.

That was what they called it.

Fear of the other.

It's the wrong word.

That ancient impulse to slam the gates against the other has no foundation in fear, nor was there terror in Bassander's black eyes. Only cleansing fire and the reflection of fires yet to come. Fires I would light myself. Would have to light.

"They are not people!" Bassander growled.

"They're as good as!" I said.

How little I knew.

It is strange, is it not, that there are always people such as I? Men who believe the stranger is always more trustworthy than their neighbor? When we were young we looked to the stars with hope, praying that what gods or kings there were in the unpastured Dark were greater than Man, and so moral and righteous beyond imagination. We imagined they might descend from heaven and bless us with their gifts, and that it was only human nature that corrupted, for evil required the black hearts of men to create it. In my flagellatory arrogance I could not conceive of evils other than our own—darker and stranger—nor could we conceive that what was evil to us was natural to others. Incidental. But Satan sprang not from Adam, and it was from the blood of Kingu that Marduk made the first men—and not the other way round. Evil is older than we, other than we—or is greater than, extending back and forward across all of conscious Time. Reader, there are other devils than Man. And by our evolved reason we may be sure of understanding human devils only.

In my youth, I believed that language might bridge the gap between our species and any other; that human reason and Truth—the Logos of Aristotle, of the Museum Catholics and the vanished Sufi—were principles greater than our human biology, and so held by all life. But now I know. And know this: every thought had by every philosopher and scholiast, every scientist and priest, is framed by the human mind.

Do not mistake me. I do not dismiss facts. But that two and two are four requires first that a mind has conceptualized two as two and four as four, and understands addition. Of this, there is no guarantee. The laws of nature do not bend, but—like the image that appears as a rabbit to one man and a duck to another—might be differently construed by one species than it is by another. Our logic, our reason, and most especially our morality—grounded as it is in the Uncreated Gods of old—have little in common with those creatures evolved on other worlds than Earth. So I might reconcile and understand, respect, admire, and love any man, be they Jaddian or Tavrosi, swart or pale, man or woman or androgyn. But the inhuman? No. They are outside our comprehension, our trust and faith. And so Bassander's zeal was justified.

I did not know this yet, to my shame. And I would suffer for it, and others would suffer for it. And worlds and peoples burn.

"They are people!" I repeated, more strongly. "They speak, they reason. They know honor. You can't just deny them their . . ."

"Their what?" Bassander interrupted. "Their humanity? They're not human."

Reader, I have seen things you cannot imagine. Things the Cielcin have done. Children—human and Cielcin alike—plated and served at table. I have seen slaves mutilated for the sake of art, partners maimed because it is a mark of status that one be made dependent on another, and the Black Feast to mark the coronation of their dark lord. The banality of that which we might consider monstrous writ casually as a night at the opera. Not because they are evil—though that is also true. But because they are not us.

Desperate and ignorant, I turned from Bassander to Otavia. To Ilex and Greenlaw.

To Jinan.

"We've come too far," I said, crossing to take Jinan's hand. "You said you had to wait to make a decision, captain. It's time."

"This is not a democracy!" Bassander said, though in a sense it was. Otavia served by contract, and like all foederati might break faith and run. Jinan served her own loyalties, to her satrap and prince. We were held together only by mutual purpose, by mutual respect. If we were to break with one another, I needed to break on the side of the mission. My mission. Promises I had made in the dark of the Chantry bastille floated back to me, rising like a chorus in my ears.

"I promised I would take them home," I said, looking Jinan in the face, forgetting Bassander. My fingers tightened about hers, willing her to see. To understand. Her lips pressed together, the flesh about them gone pale, her eyes flickering from my face and back again. "We can change this war, Jinan. We're close. March Station, then Vorgossos. Then we'll find the Cielcin."

If I had been like to other monsters and beheld the naked curves of the future, I might have turned away, for here was the crossroads. Down Bassander's path was the long holocaust. The crusade. The war. Down Bassander's path was battle and battle after battle. And death by fire and sword. For how many centuries would we have fought? On how many worlds? How many cinders? How many billion lives ended? And to what end? Whose bodies would lie upon the bonfire at the ashen end of time? War is chaos, and between our people and the Cielcin—though I knew it not, then—there could be no peace. A single tumulus lay at the end of Bassander's path, though whether it marked our end or theirs I cannot say.

I never learned.

What lay down my path, I now know: precisely that cleansing fire I felt in Bassander's eyes. There was battle, and battle after battle. And fire. And sword. But there are strange places on my road, Reader, and my turning toward them lay in Jinan's hand as she pulled hers from mine. She left me no choice, though I had already decided in my blindness. Horror and horror. Those were my only routes, though I groped unaware toward them. Knowing the future, would I have chosen at all? Or turned myself to stone as Perseus might have done to spare himself the effort?

And then she spoke, words descending like the cathars' White Sword to strike me down. "We go to Coritani," Jinan said, shutting her eyes. Dark eyes. Black like Bassander's. I forgot to breathe a moment, and for just as long it seemed my blood had stopped in my veins.

But it was done. Said. And there was no force of nature that could return the instants past. Not for want of trying. "No." I tried to take her hand, to seize it. "Jinan, no. Listen." She batted me aside in blind reflex, caught my wrist.

"No, you listen." Dark eyes opened. Not releasing my wrist, she pressed on. "Bassander . . . Bassander is right. We should return to the fleet with our new intelligence. At the very least they may wish to send ships to all these Extrasolarian outposts. It will save the time of searching them all."

"But we know it's March Station," I said, looking over my shoulder at the red markers drifting in the midst of the holograph.

"Based on the words of a criminal homunculus," Bassander said. Without looking, I felt Ilex twitch. She hated the word *homunculus* the way a man might hate the word *primate,* though both were quite correct. "That link is tenuous at best, Marlowe. Give it up."

My wrist still firmly in Jinan's grasp, I rounded on Bassander. "Every second we delay, you make yourself more *right,"* I hissed. "Each day, the Cielcin grow closer to another world. Are you so desperate to be right you'll let those worlds burn to prove me wrong? Let me go, Lin. Let me do my part, for Earth's sake."

"Hadrian," Jinan said, "please."

The breath came hard in me, and I felt my nostrils flare. It took every ounce of Gibson's stoic philosophy to keep me from rounding on Jinan and screaming. No one spoke. I was at the focus of five pairs of eyes. I might as well have been the target for five lasers, so outgunned was I. Neither Otavia nor Ilex spoke, though they might have come to my aid. They had themselves to think of, and quiet now meant they might fly beneath Bassander's notice for the moment and so come out of this advantaged. I did not blame them.

I was not angry. The emotion I felt as gorge in the back of my throat was something else entirely. Not anxiety. Some feeling at once overwhelming and eminently rational.

Disgust.

Teeth bare, I circled where I stood, taking them all in—unfairly; Ilex and Otavia had done nothing wrong. "Is this it?" I rounded on Bassander, tugging my hand free. "We're to slink off to Coritani empty-handed and mourn our dead? The men whose lives we've wasted?"

"Captain," Bassander Lin said shortly, turning to Prisca Greenlaw at his elbow. "Remove Lord Marlowe to his chambers. He's in considerable distress."

The blond lieutenant rounded the desk, raising one hand to guide me from the cabin. Bassander half-turned, dismissing me, and glanced at the bank of flickering security feeds on the wall behind him.

"Considerable distress?" I repeated, taking a step away from Greenlaw as she approached. "You're destroying my company. Of course I'm distressed."

Bassander turned back. "Your company? Yours? Need I remind you,

Lord Marlowe, that this company is a fiction meant to aid us in barbarian lands? There is no company. Lieutenant!" He directed the last word to Greenlaw, who advanced again, murmuring something about coming along now in a tone that seemed oddly conciliatory, coming from her.

"Then, if there is no company," Otavia Corvo said, speaking for the first time in a long moment, "I cannot have contracted with them." Her words stalled Greenlaw a moment. The tall Norman crossed her arms. "I will take my ship and my people and go."

"Your ship?" Lin repeated, rounding on her. "You are captain of the *Mistral* by my sufferance, Norman. The ship is Imperial property by right of conquest. You have no right . . ."

Otavia rode over him. "I will return those of your people aboard my ship to you at once, of course. And we will return those Norman personnel serving aboard the *Balmung* and the *Pharaoh* before you return to your fleet—provided they wish to leave your service. Which they will."

"Return? Provided they . . . ?" Bassander said stupidly. Shaking his head, he gathered himself. "You would declare war on the Imperium? Commandeer one of her ships? This is not a battle you can win, Norman."

Otavia's hands drifted to her sides, very near to the phase disruptor she wore at her hip. "Call me Norman one more time, Empire-man, and I will show you what this Norman can do."

"Enough!" Jinan snapped, moving between them. "We waste time! Bassander, let them take the ship. We lose nothing we did not have when we departed Emesh. Let the Normans decide if they will stay or go with Captain Corvo, but we cannot afford to fight one another." Here she glanced at me, and even still I wonder if a part of my captain's heart—which knew my own so well—knew what it was I intended, what I already had done. Greenlaw had forgotten me for a moment, distracted by the Norman Amazon's words. "In this you and Hadrian are both right: every moment we delay we give advantage to the enemy. Whatever we do, we cannot do nothing, and we cannot afford to fight among ourselves."

Bassander and Otavia glowered at one another. The captain still held Whent's highmatter sword, the blade stowed. Opposite Otavia's sidearm, I did not like his chances, but if he could thumb his shield-belt before she could draw . . . I liked hers less.

At long last, Bassander nodded. The captain—Commodore Lin—fingered the corner of his desk, looking like the portrait of some lord long dead hung upon the wall of some dusty archive, stained by firelight. In a done voice he said, "Go then."

Jinan spoke again. "It will take a day or two to survey all the active crew about their decisions."

"Any still in fugue should be shuttled to the *Mistral* immediately," Corvo said.

"Agreed." Jinan spoke before Bassander could gainsay her. "Anything else?"

Otavia bared her teeth. Very like a Cielcin smile, that expression. Her face fixed on Bassander Lin, and I wondered what she'd say. Compensation? Severance pay, perhaps? Some other artifact taken from Whent and Bordelon's men—they had been her compatriots, after all.

"An apology."

CHAPTER 13

OBEDIENCE

I FELT LIKE A man balancing on a wire. The smallest failure in any direction but forward was set to plunge me down Bassander's path: back to the war and some squalid end I could not see. I knew this: it would not be to retirement and a quiet life with Jinan on Ubar, and even if the captain kept his word and kept me from a kept life on Emesh, it would be to some poorer purpose than I envisioned for myself.

Was it greed then that motivated me? Pride? To be accounted a great hero of man, to be feted and honored by the Emperor as he who brought peace to the galaxy? Or was it—as I then claimed—a thing done out of compassion? Compassion not only for human life, but for all? I cannot say. In part because it has been so long—almost fifteen hundred years of Earth since I stood in my cabin aboard the *Pharaoh* and weighed my chances—but because also there were parts of me that were alien to my waking mind. Ancient parts, parts we humans hold in common with the ape and the whale and lobster, which are older than our words. Than all words. I knew them not and so cannot speculate as to the depth of my motivations, or their source.

Suffice it to say I felt a tragic need to do something, and to define that doing for myself. I had a talent: I could speak with the enemy. And I had a chance to use that talent. And I had legitimized that chance—if tenuously—in speaking with Raine.

Politics is a dangerous game, and I played it once before to my great peril and benefit. On Emesh, with Valka's help, I had escaped an arranged marriage and trouble with the Chantry and won my way offworld. I attribute this less to any particular genius on my part and more to a blind and scrambling pragmatism. House Mataro, the Jaddians, the Chantry, the Cielcin, the Legions. I had threaded a tight and winding way between them and emerged only somewhat burned.

As I sat on the edge of my bed in that starkly lit little room, I ran long fingers over the sparse pockmarked scars that stippled my left arm. Uvanari tried to kill me in the end, after its torment. Drops of molten lead had struck me from one of the torture implements the Chantry cathars had left to hand for use against their alien prisoner. The scars shone like slick craters in my pale skin. Like stars.

The price I'd paid for my cleverness.

With what would I pay this second time? Was it worth the price?

I had spoken to Raine Smythe, exchanged texts via telegraph from the *Mistral*, where Bassander was least likely to intercept. She'd offered me a paper shield. No comfort in extremis. She could not gainsay Bassander, whose orders came from Titus Hauptmann, himself her superior, but she might order me to disobedience all the same.

I ordered you to find Vorgossos, her message said. *If I order you to ignore Hauptmann's recall and obey me, it's me they'll court martial.*

But I'll have followed criminal orders, I replied.

That won't matter if you succeed.

"Hadrian," Gibson's voice echoed out of time. "Name for me the Eight Forms of Obedience."

As I had done years ago, again I recited, speaking to myself in the dark of my cabin. "Obedience out of fear of pain. Obedience out of fear of the other. Obedience out of love for the person of the hierarch. Obedience out of loyalty to the office of the hierarch. Obedience out of respect for the laws of men and of heaven. Obedience out of piety. Obedience out of compassion. Obedience out of devotion." I said them over and over.

Which is highest? His rough voice turned within me. *Which do you obey?*

Obey, I thought, and thought in my father's voice, and the word was like the howling of air from a shattered castle on a broken moon. My father, Lord Alistair Marlowe, the Butcher of Linon. *There are two sorts of men. One hears an order from his better and obeys. The other sees order in himself and obeys that. All men obey something, even if it is only themselves.*

I was not sure he was right, but I knew one thing: Bassander was only that first sort. He was a soldier, not a lord.

What motivated Bassander? Compassion? There was not a compassionate bone in the Mandari soldier's body. Piety? Perhaps, though what passes for religion in our Imperium is—I have learned—a small and specious thing. In any case, I did not then believe that Bassander was pious, taking him for the sort of wind-up man preferred by the admiralty in their officers. It was loyalty, of course. Loyalty not to the person of his commanders, but to their ranks. Bassander required order more deeply than I knew. He depended on it to hold back the chaos in his own spirit, for there were demons there, as dwell within us all. In the Legion there was structure, order, law. His loyalty was a function of this dependence, this need. He obeyed the office of the hierarch, the structure of his legion. His captain, his tribune, the First Strategos.

To whom did I answer? What did I obey?

CHAPTER 14

CONSPIRACY

THUS THE BREAKING OF our company was set in motion, and between the three ships went shuttle after shuttle as Norman mercenaries were separated from Imperial legionnaires and Jaddian *aljanhi* alike. Between the distances and the time required for the unloading of gear and baggage the whole process was projected to take more than two days.

I made discreet effort to spirit away those of my possessions I would not be parted with: my clothes and combat armor, the red glasses that had survived all the way out of Emesh, the dinted myrmidon's helmet, and the washing basin Jinan had given me. And my journals, of course. There were five by then, ranging in size from a folio more than a cubit high to a pocketbook no larger than the palm of my hand. Other leaves there were stuffed between their pages, depicting charcoal sketches and ink of men and cities and other things I'd drawn. They were my proudest possessions, save perhaps only my sword.

But I had no guarantee that there was a place for them on the *Mistral*, and so under the pretense of an inspection of the exchange I rode in the back of a shuttle carrying some dozen of the frozen mercenaries over from the *Pharaoh* to their new berths on the smaller Uhran-built ship.

I went alone, leaving Switch to other devices, and once the flight officers had cleared our docking I climbed up the umbilicus and followed the hall past the gallery where I'd met with Siran. The hall beyond was round as the tubes of the Quiet ruins on Emesh, though white where that strange place was black, with padded rings every few feet and brackets to assist in the event the suppression fields were turned off. I had to push past boxes left stacked in the hall, and acknowledged those as stopped to greet me. But I did not stay.

I'd foregone the crimson Red Company uniform—judging it a mistake in that moment, for my purposes, though I kept the high black boots. The rest of my kit was black, such as I had worn down to the planet, and I wore my shield-belt and Olorin's sword openly about my hips above the short tunic. My old coat I wore over all. Very dark gray it was, a gift from the household of Count Mataro when I'd left their capital after my disastrous duel. It trailed after me, flapping about my calves as I went.

"Ho, boss!" Crim's voice called from a side passage.

Stopping, I turned and saw the foederatus emerge from a room behind me. The shadow of weariness darkened the pits of his eyes, but he smiled and smoothed his unruly hair as best he could. In a quiet voice he asked, "Why are you here?"

I'd no reason to lie, not here. "I'm looking for the captain."

"She's in the ready room with Doctor Onderra," Crim said at once. "Is it true we're parting ways? You've been recalled?"

I ignored the question, asking instead, "Valka is here?"

"She means to stay with us," Crim said, his smile widening just a little. "Something about being done with barbarians and . . . I'm not going to try and repeat her words, sir."

"Valka's leaving?" I said, stunned. It made sense. She was no soldier and had no love for the Empire, and had only held on for the promise of a meeting with the xenobites and an answer to her mysteries. An odd pit like an ulcer grew at once in my stomach, and I nodded my slow understanding. A moment later it was gone, banished by need and the next thought. "Where did you say they were?"

"Ready room, lord."

"Very good." And so I hurried off without another word.

The ready room lay just off an annex that accessed the bridge and the primary airlock far to the bow. It opened at my handprint and I stepped through the circular door to a small, low-ceilinged room whose roof arced away with the curve of the hull. Valka and the captain turned as I entered, and I took it as a compliment when both their eyes widened in surprise. Before either of them could speak, I said, "Captain, I wish to hire you."

Otavia Corvo—dressed only in exercise gear, her golden hair pulled back from her teak face—frowned darkly as she said, "What?"

I waited for the heavy bulkhead door to hiss shut behind me before I said, "I want to go to March Station."

The silence that followed might have out-sat eternity if Valka had not said, "What about Bassander's orders?"

"Damn the orders. Damn Bassander," I spat back, feeling hot all at once. I planted my legs apart and faced Otavia square across the low metal console table. "And damn the Empire if they get in my way." Out of the corner of my eye I thought I saw Valka compress her lips and nod ever so slightly.

But I focused on Otavia, who settled into a low armchair bolted to the floor opposite me. As I myself was wont to do she tossed a leg over the arm of that chair, emanating a casual strength from every Olympian curve. She watched me a long moment, eyes gone narrow. At last she asked, "What else?"

Valka laughed, and I said, "I'm sorry?"

"What else do you need?" Otavia asked, brushing a crooked strand of her bleached hair from her face. "Not just a taxi service, I'm sure."

I spoke without hesitation. "I need help taking the Cielcin from the *Balmung*. Today."

"Today?" the captain repeated, incredulous. "Are you insane? We'd never get on board."

I shook my head, took the seat opposite her with a sidelong glance at Valka, who remained standing by the far wall, arms crossed, as if deep in thought. "There are shuttles passing between all three ships right now, if we sent three of the larger ones over to the *Balmung*, we might be able to come away with . . . six? Seven of the fugue units? You have hookups in the hold here. There's room."

"And how do you expect to carry out six of those fugue pods without your girl noticing?" Otavia asked. Stopping, she raised her eyebrows. "Come to think on it, why aren't you having this conversation with Jinan?"

A part of me crumpled then as if Otavia had taken an ax to it. I averted my eyes. "You heard her at the meeting. Do you really think she'd listen to me?" I'd turned the wrong way. Valka was staring at me. Those relentless gold eyes peeled the skin from me. I looked away again. "I tried speaking to her. Many times. She won't listen." Something dry and hairy crouched at the back of my mouth, and I swallowed. "Jinan and I are done. She'll have to return to her people when we return to the fleet."

"Done?" Valka said, speaking up. "Does Jinan know this?"

"Jinan did this," I said, surprised by the venom in my voice. I did not have to look at her to see the sad smile on Valka's face, the concern for a friend in pain.

Otavia offered no condolence or commiseration. "It won't work. Even if I could get three cargo shuttles over to the *Balmung* without putting your girl's hackles up or alerting that cocksucking Mandari friend of yours, there's no way we could make off with those huge pods. Not if we had two shifts and a guarantee of privacy."

"One then," I said at once. I'd planned for this, but had wanted to start big. "Just the nobile, Tanaran."

A thin line formed between Otavia's brows, and, irritable, she ran fingers through her floating hair. "That might do . . ." I could have grinned. I'd counted on her refusing to make off with multiple Cielcin. I'd started big, needed her to think she'd talked me down. I knew the way she thought. Otavia might have looked like a champion weightlifter, but she had a mind like a Rothsbank logothete and a Legion signifer all at once.

"We'd only need one shuttle."

"We'd still have a hell of a time explaining to those lovely Jaddians why it is we're walking off with one of their prisoners." Hands still in her hair, she slung her leg down and propped herself against the table. "Why am I even listening to this? I should be prepping my people for fugue and the jump out-system . . ." Her words trailed off, and she looked wistfully away past where Valka stood, as if through some window only she could see. "Find honest work to do. Sure there's got to be some little colony that wants protecting, times like they are. A nice security gig, a bit of guard duty."

"You don't mean that," I chided, attempting a smile. "Guard duty? Orbital defense? You'd be bored inside a fortnight."

Otavia snorted, crossed her arms. "Might do. But tell me this, Empireman. How is it you're expecting to pay for all this? I know where my payout was coming from, and it's not you."

It was all I could do not to bite my lip. The money had come from the Legion coffers, dispensed to our Norman auxiliaries via Bassander's signifer. I had nothing. Whatever assets had been mine as a scion of House Marlowe were gone, stripped from me by my father when he dowered me to House Mataro. Whatever entitlements I'd possessed were either stripped or granted the Count of Emesh as my future father-in-law. I never bothered to discover which it was. In any case . . .

"You're right," I said honestly. Leaning in, I flattened one hand against the tabletop. "I'm not the money, but I'm not asking you to take me to Vorgossos. Just as far as backspace. To March Station or wherever we're going."

"And to storm an Imperial destroyer for some hare-brained heist that's sure to get us killed."

"No one said anything about storming anything," I said. "I was thinking *infiltrate*. I'm at home on the *Balmung*, Switch is there. Send me with Siran and Crim—a couple others—I'll be in and out with Tanaran before Jinan even notices."

"What about the others?" Otavia asked, and there was a note of kindness in her voice I did not expect.

"What?"

"Old Pallino and the others you brought with you from Emesh."

The words choked off before I could find them. And like I'd done with Jinan already, I let them go in my heart. "They'll be happier on some other road," I said, more to assuage the guilt in my heart than out of any felt truth, though I would prove right in the end. "They can stay with Bassander. The worst he'll do is cut them loose, leave them on Coritani or some world along the way."

The Norman woman eyed me from under furrowed brows. "You're good with that?"

I bobbed my head. "Switch is coming, and Siran's here . . . a few of the others. Pallino deserves peace. He's lived long enough."

"I'm not sure he'd agree."

That pulled a rough laugh from me, and I agreed. I did not mention that Switch had already gone to the trouble of getting those of my effects I would not be parted from off of the *Pharaoh*—his old lover Etienne had helped with that—and that they were even now sitting unlooked for in the *Balmung*'s docking bay among the ammunition and the ration bars and the spare seedstock for the hydroponics station.

I don't like it, Switch had said on the *Balmung*. *Leaving Jinan and the rest behind. Don't feel right, Had.* I hadn't liked it either, and Switch only relented after I wore him down. *Don't feel right,* he'd said again, *turning on our folk.*

"Hadrian?" Otavia asked. "Are you listening?"

"I'm sorry?"

"I asked how you planned on pulling off this miracle," she repeated. "Those pods weigh a good half ton. You're not going to get Switch to carry it for you, and I think someone will notice if you turn off the suppression fields and try to float it out."

Valka took a half step forward, folded posture loosening slightly. "You're going to wake it up."

Otavia's face blanched. "What?"

Innocent, I spread my hands. "We'll move a lot faster."

The Norman captain's face contorted into a look of the utmost horror and disgust. "You want to wake up that . . . that thing? On my ship?" she spluttered, looking to Valka for support, but none was forthcoming, not from the xenologist. "For free?"

"I can't promise money. Not right now," I said. "But I need your help, Otavia. Please." She looked away, and I could see the beads of an abacus flickering in deep eyes as she chewed the inside of her cheek. "Have we not been friends?"

That stirred her, and she raised her eyebrows. "Oh, we're friends, Marlowe, but I can't fuel the *Mistral* with friendship."

"I know," I said. "I know. When we were in council you said it was your worlds that were taking the brunt of this war. Norman worlds. I still think I can stop it, but I need that xenobite on the *Balmung*, and I need a ship, and right now you're the one who can give me that." The captain thought this over, face downcast, fingers picking at some spot on the console I could not see. It was my turn to jog a response from her. "Would you do it for me?"

Her eyes narrowed. "Are you calling in our debt?"

I did not like to phrase it that way.

"I told you," I replied, "after Bordelon. You don't owe me anything. I am asking for your help. If you can't give it, I understand." I was entitled to nothing. I'd learned that in Borosevo. Everything we receive is a kind of gift, if we do not take it for ourselves. I had rid Captain Corvo of her monstrous commander and spared her life at Pharos. Were I still the boy I'd been, I would have said she owed me for my mercy. But mercy that expects repayment is no mercy at all, nor is a friendship truly a friendship that stands on debt and gratitude.

So I hoped, and ignored the stoic whispering in my soul: *Hope is a cloud.*

It is well that the human mind sees only a little of the world, and better that it is bounded by our petty senses. Had Otavia known the weight and number of the souls that hung on her words—truly hung on them—she might have bitten off her own tongue. Had I known what I asked, I would have done. Yet there were but the three of us in the close space, and so she took a deep breath. "All right. Who do you need?"

"From here? Siran, Crim—Ilex if you can spare her."

"Both of my lieutenants?"

"Just the first two, then. Them and a pilot officer and this ship ready to go the minute our shuttle clamps in. I don't think Bassander'd use the *Pharaoh*'s artillery but I'm not going to risk it any longer than I have to." I called a hand to my forehead. "And a medtech. I think I can run a thaw on the pod but I want to be sure. Has Okoyo transferred over here?"

"No." But Otavia was nodding, chewing on her cheek again. "You have to wait until my people are all secure on the *Mistral.*"

"If we do, we'll lose any benefit the chaos might give us."

"I don't care," she said, "I'm not stranding *anyone* with that stiff-necked cockatrice of a captain."

Ducking my head, I said I understood.

"And I don't like letting that . . . that alien aboard."

"You haven't met it," I said, defensive. Otavia didn't look convinced. "If we have to confine it to a cabin, we will."

She made a small noise of assent, and I did not press her further.

It had gone as well as I'd hoped. Now I had to see it through. We agreed on a time, set forth some few details. We would launch with the last wave of shuttles from the *Mistral*, arriving with those few Legion and Jaddian troops transferring back to their proper ships before those same shuttles took the last few frozen Normans back to the *Mistral.* Thence I would make for the cubiculum and with Okoyo's help thaw out the Cielcin, Tanaran. I could see it in my mind's eye already: the violet suspension fluid running out, the black blood and life restored to the Pale creature amid the frost and the dimness.

"You've overlooked the cameras," Valka said. I almost jumped clean out of my skin. She'd gone so quiet I'd almost forgotten she was there. Noticing this, she smiled, baring her teeth in that wicked way she had. "Ship's security will be on you in minutes once they see what you're up to."

"That's why I wanted Ilex," I said, "but Crim will be a bit more use if it comes to blows, so . . ."

Valka brushed her fringe back behind her ear and said, "I'll go." I froze, caught as a moving image is between frames. Valka was a difficulty, a spot in the human universe that lensed my effort and perception as a star bends light, by which I mean I was afraid to ask her—so afraid I'd not even considered the possibility that I might ask her. "I can knock out the cameras from the shuttle, I think."

"Are you sure?" I asked. The doctor's face drew into the makings of a scowl. She made an unconscious gesture for the implanted micro-computer hidden at the base of her skull, and I raised a defensive hand.

"I'm not questioning your abilities, I'm just . . . I thought you were leaving?" I gestured at the room around us, indicating her presence aboard the *Mistral* and not on either of the ships bound for the fleet.

She settled herself into one of the chairs between Otavia and myself, her sharp face breaking into a bloody smile. "What was it you said? Damn the Empire? Besides," and here she folded her hands upon the tabletop, "'twill get me my time with the Cielcin. So I'm in."

I drew in a long, ramifying breath and felt myself strengthened by each atom of it. "Right!" I exclaimed, clapping my hands. "This is going to be fun!" I had to smile, to try to make myself feel something other than the quiet, crashing panic of the necessity for action.

The faces of both women darkened, and the captain said, "You call this fun?"

"Hadrian has a strange idea of fun," Valka put in, and from the way her eyes narrowed, I wondered if she was remembering my duel in Borosevo, or when she had helped me with Uvanari and the Cielcin.

Setting my jaw, I forced myself to smile. "Oh no," I said, "it's going to be fun."

CHAPTER 15

THE FIRST TREASON

SWITCH MET US AS we landed in the bustling cargo bay. About us, the final trio of shuttles were making ready to depart with the last of the Norman auxiliaries, supervised by Bassander's legionnaires—bald-headed and in black fatigues. I wore my long coat slung over my shoulders, and beneath it fingered the catch that would activate my body shield.

"These mine?" I asked, indicating a footlocker and a couple of bags stacked against the fueling console for one of the Sparrowhawk lighters bracketed into the ceiling above. Without waiting for an answer, I added, "And did you find that mantle?"

The red-haired lictor seized the smallest packet from the pile and tossed it to me without looking. "Yeah." I turned the cloak over in my hands. Far from a perfect disguise, but it might save us an odd glance or two when we returned this way with the towering xenobite in tow.

That loading bay crouched at the rear of the *Balmung*, beneath the primary drive cluster, and its massive doors opened out the rear. It stretched for nearly two hundred yards, and was nearly fifty deep, with a full wing of lightercraft accessible by gantries above, and room enough for several shuttles to alight upon the gleaming black deck.

Turning to the young pilot officer and gesturing at the crates Switch had left upon a depowered float palette, I said, "You get these on board." I glanced round at my companions. At Valka, cold and comfortable—her strange eyes far away; at Crim and Siran in matching Red Company fatigues; at Doctor Okoyo fidgeting with her medical kit; at the two other soldiers Captain Corvo had given me, brimming with nervous tension. "You"—I pointed to one of them, a pale girl with a heavy jaw and serious eyes—"stay with the pilot, keep the engines primed. Get everything loaded."

I turned my eyes on the other. "You go with Siran and the lieutenant." And to Siran and Crim I asked, "Know where you're going?"

"Way ahead of you," Siran replied.

"Go on then," then more loudly, to be sure those nearby heard, "get the rest of what's going with the Normans and get it on board." Siran saluted and she and the others hurried toward the square door and the open airlock that led into the longitudinal hall.

Valka stepped forward and, placing a hand on my arm, said, "I'm going to get what's left of my things from my cabin." And she moved off, following Siran and Crim into the hall, leaving me with Switch and the doctor. What Valka was doing she could do from anywhere, with that Tavrosi computer lurking at the bottom of her skull. Better to split up, divide attention, dilute suspicion. We were all friends here.

"Beware Greeks bearing gifts," I said to myself in the Classical English, thinking of my mother's family.

"What?" Switch asked.

"Nothing," I replied shortly. "Careful with that!" I called to the pilot officer, making a show of our presence so as not to be too quiet.

The woman blurted an apology, and I smiled to soften the words.

The dock master, a gray plebeian with thinning hair, hurried over. "Lord Marlowe! What's all this?" He gestured at the crates containing my effects, eyes darting from myself to Switch. "You're not going with the Normans, to be sure?"

"To be sure, officer," I said, clapping the man jovially on the shoulder. "I'm returning my effects to the *Pharaoh* before we make the jump to Coritani. Just making a stop over on the *Mistral*; some of my myrmidons are leaving us."

The man's watery eyes widened, and to Switch he said, "Not you, William? Or the old centurion?" I was always startled to hear Switch's right name, but the officers all used it. Only those of us who came out of the Colosso on Emesh—and a few latter-day friends—yet called him *Switch*.

Switch shook his head. "Not me, Brux. And you'd have to throw Pallino out the airlock to get him to quit again."

"That's good, then," the junior officer said. "Did Captain Azhar sign off on the manifest? I'll need to approve it before I can clear you for departure."

Over the man's shoulder, I could see a group of black-garbed legionnaires helping a group of more wildly dressed Normans load the next shuttle over. How quickly the Red Company uniforms had vanished, as if the whole thing had been some dream. A holiday. And now it was over, the costumes and decorations packed away as if they had never been. Still, they laughed with one another, trading the hollow jokes that friends share at their final parting.

"Not yet," I said, shaking myself. "But it's me, so I'm doing things a little out of order. I'm off to see Jinan now, to . . . to say goodnight."

"That how it is," Brux said with a sly grin. "I hear you, Lord. I do. On your way, then."

If he recognized the good doctor at my elbow, he said nothing, and went about his business. So we went about ours. Leaving the pilot officer with her guard, the three of us left by the starboard door and hurried along the hall, past the odd legionnaire going about her duties or the technician at his work. I kept the heavy mantle bundled under my arm, beneath my coat. Switch and Okoyo followed hard on my heels, so that I felt myself the leader of a phalanx—an effect amplified by the rattle of our bootheels, though they were not in step.

The outer wall angled in slightly, supported by ribs of black metal. Camera eyes lurked between them, and I had to trust that Valka had done her job. She must have done, for Crim and Siran certainly had made it to the cubiculum by that time, and nothing I saw in the faces of our fellow soldiers suggested that there was any trouble. The cubiculum itself was not far from the docking bay, though it was up several floors by way of a tight lift which might fit a dozen or so men without discomfort. It hummed gently as we ascended, and the curved doors hissed open.

The *Balmung* was smaller than the *Pharaoh*, a mere sixteen hundred meters to the flagship's more than two-mile length. We had only to proceed along a quarter of that length, and so pass the alcove where I had spoken to Valka so recently after my own awakening. But for a pair of turnings that would take us from this distal hall toward the center of the ship, it was as straight a shot as could be managed. I could feel the tension in my companions the way a minstrel knows his strings, for I felt it in myself. Not the sickness one feels before a trial, but a sensation like the veins in me had gone to hard plastic or to glass, or else were stretched wide as the nostrils are by effort—and my blood would not slow down. Still, I held myself to calm, invoking Gibson's teachings.

Fear is a poison.

It was like the old bastard was there, walking beside me.

Both in fighting and in everyday life you should be determined, though calm.

Who was it said that? It drifted to me then, and I mastered my breathing, rounding with my companions the last corner that would bring us to the cubiculum.

"Hadrian!"

No bullet could have pierced me so strongly as my name did then, and in that voice of all voices. I had, like the jilting lover of so many bad Eudoran masques, planned to leave without seeing her. She would never agree to come with me, would try to stop me if she could. Love her though I did, I could trust her no more.

Turning, I bowed my head and caught Switch by the arm. "You and the doctor go on," I murmured, and stepping past him said, "Jinan! Hello!"

"Back from the *Mistral*?" she asked, referring to a conversation I'd had with her that morning—before I'd gone to see Otavia. "Did you convince Siran to stay with us?" She was still in her Red Company uniform: the belted tunic jacket, flared trousers, and high boots.

Wordless, I shook my head, and glancing over my shoulder saw Switch and Okoyo vanish around the bend. "No. After Ghen, she . . ." I trailed off, made a weak gesture with my left hand. The right stayed firmly beneath my coat, bundled round the mantle meant for Tanaran. I tried to quiet my suddenly galloping heart, but all of Gibson's stoic aphorisms were useless in that moment, for she was not alone.

"Was that Doctor Okoyo?" Bassander asked, cocking his head to one side. "I sent her to the *Mistral* not three hours ago."

"Overseeing the transfer of the last few Norman fugue patients," I said quickly. "Otavia sent her with me since I was coming over. I'll drop her off before I ferry over to the *Pharaoh* for the freeze."

This seemed to satisfy Bassander, who shrugged his lips and straightened his wide uniform belt—from which hung the hilt of Admiral Whent's old sword along with the Commodore's customary sidearm. Or, the captain's sidearm, that was. He'd donned his blacks again, like the legionnaires in the bay, and so our martial dream was ended, or would end soon.

"But what are you here for, Bassander?" I asked, trying to gather crucial information. He should have been safely away on the *Pharaoh*, not just down the hall from where my friends labored to steal away his prized prisoner.

The captain let out a long sigh. "Came to oversee the last round of shuttles separating the Normans from the rest of us. It seemed the proper thing to do."

Jinan cut in, "Alessandro told me you had Switch take away your things?" She touched my arm, moving close enough that she eclipsed Bassander. It was a question, asked as if she could not quite believe it was so.

"Yes," I breathed, looking up at her. "I was just on my way to grab a couple things he missed. Um . . ." The tallness of her was like the last glass of wine in a lonely bottle. I drank her in and might have cried, were it not for the hard captain with his flint-eyed gaze. "We're separating, aren't we? Once we return to Coritani?" I directed the question over her shoulder to where Bassander stood.

His blacks matched the black of the hall. He might have been a piece of hardware and not a man at all. "We'll have to parley with the Jaddian satrap, but I imagine so, yes. Unless we receive orders concerning the intelligence we recovered from The Painted Man." He kept his attentions fixed on a point firmly over my shoulder as he spoke. Was it embarrassment?

No. Frowning, I peered round Jinan's shoulder at the Mandari legionnaire. It was shame. Whatever else he was, Bassander was not blind. He knew the consequences of his choice, knew what he had done to Jinan and myself and what love there was between us. My eyes flickered to Jinan's, found her watching me intently. I knew that face, knew the light in those eyes moved as much for pity as mine moved to scorn. And a piece of me broke and was ashamed. Ashamed for how I had acted in council: with anger and disgust at these people who would not hear me. And ashamed for what I was about to do.

"It's all right, Bassander," I said, words slow to come. "You only did— you're doing what you think is right." Saying this, I focused all my soul on Jinan and said, "That's all any of us can ever do."

Did she know I was saying good-bye?

"I appreciate your saying that, Lord Marlowe," he said, sounding much much older than I—which indeed he was. "I will keep my word, I'll do all I can to see you're not returned to Emesh and the . . . ah . . ." He glanced at Jinan and—I swear it by all the Memory of Earth—a flush crept up his neck. Stammering, he finished, "The Mataro girl. Though . . . do you really think she's still waiting for you? It's been decades."

"I'd rather not risk it." Eyes shut against the embarrassment that ran down my neck, I said, "Do what you must." Then, "Thank you." I opened my eyes again. Jinan was looking at me with a strange expression on her face, lips raised and pressed together, as if bemused and troubled all at once to find us so agreeable. To her I said, "We'll have to talk at Coritani?" I made it a question so it was not a lie.

"Yes," she said, and the word was more breath than sound. Her fingers tightened on my arm. I kissed her, and kissing her . . . betrayed her, for it was the last kiss we ever shared—though it promised more. We broke apart, and she said, "Love you, *mia qal.*"

"Well, you're not wrong," I said, echoing her. I couldn't say that I loved her, too. It felt too much like lying, after that treasonous kiss. Mustering a little bravura to cover the screaming in my heart, I swaggered back. "Dream of me while you're frozen, my captain," I said.

She made a face, and grinning said, "I never do."

If we exchanged more words, I cannot recall them. In my mind, I simply turn and enter the cubiculum. I have no memory of the long walk up the hall, nor of the cares I must have taken to ensure I was not followed. Strange what the mind abridges, strange what it retains, and stranger still what it invents. Mythologizes. I feel sure that I did not look back at Jinan and the captain where they stood in that hall. I remember being afraid to do so, fearing that some shadow in my face might betray me as I betrayed them. And yet clearly I can see my captain standing there, tall and noble as a Chantry bronze—still wearing her reds, our reds. It is one of the peculiarities of my soul that when I think of Jinan it is to that moment I must go first, and so work either backward through our bliss and our toils . . . or forward to the heartache beyond our end.

CHAPTER 16

THE TOMB

THE COLD SHOCKED ME to myself. Thin fingers of mist like the arms of phantasms snaked out into the hall. Crim and Switch were on me at once, drew back at once when they saw it was me. Siran and the Norman trooper stood guard at the door opposite, leaving Doctor Okoyo to fuss over the huge storage crèche that housed the Cielcin.

"This is the one, yes?" she asked, keying her way through a sequence of prompts on a panel on the side of the crate.

Shrugging into my coat properly, I squinted at the name stenciled in red on its side. "Yes." I set the heavy mantle down and went to the bank of drawers fixed to the wall opposite the sleeping fugue crèches. On their feet, the Cielcin ranged from seven to nine feet tall, and so no human crèche could hold them. The eleven sepulchers that stood at intervals along the arc of that curving theater might have carried a bull auroch to some new colony. Finding the drawer I wanted, I drew it out and set it on the floor. Within was a sort of black jumpsuit of some rubbery material and a set of loose-fitting dark robes. At a strange look from Siran, I said, "Tanaran's clothes."

"Blood's mixing," the doctor said in her Norman clip. "Are you sure about this?"

"Quite sure," I said. I wasn't. I had no idea how Tanaran would react. It was no fighter, not like Uvanari had been, nor like any of these others slumbering in this hold. But for a moment I felt a hint of Bassander's trepidation, I think. His defensive coil against the strangeness of these beings. "But doctor, the minute this thing unseals I want you to step back. Switch, keep a bead on the Cielcin, will you? I don't know how it might react to the thaw."

Being mostly water, organic tissue does not like to freeze. The crystallization of water in the blood has the potential to damage the delicate structure of organs and tissues, to break blood vessels and tear arteries. And yet the long years and decades of star travel are too long to face conscious, lest all but the most high among the palatine burn their lives in transit. And so the blood had to be cycled out, replaced with the TX9, which did not freeze as it cooled. Most tanks performed the task automatically, cycling the suspension fluid out, draining the body and the space in the surrounding tank before pumping the blood back in as the body warmed. I merited special attention from the medical officer only because of my high station. It dramatically reduced the risk of cryoburn.

"Draining the tank," Okoyo said, hitting a switch on the side of the crèche. A ring of blue light glowed around one of the hoses that snaked away from the box and toward a reservoir for sterilization. That would be the suspension fluid. Arms crossed, I stalked just behind the doctor where she crouched at her ministrations, awaiting my cue like an actor hanging in the wings.

"How long?" Siran asked from her place by the far door.

Okoyo bit her lip. "I'm not sure. I don't usually work with these sorts of tanks. I'm used to people." She fiddled with another set of controls. "Temperature's rising steadily. Starting TX9 drain now." But before she pressed the final button, she turned to me. "Are we sure this will work? Their biology is different, and not cow different."

My eyes darted to the doors, as if I half-expected Bassander to burst in with an inquisition at any moment. At length I shook my head, shrugging my arms tighter against the cold. "I've no idea. Not for certain. They weren't afraid going in, so they must have some comparable technology, but . . ." I left the rest unspoken. I could only hope the technology worked as well on xenobites as it did on livestock. I knew that in the Empire there were circus troops and scholiasts and men of stranger professions who carried non-terranic life forms on their ships. On Emesh the Count's vilicus had spoken of a plan to transplant thousands of the native Umandh population to another world for labor purposes, and I knew others of the coloni races were transported between human worlds for the amusement of the wealthy. They had to be transported somehow across the dark years between the stars.

"I'm sure the Legion medtechs did everything at their disposal to keep the Pale alive," I said.

"It is alive," Okoyo replied, pointing at a set of small panels. "I'm just not sure I can keep it that way."

It seemed an odd time to be making that particular comment, given that she had already drained the suspension fluid and was cycling the TX9 out for blood. I needed a moment to understand. "I don't doubt your abilities, doctor. I know you haven't done this before." Frost crunched beneath my feet as I crossed to her and, stooping, pressed the button to begin pumping blood back into the Cielcin's body myself.

Red indicators began cycling blue with a series of faint chimes. I helped Okoyo to her feet, rehearsing my first words in my head. It had been a long time since I'd needed the alien tongue, and I was afraid of what I'd sound like.

You speak like a child. That was what the first Cielcin I had ever met said to me. *Nietolo ti-coie luda.* Like a child. I didn't feel like a child. I felt old. Aged as only a traitor can be. My mind wandered beyond the edges of that frigid room and out across our little fleet. To Valka, wherever she was, aiding our little misadventure. To Bassander, clueless, I hoped. To Jinan, whom I'd betrayed. To Otavia and Ilex and the others waiting on the *Mistral* for our return. To Pallino, Elara, and the others I would leave behind. I felt at once like one of the necromancers out of antique myth, standing above the coffin of some revenant plucked back from the void. That put me in mind of my words to The Painted Man, from Shelley.

Satan had his companions, fellow devils, to admire and encourage him, but you are solitary and abhorred. This wasn't going to be easy on the xenobite, alone among us humans. Stranger in a strange land. Pneumatics hissed, whined with recharge as the great lid of the fugue crèche was lifted up and hinged backward. Acrid vapors snaked in the cold air, smelling of antiseptic and machine oil. Under normal circumstances, the doctor ought to have approached, to check the pulse and pupil response of her patient. I did not blame Okoyo for hanging back.

Behind me, I could sense the coiled tension in Switch and Crim, their phase disruptors raised and set to stun. Siran's face and that of the nameless soldier beside her were white and drawn as corpses. I realized suddenly that I alone of all that group had been down in the tunnels at Calagah. I alone had been in Castle Borosevo and the Chantry bastille below its walls for the long interrogation and the inquest into the crash on Emesh. I alone had spoken with Uvanari and with Tanaran itself. Not Switch, not Siran, and certainly none of the Normans had ever seen a Cielcin in the flesh.

It was no wonder they were scared.

So I could not afford to be.

"Fear is a poison," I murmured beneath hearing, the words smoking in the cold air, and brushed past the Norman doctor. There was a faint violet color to the smokes rising from the crèche, and through them I could see the slick grayness of the crèche's interior. It reminded me of the paper egg cartons I have seen in marketplaces from Marinus to Jadd, wet with the undrained slime of the suspension fluid, like the snot of some fell beast. And in the center of it all—naked and dripping and pierced by several needled cords—the body of the alien. Corpse white it was, the flesh shining and bloated as if it were many days drowned and fit to burst. Yet it was thin and hard, a creature of sinew and bone, claw and horn and hide. Its long white hair—sprouting from the back of its head like a Mandari queue—was soaked and tangled beneath its crown of snarling horns. Reaching down past the lip of the crate, I peeled a sensor tape off its neck and felt for a pulse.

There it was. Faint but growing stronger as both hearts began to beat. *Ta-tum ta-tum.*

"It's alive," I said, and moving drew the long tube from its mouth. I beheld the wretch—the miserable monster I had brought with us—and my young heart filled with the milk of pity and of guilt. I said again, "It's alive." Everything that happened to it next was because of me, and I'd set its feet on no easy road. Heedless of the purplish slime on its face, I lay a hand there, feeling the slow blossoming of warmth as the black blood piped into its veins.

Ta-tum ta-tum.

"Is it awake?" Crim asked.

"It's dreaming," Okoyo replied. "The mind still has to reorient."

The muscles of the inhuman face hung slack in sleep. Its eyes shut, lips parted, it might have been a human face—carved as it were of alabaster or ivory—were it not for the absent nose. Something in the lines of its face put me in mind of those mad Italians who, by the dawn light of history, cut into corpses to understand the musculature. An artist myself, I wondered at the similarities between its face and mine: that Evolution should—beneath two separate suns—contrive two forms so alike and yet so estranged. What chance or powers had moved our two species to so similar a form I could not then guess, but I wondered, and wondering traced my thumb against the sharp line of Tanaran's cheekbone. I imagined there was a kinship between us, as if Life shared a common ancestry with Life—as indeed is the case for all terranic life forms. I ignored our differences out of necessity and the necessary idealism of youth. I needed to ignore them, and so imagined that it was Humanity I saw in the inhuman lines of its face.

It jerked as if electrocuted and I yanked my hand away. Behind me, the others all gasped, and I heard at least one stunner ping as it was primed. Switch's, at a guess. With a wet and rattling gasp the Cielcin lurched, trying to find its feet—its knees. Tanaran scrabbled instead and collapsed, pulling at the tubes that still fed its blood like ink beneath the wrinkled paper of its skin.

"*Paiwarete,*" I breathed, laying hands on its arm and shoulder. "Careful now." I spoke its language softly, almost crooning. "You've been asleep a long time."

It pawed around blindly, hand finding my elbow, my shoulder, the front of my shirt. Hard fingers closed on my tunic, and it pulled me down. "*Yukajji-do,*" it said, looking around. Its black eyes opened, large as my fist, and cast about the cubiculum. It took in Okoyo and the others before at last settling on my own face. "Hadrian."

"Yes," I said, still softly. "It's me."

"Is it the day?" it asked, raising its upper lip to show those horrible, glassy teeth. "Aranata? Did you find . . . my . . . master?"

I had thought long about what I would say to Tanaran when I awakened it. Nothing seemed sufficient, given the circumstances. One thing alone was clear: there was very little time, and the truth—in my experience—is always a long story. So too are lies. "*Namne deshu civaqeto ti-zahem gi,*" I said.

"When we get where?" it asked.

"Can you stand?"

"I think so. Yes."

"I'll help you."

When at last it found its feet, Tanaran stooped over me, leaning on my shoulder, naked and covered in slime. It showed no particular shame at its undress—neither had Uvanari in the throes of its torture—and not for the first time I wondered if the xenobites had a nudity taboo. And why should they? The Cielcin were hermaphrodites, and had no special modesty to hide from one another as we.

Extending a hand to Okoyo, I said, "Towel." She tossed one to me rather than handed it. I could see the whites in her eyes, like she was a racehorse spooked by some uncommon noise. Tanaran understood implicitly what the towel was for, and began to wipe itself off. "There isn't very much time," I said seriously. "I need you to come with us."

"*Iagami mnu ti-perem ne?*" it asked. *Where are we going?*

"To another ship," I said tersely, pointing it toward the drawer I'd removed that held its clothes. "I'll explain once we're there."

If it understood at all what the urgency in my voice meant, it gave no sign, only continued to wipe the violet slime from its pale limbs with the rag. Presently it stopped, cast about the cubiculum, taking in the crèches where lay interred the others of its kind. It swayed there, narrow as a reed. "What about the others?" it asked, turning to look straight down at me.

I rolled my head in rough approximation of the gesture the Cielcin use to signal *no*. *"Usayu okun."* Just you.

"You are taking me to torment," it said, "like you took the captain."

I had nothing to say to that. There was nothing I could say. Except, "Get dressed."

Crim and Switch led the way, with myself and the hooded Cielcin close behind. The black halls had transformed themselves while we tarried in the cubiculum. I kept my hand on my shield-belt beneath my coat, shoulders tensed as if expecting at any minute a knife might plunge between them. But it was only Siran and the doctor behind me.

"The lift's just ahead," I said, speaking to the Cielcin. "Keep your head down." The hall was lower than the cubiculum had been, and Tanaran stooped as it followed on.

Tugging the deep hood further down, it said, *"Oreto yagiara. Raka hassu-iuna."*

"What's it saying?" Crim hissed, pressing himself against the wall before Switch moved round the corner.

"It can't see," I said.

"Cryoburn?" the Norman asked over his shoulder as we moved quickly down the hall.

Shaking my head, I said, "Not sure. The Cielcin aren't fond of light to begin with." The tall xenobite shrugged its gray mantle about itself, and were it not for the hands—too white and with too-long fingers—one might have thought the creature the specter of some itinerant, bent by time and toil. It slumped against the wall, bent so that its head was almost at a level with my own. Remembering well the struggles of waking from fugue, I caught it. "Not far now. Not far." Helping the creature to stand, I looked up at the ceiling, at the hemispheres of black glass studding the dark roof at intervals, each housing a camera. They must be quiescent, depowered by Valka's will, but still I felt the weight of them, the lidless eye of the Imperial conscience. "Come now."

We'd not gone three paces when Crim cried out in Jaddian and fired his stunner. I left Tanaran leaning on the wall and hurried forward. I had seen no one, but had been distracted helping the hulking alien to walk. Without having to be asked, Switch said, "Technician saw us. Don't know which one."

"Black planet!" I swore, grinding my teeth. "To the lift, then. Double quick." I turned back and snatched Tanaran by the wrist. Switching tongues, I said, *"Liara doh!"* Quickly now!

Only the Pale's silver-glass teeth were visible beneath its cowl. "What is happening?"

"We have to hurry," was all I said. *"Liara!"*

It didn't move, save to straighten as much as the hall would allow. Its mouth hung open for a moment, and it said, "You are fighting your own people. For me? Why?"

"Liara!" I said again, tugging its arm.

"You are a fool," Tanaran said.

"Granted," I said, "but if you want to see your people again, you'll come with this fool now."

Have you ever walked by night for the first time in a place too familiar to you by day? Have you felt the darkness and the light of stars and moons transmute that comfortable place into somewhere threatening and strange? Thus it was for that hallway. It was as if I had never walked that way before, who had walked it a thousand times. The ribbed walls and trapezoidal profile and the winking camera blisters felt as if they contained some unspoken threat.

We piled into the lift, Crim and Switch coming up last to take a position nearest the door. Tanaran had to lean, lest its head scrape the roof of the carriage. The door sealed, and we seven plunged back down several floors.

"Odds on there being a party waiting for us at the bottom?" Siran asked, triple checking her own disruptor was set to stun.

"Too soon," Crim said. "But it won't be long."

The doors cycled open with a hiss, revealing a pair of haggard-looking fugue techs—bald-pated and pale in their gray-striped blacks. Crim didn't hesitate, and so they had only the barest instant to register confusion before the stunner bolts felled them. They collapsed like a stack of wet rags.

"Don't seem right," Switch said, lingering by the nearest of the stunned men. "They're our people."

Tanaran's distended form drew my attention as it emerged from the lift behind me, and I said, "Our Cielcin friend would agree with you." Switch made a face, eyed Tanaran with a look of mingled horror and disgust, and when the xenobite had passed, the myrmidon made the sign of the sun disc, thrust it toward Tanaran as if the creature were a hedge witch Switch meant to ward against. I squinted at him, but was glad he did not see me shake my head as I added, "Leave them. They'll be all right."

All the same, Switch stooped and untwisted the man's leg out from under him and moved off with a punctilious little nod. I smiled after him. What was it I'd said to Jinan—it felt like years ago? That it was intolerable such good men should spend their lives in battle? I felt that sense again, and with it the sense—too common in me—that I deserved neither their loyalty nor their friendship. I confess I tarried there a step, watching Switch and Crim and Siran fan out, the latter dragging Tanaran behind her, moving from support strut to support strut. I did not stand there long—just a moment—and despite the urgency of our moment I smiled.

"It's not far," Crim said, unhelpfully. I repeated the words to Tanaran. "Going to get more crowded the closer we get to the bay."

He could not have said it at a worse time.

"Lord Marlowe!"

There was the knife I'd been waiting for, plunged right between the shoulder blades, just east of the heart. My name seemed pulled from me like a shard of ice extracted from my back, and turning I saw Lieutenant Alessandro Hanas standing with six Jaddian *aljanhi* in their striped blue and orange tabards.

They had phase disruptors trained on us.

Even as I turned, I thumbed the catch on my shield-belt and felt the energy curtain collapse around me, skin tightening as the static charge forced hairs to stand on end. Trying to speak casually, I slid my arms into the sleeves of my coat. "Lieutenant, hello."

"I'm not sure what it is you think you're doing, sir."

"Sir," I said, checking that Tanaran was still standing there, "I'm taking this Cielcin to its leader." No sooner had the words left my mouth then I realized the cliché they contained, but I set my jaw all the same. I did not draw my stunner. Hanas was shielded himself, and though the *aljanhi* were not, I did not want to provoke them, for my companions' sake. Solutions began to spin off in my mind, ways to get my people safely down that hall and out. It was a straight shot to the bay a couple hundred meters away, and turning our backs would only expose them to fire.

The Jaddian lieutenant scratched his beard. "Surrender, and I'm certain the captain will treat you fairly." He shut his eyes, and for a moment the man spoke and not the officer. "After all she did for you."

"Don't talk about her, Hanas," I snapped. "I know what I'm doing."

The officer did not raise his hands, but his jaw worked as he glanced at the soldiers at his either side. He seemed to chew on some sour gristle, as if some foul taste had poisoned him. "I hope for your sake that you don't." The muzzles of six stunners glowed blue like the slitted eyes of a half dozen jeweled serpents. Crim had a shield. And Siran. And Switch. But the doctor, the other soldier, and Tanaran were not so fortunate. Tanaran might take a stunner bolt or two before it fell—I had seen its kind endure thus on Emesh—but I didn't like the risk. And Tanaran *would* draw fire. There wasn't an eight-foot-tall xenobite in the galaxy that wouldn't draw fire from a cluster of human troopers in a narrow hallway. No matter how I turned it over in my head, I didn't like our odds. I toyed with the idea of drawing my sword, but these men were—had been—my comrades. My friends. And they were Jinan's people, and despite all that I was doing and had to do I could not bring myself to cross that line. Attacking those soldiers seemed too much like attacking her.

"Surrender!" Hanas said, placing his own hand on the stock of his phase disruptor where it remained slung on his hip. "For the last time! Throw down your arms and kneel!"

As he finished his demand, a stunner bolt from behind felled one of the *aljanhi* to his right, then another. A third. The lieutenant turned, drawing his weapon as two of the soldiers fired. One of their shots went wide, striking the ceiling, while the other struck me full in the chest and dissipated against my shield curtain. I moved forward, shouting at Tanaran to get down and out of danger.

The shielded lieutenant lurched sideways, staggering for the wall. I drew my own stunner and fired uselessly at him, watching the energy curtain coruscate as the field exchanged with my weapon's discharge. The lieutenant's square shoulders hid what he was doing, but I knew well enough.

Vwaa! Vwaa!

The standard Imperial alarm blasted through that corridor, urging the ship's response division to our location. Red lights flashed. I heard a coarse oath from Switch behind me, and another set of stunner bolts whistled from a side passage behind Hanas's men. Catching on, Crim fired at the remaining *aljanhi*, catching one full in the face.

"What the hell is going on?" Siran shouted, words half-drowned by the alarms.

Vwaa! Vwaa!

I had much the same question.

I did not have it long.

There ought to be a word, I think, for the opposite of a catastrophe, though such moments are rare. Two figures emerged from the side passage, still in their Company reds. Elara caught one of the remaining soldiers full in the face with her stunner and Pallino followed, weapon at his side. The lieutenant was still on his feet, and whirling to face the newcomers, he tugged his disruptor free from its holster. The silver stock gleamed in the harsh light. Knowing the officer was shielded, Pallino threw his stunner square at Hanas's face. The lieutenant's shot went wide, and Pallino dove in past Elara before I could so much as adjust to the myrmidons' surprise appearance. He threw a vicious hook—following through fist-to-elbow—that clipped the square Jaddian's temple and snuffed him out like a candle.

Vwaa! Vwaa!

It happened so fast you could be forgiven for thinking it hadn't happened at all, or for disbelieving that the aged and wiry old man had done it. Pallino looked at me with his one blue eye and through clenched teeth said, "I should have guessed you'd try something like this, boy."

"Guessed?" Clearly he had guessed; he was there, after all. "What do you mean?"

"I told him, obviously," said the voice, and it was only then that Valka appeared in the doorway, carrying a stunner herself. She looked a little gray, as if she'd somehow gone days without sleep in the hour or so since we'd parted ways in the hangar. "Once I had the security under control, I thought I'd fetch them."

Pallino's one eye narrowed at me. "Going off on your own, is it?" He seemed not to notice the tall Cielcin standing right behind me, or else Tanaran was just another part of the furniture in its graying robe.

Vwaa! Vwaa!

"It is," I said shortly.

"Not without us, you're not."

I swallowed, and we teetered there a full moment before I nodded and gestured on ahead. "We can fight about it later."

"You're damn right we will," Elara said, brushing past. "Leaving us like that."

"Save it!" I snapped, a little too palatine in that instant. "Let's move it, people!"

They hurried past me—all except for Valka, who stood still framed in the door from the side passage. For a moment I thought she was staring past me, watching Tanaran. It was only after a pregnant instant that I realized she was looking at me. The red light of the alarms flushed her pale face, and she offered a curt little nod. I mouthed a silent "thank you" to her, and together we turned and followed the others down the hall.

CHAPTER 17

THE BREAKING OF
THE COMPANY

WE'D GONE MAYBE A hundred paces when the others found us. Security was still disabled, per Valka's interference, so the men and women who came hurrying around corners were not all spoiling for a fight. The technician we'd seen upstairs must have alerted Hanas, but word had clearly not spread to everyone on the ship. We ran directly past them, not firing. Most were unarmed. Not security at all. Shouts followed us up the hall, followed by a deep human silence when they realized just *what* was moving under that heavy mantle. Twice Siran fired on an armed legionnaire, reducing them to a ragdolled puddle of limbs dribbling sleepily down the walls. She led the way now, her long legs carrying her ahead of the shorter Crim, and she offered little quarter. I kept my eyes on the side passage, ready for proper security to arrive.

Vwaa! Vwaa!

"Can you do anything about that alarm?" Switch called to Valka. "I can't hear myself think!"

"In a minute!" the doctor shot back, waving him to silence.

"We're nearly there!" Pallino interjected. "Nearly!"

The door to the bay was closed—though whether by alarm protocol or some will set against us I did not dare guess. I had reviewed the design schemata for the *Balmung* years and years ago, and knew those bulkheads were more than a foot thick and solid titanium. The walls were worse: a honeycomb of titanium and carbon fiber threaded with all manner of wiring and fluid conduits. I might cut through it with Sir Olorin's sword, but sharp as the highmatter edge was, that would take time.

Vwaa! Vwaa!

"Forget the alarm," I said, touching Valka's arm and pointing. "Can you work that terminal?" To my surprise, she said nothing, but turned toward it just as a stunner bolt crackled past me. I went with her, moving in front of the Tavrosi scholar to cover her with my shield. "Take cover!" I shouted, and aimed at the nearest of the black-clad men emerging round a corner midway down the hall. The blast caught him full in the chest, and his feet skidded out from under him, prompting his neighbor to dive sideways for the shelter of a support column. I clenched my teeth.

Behind me, Valka stooped over the security panel, tapping her way through the user interface. She grunted, brushing a fall of hair from her eyes, and drew back.

"Did you get it?" I asked.

Vwaa! Vwaa!

She shook her head, stunner fire burned past us—one shot clipped my shield. I heard Pallino swear and Crim call, "You all right?"

I had never seen Valka work her magic before—save on lighting systems—and had no idea what to expect. Some believe, outside the Empire, that we know nothing of machines, that the Chantry keeps us in embalmed Dark and ignorant. It is so for the plebeians and the serf classes—for whom a groundcar is a great luxury—but we palatines are surrounded by machines. The Chantry only keeps its vigil to ensure that none of those machines betrays a glimmer of self-concept, of intelligence. For even fifteen thousand years dead, the ghosts of the Mericanii haunt human nightmares. In the Imperium, at least. And in Jadd, and in many places among the Normans where the Memory of Earth is sacred. Even among the Lothriad where the minds of men are overthrown. I say this because I knew enough to know that Valka was not like to open a vein and daub runemarks on the console in her life's blood. Still, I had expected a flash, and the part of me that was my mother's son hoped for the rattle of offstage thunder.

Vwaa! Vwaa!

The panel just went dark, and Valka's eyes shut tight. Whatever happened next I missed, because a pair of stunner bolts dug into my shield and I was forced to redirect my attentions. Switch crouched in the shadow of a bulkhead with Tanaran against the wall beside. My lictor's face had gone white almost as the Cielcin, and he bared his teeth. I squeezed the trigger—there was no recoil—and another of Bassander's legionnaires fell in a heap.

"*Dex!*" Valka said, lapsing back into her native Nordei. The heavy bay doors began grinding open, and Crim barreled across the hall, dropping to his knees to skid across the polished floor beneath the level of the next stunner burst.

"You go on," I said, giving Valka a small push, then, *"Tanaran-kih, civaqa ti-kousun."* I gestured for the xenobite's attention, and indicating Valka said, "Go with this human. She can understand you. I'll follow on behind!"

Valka caught my wrist as I began to move. "Where are you going?"

"Nowhere!" I said. "I'm shielded."

Vwaa! Vwaa!

I brushed her hand off and moved to the middle of the hall, my weapon raised. I had a vague notion of drawing any fire while the others crossed the hall, counting on my shields to hold through a round of stunner tag. The weapons *were* relatively low energy, and someone had to make sure the way across the hall was safe.

"Shit," I heard someone say down the hall, "that's Lord Marlowe."

Had they just noticed? Did they understand what was going on? Or was the speaker only new to the party, so to speak? I stood there, shielded, bathed in the pulsing light of the alarms. It couldn't have been more than three seconds' peace. It felt like centuries. I was aware suddenly of the tension in my shoulders, the way I carried myself as if hung by two hooks beneath my arms. I allowed my posture to relax as I cried out in my best palatine sneer, "Let us pass!"

No one answered. The alarms *vwaaed* again.

"Let us pass!" I cried, holstering my stunner. Shielded as I was, there wasn't a thing they could do about it, not without escalating from non-lethal force. I heard footsteps behind me, my people crossing the hall.

"Hadrian!"

Behind me.

I whirled, the soldiers in the hall forgotten. Stunner fire arced from within the hangar, and rounding the door I found a full complement of thirty soldiers—not proper decades, but the disorganized servicemen who had been in the hangar when the alarm sounded—scattered among the crates and the grounded shuttlecraft.

Vwaa! Vwaa!

And there was our shuttle on the far left end, unmolested during this whole affair. And why should it have been? If the soldiers in the hall had been surprised to see me, then surely the ones in the hangar were as well. Valka, Switch, and Tanaran crouched behind a forklift; Pallino, Elara, and the rest were spread behind crates. I was the last through, and smashed the door controls behind me. The hall door cycled closed with a groan like some chthonic thing.

Drawing my stunner again, I ducked as I hurried to where Valka waited with our Cielcin prize. "Can you stop them closing the bay doors?" I asked, voice low.

Vwaa! Vwaa!

She blinked at me. "Probably, yes."

Beyond the line of shuttles was only an empty space of floor leading to the open mouth of the bay. Only a static field sealed the massive opening against the black of space. Impermeable to gas exchange and so strong enough to trap the atmosphere while permitting shuttlecraft to exit unmolested. Beyond that there were only stars. We could not see Rustam from the angle. It must be in the sky above us, I thought, uselessly.

"We're going to need it."

A muscle rippled in Valka's pointed jaw, transmuted to steel there.

"Lord Marlowe!" It was Brux, the deck officer I'd spoken to before ascending to the cubiculum. His easy voice had found an edge of cold fire. "I don't know what's going on, but you need to lay down your arms, son."

Not poking my head out from behind the forklift, I called back, "I can't do that."

"Captain'll be here in a minute, lordship. Both of them. Put down your arms!"

"Hanas said the same thing!" I returned, catching Pallino's eye across the way. The old man cocked his head once, recalling so many Colosso melees, dodging amongst the pillars of the killing floor. "He's asleep in the hall just now."

Vwaa! Vwaa!

With a *stay here* gesture to Switch, I burst out and to the right, drawing a barrage of stunner fire. I couldn't see Brux—decided he was up in the bay's panopticon overlooking the action. My shield ate a full five of those stunner rounds, and I returned just as many. Must have dropped three of Brux's men. Glancing back, I saw Pallino break for the shuttle, pushing Doctor Okoyo ahead of him, their heads low. Elara half followed with Siran, Crim, and our Norman tag-along, the four of them strung out between the storage crates. It was a start.

I dove behind one of huge support pylons that held the Sparrowhawk lighters in place above us, firing wildly at Brux and his men. Valka, Switch, and the Cielcin were still pinned down behind the forklift, and with my momentary distraction's usefulness played out, the others were stuck. We should have all worn shields, conspicuous as that would have been. It did no good now.

Vwaa! Vwaa!

The rest of the hold was acclimating to the chaos, and more and more legionnaires in their black fatigues hurried from where they'd been at work loading the other shuttles. I poked my head out around the pillar. At least they weren't shielded, either. That was something. There were too many of them. They would outmaneuver us, flank the others where they hid and stun them down, unless . . . unless . . . I looked round, casting my attentions about the crowded hangar, at the stacked crates, the lifting equipment, the stowed gear and half-packed shuttle craft. At the Sparrow-hawks neatly stowed overhead like so many sleeping bats.

Ignoring the alarms, I scrambled round the pylon to where a red-painted ladder ascended to the grillwork catwalk that serviced the attack lighters. The pylon offered some small protection from Brux and his men and hid me from their eyes and the blue glow of their stunners. Holstering my own weapon, I climbed.

"I'm not sure you know what you're doing, Marlowe," Brux said in his kindly plebeian drawl, "and I'm sure you think it's right. But you best come out now."

I didn't answer. Any second now one or two of the legionnaires would round the base of the pylon and figure out where I'd gone. The gangway rattle gave me away instead, but there was nothing for it. Stunner bolts spun about me, and I surprised a flight tech as she hurried out of a service room to my right. She staggered back as I barreled past her, and I felled her with a stunner bolt and a curse as I flew by.

"He's on the gangways," I heard a trooper call.

"Come down, Hadrian," Brux said coolly. "You're palatine, so they won't have you hanged or nothing. You're only hurting your friends with this."

That gave me pause, and I slowed my advance for half a step. It was true enough. I wouldn't be hanged—the Indexed punishment for treason on the part of an Imperial palatine in Legionary service was decapitation on the White Sword, following the shattering of both hands. Such are the privileges of the nobility. But he was not wrong about the others. Valka might escape unscathed—she was a Tavrosi national, and therefore a member of their mad government. The others would hang. The others would at least hang. Provided I didn't do something terribly clever.

Or stupid.

The *Balmung* housed a dozen Sparrowhawks, each massing thrice the size of the standard groundcar, each perhaps eight meters end to end, each secured by a set of electromagnetic grapnels that could be deactivated once the ships had repulsors active and were under thrust—or when someone cut the power.

Which is precisely what someone did.

Lacking Valka's faculty with machines, I drew Olorin's sword and slashed the power conduits for the first lighter cleanly in two. The fiber optics and the fuel lines parted with ease—and the support pillar, too. There was almost no sound as the electromagnets fell dead, no cracking as of timbers in the shipyards of old, no clangor of metal. The lighter dropped like an anchor in the *Balmung*'s heavy gravity and fell like the hand of God. I tried not to think about the men on the ground as the machine fell, banging into the catwalk on its way down. Its huge dart shape smashed atop a stack of crates, alumglass cracked, and a sound went up like the roll of awful thunder. And men screamed.

"Bring him down!" I heard Brux call, voice amplified by the public address system now. I hurried to the next lighter berth, sidling now to watch as Crim and Siran moved toward the shuttle. Valka had pushed Tanaran on, and the two had found cover just as the soldiers on the ground opened fire again.

No more words from Brux on the comms. No more placating or reasoning. No gentle attempts at peace. The line was drawn—as lines are always drawn—in that shade of red which no careful scribe may wipe away. Thus I dropped a second lighter on the floor below. I did not slash the next in line, nor the one after that. I aimed to break up a cluster of Brux's men below, and break them I did. They scattered as I shouted a warning, and a breath of relief escaped me when the shouts this time were of fury and not of pain. As I turned from my work, my eyes scanned the opaque windows of the deck office panopticon, an armored observation blister high in the far wall. I fancied—as it were—that I beheld the Imperial eye, unveiled, and that it beheld me with all the scorn of the funeral masks that hung about the entrance to the Dome of Bright Carvings. It saw me. And it knew me. And it loved me not. So observed, I deactivated the highmatter sword and slipped the hilt back into the pocket of my long coat.

"Hadrian!"

The voice slashed across my impression of the eye, buried by and yet somehow louder than the constant bleating of the alarm.

Rarely does the universe match my capacity for drama.

Rarely is not never.

Bassander Lin stood alone on the catwalk behind me, blocking my way back to the pylon. Where he had come from I wasn't sure—whether from the other end of the bay while I was out on the finger of metal beside the smaller ship, or else from one of the side hatches opening onto the upper hall. But there he was, glittering in his officer's blacks with their silver rank insignia. He took a step forward, and from the shimmer about him I detected the faint curtain of a shield.

"Captain." I holstered my phase disruptor. The stunner was useless with his shield up.

"I should have known you'd do this."

Below, I watched Valka help a limping Tanaran dart from cover to cover. Switch was nowhere to be seen. I spread my hands. "And yet here we are." I put my hands into my coat pockets, fingers closing about the hilt of the knight's sword, momentarily deaf to the shouting from below. "You're in my way."

"You're not going anywhere," Lin said, taking a step forward. "You're done, Hadrian. The only place you're going is before the admiralty."

There was no one on the walk behind me. I might have turned and run, made a break for one of the other ladders. Not before Bassander could catch me. Nor could I throw myself over the rail: the fall was too far in the *Balmung*'s higher-gee environment. This was not Rustam, not The Painted Man's palanquin of an office.

Bassander took another step forward, then another.

I drew Olorin's sword, held the hilt forward with the emitter end up. "Get out of my way."

That gave the captain pause. He raised a hand and said, "Why are you doing this?"

"Because someone has to."

"You killed three of my men," Lin said, and pointed down to where the first Sparrowhawk had surprised the soldiers. In the red flashing of the alarms, Lin's eyes gleamed with a wild light hinting—not for the first time—that here was a man who had seen things beyond retelling and done them, too.

He didn't wait for an explanation. My actions were explanation enough. He lunged, and as he did so he snapped Admiral Whent's sword loose from his belt and thrust it out even as the blade coalesced, the exotic matter rippling pale and bloodless in the bloody light. I leaped back, my own blade springing forth like a shard of lunar crystal to snap his lunge aside. There we stood a moment, the line of fire drawn again between us, eye to eye, swords like shards of ice glowing with a light of their own. Bassander recovered forward, and I swept my sword around my head and down through a rolling cut that should have cleaved him from collarbone to hip.

It felt strange to meet resistance with that highmatter sword. The blade would cut almost anything: stone, metal, wood, and flesh. It parted those power couplings easily enough, and would part me as if I were a piece of the air. It had never known resistance, much less a weapon like itself—not since it came into my hands, at any rate. Bassander slashed at my face, and blocking it I stepped inside, moving smoothly to heel-stomp the arch of his foot, unbalancing him as I pushed past. He snarled, chopped down as I moved so that his blade sliced clean through the rail at the edge of the catwalk. Whirling, I managed to recover my guard in time to block an overhanded swing.

Bassander was an Imperial officer, and fought like one. Broad movement. Power in precise application, lacking in the finesse of the palatine tradition. He was trained, that couldn't be denied, but he lacked subtlety— nor did he need it. His teeth flashed as he snarled, forcing me back a step. His hair—loosed from its smooth order—fell rough across his face. I could hear shouting from below, knew there wasn't much time.

The fluid metal of the blades rippled as I took a parry, lunged into the riposte. Bassander beat the thrust down and the point of my sword carved a notch in the metal floor. I leaped back, catlike, glad that none of the legionnaires had found their way up to our level. I gave ground all the same, fading back toward the pylon and the ladder I'd ascended. Bassander came on like the tide, each step a blow, each blow a step. Whent's sword was cut differently than my own: broader, flatter, squarer, without the finger-loop by the rain guard or the quillions of gleaming crystal. It seemed unsafe, without the hand protection mine afforded, and rough without the delicate point control. But it was heavy, not usually a quality that mattered in a blade that cut without resistance.

It mattered then.

Bassander battered my weapon aside, and before I could recover smashed me across the face with a haymaker that sent me reeling. He'd overbalanced in his attack, and so I had enough time to spin away, staggering as I rubbed my jaw with my free hand. I'd not lost a tooth—which was fortunate, as I was not like to grow new ones for another thirty years or so. He followed on fast, swinging broad so that Whent's sword cleaved the wall at my right hand, carving a cold bite in the titanium. Wrapping my finger though the loop, I took the weapon in both hands and so blocked his remise even as he redoubled his attack, thrusting at my eyes. I thrust upward, using the highmatter crossguard to push his weapon up and away. Then I slammed my sword down. The flowing metal hissed as the blades clashed, and spat strange vapors into the noisome air. Bassander got his head out of the way just in time, but I nicked his shoulder and he winced, recovering back.

"Blood," I said, meaning I'd scored against him. The captain touched one hand to his shoulder where I'd cut through epaulet and tunic and shirt. It came away red. He said nothing, only snarled and threw himself at me. I leaped back as he swung—blade slicing the floor. Sharp as they were, I was not about to risk any sort of infighting with Bassander, not again. He chased me backward along the catwalk while stunner blasts fell around us, sparking in the air and off our shields.

He rolled his shoulder, air hissing past his teeth. Memory of another duel welled up in me, of Gilliam dead on the white grass field in Borosevo. I had hated him, hated that he was a priest of the Chantry, hated him for trying to get Valka killed, hated that he was an intus, a genetic defect. A cacogen misborn. Though I regret his death now—I did not regret it then, though it haunted me. And all that surety, all that disgust and contempt ran through me and from me and left me in the grip of one clear and stunning thought.

I did not hate Bassander. I did not want him dead.

"I should have liked to work together, Lin," I said, shouting past the alarm.

"You had your chance!" he called back, and leaned into a heavy slash that might have cut me cleanly in half even if the blade were common steel. He overextended, and I was accorded a clean opportunity to stab the Mandari in the back.

I didn't take it.

As with Gilliam—so long ago—I hesitated in the final moment. With the priest, it was my own cowardice that slowed me. Now it was something else. Something deeper, truer. Respect? Pity? Compassion? I did not want to kill the man. But the swords were out, the decision made. The time for speech was done. I'd made my choice when I dropped that Sparrowhawk on the deck workers, when I'd opened Tanaran's crèche. I'd made my choice in Otavia's ready room.

And on Emesh, years before.

Bassander charged forward, the blood soaking his uniform shoulder. I stood my ground as Sir Felix taught me, years and years ago, and turned each blow aside. Weakness crept into Bassander's arms. I could sense it. A slackening of the fingers, perhaps it was, for his blade sagged in his hand.

I pushed my advantage, threw a cut at his head, his wounded shoulder. The captain raised his sword to block, caught himself on the rail as he stumbled. He swung low, and I trapped his blade with mine. There we stood. Locked. Strength for strength, the long bones of my right arm seeming to wheeze and spit within me. But I had the leverage, the control. Slow as geologic time I pressed his arm down, kept his blade prisoned there. Just a little further and I'd drive my elbow into his chin. It was all so plain.

Bassander slammed his forehead into my nose.

For a moment, I forgot to think, forgot to breathe. The move was so utterly surprising that I fell fully to the ground before I could so much as scrape a thought together. I hit the floor square on my back, the wind knocked out of me. Hot blood dribbled down my face from my shattered nose, and the whole region felt warm and soft. The pain came after, distal—as though it were some other Hadrian who ached.

Good, Crispin, Sir Felix's voice cracked, whip-like, in the vaulted space of the training hall of my youth. *Again!* I had been knocked down before. At Colosso in Borosevo, on missions with the Red Company, on black nights starving in the streets. And by Crispin, my brother, time and time again. Almost I fancied it was my brother who loomed over me. The black uniform of the Legions was so like unto the uniform of my house: the belted tunic glittering with badges of rank, the piped trousers tucked into high boots.

"This isn't one of your stories," Bassander said, stopping just out of the reach of my sword. He looked down at me, and with steady fingers combed back his ridiculous fall of hair. "You're not some sort of hero. The Empire's fate is not in your hands. This is not a play. Put up your sword. It's done."

To my inward self it seemed I lay again on the floor of the Colosso, as I had many times in life, beaten by some gladiator or gladiatrix of the Count's. Beaten I knelt at their feet while they pressed the point of their sword into the hollow of my shoulder, awaiting the judgment of the crowd and of Lord Balian Mataro. Ever had I fought well, and so their judgment was good. Thumbs back. Life spared.

No crowd on that lonely catwalk. No cheering, no jeers. Only the howl of the alarm and shouting from the bay below. I made no response, for even then I fought for a way free, a way to win. The vision faded, and the ghostly coliseum in my mind's eye gave way to my grim reality. There was only Bassander, sword ready to fall. No gladiator. No crowd.

We were alone.

We were not alone.

The shot caught Bassander full in the face, and the azure light of stunner fire twisted the energies of his shield and shocked him back a step. He was not harmed, but he was momentarily distracted. It was enough. Calling to mind Crispin and the Emeshi gladiators both, I rose, and it was Hadrian the boy who rose with me, and Had the myrmidon, and together with the man I was we three slashed Bassander's sword hand from his wrist and plunged forward, cracking his own nose with the heel of our hand. Two times we struck him, then a third, and he staggered back nerveless and crumpled like a wall of stones whose mortar had long gone to dust.

I fell atop him, one knee on his chest, one hand at his throat. There was nothing to say, no argument to make. We had argued with a language other and more honest than words. "Yield." For a moment it seemed he might argue, and my fingers tightened and almost I heard my father speak in my own voice: growling, imperious. "I said yield."

The good captain was bleeding badly then from wrist and shoulder, and weak he seemed and shrunken, his nose cracked even as was mine, his almond eyes starting to swell. He moaned, but said no word, nor offered any objection. "The medica will find you," I said, releasing him. "They should be able to reattach the hand." I tried to stand, but my legs gave out.

Strong arms caught me, and a familiar voice said, "Careful, man." His hand closed over mine and depowered the highmatter sword, lest I maim us both. Switch pulled me to my feet and steadied me. It had been him with the stunner, I realized. The one who'd shot Bassander in the face.

I looked round. "Switch, I . . ." My friend, my oldest friend. "I . . ."

"Yeah, it's me," he said, cutting me off. "You look like the last hell. Earth and Emperor . . . Come on."

"It's not so bad. I can walk." And brushing him off I staggered to where Bassander's sword had fallen. The blade still rippled, the bronze hand still closed around it. Stooping, I plucked the sword free, and turning to the fallen soldier I held it up. "Mine, I think." Perhaps it rightly should have been Switch's, but I wanted to cut Bassander one last time. It was petty. I knew it was petty, but I slipped the weapon into my coat and went with Switch down the ladder for the shuttle.

He hurried on ahead, flitting from cover to cover, unshielded as he was. I took care, but moved more slowly. Stunner in hand, I did not shoot, and the shouts of the others were far away. I could see Valka and the rest in the shuttle bay ahead, but the light and the howl of the alarms crowded my sensorium as water crowds the lungs. I staggered, and might again have fallen if there had been no crates to fall against. I could see black-sleeved arms beneath the fallen Sparrowhawk, and red blood run black on the darkling floor. My vision blurred, and the blood came as thunder in my veins.

Thus heaven gives its favorites . . . early death, I murmured, or I thought. What does that say of me, Byron? What does that say of me?

The shot knocked me to my knees. No stunner blast, that round.

"Ios di puttana!"

Jaddian. The words were Jaddian, and sharp as a Maeskolos's blade.

You son of a bitch!

I knew she was there, knew she had shot me. But I did not look back. Instead I threw myself forward, scrabbling for the landing ramp. On hands and knees at first, then again on my feet. The second shot went wide, cracking against the armored shuttle ahead of me.

"Meta tutto che mararna!" she shouted, *"Ti itantre mia qal!"* After all we've been through . . .

The third shot caught me in the shoulder, and this time I kept my feet, lurching onto the ramp. "Pilot!" I screamed. "Fly!" Only then did I turn, only then did I see her standing with bloody-faced Hanas and a coterie of Jaddian soldiers. Jinan. My Jinan. My captain. There were tears in her eyes, but no sorrow. The shuttle lurched beneath me, and Elara rose to steady me, and Switch. The ramp began to fold up into a hatch. She aimed her rifle again, and the muzzle of that barrel was the darkest black I'd ever seen. The weapon flashed, the bullet tagged me in the shoulder, crumpled as it broke against my shield.

"Ti abatre!" she yelled. *I loved you.*

Loved.

The hatch sealed. Our shuttle tore out past the static field and into the long and silent Dark.

CHAPTER 18

THE OTHER EDGE

AT WARP, SPACE IS a confusion of violets. The onrushing stars Doppler to azure and indigo, become delicate fingers of light, transformed thence by the contortion of spacetime to geometries without name. I stood upon the bridge of the *Mistral*, wrapped in a heavy blanket—still shuddering and fuguesick—and watched the wild weft of the universe flex about us at eight hundred times the speed of light. That was only an illusion, of course. We moved not at all, were buoyed in a bubble of space itself, carried as a gull is carried by a wave.

Otavia stood above the center console, on a catwalk overlooking her officers in the control pit below, snapping orders and replies to her men with the casual grace of long practice. No one spoke to me, and so I was allowed to stand, barefoot and hunched and watching the glimmer of ionized particles caught in the membrane of rippled space at the edge of the warp envelope. How they shone! Like Cat's faeries in the forests of Luin.

"Thirty seconds to reversion, ma'am," said one of the junior officers. I don't recall his name.

"Prime scoop for reversion. I don't want a messy warp wake giving us away." Otavia gripped the edges of her console, muscled arms flexing as they took her weight. "Heat sinks prepped?"

"Aye, ma'am."

"You think they'll attack us?" I asked, then clamped my jaw shut to stop my teeth from chattering.

The captain only glanced at me. "I don't want to risk my ship."

"Fifteen seconds, ma'am."

Feet scuffing the deck plates, I shuffled further along the catwalk. Otavia relayed a few terse orders to her people, but I held my silence again, watching. Unlike the *Pharaoh* or the Sollan-built *Balmung*, whose bridges were all technical readouts and holograph plates, the *Mistral* had proper windows on the sloped and arching canopy above and along the tapering length of her nose. Through these I watched, hugging my blanket to myself like a toga.

"Five seconds," said the junior officer. Violet light poured through those windows, rippling as sunlight does through deep waters. "Mark."

Darkness.

The light was gone, replaced by the star-dusted vastness of space, and distant could be seen—below and away—a frigid blue sun, a supergiant. The windows cut the solar glare to manageable levels, and beneath that glow I beheld the gleaming nimbus of the accretion disk. Planets yet to be formed circled in the dust of that star. Dust motes vast as empires—as moons—orbited and impacted, growing and shattering in turn. I had never seen such a thing before in all my life and travels. The birth of worlds. Long would that star—that titan—labor to craft his children of clay, but in a billion years or three perhaps out of all that chaos might march stately worlds: planets fiery and unfinished.

We had the precise frequency for communicating with the Extras. It had been on The Painted Man's terminal with the coordinates for March Station. Otavia went about preparing the signal, using the precise message I had written her before we went into the freeze after we escaped the *Balmung.* That had been nearly seven years before.

I did not hear her.

I leaned against one window at the starboard side of the ship, looking out and down at the red churning and cosmic nursery of the disk. *The birth of worlds,* I thought again, feeling that sense of wonder I had known in the black tunnels of Calagah. Four hundred billion suns drifted in the galactic Dark. And though the Empire filled an appreciable volume of that space—millions of such star systems—we covered the galaxy only as a spiderweb blocks a window. We were so small.

Quite by chance I saw a blue spark leap out from the disk below. Had our window been a holograph plate I might have zoomed in, but as it was I squinted. "There's something there," I said over my shoulder, not taking my eyes away. How I'd seen it I cannot say, so remote was it, as an insect atop a distant hill. It sparked again, flaring against the blackness. The drive-glow of a fusion torch. A ship.

"We're picking up multiple contacts in the disk below!" one of the junior officers said.

"Are they moving to intercept?" Otavia asked, defensive. I glanced back at her where she stood, a bronze goliath hunched at her controls, bleached hair drifting.

"No," I said, and again from the officer.

"No, they don't care about us. They're sticking to the ecliptic."

"They're mining," I said, recalling holographs my father had shown me as a boy of our mining operations in Delos's asteroid belt. "Trawling the disk for heavy elements, I imagine. It must be easier than planet-cracking." As I watched, more blue sparks rose from the disk, from the deep-cut shadows cast by planetoids in the light of that frigid sun.

Otavia had called up images in the air before her, relayed from cameras on the ship's outer hull. "Looks like, aye. Word from this station?"

"No ma'am," the comms officer said. "Send again?"

"Send again," Otavia confirmed. "But stay on course."

I nearly tripped on my trailing blanket as I turned from the window. "I'll go check on the others. Okoyo should have everyone awake by now."

I found Siran and Pallino still shivering in the medica, wrapped in thermal blankets and drinking the customary post-thaw glass of orange juice. Ilex was with them, and Crim. "Where's Switch?" I asked, checking to make sure my collar lay flat. With the Red Company disbanded, I'd donned simple black shirt and trousers again, the side-closure hanging open to expose the paisley lining.

Pallino fixed me with his one blue eye. He'd not yet donned his leather eyepatch and the scarred ruin of his eye socket yawned at me. "Coming out of thaw now."

"And the Cielcin?"

The old myrmidon shrugged. "Not here."

"Been awake a couple weeks," Ilex put in, helping Siran to stand. "It and Doctor Onderra. She's been speaking with it."

My head must still have been fuguesick and fuzzy, for I said, "I'm sorry?"

The dryad jerked her head. "In one of the holding cells. Otavia's had it done up like a proper room." She moved Siran toward the showers, ensuring the blanket stayed on. The homunculus always seemed to come out of fugue more readily than us mere mammals. Some trick in her blood chemistry, I didn't doubt.

Hands on my hips, I nodded and turned to go.

"Had." Pallino's voice coiled out and turned me round. "You all right?"

I looked down at my boots, unsure whether looking at Pallino's empty socket or his piercing eye was the harder task. I could still hear Jinan screaming at me as I staggered onto the ramp, could still see the tears in her eyes, the fury. Seven years we'd been frozen, but it was only yesterday. *Time, Ever-Fleeting, forgive us . . .* I thought. It was not one of the scholiasts' sayings. It was a prayer, dredged out of childhood. At once I inhaled sharply, stood a little straighter, a little taller. "Yes, Pallino. I'm . . . I'll be fine."

The empty eye and the blue both narrowed in suspicion, but he smiled—baring yellowed teeth. "Aye then. You be on your way. I'll tell the kid where you've gone."

I saluted the old centurion, pressing my fist to my chest, and hurried smartly from the medica. I passed beneath the battle standards where they hung limp from the mighty bulkhead. No one troubled me, not even the two Normans Otavia kept posted on the stair or at the door to the brig. They only bowed their heads and murmured, "Commandant." I longed to correct them, to tell them that dream was over, but I did no such thing. They keyed the door at request, despite my lack of a bodyguard, and I stepped over the threshold.

For all the talk of its being a cell, the chamber was cheery enough. The walls were of the same padded white as the round halls, the ceiling too low for the tall xenobite, the bed too short. But there was a bed, and indeed a toilet and a sonic wash closet. The lights were low, were tuned far into the red spectrum to protect the Cielcin's delicate vision. Tanaran itself sat on the edge of the bed, its head bowed. Its queue of white hair had started growing back and hung draped over one shoulder, and its dark robes looked clean and good as new—so much so I wondered if someone had ordered new clothes printed while we were dreaming. It turned as I entered, breaking off its conversation with . . .

"Valka!" I said, feigning surprise.

The Tavrosi xenologist smiled and in perfect Cielcin said, "Hadrian! Glad to see you up and about. We were just talking about you."

Tanaran bared its glassy teeth in what passed for a smile among its kind, but said nothing.

Valka smiled at me as the door cycled closed. The expression faltered as her eyes lighted on the sword clipped to my belt, and she said, "Did you just wake up?" She didn't have the hangdog look of fuguesickness about her.

"I . . . yes," I said in Galstani, clasping hands behind my back. "You?"

She shook her head, replied in the Cielcin tongue for the benefit of the xenobite. "Tanaran and I have been out for a couple weeks now. I've been practicing my Cielcin."

"She speaks it well," Tanaran said. "Better than you."

"Indeed." I did not have the energy to smile. "The second freezing was not too bad, I trust?"

Tanaran let out a rush of air that I realized too slow was the alien word for *yes*. We'd had to improvise, modifying the medica's rejuvenation tank to work as a fugue crèche. It had been risky, but it had been our only choice. None of the fugue crèches were large enough to hold the tall Cielcin. *"Yukajjino-do uledatolomn yumna ti-ereshinan gi buradi."*

"Yes," I said, adding the air-rushing sound belatedly. "We have to freeze ourselves for long journeys."

Did I imagine it, or was that fear in the xenobite's eyes? The impression passed, and I was left again with a face whose gross musculature was wholly unreadable. *"Okun'ta naddimn,"* it said at last.

You are insane.

I snorted.

"But perhaps your ships are slower than ours," Tanaran said.

An objection snapped to the tip of my tongue, pushed there by two decades' aristocratic upbringing and a native human and imperial pride I felt like a knife at my back, but I said nothing.

Valka spoke instead. "Did we find the . . ." She switched to Galstani: ". . . the Extrasolarians?"

"We did," I said, replying in kind. "At least, Otavia thinks so. There's something here, at any rate." And briefly I told her about the mining ships I'd seen away and below us.

By the end, Valka was nodding. "'Tis them. Or sounds like them."

"No sign of the station, though."

"Sta . . . tion?" Tanaran said, in halting Galstani. "What . . . is . . . sta . . . tion?"

I blinked in astonishment. Eyes darting to Valka I said, "You've been teaching it?" She shrugged.

"'Twas a fair trade," she said. "We have been talking of its gods." The Quiet. I supposed I couldn't blame her. Valka had traveled with us for decades—spending much of that time awake, waiting for an interview with the alien baetan. Tanaran was some sort of priest or . . . historian. If its people did worship the Quiet—as indeed seemed to be the case—Valka could not afford to squander such an opportunity. To be the first human to interview one of the Cielcin noble-born about their religion and gods . . . it was an honor and dream.

Not knowing what to say or how to react to this piece of news, I said, *"Oscianduru,"* using the word the Cielcin used to refer to their great world-ships, though I had no notion what to expect from the Extras. Mother's operas led me to suspect some dim industrial hell, a place of grinding machines and shadow. Still other tales spoke of crystal palaces, like those on Jadd. Vorgossos itself was meant to be a palace of ice and diamond, a faerie city peopled by demons such as the legendary Kharn Sagara had tamed when he cast out the Exalted.

My terminal chimed. Turning away from the woman and the xenobite I tapped the conduction patch beneath my right ear to accept the call. "Marlowe here."

Otavia's voice ran through the bones of my head, making it sound like she was in the room with me. "We have contact."

"With the station?" I asked.

"Aye. You should see this."

"Very good," I said crisply, "I'll be along in a moment." I turned, glancing back at Valka and the Cielcin. "And alert the bridge I'll be bringing our guest." Not wishing to be rude but not wishing to argue either, I terminated the link.

The bridge fell silent as we entered. All work and chatter ceased—even among the flight officers in the tactical pit beneath Otavia's catwalk and central chair and console. It was no matter. Though I did not know it, we were locked into our approach vector, and the *Mistral* was under the control of the port authority . . . or of what passed for port authority in these trackless wilds. One might almost have heard the sweat beading on Bastien Durand's upper lip.

He brushed it away, adjusting his cosmetic spectacles to hide some paroxysm of fear. He needn't have bothered. He might have been a ghost, despite his Norman complexion. He was not alone. The Norman officers all eyed the eight-foot xenobite with suspicion as it entered—bracketed by two guards with stunners drawn, seeming more lictor than gaoler.

Whatever fear was in them, it was not in Otavia. I do not think that she had seen one of the Pale before, but you might not have known it to look on her. Arms crossed, chin up, the captain strode straight toward Tanaran, biting the inside of one cheek. She advanced well within arm's reach. Standing at her full height she was nearly so tall as the creature, particularly as Tanaran had taken to stooping in fear of the low bulkheads we had passed.

"You're the one, then, eh?" she asked.

"Raka ichaktan," I said.

"Cap . . . tain?" Tanaran repeated, speaking its broken Galstani. "You are captain?"

Corvo's eyes did not widen. I supposed she must have been watching the Cielcin's conversations with Valka since the beginning. Monitoring them through the ship's internal comms. She'd grown used to the idea of the alien thing on her ship in ways her officers had not. Ye Gods, there was iron in the woman. And more than iron.

"Corvo," she said, "Otavia Corvo." And I swear by Earth's stone she extended her hand.

In its halting human speech, the creature said, "I am Casantora Tanaran Iakato, Baetan in . . . Baetan of Itani Otiolo, of Aeta Aranata." It did not offer its hand. I cannot say if it understood the gesture—as I had not, being born palatine—or if it did and spurned it.

Otavia let her hand fall and—not to be outdone—added, "I am captain of the starship *Mistral* and . . ." and here she glanced at me, "and ranking Commodore of the Meidua Red Company." I almost smiled. I supposed she was Commodore now, such as it mattered. Sham though the Red Company was, it was legally recognized on Monmara, Pharos, and several of the Norman Freehold worlds. It remained a legal entity. If Otavia wanted the name, so be it.

Valka softly translated this for Tanaran, whose human speech went only so far.

I could feel the eyes of the others shifting to me, and I stepped forward, one hand on Olorin's sword to keep it from swinging. "What is it?"

Otavia Corvo adjusted her tight jacket, waved a hand in such a way as summoned a holograph in the air above her central console. "The station? Here." She stepped a little to the side, revealing an enhanced, false-color image of the space out in front of the ship. Nestled against the backdrop of the accretion disk—orbiting just above the plane of the ecliptic—was a ring. From the holograph, I had no way of estimating whether the ring was a mile across or ten thousand, and the massive, nameless blue sun offered no frame of reference my human eye could grasp. Even enhanced, the image was faint, brought to light by only the faintest emission of infrared and ultraviolet.

I looked through the holograph, out the window. There was nothing ahead. Only darkness. "You've communicated with them?" I asked. "Successfully?"

She nodded. "We're under pilot control. They're bringing us in remotely."

"With a daimon?" I asked, unable to help myself. Behind me, Valka scoffed.

Corvo shrugged. "Could be. Don't know."

"How long until we dock?"

"Nine hours," the captain replied. "Long enough for you to sleep. You look like you need it after the freeze." I acknowledged this with a slow nod, returned my attentions to the holograph. Something of my thoughts must have shown in me, for Otavia said, "It's an Extra ring city."

Valka approached, Tanaran close behind. In her bright-edged voice, she said, "I've never seen one. How large is it?"

The Norman woman didn't have to check a readout before answering. "Some six hundred miles."

"The diameter?"

"Yes."

Valka made an appreciative sound. "They must have been building it for centuries."

And what centuries those must have been! I could scarce imagine them, clambering in the Dark, hoping the Empire or some Mandari prospector would not find them at their work. How many such stations were there between the cracks in the Imperium? How many cities? How many million souls? How tempting it was to imagine our Empire lay thick upon the stars. I thought again of the spider's web, our Empire like gilded filaments veining the settled universe. Tenuous, delicate.

The ancients used to people the edges of their maps with monsters. Leviathans and sea serpents. The world was strange. Grew stranger as you traveled farther and farther from the walled cities of civilization. Yet maps had other edges. Inner edges. Cracks.

Here there was one.

Here there be dragons.

CHAPTER 19

THE GATES OF BABYLON

THE MIST—WHEN IT THREADED its way from between the teeth of the hangar gate—looked like smoke from the mouth of a dragon, and I raised the collar of my long coat. I felt Switch stir beside me, retreating with Siran half a step. I kept my hands in my pockets, one of them clenched around the hilt of my sword. Cautious, I took a step toward the opening portal, mindful of the bluish light ahead and of the docking umbilical behind us that led back to the *Mistral*.

I'd no notion what to expect, and not knowing conjured monsters. I remembered my mother's operas, and expected some nightmare to come crawling out of the fog. Some rough beast, once human perhaps, with metal legs and dripping hoses. Some shambling nightmare like the SOMs we'd fought on Rustam weeks and years before. The blue light changed to pink, and golden points flared through the fading fog, and faintly could be heard the sound of voices.

And beyond them—the crying of birds.

The fog vanished, turned—I think—to dew upon the metal walls where the air of the docking bay brushed the air of the city, the world, beyond. Crim moved past me, and I followed, without track or plan, my own words echoing after me.

"Otavia," I had said, "if this doesn't work. If we don't find anything. You have to leave me here."

The thought had come to me in the hours of waiting, while I'd watched our approach to the ring station. March Station had emerged from the darkness, twisting like the ouroboros from its bed of chaos. I could not go home. If I did not return victorious, not even Raine could save me.

I could not go home.

"What?" She'd looked at me like I was very mad or very stupid. "Why would I do that?"

"It's not you they'll come after. Bassander. The Empire." I'd watched as running lights like false stars studded the surface of the great ring. "Any of my people who want to sign on with you can do so. They're not sworn to me. But I can't leave here except by Vorgossos." I had money, credit left me from the Pharos affair, enough to book passage . . . somewhere. Suddenly the absurdity of what it was I was doing impacted me. The madness of it. Here I was, past the end of the world. Chasing a place out of legends on the word of a creature out of nightmare. I'd become like the mad pirates of Old Earth, drunk on stories of the golden city and the waters of life. Like those pirates, I'd lost much of what I had in pursuit of my goal— my title, my position with the Mataros, my place with the Legions . . . Jinan. Like those pirates, I knew what I sought was real, even when the world did not. I wonder if old De Leon still believed—dying of poison in his promised land—that there was yet some power to save him. I like to think he did.

"I couldn't make your people leave you if I held a gun to them," Otavia said, "but I'm not going to leave you, either." I'd tried to argue, and she said again, "It's my worlds that are burning in this war. My people."

Burning.

We stepped out into pouring rain. Rain. On a station.

I froze.

Above and around us rose the obscure figures of gray buildings, some short, some rising through the clouds above, looming like the pillars of some drear and dreadful hall. I cannot say how far above that ceiling waited, but I felt it. Felt it the way a man feels the thunderhead. The roof of the world. Like Damocles' sword aimed just above the shoulder blades. I heard Switch swear, and forced myself to look up into the oily rain. As in Rustam, the buildings here were dominated by holograph advertisements, text shining out in Galstani and Nipponese, in Lothrian Cyrillic and the right-to-left scrawl of Jaddian script. The image of a vate in the saffron robes of a Theravada bhikkhu glimmered in the rain, and I heard a mighty droning carried on the wind. His image faded, replaced by that of a woman with a white-painted face. She smiled as words appeared in Nipponese beside her and she too faded into the rain.

Almost I failed to notice the people beneath the crush of that city and the blue-white light glowing through cloud from the roof above. They emerged from the ultramarine twilight, crouched beneath umbrellas, huddling in slick coats, untroubled by the holograph advertisements. In among them, a man as tall as a Cielcin lumbered, leaking steam from some huge device on his arm. Only when it moved did I realize the thing *was* his arm and shrink away. We were among the crowd, then, and though none paid us any mind, I could see the indicator lights glowing beneath their skin; the white porcelain of hardware contacts gleaming behind ears and on hands; and false hands of ceramic or jointed steel or polycarbon. One woman wore an armored suit with a collar up to her jaw line, and only as she passed did I see the exposed fibers—black and blue—that stood beneath in place of sinew and cord.

Even I—who am not a religious man—prayed.

Holy Mother Earth, keep us and protect us in Darkness and in the land of strangers, I thought. *From the grip of the machines, O Mother deliver us.*

Where was Switch? Where were Crim and Siran?

From the perversion of the flesh, O Mother deliver us.

There was no face, but six glowing apertures like camera eyes in a sheet of black glass. A helmet? And there was another whose jaw was of gleaming steel, his teeth chrome.

From the destruction of the flesh, O Mother deliver us.

That was a glass cable shining with light strung between two girls, their eyes like empty windows. One bumped into me, but said nothing and moved on.

From the replacement of the flesh, O Mother deliver us.

From the dominion of steel, O Mother deliver us.

From the tyrant in silicon, O Mother deliver us.

From the ghost in the machine, O Mother deliver us.

I thought of Valka, of the machine that crouched at the base of her skull, reminded myself that here were no monsters. These were only men. Mutilated and transformed by their machines, yes, but men underneath. This was a city, whatever else it may be. This was only rain. Yet I could not quiet my thundering heart, only seized it and forced it down. I could not make myself believe the shapes around me were men, but steadily I acclimated to the horror, and my pulse slowed.

No one hindered us or barred our way, nor plied us with questions. No port authority had come to us, no guard received us. That we were marked known by things alien I'd no doubt. Growing up as I had in Devil's Rest beneath the watchful eye of uncounted cameras, I knew the sensation on the back of my neck for what it was. A lumbering trolley made its way up the dark street, throwing out plumes of white vapor even as a crowd of men and women in clear plastic raincoats tried to cross the street.

Bereft of any clear goal, I permitted myself to be led, to follow Crim into the city. The Norman-Jaddian looked out of place in his garish red and white kaftan, so bright against all that gray. "You walk like you've been here before," I said.

"That, lordship," he said with a pointed smile, "is because I am a liar." He tapped his nose, leaned toward me conspiratorially. "But I've been among the Extras before. We are not so afraid of them as you."

I wanted to deny this, but I caught the glowing red eyes of a young man across the street and only grunted. Pivoting topics, I said, "You probably shouldn't call me that here."

"Lordship?" Crim repeated, shaking his head. "Wouldn't do much good. You have 'lordship' stamped all over that face of yours."

"True at that!" Switch agreed, unhelpful.

"No no, don't worry!" Crim said, clapping me on the shoulder. "No one here will care. It's freedom they love, Marlowe. Not bloodshed. Free people, free markets. Not so different from we Normans."

"Not so different?" I repeated, looking at a woman with glittering wires woven beneath her skin.

Crim watched the woman go by with appreciation. "Chantry has it wrong. Human blood doesn't thin so easy as that. Their machines just make it easier for them to be what they want to be."

I let this go without argument. It was neither the time nor the place. Somewhere about, the droning sound returned, and I guessed the holograph of the bhikkhu had returned with it, advertising who knew what. Points of light like stars shone through the roof of cloud, and between clouds I saw the faint lamps which lighted the azure gloom of that city and portholes opening onto rooms in the ceiling above. How many people lived here? How many thousands? The *Mistral*'s sensors had said the ring stretched six hundred miles across, fifty from edge to edge, and five high. Many years and decades later—when I would stand as guest to Aldia, Prince of Jadd—he showed me the Celestial Gardens in the Alcaz du Badr. There, sealed in floating crystal spheres three meters across were little worlds. Perfect microclimates like a child's snow globe, replete with bonsai and living flowers and tiny animals designed and bred by the bone-cutters and chiromancers of that strange kingdom. Perfect little worlds. I was reminded of the ant farms kept by peasant children and the bottled ships built by enthusiasts given the benefit of too much time.

March Station was that on an extraordinary scale.

"Still," I said, "I'm not sure trumpeting my name is the best approach."

"On the contrary," my companion said, "you palatines are always running out to backspace seeking some bonecutter or gene tonic."

The four of us stopped in the shadow of one building, out of the rain. Switch and Siran were quiet, eyeing the crowd with that same religious suspicion I felt. Crim's words had shaken a memory loose in me, words I'd heard in a cable-car office above the streets in Arslan. "On Rustam, The Painted Man said that palatines would go there seeking . . ." I almost laughed, thinking again of ancient pirates and the waters of life, "life extension. The sorts of therapies the Chantry's forbidden." There were techniques available to those willing to flout the Chantry. Cloning. Machine implants. Certain retroviruses. Things that went beyond the precision genetic tailoring we palatines receive. Things that could bring a man before the Inquisition and beneath the White Sword. I felt myself reconsidering Crim's suggestion about using my name, but suggested, "I could be in the market."

I felt Switch's face darken without having to see it. My friend and lictor knew enough of the decadence of Sollan palatines to fill a lifetime. As a child, he'd been sold into indenture on a Mandari brothel ship, forced to work as a catamite, to service those men and women who came to treat with his masters. He took a dim view of the upper class, knowing well what the worst of them were like. Those casual dealers in other men's sorrows, spending blood or spilling it like wine. Though it is a mistake to imagine all aristocrats are thus, I could appreciate his disgust.

"We could just say trying to sell the Pale," Siran said, meaning Tanaran. "These Extras are slavers, yeah?"

"But there'd be buyers *here*," I said, looking round with a grim expression at the gloomy city. "No good."

"We could ask," Switch said, crossing his arms so that his hand rested just beneath the handle of his nerve disruptor where it hung inside his jacket just below the shoulder. "Someone's got to be sailing for Vorgossos."

Siran bobbed his head. "Could do."

Teeth clenched, I shook my head. "I don't think it'll be that easy. The place wouldn't be a myth if it were." I tried not to think about what The Painted Man had said, that Vorgossos was only ever found by those people its ruler wanted to find it. The words had the flavor of a cultist's invocation. Of a prayer. A promise. I shook my coat to clear away what drops remained on its hydrophobic surface, feeling suddenly cold.

"We have to start somewhere," Crim said.

CHAPTER 20

THE BONECUTTER

IT DIDN'T LOOK LIKE a clinic, leastways not any more than the flophouse had where I'd first awakened on Emesh so long ago. The words *Cento's Biotechnic* spat in neon frames above the corner door, the letters red in Galstani and blue-green in Lothrian. There were no windows, as there had been no windows on most of the street-level buildings in that dark city, and piping and heavy ductwork crowded about the entryway and along its walls. The place hadn't been hard to find, was only the fourth or fifth such establishment we'd entered that day. The bonecutters were everywhere, peddling tonics to change the color of skin or eyes or hair, to enhance hearing and sight beyond the normal range, or to implant terminals or praxis stranger still. One peddler advertised the regrowth of fingers—or the growth of additional ones. Still more focused only on genitals, complete with dancing holograph displays of the improvements on offer, and advertised their ability to change one's sex completely, rebuilding the body from new cells.

The whole show disgusted me, filled me with the same contempt I'd felt for Crispin and for my own mother with the way they used their concubines. Indeed, I'd felt a similar distaste for Valka, who for all her talk of equality and of the dignity of life had used the body servants on offer at Borosevo Castle. The commodification of the flesh. To reduce to transaction and whim one's own life and body seemed to me a violation sure as any slaver's whip. And worse, for it was one's own hand that held the lash. *You are a body,* all of it screamed. *Nothing more, and it is not enough.*

From the perversion of the flesh, O Mother deliver us.

But we are not bodies. We *have* bodies. And though who we are is rooted in that animal matter we rise higher, growing like a tree toward heaven. I can think of no greater evil than the insistence that we are only meat. How many lives have been demeaned—*destroyed*—by that insistence? How many millions? That city, what it offered, suggested that we were nothing more, and so the men who traded in flesh—offering surgery, therapy, and replacement—offered people a vision of their best selves. As if identity were fluid. As if who we are is only granted to us by others and is by others taken away. As if no part of us is our own. I saw signs selling memories and offering dreams, selling experiences and emotions wholesale. Those buying such services imagined they improved themselves, when in truth it was their selves they destroyed. Their souls. Traded piece by piece for pieces unrecognizable, until, like the ship of the legendary Theseus—who replaced his vessel part by part until all of it was changed—they had replaced all of themselves, and who they were born was dead.

As a man who suffers a stroke is forever changed by the event, so too the addition of arms or of a new kind of sight or the complete transfiguration of the body was not the actualization or purification of self, but a kind of death. Not the caterpillar becoming the butterfly, but the spider devoured by her own children. No mind could undergo such changes to the body and remain itself, any more than an uprooted tree can make its home in hostile soil.

Yet it was to one of these flesh peddlers, these surgeons of the human soul, that I had turned. For the road to Vorgossos, it seemed, was paved with such depredations. I combed back my wet hair, shook the spare droplets from my clothes. Crim and the others filed in behind me.

The room shone a polished white, starkly lit in contrast to the urban gloom without, the age of the place belied only by the deep scrapes and scuff marks etched into walls and floor. For all that, a pleasant music softly played, and under it the sound of water falling, though there was no fountain to be seen. It had every appearance of a grubby place trying to be pleasant, and so disarmed my trepidations after the casual inhumanity of the street.

There was no one there to greet us.

"Are they not open?" Switch asked, visibly tense.

"I don't know . . ." Crim said, drying his hair on a kerchief produced from a pocket in his quilted kaftan.

"Welcome!" a bright voice interjected, speaking in perfect Galstani. "Here at Cento Biotechnic, the number one leader in genetic recombination therapy and organic implant technology, we pride ourselves on—"

"Hello?" I said, speaking over the artificial voice, which dropped its volume in response to my voice—though the message kept playing. "Hello, is anyone here?" Crim had been acting as my herald, but the lack of any human person wrong-footed me, and I'd spoken out.

"Someone will be with you shortly," the voice replied, not changing its cheery tone. "If you do not have an appointment, or are here for one of our free consultations, kindly seat yourself by the dispensary. Someone will be with you shortly."

Looking round, I caught sight of the beverage dispensary. We'd not made it halfway to our seats before another, rougher voice called out, *"Dobra! Dobra dovarishka!* And welcome!"

The speaker was a small, rat-faced little man with a pigeon chest and round shoulders. Not a visage to inspire confidence in a genetic surgeon, though I supposed the strange man had his reasons. He wore a device like a jeweler's glass over one eye, though whether it was only a device or part of him I could not say, and when he smiled—which was constantly—it was to reveal teeth the color of gunmetal. Seeing me, he stopped. *"Solnech?"* he asked aloud. "This is Imperial, yes? No mistaking it. The height of this!" He raised a hand above his head to indicate how tall I was. "Patrician? No no. Palatine!" His one visible eye widened. "What is bringing palatine to Cento?"

I flashed Crim a look. No use trying to hide what I was from a geneticist, after all.

"You're Doctor Cento?"

"Yevgeni Cento, geneticist." He thrust out a hand, and it was only after I'd taken it that I realized the skin there was smoother and more pink than the weathered dun of his face. Younger. "What is it the palatine wants?" He was clearly Lothrian, or had been, and had that disconcerting Lothrian habit of eliding pronouns from his speech. "And is the palatine having a name?"

"Gibson," I said at once. "Just Gibson."

Cento's eye narrowed, but his expression did not falter. "An honor! An honor, sir. Few palatines come so far from home." He leaned forward, a conspiratorial hush overtaking him. "But what can Cento give man who has everything Empire can give?"

"I was told"—I did not say by whom—"that you might be the man to help me." I took a step closer to the short little man, tipping my head so that I spoke to him from the corner of my mouth. "There are things the Empire cannot cure."

"Eh?" Cento looked at me more closely, and I saw the lens in his monocle focus as his brows furrowed. "The palatine is not intus, yes? This can be cured, but . . . is costly. Intus . . ." He waved a hand. "Complicated."

Trying not to think about Gilliam Vas and his mismatched eyes, hunched shoulders, and twisted back, I suppressed a shudder. "No, no I'm not." The inti were palatine bastards, born without the intervention of the Emperor's High College, damned to a life of disease and mutation by engineered genes so complex the fetus required constant medical intervention to ensure proper development. Development I had received—as all trueborn palatines must—by medical technicians while I grew in my father's tanks.

"Then . . . is children?" He paused a long moment, pointed at me. I could almost see his brain seizing on the difficult word: "You. This woman?" He pointed at Siran. "High College makes children difficult for palatines, yes? Makes intus?"

"What?" I practically blurted the words out, glanced in horror at Siran. "No!" My myrmidon friend smiled wryly, making me feel a little safer. "It's nothing like that."

Cento frowned. "Nothing like that . . ." His voice died off into vague mumbling. "Cento sees. Yes. What is thing Cento can do for the palatine?" Here he affected a mocking bow. "Assuming the palatine can pay, this is." His human eye and the monocular swept over my scant escort, as if to criticize them for not being a proper guard. I wondered how often—if ever—a lord of the Imperium had been in his grungy little shop. We'd had similar experiences in the other clinics we'd entered, and on the docks before that. It was disarming, being doubted. Here, it seemed, blood meant nothing at all, and it was only my coin that mattered. It was almost refreshing, being treated as a man among men and not a lord at all. In the Empire, my credit had been assumed good on principle—it was how I'd nearly bought a spaceship with no income by merely flashing my ring.

My ring. Thinking of it drew my hand to my left thumb, to the wheal of burn scar that wrapped its way around it. I'd thrown the old thing away after my father stripped me of my title and holdings. I had gone into exile with it on my finger, into cryonic fugue. The metal had burned my skin in suspension, and the thick scar shone waxen in the harsh light of the clinic. Cento saw the gesture and darted forward. "Cryoburn," he noted, taking my hand. Something in the shift of the light revealed the faint spots of other scars on the back of my hand, relics of my battle with the Cielcin captain, Uvanari, after it escaped on Emesh. "More burns." His human eye darted up, inquiring, even as the machine stayed focused on my hand. "Cosmetic, then? Cento can grow new skin—entire new skin! Twenty thousand marks!"

"No!" I said, tugging my hand away. I cannot say if it was a fighter's sentimentality or the same disgust I'd felt of the street outside, but the thought made my skin crawl, as if the skin itself feared to be replaced. Summoning then a portion of my lordly hauteur I said, "Instead of pawing at me and guessing, doctor, you might allow me to answer your original question."

Cento stepped back, smiling to reveal his gray metal teeth.

Tired by my failures with the other clinics and by all that strange day and place, I said, "It's life I'm after, doctor." I felt suddenly foolish, standing there.

"Life?" Cento frowned. "The palatine is young, yes? Cento can lengthen telomeres, regenerate organs, remove plaque from brain, but so soon? We . . ." He paused again, pointing from himself to me and back again. "We can take look, yes?" He made an expansive gesture, indicating that I should follow him down the hall. "Guards wait here. Clinic very safe. No one bother Cento . . ." His words devolved into a patter of indistinct Lothrian, thick and guttural.

Switch pulled a face that seemed to say he'd rather leave me alone with a foaming azdarch than with the chiromancer, but I waved him back. "Watch the door," I said, allowing myself my crookedest smile as I patted the hilt of my sword through the coat, reminding both Switch and myself that it was there.

Cento led me into an exam room. A doctor's bench stood against one wall, and a round platform stood in another corner, an array of sensory apparatus hanging from the ceiling like the legs of some waiting, pregnant spider. A console stood at the far end of the room, screens a quiescent black, indicator lights blinking a pleasant blue-green.

"Palatines already have life. Much life," Cento said, gesturing that I seat myself on the bench. I leaned against it instead, not removing my coat. If the gesture annoyed the doctor, he made no sign. "Sometimes Cento can do much, sometimes little. Human genes only stretch so far. May be the client need seek abstraction."

"Abstraction?"

"Machine!" Cento said, tapping his monocular implant. "Kidney fails, say. Can replace this. But as get older, humans begin fail systematically. On cellular level. Cancer happens. Palatines age less. Less plaque on brain, in blood. Less organ failure. More cancer. Die quickly at end. Machines . . . no cancer. Other problem, maybe. But no cancer."

I shook my head. "No machines."

"No machines!" Cento repeated in exasperation. "Of course. *Solnechni*. Already breaking law coming to Cento but not break this law." He snorted. Approached me with a needle. On instinct, I backed away, pressing myself against the bench. "Is only sample. Cento must see what is working with, know how can help."

Old stories returned to me, tales of how fools and desperate men seeking life or knowledge had traded for it with a cupped handful of their own blood. I had to remind myself that however like an ordinary medica this place seemed, I was among the Extrasolarians, and the Extrasolarians were little better than demons. I was too well-educated to believe that giving Cento a vial of my blood gave him power over me, the way one might overpower a demon with his name, but I could imagine other things. A virus designed to kill only me; clones of myself made and sold into slavery, sold as soldiers or catamites; pieces of my genome cut up and turned into products—those Marlowe eyes shining out of other faces, that Marlowe smile grinning with other delight.

The commodification of the flesh.

Suppressing an instinct to smash the man and flee, I said, "You misunderstand me." And here I reached out a hand to stay the doctor's own. "It is not more life that I seek. It's another life. I am a foederatus, doctor. A mercenary. Mine is dangerous work. I might die any number of ways. I have heard among the Extrasolarians that there are ways to cheat death. That even if my ship were lost I might survive."

Cento frowned, stopped. "This Cento cannot do."

"Who can?"

"On March Station? No one." Cento closed his hand around the needle and drew away. Only then did I release his hand. "This thing cannot be done. Not by Cento. And if Gibson not pay Cento, Cento not work for Gibson."

I reached into my coat, hand gliding over the sword hilt there for the zippered pouch in the lining. My fingers found the universal card and waited there. "I'd be willing to pay for a referral. I understand if there is no one here, but I hear that on Vorgossos—"

"*Chern zashich nme!*" Cento swore in his native Lothrian. "Say no more!"

"You're the fifth clinic I've been to today," I said coolly, expecting this

reply and no longer impressed by it. "None of the others could help me."
I drew out the black universal card with the three golden helms of the
Rothsbank glittering on its surface. "I am willing to pay for information,
doctor."

The doctor put his syringe into a pocket of his gray smock and stood
silent a long moment. He seemed to deflate, to sag to the polished white
floor. "You do not know what it is you ask." His accent, which before had
been thick almost to the point of opacity, slipped. After the spirited performance of minutes before, the man seemed almost undressed. He used
Galstani pronouns without hesitation. Understand, it was not that he was
not one of the Lothriad, but that some exaggerated performance of his
slipped away. Seeming at once very tired, he reached up and unscrewed his
monocular. The lens housing came away, revealing a naked socket that
sank deep into his face. Dark metal glinted there, and a red light pulsed far
back in the recessed hole. Cento drew a dirty kerchief from another pocket,
polished the lens before screwing it back into his face. "Vorgossos . . . no
one gets to Vorgossos except through his Exalted."

"His Exalted?"

"The Undying who rules Vorgossos," Cento said, pressing his lips together. "This is the story you hear, yes? The Undying who shares his gift
to those who pay for it. A cure for death. This is why you seek Vorgossos?"

A cure for death. That was true, in a sense. Only it was not my death that
concerned me, for I was young and not then afraid of my fortified mortality. Unbidden, the black scar on Rustam's surface filled my vision, that
aching ruin of a city. I heard again Uvanari screaming under the cathar's
knives, and saw men writhe in the dark as Cielcin stooped over them,
blood on their faces like vampires.

A cure for death.

"Yes," I said, swallowing. "I was told you Extrasolarians had such a
thing."

"Extrasolarians . . ." Cento almost laughed. "We are not a people,
Gibson. We are people. There are Extrasolarians and Extrasolarians. I am
only a doctor. The Exalted . . . you have heard stories."

I had. My mother was fond of them. The Exalted had appeared as vil-
lains in some bad Eudoran masques, in so many great operas. It was against
them that the legendary Kharn Sagara had fought after they destroyed his
home. They were beyond humanity, it was said, creatures who had given
so much of themselves to their machine daimons that almost there was

nothing left. The very word conjured impressions of bloody fangs in metal jaws, of eyes dead as old metal, and vague shapes lurching about the dark corridors of the mind.

"The Exalted serve Vorgossos?"

"Some of them do," Cento said. "They are not an order; they are not a people. Some of their captains answer to the Undying, but not all. Only they know where the world is."

"How is that possible?" I said. "It's a planet, isn't it? How does one hide a planet for . . . centuries?"

Cento's human eye wrinkled in amusement. "No one knows, and yet no one will tell you where it is."

"You know, then?" I took a step forward, emphasizing as I did so my height advantage. I towered head and shoulder over the little Lothrian, and the gravity on March Station was not so strong as on Emesh. I might have lifted him with one hand if I wished it.

"No! No!" Cento raised his hands. "You need to ask right people. Vorgossos has contacts. Traders. Men who know right ships. Cento is not one of them. Cento does not know. You have to go to the traders. To the docks. Not ships captains. Shipping companies. The Exalted have people on March Station. Some are Vorgossos. Some not."

I brandished the universal card again. "A name, Cento. I need a name."

CHAPTER 21

A MATTER OF PRICE

GREEN WATER LAPPED AT concrete pilings, the waves generated not by the pull of some moon, but by huge pumps deep in the vast fishery. The algae stank, and the fish disturbed that verdant surface only sparingly, afraid—perhaps—of the hunting gulls. Gulls. I had not seen a true terranic gull since I'd left Delos, nor heard their cries. How strange to find them in that grim city, on that dark station so very far from the light and silver sky of home. The rain had fallen, and the misty clouds had gone, leaving only thin tendrils of fog crawling over the waters and among the utilitarian ugliness of the dark buildings.

What must those birds be thinking, wandering those sunless airs? I imagined them striking the ceiling of the ring station, or confused by the pseudo-gravity of March Station's spin. I felt for them, who was himself very far from home. Peregrines were we, and not gulls at all.

The azure lenses of camera eyes watched from crooked pillars, hung from cables threaded on the causeway that ran out over the green waters toward the freight lift tower and the warehouses that clustered like limpets about its base. Even here there were holographs. An advertisement for T-free cigarettes blew imitation smoke across our path from lips too full and too red. A bearded man with a mace battled a massive, green-skinned homunculus in a bas-relief hawking some Colosso match. Food vendors lined the row, selling kebabs and fish rolls and sandwiches wrapped in colored paper.

"This the place?" Switch asked, voice close behind me.

"Looks like," Crim replied, pointing.

In huge block letters—white against gray—were the words: FREIGHT LIFT 013.

Ships docking with the station did so by clamping onto the outer hull, and so ascended through a lift umbilical to platforms like the one from which we'd entered the city. Most of these were small, passenger conveyances, but some were larger. Freight exchanges meant for the loading and offloading of bulk goods. Many goods were destined for the markets in March Station's one, long city, still others for her manufactories, still more for other ships. I dared not imagine what foul contrivances might be traded in a place like March Station. Not merely food and mineral wealth, not only livestock, hardware, and media goods, but things not dignified in the light of Sol. I tried not to think about the street outside Doctor Cento's medica, about the grafts and body augmentations on offer. I tried not to imagine that in those warehouses ahead of us might sleep thousands of human fetuses, awaiting sale into slavery or transformation into SOMs.

I walked on instead, pressing between two men nearly ten feet tall, their bodies encased in suits of armor. One swore at me in a language I did not know, but we kept on past a group of green-skinned dryads in the orange jumpsuits of some work crew and into the warehouse complex.

The office whose name Cento had given me was not hard to find. The round door rolled open as I approached, admitting the four of us into a low-ceilinged chamber. It was less a formal lobby than it was a private office, but there was a desk opposite with a receptionist smiling prettily—too prettily—at us.

"Good afternoon!" she said, settling some private guess I'd had about what the local time exactly was. "Did you have an appointment with M. Brevon?"

Glancing sidelong at Crim, I smiled. I was playing the part of the Imperial palatine, of the mercenary commandant. Better to have a herald.

"I am afraid not," Crim said, affecting his deepest, most respectful bow. "But his services come to us highly recommended." Straightening, he executed a half turn, indicating my person with an expansive gesture. "I have the honor of representing Lord Hadrian Marlowe, formerly of the Sollan Imperium, Commandant and Captain-Owner of the Meidua Red Company, operating out of Monmara."

The woman stood primly, moving with almost clockwork precision. She wore a pinstriped suit of some synthetic material cut so tight I marveled that she could breathe at all. "It is an honor," she said, smoothing down her wine-colored hair with a gesture. She wore it up, coiffured into a severe style pinned at the back of her head. "Might I inquire as to the purpose of your visit?"

Her eyes were too large. Too green. The nose and chin too small. She was a homunculus, I realized too slowly—a fact which explained the hypertrophy of her shape and the mincing way she moved. She'd been made that way, designed like some sort of living sculpture. Docile, obedient . . . unable to run even if she wanted to.

I felt sick.

Crim still spoke on my behalf. "We've been given to understand M. Brevon is in contact with the Exalted. That he trades with them."

The woman smiled, revealing pearlescent teeth. "And you are seeking . . . ?"

"Transport," I said, stepping forward. "Passage."

The homunculi's smile did not falter—nor did it reach her eyes. She gave me a long, appraising look. "Is that so? I shall see if—" She broke off abruptly, those large eyes glassed over, focused on something only she could see. Her lips moved, mouthing silent words, and she nodded. I caught the brief pulse of light in one of the earrings she wore, and guessed someone was communicating with her. "This way, please."

With a discreet gesture, I ordered that Crim and Siran remain behind. The woman clasped her hands before her in a gesture clearly designed to accentuate her artificial charms and led her mincing way through another round door and along a hall, clothing groaning with each small step. I looked dutifully at the floor, at the patterned Jaddian carpet too rich by far for that close, low-lighted space. There were rust stains on the walls, and old ductwork clustered along the ceiling above, here dull, here bright-painted with warnings and access instructions. Several doors we passed, many of them open on dull offices whose dull occupants paid us no more than cursory attention.

The doors at the end of the hall irised open onto the strangest office I had ever seen. The far wall was an arc of alumglass that opened onto the vast fishery outside. Somewhere in the warehouse tower, we had descended beneath the level of the waves, so that fish swam past the glass and green-tinted light streamed in, casting sick and turbulent shadows on the chamber floor. Books stood piled—not on shelves, but stacked like a child's building blocks, like the stones of a cairn—about the walls of the chamber. There were no tables, no desks. Only a single, high-backed armchair near the far wall, giving the place more the air of a throne room than an office. The room's only other furnishing was a large perch right beside the chair, a gilded piece of scrolling baroque woodwork on which squatted a raven of enormous size.

"Welcome, welcome!" said a jovial voice from that single chair. "Come forward! It is so rare to have a visitor from the Imperium, and a palatine no less! Which of you is Marlowe?"

"I am he," I said, pressing past Switch.

The man in the chair rose, smiling. I was not sure what I expected, but it was not the affable grandfather before me. His white hair flew in untidy waves above a face somehow somber despite the smiling expression, a sobriety made more so by the dark glasses he wore over his eyes, hiding whatever warmth they might have contributed to his smile. His clothes ill fit him, at once too baggy and too tight, cutting into him at the shoulder. He looked like nothing so much as a boy still dressed in his father's clothes: a gray suit cut Sollan fashion, with a black toga fastened at the left shoulder.

He extended a gloved hand. "Antonius Brevon."

Smiling, I clasped his hand. It felt wrong through the glove, did not give like the flesh of other hands. It felt . . . solid. A construct as of horn and leather. Plastic and steel. It was like shaking a skeleton's hand. I felt the blood drain from my face even as Brevon's grandfatherly smile widened, not reaching his eyes behind those dark glasses. "Hadrian Marlowe," I said at last, remembering myself.

"What can I do for you, M. Marlowe?" He released my hand, clasped both before him. "You told Eva here you seek passage? Passage where?"

Behind him on its perch, the raven ruffled its feathers and muttered something that sounded like, "No."

I glanced sidelong at the homunculus in her tight suit, thinking of the skeletal fingers beneath those black silk gloves. Brevon's smile did not falter—his expression did not change. He was . . . impossible to read, a smiling, somber cipher in mourning black and gray. "I'm told you know the way to Vorgossos. Or know those who know."

"No! No!" the raven said. Sidling back and forth.

"Vorgossos . . ." Brevon repeated, turning his back. He returned to his chair, to the raven hunched on its perch. The bird cocked its head as he approached, croaking softly. "May I ask who referred you?"

"A Lothrian bonecutter."

"Yevgeni Cento, was it?" Brevon laughed. "And how is the little cyclops?"

Not wishing to answer that, I took a step forward. "He said you have dealings with the Exalted, that you charter freight and passengers on their ships. He said you have ships that make the journey to Vorgossos."

"No!" the raven cried, thrusting its head forward.

"Quiet, Hrothgar!" Brevon said, waving a hand at the animal. "I do, yes!" Still not looking at me, he drew a small bag out of a pocket and—opening it—offered it to the raven. Stooping, the bird dipped its beak in, withdrew it with some morsel clasped there. "But before we go any further, M. Marlowe, let us be clear. You Imperials come out here often enough. And often enough it's with tales of Vorgossos. It's the best, you hear. The darkest corner of the firmament. You think that's where you need to go, because you don't realize that what you're seeking—no matter how illegal it is where you come from . . . where there *are* laws—is commonplace here. You've met Cento. You know what he's capable of. And yet here you are."

"And yet here I am."

"No!" the raven said. "No!"

"Hush, Hrothgar. Hush." Only then did Brevon turn, restoring his pouch to its pocket somewhere beneath the black toga. Idly, he reached up and scratched the bird on the white spot under its chin. "I don't want to waste your time. I'm happy to arrange passage to the City, but if what you seek might be more easily attained here or elsewhere, I would recommend it. Passage does not come cheap."

Picturing my father, the way he would stand unmoved like the image of some Hellenic pharaoh lost in desert sands, I said nothing. He expected me to brush off the matter of payment as a trifle, as any pampered lord of the Imperium might do. I was not about to give him the pleasure of predictability. Brevon was not a talker, it seemed, and at length he turned his eyes from me to his raven.

"Vorgossos, then?" he said at last. "You're certain?"

"I am."

"Immortality, is it?" He lowered his hand from the bird's neck. It hopped a little closer to its master, deprived. "You know that's only a dream? The way you're picturing it?" He took a step closer, and even through those heavy lenses I could sense the weight of the gaze on me. "You don't even look old. You palatines are hard to age, but if you're a day over fifty I'd eat Hrothgar here." He jerked a thumb at the raven. "Not that I'd do that to the old boy." He resumed his seat. "Not immortality, then? Body servants? Homunculi? You can have those here. You could have those back home, as I understand it. Your Empire is backwards but you allow biofacture." At this his vision tracked toward where the woman, Eva, stood demurely by the door. "Do you like her? I designed her myself."

"No!" Hrothgar croaked, speaking for me. Brevon smiled. The homunculi's eyes were far away.

I clenched my teeth, thinking of Ilex and the razor-thin line that separated her—a woman free and free-willed—from this shuffling puppet bred to servility and submission. "She's lovely."

"I'd be willing to sell the genome, if you're buying," Brevon said. "I know a natalist uptown who could have you one grown in a couple of weeks. The model is *very* obedient, I get a lot of use out of her."

"No. Thank you." My stomach turned.

"Pity!" Brevon's smile lingered a moment too long. "Eva! Tea!" He clapped three times—the snap of it unlike the sound of hands. The homunculus bowed and shuffled from the room. With a gesture, a chair descended from the ceiling, floating a good two feet above the Jaddian carpet, suspended by a metal arm from the dark above. I took my seat without comment while Switch took up a position beside me, thumbs hooked in his belt.

The merchanter curled his hands on the arms of his chair. "Truth be told, I don't much care why you want to go to Vorgossos. I am a businessman. If you want passage to the City, it's in my interest to provide it. But there is the matter of price."

"That shouldn't be a problem," I said. "How much?"

"For a place on one of my ships?" Brevon adjusted his glasses. "One hundred."

"One hundred thousand marks?" I repeated, aghast. "I could practically buy my own ship for that."

Brevon leaned as far back as his chair would allow. "I would love to see the ship you could buy with a hundred thousand marks. Be serious."

"I have my own ship already," I said. "I need only coordinates."

The tea chose that moment to appear. Eva returned, following a table balanced on a spherical wheel. This rolled to Brevon's side and stopped there. Eva poured judiciously, in silence, leaning over as she did so, one porcelain hand on the porcelain teapot.

"Thank you, Eva," I said, accepting my tea. No expression from her, no tea for Switch.

"Coordinates?" Brevon repeated. "That isn't how this works. Vorgossos's location is secret, as are many of our places. All the better to keep them safe. No one comes to Vorgossos except by our way. You've never seen an Exalt Sojourner before, have you?" When I didn't answer—I didn't know what he meant—he said, "I thought not. You Imperials . . . your dreadnoughts are something, but . . . a Sojourner is something else. It'll tuck your ship in one little corner and no one will even care you're there. That's why the price is so high—it's for your ship, not for you, in which case the price is quite low." His smile was starting to turn to something septic. "Unless you'd like to make another deal."

"Excuse me?" I asked, holding the tea. I did not drink. The steam wafted over my face, carrying with it a fresh and grassy scent. Green tea, such as the Nipponese prized most highly.

Placing his tea back on its saucer, Brevon passed the drink to Eva, who held it without comment. "Blood is the ultimate currency. You are a palatine of the Imperium. Whatever else they may be, your High College has tricks even our bonecutters have not thought of."

Blood again.

Again I imagined my eyes in other faces, my genome—the language of me—spoken in new sentences, writ in new blood. Parts of myself or the whole sold and itemized. I looked at Eva, her distant expression and the ecstatic shape of her, in the smoky pigment about her eyes and the luster of her hair. There was a horror in the fact of her design. That it should be done to anyone sickened me; that it might be done to parts of me turned my stomach. And yet . . . I did not have a hundred thousand marks to spare.

"I am not for sale," I said, my spirit speaking and not my mind. "Nor any part of me."

Antonius Brevon leaned forward, hands folded between his knees, and appraised me as a jeweler might a diamond. After a moment, he reached up and removed his glasses. I started.

Once when I was very young, Gibson had showed me a film about the funeral rites among the adorators who yet live in the highlands above Meidua. Those pagans with their one god placed coins—kaspums stamped with an imprint of the Imperial sun—on the eyes of the deceased. Brevon's eyes were little different. Blank curves of dead metal the precise color of those old coins. They were not the eyes of a man. What they saw I cannot say, nor dared imagine.

"Everyone is for sale, M. Marlowe," Brevon said acidly. "It is only a matter of price."

"I've been sold before," I said, thinking of Anaïs Mataro. Of my father. "I won't be sold again." And to be sold to Brevon was worse than being sold to the Mataros. In selling my genes I would be complicit in the creation of lives bred into slavery like the woman beside us. I would be complicit in their suffering, and for what? Money? Convenience? A little time? And that they would be in part myself made it seem a kind of prostitution.

That made me think of Switch and all he had endured as a boy, and so I set my jaw and resolve with it.

Brevon sniffed, sat back in his chair. "Pity." He took his tea from the homunculus, drank it down. Those dead metal eyes narrowed. "Your College is always finding new ways to stretch the human lifespan. I'm sure we might have made some use of you . . . And I'd have liked to wear your eyes. What a color!" I was glad I'd not had any of the tea. I wished I'd had the sense to refuse.

"I don't suppose you could make the journey for seventy-five?"

"I am not a fishwife, Marlowe," Brevon said coldly, and at his words twin points of light like cold stars flared in those dull orbs he called eyes. "And this is not a bazaar. I have told the price. You may pay it or you may leave my office." Startled by the sudden edge in his voice, the raven jumped, agitated, and fluttered to the back of its master's chair. Brevon paid it no mind, but handed the teacup to Eva, who placed it on the little table service.

Switch took a half step forward, and I had to put a hand on his arm to stay his advance. "One hundred is too high."

"Then book crèches for yourself and your fine friend here."

"And leave my ship?" I snorted.

The merchanter polished his glasses on his toga and—blessedly—replaced them on the end of his long nose. "I thought you Imperials trusted your own people? Are they not loyal to you?"

The raven croaked, but no words were forthcoming.

"That isn't the problem," I said coldly. "It's a question of cargo."

"You intend to take something away from Vorgossos?"

"I intend to take something *to* Vorgossos. I . . ." At this I held my tea out, untouched. "I'm sorry, I'm afraid it's not to my taste."

Eva advanced smoothly and took the drink from me. "May I fetch his lordship something else? Water? Wine?"

I shook my head. "No, thank you. My apologies."

Through the thick glass of Brevon's spectacles, two points of blue-white light flared. "Your cargo?"

"I'm sorry?" I asked, feigning ignorance. "Only passengers."

"But you said . . ."

"One of our number cannot travel by standard fugue crèche . . ." I trailed off, struck by a sudden idea. "I cannot make the journey, not for one hundred thousand." Most of the Red Company's funds had been with Bassander's payroll officer. We'd come away with only the *Mistral's* small treasury—and my own small accounts. The price Brevon asked for transport to Vorgossos would drain our treasury, leave us with almost nothing left for food or fuel, and in any case the money was not truly mine to spend. Bribing Cento had been a small thing, a paltry thing. But a hundred thousand marks? What right had I to strip Otavia and her people what little money was left them? Poor payment that would be for their loyalty.

The merchanter drummed his fingers on the arm of his chair. "Then you have wasted enough of my time for today, M. Marlowe." He raised a hand to dismiss me.

I held up one finger, and—consciously parroting the other man's word choice and tone from earlier, said, "Unless you'd like to make another deal."

The blue points flared again through the heavy glasses, and Hrothgar the raven croaked from its place at the top of the chair. "Go on."

"Blood is the ultimate currency, you say?" I said. "I have in my possession a sample of Cielcin blood, belonging to one of their upper caste."

The merchanter's lifeless eyes observed me over the rim of his spectacles. "You mean you have one of the Cielcin upper caste in your power. This is your passenger, then? The one who can't be accommodated by standard fugue crèches?"

I gave Brevon my crookedest smile.

I am not proud of what I did. I knew what it meant—what it might mean. I had, after all, been in fear of just such an outcome for myself and my own genes. But it is always easier to spend what is not yours to give. I told myself that Tanaran was not human, that this lessened my trespass. I told myself the Extras might not know what to do with blood that was not human . . . that this lessened my trespass. I decided—as youth so often decides—that the ends justified the means . . . that my path was righteous because the place it led was righteous. That calculus has led to darker places than Brevon's office in human history, and for worse reasons. To Gibbeah, to Bannatia and Rustam and every world sterilized in our wars, by our weapons or the Cielcin's. To mass graves on asteroids without name. To the billions dead on Atlanta and the other old Mericanii worlds, victims of their machines' utopian vision, and of the avenging fire of man. To Earth. To quiet fields in forgotten Poland or buried beneath Siberian snows. To Beijing. Nanjing. Hiroshima. To the ruins of Constantinople and of Rome before it.

To Emesh, and to Gododdin yet to come.

But I had to make a choice. Go forward or go back. Tanaran's blood or mine. Call me a coward, call me a villain, but I could not put my blood in the hands of that Extrasolarian merchant, knowing how it might be used. With Tanaran's at least, I hoped it might be otherwise.

I made my choice.

"Would you be interested in it?"

"Research into Cielcin genetics is . . . rather new." Brevon frowned. "It may be I could find a buyer. Some pharmaceutical company, perhaps. One never knows what sort of compounds extraterranic life might produce."

This caught me by surprise. "You wouldn't just sell it to the natalists?"

Brevon's lip curled in disgust. "Is that what you think I am? What we are?" He shook his head. "The market provides for people's appetites, and I do not stop it. But it provides opportunity. Invention. For all I know there's some protein in Pale blood that can cure diseases, regenerate tissue. Maybe it will be compatible with humans, maybe not. We do not only deal in flesh for flesh's sake, Marlowe. Half the terranic species still in circulation are only alive because businessmen like myself elected to save them during the first waves of colonization, because we saw a market for them. The ossulum vaccine was produced out here. We sponsored the eradication of AIDS-3, not your government. They just quarantined affected worlds and let their people die. They were peasants, after all. So don't moralize at me because I profit by my work."

I had no idea what he was talking about. Ossulum, I knew, was an ancient disease—alien in origin—that had wasted the Empire millennia ago. What AIDS-3 was I could not guess. "I meant no offense," I said.

"No!" Hrothgar cawed. "No!" I half-wondered if the beast was mocking me.

"I have a ship leaving for Vorgossos within the month," Brevon said, steepling his hands in front of him. "If you can deliver what you promise, I'll see you aboard."

CHAPTER 22

BLOOD AND WATER

"YOU PROMISED THEM *WHAT?*" Valka asked.

I'd known she would object, from the moment I made Brevon my offer. I'd known, and spent the entire return to the *Mistral* pondering what it is I would say. I would not argue, nor make excuses. Nor apologize, either. I braced myself for the tirade, pictured the way Gibson might sit placidly and weather my father's storm.

It never came.

"A blood sample!" Valka exclaimed. "Truly?" And then she did the last thing I could have expected of her. She laughed. I felt every thought flee me then, my mind gone blanker than any scholiast dared dream. I had no idea what to say.

Fortunately, Captain Corvo rapped the table with her knuckles. "I think you did well. You got us what we wanted and at no cost."

That brought me back to myself, and I looked round at the others: Corvo, Durand, Ilex, Valka, Switch, and Crim. "Not at no cost," I said, soberly. "I shudder to think what those flesh peddlers might do with it, but didn't see another way." I did not mention that I had declined to sell my own blood instead, and Switch did not sing out. Valka and the others seemed not to be troubled as I was by what I had done, but I did not wish to give them more reason to think ill of me.

We were seated in the same little conference chamber where I'd first asked Otavia to help me with Tanaran. The low ceiling curved overhead with the shape of the hull, and the round door was sealed.

"What are you so gloomy about?" Valka asked.

How could she not see? Not understand?

"Do you not know what these people do?" I looked round at them, at their unfeeling faces. Even Crim's usually jovial face was confused.

"Blood is blood, Hadrian," Valka said tartly. "It's not a person."

I shook my head. "You don't understand." I was picturing Eva again, the shape of her and the foot-bound way she walked. More faintly, I heard my brother's stupid laugh and the way he'd described a homunculus my mother had owned on Delos. I shifted uncomfortably in my seat, but let it go. "In any case, I should speak with Tanaran myself. Let it know what we mean to do and why."

"Will it be a problem?" Otavia asked.

"I don't think so," I said, "but I don't know if the Cielcin have any taboos about drawing blood. Some of the old religions did."

Switch cleared his throat. "If it comes to it, we can knock out the creature out and take it."

"I would prefer it not come to that," I said, rubbing my eyes. "Tanaran is our only ambassador at this point, and our only bargaining chip. We should do all we can not to compromise that." Murmurous agreement flowed across the table like water. "In any case, this merchanter . . . this Antonius Brevon, says his ship won't leave for Vorgossos until the end of the month. That gives us a little over a fortnight to prepare."

Commander Bastien Durand shuffled through a stack of notes in front of him—he was always printing hard copy for review—but before he could speak Ilex said, "This is an Exalted ship, yes?"

"It is," I said, toying with the cuff of one sleeve. "Brevon called it the *Enigma of Hours*." I broke off, having never said the name out loud. Distantly, I thought I heard old Gibson chiding me about melodrama. "Are all Exalted ship names that pretentious?"

Under her breath, Valka muttered, "They're called the *Exalted*."

"Fair point," I said. "But there's no reason to dawdle with Tanaran. I'd prefer to have this sorted out well in advance of the . . . the *Enigma*'s arrival. Unless any of you objects, of course." I did not expect to meet resistance, and found none. In the brief quiet that fell between us, the desire for a shower overcame me. I'd not washed since returning from our expedition to March Station, and I could feel the faintly oily sheen of the city on me. The smell of the algae-choked fishery still clung to my nose, and the rain—though it had not afflicted my clothes—had fouled my hair awfully.

The streets, Cento, Eva, Brevon, and now this vial of Pale blood . . . the whole thing sat badly with me. Made me feel dirty. I had done horrible things before. To Gilliam, to Uvanari, to Emil Bordelon and Admiral Whent. But this was different. On Emesh—in the Empire—and even on Pharos and the other Norman worlds I'd visited, I'd known where it was I stood. I'd understood the system of the world around me: what I was and what everyone around me was. But out there the true path was lost.

Leopards, lions, and wolves . . .

"What do you think, Hadrian?" Durand asked.

"What?" The bookish First Officer had been rattling his way through something about the freeze schedule—putting all but essential personnel back under the ice as our fortnight drew to an end. "Oh, yes." A thought occurred to me, and I added, "Captain Corvo, if it's all the same, I should advise against granting shore leave while we're here." Even as I spoke, I wiped at the back of my hand. A thin layer of grime—greasy and invisible— came away. I rubbed it between my fingers, unsure if my unease were grounded or merely Imperial superstition. "I don't like this place."

"And what exactly is your problem?" Valka asked, catching up to me as I left Doctor Okoyo in the ship's medica. Her heels rang on the metal grating, and she had to catch herself on the white-padded wall to steady herself—she was not yet used to the centripetal force that passed for gravity on March Station. Here in the ship, beneath street level, the pull was heavier than it had been in the city above, and I felt dragged down by my own feet. I wondered how fast March Station had to spin to maintain such drag. I'm sure Durand could have told me, but I never knew.

I stopped, clutching the ampule and syringe kit in one hand. "I'm sorry?"

The xenologist seemed a bit breathless, as if she'd been running all over the ship to find me. There was a flush in cheeks and her red-black hair was askew from its customary bun. "You were strange through that entire meeting. Like you were somewhere else."

Unsure of what to say, I rubbed my eyes with my free hand. "It's nothing. Just this business with the blood." I held up the ampule and needle for her to see. "The whole thing has me unsettled."

"Why?" She pushed loose hair behind one ear and walked with me, heading aftward for the brig.

Briefly, I told her about Brevon and his homunculus, about what I feared might be done with the blood we were selling him. "He says they do pharmaceutical research, but you didn't see this . . . slave concubine of his." I must have walked three paces before I realized Valka had stopped walking with me. "What?" There exists no word for the expression she wore. Puzzlement, perhaps? Or pity? Anger? It was all of these and none. The way she pressed her lips together, brows raised but drawn together. I could not read those golden eyes, nor guess what lay behind them. I never could. When she didn't speak, I asked again, "What?"

"You're a strange man, Hadrian." She put her hands on her hips, looked briefly down at my feet—as if she were unable to look me in the eye. "You've done worse things—owned slaves, even—and this is what gives you pause? This is nothing." Valka made a gesture like she was throwing something away. "'Tis blood. Not a person."

Without thinking, I thrust a finger in her face. "I have *never* done *anything* like that. This man tried to sell me a woman by talking about how *obedient* she was and how much *use* he gets out of her. Think of me whatever you like, but I am *not* that kind of man."

For once, Valka was speechless. She opened her mouth. Closed it. Opened it again. At last she said, "I'm sorry, I . . ."

I cut her off. "And I never owned slaves, Valka. Never!"

"Your family . . ."

"Is not *me*. What could I have done? Ordered my father to change his ways? My grandmother? Please. I was a child. But this . . ." I let the hand holding the ampule drop. "Whatever comes of this will be on me. Whatever creatures these Extras . . . produce, they'll be alive because of me. Suffering because of me."

Valka sighed. "You put a lot on yourself."

"I just don't want to make a mistake," I said, forcing a thin smile, "not again."

"Listen to me," she said, and there was an edge to her words I'd not heard in a long time. "You've made mistakes before, but this?" I could feel her eyes on me, but it was my turn to look away. "'Tis not one of them. Have you forgotten why 'tis we're doing this?"

I hadn't.

Valka was smiling.

"Stop that," I said, half-turning away.

"Stop what?"

"You're making me uncomfortable." I started walking again, eager to have this final task over and done with. "Come on then, we've got work to do." Valka hurried after me. Unseen by Valka, a small but genuine smile forced itself onto my face, without irony or bitterness. Almost I did not notice it was there. Almost.

The brig was dark as ever, what light there was keyed far into the red to protect the xenobite's delicate eyes. Tanaran crouched curled on its bed, the sheets rumpled, the ruins of a meal beside it. It raised its eyes as we entered, bared its teeth in that threatening gesture that passed among its kind for a smile. "Hadrian-do."

"Tanaran," I said, and nodding at the plate asked, "They're feeding you well?" I knew full well the meal was only a kind of protein paste, slightly altered to accommodate the Cielcin's alien biology. It would serve the carnivore, but it was no feast.

"It is enough," the creature said, speaking in stilted, painfully lucid Galstani. With patient slowness it stretched its legs before it until its feet touched the ground. It was too large for that cramped, human living space. It's prehensile toes flexed against the metal floor, and it cocked its head to one side. Switching to its native language, it asked, "Have you news of my people?"

Sighing, I placed the ampule and the needle in the pocket of my coat—no need to start in just yet. "We're working on it. I think I've found someone who can get us to Vorgossos, this planet Uvanari spoke of." At the sound of its dead captain's name, the xenobite's face twisted into some emotion I could not recognize.

"Tutai," Tanaran said at length, twitching its head in the affirmative. After a space, it said, still speaking in its native tongue, "And you think these *yukajjimn,* these other . . ." It broke off, spoke in Galstani. "These other humans. Do you think they can help me?"

"Your captain thought so," said Valka, speaking the xenobite's language. "Uvanari said it had had dealings with these people before."

Tanaran opened its mouth, ran a hand over the short horns growing from its crest. *"Belutoyu o-tajarin'ta,"* it said. *I do not know them.* "I have never been to this place. I do not know what good I can do you."

"You won't have to do anything," I said. "Not until we reach your people. Except . . ." I drew out the ampule and the needle, cradled them in my hands. "Tanaran, I do need one thing from you." I held the device up for it to see. "The men who have agreed to ferry us to Vorgossos asked for payment."

The Cielcin cocked its head again—toward the other shoulder, making me wonder if there was some coded subtlety of body language lost to me. *"Biudate?"*

"Payment," I repeated. "They asked for a vial of your blood." I did not look at Valka, though I felt her standing there. I wondered if she knew the effort that statement had taken from me.

The Cielcin sat there a moment, uncomprehending. *"Tussun . . . ti-koun ne?"* it asked. *My blood?* "Why?"

How to explain? I bit my lip.

Valka spared me the trial. Speaking in her now nearly flawless Cielcin, she said, "There are some of us who make a study of blood, of . . ." She cast about, searching for a way to translate the concept of genetics. Did the Cielcin even have such a science? It seemed incredible that they might *not*, but it was irresponsible to make assumptions. "Of *heredity*." Valka seated herself in the room's only chair, scooting as near to Tanaran as she was able. "They are men of learning. Men who want to understand your kind as we understand ourselves. How you are built." She pressed a hand to her chest. "On the inside."

Tanaran seemed to mull this over, its mouth open to reveal its glass-shard teeth. "They mean to study us? To make weapons?"

"That is a possibility," I said, thinking of the Chantry. Of the biological weapons the Inquisition held as club over the heads of disobedient lords. So exact were they, so terrible, that they might decimate a local population—precisely decimate it—to punish such a rebellious lord. Indeed, I recalled that I had heard such whispers on Emesh, when the Gray Rot was thick on the streets. There had been those who said the illness was not chance-brought from offworld, but the Chantry's punishment for some crime on the part of House Mataro. What crime that was none had said, but rumor dies a slow death, and is born—as mice were once believed to be—of the very earth itself.

It blew air through its four slitted nostrils. Derision? Surrender? "Most would deny such possibilities."

"I will not lie to you," I lied, though this at least was true. "It may be that they will do exactly that. For what it's worth, I don't like it either." And here I did glance at Valka, wishing she did not understand the xenobites' tongue. I did not mention how I had refused to offer my own blood.

By some miracle I had come through this episode in Valka's good graces, and with all the rest of my experience piled upon me like a yoke, I was in no hurry to add to my burden. "But it will get us where we want to go, and it may get you home."

Tanaran jerked its head toward its left shoulder. *No.* "*Rajithatayu,*" it said, then in Galstani, "I will not sell myself to your people." It wrapped long arms about itself. "They will have a piece of me, and it will be theirs. And I will be theirs."

Some part of me wanted to turn to Valka, to spread my hands and say, *See! It understands!* But I did not gloat. Too dire were the circumstances, and I would only weaken my position.

"We could take it from you," I suggested, "by force." I tried to soften the threat with a smile, forgetting that the expression meant almost nothing to the xenobite. "So that you will not have been dishonored."

Tanaran blew air through its nostrils once again. "Dishonored," it said. *Dishonored.* Literally *to lose one's place.* "*Veih.* No."

Valka cleared her throat. "'Tis only a little blood. You let us draw it to put you in fugue."

"That was different," Tanaran insisted. "I am in your power already. Your prisoner. Yours. This . . ." It tugged its head down to the left shoulder once more. "You would sell me to new masters."

"We would have you return to your old one," I said.

"We would have you go home," Valka corrected, softening my words.

The xenobite puts its hand on its head, on the place behind its saurian crest where the white hair sprang thick as a dog's fur. So like human hands they were. Like—and yet unlike. Those too-long fingers, tipped with black talons in place of nails, kneading the flesh beneath. The moment those fingers moved, the illusion of their humanity was broken, and they were transformed to something more akin to the twitching legs of spiders. The lines of muscle beneath that milky flesh tied themselves to bone in ways strange to any human anatomist.

"Tanaran," I said into the stretching silence, unable to take my eyes away from those awful, twitching hands. "There's no other choice. I'm sorry."

I am told that the hunter who enjoys his time alone in the wilderness does so because in his solitude—an animal among animals—he is not a man but Man. The face he wears then is that of our species, his actions our actions, his hand our hand. I had felt a glimmering of that feeling once before, when I'd been left alone with Uvanari in the cell beneath the

Borosevo bastille. I wondered if the xenobite before me had a sense of that same feeling. That in that cell it was not *Tanaran* at all but *Cielcin,* and that the Cielcin would fight to the last. I had to remind myself that this was no warrior, no officer like Uvanari had been.

If only it had still been frozen. If only we'd had the other Cielcin to spare. We might have avoided all this unpleasantness and taken the blood directly from the medica. Tanaran would never have had to know. But our departure from the *Balmung* had left no time for such planning, even if I could have foreseen such an eventuality.

"Promise me something," the alien said. "When we find my people, do not tell them of this."

I pretended to mull this over a moment. I could think of no reason why this would matter to Tanaran's superiors, but I couldn't think of a reason not to do as it asked, either. After a moment, I said, "As you wish."

Valka stirred in the low seat. "Why? What does it matter?"

"I am baetan," the creature said. "I belong to my master. To my people. And to no other. I am theirs, and keeper of their sacred past."

Baetan. The word acquired a new and special sharpness for me then. *Baetan.* Literally it meant *a root.* Not as trees have roots—to the best of my knowledge, there are no words in Cielcin for anything resembling trees— but as mountains have roots. Roots. Traditions.

"You are . . . a priest, then?" Valka asked, using the Galstani word. We did not know if the Cielcin had a word for *priest.* She clarified quickly, saying, "You serve the gods, the . . . Watchers?" We had been a ways down this road before, Tanaran and I. The Cielcin had some sort of relationship with the Quiet, the ancient builders who had left ruins on a hundred worlds. What that relationship was I could not say, though I longed to understand. It was the answer to that same question that had bound Valka to our strange expedition.

"I serve my people," it said. "I remember what they were, and what *they . . .*" and here it used a variant of the pronoun I had not heard before, and used it with gravity, "made us." Tanaran sat a little straighter, tucking its chin defiantly in a way that aimed its horns at Valka and myself. "If I am defiled, they are defiled."

Showing a species of that same exasperation she had used on me, Valka said, "This is a medical procedure."

"A door is many things," Tanaran replied, speaking with the gravity of a proverb, "and once opened, many things may enter."

"Peace, in this case," Valka said dryly.

Tanaran tucked its chin, worried at the collar of its skin-suit beneath the gray wraparound it wore. I did not press it. Not about the blood, not about its people, not about the Quiet. I was quiet myself, done in by that long day clambering all over that strange and unpleasant city. Just as wordlessly, the xenobite bared its throat to me, turned its head away. There we stood, two pieces frozen on a chessboard while Valka looked on. I did not understand at first that this was a surrender. *"Mnada!"* Tanaran said. "Do it."

Shocked to motion, I stood, fumbling with the ampule. I screwed it into the needle and approached. The Cielcin's vein was not hard to find. Its skin was translucent, like fine china, traced with delicate black lodes and beneath it all the faintly purplish stretch of muscle. I pressed the muzzle of the device against what passed for carotid on the creature—much farther out to the side than on a human neck—and squeezed the trigger.

Tanaran winced, but offered no complaint.

Blood black as ink—as water at night—filled the ampule. My task done, I drew the device away, snapped the ampule out of the injector. The stem of the phylactery was still hot where the injector had sealed the glass shut, and I placed the sample with care in the inner pocket of my coat.

"You have my word," I said, "that this will see you back to your people." As I spoke, I watched the faint dribbling of blood snake down Tanaran's neck. Valka approached and handed the xenobite a kerchief, helped it press the thing to its wound.

Tanaran fixed massive eyes on me, black as space, and—imitating a gesture that perhaps Valka had taught it—nodded. "I believe you."

CHAPTER 23

THE PILOT

FOLLOWING A DEPARTURE VECTOR given us by Antonius Brevon, the *Mistral* unclamped itself from March Station and fell away, at first using only gas jets, then the ion drives, then the big fusion torch as we peeled away from the station's local space and out into the unquiet dark. The light of the sun and the accretion disk shone through the viewports to front and sides, and the bridge was alive with the soft back and forth of voices as the crew spoke updates to one another. I have always admired sailors, though I never learned their trade. The dizzying array of readouts and holographs dancing above and about their stations defied my understanding, though the progress map showing our plotted course was plain enough.

"Where are they taking us?" Valka asked, craning her neck to look down at the navigation console beneath the captain's platform.

Otavia turned her head, hands not leaving her console. "Not far, but about straight down from the ecliptic, out-system."

"Strange place for a rendezvous," Valka said. "I thought this Brevon character said this Exalted ship was docking with the station?" Otavia and I had already had this conversation the day before, when a message from Antonius Brevon had arrived via the station's datasphere. It had contained only a string of coordinates and a time stamp.

Ilex emerged from the hall, wiping her hands on a rag. "Exalted ships almost never dock with Extra stations. Too big." The dryad had grown up on ships. On stations. Until that moment it hadn't occurred to me that some of those stations might have been Extrasolarian, or have had dealings with them.

"I still don't like this, captain," said Bastien Durand. The First Officer sat at the console immediately to the right of and beneath Otavia's platform.

"Ships get captured this way, and this whole thing's been too easy. Passage for a vial of blood? It's a bit storybook, isn't it?"

"Storybook, commander?" I asked, leaning against the rail of the captain's platform.

"A bit." Durand pushed his spectacles higher up his nose. "When we were with Whent, we dealt with the Extras all the time. I know their reputation as cloners and natalists, but this?" He made a dismissive gesture.

I was spared the need to argue with him, for Captain Corvo said, "Keep the warp drive primed. I want us ready to make the jump plus-c at the first sign of trouble." She keyed a button on her console. "Lieutenant Garone"—it took me a moment to recall that this was Crim—"have our security team readied. I'm not expecting trouble, but these are the Extras we're dealing with." If Crim replied I could not hear him, but Otavia said, "Acknowledged. See it done."

"They'd not try something so close to the station, surely," I said, compulsively checking that Sir Olorin's sword yet hung from my belt.

Even with her back to me, I could hear the frown in Otavia's voice. "Why not? This isn't the Empire, Hadrian. There's no ODF, no patrols. So long as they leave the station alone, the Extras can do whatever they like." She half-turned to continue speaking, but an indicator light on her console drew her attention, and she turned away.

Far away and above us, I could make out the violet glow of other fusion drives in the accretion disk above. I put two fingers on the window glass, spread them apart. The image magnified, showing me a vessel with great wings and blue-glass sails standing high on masts perfectly still in the airless stellar winds.

"I worked a rigger like that when I was little," Ilex said. "We dryads are meant for Dark-work. That's why we were made."

"I'd read that," I said, glancing at her. There was something distinctly fey about her, as if she or someone very like her had tended the infant Zeus in Rhea's cave. Would that it were so. The dryads had been designed as slaves, meant to sup on air and sunlight instead of encumbering their masters with the cost of shipping food on long, early expeditions in the bright Dark of space. One of the Emperors—Titus III, I believe, or Titus V—forbade the creation of new dryads as slaves. Not from any warm feeling toward the homunculi, but because their use had put honest citizens out of work. Realizing that I'd been quiet for an uncomfortable period, I said, "What was it like? Growing up out here?"

Ilex thought about this a long moment, blue-green lips pressed dark together. "Quiet," she said at last. "Except for the stardrives. Ships I grew up on were in worse shape than this. Used to shake." She mimed shaking with her hands. After another moment, she added, "You've never met the Exalted, have you?"

"No," I admitted. "Have you?"

"Mm." She bobbed her head. "Once or twice."

"Is it true they're like the Mericanii were of old?" I asked, conscious of the eyes of the bridge crew that might be on me—and of the ears that certainly were.

The dryad shrugged slim shoulders. "I'm not sure what that means, but Crim says you saw chimeras on March Station?"

"Chimeras?" I asked, thinking of the hybrid creatures that so frequently battled gladiators and slaves in Colosso.

"The augmented. Men with machine parts," Ilex clarified.

I chewed my lip, looking back over my shoulder to where Valka and Otavia were speaking in close tones, the latter hunched over the console, the former in her low seat at the center of the platform.

The dryad continued. "The Exalted are worse. They barely leave their ships. They're barely even human anymore."

"I've heard," I said slowly, angling away from her to look out the window again. The zoom I'd initiated had reset, the image out the glass reset to one of the rosy light of the accretion disk orbiting that distant blue star. "But they are human."

"More than me," Ilex said, and though I did not look I sensed her duck her head.

"Don't talk like that," I said, thinking of Eva. "You're as human as the rest of us." Ilex had a freedom of will Brevon's slave never could, as free to make her own choices as any natural-born person. She was hampered, hindered, crippled by her very genes.

"Just a little more tree than the rest of you."

A short laugh escaped me. "As you say."

Hours passed before we made Brevon's rendezvous. According to ship's telemetry, we'd traveled some three hundred thousand miles—more than the distance between Old Earth and her Moon—but the accretion disk seemed no farther away above us. March Station was lost in the glow. I never saw it again, nor wished to.

All was quiet on the bridge; even our breathing was stilled. Space travel, I've often found, is a hushed experience. Not only for the great quiet of the endless Dark, but in the way that quiet oppresses you, impresses you to silence. To stand beneath the bottomless sky and above and among its stars is like standing amidst the pillars of a great cathedral—afraid to speak, lest God may hear.

Or devils.

"Initiate deceleration burn, bump inertial dampeners to compensate." Otavia stood again on her platform like a maestro at her orchestra, hands on hips, back straight. Her low chair sat behind her, forgotten. Forgotten as well, I stood at the back of the bridge with Valka, quietly out of the way. "Scanners?"

"Nothing, ma'am," said one fresh-faced ensign. "No sign. Shall I deploy light-probes?"

"See it done."

A wire-frame schematic of the *Mistral* drifting in the air to the captain's right flashed, showing the deployment of half a thousand tiny sensors from an array clustered along the ship's ventral hull. Pushed by a rapid spray of laser fire to tremendous speed, they spread out from the *Mistral* in a growing cloud, relaying signals back to the ship in as close to real time as that growing distance and the stubborn speed of light allowed.

"Big as these ships are meant to be," said Bastien Durand, removing his ridiculous glasses to rub his eyes, "we should see it from half a system away."

"There's nothing," the ensign said. "Nothing on light-probes. Nothing in infrared, no reactor leakage, none of the usual telltales."

"It's a trap," Durand hissed. "I told you, that bonecutter set Marlowe up."

"We don't know that," Valka put in, oddly leaping to my defense.

"Stay vigilant," Otavia snapped, pivoting toward a different set of consoles at her left. She tapped at a few controls, head bent over the display.

The whole ship bucked in that moment, and a great roar carried through the metal and carbon superstructure of the old Uhran starship. Old supports groaned, rattled like an old tramline barreling into station, like the damned out of some hell. Caught unawares, I stumbled into Valka, who might have fallen but for the wall at her back. I tripped my way through an apology and turned just in time to hear the helmsman say, "Decel burn initiated."

As always, I tried not to think about the crushing force of that acceleration. Were it not for the inertial dampeners, every one of us would be a smear of bloody pulp and bone paste plastered against a bulkhead or the outer hull, so rapidly had we bled speed. I hadn't felt anything but the initial shock as the *Mistral*'s retro-rockets engaged, working opposite the primary fusion torch. We'd been delivered by forces less substantial than the wind.

I shuddered.

"Keep that warp drive primed," said Captain Corvo to the helmsman. "First sign of hostile contact you micro-jump." She looked down at First Officer Durand where he sat just below and beside her platform. "Bastien's not wrong, there should be something here."

As if on cue, the ensign spoke up. "Still nothing from the light-probes or primary sensors. I'm not even picking up anything on gravimetrics."

A blue light flared on Otavia's console, and she slapped at it at once. "You're go, Centurion."

A holograph panel sprang into being above the arc of Otavia's console, showing an image through one of the ship's internal cameras. The holograph was slightly blue where the projector hardware had degraded over time, but it was clear enough. It showed one of the lateral airlocks near midships, a low-ceilinged, round corridor, padded as the others were padded. Pallino stood there, one hand to his ear, dressed in full combat kit: black ceramic armor done Imperial fashion in the shape of a sculpted torso, segmented shoulder and arm guards. He kept one hand on his holstered nerve disruptor as he spoke.

"Captain, we've something strange down at the port airlock."

"Strange, Centurion?"

The old man looked right up into the camera. "Aye. It's—"

Bang.

The men around Pallino jumped, but the veteran's alarm was confined only to a turn of his head, as if to reproach the sound.

Bang. Bang.

"It's coming from outside, ma'am. Took us a moment to realize it wasn't the ship settling from that burn."

Bang. Bang.

"It sounds like someone's knocking," I said, moving up behind Corvo.

The Captain called up another holograph, cycling through camera feeds. The ensign running the sensor suite spoke up. "That's not possible. I'd have detected anything larger than a rations can on approach."

"Unless it were cloaked somehow," another voice suggested.

"There's no heat sink small enough to mask a person."

"You're assuming it's a person," Ilex suggested, voice cold.

Corvo had found the camera feed she wanted, pointed back at the round swell of the airlock from where the wing section began to swell along the *Mistral*'s vaguely deltoid profile.

There was nothing. Only gray metal and white ceramics pitted and scored. Nothing.

Bang. Bang.

"Can we get eyes out that airlock?" the captain demanded, knowing full well the answer was no. The interior doors had windows looking in on the airlock itself, but the exterior doors were titanium, without slit or porthole.

Pallino's voice crackled over the internal comm. "No ma'am. Not without opening the outer door."

Bang.

Had she been born in the Empire—no matter her caste—I felt certain that Otavia Corvo would have retired a Strategos of the Legions. Faced with this situation, with data that made little sense and less, she wasted no time. "How many men are with you?"

"Two decades, ma'am."

"Take defensive posture, I want clear lines of sight on that inner door. Hoplites in front, I want shields up and NDs set to stun. Then open the outer doors."

"Ma'am." Pallino thumped his chest in salute and turned to go about his business.

Bastien Durand rose from his seat and, turning, gripped the lowest part of the rail on Otavia's platform. "I don't like this."

Corvo acknowledged this with a curt nod, but spoke to her other officers. "Why are our cameras showing us all clear on the airlock exterior?"

Ilex was the first to respond, craning her neck from her station in the pit below. "Could be some sort of virus showing us a looped feed."

Before this conversation about the defense of the ship's datasphere got too far along, Pallino's voice came back in over the bridge's sound system. "Everyone's in position, ma'am. Shall I proceed?"

"See it done."

"Wait!" I said, shrugging out of my coat. "Hold for five minutes. I'm coming down. Is Switch there?"

"Aye!" Switch called over the same feed—I couldn't see him on the internal camera.

"I'd rather you stayed here, Hadrian," Corvo said, turning to look at me, one hand still on her controls. "God knows what's making that . . ." *Bang.* "That sound."

Tossing my coat onto one of the crash seats at the rear of the bridge, I said, "Those are my people down there, too. I'll be damned if I'm up here sitting on my hands and something happens, captain." I didn't wait for an argument, but turned and promptly hurried from the bridge, thumbing my shield on as I went. The light distortion and static cling of the shield curtain collapsing around me was like putting on an old suit by then. I could feel my mindset change, feel my walk change from its usual cadence to the conscious tread of a man at war. The hall—invisible to me a moment before as a familiar place, an artifact of memory and my everyday life— transformed into a theater for action. I was acutely aware of the rounded walls and the way the grated metal floor gave just so with each footfall.

"Hadrian, wait!"

"Stay on the bridge, Valka!" I said, hurrying on.

She followed. "I'm coming with you."

"Please stay on the bridge!"

I could still hear her feet on the decking behind me. "I can handle myself!"

"I know you can handle yourself. You don't have a shield!"

Her footfalls stopped abruptly. I did not.

Pallino and his twenty men lined the hall approaching the starboard airlock. They knelt in side doors, stunners trained on the heavy door.

Bang. Bang. Bang. Bang.

The knocking was more insistent now. Louder.

"Hadrian! Stand back," Switch said, holding out his arm to bar my passage. Switch. Ever the faithful friend and lictor.

I unclipped Olorin's sword from my belt and held it ready, but did not activate the blade. Unwilling to waste time on pleasantries, I said, "Open the door."

Pallino didn't hesitate, slammed the button to begin the airlock cycle. Switch tried to keep me from the door, but I pushed his hand gently aside, kept my eyes trained square through the door's porthole. An alarm whined, announcing the decompression of the space beyond. Red light flooded the airlock and—silently—the doors opened.

I leaped back, animal instinct tugging my sword arm up before me. Switch swore and made a warding gesture before bringing his stunner in line. Calm as ever, Pallino took two steps back, squared his shoulders to better cover the door. *Something* entered the airlock, pulling itself forward with too many hands. The doors shut behind it, and it regarded us with too many eyes. I felt cold like a knife between my shoulder blades.

"Holy Mother Earth, keep us and protect us in Darkness and the land of strangers . . ." Switch breathed.

From the dominion of steel, O Mother, deliver us.

The airlock light cycled blue, and the inner doors hissed open.

"Hold!" I cried, to myself, the creature, and my men. "Hold!"

A walking engine of glittering metal it was, standing on arms like articulate ropes of steel, arms which supported a head—for head it seemed—bullet-shaped and large as a man's torso. With eyes red as coals and glittering as a spider's it watched us, unmoving.

No one spoke. Not for a long time.

How many arms were there? Seven? Eight? Each terminated in four jointed fingers like the petals of some grotesque flower, and each was splayed on the floor.

"Permission to come aboard, sir?" When it spoke, it was in a curious high voice, strangely accented, lilting almost as a Jaddian's. It sounded . . . young. Like a boy newly at his post. Somehow that made the effect more terrifying.

I did not lower my sword.

"What are you?" I asked, ready to squeeze the trigger on my sword at the slightest provocation. The creature's arms looked to be of some common metal, aluminum perhaps, or steel. "What are you? Man or daimon?"

The creature's body jounced as it laughed. "You're from the Empire, aren't you?" An image formed on the blank, black metal space between the two largest of the creature's glowing eyes. The image of a young boy—no more than twenty—brown skinned and smiling. "I'm called Nazzareno, sir. At your service." The image smiled and flicked out. It—he?—seemed to hesitate a moment, regarding the others. "I didn't mean to frighten you. I'm meant to ferry you into the *Enigma,* sir. The *Enigma of Hours.* I'm your pilot."

CHAPTER 24

THE ENIGMA OF HOURS

WE HAD OUR CHARON with eyes like coals, our ferryman of souls. The Exalted followed with an oddly demure politeness, clanking slow but heavy on its metal paws, body lurching with every step. Here and there it steadied itself with a claw braced on wall or on ceiling, each time causing our guards to flinch and raise stunners I thought worse than useless.

Nazzareno's arrival on the bridge was worse than Tanaran's had been. Even among the Normans the fear of machines ran deep, and though they walked at times among the Extrasolarians, the creature I led onto the bridge was something else entirely. We did not even know if it *was* human, if somewhere deep in that carapace there lurked a heart or brain or face. For all we knew, we had admitted a machine—a daimon—onto our ship. That face that had formed on Nazzareno's body might be only a simulacrum, and not the face of some boy that was or had been destroyed.

I shall not linger on the tense discussion that followed, the horror even on Valka's face. Suffice it to say that Otavia took convincing—and what captain would not?

Nazzareno's many arms—eight of them? Nine?—clamped onto the rail of the captain's platform, onto the ceiling above, supporting the body as though it were an egg sac in some spider's unholy web. From the way it moved, I guessed that Nazzareno was unused to gravity, and discomfited by it.

The talons at the end of one of its paws moved, rearranging themselves into fingers. These worked the controls with deft familiarity, as if it had piloted the *Mistral* every day of its life.

"Captain." One of Nazzareno's eyes swiveled full round so that it could look at Otavia straight from the back of its own head, "With your permission, I would like to route control for your ship directly through my chassis."

"And give you access to our datasphere?" Otavia took a step forward. "Small chance."

"Respectfully, captain." The Exalted bobbed its whole body in some weird approximation of a bow. "I have had access to your datasphere since before I was brought on board, as is only proper in my capacity as customs officer. Please rest assured, your safety and conduct are guaranteed by Captain Eidhin and our contract with Brevon Imports." When Otavia said nothing, Nazzareno repeated its question. "May I assume control of your ship?"

For a moment, I thought Otavia would balk. But she had not so much as blinked when Tanaran appeared on her bridge, and she was not going to back down now. She thrust out her chin. "See it done."

Nazzareno's one eye rolled back to the front of its outsized head and it resumed its work, one jointed steel hand fidgeting with the controls. A series of red indicator lights flickered along its right side, and all around it the diagnostic panels and holographs flickered and went dead.

"What are you doing?" demanded Bastien Durand.

In answer, the drone of ion drives reverberated through the *Mistral*'s superstructure. Nazzareno did not swivel its attention, but said, "T-minus six minutes to rendezvous."

"Six minutes?" the ensign in charge of the sensors asked. "There's nothing out there."

I had to applaud the young officer for bravery. Not anyone would have the courage to look something like the Exalted in the eyes and call it a liar.

"Bring our instruments back online," Otavia said.

"Respectfully, captain, I have put a freeze on your instruments until you are safely aboard the *Enigma*. I have a duty to protect my ship and my employer's privacy."

Looking back, the situation was absurd. A demon out of mother's operas—with tentacles and glowing eyes—speaking of privacy and with the manners of a Forum courtier. Still, I found I could not look at the Exalted for long. The ordinary human motions of its one steel hand contrasted with the supreme inhumanity of its construction chilled me, and I moved again toward the window to clear my head.

It was the same window I'd looked out not two hours before, the same stars wheeling in the same deep Dark. The same rosy accretion disk orbiting the same distant, blue-giant star. I could still make out the distant, violet flare of fusion torches against that blackness . . . the mineral trawlers at their work so far and far away. Where had Nazzareno come from?

Surely it had insinuated itself into the *Mistral*'s datasphere. That was how it had concealed its presence from our sensors, and not through any camouflage. I glanced at Valka. Had not the Tavrosi woman done the same thing on Emesh, concealing our conversations from the watchful eye of Mataro security and from the Holy Terran Chantry?

I shuddered, eyes skating over the machine creature where it nested among the controls. The bridge crew all looked on helplessly, unable to do aught but watch their ship piloted into darkness.

Into darkness.

A shadow fell across the stars, and—falling—cast a quiet deeper still. Deep gloom filled the space around us, turning the red glare of holograph plates and viewscreens to the glow of hellish embers in a threatening night. I looked out the window, and could not find the stars. The accretion disk was gone, and the trawlers with it. All we beheld was Dark. Never had I seen such blackness, unless it was in the dark beneath Calagah, in the temple-hushed gloom beneath the surface of the world. It was not that we were at warp: the whine of ion drives still carried through the *Mistral*'s yawning superstructure. It was as if we had flown into the mouth of some cave vast as moons.

"What's going on?" Bastien demanded of Nazzareno. When no answer came, he said, "What have you done to us?"

Sharing the First Officer's disquiet but not his fire, I squinted out the window. Almost I imagined it was not space I looked upon, but the pelagic dark of the sea. I half-expected the blur of some fin or tentacle to pass my window, or to hear the cry of some leviathan or the song of whale. But the abyss stood lifeless, silent, and so screamed. Darkness filled me, and filled me with a sense of foreboding such as the old Florentine must have felt standing at the gunwale of Charon's ship as they crossed the Acheron. Almost I felt the boards groan beneath my feet. I found myself thinking of Demetri and his crew—the Jaddian merchanters who had meant to take me to Teukros when I left home—and of the untold billions lost in that endless Dark. Perhaps the ancient spacefarers were right—perhaps the Chantry was right—perhaps hell was in the deep of space. Perhaps it was not sea life I might see out my window, but the faces of the dead looking back me. Not just Demetri and his crew, but Uvanari, Gilliam . . . Cat. Even Gibson with his slitted nose.

Light.

There was light, running in the darkness as sparks run from flame. From another window another voice rang out, "I see something!" The more curious joined us at windows, and I was jostled by a lieutenant whose name I no longer recall. Like the lights of stars they were, and yet unlike, coming from a great depth, as though it were from the bottom of some trench. Several trenches. They spidered across that blackness, and as I watched my understanding shifted. They were not sparks flying in the night, but orderly candles lighted in deep alcoves, flickering. Lighting great rings around us and above us and below, as if someone had taken all the dimmest stars of heaven and ordered them to march rank and file.

They were not stars, for they vanished or were hid as we moved. And they moved, flashed or flickered or danced, changing color in accordance with patterns I could not decipher. I gasped, and was the first to say, "It's a city."

Smaller than March Station it must have been, but grander because we could see it all at a glance. The candle flames were the lights of buildings, obscured by the height of those structures built around them. For how many miles it stretched I could not say.

"'Tis a ship," Valka corrected.

The lights above us grew closer, and pressing two fingers to the glass I tried again to magnify the image as I had before. It wouldn't work. The glowing chasms whence the faint light shone took on dimension: the surrounding darkness reaching down to meet us like so many black hands. They were towers, and the lines of colored light were streets. I could just make out the movement of what looked like groundcars or trams in those deep places. Overcome suddenly by the sense of vertigo, I shut my eyes and turned away.

A ship.

Given what I'd seen, I guessed the ship was like the great spinships of the sort the Mandari used, though on a scale that dwarfed any the Consortium and its ilk had. The *Enigma of Hours* was cigar-shaped, perhaps a hundred miles from end to end, perhaps longer, and perhaps a tenth that across. I never saw much of it, but deduced from those parts I did see that her front end was open to vacuum. The crew section and drive cores were in the aft, separated from the docks and the city by a vast bulkhead that sealed the back end as surely as the front was open.

"We are now on final approach." Nazzareno's lilting voice filled the silence disquietingly. There was something artificial about how natural the chimera sounded. The Exalted swiveled its bulk to look at Captain Corvo, but even as it did so several of its secondary eyes turned to look at different people: at Bastien Durand, standing nearby with his jaw set; at

Valka, listening raptly by the window; at myself. "On behalf of Captain Eidhin and the rest of the *Enigma*'s crew, I am instructed to remind you that for the duration of your stay with us you will be expected to abide by the ship's rules. Passengers are to remain in the visitor's port and are not to attempt entry into any of the restricted zones, or to carry weapons in the visitor's port. Any passengers found in violation of these policies will be subject to summary disembarkation. Similarly, all passengers will remain aboard their ships until such time as the *Enigma* is at warp. Anyone found attempting to interfere with the *Enigma*'s physical or datum-plane integrity will be subject to summary disembarkation . . ." The list went on. About halfway through it I had the uncomfortable realization that the Exalted wasn't speaking to us, not exactly. Its words were canned, pre-recorded, so that instead of having worn out the tired speech, it simply repeated statements it had made before, played back in bored bemusement.

When it was done, Bastien Durand stepped forward and asked, "To be clear: what is 'summary disembarkation'?"

All of Nazzareno's eyes twitched forward to refocus their attentions on the Norman in his fake spectacles. "Your ship will be ejected from the *Enigma*'s central hold without warning or review, without regard for your fuel reserves."

The First Officer made a small *hmm* noise, but offered no other commentary.

"It won't be a problem," said Otavia Corvo. "The minute we're clamped in for the long haul, I'll be reducing my active crew to a minimal complement and putting the rest into cryonic fugue for the journey."

The big Exalted unclasped its metal hands from the ceiling and the rail beside it, turning its whole bulk around so that it half-loomed, half-crouched before the Amazonian captain. "That will not be necessary."

"I'm sorry?" Otavia tilted her head, clearly confused. "How's that?"

"You're for Vorgossos, yes?" The creature raised its chassis above the level of Corvo's head, red eyes growing dim, as if hooded. "That journey won't take but three standard weeks."

You could have knocked any of us over with a breath. *Three weeks.* There would be no point in putting anyone on the ice for so short a time.

The Captain was a moment regaining her footing and voice. "V-Vorgossos is that close?"

"I cannot answer that," Nazzareno said, and began clanking its way back toward the door. "Suffice it to say the planet is several kilolights from here."

"Several . . ." Her voice trailed off, calculations turning over in her mind. "That's not possible. You're talking about speeds several thousand times light."

"'Tis possible," Valka said coolly. "I did time on a Demarchy courier when I was younger that averaged three thousand *c*."

Nazzareno shook with silent laughter, pointed a claw at me. "The Empire keeps such craft as well. None could keep pace with us if they had a mind." He was boasting, and I caught myself wondering if he really was so young as he sounded. A boy. What sort of person could put a boy in a body like the one before me? Carve a child's flesh and pack it into cold steel?

A resonant, metallic boom resounded throughout the ship. Another clang followed a moment after, and the lot of us looked round, muttering in confused alarm. Several of the holograph panels flickered, returned to their original states, showing ship's diagnostics and astrogation as if nothing had happened. Several of the techs scrambled to their stations even as the gravity began to shift beneath our feet. Centripetal gravity bled over me, rising up under the constant pressure of the suppression field, dragging my innards down to their proper place. I could see from the way the others moved that they had felt it, too.

Nazzareno bobbed its head again, eyes bright. "An inspection team will be aboard presently to assist me in making sure you've brought no dangerous substances onto our ship. A lock has been placed on your ship's weapons systems for the duration of your stay." It turned to go, gripped the door frame with three clawed hands to steady itself. Nazzareno caught himself and turned his turret of a head back to face us. "Welcome to the *Enigma of Hours.*"

CHAPTER 25

BECALMED IN MOTION

"THINK THEY'LL SOUND THE all-clear soon?" Switch's voice carried down the steps from the observatory. I was supposed to be meeting Valka there. She had gained permission to let Tanaran out of the brig for a time, to show it where we were and what we were doing. I shouldn't have been surprised the captain was there, nor shocked to find Switch at the ready.

Otavia answered, her voice frayed by exhaustion. "Not sure. Instruments say we're at warp, pushing nine thousand *c*."

"Thought that squid man said we'd be let out once we were at warp?"

I'm not sure what made me do it, but I stopped on the stairs. The well spiraled up and to the left, ascending from an access off the central hall between the rear section and the bridge, up to a semicircular chamber that looked out and down on the tapered Clovis point of the *Mistral*'s prow. I was alone a moment, unseen by either anyone in the hall or anyone in the room above. I might have been the only soul in a million light-years, were it not for the voice flowing down from above.

Captain Corvo replied, "That's what he said, William. Nothing we can do about it in any case."

"I don't like it," Switch said. "Feels like a trap."

"If it were a trap, why'd they drag it out like this?" I heard the thud of a glass—wondered at the early hour. "We've been in their power for three days."

Switch conceded this point quietly, but even still I did not move. The outer wall of the stair was cold beneath my fingers, and I was aware suddenly of the faint hum of the ship, and of the distant, more noisome sounds of the world beyond. "Still feels like a trap. And we got the Pale to worry about."

"Tanaran?"

Switch seemed to take ages before he answered. "I think Had's making a mistake. Sticking his neck out for this demon, betraying the Empire. It ain't right."

"I didn't think you the patriotic type." Otavia's voice was almost wry.

"I'm not," Switch said, "but human is human. Sometimes Had forgets that. Doesn't feel right, turning on the others like that. Lin and Jinan."

"I don't like it either," she said, "but I owe Hadrian for Bordelon, and he thinks this plan of his to parley could open peace talks, so . . . if Hadrian wants to go to Vorgossos, we'll go to Vorgossos."

"Sure." Almost I could see Switch nodding in that slow way he had. "Then what?"

I was listening to something I shouldn't have been, and I knew it, but of all my sins this was perhaps the least. Otavia spoke, and you could hear the shrug in her words. "More of the same. Murder and violence, I expect. If you and Marlowe and his lot don't stay on, you don't stay on, but a girl's got to make a living, doubly so if she's got a crew. And this ship ain't small. I've got a lot of people to watch out for."

"If the Extras don't grind them up for fodder, sure."

"You don't know them like I do," she said. "Granted, I never saw an Exalted ship like this. What did they call it? A Sojourner? But I know the types like on March Station. They may look different, break rules you have they don't, but they're still people like the rest of us."

Switch was quiet a long while. "That's what scares me."

"Well, it's like your Hadrian always says," the captain said with a sigh. "We're off the map."

Switch snorted. "Here there be monsters."

They both laughed, and even I could not help but smile. Seeing my opportunity, I climbed the rest of the stairs and entered the top chamber. The observatory was small, little more than twenty feet across, with an arc of window that overlooked the gray-white, pitted hull of the old Uhran cruiser and opened on the sky above. It still looked like night. The gold and violet veins of the far side of the ship made an orderly impersonation of stars, sunk as they were deep in the grid of city blocks. Otavia herself and Switch sat on a low couch looking out at the gnarled and knuckled structures of the docks and the city beyond.

Switch raised his glass when he saw me, careful not to spill a dram of the clear spirit he was drinking. "Evening to you!" There was nothing of the disquiet I'd heard in his voice on his face. He was a good actor.

"It's morning," I said wryly, taking a seat opposite the red-haired man.

"Not on the *Enigma!*" Switch said. "It's evening."

"Valka and Pallino went to get the Cielcin," I said. Nodding at the bottle and the glasses on the table, I added, "Are we drinking before work now?"

"We drank before work in Colosso all the time!" Switch grumbled. "And I'm going to need it to look that Pale bastard in the face. Gives me the chills."

I glanced at Otavia, who shrugged. "We're not exactly *in* Colosso now, are we?"

Before I could carry this line of conversation forward or really settle myself into my chair, Otavia said, "We were just looking at the other ships docked here, see?" She pointed. Through the arc of alumglass I could see the crouching forms of other ships, lain down like the statues of antique kings atop their sepulchers. Their white hulls and gray contrasted with the blank sable of the Exalted craft, marching around the gradual turn of the *Enigma's* circumference. "Those two are Durantine galleons, there and there. You can see the sail housings there around the forecastle."

"Those spires?"

"Yeah!"

Switch drained his glass. "They're far from home."

"More than thirty thousand light-years," I agreed. The Republic was on the far side of the Imperium, in the Outer Perseus near galaxy's edge. "Those Jaddians came even farther." The Jaddian ship was even easier to identify: whale-like, all organic curves, its black ceramic hull accented with a heat-treated titanium brass; its photovoltaics gleaming like graceful fins. There were even Imperial ships in among the passengers, their heraldic crests bright-painted on their gunmetal hulls, displaying all manner of devices strange to me. I had never had a head for heraldry. Crispin had memorized nobile crests with an avidness I couldn't share. He could have told you the symbols and mottos of every house major in Auriga Province. I could only wonder who they were, what strange circumstance had brought them out so far and on so strange a road, and whether they—like myself—would have chosen to be somewhere else.

Somewhere else.

"Drink?" Switch asked, proffering the bottle. It was from the same case of vodka Crim had sent up from Rustam before our meeting with The Painted Man, the same vodka Siran had drowned herself in after Ghen's death. The label had a spaceman in an antique-style suit with a gold star on his black visor. He had one foot planted on a red planet, and his arms were thrown wide.

"A small one." I took the bottle grudgingly and took one of the drinking tumblers Switch had brought with him. There was no reason to be hard on Switch for drinking.

Following on from their conversation—their real conversation—from before I'd climbed up the stairs, the captain said, "Say, Hadrian, have you given much thought to what you'll do after Vorgossos?" I didn't reply at first, was focused on pouring just enough of the vodka to seem social—I did not care for the stuff. When I didn't answer fast enough, Corvo added, "William and I were just talking."

Still I didn't answer a moment, held the vodka on my tongue. It tasted medical. Metallic. Far out the open front of the *Enigma* the violet weft and ripple of spacetime whorled and rioted. So far off it was—dozens of miles away—that the open end of the great cylinder was no larger than a gold hurasam. At last I sucked in a deep breath. "No. I can't see past Vorgossos, not yet. This place . . . the past few days . . . it's been a lot to take in." Nazzareno's metal hand twitched across controls behind my eyes. Bassander's hand fell lifeless from his wrist.

"You're not having second thoughts."

"What? No. Of course not." I cradled the vodka in my hands, looked from the blond Norman to the red-haired lictor. Both still wore their Red Company uniforms. That made me smile. "But I did commit treason." I did not mention my conversation with Raine Smythe. I was not sure it would save me. "I left three of our own people dead on the *Balmung*. I assaulted an Imperial officer. Those charges alone . . ." I slammed the vodka back, but would not pour another. "I'll be crucified for sure."

"Blown out an airlock, more like." Corvo smiled thinly. "Your Legion's efficient, won't waste time on theater." I did not have the heart to tell her how wrong she was. There was no doubt in my mind that Bassander Lin would have me on a cross given the opportunity, and the gods only knew what Strategos Hauptmann might do if he got his hands on me.

But I knew Otavia's intentions, knew where she would drive next, and I saw no reason to stop her. "You could always stay with us. Best place for a fugitive is on the move and we're always moving."

"May come a time I take you up on that," I said, perhaps too dryly, looking back out the window. There had been a time, when I'd been a myrmidon in the Borosevo fighting pits, when I'd thought about turning mercenary. Switch and I and the others had talked of buying our own ship. If I stayed with Otavia, with what was left of the Red Company, I could have my own ship, in a sense, but only in a sense. "If I did, it wouldn't be as Commandant or anything like that. I'm no real commander . . . I'd never really been in space until I left Emesh. Besides . . ." I turned back and smiled, looking down at the table between us. "I'm going to be in *your* debt after all this, anyway."

"I've got decks that need scrubbing." She grinned.

"Maybe tomorrow." I smiled weakly.

Switch cleared his throat. "They on their way up?"

"Valka, do you mean?"

Even in the dim light, I could see the way the color drained from Switch's face. "And the alien."

My fingers gripped my knee, knuckles white against black fabric. Presently I nodded, licking my lips. "Yes." I don't know why I was nervous. I had spoken with Tanaran dozens of times. I did not fear it. Valka certainly did not. But having it walk about the ship—even under guard—seemed like tempting fate. I couldn't blame Switch for being scared, if scared was what one called it.

"We should have put that demon back on ice and no mistake," Switch said, glowering.

I released my knee, sucked in a rattling breath to calm my nerves. "Even if we had the hardware, we have to put our best face forward. Diplomacy, Switch."

"Diplomacy? You seen the fangs on that thing?"

"Quite close up, thank you," I said in a cold rush, not wishing to continue the line of conversation. I had enough concerns in that moment without borrowing my friend's.

Footsteps on the stairs. The clack of hard soles and the slap of naked feet. A clicking of talons. Turning, I saw the crouching figure of Casantora Tanaran Iakato emerging from the stairs. The Cielcin seemed to unfold into the room, so tall was it and so compressed by the narrow stairwell. Its horned crown nearly scraped the ceiling and it looked round with eyes wide and hollow as the pits of a skull. Pallino entered right behind, dressed this time in simple shirt and trousers—though he wore a shield-belt inactive about his waist. Then came Valka, bare arms crossed, eyes lit with anticipation.

I stood, steadying the swing of my sword against my hip. Like Valka, I watched the Cielcin in numb anticipation, wondering what it would do. Tanaran didn't speak, but shuffled toward the window, ducking its head to keep it from banging into the low ceiling. Switch made a warding gesture, clambering to his feet to put distance between himself and the xenobite. Otavia didn't move.

The Cielcin's hands were unbound, and it pressed its fingers to the glass, tilting its head to look out and up at the tableau, its overlong shadow dancing across the floor in the light cast by the *Enigma*'s warp. At last it spoke, using the halting Galstani it had learned from Valka. "This . . . reminds me of home." Its words were hushed, as if it spoke in temple. "Almost . . . as large."

Valka moved to stand beside the xenobite, passing Pallino where he stood attentive, watching the creature for any sign. "You grew up on a ship like this?"

"Like this?" Tanaran repeated, taking its hand from the glass. A filmy print remained there, six long fingers standing out against that blackness. "Not exactly like this. We . . . the People I mean, we . . ." It broke off, unsure of the words. Switching to its native language, it asked, *"Nietolo dazen ne: 'Eatabareto o-velegamaya.'"*

"We hollowed out asteroids," I supplied, insinuating myself between Valka and the tall creature. Tanaran had given no indication of violence, nor any sign that it was capable of violence, but those were still claws on its fingers and toes, still horns on its head.

The Cielcin cocked its head, making the twitching gesture that signaled that it understood. "Hollowed . . ." it repeated, mulling over the word. Presently it turned, looking up through the observatory's skylights toward the lights of farside. "We do not have such spaces. We build deep, in layers. Not open, not . . ." It made a circular gesture with one hand. "Around." It fell silent for a moment, hands slack at its sides. "How . . . large is this place?"

Valka glanced at me, and from the look in her eyes I knew we were having the same problem. Neither of us knew a thing about Cielcin measurements. How could we answer a question like that? The xenologist found an answer before I did, saying, "'Tis only an estimate, but some forty thousand times as tall as you."

"Estimate?"

"Guess."

Tanaran tucked its chin, lips pressed together in what I realized was contemplation.

It looked like anger.

Slowly I became aware of the way Otavia Corvo's dark eyes were studying the creature, as though it were a leopard in our midst, one that might suddenly strike. However diplomatic she had been at her first meeting with the creature, she was not asleep.

"Raka yumna velatate, ne?" Tanaran asked.

"This *is* a ship," I said, conveying by my tone that I was translating for the benefit of my human audience.

Valka chimed in, "It won't be but about twenty of our sleeping cycles, and we'll be at Vorgossos."

"If these Exalted are to be believed," said Otavia Corvo to no one in particular.

Tanaran flexed its fingers, looking round at the lot of us through slitted eyes. It was dark in the observatory, with only running lights on about the edge of the floor and the lights of the *Enigma* beyond, but I gathered it was still too bright for that creature of the night. "These others . . ." it said, raising a hand to the ships around us, "they sail for Vorgossos, too?"

"Vorgossos, yes," Valka said, moving back into the xenobite's line of sight, "and other places. That one there . . ." She pointed at a knobby, silvered vessel with green markings and a squat, wedge-shaped hold. "That's from my own people. From Tavros."

Never having seen a Demarchist ship before, I craned my neck to look. It had a polished, clean look to it, unlike the pitted, industrial blackness of the *Enigma* around us, looking like a new fixture in old armor. I wondered if it was piloted by a daimon, a true artificial intelligence. The Tavrosi were said to use such, free as they were of the Chantry and of the memory of the Foundation War, living as they did so far from those worlds the Mericanii had deformed—so far from Earth and old holocausts of ancient days.

"Tavros . . ." Tanaran repeated. "This is your tribe? Your *itani?*"

The word *itani* meant something more like *gens* or *clan* or *constellation* than *nation,* but Valka nodded, smiling. "They are."

"These people," the xenobite began, waving its hand at the other ships, fingers spread. "They are here . . . *detu?* Why?"

"*Rajithiri.* To trade. The Exalted, the people who own this ship, they're merchants."

The Cielcin swiveled its head, looking from Valka to myself. "Merchants?"

"*Mnunatari,*" I said.

Tanaran shook its head, ducking its horns in what seemed to me some sort of threat display. Valka retreated, and even I took half a step back, half-sliding into a guard to defend myself. "*Mnunatari,*" it said, making the word a curse. "*Hasimnka.*"

I knew the word, though I did not then fully understand it. There were human groups who shared a status comparable to that borne by the Cielcin *Hasimnka:* the Dalits among the Museum Hindus, the Nipponese Burakumin farmers, the Eudoran out-castes in their migrant fleets—even the homunculi. To the Cielcin, nothing was so unclean. They were without station in the *scianda,* the fleet, belonging to no one, owning no one. But why should merchants figure among their number?

Valka, who perhaps had missed the significance of the gesture or the xenobite's strange tone, said, "Once we're there we'll go about contacting your fleet."

"*Tutai,*" said Tanaran, and again, "Good."

CHAPTER 26

THE ORACLE

ON THE SIXTH DAY, they let us off our ships. They did not speak to us, nor send any message, only extended docking umbilicals to ours and the other ships, allowing us out into the concourse and what Nazzareno had called the visitor's port. Otavia had insisted that everyone remain aboard. I had insisted that I be allowed off. I won.

It was always night on the Exalted's ship, always the black day of space. Pale white sconces flickered high on fluted, black metal walls and from recesses in the ceiling. I had donned a full combat suit for the occasion: sculpted breastplate and segmented arm and shoulder guards, tunic, gauntlets, and greaves above the nanocarbon underlayment. The armor had been Imperial issue, and gleamed bone white beneath the heavy lacerna I wore fastened at the right shoulder in place of my customary coat. Despite all this, despite even my shield-belt, I felt naked without my sword—without any weapon at all. But such was the law as Nazzareno had explained it, and one had to allow for differences in culture.

"What exactly are you looking for?" Switch asked for the dozenth time.

"I just want to get a sense of the place," I said, twitching the heavy cloak over my shoulder. A piece of me wished then that I'd worn simple clothes on the occasion—valuing secrecy over protection. But I saw a creature, a beast with spider body and the head of a man, move past the opening at the end of the hall, and I changed my mind. "The . . . people."

My friend and lictor swore, moving back. "What in the hell was that?" Other shapes moved up ahead, most of them human, thronging along some path ahead. When I didn't answer, he breathed, "Black Earth, Hadrian. Did you see that thing?"

"You can go back if you want," I said, not unkindly. "It should be perfectly safe. I can handle myself."

"Unarmed?" Switch said, brows contracting.

"I can handle myself," I repeated, shrugging ineloquently. "I used to put Ghen out on his ear when we sparred." Mentioning the dead myrmidon sent a spasm through me, and I saw an echo of it twist the other man's face. There was a piece of Ghen in each of us, lodged there like shrapnel.

A brief, forced smile cracked the ice in Switch's face. "Ghen wasn't an eight-foot metal spider, though."

"No, he was not . . ." I half-turned back toward the street, made a gesture. "Are you coming?"

For a fleeting instant I saw the boy he had been recoil beneath the man he was. The gawky, large-eared boy who had frozen up in his first Colosso melee. It was that child who hesitated, open-mouthed and wide-eyed, plagued with indecision. The man shut his eyes, set his jaw, and nodded. We believe our fear destroyed by new bravery. It is not. Fear is never destroyed. It is only made smaller by the courage we find after. It is always there.

The visitor's port was a single road, proceeding left and right in a great loop so that it made a circuit around the *Enigma*'s entire circumference, with ships docked in berths to either side. The concourse lay open to the air, which hugged the rotating inner surface of the Sojourner or else was contained by the static fields that guarded the ship's open mouth. I realized on stepping out from the shadow of the umbilical hall that my original understanding of the ship had been wrong. This was not March Station. Not a city at all. There were very few other people on the concourse, and most of them seemed to know exactly where they were going and why. They moved ship to ship with the determination of executives on the cusp of some business arrangement. Perhaps that's what they were. A coterie of women in the gray and violet uniforms of the Wong-Hopper Consortium filed past, and I marveled to see something so commonplace in that strange land as the Mandari in their tall hats. A Durantine ship's captain in doublet and hose hurried past, accompanied by a gaunt man with papery skin. Some emotion in the face of the latter one drew my eye, and it took me a moment to realize that it was no emotion at all.

"That was an android," I whispered to Switch, looking back over my shoulder like the rube I felt. I had heard the Durantines kept androids aboard their ships, trusted them to watch their crews while they slept the long sleep between the stars. I shivered. It sounded like a recipe for horror, like the premise of some grim Eudoran masque.

Switch made the sign of the sun disc discreetly, whispered, "What are we doing out here, Had?"

"Just getting a sense for the place," I said, resuming my walk, checking the drape of my lacerna over my armor. "Get a sense for what Vorgossos is going to be like. I don't want to be wrong-footed when we get there."

"Should have brought Doctor Onderra," Switch said, sticking close to my side. Up ahead, a box like an upright sarcophagus floated on repulsors, flanked by guards dressed in deep blue cloaks with black feathers adorning the crests of their helms. I did not recognize the livery. They held a silk awning on tentpoles over the top of the sarcophagus, and as they approached I could see the metal arms extruding from the sides of the artifact. It had four faces, front and back and either side, carved of some pale wood that contrasted with the black metal. We had to step aside as the strange procession passed. I wondered what it was. Some religious item? Or else some fey Exalted from the depths of space. "She knows about demoniacs."

"She *is* a demoniac, you know," I said, continuing forward.

I didn't have to look to see the fear in my friend's face. "I know that, Had, I do. But she's not an eight-foot metal spider, either." He stopped, forcing me to stop with him. Opposite us, a man with four arms of jointed bone clung from the underside of a starship, working at some instrumentation panel with tools I did not understand. "I'd take the Pale over this lot. The God Emperor did right to wipe out the Mericanii. Can you imagine if this were everywhere?"

I was seeing the dead eyes of the SOMs in that cafe on Rustam, the way their shattered bodies still moved, severed limbs writhing, clawing after me. The memory smoldered, the light of it reflected in my friend's drawn face. A little girl hurried out of the ship the four-armed man was working on, carrying a pocket plasma cutter. Her greasy coveralls swamped her tiny frame, and she stomped a bit in boots too big for her, but she laughed, and held the plasma tool up for the chimeric man harnessed to the hull of the ship above her. A father and child, I realized with a start, or else something very like it.

Far above our heads, the far side of the Exalted ship glittered in the dimness, distinguishable from the native stars only by their regularity—the grid pattern of them. The crowd grew thicker as we pressed on, dozens of people and creatures of all descriptions crowded into what seemed suddenly a narrow lane. The too-familiar glisten of holographs danced above our heads, recreating the feel of the streets on March Station and in Rustam, all of it shouting for a shard of my attention.

Long ago, Sir Roban, my father's lictor, would take me to the Meidua bazaar that I might see the people whom I might one day rule. Rushes had littered the ground outside, and livestock shipped in from upcountry snuffled in pens beside parked shuttlecraft. The air was close inside, thick with smoke and the sound of voices, unwashed bodies pressing, moving through a dance as old as Ur. In a way, that concourse reminded me of nothing so much as the Meidua bazaar. Not a proper streetfront as in Borosevo, but a riot of informality pressing all around. It was as if all those strange persons had unburdened their ships' holds and spilled their contents upon the concourse, so that Durantine electronics might be had alongside Imperial cloth and genetic sculptures from the aesthetes in Jadd.

We passed by a Nipponese man with tattooed arms holding court with a pair of Tavrosi clansmen haggling over the price of solar sailcloth. Beyond them an Extrasolarian—her body replaced with white porcelain—sold some things sinister in tiny vials. Some of the contents moved.

"Why the marketplace?" Switch asked. "Don't these Extras use their dataspheres and whatnot? Communicate that way?"

I stopped to admire a caged bird standing among a collection of animals being sold by a Jaddian man in a turban. In a quiet voice, I answered, "I suppose they want the company. It's not easy being locked up on these ships for so long, and most of this lot don't make landfall." I stooped a little, putting my face on a level with the bird's. I'd never seen its like before. Not graceful, slender like the raven Antonius Brevon had kept, but squat, large-eyed, its snow-feathered crest evoking horns.

"You like our owl!" the Jaddian said, accent thick on his tongue. He tugged at his beard. "Jacopo designed it himself. It's good?"

"*Innino formoso*," I said, speaking Jaddian. "It's artificial?"

"He speaks Jaddian!" the merchant said, throwing up his hands. "Artificial, yes. Jacopo designs the finest pets in the galaxy. Prince Aldia himself is owning two of Jacopo's cats. You like cats?"

I raised a hand. "Perhaps later, sirrah." And hurried off, ignoring the merchanter's attempts to sell to my retreating back. Switch and I proceeded along the curving road, the metal decking rising to meet our feet. As I have grown older, I find I like the simulated gravity of spinships less and less. I did not like it then. But what disquiet I felt on account of the centripetal gravity was lost beneath the foreign wonder of that place: the dark structure, the flashing lights, the confusion of forms familiar and bizarre. It was all my eye could do to soak them in, to commit to memory the impressions of machine and flesh and the conjunction of the two.

Never before had I attempted to draw such a thing in my sketchbook. I longed to try.

"We should head back," Switch said, gripping my shoulder.

"Soon," I said. But I had seen something. Up ahead, moving through the crowd, there was a shape. Man-like but not man. Shorter and rounder in the shoulder, huddled in a hooded orange mantle. I don't know what had recommended it to my attention, obscured as it was by the press of forms around. Something in the movement of it, the waddling gait. The sleeves of its mantle were dressed in green feathers big as swords, and they fluttered as it walked beside a tall woman in a cloak the color of pale seas. Presently it turned, and I started, transfixed and transfigured to the boy I had almost forgotten I once was. "Switch," I said, reaching blindly for my friend, unable to take my eyes away. "It's an Irchtani."

"A what?" he asked. Then he saw it and grew silent.

The xenobite whose people Simeon the Red—my childhood hero— had befriended opened its long beak to speak. I could not hear it through the crowd, but could see the shadows of a green-feathered face beneath the cowl, and a hooked, black beak failing to red. The feathers I had taken as sleeves were on bare arms, and its elbows almost touched the floor, most unlike a terranic bird. It held its hands clasped before itself, scaled digits at the end of arms longer than it was tall.

All the old stories came rushing back to me, kindling in my chest a kind of glee I had not known since . . . since those first days with Jinan after Pharos. I lurched forward, thinking that I might speak with one of the heroic birdmen out of childhood legend, and so touch a piece of Simeon's story and the sacred past. I little thought that this was a stranger, and like as ignorant of Simeon as I was ignorant of its own name. As children we imagine that there is a secret mythology in nature, and that everything in nature is a party to it. As we grow, we experience enough of nature to know there is no such magic, and are forced to inhabit the everyday. We trade the mythology of childhood for knife-edged reality and call it truth, forgetting that there are deep truths, and deeper magics in our universe.

Someone banged into me, and I lost sight of the xenobite and its human companion. Someone shouted something in a language I did not understand. An insult I thought it was, and turned. Where was Switch? I looked around in confusion, lost for a time. Whoever had accosted me was gone, melted back into the throng. I called for Switch, cast about for his fiery hair. Saw nothing. A woman in dyed cerulean, concealed but for her eyes, loomed up, and a hulking man in a pressure suit laden with hoses and knobs. Behind them a pair of dryads green-skinned as Ilex with flowers in their hair passed in the company of a saffron-robed priest. Faces. Faces. So many faces and colors. Men and machines and homunculi passing by. Despair gripped me; I had lost sight of the Irchtani. Someone tugged my cape, the lacerna pinching where it was clipped onto the breastplate of my armor.

Spinning, expecting to find Switch, I found no one, only the crowd still flowing around me like a sea. For the second time, I froze, seeing among those faces a face familiar to me. Skin the color of old parchment and just as wrinkled. The nostril slitted by a cathar's knife, the hair and sideburns wild and leonine. The eyes green as the scholiast's robes he wore.

"Gibson!" I cried, uncomprehending. It wasn't possible. I pushed through the crowd, so certain of what I had seen. He went down a side street, beneath the shadows of two ships, and I followed, seized him by his arm, turning him to face me, the beginnings of tears in my eyes.

It was only an old man in a green jacket. He watched me with eyes half confused and half afraid, and I—embarrassed—turned away. Deep truths there may be, but none is deeper than this: Those lost to us do not return, nor the years turn back. Rather it is that we carry a piece of those lost to us within ourselves, or on our backs. Thus ghosts are real, and we never escape them. Turning and turning about, I realized I had lost my place, having taken some turn in all that warren of black iron and cold neon. People still moved about, walking with purpose or wandering among the stalls.

"You, sir! You've the look of a man with *purpose!*"

The speaker was a man in a tall hat, such the Mandari often wear. His eyes were concealed behind a pair of spectacles—or perhaps they were that pair of spectacles—though he was elsewise only human, unless one counted the white light blinking under the skin of his left ear. Shaking my head, I said, "Only a man who's lost his way."

"Haven't we all, sirrah?"

"Which way to the concourse? I mean."

"But, sirrah! You are in the right place! You have found the only oracle on the *Enigma of Hours!*"

"Oracle?" I said, confused, still scanning the street for Switch and growing angry with myself for running off as I had. How could I have believed it was Gibson I saw? Yet I'd been so sure of myself.

The man with the spectacles and the tall hat smiled, revealing gold teeth the like of which the ancients once wore. "Sees the future, sees the past. Took a dip in one of them Deeps, he did. Nearly killed him. Only drove him mad. All that Time laid bare as houris in the Emperor's harem to his eye. Might see things worth seeing in Time past or future. Things you ain't seen. Things you ain't known. Only a kilo to see him. Three to ask a question. Five to speak a time."

I am not a man given to superstition. Less so in my youth. Even having seen those things I've seen since, I cannot say what held me there. I might have dismissed the charlatan as easily as I had Jacopo the gene sculptor. But something held me in place. Maybe it was having imagined I saw Gibson on that street, maybe it was the inhuman Irchtani, I don't know. But I did not dismiss the nuncius out of hand. Something in his story snagged on a corner of my mind, and I asked, "What's a Deep?"

"He doesn't know?" the man said, sweeping his hat from his head. The bare scalp beneath peeled like aging plaster, and beneath that pallor wires twined against bone. "Wells, they are. Cisterns built by those as came *before*. Those as drink their waters come back changed." He leaned toward me, raising one painted hand to whisper conspiratorially, "If they come back at all."

"Those who came before?" I repeated. "You mean . . . do you mean the Quiet?" Switch was right, Valka should have come with us. I still did not know what a Deep was.

The nuncius only smiled. "The man within sees time as a kind of space. Sees the past, sees the future. All he has to do is look at you."

"But how?" I said, growing colder. "Do you expect me to just take your word for it?"

The nuncius frowned. "He has drunk of the Deeps on Apas. The Deeps changed him. Their waters contain a xenobite, an animalcule that changes the blood. Breaks the helix and remakes it. Jari came away changed."

"Jari?"

The Exalted nodded. "My crewman. Jari asked the Deep to show him his future, but the human mind can handle only so much. He sees!"

"What does he see?"

"Everything."

The door I'd been ushered through opened onto a rusted hull, and it was only then that I considered the possibility I might be kidnapped. I told myself that whoever the nuncius was, he wouldn't jeopardize his place on the *Enigma* over one captive. And I still had my terminal, and it still drew a signal. Standing in the entryway, I keyed a message to Switch, explaining where I was—but not what I was doing—and left orders to wait for me.

I'd thought I was entering a ship, one of the many moored along the *Enigma*'s concourse. I hadn't. Pipes bracketed the walls of what seemed a kind of service tunnel, flowing like the sinews of a man's body around a bend and down, recalling for me nothing so much as the black pits beneath Calagah.

The door at the end of the passage stood open, revealing a round, low-ceilinged chamber whose metal-grated floor opened on a blackness whose depth could not be guessed. I thought it a blast tunnel to direct the flame of fusion drives for ships lifting off from the visitor's port, though I knew enough of starship design to doubt such a thing would or should be built so close to a crowded street. The pipes that flowed along the hall rose here, hurrying along further halls, over bulkheads permanently opened, and up along the domed ceiling through a narrow sort of oculus through which the room's only light fell.

The Exalted—for Exalted he must be—sat like a smashed statue. What limbs remained were fragmented, one metal calf removed at the knee, both arms gone to the shoulder. Exposed wires and fiber optics twisted, and but for hoses I guessed were for nutrient delivery and waste removal, it stood apart on a stack of old pallets draped with a starry cloth.

This rusting carnival twitched as I approached, turning a single red eye on me from the center of its forehead. Laser-bright it was, and I shielded my own eyes as its point tracked across my face. I could still see its face— the only human thing in all that nightmare of steel. The dark skin gone ashen, as though there were no blood and little fluid beneath its surface. The human eyes were closed. But it moved like a human face, and spoke with a human voice, deep as darkness.

"Marko? Is that you?" One of the dismembered metal arms twitched.

All I could think to say was, "No."

The oracle's head jerked up, cocked to one side. I could see milk-white polymer beneath the ashen skin, blended with the flesh of the neck. I shivered. It was less human than Brevon had been, nearly all machine and monster. "A guest? A guest. Why does Marko disturb him?"

"Who?"

"This." The dismembered hand curled into a fist, flopped as it bent at the elbow. "Jari."

"He said you were an oracle. That you see time."

"Time." The Exalted turned its head away. "Time yes, we see."

"The future?" I asked. "Can you see the future?"

"There is no future," the seer replied. "Everything already is. They have only to choose."

Circling the dais so my back was not to the tunnel whence I'd came, I said, "I don't understand."

"Jari drank dark water," the Exalted said. "Jari died." I kept my silence, watching the dark face nestled amid steel. "Jari wanted eyes to see." Its eyes were closed. In a sing-song voice he wheezed, "The water gave us eyes." The words had the weight of prayer. "The water gave us eyes." It made a racking, wheezing sound, the metal plates of its body flexing as it moved.

There was nothing in my experience at Calagah or in all of Valka's literature to suggest a connection between the Quiet and water. Nothing of these Deeps. The nuncius, Marko, had said they were a species of xenobite. A microorganism that altered life.

"You can see time?" I asked.

"With my own eyes," Jari said, not looking at me. "With my own eyes." The oracle jerked its head. Its dismembered limbs writhed on the floor. I felt a twinge of pity for the creature, alone and insane, its humanity long gone. "The water took him. Took his eyes. Gave. Us. New. Ones."

Forgetting my trepidation, I approached the dais. "Who did they take?"

"Jari. We took Jari."

"Then who are you?" I asked, placing one gloved and gauntleted hand on the prophet's shoulder. When it didn't answer, I said, "Look at me, please. There's something I need to know."

Maybe it was my tone—as calming as I could make it. Or maybe it was the hand on its shoulder. That fleeting human contact in this world of wire and steel. Jari opened its eyes, and they were only the eyes of a man. Perhaps his humanity was not so far gone as I'd thought. They were not flat obols as Brevon's had been, not the glassy spectacles of Marko the nuncius, or Cento's monocular. They were only human. The red light in the center of Jari's forehead dimmed, and its fleshly eyes went wide, as if it were the Exalted who saw a monster and not I. "What are you?"

"What?"

Jari tried to push itself backward, but it had no limbs to escape on. "What are you?"

"I don't understand," I said, looking round. "What do you mean?"

The oracle looked at me, struggling to control its breathing. "It's . . . broken. Behind you."

"What's broken?"

"Your river!" it said, and the dismembered hands pointed accusing fingers in random directions on the dais beside it. "Your beginning. You have no beginning."

I laughed, ran hands back through my hair, cast my gaze up at the ceiling. "Excuse you?"

"In Earth's name, girl, get a fucking mop!" I froze, hands stopped halfway between my head and my sides. The way it'd said those words . . . he had imitated in tone and cadence some of the first words I had heard on Emesh. I could almost smell that horrid flophouse by the starport. The old woman. Her ragged voice and the alkaline bite of verrox on her breath. But Jari wasn't done. In a small voice, barely to be heard, it said, *"Tell me a story, would you? One last time."*

I felt my blood beat against my ears, forgetting myself. My feet advanced on their own, closing the distance between me and the shattered hulk on its platform. "What did you say?" I breathed, knowing full well what it was. *Tell me a story, would you? One last time.* Cat's words, whispered in a storm drain beneath Borosevo's White District, her body consumed by rot. "What did you just say to me?" I mounted the dais again, less concerned suddenly for the terror in Jari's eyes.

"You buried her in a canal, just like she wanted. Just like so many others. But you never went back."

"Don't speak of her! Don't you ever speak of her." I had never spoken of Cat to anyone. To speak of her was to trouble her memory, and she had suffered enough. "Was it the Quiet that made you this way?"

Jari looked at me, and for a moment it did not speak. When it did, it was in a voice I have never forgotten, with words that have never left me. "Leopards," it said. "Leopards, lions, and wolves . . ." I did not understand.

"What does that mean?"

"We are not them." Its eyes did not move, yet I perceived it turned them another way, as though it looked over my shoulder and around some corner only it could see. I felt something cold seize my guts. I was sure then I was not talking to Jari at all, but to some . . . *colony.* To some *thing* that had crawled inside the Exalted that wore it like a skin. I should not have touched it, even with my gloved hand. Having forgotten my question, the thing that wore the face of a man said, "Your past is broken. There is a hole in it through which we cannot see. The ship . . . your ship was taken. Wiped clean." He looked at me the way common men look at a flier crash, the way new soldiers look at a battlefield. At length he said again, "Your past is broken."

"And my future?" I asked the question reflexively, not knowing what I meant by it, not understanding any of this strange conversation. It seemed some dream, some mad fiction I'd stumbled into.

The seer's eyes moved again without moving—as if the light hitting them had changed.

The pupils shrank, and the whole great metal construct of him shook and fell backward with an almighty crash. "Light!" it shrieked. Its disconnected limbs flailed. One hand seized the hem of my cape, and I staggered back. Jari kept screaming. Fans whirring in its chest kept air flowing through its throat. "Light! Light! Light!"

Marko appeared as if from nowhere. I expected him to barrel past me to see to his asset, but the other Exalted seized me above the elbow, kicking Jari's arm free of my cloak. "What did you say to him?" he demanded, spittle flying past his gold teeth.

"Nothing!" I said. "I asked him to look at my future. That's all."

"Light! Light! Light!"

I was speechless. I didn't know what to say, only stood there in numb confusion, remembering. *This must be.* Words in an unheard voice echoing out of Calagah. A black ship vast as cities, her surface bristling with the forms of men and gods and angels. How she turned sunwards and plunging down drowned in light.

I remembered, but did not understand.

Marko shoved me back the way I had come. "Get out of here! Go!"

"But . . ."

Bone-white scalpel blades clicked out from beneath the nuncius's fingernails. "Leave!"

I fled. Jari's words followed me, rebounding off the metalwork.

"Light! Light! Light!"

CHAPTER 27

VALKA

MY ENCOUNTER WITH THE oracle left me rattled, and I spent much of the next day alone on the *Mistral*. I found I could access the *Enigma*'s datasphere and—if I was willing to foot the bill—I could have access to all manner of information. I read what I could on these Deeps, found little more than Marko had told me. On certain worlds, there is a certain animalcule that grows like algae in water. Where it came from none knew, whether it was some bastard child of Red-Handed Evolution or the artifice of some antique intelligence greater than man's none could say, nor did any know how it was the creatures had found their way to nine disparate worlds. There was no reference to ruins in any of the short documents I could find, nor any help to be had on the datasphere fora.

I'd said nothing to Switch, not knowing what to say. After Valka had not believed me when I told her about my vision in Calagah, I had said nothing about the experience to anyone. I decided that this, too, would go on the list of things I did not talk about. But for many days after, and many years, I would awake to the image of Jari's eyes, mad in their bloodless face, and to the haunting words he'd spoken.

Your past is broken. There is a hole in it through which I cannot see.

What does one say to that? What did it even mean?

A knock sounded at my door, and I keyed it open without getting up from my desk.

"Here you are!" Valka said, entering. "Are you all right? Switch said he hadn't seen you in days."

I shut my journal before Valka could see the charcoal I'd done of the oracle, Jari, and—smiling—turned to face her. I'd had an excuse forming but on seeing her could only manage, "Are you going somewhere?" She'd donned a jacket over her customary vest and sleeveless blouse, and swapped her shipboard slippers for the high boots and jodhpurs she'd so often worn at Calagah. An awful thought struck me and I asked, "You're not leaving, are you?" My thoughts jumped to the Tavrosi ship we had seen moored from the *Mistral*'s observatory.

"What?" The xenologist frowned at me. "No! Corvo's letting me out on the concourse. I thought I might go look around. 'Tis all manner of strange folk out there—I saw through the window. And one never knows what one might find. Besides!" Valka put her hands on her hips and stood a touch straighter. "I thought I could use an escort. That's what you big, swaggering Imperial lads are for, is it not?" I think she expected me to rise to the bait, for when I did not immediately punch out with a response, she rocked back on one heel and said, "Are you all right?"

My attention had drifted, eyes wandered to somewhere over her shoulder. Shaking myself back to myself, I said, "Hmm? Yes, I'm fine. I'll be all right." Not my best performance.

Valka was not convinced. I could see it in the brittle quality of her smile, held on her face long after the feeling that had put it there was gone. "Shall we, then?"

The concourse was more crowded that day than when Switch and I first ventured out. A piece of me wanted to return to the alleyway where Marko lurked and sold his companion's visions. I stuck close to Valka, walking slightly behind to better keep an eye on her. The people were nominally unarmed, but Marko's talons had demonstrated just what *unarmed* meant to these people. I didn't trust them. Not with my own life, certainly not with Valka's.

"You know there are other Tavrosi aboard?" she asked, pointing up in the air where the road curved in a great arc ahead of us, ascending into the dimness. Following her gaze, I beheld a sleek ship, porcelain-white save where the ceramic was scored black or stippled by micro-impacts. "That ship there's the *Jayavarman*, out of New Angkor. I spoke to her captain a couple days back over the net." Here she tapped her head to indicate the computer enmeshed beneath her skull.

"Is that where we're going?" I asked, keeping close.

She didn't answer at once. "Mayhaps. I only wanted to see what we were getting into. Corvo wouldn't let me ashore in March Station, and I'm curious to see what I can of these people before we get where we're going."

We had to stop a moment to allow a street sweeper to pass us by. The massive vehicle huffed steam into the damp air, holograph plates to either side blue-flashing the words *KEEP CLEAR*. Once it passed, we proceeded along the road in silence for some time. Privately, I was glad to be going in the opposite direction from the way I'd gone with Switch, climbing the road toward the Tavrosi ship and not toward Jari's sideshow. Valka spoke again. "Why so laconic? 'Tis not like you. We've been out here more than an hour and you've not so much as disagreed with me once."

This remark stuck to me, and I was a minute shuffling it off. "You . . . want me to disagree with you?"

Briefly, Valka looked back over her shoulder, a wicked smile on those cruel lips. "No, no! I want you to roll over and surrender, Hadrian—of course I want you to disagree with me! That's why we're friends."

That wicked smile softened so quickly it was like the cracking of ice in spring. I felt its warmth, said, "Are we?" All these years and I'd never really asked. Why was I afraid of her answer?

"Friends?" Valka turned away. "Of course we are!" Not knowing what to say to this, I held my silence, which must have vexed Valka, who asked, "What's up ahead?"

"I'm not rightly sure. Switch and I went the other way last time," I said darkly, scowling as a woman moved past, a queue of glowing wires dangling from a socket in the back of her head. I could see hollow space inside that socket, as though her skull was empty behind her face. "I don't much like it here."

The Tavrosi made a small *oh* sound, before half-turning to say over her shoulder, "Is it the machines?"

I tried imagining what it must be like to be Nazzareno, or Jari trapped on his dais, unable even to stand on his own. To be anything other than I was. To be inhuman. I felt ill. "Yes." Anticipating her next comment before she could make it, I added, "And I know you have a neural lace, Valka. You don't have to mention it. It's . . . you're different."

"Am I?" she asked, slowing a moment that I might catch up. "How am I different, exactly?"

I stopped, not sure how to answer, sensing—as I often did—that the waters around the Tavrosi woman were dangerous ones. Echoing Switch, I blurted out, "You're not an eight-foot metal spider."

The doctor turned and looked at me, an unreadable expression in her eyes. Then she laughed, and the music of it drove away a piece of the shadow hanging over me since last I'd walked the concourse. "What?"

She hid her mouth behind her hand—the way Nipponese women are wont to do. "Do the Exalted scare you? Did they frighten the Lord Commandant of the Meidua Red Company?"

She meant to shame me. I was not going to be shamed. Swallowing, I stood a little straighter. "Yes. They do."

"They're more human than Tanaran."

"Tanaran I can read," I said, shrugging my shoulders. "These chimeras . . ." I could only shake my head.

Valka and I lingered a moment beside a ship that seemed to be selling nothing more exotic than clothing. Not looking at me—her attention rather captured by a black silk shirt—she said, "I'd not be so sure you can read Tanaran."

"No?" I stepped out of the path to stand beside her, watching her as she studied the fabric with her fingers. "I think we understand each other."

"I think you have an understand*ing*," she corrected, arching her eyebrows for emphasis. "'Tis not the same thing. I spent a long time with Tanaran while you were in fugue. Its facial expressions are unreadable."

Pressing my back against the rack of clothes, I looked at her. "Not completely. I can understand a few of them. The way they smile is very obvious."

"You're sure 'tis a smile?" She smiled at me, though there was no amusement in the expression. "As if smiles were all the same."

"You think I shouldn't trust Tanaran?"

"I think you shouldn't be afraid of the Exalted."

"Afraid is an ugly word."

"It's an ugly thing."

"It's the wrong word," I said, tugging the collar of my old coat up around my face. "I'm horrified."

That stopped our conversation a time, and we walked on in silence. The ground felt always to rise up to meet our feet, and the great chatter and haunt of human voices filled the air of that long bazaar. I tried to imagine the place empty—as perhaps it never was—stripped of all that light and color and the thrum of human activity. Only bare, black metal remained. Rusted grates and fluted ironwork, puddled coolant in dim corners. The drip from unseen pipes.

"Otavia is right, you know," Valka said at last. She said *Otavia*, not *Corvo*. Somehow I did not think that a good sign. I got the sense she had been screwing herself up to say that since she'd entered my cabin earlier that day.

"About what?"

We had stepped off the main concourse and out under a striped awning set up in front of an open hold that sold—to my amazement—a collection of printed books. The smell of them! The smell of pulp and glue! Of paper aging in yellow light, turning from white to that species of gold which is to me more precious than gold itself. I could sense Valka looking at me, and so I replaced a heavy volume of Golden Age Classical English poetry on the shelf where I had found it.

"About how you need to be thinking past Vorgossos, about what you're going to do if this doesn't go the way you think."

"Ah." I turned away, finding it easier to examine the curling letters on the displayed spines than whatever emotions curled in the doctor's face. "Switch told you about that."

Without having to look, I could see the small, sad smile on Valka's face. "He's worried about you. I'm worried about you."

I let my fingers drop—having been about to pull down a biography of Emperor Winston the Good, thinking it strange to find such a thing in an Extrasolarian bookshop . . . thinking it strange that there was such a thing as an Extrasolarian bookshop. A piece of me hoped I might find a copy of the old book Gibson had given me so long ago, *The King With Ten Thousand Eyes*. But it did not appear. "She wants me to stay on. Rebuild the Red Company. Figures it's better if I don't set up in any one place. Stay ahead of whatever Bassander or Smythe or Hauptmann send after me."

"You think they would?" she asked, leaning against the bookshelf beside me. I could just see her eyes from the corner of my own. I didn't want to look.

"Send someone after me?" I made the mistake of glancing her way. "Are we talking about the Sollan Empire here? No. Otavia's not wrong."

"Where do you think Bassander and the others are now? You don't suppose they could have followed us to March Station? They had the coordinates."

Crouching, I pretended to examine a row of colorful volumes that turned out to be an encyclopedia of erotic Jaddian poetry. I made a face. "No, no. Bassander's gone to Coritani, I'd bet my life on it. Regrouped with the 437th." I knew for a fact that that was what he had done. He'd told me as much before I stormed the *Balmung* and made off with our star prisoner. Straightening, I turned to look at her, smoothing the fronts of my greatcoat. "Smythe will have recommended no pursuit on the off chance this little gambit of mine succeeds."

"And if it does not?" Valka's eyes hadn't left my face. "'Tis all you want? A life of violence?"

Unable to suppress a weak smile, I said, "If you're asking me to go with you when you leave, you could just ask."

That did it. Valka stood straighter—coming off the rack of books—and crossed her arms. "I said nothing of the kind."

"Ah, but you were thinking it!" I said chidingly, wagging a finger at her. Lacking the courage to hold her gaze, I pivoted and continued down the aisle of books. The stacks rose high to either side, higher than even my palatine advantage could aid me. I'd seen hovering drones with dangling claw-arms flying among the shelves, retrieving books—I guessed—for customers not interested in the hallowed rite of browsing.

Valka clutched her left arm just above the elbow, massaging the tattoo that covered her left arm as if it hurt her. I broke off my half-hearted perusal of the bookshelves to look at her. At last she said, "I told you once I wanted to be a pilot. I was one for a time. Did five years in the Orbital Guard back home. Everyone has to put in their time, but I stayed. Renewed after my three years were up." As she spoke, her sentences grew shorter, voice drifting further and further away. "'Twas before my father . . . well . . . He was so proud. Not many in the Demarchy stay in the Guard once their term's up. He always joked that I'd be chief of defense in a few decades." She smiled, eyes far away as her tone. "He used to talk a lot of nonsense like that."

Getting the sense that this was going somewhere I didn't want to hear, I asked, "What happened?"

"Prachar terrorists took control of a Durantine trading cog out past lunar orbit."

"Prachar?"

"Religious nationalists." She waved a dismissive hand. "Edda orbits pretty far from her parent star, uses mirrors to keep the surface habitable. The Prachars meant to smash the mirrors, force the rest of us to negotiate." Valka looked at a point just over my shoulder. "They had captives on that ship. Foreign captives. More than two thousand of them. Most of them in fugue. We had poll data flooding in over the datasphere, everyone on the surface saying 'twas only a mirror. We could rebuild it, better to negotiate. But the orders came from Command. Told me to take the shot."

Her eyes were very far away.

"Did you?" I asked.

"To my everlasting shame," she said, and blinked for the first time I think in all her narration. "I did." She swallowed, turning to the rack of books behind her. "None of them survived. I resigned the next day, moved offworld to get away from the datasphere—the things people were saying about me."

"You saved their lives."

"I saved their *quality* of life."

"Don't be absurd," I said. "I've seen orbital mirrors. Any part of that could have dropped from orbit and leveled half a city. You did the right thing." For once, Valka didn't fight back. She just stood there, her back to me, shoulders drawn together the way a prisoner's did before the cathar struck off his head. Not knowing what else to do, I placed a hand on her shoulder. I felt her tense, but did not move my hand away for a long moment. "Why are you telling me this? Do you want me to stop all this? Now?"

Valka inhaled sharply, as if banishing the beginnings of tears. Presently she turned, and whatever hole there had been in her armor was closed. "No, I . . . never want to be in that position again."

"You won't be," I said.

"No one should have to be in that position."

It was my turn to look away. "Valka, I had no idea."

"Of course you didn't," she snapped, sounding herself again. "I didn't tell you." She lifted her chin in defiance, as if expecting some judgment from me. I only managed a weak smile, seeing her—as it were—by the light of a new sun. Her cold disdain for my life as a myrmidon, her dislike of the way Imperial life codified violence, her displeasure at being the subject of a duel. Even the stiffly formal way she carried herself, ramrod straight and square as laser-cut crystal; the stance of a soldier at attention, or at parade rest, proud as any queen.

"I'm glad you did," I said, one awkward hand plucking at the frayed jacket of an old tome on the shelf beside us. "For what it's worth, I understand." The harsh silence of the comms channel going dead as I ordered Emil Bordelon and his ship wiped out of the sky thundered in my ears. Valka knew what I meant. Whether she was thinking of Bordelon or of Uvanari—or even of Gilliam—I could not say, but she pressed her lips together and did not contravene me. It was a strange conversation to be having in a place so open as that one, but we were deep in the stacks and alone.

"No one should understand."

Something Jinan had said to me came drifting back, and I said, "It's better if good men do what we do than bad ones." I have told you I once believed that wars are fought with words, not soldiers. I have told you I was wrong. Here was my first glimmering of that realization. For when a war is done, no matter how small, pieces of it remain. Most of this *shrapnel* is carried in the hearts and souls of those who visited that strange country we call *battle*. Wherever such people go—be it to the brightest garden— they are at war. To say that such people do not fight wars, as I had, to say such do not win them, was a dishonor. A dismissal of their struggle and pain. I understood that then, as one can only learn by experience.

"Are we?" Valka asked. "Good?"

I thought about that a long time, distracting myself with the labels on the shelves, finding it easier to look at my hands than into her eyes. I realized then that I'd long ago stopped thinking of myself as good or ill, as if those bright categories had dimmed, one flowing softly casual into the next. When had that happened? I knew. It was in a torture cell in the Borosevo bastille, and before that: tormenting a Cielcin prisoner in the dark beneath Calagah.

"I think the fact that we're asking that question is a good sign," I said, not fully confident in my answer. Perhaps I was troubled by some presentiment of my future—recalling the horror in Jari's eyes when he looked upon my future and my past. It did not take an oracle to know that violent lives end so often violently. In lonely places. Down lonelier roads. "In any case, someone has to keep me from making a fool of myself."

"That's my job, is it?" She thrust out her chin, all *herself* again.

I smiled. "Well, someone has to do it."

CHAPTER 28

THE DARK WORLD

WITH MY OWN EYES I beheld the white curve of her beneath the black and baleful eye of her dead star. Never before had I seen such an undead sun. Stillborn, a pitiful brown dwarf glowing less than the meanest ember, vaster than the vastest world. The planet itself was almost as dark, illumined only by the ghastly white lights of what I took for cities. Many times I have read of sailors lost out airlocks or through fractured hulls, their bodies burst by vacuum, faces drawn and pale as the faces of men drowned at sea. In the tales, these ghouls cry out to torment their living crewmates. I have seen many such faces myself, and heard their silent song. The planet cried out to me the same.

Dim Vorgossos.

We were not permitted to land, nor to pilot our vessel ourselves. At first, I believed that a pilot would come aboard to take us out of the *Enigma of Hours.* Nothing of the kind happened. Our systems gave no sign of interference, but without warning we unclamped from our berth in the Sojourner, drifted out into the naked center of the massive starship's main hold, joining a slow procession of ships leaving the *Enigma*'s drum.

Around me, all was chaos as Corvo and her people attempted to ascertain what was happening. Clearly some power had seized control of our systems and was piloting her and the other ships in grim parade.

We came in time out beneath the stars, and then it was I first beheld that whited sepulcher of a world beneath her black-dead star. The surface of that dark world drifted mere dozens of degrees above absolute zero, and whatever atmosphere there might have been was choked to frost. Words were said, but I do not now remember them, recalling only the vision of the strand ahead of us. The hightower.

A single spar of adamant, black as hell, reached up from that pale and shadowed planet like a pillar of smoke, like an accusing finger aimed at heaven. Impossibly thin it was, hanging like a thread of evil gossamer between the planet and the stars, rising mile upon thousandth mile into the Dark. It was toward this tower we sailed, each ship silently guided into its berth about a station platform which sat atop the lift column the way an insect sits atop an antenna. We did not see the *Enigma of Hours* vanish behind us, disappearing with the telltale glimmer of warp before it vanished into the superluminal. We had a mind for nothing but the sound of docking clamps seizing the hull.

We had arrived.

Pallino was first through the doors when they opened, body shield shimmering about him. Crim went after, one hand resting casually against his sidearm in its holster.

There was no one to greet us. No customs officer, no police. There weren't even other merchants in all that bare and echoing hall. Stars shone through massive windows, and the smoldering wheal of the brown dwarf smote above and near at hand, larger than any true star I'd ever seen. It filled half the sky above and beneath us. And beneath it? Forty thousand miles below our feet? The lone and level snows stretched far away.

"I get cold just looking at it," Ilex said from behind me.

"This feels wrong," Pallino said, as if in answer. Around us, dark metal scrolled like vines and distended human statues buttressed the arching ceiling, great chunks and stripes chewed out of their time-eaten surfaces. I wondered how old they were, and for how long this ancient elevator had stood high above the surface of this planet. "There's no one here."

Crim—ever bravest—hurried on ahead, soft boots padding on the marble tiles. "Hello?" he called, raising his clear, richly accented voice. "Hello?"

Nothing.

Switch pressed out of the airlock behind and around Valka and myself. "Had, you and Doctor Onderra stay here, we'll look round."

"Rot that," I said, throwing out a hand to bar his way. "We'll go together. Everyone, shields." Those who had not activated body shields did so then.

"Why wouldn't there be anyone to greet us?" Pallino asked. "This place is for business, isn't it?"

"They don't need anyone," Valka said coolly. "We're being watched."

I'd felt it, too. Raised as I was in a castle, I'd known what it's like to be observed. One could feel the pressure of the cameras in the way our ancientmost ancestors sensed wolves watching in the forests by night.

The entry hall opened without ceremony or corporate distraction onto a high, domed place. There were no holographs, no advertisements, no booths. No vendors selling food or religious icons.

Nothing.

A battery of several dozen lift carriages stood waiting beneath fluted pillars and the protective arms of giant statues. Three of them, with arms longer than those of any man and faces blank and pitiless as the dead sun seen through the glassy dome. We were the first to enter—or else the last—for no others appeared by the other doors, and many a lift carriage was absent, having descended through the floor and out an airlock.

"I have a bad feeling about this," I said, looking down at the floor. White stars, five-pointed, studded a ring which encircled that mighty hall, fringed with brass inlay in marble so black it was almost blue. Why was that familiar? I cursed myself for never becoming the scholiast I wanted to be. A scholiast would have remembered and trembled. I trembled all the same, and murmured one of Gibson's aphorisms to quiet my nerves.

"We should head back," Switch agreed. "Get a decade together. We should have done in the first place." As if in answer and proving Valka's suspicion and mine, the door back to the loading dock irised shut. Switch whirled, roaring, "Black Earth and damnation!"

"Steady, boy!" Pallino said. "Steady on."

I pressed a finger to the comms patch behind my ear. "Captain Corvo, this is Marlowe. We've been locked in. Repeat: We've been locked in. Do you copy?"

Nothing.

I shouldn't have been surprised. I imagined there were no signals getting in or out of a place like this.

"I guess we're left with no choice then," Ilex said, sounding completely unafraid. The dryad checked her weapon calmly and, satisfied, awaited instruction.

Shaking my head, I said, "We never had a choice. We've come this far already." I pushed past companions and lingered a moment, looking up at the three faceless statues that stood above the lift carriages. Almost they seemed women to me, so slight were their forms. Almost the figures of Furies, so horrible were they. What hand had wrought them? And in what age? To what purpose? Like Cielcin they seemed, so tall and frail-seeming . . . and like the Exalted, crafted all of jointed, flowing steel. They made me think of Jari and his prophecies, and of one prophecy older still, words in a wordless voice whispered in the dark.

This must be.

I steeled myself, squaring my shoulders. I drew Olorin's sword, held the handle quiet at my side and ready.

"I am not afraid."

CHAPTER 29

THE PROFANE CITY

LONG WERE THE HOURS of our descent, and little of them shall be writ here, for there is little to say. We sat on couches, or stood in numb anticipation, watching the witch-lights shine from the depths. Pale green they were, or white, or sulfurous yellow. We were alone in our descent, climbing down our cable with all the patience of a spider at her web, un-accompanied by the lights of other lift carriages. Switch sat sweating, sick at his guns, staring at his hands more than out the windows. Ilex and Valka exchanged quiet words with Crim. Pallino stood by the window, said, "In all my years in the Legions, I ain't never seen a place so desolate as this," and was silent.

I must have dozed a while, and dozing dreamed. I was lost in dark waters, with no inkling where light or the surface might be. All was dark as space, as our approach to that lightless world had been, without even the unfixed stars to ameliorate. I did not know which way was up, and so fancied that perhaps I *was* in space after all. I could not breathe but . . . did not need to. For a moment, I thought I saw the funeral masks of my fore-bears shining like swamp gas.

Hadrian . . .

They seemed to speak in voices dry as desert sand.

Hadrian . . .

Those white faces . . . each in turn opened like the lid of some horrid eye. Vanishing . . . vanishing until none remained, leaving me alone. Only then did I realize I could not breathe, and realizing—panicked. I tried to swim, to fly, to cry out. No words came. Then the hands came, emerging from the inky dark beneath me on arms long as lift cables. Fingers hard as iron seized me, closing over my mouth, around my wrists and ankles.

Hadrian . . .

I awoke with a start, glad none of my companions had seen. I could still hear the awful voice ringing in my head.

Hadrian . . .

It spoke again.

Listen!

I shook myself and ground my teeth.

How fast we descended I couldn't say. There was no wind, no atmosphere to slow our descent, and so we fell like a meteoroid, buoyed by the protective curtain of suppression fields. Most hightowers, I knew, took days to make their climbs. Ours took hours. In all that time we couldn't get a communication through to the *Mistral*, no matter what we tried. As we sank lower, the ghost-lights revealed themselves as markers on the doors of sealed blast pits, half-concealed by snow so that the ice itself glowed ethereal in the deep and endless night.

I don't know what I expected. A city perhaps, sprawling and strangled, with buttressed walls and high towers. A piece of me, I think, suspected the place out of the vision I had seen in Calagah: that ancient city, Gothic in its ruinous splendor, limitless in scope, its halls echoing to the sound of that terrible infant I had heard in the dream. But on the surface there was nothing, nothing but the trackless snows and a single obelisk of white stone—more than a mile high—through whose open summit was threaded our lift cable and all the others. All was dark within, lit by faint service lights that recalled for me the crimson lamp in Jari's forehead.

We stopped.

"Are we down?" Switch said, voice high. He sounded almost the boy of seventeen I'd met in the Colosso.

Ilex shook her head. "Airlock."

Sure enough, the whole lift carriage rocked on its cable a moment after, and the sound of rushing wind overwhelmed us. Then we resumed our descent, more slowly now. Down into darkness.

Boom.

A deep sound reverberated up the shaft around us. Light—soft and with the faint gray of rainy sunrise—rose from below us.

Thus we entered the unholy City: through an oculus near the side of a massive concrete dome. I tried to imagine the building of such a structure—whose mad hands had hollowed such a space beneath the surface of a world. It must have stretched for miles, and from our great height I could see the arched mouths of great tunnels leading away to what I guessed were other domes, other chambers. It must have been two miles from the apex of the dome to the ground. A river ran through a sluice gate high in the dome wall and through streets and plazas of white stone. Crumbling tenements of gray concrete stood in grim file along one wall, dwarfed by the great turrets and pyramids that looked almost childlike next to the massive scale of the ancient dome.

"Well," Pallino said, crossing his arms, "there's a thing you don't see every day."

Even I was speechless, watching as a pair of albatross dove past us through cloud—*cloud*—toward the tops of towers below.

"It must have taken centuries to build all this," Crim said, pressing himself against the glass. "The dig alone . . ."

Ilex stepped up to join him. "They could have built the dome over a crater. Ice might have stacked up over the years."

The Norman nodded. "Fair point."

"I see people!" Valka interjected, pointing.

She was right. Far below, the insect shapes of men and women moved along streets and about fountains, or else stood in the shadow of a street corner or leaned against a column. The relief I felt at the sight of them! To know this was a true city and not some grim necropolis of pale white . . . I felt tension ebb from my shoulders that I had not known I had.

"Stay sharp, everyone," I said, watching the tops of the towers sink past our eye level. "And stay close."

The air smelled damp and mossy, and everywhere was heard the cry of birds. A deep-throated warbling greeted us as we left the lift carriage, stepping out onto a marble plaza not unlike that in the station above. Here the tiles were cracked, or worn by the passage of uncounted feet, and the bronze statues were green with time. Every building was of the same white stone, or fronted by it, and the very air seemed faintly to glow with reflected light.

Our passage across the square disturbed a flock of pigeons, and it was they who led our procession down a short flight of stairs to what I took for the main street, which rose smoothly up an incline and across an arched bridge toward a massive gate in the wall of the dome. A great many people hurried along the street, many of them only human, still others homunculi or chimeras. Almost instantly I felt the old hair-prickling sensation steal over me, as though my every inch was begrimed by a thousand grasping hands.

We were being watched.

"Do we have any idea where we're going?" Valka asked, stopping beside me at the base of the stair. She had insisted she be allowed on *this* expedition, who had missed March Station and Rustam before it. Otavia had refused, but I'd supported her. Valka had never been a ground soldier, never a legionnaire, but she carried a plasma pistol all the same. Not an arc burner, but an actual, cartridge-fed repeater. I'd never seen the weapon before.

"I don't even know what we're looking for," I said. "The Painted Man said the ruler of Vorgossos calls himself the Undying. I've no idea if that's to be taken literally or if it's warlord pretension."

"It could be literal," Ilex said, "if he's Exalted. Earth knows how long they live."

"People who speak of this place speak in terms of needing something," Crim said, hooking his thumbs into his shield-belt. "Gene tonics. Abstraction. Cloning. Xenobite genetic augmentation. The sorts of things they won't do even among the Extras." Pointing with his chin, he took in the buildings around us. All were laser-cut of the same pale rock, quarried—I did not doubt—from the excavation of that massive dome. "This look like any Extra city you've ever seen?"

He wasn't wrong. Whatever horror I had felt on our approach and descent was fading behind the voices of the crowd. On the *Enigma,* on March Station, even on Rustam—where Imperial law was faltering—the streets had been littered with holographs, massive advertisements selling everything from cigarettes and sim games to body modification. They'd even sold religion, or the religions had sold themselves. There was a debasement there, as I have already recorded, but there was a freedom, too.

And perhaps it was better to buy debased things if that meant one was free to choose. Perhaps having that very choice—that freedom—is what debases the things we choose. The Cid Arthur teaches that life is suffering and called that a noble truth, and the Christ of old says that nobility comes in bearing that suffering as he did, out of conscious choice. Perhaps that was why the advertisements on March Station had so offended me.

All that choosing rendered a noble choice impossible.

But here there were no advertisements. No holographs of women or of smiling cartoons. No vendors hollering from street corners. The City beneath Vorgossos was somber as a sepulcher. What people there were—and there were a great many people—moved quietly about their business and did not look up.

"It reminds me of home," I said suddenly, only realizing as I spoke that it was true.

Switch looked at me, aghast, and even Pallino raised an eyebrow. "What sort of place did you grow up, exactly?"

Father had forbidden the installation of advertisements—even printed ones. The streets of Meidua had been kept clean, and if a banner or device was shown it was only the sable banner of my house with its capering devil cackling in crimson thread, or the red sun of the Empire. The buildings there had been of white stone, too, and the great thrust of our acropolis whence rose the black tower and citadel of my birth.

"We kept it clean," I said.

"'Tis unnatural," Valka put in, and there was a species of despair in her voice. "It takes force to keep a place like this." She was not wrong; by Father's word vandals caught writing on the walls or putting up posters were given to the Chantry for torment.

No one accosted us as we moved deeper into the City, or paid us any mind. Those persons we passed averted their eyes or went on as if we were not there. Only the rare dram of attention stuck to us—on Ilex more than on any other member of our company. At any moment I expected some sinister figure to come lurching around a street corner or from the shadow of a door. But neither the likes of Jacopo the gene sculptor or Marko the Exalted spoke to us. None did.

"'Tis like being in one of your cities," Valka said to me, unable or unwilling to hide her sneer. "Like everyone's afraid." I let this dig at my home and empire pass by, having already admitted that I was reminded of Meidua and Devil's Rest. When the doctor noticed she'd failed to get a rise from me, she added, "Did you notice the guards?"

I had. I could see two of them standing in the shadows of a fat concrete stair that corkscrewed up along the outside of a cuboid building, holding shock-sticks tonfa-fashion. Even at a distance, they seemed curiously face-less, their features blurred and indistinct.

"They're SOMs," Ilex interjected.

Switch swore. "You're sure?"

"She's right!" Valka agreed. "They're standing too still."

The guards wore a sort of khaki uniform that recalled for me the jumpsuits worn by the Umandh slave douleters on Emesh, more akin to the uniforms of an urban prefecture than the armor of house hoplites or peltasts, with high boots and long gloves done in brown leather. Without being certain, I could sense that Ilex and Valka were right. They might have been graven from stone. Oft I have witnessed such decorum, in my father's soldiers—in the Emperor's own Martian Guard—but these crea-tures seemed not even to breathe.

"You!" a soft voice said. "You are visitors!" Turning, I found a woman in a dull blue suit near at hand. She had the soiled look of one who lived without the comfort of bed or shower. It was a look I knew all too well, having worn it for years. And like the beggar I had been—once—she reached out a hand, palm up. "What you here for? Ol' Shara knows the way. Knows all the best magi, she does. Knows where to find them. Is it slaves you come for? Soldiers? Weapons?" She screwed up her face, cring-ing. It took me a moment to realize that this woman, this brave woman, expected that I would strike her. I wondered at the sorts of people who often came down those lifts. I did not have to guess. She had come to me of any of the six of us. The only palatine.

I waved Switch back, not needing a bodyguard against an old woman. "Shara," I said, using her name. "Have you ever seen one of the Cielcin? The Pale?" I raised a hand above my head, indicating the height of the creatures I meant. "Here?"

"What?" She shuddered, not looking at me. Sparing a glance round I saw others like her, dirty men and women in once-fine clothes. There were many of them, coming toward the main street and the lifts like pen-itents to an altar. "Not here," she said, "not here."

"I have come a long way to speak with them," I said, fumbling in my coat. "I am told the master of this place has business with them. That he speaks with them."

The woman had twisted herself as far from me as she could without running away, but still she kept that one hand extended, palm up.

Sighing, I placed a single coin in the palm of her hand. It was golden. A single Imperial hurasam stamped with the profile of Emperor William XXIII, the living Emperor. Her fingers closed about it, and she looked at it, looked at me, eyes wider than the coin. It was not a small price. For such as she, it was a fortune. In all my time as a beggar in Borosevo, none had given me so much. Not once.

"The Master?" she breathed. "The Undying?"

Stooping so that I looked her in the eye, I said, "Where can I find him?"

"He's all around us, lord." She raised a hand. How it trembled! "He sees all around us! He knows why you are here. It is why you are here. It is why we are all here. He leaves Shara to mind the gate . . . poor Shara. Her and the others." That rocked me back on my heels. This was a performance, of a kind. An Attic chorus dressed in rags. Did they greet all visitors in this way? Perhaps so.

"What the hell does she mean?" Switch asked, and without turning I knew he had a hand on his plasma burner.

I raised a hand to stay him, thinking of the ghostly way our ship had been piloted from the *Mistral.* On Emesh, Valka's neural lace had allowed her to see through the eyes of the castle's security system. She had controlled the lights and the power grid and helped me . . . helped me to deliver Uvanari from its suffering. But she had *seen.* I did not understand much about datasphere communication networks, but I knew enough, for the hair-prickling sensation I had felt took on a special sharpness. Turning, I beheld the two officers I had seen standing in the shadow of that spiral stair. Their blurred faces had turned and were looking at me. Was it my imagination? Or was there a light shining through them?

"I'm not here for slaves or soldiers," I said. "I need to speak with him."

"Hadrian . . ." Pallino cautioned.

Again I raised my hand, a fist this time, for silence.

"Lords come to him, wanting to be young again, wanting things no one else can give."

I'd heard the stories, had told pieces of them in my quest for this place, but I'd never really believed it. Everyone knew immortality was impossible. If it were not, then surely the Emperors would be immortal. The human mind could only endure so long, could only shoulder the weight of so much memory.

"He's really immortal?" I asked, taking a step closer.

"He does not die," she said. "He raised these stones. Built them on what was before. Drove the demons out."

A piece of me froze a little, and I said, "You're not serious."

The woman looked at me, affronted, and backed away.

"You're talking about Kharn Sagara," I said, remembering the story. "The King with Ten Thousand Eyes?"

Shara's face went white. "Say not his name!" She staggered back.

"That's impossible," I said, following her.

"Hadrian!" Crim interjected, more sharply than Pallino.

"He would be ten . . ." I trailed off, trying to remember. "Fifteen thousand years old!"

"Hadrian!" Valka this time. Her voice—the bright urgency of it—stopped me cold, shook me from my myopia.

I had been so focused that I did not hear—that I did not see—the guards emerging all around us. Dressed all in dun they were, jackbooted and gauntleted, with peaked helmets and indistinct faces. Shara staggered away, and the other beggars with her, one Attic chorus fleeing the advance of another, leaving us six alone in a ring of faceless men.

Faceless.

They had faces. Once. If you have seen a corpse—as all of us do eventually—you have seen the guardians of Vorgossos. The dead do not have faces, not truly. They have objects that *used* to be faces, but whose cheeks and jowls are animated by no will, and so hang like old meat from hooks in an abbatoir. And a light shone through them, gold and faintly green, so that the dim contours of the skull showed beneath the servile flesh. Ilex was right. SOMs indeed, and far more unsettling than the ones The Painted Man had wielded against us in Arslan.

"I see them!" I said, reaching beneath my coat to draw my sword.

The guards made no threatening sign, only tightened their cordon around us.

There were nearly thirty of them. We were surrounded. I did not activate my sword, but kept my thumb on the trigger as the other hand drifted for my shield-belt. Glancing over my shoulder I saw the others. Switch had drawn his weapon already, and Ilex. Pallino stood on guard, Valka beside him. Crim looked unconcerned. I envied him that. "Steady on!" I said, taking a half-step forward, settling into a proper guard. "No one move!"

One of the guardians moved forward, head tilted to one side. It stopped five paces from me, watched me with that unholy light glowing its flesh. It had been a man once, pale-skinned and hard-boned, with a subcutaneous growth of beard that colored his jaw blue. Something moved behind those dead, unfocused eyes. The pupils tightened, and a moment later the slack and atrophied muscles of that rubberized face pulled tight, until almost one could believe the thing a man. I imagined unseen strings tugging at the creature, as though it were some ghastly marionette.

"Put down your weapons, and you will not be harmed." Its voice was flat and dead. Lifeless, as though it were a statue that spoke. A golem. A machine.

Taking my hand off my shield catch, I said, "I am Hadrian Anaxander Marlowe of Delos, a cousin of the Emperor. I am come on a diplomatic mission on behalf of His Radiance and of First Strategos Titus Hauptmann."

"Put down your weapons, and you will not be harmed," the SOM said again.

"'Tis not listening, Hadrian," Valka said. "There's no one home."

I couldn't afford to listen. "I bring with me a baetan of the Cielcin Itani Otiolo. I am told the Undying has had dealings with the Aeta of that clan in the past." The SOMs began to advance. Suppressing a howl of frustration with a mental effort and one of Gibson's platitudes, I clipped my sword back to my belt and stepped forward. "I must speak with . . . with Kharn Sagara—if that is your master."

The SOM's head twitched, and almost I believed there was *something* in its hollow eyes.

Eyes I dare not meet in dreams.

But it was a dream, and what recognition I'd thought was there vanished a moment after.

"Put down your weapons, and you will not be harmed."

The creature raised its stun baton . . . and struck.

CHAPTER 30

THE SUPPLIANTS

I AWOKE TO THE sound of voices.

Not rough voices, not the braying threats or coarse humor of prisoners; nor the cold, businesslike patter of the Inquisition, clinical at its work. Quiet voices. Polite. Fighting stun-fatigue and the leaden numbness that is ever its companion, I struggled to sit up. Young as I was then, already I had grown accustomed to waking up in strange places and to dungeon cells. I had made quite a habit of frequenting such places during the brief period wherein I called myself a mercenary. And yet, as I fell back against the cushions, it was only with the glum certainty that this time Jinan was not coming to save me. Jinan was far away, with Bassander and the Centaurine Legions at Coritani, regrouping in their defense of the Veil.

Cushions . . .

My second thought was that no prison should have cushions, nor so fine a couch as the one I reclined upon, upholstered in rich and patterned velvets of red and gold. It had the feel of an antique. The gold leaf upon its woodwork peeled in places, and its fabric faded, marking the splendor of some other age. The ceiling above could not have been more different. Pale concrete it was, cracked in places, and in others exposing naked steelwork gone to rust. The walls were the same, but hung with paintings and with tapestries fine as any lord's.

"You're awake!" said a quiet, measured voice, polished as old wood. "The guards brought you in some hours ago. They stunned you, yes?"

My new acquaintance was an elderly man, liver-spotted and with thick white hair and a pointed chin-beard. High-cheekboned and with a touch of epicanthic folding about the eyes. Nipponese? He wore a pale suit with a high collar and gold-fringed red toga, and his long fingers were heavy with rings. I knew at once he was palatine, and from that guessed that he was very, very old. There were liver spots on his hands as well, which struck me as a sure sign that he was near the end of his long life. Of all the people I had met, only Gibson seemed older to me.

"They did," I said, nodding best I could while lying down. "My companions?"

The old man shook his head. "You were brought in alone. We all were." He waved a hand, taking in the room at large. Several dozen others sat or stood or milled about in the hall behind him. Men and women, all haggard-looking but finely dressed, all with the tall, too-symmetrical look of palatines—or of the similarly well-endowed—about them. The man pressed a hand to his chest. His nails were very long. "I am Kim Hae Song, Baron . . . I *was* Baron . . . of Munshin." Not Nipponese, then. Mandari, perhaps?

I mirrored his gesture, astonished to find a planeted nobile tending to me in my unconsciousness. "Hadrian Marlowe. My father is an Archon on Delos."

"Delos!" The man's eyes went wide. "You're an Orionid lord! What constellation?"

I saw no reason to lie. "Victoria."

The man's face paled, and he stood quick as his old bones were able. "You're one of the Peerage?" He bowed. "Lord, I . . . I did not know."

"I am the very least of the Peerage, Baron Song," I said. "Indeed, I would bow if I could move."

"Nonsense, nonsense!" The old man regained his seat on the ottoman. "A cousin of the Star Victoria and His Radiance ought not to bow to me. My great-grandfather was a starship manufacturer." He pressed a hand to his chest, to the ruby pin securing his frilled ascot. "But you're so young! So young to be . . . here?" He made an inquiry of that statement, casting eyes about.

Following his gaze, I saw naught but gray heads around me, and realized with a start that every other person in the chamber was old, though most were yet tall and lordly. "What is this place?" I managed at last, not able to think of a better question. "What sort of prison is this?"

"Prison?" Lord Song repeated, "Prison? No-no-no, dear boy, no. There are no prisons on Vorgossos. Should one offend the Undying, I hear he offers them a choice: to be turned into one of his soldiers or, ah, exile."

"Who chooses the former?" I said seriously.

"The, ah . . . the ones who don't want to freeze on the surface." He flapped his hands, a gesture which only intensified when I began to stand. "You must not! The stun fatigue, Lord Marlowe, you'll fall."

I *did* stagger, banged my hip against the couch. My oath drew the attention of several of those well-bred personages nearest me, and a thick silence fell about me.

"Is he all right, Kim?" asked one nobile lady, her face wrinkled as sand-etched teak.

Lord Song held up an acknowledging hand, but moved to put his shoulder under my arm. I swayed there, steadied by the old man's weight against me. "Where are the guards?" I asked.

"Guards?" Song said, uselessly.

"I need to know what happened to my friends," I said. "I had five companions. Three men and two women. They must have been taken with me."

Kim Hae Song patted my shoulder in what I assume was meant to be a fatherly way. "They'll have been quartered appropriately. They're fine. You could probably have a message carried to them. They have to wait separately."

"Wait?" I snapped.

"Well . . ." The old man blinked. "Yes!"

"Wait for what?" I began stumping toward the door, conscious of the plush give of the fine carpets beneath my feet.

Song tried to dig his heels in, but I brushed him off, stumbling only a little before I fell against the wall. There I remained. It was all I could do not to slump over, and I struggled to stop my knees from shaking. "Surely you're here for the same reason we all are? To petition the Undying? This is where to meet him."

"Not a prison?" I asked.

"You're free to leave, boy!" shouted another, older man. "Looks to me you've more time than the rest of us, and the golem doesn't take us in any sort of civilized order. I've been waiting two weeks for an audience."

A silver-haired woman in a white evening gown spoke up. "Two weeks, Archibald? I lost count of how long I've been here at six weeks. That was weeks ago!"

"And I've been here the better part of a year," called another whose face I could not see.

Baron Song leaned toward me. "We've all been waiting a long time. The Undying sends his golem for us when it pleases him." The old Mandari wrung his hands. "It pleases him for us to wait."

"I am the Marquise of Sarmatia!" the woman in the white dress announced, banging her cane undramatically against the thick carpets. "It's an affront, I tell you! An affront!"

A hulking man, reduced only somewhat by age, said, "And I am the Grand Duke of Milinda, Marquise. What of it?"

"We are all lords here," said Baron Song diplomatically.

"I am only a spice merchant!" said another man whose gray-faced complexion reminded me of the old vilicus on Emesh. "And Pardos here is an artist!"

"Who are you, newcomer?" asked the Marquise of Sarmatia.

Trusting my knees at last to stop shaking, I stepped forward—only then becoming aware that my sword was missing—and said, "Hadrian." I was patting down my coat pockets reflexively, searching for the lost weapon. The guards must have taken it. Remembering myself and bolstered by the effect the information had had on the old Mandari Baron, I said, "I am Hadrian Anaxander Marlowe, of Delos and the Star Victoria."

"Nonsense!" said one of the lords. "And what's a stripling like you doing in a place like this?"

"It's not nonsense, Frederick," said the dark-skinned woman. "The Viceroys of Delos are Star Victoria, the Auriga branch . . . some Princess Imperial married one of the Delian Viceroys millennia ago. If House Marlowe was a local house, married to the Viceroyalty, it could be the boy's of the Peerage."

"He has the look . . ." said the Grand Duke of Milinda, adjusting his saffron cape.

I clenched my jaw, not terribly thrilled to have my family history debated before my eyes. Only it seemed very trivial to me after so many years a mercenary, though I knew it was not. Of old, perhaps, it was so. In ancient days a king was only a man who believed himself king and made others believe by the strength of it until the people took that strength on faith even after it was gone. It is said that no less than Alexander, considered by many the forefather of our Empire, once asked the scholiast Diogenes why it was he searched through a pile of bones. Diogenes rebuked the young Emperor, and sent him away saying that he sought the bones of Alexander's father, but that they looked no different from those of a slave.

It is not so any longer.

We believe our civilization the product of our struggles, when in truth we are its products. We are its children, raised behind its walls. When the first magi of the High College altered the genetic makeup of the first palatines, it was in the spirit of Imperial civilization: to answer the demands of their age and to reward the heroes who conquered the Mericanii. When it came time for those new palatines to conceive children of their own, it was in that same spirit they acted, until that tradition was as ossified as natural law. Until it *was* natural law. Humanity parted ways with our cousins, the late, lamented chimpanzees, because the differences in our behaviors—our cultures—drove us apart.

How long, I wondered, before we palatines are similarly sundered from native man? Forget Diogenes. How long before even blind Homer could tell the bones of our Emperor from those of a slave? Not long. There are many amongst the old houses of the Imperium—dowagers, mostly—who make a study of the genetic markers that define our constellations. These old women can identify a nobile's family from the smallest detail of body or face. In my youth, I'd believed it a kind of game. I am wiser now. Nothing old women do is a game, and it is a profound mistake to believe that one must care about a thing to be subject to it.

"He does look Imperial," said the Marquise of Sarmatia. "A bit on the severe side, but he reminds me of Prince Faustinus—did you ever meet him, Sendhil?"

The Grand Duke of Milinda shook his head. "What's he, then? The Emperor's eighty-third son or the eighty-fourth?"

"Seventy-eighth."

"Well, excuse me!" The Grand Duke threw up his hands. "How am I supposed to keep track of a brood like that? Ye gods, Marietta, who has the time?"

It was like they'd forgotten I was there.

In time, food was brought to us, and what strange food it was. No proper meal, no feast. Two homunculi: one with skin like milk and hair like onyx—the other reversed—escorted a train of several carts through the chamber. Briefly I saw four guards without. Dun-uniformed SOMs with their blurry faces. They held the massive doors for the serving girls, but otherwise were unmoved. The homunculi went about with trays bedecked with canapes and airy vols-au-vent. Coffee was to be had in abundance, and tea, but no wine. No water. I watched as the others all took fulsomely from the trays—none speaking to the girls who carried them.

"Take what you can," Song advised, plucking a round dozen of the things onto a small plate. "There's never enough . . . Tea please, there's a good girl." The homunculus with skin whiter even than mine curtsied and returned with a ceramic cup.

"Do you know where my companions are?" I asked her.

She watched me with eyes amber as her thin robes, but said nothing.

"They would have been brought in with me."

"Don't waste your time, Lord Marlowe, they don't speak," said Baron Song. "Let's resume our game, shall we?"

I teetered a moment, keeping eye contact with the pale homunculus, who after a moment bowed demurely and moved away. Given no choice then, I returned to the couch and the table beside it. *Druaja*—labyrinth chess—is a very old game, played as much with the board as the pieces on it. I'd never mastered it, having not the patience or the puzzle-solving mind for such things. But Song had invited me, and I'd seen no other choice.

"Your move, I believe," said the old baron, popping a piece of salmon pastry into his mouth.

In Druaja, one races one's opponent to the center of the labyrinth, all the while trying to capture your opponent's emperor. The labyrinth shifts—or can be made to shift—depending on varying arcane rules. I moved one of my centurion pieces round a corner, blocking one of Song's cataphracts from advancing further toward the center. Myself eating a roll stuffed with onions and some fine cheese, I asked, "How long have you been here, Lord Song?"

"I don't rightly know," he said. "My terminal died a long time ago, and those delightful serving girls don't come to any schedule I've noticed, so I can't use them to keep time." With a ringed hand, he captured one of my legionnaires and—having taken a piece—used it to depress a switch on the edge of the board. This altered the shape of the ridges running between the board's hexagonal tiles. My centurion was cut off, freeing his cataphract. "But I should think several months now."

"Several *months*?" I repeated. "Sitting in this room?"

"Where else can I go?" he shrugged.

"Earlier . . . one of the others mentioned a golem?" I said, studying the board.

The Mandari looked at me a long time. "His servant. Yume."

"Yume?"

"It's a daimon. An android," Song said, responding to my next move with a quickness that made me feel inferior. "The Undying keeps an android majordomo. When it is our time for an audience, he sends it for us."

"But . . . months?" I said, confounded, forgetting the Druaja board for a time. "I don't have that kind of time."

The Baron looked at me seriously, folding his hands across his chest as he leaned back. "What's this, then? Are you ill?" His face darkened. "Are you an intus? Is that it? You don't look like an intus . . . unless it's your mind that's afflicted. That's something only the Undying could cure?" He made this last a question, though it seemed to me not to be so.

Chewing on another of the canapes, I was able to bite back a harsh retort. Doctor Cento had asked me the very same question, and I found it grating. The Baron, too, should have known that back home such an insinuation would have been grounds for a duel.

But I checked myself. "I'm not an intus," I replied, moving my hierophant to capture one of the Baron's knights. I held the captured piece in my hand, feeling the weight of it. The fine details of the knight's medieval shield were worn down, and his face was a dull, featureless oval. It was old. Very old. I wondered just how old it was, and for how long it had moldered in this hall, a part of the furniture.

"Why are you here then?" the man asked.

Kindly or no, I was not about to tell the old Baron about my mission, about Tanaran and the battle at Calagah, about Raine Smythe and Bassander Lin. I smiled my thinnest smile, but said nothing. I slammed the knight down on one of the buttons, shifting the labyrinth's shape again, trapping three of the Baron's pieces.

The Baron swore, changed his plans, his question momentarily forgotten.

Eager to push the conversation away from myself, I asked, "You really think it's true, then? That they have a cure for dying here?"

Song's eyes lit up like those of a fanatic. "Oh, yes. Without a doubt."

This shocked me, and I fear that I recoiled slightly at the vehemence in Song's words. I had heard the stories, of course. Dim Vorgossos, where dark sacraments are performed to twist the blood. Lost Vorgossos, where of old Kharn Sagara revenged himself upon those who'd murdered his family. That bit of the story seemed true, if what I'd learned could be believed, and yet . . . and yet the rest of it still seemed to me a black fable.

"If immortality were possible, surely the Emperor would possess it," I said. "It was my understanding that we were pushing the limits of the possible anyway. Something about the brain."

Song rocked back in his chair, our Druaja game forgotten. He took a drink of his tea, smacked his lips. "Memory." He smiled. "The brain struggles with memory as it ages—among other things. In we palatines this is stretched to the very limit, but we cannot go much beyond seven or eight hundred years, even if the heart and other organs can be kept young." He smoothed his velvet jacket, darkening the green fabric.

I saw where he was driving, and frowned. "What's the solution? A new brain?"

"A new brain! A new body! That is what the Undying offers. A new you." He leaned forward again, leaping his hierophant over one of the walls to threaten my emperor. This done, he raised his eyebrows at me. "This is why the others are so confused to see you, young as you are, ah . . ." He looked me up and down. "How young are you, exactly?"

"Thirty-five," I said evenly. "I was born in '117." That was more than a hundred years ago, I realized with a start. I'd spent more than two-thirds of my time alive frozen in cryonic fugue. This moved me to silence, and I looked down at my plate, selected another of the dainties on offer and ate it, hoping the food would drive away this existential crisis.

Song was still speaking. "Thirty-five! Why, you are only a child!" He smiled. His teeth were very white. "No wonder you are such a poor hand at labyrinth chess!"

The serving girl chose that moment to return, offering me a selection of small fruit tarts. Recalling Song's advice that I should take what I wanted while I had the chance, I selected a pair of raspberry ones with chocolate and thanked the homunculus. She departed in a swirling of bronze silks.

"Thirty-five . . ." the Baron said again, shaking his silver head. "You know, when I was thirty-five, there were no Cielcin? No Crusade!" He made an expansive gesture, nearly upsetting his tea. "It was different in those days . . . ah, but where were we? Your move?"

Days later, I had very much improved at labyrinth chess.

CHAPTER 31

TARTARUS

THE LEGIONS HAVE A code regarding the treatment of prisoners. They are to be fed twice daily and to a schedule. They are to be provided a place to sleep—even if it is only a blanket and a patch of floor—and they are to be provided some semblance of day and night. There are other rules, but it was upon these I meditated in that concrete vault of a chamber. As I have said, the twin serving girls appeared at random intervals. I timed them. Sometimes they would appear within hours of one another, sometimes almost a standard day would pass without their arrival. And each time they did appear, the crowd of old men and women would stand and turn in expectation of something other than the food carts . . . of this golem Yume who served the lord.

Through all this, the yellow light in the chamber went on unchanged. And, but for the varnished paintings so dark as to be almost opaque and the dusty velvet hangings, there was nothing to look upon, no change in the environment. It was enough to drive one mad, to be so deprived of darkness. I could handle the irregular eating schedule. The darkness was harder, but I made do, using my coat as a kind of tent.

No one bothered me. Not even the Grand Duke of Milinda.

On the ninth day or the tenth of my soft captivity, the doors opened. The palatines all stood and flocked to the doors like cats at the arrival of their master. Even I stood—canceling the holograph I'd been reading off my terminal, a bit of Impatian's *History of the Jaddian Wars*. I meant to try again to implore the serving girls to have a message sent to Valka and the others, as, contrary to Baron's Song's assertions, I had not been allowed to send a message to my companions.

But the food carts did not appear, nor the twin girls in their translucent gowns. No one appeared for a good five seconds, prompting a wave of excited muttering from our herd of cats. The palatines all muttered, equal parts nervousness and expectation, and moved toward the door.

The figure that entered did so with a quiet whirring. There should have been hissing, clanking, the grinding of awful gears.

Far from the nightmares I had seen on the *Enigma of Hours*, the creature that entered the waiting room was elegant in its design and execution. Perfectly human in its mechanics, of androgynous design: narrow-hipped and narrow-chested. It wore no clothing, having no flesh or shame to cover. Much of its form was dull gray, with here and there a band of bright electrum reflecting the light around it. Crystal panels in hip and shoulder exposed glittering brass clockwork.

"Yume . . ." Baron Song whispered, shuffling up beside me.

The golem turned its head back and forth—pistons and chords in its neck stretching. The face was a convex arc the color of bone. It had only one eye: black and painted on the surface where the left eye ought to be, gold filigree playing about its edges. It would have looked hardly out of place at a masquerade ball on Renaissance.

Smoothly—moving with the grace and poise of a member of the Avalon ballet—the machine raised an arm. "Would the Lady Catherine Domitia Harfleur, the Baroness Varadeto, please step forward? The Master will see you now."

A pulse went through the crowd, murmurs intensifying. The elderly black-skinned woman stepped forward as the group stepped back until she stood in a sort of no-man's land between the crowd and the android. She looked very small, stooped as she was by age in her soiled finery, glittering though it was with jewels. Yet despite the silver cane on which she leaned, she hurried, and despite the native trepidation I felt at the sight of the golem and its one black eye, she seemed unafraid.

The android pivoted smoothly on one heel, offering the nobile lady its arm. Being less affected by a Sollan fear of machines than she was an eagerness to be getting on, she took it without complaint.

"Sir," I said, stepping forward. I didn't know what else to call the thing. "A moment." Servos whirred as the android Yume turned its head—a little too far, I thought—to look at me. It did not speak. Only then did I realize that the filigree rimming that mask's one eye described a stylized tear running golden down the robot's blank cheek. "I was . . ." I would not say *arrested*. "I was brought here with five companions. Three men, two women—one of them a dryad. I have been here for more than a week. I do not know what's become of them. I do not know how they fare. The others here say they are permitted to send messages to their entourages. Might I not send one of my own?"

A dim red light, like a cinder, burned in that black eye. In its polished court accent, the android replied, "You are not permitted." It swiveled its head away.

"Why not?"

The machine very gently released the Lady Catherine Domitia's arm and turned to face me. Its head pivoted first, one hundred eighty degrees. Its body followed. "I can assure you that your companions are quite well."

"May I see them?"

"You are not permitted," it said again, speaking with the precise tone and cadence it had employed mere moments before. I wondered if it was truly intelligent, or if it was only a puppet, force-fed a list of prescribed responses. It clasped its hands before itself like a cantor preparing to sing and added, "You will have your time with the Master."

"When?"

"When you are sent for," the machine said. "There are others here whose needs are far more pressing than yours. You will be attended to in time, Lord Marlowe. Do be patient . . . although . . . if you cannot wait, you are welcome to leave." And with that, it turned, offering its arm again to the Lady Catherine Domitia.

Baron Song whispered, "You shouldn't have done that. You'll wait longer now."

Another week passed. I read all four volumes of Impatian's *History of the Jaddian Wars* and half the collected works of the playwright Bastien. Incisive as the old comedian was, I found his old-style comedy too much like farce, and gave it up. There was no datasphere to access, and so I found myself limited to the contents of my terminal. No small library, to be sure, but much of it was review. Not being a trained sailor, there'd been little for me to do on the *Mistral*, or on the *Pharaoh* or *Balmung* before it. I'd read a lot. I reviewed Valka's notes and holographs on the Quiet ruins at Calagah on Emesh, on Ozymandias, on Sadal Suud.

I caught myself thinking about my vision again. And about the Jari and his words.

I wished I could speak to Valka, wished I could make her believe me.

For that matter, I wished I could make myself stop thinking about it at all. I had larger concerns: the Cielcin, the war, my treason, Ghen's death, the deaths of the three aquilarii I'd left on the *Balmung*. And that place: that whited city, its haunted guards, the Undying's pet machine, and the Undying himself.

Kharn Sagara.

It wasn't possible. It couldn't be. He was a myth, a fairy story as surely as were Apollo and the Moon, as Genghis Khan and the Cid Arthur. I knew his story, had told it to Cat a hundred times in Borosevo. If any of it were true, he would be old almost as the Empire. It could not *be*. And yet the Quiet, too, had been a fairy story—whispers of ancient aliens told by serfs and spacers alike, none too well believed. I had not believed, not until Valka showed me better.

Perhaps that was why I dwelt upon Jari and my vision. The rational foundations of my universe were blown out from under me, and I twisted in a fell wind. As when I'd first learned of the Quiet, this revelation about Vorgossos and its ruler had shaken me, left me without a box with which to frame my universe. And so my mind, frantic, had revisited those older, unincorporated parts of my experience, trying to build a new whole from the pieces.

Light! the seer had said when I'd asked after my future.

I have never forgotten my vision: the image of that black ship descending, plunging dagger-like into a whiteness that drowned the stars. Nor have I forgotten the host of the Cielcin, glittering where they stood arrayed like some great leviathan.

Light . . . How had Jari known? I knew little of his Deeps, but the oracle had said that he—or the *things* that had consumed him—were not the Quiet. *Leopards,* he had said, using my own words. Words I had not yet chosen. *Leopards, lions, and wolves.* The light had been in his vision and mine. A harmony. Did that make it true? *There is no future,* the seer had said. *Everything already is. They have only to choose.*

To choose what?

"It is well to see a young person like yourself reading."

"What?" I looked round, found an elderly woman—the Countess of Somewhere I did not doubt—smiling at me. She was dressed in crushed and ruined velvet, soiled by her long stay here, but her face was kind. She proffered a plastic plate at me. There was a single fruit tart on it. The serving girls had not been for ages. She'd been saving it. Crushing my terminal's floating holograph to close it, I sat up properly, declining the dish without comment.

"Reading," the grandmotherly woman repeated. "Most oft these days you only see young people reading printed books. Antiques, you know? Or counterfeit ones. They like to be *seen* reading more than they like to read. What are you reading?"

Self-conscious, I pulled my sleeve back down over the short terminal gauntlet. "Travelers' tales." It had been an account of the first excavations of the tombs on Ozymandias, written by an aide to the scholiast who had led the excavation. How Valka had come by the text I'd no idea. It was the sort of thing the Inquisition would kill one for having, full of references to other xenobite sites on other worlds.

The Countess of Somewhere set her plate aside, leaned forward. "Really? I used to love such things. What's it about?"

I was in Vorgossos. I saw no reason to lie about the Quiet. "The colonization of Ozymandias in the Thirteenth Millennium. In particular the excavations beneath the Great Arches at Panormo south of the capital at Merenhor."

"The Arch-Builders, do you mean?"

"The very same." I returned her smile. "The author has this notion that the Arch-Builders did no such thing, that they were only inhabiting the constructions of an older, far more advanced civilization." When she said nothing, I added, "The same has been said of the Judeccan Irchtani, and of the Cavaraad on Sadal Suud."

The Countess made a face. "Are you talking about the Anunna stories? I haven't heard those since I was a girl!" I must have made a face, for she pressed on. "I suppose you are a bit . . . *young* for them. There were a bunch of operas about them. Ancient xenobites out among the stars, greater than us."

"The Chantry didn't repress that?"

"They weren't so stodgy in those days, you know? Weren't so concerned with propriety or the dreck artists cook up, you know? They were different times." Her eyes—blue eyes—seemed far away after that peculiar fashion unique to the very aged. "But I suppose the war's changed things. Stories about fearsome xenobites must have fallen from fashion once we had the real thing."

With nothing to say to that, I studied my hands, nodded primly.

"You're not like the rest of us," the Countess noted. She was only the dozenth since Song to make that determination, and I felt my smile calcify.

Brittle as my smile, I said, "I suppose I'm not."

"You can't be here for the same reasons as we."

"And why not?"

She shifted forward in her seat. "You're too young to be thinking of dying. Especially for one of the Peerage. Baron Song said you were one of the Star Victoria? The Emperor's own? You must have . . . centuries. Centuries before you would think of coming to a place like this."

"That's why you're all here, then?" I asked. "Life extension?"

"Life extension!" She showed her teeth. A couple of them were missing. "We have nothing left to extend. The Undying offers us a second life."

Baron Song had said much the same thing. A new brain. A new body. "But how?"

"He grows them. Raises them. Until they're ready."

"Raises them?" I looked her squarely in the face. "You're talking about children."

The Countess of Somewhere's face might have been a graven mask. Whatever else she was, she was Sollan nobile, and had learned long and long ago to control herself. "I am talking of another me."

"Cloning?" I said, disgusted. Cloning was one of the Chantry's Twelve Abominations, the most mortal of sins. It was added to the list later on, if memory serves, after clones had been used too often to cheat in matters of succession.

The Countess didn't answer. She didn't have to.

"The young man bothering you, Countess?" said Baron Song jovially, appearing at my elbow. She *was* a Countess, after all. Ordinarily, this synchronicity might have amused me, but there was a sucking hole where my stomach ought to be. Gone was the kindly old Mandari with his frilled necktie and pointed beard. Gone too the elderly woman with her grandmotherly smile. The faintly funereal texture of the room with its trace geriatric musk and the smell of old upholstery and oil varnish took on an aspect of brimstone and salt smoke. Static and charge.

There is a chamber in the Peronine Palace on Forum where are kept a great many paintings and artifacts recovered from Old Earth. Among them, kept in a windowless room lighted by glass candles, were nine of a series of fourteen murals. The *Pinturas Negras,* painted at the end of Earth's Golden Age by an artist called Goya. The other paintings—and the rest of Goya's work—are lost. Victims of the Advent that claimed our homeworld, or else lost in the Peregrinations that followed.

The Emperor himself showed me the paintings, and but for three of his Knights Excubitor and a detachment of his own Martian Guard at the door—we were alone. He was shielded . . . the Emperor is always shielded, and the Royse field flickered in the light of the glass candles.

"Saturn Devouring His Son," the Emperor said, gesturing with one beringed hand.

It was an ugly painting, but unforgettable. It showed a naked man with tangled hair and beard, a giant clutching the mutilated corpse of a headless man, his teeth tearing an arm off at the joint. There was self-aware horror in the eyes of the mad Titan. He knew what he was doing was wrong, and yet would not stop himself, so hungry was he for life.

So old was that ancient canvas—rotted through in places—that the bright crimson of the blood covering Saturn's hapless son had gone to clotted brown. Seeing it, I remembered the eyes of those people in that grim hall. Lord Song and the Countess of Somewhere. The Grand Duke of Milinda and that Norman spice merchant. They knew. They knew what they were.

The very foolish might look upon such creatures and, sneering, say their wealth had corrupted them. It is easy for those without wealth to pretend at morality, as if they would not themselves make depraved choices given the means. There is no morality in poverty. It is only that wealth gives the immoral greater opportunity for abuse. Given the means, how many souls would make pilgrimage to Vorgossos? How many trillions?

"He's not bothering me at all, Kim!" the Countess said. "Quite the opposite! I've interrupted his reading."

"Not at all!" I said, scrambling to maintain a mask of politeness to quash the screaming in my head. "We were just discussing the, um . . . the procedure."

Baron Song seated himself in the chair opposite my couch, so that he surveyed me across the empty Druaja board. "I do hope I'll be taken below soon," he said idly. "I've been here ever so long." He opened a drawer on the side of the table and began pulling out the worn marble pieces. "Fancy another game, Lord Marlowe?"

CHAPTER 32

SATURN OR DIS

ALL THAT WHITE STONE recalled for me the great caverns of our necropolis. As I followed the golem Yume through that labyrinth of drab corridors, almost I thought I could hear the faint drip of water falling from stalactites into the black pools about the sarcophagi of my ancestors.

There had been outrage when I was taken. Song and his fellow Titans had snarled that I was only a child, that they should be taken instead. Yume had ignored them, and so cowed were they by their unholy desire and their lust for what the Undying alone could give that none raised a hand against the automaton.

I never saw them again, nor learned if they received their inhuman sacrament.

I did not want to learn.

I had found my Virgil, and quiet followed it down windowless halls of blank stone, past sealed metal doors and square columns supporting ceilings lost to clinging shadow. The machine responded to none of my queries, and I soon stopped asking questions. We saw no servants, no guards, no cameras on our descent, not along colonnades or winding stairs, not in empty galleries or the vacuous dining hall through which we passed, its brushed metal tables bare and bolted to the floor. We descended by many hundred steps, round many dozen corners, through uncounted levels. I could not have found my way out if I'd wanted to.

A great metal door barred our path. Three times the height of a man it was, and three times across, being round, and sunken slightly so that the hall floor might pass unbroken through it. Some nameless artist in the deeps of time had taken a plasma torch to its thick surface, and fashioned there in flowing metal the bas-relief image of a boy enthroned atop the shattered ruins of monsters. Machines, I took them to be, the Exalted, and so guessed the seated boy was Kharn Sagara. He clutched something in his hands. A bottle, perhaps?

"It's true . . ." I breathed, stopping. "He really is Kharn Sagara."

Yume's head swiveled full round, though it kept walking forward. "You did not believe?"

"No."

"None ever do."

The door rose up and admitted us onto a raised platform where an open monorail cart waited hanging by a rail above our heads. The tram was accessed only by a single stony strand reaching out into absolute blackness like a warning finger. Glowspheres hovering above its length did little and less to illuminate that blackness, and beyond their light I sensed an abyss infinite almost as the black of space.

But here there were no stars.

The tram rattled as it advanced, and the gentle wind of its passage carried the briny stink of salt and alien planktons. "What's that smell?" I asked.

"We are beneath the original installation," Yume said, mounting the stairs to the tram car. "The builders placed their city above the underground sea, whose surface is more than five miles below."

Ahead through the gloom I discerned a shape, hanging from the cavern above like the stalactites in my memory. Only as we approached did I see it more clearly, not a stalactite at all. A pyramid. A great, square pyramid done all in white stone. Two sentry towers decorated with golden cartouches hung to either side of the track. Their glowing faces showed sculptures in the same style as those on the massive door. What they depicted, I could not say.

The tram ground to a halt, and Yume led the way down from the tram onto a white marble platform. Light shone from hidden sconces high above, illuminating a vault decorated with an image of the heavens. We descended a steep stair, Yume careful to check its pace that I did not stumble or fall. I sensed we must be approaching the base of that terrible structure, though how I knew that I could not say. The air grew colder. Dry. At the base of the stair was a short hallway, perhaps ten yards long. I could almost taste the silence.

Yume seized the great bronze ring in the doors and knocked. Once. Twice. Three times. They creaked as they swung inward, though there was none to open them. I pressed on, aware only after I had done so that I was alone. That Yume had left me.

And the doors were closed.

No stir of air was there, and but for the sound of water the place was quiet as a temple. As a tomb. Not speaking, not knowing what to say, I stepped forward. The place was all in shadow, and dimly I was aware of great pillars of pale stone rising like ghosts about me and of the statues that filled the space between.

One such pillar rose ahead of me, greater than the rest. At its base—upon a dais of many steps in the very middle of the chamber—stood a massive chair. A great tangle of cables flowed toward it, gathered from every dark corner and falling from the ceiling above like garlands. A great horror was on me, and a sense of awe and of terror unlike any I had known. The fear of the shepherd before Pharaoh, of the merchant before Caesar. Of man before god. Still not speaking, I approached to within five paces of the lowest step, turning my face upward to look upon the man seated there.

The Undying's face was ageless, neither old nor young, though his dark and wild hair was touched with gray at temple and forelock. A heavy cloth-of-gold robe lay upon his shoulders, tiny dragons picked out in black against that shimmering garment. It stood open, and beneath he was bare-chested, and I could see the hoses and sensor tape wired to sockets in his flesh. What trousers he wore seemed to me part of a spacesuit's under-layment, black and padded. His feet were bare, calloused almost as much as my own.

He did not speak, and for a time I honored his silence, standing placid at the foot of that mighty seat. His eyes—black as coals—were far away, nor did they seem to see me.

> *Deep in the shady sadness of a vale*
> *Far sunken from the healthy breath of morn,*
> *Far from the fiery noon, and eve's one star,*
> *Sat gray-hair'd Saturn, quiet as a stone.*

Thus he seems to me in memory: King of the Titans in all his ruinous glory, couched in numb contemplation of the Dark. How long he'd been

seated in that awful chair I could not imagine, nor imagine the well and
depth of years in his experience.

"Lord," I said when minutes had passed, "I am Hadrian Marlowe,
grandson of the Vicereine of Delos and a cousin of His Radiance, the Emperor William XXIII. I am come on a mission of special significance, to
the Imperium and to all Mankind."

Nothing.

Not even the eyes moved. My words died in darkness, and the silence
which followed was total and absolute.

"Lord," I said again, "I come at the behest of an Ichakta of the Cielcin
Itani Otiolo, and on behalf of a baetan of the same."

Nothing.

He did not seem to breathe, and I would have thought him dead but
for his reputation. All that chamber was still, the fixed center of an unfixed universe, dead as the dead sun about which that frigid world turned.

"Lord," I said a third time, "you brought me here in your own time, of
your own will. I've been waiting the better part of a month."

Again, nothing.

Frustrated, I turned, looking round, half-expecting Yume to appear
behind me and take me away. From my vantage near the throne I saw the
statues were not alone in decorating that dim chamber. There were paintings. Some ancient and others less so, paintings of the sort my father or
any great lord of the Imperium might slaughter to keep. Some, I think,
were artifacts from Old Earth, so faded were they and time-stained. I approached the nearest statue where it stood on a plinth at the base of another column, aware of how the ceiling seemed not to exist above me. It
was of a woman in a great cloak, and beneath that cloak she opened on
hinges to shelter and reveal a bearded man who himself comforted a broken figure. The statue's hinged doors opened to form a kind of triptych,
and on the left the same woman cradled an infant, and on the right the
broken man stood renewed, as if whatever torment was in the central
frame was undone and forgotten.

"Beautiful, is it not?" asked a voice deep as the darkness.

I had been just about to touch the sculpture, and so turned sharply out
of guilt.

Kharn Sagara—if that was who he truly was— had not stirred. A tiny
drone, leaf-shaped and smaller than my fist, sped back and away from me,
its one blue eye gleaming. "It is," I said, unsure whether I should address
the little drone or the man in his chair. Between Brevon and Jari I felt I

had grown accustomed to speaking to strange creatures in strange rooms. And yet this was different. Brevon, for all his mechanical abstraction, had been a man, and Jari had been a monster inside and out, hardly human at all. This was different. I felt . . . I felt as I imagined some ancient Achaean might have felt, standing in the shadows of the temple at Olympia before the gilded statue of Zeus. Waiting for the god to speak.

"She is a tree of life to them that lay hold on her: and he that shall retain her is blessed."

"What?"

"That is why they come here. Your . . . ilk." The voice was all around me, emanating in chorus not from the mouth of the man in the chair, but from a swarm of little, blue-eyed drones descending in formation like comets from the dark above. "They wish to live again. Anew." His words were halting, fractured, as if each was painstakingly selected and not without cost or pain. "Not you."

"You clone them," I said, accusing—knowing I should not accuse. "You clone them and . . ." And what? "You destroy the clones so the original might live."

Nothing.

I walked around so that I stood in front of Kharn, looking up into his hooded eyes. He might have been Mandari, or perhaps Nipponese, though he was pale almost as I. He had the eyes. He did not speak again for minutes, and when at last I could bear it no longer, I said, "I wish to make contact with the Cielcin Prince Aranata Otiolo. I am told you've had dealings with its kind."

Kharn's eyes—his human eyes, which were black and not blue at all—swiveled to regard me. The light in them was very far away. Remote as the faintest stars. His voice coming like the grinding of stones beneath the earth, he said, "Knowledge, then. Not life." Then in a voice barely more than a whisper, a voice which came only from his human lips, he added, "But of the tree of knowledge of good and evil, thou shalt not eat. Did no one tell you?"

He was quoting, I realized. Quoting from an antique religious text, one with which I was not at the time very familiar. But Gibson had been a thorough teacher, and I'd a fair grounding in the literary canon of Earth's Golden Age, and so replied, "The day thou eatest thereof, my sole command Transgressed, inevitably thou shalt die . . ."

"Milton." One of the drones orbited smooth and silent about my head, a mere hand's span from my face. "I see you are a man of culture." I angled my chin, determined not to shrink or scrape in the face of this dark lord. Kharn sat up straight, hands gripping the arms of his chair. "But what else are you? An emissary? An apostol of the Empire? Speak your words, ambassador."

"The war has gone on long enough," I said shortly, holding my hands out in formal entreaty. "Nearly four hundred years of conflict now. Dozens of worlds lost, billions of lives. It has to end." I paused, expecting the other man to interrupt, but he never did. The black drones moved in slow spirals, all watching. *The King with Ten Thousand Eyes*. I wondered what perverse God there was to have chosen that book of all the books Gibson owned to give to me. "A Cielcin captain surrendered to me at Emesh. I have hostages, among them a priest-historian of their kind. I am trying to arrange contact with their leadership. To make peace."

That xanthous king surveyed me with eyes like coals. He reached inside his robe and adjusted the drape of one of his many hoses. I'd had my next series of remarks prepared, but they fled me. What I had taken for flesh beneath Kharn's yellow robe was paneled, segmented like a carapace, so that his ribs were separated from the flesh beneath. The hose he'd rearranged ran up under his ribs, toward whatever organ there passed for a heart.

Still he did not speak.

"The Cielcin captain itself informed me that you have had dealings with its kind in the past, that you might be able to arrange a meeting with them."

"An interesting design, this," Kharn said, lifting an item that had lain unseen in his lap. "Jaddian, I believe." It was my sword. Olorin's sword. I'd lost it when I was taken, brought to the waiting room with Song and his fellow Titans. Her silver fittings and emitter shone brightly in the dim air.

I stood a little straighter, braver now I was growing used to that strange room and the man before me. "It is. It was a gift from a Maeskolos of Jadd."

"Ah," Kharn said haltingly, "only a Maeskolos?" He triggered the blade, turned the weapon in the air before him. It shone its familiar lunar blue, star-bright in the gloom. The highmatter surface rippled, flowing like quicksilver. "I have always admired their order. The Maeskoloi understand the art of violence because they understand that violence *is* art. It is a lovely weapon. I don't suppose you would part with it?"

The question caught me by surprise, and almost I stumbled. "I'm sorry?"

"I've a collection of Jaddian weaponry; yours would make a fine addition," Kharn said. "I would pay you, of course."

"It's not for sale," I said, a touch too sharply, I think, for the Undying raised an eyebrow. Backpedaling, I said, "The Maeskoloi do not sell their arms."

"*Si fueris Romae . . .*"

"Do as the Romans do."

"He speaks Latin as well!"

"*Modo paulo,*" I said. *Only a little.*

The Undying's flock of eyes all orbited me by then, disregarding the chamber and the art around. When Kharn spoke again, it was from everywhere, as if all the air of that immeasurable hall trembled by his word. "You have come by a long road to find this place. Why?"

"I've already told you," I said. "To make peace."

We stood thus a long while, like two pieces on Song's Druaja board, though how close we were to the center of the labyrinth I could not say, nor could I guess what sort of piece I was. *Kings and pawns,* I thought. *Kings and fools.*

After what seemed a very long time, Kharn said, "But why?"

The reasons were so self-evident that I could not articulate them. I tried to remember, to recall what it was I had said to Sir Olorin and Bassander that night by the wreck of Uvanari's ship. I could not quite recall, and so said, "To end the war. To save lives. To make a better world . . . and because there is room enough in the galaxy for both the Pale and us."

"Is there?" Kharn smiled, his human eyes still fixed on the blue glow of my sword. "A tiger might prowl over miles and within her bounds, and no lamb is safe, though their flock asks only for one pasture."

"How many worlds should burn?" I demanded. "How many billion lives? We could end this war."

"War," Kharn repeated, and leveled my blade at me like some medieval judge. "There is always war. As well struggle against it as against gravity. You will fail."

"Wars end," I said coldly.

"Wars end," Kharn agreed, more coldly still. "*War* does not. And I am not much troubled what form our wars take. For over fifteen thousand years now your Empire has warred across the galaxy. I have watched your sun rise over half a billion worlds. And before that, before me, it was the same, only it was smaller." He lowered the weapon, and lowered his eyes. I would have thought them closed, but Kharn Sagara never seemed to blink, only to stare sightless and all-seeing and at all times. "What is it to me who sits on your Solar Throne, or how long is its sway?" With a click,

the King of Vorgossos deactivated my sword and turned the hilt over in
his long-fingered hands. The nails were long, neglected, claw-like.

I took a step forward, forcing his eyes to widen their orbit. "What is it
to you if the Cielcin come here? What if they decide they've *dealt* with
you enough? What if they decide to *deal* with you instead?" The ageless
face only smiled. And with painstaking care he lay my weapon on the arm
of his chair. He did not blink, nor turn his eyes away. "The war is spreading, lord. How long until you are yourself affected?" Somewhere between
the start of this sentence and its ending, Kharn's black eyes glassed over, as
if the man had vanished from whatever room the soul occupied behind
those eyes. "The war affects us all."

Distantly, a fountain burbled.

The Undying did not move, and again he did not seem even to breathe.
The man had the patience of a statue. And why should he not? Every
statue in our necropolis underneath Devil's Rest was younger than the
man before me. Small wonder Song and the others were left to wait so
long in that chamber far above.

To Kharn, it wasn't long at all.

"Once," Kharn said at last, speaking only with his own lips. His chest
rose and fell. "Once it was so. Once mankind had but the one neck and
war the hands to squeeze. No more. The Cielcin may pillage as they
please and not destroy mankind. This storm shall pass like all the others."

Recalling his earlier quotation, I marshaled myself and—speaking, it
seemed, to Dis himself—said, "The hottest places in hell are reserved for
those who maintain neutrality in a crisis."

"And if you had truly read Dante, Marlowe," Kharn said, voice issuing
once more from the drones around me. "You would know the deepest pit
of hell is cold." He lifted his chin, staring up into the darkness at things I
could not see. I wondered then what else he saw, and through what eyes. I
thought of his SOMs, of the light shining through their dead and sagging
faces. I felt certain then that there was no place on that dreadful world
where Kharn Sagara could not look. From the highest dome through caves
of ice and down to that sunless sea, every square inch and stray atom passed
beneath Kharn's lidless gaze. How his mind endured the strain I cannot
say, but I had not then seen the ceramic shine of implants beneath his ear
and that wild fall of hair.

"So you will not help?"

"Five hundred standard years I've traded with the Cielcin. With Otiolo,

Hasurumn, and Dorayaica," Kharn said. "I see no reason to jeopardize these arrangements in the name of your Emperor."

I blinked. "Five hundred years is . . . before first contact." I meant the Battle of Cressgard in ISD 15792, when the Cielcin attacked our colonial fort settlement on the edge of the Marinus Veil. The loss of that colony had sent its horrible message careering across the Imperium, the temple fires burning on every world and the priests beside them crying out those fateful words: *We are not alone.* I had come too far to give up so lightly, and stepped forward, placing one boot on the lowest step of Kharn's white dais. "Do so many deaths mean so little to you?"

"Yes," Kharn said, speaking for the first time without hesitation. "When you've seen as many lives as I have, you learn how little they are worth."

"Then why do you cling to yours so tightly?" I demanded. "Or is it only other lives that are meaningless?"

Kharn's lips twisted into some septic impersonation of a smile. "When you have seen enough of other people, you will learn that it is they who believe their lives are meaningless. Why should I value them, who do not value themselves?" I had no answer to that, only a vague sense of righteous indignation. "Flesh is the cheapest resource in the human universe, Lord Marlowe. It spends more easily than gold."

"I don't believe that."

"Because you are a child," said the Undying. "Thirty-five, was it? Thirty-five . . ." He meant my age. He had heard my conversation with Song, of course. "I have lived more than four hundred of your lifetimes, boy. Your *belief* means almost nothing." He lifted my sword from the arm of his chair and—leaning forward—presented it to me pommel first. "Take your Jaddian weapon."

I had to climb the dais to accept it, and so came close enough to really *see* the man. The myth. He stank of unwashed flesh and hair, of machine lubricant and something . . . sweet. Myrrh? Blue lights pulsed beneath his left ear in time with some unheard signal. It was the chest, I decided, and his ribs that were prosthetic. The flesh there was not flesh at all. Veins stood blackly out on his neck, and again he did not seem to breathe. Some mechanism, buried perhaps beneath the flange of his ribs, breathed for him.

"Thank you," I said, taking the sword. I was eager to be away. Sagara frightened me, I am not ashamed to admit. Halfway down the nine steps—sword yet in hand—I turned. "This is not like other wars, lord. Unless we can communicate, our two sides will tear one another apart."

Kharn did not look at me, but folded his hands in his lap as he contem-

plated the dark above. "You may have the hospitality of the palace, naturally. It wouldn't do to turn so august an ambassador away at the door
when he has only just arrived. Yume will find rooms for you. Yume!"

"Here, Master." The golem appeared from the shadows—the red light
in its black eye leading. I would have sworn the door had not opened. It
padded forward, silent on metal feet. Without being given instruction, the
android placed a hand on my shoulder and prepared to lead me away.

I turned to go, sick with the weight of my failure. But I did not protest, I did not grovel. *So august an ambassador . . .* He was mocking me, and
I had no choice but to be mocked. I'd not come in a strong position, had
nothing to trade. I had counted on the humanity of the least human man
I have ever met, a man whose consciousness perhaps resembled my own
even less than those of the Cielcin.

"A moment." Kharn's voice was like flint. The golem stopped beside
me, and shrugging free of its iron hand I turned. "Approach."

I did, aware that—surely—I was a pawn in some dominance display
but not caring. If this man, this creature, wished to humiliate me, I could
not stop him. Nor would. I had need of him and his connections, and
though I'd already thought them closed to me, I was not about to make
matters worse by arguing. So I stopped at the base of the dais, mindful of
the automaton at my back. It was my turn not to speak, and so I waited.

"Your Cielcin prisoner. You said it was one of the baetan?"

"Yes."

"Bring it to me. We will hear its case." Kharn's flock of eyes dispersed,
each vanished up and into the darkness, and lonely Saturn's head drooped.
He must have sent some silent communication to the android behind me,
for now I heard its quiet advance. In the scant seconds before it took me
by the shoulder, I found myself moved again by that same awe and fear I'd
felt on entering. Not even the halls of our Sollan Emperor would later fill
me with such disquiet. I felt again that sense of time, and the sense that
here was the oldest man in existence—perhaps the oldest ever to exist.
The silence that fell and folded about his throne comprised millennia.
There thickly lay the frozen years, so that the very air seemed a kind of
amber, and I the prisoned fly.

CHAPTER 33

DIVIDE AND CONQUER

"HADRIAN!" VALKA HURRIED FORWARD the moment after Yume opened the doors. "What the hell's been going on?"

Switch leaped to his feet, Crim and Ilex looking up from where they'd been watching some holograph opera off the latter's terminal. Only Pallino was unmoved, leaning against a pillar against the far wall of the suite. I was glad to see they'd been left together. For the many days of my imprisonment I'd imagined each of them locked in separate cells—or worse. But all things considered the rooms were comfortable. Void of decoration, yes, but richly appointed after a fashion identical to the waiting room where I had met so many monstrous lords and fine people. The remains of a meal stood on a large service cart, the used plates still fragrant with the smell of rosemary and thyme.

"I only just spoke to him," I said, putting a hand on her shoulder. "I'd been trapped in a sort of holding pen the past . . . how long has it been?"

"Twenty-three days, standard," Pallino barked. "Thought they'd turned you into one of those . . . hollows."

Squaring his shoulders, Switch said, "We were thinking of a way to come rescue you . . . only we couldn't get out ourselves."

Ever attentive, Valka said, "With whom did you speak?" Her brows contracted. "You said you spoke with someone?"

"The Undying," Crim said.

"Was it Kharn Sagara?" Pallino asked. "Was it *really* Kharn Sagara?"

I pressed my lips together.

Ilex shook her head. "Impossible."

His voice still shook in me, emanating as from the very air. I could still smell the antiseptic stink of him and the fragrance of myrrh; see the gruesome patchwork of his flesh and the black eyes so very far away. "You would not say that," I told the dryad, "if you had seen him."

That stopped her doubting, and something in my face stopped all questioning on the subject of whether or not it was the real Kharn Sagara whom I had met. I supposed it was possible that the creature in the pyramid was some usurper, some pretender to Sagara's name, but I did not believe it was so.

"Can he help us?" Valka asked, looking from me to the machine still waiting in the door. "Can he set up a meeting with Tanaran's chieftain?"

I did not say *no,* though Sagara had as good as done so. The truth was, I'd come away from my audience not knowing where I stood. Kharn had rebuked me, mocked me, and left me no way forward, and yet . . . "He wishes to speak to Tanaran. We have to go retrieve it from the *Mistral.*"

"Can't we wave the ship from here?"

Yume spoke up. "No electronic or quantum communiques are allowed in-system save at the Master's behest."

Unafraid of the machine, Valka rounded on it. "Then tell your Master we wish to send a message to our ship."

"I am sorry, madam, but I am afraid that will not be possible."

"And why not?"

"The security of this installation and the privacy of its people is paramount."

"The security of . . ." Valka trailed off. Under her breath, she added, "You can't be serious."

The android said nothing, implying by its silence that it was deathly serious.

Switch shifted uncomfortably where he stood, torn—I think—between fear of the android and a desire to put himself between the machine and me. In a small voice, he said, "I'll go. I can explain everything to Captain Corvo and return here with the Pale. I . . ." He broke off, realizing the gap in his planning. "Had, I'd need you or the doctor to go with me. I don't speak monster and I don't trust its Galstani."

Valka and I exchanged a look. I did not wish to volunteer her for a trip back up the orbital lift to the docking platform and the *Mistral,* but neither did I wish to leave her or any of the others behind in that awful place. Having so recently dealt with Kharn, I was content to wait Valka out, sensing her impatience.

I was not disappointed, for not a moment later she said, "I'll go."

"You should all go," I said, crossing my arms. "I'll remain behind and see if I can't make progress here." To my astonishment, Switch did not argue that he should remain behind. He would not meet my eye. I thought him only tired, strung out on the weight of his imprisonment and eager to be gone.

Still unmoved from his place by the wall, Pallino said, "You sure you'll be all right?" He glowered at the machine, one cyclops to another. Yume did not seem to notice, or care. It was hard to remember, when it was not moving or speaking, that the android was animate at all. One might have imagined it only another of those misshapen bronze statues. But I knew whose eye it was in Yume's face—one eye in ten thousand—and knew that Yume was no statue at all.

"I'll be fine," I said, dismissive, and clapped the other man on the back. Turning back to Yume, I asked, "How long will it take to return to orbit and back?"

"The orbital lift takes just over fifteen hours to ascend," Yume replied.

"So two days," I said, stifling my surprise. The descent had not felt so long on our way into Vorgossos, but then . . . fear does strange things to time. "Permit me a word with my people and the time they need to gather themselves?"

The golem bowed its head and withdrew. The heavy metal door grated closed behind it, and we found ourselves alone. I was a moment banishing the morbid thought that the grinding of that heavy door was the moving of a temple slab to seal us in our tomb. The impression faded, retreating like Kharn's flying eyes into the dark of the pyramid chamber.

"I do *not* like this place," Switch said darkly, looking at me for the first time.

"If you had seen what I've seen," I said, more darkly still and meeting his eye, "you'd like it even less." I did not tell him about Lord Song and the others, about the Titans waiting in preparation for their youthful feast, or about the dark ocean beneath the city, or the surgeries I imagined taking place. I did not describe Kharn Sagara. His flashing eyes! His floating hair!

My lictor and dearest friend half-turned away. "That golem . . . and the fucking guards. It's sick. It's all sick."

"We know," Ilex snapped, hugging herself. "That isn't helping."

"The Chantry should lance this place. Burn it to the ground." I could see him working himself up to some kind of frenzy, his words all tumbling one over the next. "That was a daimon!" He pointed at the door. "A daimon!"

"That's enough!" I said, conscious of the fact that we might be observed, and that such talk would not endear us to our host.

"But Hadrian!"

"Enough, I say!" I threw up one hand, and hoping to cut off the conversation before it could worsen, I turned to Valka. "Are we being watched?"

The doctor bit her lip, "I'm not sure."

"What do you mean, you're not sure?" I asked.

Valka flicked her red-black hair back and pivoted, turning on one heel. "I mean I'm not sure, Marlowe. There must be a datasphere here—they took over the *Mistral* somehow. But I can't feel a thing."

That took me aback. Understand: I knew and know next to nothing of networked machines. I am as I was born: a son and soldier of Sol, of the Empire. But I knew enough to know that that couldn't be right. Sagara must have communicated remotely with his android. For that matter, Sagara must use some kind of network to control his SOMs, to see through all the City's camera eyes. "Not even on the golem?" I asked, jerking my head toward the door. "Not even on the door lock?"

"Door lock's mechanical," Crim said. "That was the first thing we tried."

Valka worried at the back of her neck, massaging the implant at the base of her skull. "'Tis all very strange. I can sense the android in the hall, but 'tis behind layers of encryption I don't think I could decipher if I had a hundred years to try." After a long moment, she tossed her head, took her hand away from the base of her skull. "No."

Letting the subject drop, Crim asked, "Not that it's my place to be asking, but what do you hope to gain by staying behind?"

I turned to regard the Norman-Jaddian man in his padded red kaftan. Alone of the company Crim remained seated, one long leg crossed over the other. He might have been by a poolside in some Jaddian satrap's palace. Absently I massaged the hoop of cryoburn scar about my left thumb, addressing some phantom pain. Half-shrugging I said, "It took three weeks to get a word in. I'm afraid if we all leave it will look like we're beaten." Conscious of my posture, I squared my shoulders and stood straight, imagining as I often did that I stood upon an amphitheater's orchestra, speaking to a crowd. A thought struck me, and I said, "Sagara didn't believe we want peace." I had not realized it was true until the words were spoken. "He thinks we mean to jeopardize his relations with the Cielcin. He thinks he's called my bluff, and if we all leave that will as good as confirm his suspicions. If I alone, if I put myself at his mercy, it demonstrates good faith."

As if on cue, the door scraped open again and Yume appeared, entering like the messenger he was onto my stage. Without pretense or preamble or a clearing of throat it said, "I will escort you all to the tramway."

"I'm staying," I said, bowing ever so slightly. "I will take your Master up on his offer of hospitality. My people here will repair to my ship and return with our Cielcin emissary." The golem gave no sign but to tilt its head to one side. "If that is still allowed, of course."

"Of course." Yume pivoted, sweeping one arm to indicate that the others should lead. "This way, please."

The tramway by which the upper labyrinth of the Undying's palace was accessed, like the tramway far below, hung from a single rail embedded in the roof of what once had been a lava tube. The tunnel ran straight for what looked like several miles—broken and jagged in places from millennia of tidal stress—to a faint, white haze in the middle distance. The City dome, I guessed. White lights stood at irregular intervals along the tunnel, and the metallic shine of artillery stood guarding the approach.

Behind us, the great door of the palace stood open. Two meters thick it was, and solid steel. The bunkers which honeycomb the earth beneath many a palatine castle had such doors, proof as they were against orbital and atomic bombardment. I imagined our Legions breaking themselves on this approach under the command of Chantry Cantors, imagined Inquisitors calling down fire with their superweapons. The fortress—like Kharn himself—could out-sit eternity.

We had not brought anything by way of luggage, and my friends' departure was a thing totally devoid of circumstance. The air in the tunnel was still as a sea becalmed, damp and chilly. A single brazier stood at the end of the concrete pier. Like the graven metal door below it was: an after-market addition, a thing not of the original construction. Its base was an inverse pyramid of white stone, graven with the image of a weeping eye like the one Yume wore on its face. Blue flame burned without flickering from it, fed by some gas from below. I could not shake the sense that I stood now on the opposite bank of the Styx, looking up and out from Hades toward the living world.

"He's ignoring us!" Crim said, and jostled me in good humor.

Coming back to myself, I said, "I'm sorry, what? I was just thinking . . ."

"The hell sort of name is *Anaxander*?" Switch said, repeating his joshing question a second time.

I grunted, not especially ashamed of the old name. "What sort of name is Switch, eh?" I riposted, knowing full well.

"Anaxander . . ." Pallino repeated, squaring his own shoulders in what I must admit was a credible impersonation of me. "Hadrian Anaxander. How is it in all the years I've known you you ain't dropped that gem on us?"

"I should think the reason for that's obvious," I said acidly. But even Valka was smiling, and I did not bristle to defend my name, or to explain that Anaxander had been a king on Old Earth, long forgotten, and the eleventh Lord Marlowe of Devil's Rest. It did not matter.

Crim, Ilex, and old Pallino filed onto the tram car—the last pausing to clap me on the shoulder. Valka went behind them, but stopped on the platform to adjust one of her high boots.

Switch turned back, caught my arm. "I don't like this. You staying here."

"I've stayed here three weeks already!" I replied, tapping his arm to release me. He didn't. His grip tightened and his eyes fixed on the android behind.

"This is wrong. Shouldn't be dealing with daimons like this. Cielcin's one thing, but this?" He broke off, made the sign of the sun disc discreet at his side, thumb and forefinger encircled. "We shouldn't be here."

Valka was still fiddling with her boot on the loading platform, and with the golem standing just behind me I was finding it difficult to think. "We won't be here long."

"How do I know it's even you anymore, eh?" He jabbed me in the chest with a finger. "How do I know you ain't some . . . *replicate*? Some changeling?" Decades of being around me had sanded a portion of Switch's plebeian dialect from his speech. That he was using it again was not a good sign. His eyes were wide as ever I had seen them, and his freckled face stood white as Tanaran's.

"Switch." I reached out and embraced my oldest and dearest friend. "It's me." I didn't argue or try to reason with him. He was beyond reason, and perhaps justly so. We'd come to a house of horrors, to the deepest corner of the Dark.

Switch returned my embrace. "I know, man. I just . . ." He broke off and drew away. "We shouldn't be here."

I looked around the cavern—listening for the sound of birds that would not come, for the crash of waves, for any sound beyond the quiet guttering of that single blue flame. No sound came, no shout of human voice, nor groan of the damned. No cock crowed. At long last I said, "No one should be here." Switch looked on the verge of a response, but I waved him on. "The sooner you go the sooner we can all go. Go on!"

He said nothing. That was the worst part. Only bobbed his head and turned, matte-black armor dull against the deep red of his uniform. With a leap he bounded the steps to the tram platform—passing Valka as he went. His disquiet lingered like a phantom haunting the platform. Disquieted myself, I turned to go, not willing then to watch them depart.

"Hadrian."

Valka caught my elbow and turned me around. She had doubled back from the tram car—lacing her boots indeed! An echo of Switch's discomfort showed in her austere face, betrayed by furrowed brows and the way she pressed her lips together. She did not speak at once, and I sensed she was choosing her words with exquisite care.

"I'll be back with Tanaran before you know we've gone," she said at last, lamely. I closed my mouth and gave a sharp little nod, sensing that it was unwise to interrupt her. She looked away, and for a moment the light of those golden eyes was quenched. Then something happened I could not have expected in a hundred years.

She embraced me.

I confess I froze. It was so unexpected—from her, there, in that hideous place—that my thoughts all fell to pieces. I stood numbly a moment, long enough to hear her say, "I'm glad you're all right. I—we were all worried about you." Some part of me was acutely aware of the golem at my back, of Yume watching and of Kharn Sagara watching through its eye.

She'd withdrawn before I could return the embrace, retreated up the steps to the tram.

At once it seemed very cold on that platform.

I watched the monorail glide away on casters, its running lights seeming so much like the ghostly lanterns of a gondola poled on black seas. It shrank into the middle distance, leaving me alone with the android. In the torch-lit gloom, I drew my coat around myself and turned up the high collar.

To no one in particular—to the memory of the moment past—I said, "I was worried about you, too."

CHAPTER 34

IN THE HOUSE OF
KHARN SAGARA

"I SHALL HAVE A meal prepared and brought to you at once, Lord Marlowe," Yume said when I was returned to the suite my companions had previously occupied. All signs of its previous occupation were gone: the food cart was cleared away, the bedclothes changed, the furniture ordered, the bathroom soaps recharged. "You've been waiting a long time."

"Three weeks," I said under my breath, suddenly eager for a shower.

Undeterred by my tone, the android replied, "And two days, four hours, and thirty-seven minutes." It pointed. "There is a sonic cleaning unit for your clothes in with the bath—unless you would prefer that I take them?"

It waited, and realizing that I might be expected to disrobe then and there, I said, "No, thank you. I can see to it myself."

"As you wish, sir," Yume said, continuing my tour of the chambers. "You are free to explore the installation and its grounds, so long as you remain within bounds."

"Will I be able to speak with Lord Sagara?"

The golem stopped midway through a demonstration of the laundry service unit.

"You already have." If I didn't know better, I might have said the creature was perplexed. It tilted its head as a dog might, and almost I imagined a frown on that blank curve of metal it called a face. I could see its gears whirring through the crystal windows in its shoulders. I caught myself making a warding gesture with my first and final fingers. How strange that I who did not believe should fall upon religion in the face of that machine.

"I had hoped to speak with him again."

"The Master will speak with you in his own time," the golem said.

"When my friends return?"

Yume's single eye studied me a moment. Talking to it was not like speaking with any human in my experience. There was no presence to it, nothing of the sort that might cause the hair to stand on end, the skin to crawl. It was dead space. Shape without form. Shade without color. In its polished, patrician accent, it said again, "The Master will speak with you in his own time."

In my own time I washed and laundered my clothes, and so newly ordered I set myself to exploring that strange palace. The *installation* Yume called it. The word implied a sort of military order, and indeed the heavy blast door and the spartan geometry of hall and stairwell spoke to me of some ancient fortress built beneath the surface of that lightless world. How many hours I lost in those barren corridors I could not say, nor count the number of sealed doors that barred my way.

In my time since that first sojourn on Vorgossos—and before it, on Emesh—I had the privilege of standing amidst the ruins of ancient civilizations. The black-walled tunnels of Calagah with their walls smooth as glass; the Marching Towers on Sadal Suud, broken fingers rising above the fungal forests; even old Simeon's tomb on Judecca. Old though they were—their histories measured in scores of millennia—none felt so old to me as that blasted labyrinth. There was a humanity in its bones unlike that in those strange structures built by alien hands. Familiarity aged it. I knew concrete, and so marveled at what depth and span of years must pass to crack and weather those walls. It was not—as the pyramid below—the palace of a great king or emperor, but something else.

Installation.

Who had built it in the deeps of time, and to what purpose? Who had quarried out these caverns and raised these halls? Whose hands had placed those chipped, square columns in the vast and empty spaces, hangar-like, that processed down one arm of that seemingly endless complex? One could yet see where the mark of some ancient trowel had smoothed the cement and badly.

And I was alone.

Yume did not reveal itself as I wandered, nor any of Kharn's ghastly guards, nor the homunculi who had served us in the vestibule. Once or twice I passed one of Kharn's blue-eyed drones, floating like a small and lonesome fish in the dark airs. I tried to find Lord Song and his companions, but after some time decided that—wherever they were—they'd been left behind a locked door. Once or twice I thought I heard a human voice and ran to meet it, only to find an empty hall. As I walked, at times one of the great bulkheads would open or close of its own volition, and I thought about what Valka had said: that this place had no datasphere. Not one she understood. Then I remembered older stories, ones I'd told to Cat in another lifetime. They said that when Kharn Sagara took Vorgossos from the Exalted and drove them out, he took from them a demon of the ancient world, a daimon such as the Mericanii had made.

Switch was right, the whole place stank of sorcery. On Emesh, Gilliam Vas had called Valka a witch. He'd been right, in a sense, for the implant in Valka's brain had allowed her to access and control the castle's datasphere and power grid. But the more I understood what Valka could do, the less I thought it magic.

Not so in dim Vorgossos.

My first journey to Kharn's pyramid had left me with the impression that all his palace was empty, a desolate warehouse of drab concrete. It was not so, it was only that the halls were barren. Many doors opened to me, and within I found rooms richly appointed as my own quarters, and the vestibule had been that. Sumptuous carpets covered the floor, and the walls were hung with many priceless things: tapestries and paintings, art and arms and artifacts of all descriptions.

I tarried a while among a collection of ancient legionnaire armor, bone-white and red. The earliest suits were bulky things, the armor hid beneath the baggy environment layer, hoses wired in from the air and plasma packs worn on the back. The helms of two centurions bore the transverse horse-hair crests still worn in formal parades. One proud example wore the high, plumed chevalier's helm of an Imperial Martian Guardsman, his great shoulders draped in a red cloak, with pteruges hanging at shoulder and hip to recall the image of vanished Rome. Many of the pieces were scarred, many broken, many bearing the proud sigils of the House Imperial, or the standards of legions or houses of great renown. Other examples there were: the mirrored masks of Jaddian *aljanhi*, their bright blues and greens and oranges resplendent beside the drab and ugly ironwork of the Lothriad.

There were smaller pieces under glass, epaulets belonging to famed commanders out of history, a roundel showing the Imperial sunburst that had purportedly been part of a suit of armor made for Prince Cyrus the Golden . . . the shattered remnants of the White Sword that had executed the pretender Boniface in the fifth millennium.

I could hardly believe it.

Kharn had not exaggerated when he called himself a man of culture.

Clang.

A metallic sound reverberated down one colonnade, undampened by any carpet or tapestry. I halted, drawing my sword. Torn between curiosity and the terror of the unknown. But Kharn had offered me the hospitality of his palace, and Yume treated me with every courtesy. I recalled my own words from the landing platform high above and murmured, "I am not afraid."

Fear is a poison, the part of me that thought in Gibson's voice said.

Buoyed by that thought and the memory of the old scholiast I turned, following a side passage as it curved gently down a kind of horseshoe bend. It emptied me onto a curving hallway, a circle along whose inner wall stood several round doors. Above I heard the roar of a big machine, great turbines turning in the stone above. I'd heard such things in several places about the palace, and reasoned they were part of some great network that powered the installation—though I confess I knew little of such things.

The inner door opened at my touch, and a blast of warm, wet air rose to greet me like a breath. A shout. Light poured in, not cool and bloodless like the lights in the hall, but true and proper light, such as a sun might make. I thought to turn back, thinking that it must be some mistake, that the door should have been locked and wasn't, but I heard something then that urged me forward.

The sound of birdsong.

Sword in hand but unkindled, I stepped gingerly forward, placing my feet with silent care. The door had opened onto a short hall—and airlock, I realized, though it had not cycled—and I followed it out into golden sunlight. I gasped. I'd emerged onto the uppermost of a series of round terraces that descended—layer by layer—ever downward. Every layer bloomed with flowers and fruit trees and all manner of greenery. Hummingbirds flitted among the branches, and squirrels. And what at first I took for bees I realized with a start were tiny drones.

I stood a long while by the rail, looking out and down upon layer upon layer of greenery. A strange bird—red and blue, with a hooked beak—fluttered down and sidled up to me, watching me with one beady eye. I tried to imagine Kharn Sagara walking in these gardens, trailing hoses and fiber optics from beneath his yellow robe. I almost laughed aloud. It was a strange vision.

It was a strange extravagance. Kharn had seemed to me so like one of the kings of ancient myth, lord of a tyranny of stone and not the sort of man to love gardens. There was a clinicism in the way he studied his art and kept it in that place, the way a scholiast kept organs and little animals in jars of greenish fluid. A single flight of steps descended, spiraling ever down and in ever tighter orbits, for each garden terrace had a smaller diameter than the last. Water fell in irregular streamlets from the roof above, and looking up I was astonished to see not the blank concrete so abundant in that hideous place, but the naked limestone of the living rock itself.

Perhaps it says a thing of me that I tarried here less long than in the museum halls. I do not know what it says of a man that he might linger for hours before a painting of a garden and yet ignore the flowers themselves—but such am I. Perhaps it was only that I expected a serpent to spring from the bushes and strike at my heel, or for one of the infernal SOMs to at last make an appearance. Down nine levels I descended, and so came in time to the very base of the garden, which was shaped like a keyhole: the stairs emptying onto the round center while the single hall stretched on away, cutting under the terraces above.

Orchids clung to branches above my head, and somewhere a lark cried. The imitation sunlight shone from tiny fixtures bracketed to the roof above, and the mosaic on the floor was treacherous with false rain. The air wafted thick with the smell of flowers, of fruits I could not name. I looked back and up past ascending levels of foliage, and then—sure I was alone—returned my sword to its clip.

The hall that stretched away, like the rough ceiling high above, was all of native rock, and the pale stone sweated with the hothouse moisture of that garden. I'd come so far down I thought that surely I was approaching the level of the subterranean sea Yume had spoken of, and half expected the tunnel would lead down to some Plutonian shore.

There was only another door.

Like the door to the pyramid it was: sculpted of floating metal. It depicted a great, spreading tree, and two great snakes descending from that tree. Their bodies twined into a double helix, tails twined around the stem of the tree, fangs sunk deep in the flesh of a man kneeling about the bowl of the tree. The image filled me with a perverse fascination, and I stood a long while, tracing the contours of the image with my fingers. A light at the corner of my eye caught my attention, and turning I saw a key panel gleaming. It was different than the others. No mere mechanical switch, but a holograph plate. Without much hope, I called it up, was met with an authentication request.

Disappointed but unsurprised, I turned back, returning up the hall to the stair.

Yume was waiting for me.

Or, I thought it was Yume. In truth, I cannot say if the Undying kept but one of the golems or several. The dull gray and unsexed body was the same. The brass clockwork identical. The white mask with its one black eye and weeping golden filigree. In those same cool, patrician tones, the android said, "Lord Marlowe, your meal is ready." That was supper on the day my companions had left to return to the *Mistral*.

A pretext? Surely it had appeared in time with my discovery of the Well and its gardens. I could not help but feel that I was being herded away like some irritating child. That I had seen enough and too much of Kharn's palace.

"What is this place?"

Yume did not look round. "The Orchid Stair. The vestibule to the Garden."

"This is not a garden?" I asked, confused.

"It is not *the* Garden," the creature replied, still a statue but for the winking of the light in its black eye. "The Master maintains extensive gardens. For the children, you understand."

I did not understand, though I had a sinking suspicion in my bowels that was worse than true knowledge. Thinking of the snakes carved into the doorway, their heads facing one another as they devoured the helpless man, I asked, "What children?"

Still the android did not move. "You know what this place is."

The creature had a disconcerting habit of not answering questions, as if by avoiding answers it might avoid a lie. Could it lie? I wasn't sure. It is said that the daimons of old were incapable of mistruth, that the ancient laws which bound and governed their kind prevented it. That had never seemed sufficient safeguard to me, for truth is sharper than falsehood, and just as poisonous. Still, Yume's omissions were louder than its words. *The children.* I thought about Baron Song, about the Grand Duke of Milinda and the others. I could imagine a pack of their younger selves living sheltered lives in these gardens, feral as troglodytes, as the children of plebeian families so often are. Each unaware of his fate, of her destiny: of the end that awaited them all.

The warm garden felt very cold.

Thus I permitted myself to be led away, back up through the concentric rings of the Orchid Stair, beneath hanging bowers thick with the delicate fragrance of that eponymous flower. When we'd climbed halfway to the top, I asked, "How far down are we?"

"The entrance above is twenty-seven levels below the outer gate."

"We're near to the sea, then?" I asked, meaning the subterranean ocean beneath Kharn's pyramid.

Without breaking stride, Yume pivoted its head fully around to watch me as it ascended the steps. "Oh no, lord. The sea is much farther below."

Below.

Song and the others had talked of being taken *below,* as well. Had they meant only some deeper level of the installation above us? Or was there yet some deeper hall? Some darker theater where the medical labors that gave Vorgossos its dire reputation played out in grim burlesque?

I gave up trying to speak to the machine. Its unwillingness or inability to lie made it a difficult interlocutor. But it was comfortable in silence, and I was happy not to speak to it.

By several stairs and empty corridors we returned to my chambers, and Yume left me at the door. I entered, the heavy portal clanging shut behind me. I left my coat on the back of a chair and found the food trolley waiting by the table. Trusting myself to my solitude, I unclipped my terminal from its gauntlet and set the device on the tabletop, calling up the text of Impatian's *The First Emperors,* a biography of the first eleven emperors. I'd finished his *History of the Jaddian Wars* while locked in Sagara's vestibule. I set the thing to playing and soon a cool, artificial voice began reciting the text aloud. Forgetting myself, I returned to my coat and pulled my small journal from an inside pocket and returned to the table. That done, I lifted the tray off the trolley and carried it to the table. Beneath the steam lid was a species of strange silver fish, fried in oil and delicately spiced beside an arrangement of red-cap mushrooms stuffed with cheese and onions. A soup there was, too, sweet and smoky, and wine.

Wine. How long had it been since I'd had wine? Since before Rustam, at least.

I took a sip. The torpor that had overtaken me during my time among the client lords was gone, and I found it impossible to relax. I doubted even wine could chase my anxieties from me. Still, I meant to try, though I placed my sword on the table as if it were a piece of cutlery.

Eating slowly, I studied the painting on the wall opposite me while I listened to my terminal read Impatian's histories. It showed a stone cottage beneath a whorling blue sky. Twining trees and yellow fields. Clumsy brushstrokes and heavy lines captured not the image the artist had seen, not his eye, but some piece of the soul of him. I wondered at it a long time, and so failed to absorb much of the reign of Emperor Victor I. The clear voice seemed a kind of curtain, a pall that drowned the world and drowned myself, so that I sat—like Kharn himself—in contemplation of that image of another age.

Cottages at Cordeville. A replica, the original had died with Earth. I opened my little journal casually, thumbed past black ink sketch after sketch. How poor they seemed by comparison, how crude and unpleasant. How . . . forgettable.

Eternity is the chief quality of high art. Depending on no moment, such art belongs to every moment, and so takes us for a time from our time—allowing us to touch eternity for our fleeting instant. I was there, transported by that painting, my reading, my food. Hidden from the world a time, from my cares. From Uvanari and Gilliam. From Bordelon. From Bassander Lin and three aquilarii dead on the *Balmung.*

From Jinan.

Transported as I was, I did not hear the approach of feet behind me.

Not until soft arms closed about my neck.

CHAPTER 35

THE GORGON

YEARS OF BEING ATTACKED by night in the streets of Borosevo had taught me panic, and taught me the strength to overcome panic. Exhaling through my nose, I tucked my chin and—gripping the thin arms about my neck with one hand—reached back with the other to seize my attacker by the scruff of the neck. I tugged downward, pulling his chin over my shoulder that I might strike his face.

"Please!" The voice startled me. It was not a man at all.

Her arms slackened, and I released them, turning quickly and snatching up my sword. I did not conjure its blade, but stood ready, processing. The woman—for woman she undeniably was—stood a head shorter than I. Where she had come from I could not at first guess, for the hall door had not opened, nor any of the doors to the secondary chambers. Only the door to my sleeping room was open, and I'd a sudden, horrible feeling that she'd been waiting there for me. In bed, to judge by the disheveled nature of her raven hair and her gauzy white dress.

"Who are you?" I asked, not lowering my sword. Completely oblivious, the unthinking circuits in my terminal continued translating Impatian's text into placid tones. Emperor Victor's biography filled the silence.

The invader massaged the back of her neck, eyes downcast, reproached. "Naia," she said, voice rich as candle smoke. She looked up suddenly, and I felt a lurch. Her pupils were twice the proper size, the irises large and blue as ice. They gave the look of one permanently startled. Or permanently aroused. With exquisite care, she removed her hand from her neck, raked fingers through her fall of black hair "You hurt me."

I did not apologize. "You startled me." Whatever chivalric impulse had made me free her at the sound of her voice was gone, and I was on my guard. The eyes betrayed her. She was a homunculus, and so designed . . .

but designed for what? She was a bed servant, the full and perfect shape of her announced that plain as sunrise. But was that all she was? My own grandfather, Lord Timon, had been killed by a concubine homunculus. And there was always a vague inhumanity to many of them. Something of the machine in the way they were tailored, cut to fit a purpose and design. I supposed that I—a nobile of the Peerage, a palatine—was little different. But like Ilex, I had the freedom of my own thoughts, whereas who knew what impulses had been built into the deep structures of this woman's brain? No doubt she had been designed to be the perfect courtesan: coy, alluring, but ultimately pliant. She could not choose, could not say no.

That she *might* say no would never even occur to her.

"I did not mean to," she said, still clutching at her hair as though it was a lifeline. "I only wondered when you would come to bed. You were in here so long." She took a step, fine gold chains tinkling at wrist and throat and ankle.

I took a measured step back, circling to put the table between us. "Why are you here?" I asked, as though the answer were not obvious. With my free hand I silenced the chattering terminal.

"The Master sent me," she said into the fresh silence, fingers worrying at her neckline, tugging the fabric lower. Her skin was paler even than mine. It shone like milk by moonlight. "He thought you would like me." I did. There was something in the hard bones of her face, a hawkish severity softened by full lips and that pouting expression, that reminded me of . . . something. I could not put my finger on it. She took a step closer, following me round the table, one finger trailing on its surface, hunting, teasing. "Do you not like me?"

Like those brave and foolish men who came before the Medusa, I was transfixed. My sword was at the ready, fingers on the trigger. How small she was, how slight—though in her kind smallness was no guarantee of weakness. She might have overpowered me if she wished, or torn my arms from their sockets for all I knew, or strangled me just like my poor grandfather.

Her robe vanished, and I realized it was no robe at all. Only a holograph shell: gossamer light spun to conceal what lay beneath. A marble sculpture of a woman, perfect as Pygmalion had made. Dark hair and soft curves and eyes like frozen stars. An anklet she wore—fashioned in the likeness of a gold snake devouring—and gold were the chains that hung between her breasts. Silver would have suited her better, so pale was she. A creature of the night, and with those terrible, frightened and furiously loving eyes she might have been a vampire out of some antique fable. Some monstress to frighten and allure, to teach men fear. How could I have thought her reproached by me? Shrinking? I have seen demons less frightening.

I did not move, not even when one cool hand closed over mine, or pressed my sword's emitter to her breast. "Are you going to kill me?" she asked, breathless, mouth open and turned up to my face. "Do you want to? You can." Her breath was hot in my ear, her voice gone all husky. "It would not be the first time." She seized me between the legs, and a grunt escaped me.

My hand moved of itself, shoved her away. I tried not to think on what she'd said about dying, about being killed. Repulsed, I put the sword down on the table, keeping my eyes on the homunculus. She tossed her hair and smiled. I was relieved to see only ordinary teeth. "Are you frightened? Of me?"

I was. My hands burned where she had touched me—where I had touched her—as if with fever, and my breath came in ragged gasps. "Of this place," I said, "of your master."

"Why? He likes you. He must like you—else he'd not have sent you me." She advanced, leaning—*leaning*—over the table. "I like you, too—but then . . . I like everyone. It's . . . my nature."

"What do you mean?" I asked, though I had a suspicion. "You mean you don't have a choice?"

She showed her teeth again, knowing too well whence my treasonous eyes were drawn. "Ooh . . . none of us has a choice. We like what we like. We can't explain it. We can only . . . explain it away." Advancing, she pressed her hands against my chest. "Take off your boots, soldier. Stay a while." She was very close. One arm snaked back behind my head and bent it down. Lips pressed against mine. Tongue. I'd forgotten where I put my hands, forgotten where to find them. She broke away, stepped back so that she could look over the length of me. I wore the same belted black tunic, high boots, and piped trousers I had worn on Rustam. "You look fit for the parade ground and I'm not wearing a stitch." She pouted, then did something with her hand that pulled some howling animal from the lowest dungeons of my brain. "Doesn't seem fair, does it?"

It didn't seem fair at all, put that way. My tongue felt thick, and a red mist was rising in my mind. But there was yet a piece of me—the piece that drove me to write this account, I don't doubt—which replied, "What makes you think I'm a soldier?"

"Ooh"—Naia bit her lip—"the shoes mostly. Those boots. Like I said. I bet if you took them off you wouldn't be a soldier, though. Only a man. Men are only men when you take their uniforms away."

I had no intention of allowing such to be done to me, and hurried past Naia to the door. As I did, I brushed up against my journal where it lay on the table's edge and knocked it to the floor. "You should go," I managed to say, fumbling with the locks.

I wanted her to go. I wanted her to stay. I didn't know what I wanted. We like to imagine that we are ourselves a unity: one mind, one spirit. Not so. In truth we are each a little legion, a pack of little personae—each one-eyed in its attentions and single-minded in its aim. I pulled in two directions, and so fumbled the door controls even as her hand seized mine and pinned it to the wall. I might have resisted, but resistance seemed wrong, somehow. Surely there was no harm in letting her stay? She wanted to stay.

"Don't say that," she said, putting a hand on my cheek. "What's wrong? Don't you like me?" She took my hand and dragged it to her breast.

I kept seeing Brevon's secretary in the corner of my eye. Her dumb obedience. Her hobbled gait. The way she simply stood there, waiting. How many were there in her inner legion? How many had she been allowed to have? Brevon had made her that way to suit his own purposes. Kharn had made Naia, or bought her, to be precisely what she was. She'd said it herself. She could not choose, and my choices were narrowing, drowned by the red fog behind my eyes.

A chill went through me even as she kissed me again. I felt her pressed against me. Her breasts, her hands in my sweating hair. What had been done to me? I could feel the resistant piece of me fading and threw up my hands to knock hers away. I told myself it was thoughts of Jinan that stayed me, some nostalgia for our shattered romance. I told myself it was principle, what I learned from Kyra. What I'd loathed in Crispin. In Bordelon. In my own mother. The tendency of power to corrupt and abuse. But I still wonder if it was only terror, fear of that place and its dread lord. Fear of the woman herself. Aching, I pushed her away.

There was no hurt in her eyes. Laughing, she danced back. It was like she didn't understand, like I was speaking to someone in the wrong language, communicating by the wrong signs.

"Did you draw these?" she asked, stooping—legs apart—to collect my journal where it had fallen. From her smile I knew she'd acted deliberately.

Relieved to have her off me a moment and to be able to marshal my thoughts and smooth my tunic, I said, "I did, yes."

Naia flipped through the little journal, images fluttering by one after another. She did not linger on any of them, not even on the images of Jinan that no eye was meant to see. She doubled back once or twice, shoulders folding in as she studied. After a moment she shut the book with a snap and fully turning said, "Do me." She thrust the book at me, and I took it, studying it for damage. I don't know why I bothered. The old thing had traveled in my coat through many dangers, and there wasn't an angstrom of it undamaged. I must have studied it too long, for the woman said, "*Draw* me."

She didn't wait for a response, but threw herself on the fainting couch, arching her back in a display worth commemorating. I could *draw* her, couldn't I? Just *draw* her? Keep her off me, keep her at arm's length long enough to gain a measure of control over the situation. So I seated myself opposite her and took out my stylus, pausing only long enough to master my breathing.

I could hardly think, hardly hold the pen. My hand was shaking, but I began to draw her. Broad strokes, just taking in her shape. I did not speak, for to speak seemed too much an invitation, and I did not trust myself. She did not speak either, only watched me with unquiet intent, those dusky eyes alert and alive.

I never finished that drawing. I tore it out after, contaminated by the event. She moved quickly—more quickly than I could have believed. She brushed my hands away, knocking my journal again to the floor, and straddled me, grinding her hips against me. Her lips found mine as she forced my head back, making me think again of the vampire. There was a strength in her clean limbs and an urgency that scattered my legion and left a single, one-eyed soldier at attention. Her breath came hot across my face and on the hollow of my throat and all my thoughts were drowned in that red and fevered fog. Her tongue was in my mouth. I remember the taste of spiced wine and the mint-like tang of hilatar.

Naia let out a little moan and pressed herself closer to me. My hands traced up along her sides until I held her face between them, fingers in her hair.

That was when I felt it, and froze.

There was a metallic spur behind her right ear. At first I thought it jewelry, but with the cymbal crash of memory recalled the gleaming implant behind Kharn's own ear. Nausea turned in me, and I stood, lifting Naia to throw her bodily on the couch.

Boots still on, I towered over her. Those dark eyes turned to look at me, and I was unsure whether it was terror or longing in them. Her designer doubtless had not wanted me or any man to know. She laughed, thinking it some species of game, that I'd revealed myself—my soul—to her at last. Squirming, she spread her legs, small teeth playing against one lip.

She did not speak.

I did not stir.

Words at last. Hers. Not mine.

"What's the matter, soldier?" she said. "Going to keep your boots on after all?" One hand descended, finding herself. "Fine by me."

"You're *him*," I said, hands clenched. "You're a SOM."

Her brows furrowed, but she did not stir. "What?"

"Don't lie to me!" I snapped. "There's an implant behind your right ear." Here I lifted a finger and tapped my own head with a finger. "Don't deny it."

Her hand stopped, whole body gone stiff. *Something* shifted behind those black and open eyes. The thin blue iris grew, pupils narrowing—as though she were coming down from some drug. Her posture shifted, and she crossed her arms, sat with knees apart, as a man does. The thing behind her eyes smiled up at me, mouth open. In a voice which was a parody of her voice, he said, "You are a strange one."

"You should talk." I wore my anger like a cloak, clung to its folds with a desperation to fend off the sense of violation stealing over my bones. Naia—Kharn—bared her teeth in a wicked grimace. She stood, and tapping one golden earring restored the gauzy holograph shell she had first worn. How I had thought it cloth before I couldn't say. It shimmered, floated to a wind that was not there. She paced round the dining table, her back to me, her every contour yet visible through the cloth. "Why?"

Kharn's characteristic silence answered me. I was suddenly too aware of the highmatter sword resting on the tabletop. The concubine stood between it and me, and I stood like a fool with his tunic unbelted. "Did you not like her? Our Naia?" He traced a hand down her flank, turning as he did so. The gesture was obscene, as though her hand belonged to someone else . . . which I suppose it did.

"Get out."

"Does she not look a bit like that friend of yours?"

"Get out!" I almost shouted.

Kharn grinned at me. "You must care for her." Valka. He was talking about Valka. My sense of violation sharpened, deepened in that now I was not the only one violated.

"Or else I'd have thrown myself on your slave?" I retrieved my journal from the floor. "You don't know me, Lord Sagara."

"I might have."

I suppressed my creeping sense of horror and stood as before a firing squad, hands clasping my journal behind my back, chin raised. "You won't." He watched me with her eyes. I could see the light behind them. The shadow. Almost I could see Kharn's ruined body on its pale throne, his craggy face upturned, staring into the darkness above him, peering out from Naia's face. "Do you abuse all your guests?" I asked when I could stand his quiet no longer.

"Is that what you call it?" He frowned. "She was meant to honor you."

"She was meant to amuse you," I countered. "And what have you done with Naia?"

"She sleeps with the others. Until I call for her."

"And she's asleep now?" I had no idea what he meant, but decided that I did not want to know.

"Yes," he said. I tucked my chin to shade my eyes from Kharn's pitiless examination. "You know, I thought for certain you'd flee with your companions." He moved Naia's body all the way around the table, so that she stood beneath the replica of *Cottages at Cordeville*. The painting struck an odd contrast, so bright and wholesome beside the devil in her white dress.

I advanced to stand opposite the puppet homunculus across the table, placing my journal beside the half-finished remnant of my meal. My sword was still closer to Kharn, but I felt I stood a chance now if it came down to it. Trying to keep this concern from my face, I said, "I have a job to do."

"Indeed," Kharn replied. "You know . . . I almost believe you."

"My companions will return the day after tomorrow," I said with all the candor and sobriety I could muster. "You'll soon see."

"I expect I will." He turned her back on me, regarded his painting a moment. "They said the artist was too intense. That he frightened people. Seem it strange to you that such a thing might be said of he who made so innocent a painting?"

I half-rounded the table, taking the opportunity to reclaim my sword, which I held carefully in one hand. A little closer now, I said, "It's the color. People are afraid of color. Your painter saw too much of it."

"Is that why you only work in black and white?" he asked. "Because you are afraid?" I did not rise to the bait, and so Naia's voice added, "An artist afraid is no artist at all."

"Is that why your palace is all gray stone?" I countered. "Because *you* are afraid?"

Kharn Sagara watched me out of that woman's face, eyes old as empires. "And do you abuse all your hosts?"

"Is that what you call it?"

The Undying barked a laugh—an astonishingly rough sound from so fine a throat. "You argue like a Eudoran actor." He paused a moment, then without warning said, "I will take my leave of you." He turned and on bare feet moved toward the door. Halfway between painting and portal he stopped. "Shall I leave the girl with you, Marlowe?"

"Get. Out."

CHAPTER 36

THE DEVIL AND THE GOLEM

I COULD NOT SLEEP in my bed that night, nor upon the couch or in the winged armchair. Instead I spent an hour on the floor of the shower there, scalding myself, as if heat and pain could wash out the memory of her hands. I tried washing my mouth, but the taste of soap only reminded me of what had been done to me. The memory of Naia lingered with her perfume. I wrapped myself instead in my old coat in a corner of the room when the suite's other doors would not unlock. It would not hide me from Kharn should he return—in one guise or another—but I was as far from the memory of the homunculus and her white arms as I could manage.

I missed Jinan. And missing her made it worse.

When I did sleep, I dreamed again, and dreaming was conscious of a wet wind blowing out of darkness and the sound of waves. I was not in my body. I was only a mote, like an ember cast from unseen fires, hurtling through the night. I sensed deep water below me, and the sky above was clouded and close as the roof of some limitless cathedral. Witch-lights the precise, greenish hue of those I'd seen on our descent from the orbital platform shone in the depths. They illuminated a round and broken arch, like the ring of some giant shattered but standing still.

Hadrian . . .

I stopped, hearing the voice—the same voice I had heard in my dream when we first arrived on Vorgossos—and called out, "Who's there?" But I had no voice.

Listen.

The word echoed in eternity. Infinity.

Listen to me.

"Who goes there?" I tried to say.

Listen!

I had a body then. Without warning. Mass and weight. I fell like a stone, like a turtle dropped by an eagle. Plunging into the depths. I woke with a start before I hit the water.

I did not explore the palace the next morning. I awoke to find food laid out for me—and the remains of the last night's unfinished meal cleared away. I tuned my terminal to read to me and tried to pick up where I'd left off with Impatian's *First Emperors,* but the life of Victor Sebastos held little shine for me, and I soon surrendered to the quiet.

Somewhere far above, Valka and the others were returning to the *Mistral,* beyond the misshapen statues of the Furies at the top of the high-tower. I imagined them stepping through the airlock back into known territory. Back onto familiar ground, back with familiar faces. I longed to leave with them, to take Otavia Corvo up on her offer: to leave this place and this foolish mission and never look back.

Who did I think I was?

I was no great hero—am no great hero. I was only a foolish young man very far from home. Forget the *Mistral,* I'd have given all I had to wake up in my room at Devil's Rest, beneath my painted stars. This was all a nightmare, it had to be. I was in the palace of *Kharn Sagara,* a myth old almost as the Empire itself. I had seen demons and xenobites and imagined I could contend with them.

Kings and pawns, I thought again.

We're all pawns, my boy. Gibson's words echoed back to me. *But remember, no matter who moves you, your soul is in your own hands. You have a choice.*

None of us has a choice, Naia said. Or was it Kharn? Had the Undying lurked behind her eyes from the very start?

Choice.

That is the question, is it not?

Those who say we are only flesh must reason that we have no will of our own, that we serve our impulses, which are rooted in our brains and nowhere else. Such thinking gave rise to the homunculi, who are made happy in their servitude. After all, to such thinking we are all slaves, if only to our breeding. Thus it is no crime to create creatures such as Naia. And yet it is clearly a crime. Evil needs no explanation. You know it by its smell. That knowledge—that apprehension of the Truth which is there and obvious—spoke to me of something *more*. To us. In us. A quiet thing.

I wonder now what I looked like to Kharn. He who had lived so long and so variously, who was no longer truly human. I suspected then and know now that much of his mind was given over to machines. That they sustained him in his old age and ordered what flesh and chemistry would have long ago destroyed. Being so old and so much machine, I think we must look to him as dogs do to us. Animals do not think as we—cannot be said to think at all. Rather they inhabit their world and respond to it.

They do not create.

They do not choose.

What Kharn had done was clear. Create a sealed environment. Introduce a stimulus. I'd been a lab rat and my sleeping chamber the maze. It had not gone as Kharn expected . . .

However precarious my position, I had yet the will to choose. I was there, after all. Who would come to Vorgossos except by choice? Who would stay? I had made my choice, and had only to wait. My friends would return soon.

The door cycled open, and Yume appeared, leading a laden food trolley. Some part of me expected that it would be Naia again, or one of the girls who served the lords and ladies of the vestibule. The android smoothly deposited the steam tray and a pewter carafe and drinking cup on the table, making no comment. I watched it work, sitting with my back against the wall on a cushion in the corner. Yume cleared away the remnants of that morning's breakfast—and with it the torn-up image Naia had forced me to draw.

It had been quiet a long while, and looking up I saw the golem watching me, unmoving.

The moment my eyes found its one, Yume's head twitched to one side. "You are on the floor."

"Well spotted," I said, massaging beneath my terminal gauntlet with a finger. After the incident the night before, I'd kept my sword on my person at all times. It lay by my cushion then, near to hand, though I'd no notion how quickly the inhuman butler might move.

The gears visible through the glass at Yume's hips and shoulders turned over, filling the silence with the ticking of jeweled mechanisms. In its clear, patrician tones, Yume said, "The Master has asked that I apologize for the events of the previous evening, and he hopes no offense was given."

"Offense?" I repeated, half-rising from the cushions. But I thought about Tanaran, about Valka and Switch and the others. They ought to be on the hightower, descending. "No," I said at last, unable to curb all the sarcasm from my voice, "no offense."

Yume clasped its delicate hands before itself. "The Master was worried when you did not leave your chambers."

"So he sent you?" I asked. "Surely he knows where I am." I raised a hand, described a circle with one finger to indicate the cameras I felt sure were everywhere. "The King with Ten Thousand Eyes and all."

"If you mean to imply that you are under surveillance, I can assure you there is no monitoring equipment in the diplomatic suite."

I confess I snorted. "You expect me to believe that?"

"Belief is not required."

"Is that so?" I said, struggling to my feet. "You'll forgive me if I'm not convinced."

The golem said, "I cannot lie."

"I'm supposed to believe that, too?"

"Belief—"

"Is not required, yes." I turned my sword over in my hands, recalling how Kharn had done that very thing on our first meeting. It had a pleasant weight, and the wine-dark leather grip was sweet to the touch, her silvered fittings only somewhat tarnished by time and hard use.

"The Master considers it unwise to provide me with counterfactual data. It introduces error." *Something all liars should take into account, and something each of us forgets.* Yume was not finished speaking. "In any case, indulging mistruth violates the laws which govern what you think of as my persona."

I stared at the creature. "You mean to say that you do not truly think."

"I am only what the Master made me. A high-order virtual intelligence and personal assistant. Genuine cognition is not required. Pursuant to which, I was asked to attend to any desires his lordship might have."

The couch loomed beside me, and it was all I could do not to turn my eyes in that direction, for I knew all too well just what Kharn Sagara had in mind where the matter of desire was concerned. Instead I asked, "Where are my friends? Are they on their way back down?"

"They are still aboard your ship at the marina. We expect they will be underway shortly, provided we do not occupy the nine-percent-probability space where they leave without you."

"Nine percent," I repeated, not impressed. "And what data are you working off, precisely?"

"Only what is available."

"Hmm." If it were really true, if Kharn did not monitor my rooms, what a statement of power it was to permit his *guests* their privacy. All the same, I knew well that the single eye in Yume's face was one of Kharn's Ten Thousand, just as Naia's two had been. For all I knew, the Undying lurked even then behind his servant's face. And watched. And listened.

Tanaran's arrival could not come soon enough.

CHAPTER 37

TANARAN

TWO MEALS PASSED AND the better part of a day, and in all that time no word from Yume as to my companions' whereabouts. On its twin appearances, the golem only said what it had said before.

The door opened a third time, hours before I expected the golem to return.

"Still here?"

Valka stood in the doorway, Yume behind her with a towering figure in a hooded black abolla. It seems strange to say that after so short a time apart seeing a familiar face was like seeing the sun after weeks underground, but it was. I rose from the table at speed, glad not to be alone in that awful place.

"Where else would I be?" I said, and turning to the hooded figure added, *"Asvato o-renimn ti-okarin yelnuri mnu shi."*

In its native tongue, the tall xenobite replied, "You are most welcome."

Looking round, I asked, "Where are the others?" Valka and the Cielcin priest were alone. Pallino, Crim, Ilex, and Switch were nowhere to be seen. It was Switch's absence that seemed the strangest to me—as indeed it was—and his absence I felt most sharply.

"I suggested they stay behind," Valka said. "'Tis no danger here." Despite this she was still wearing her sidearm strapped to one thigh.

Switching to Valka's native Panthai, I asked, "You came alone? With it?" I suppressed an urge to glance at Tanaran, who stood impassive, but must have guessed we spoke about it.

"'Tis perfectly safe," she replied in the same language. "I told Otavia I could handle it. You know, I think if you'd come back as well she'd have done all she could to leave this place."

That did not sit right with me. Captain Corvo must have been greatly unsettled to have allowed such a thing. If that were so, I could understand her wanting to keep Crim and Ilex aboard the *Mistral*. They were her people, after all. That Switch or Pallino had not come either filled me with a deep foreboding, and the blank loneliness I felt before Valka's reappearance asserted itself again.

"What's it like on the ship?"

Valka's eyes turned toward the watchful Yume. The golem stood impassive, waiting to be acknowledged. She brushed hair from her eyes as she returned her attentions to me. "Unsettled." She raised a hand to touch my arm, but seemed to think better of it. "They still can't access the ship's communications or navigational readouts. They're locked out. It has Otavia and Durand nervous. I'm sure it's just the Vorgossene protecting their privacy. She's sent people around the landing platform up there. All the ships are locked down the same way."

"I'm sure this place hasn't kept its secrets for so long without being careful," I said, looking away.

"What's wrong?" She did touch my arm then, for only a moment.

"Nothing," I said, too shortly. "It's nothing."

"This place . . ." Tanaran's Galstani was still halting, still thick on its alien tongue, but it spoke clearly. "It is like the ships of my people." I noticed then that the Cielcin was not squinting. Beneath the shadow of its hood the black eyes—large as fists—were wide and staring.

Valka turned to the silent golem, thrust out her chin. "Will your master see us now?"

"He will," Yume said, gesturing. "This way."

I had expected Kharn to delay, to let us fester for weeks again as I had the first time. But the Undying seemed to have found for himself some scrap of urgency, and his pet golem led us down to the dark tramway about that lightless ocean. Ahead, the white shape of Kharn's inverse pyramid shone like the face of some blank specter by night.

"There are buildings," Tanaran said. "Far below."

"There!" Valka pointed back the way we had come, down and down.

I could see nothing in the darkness. What Tanaran's alien eyes saw I could not say, and I had to remind myself that these deep caverns must have been like daylight to the xenobite. It seemed at once incredible to me that Evolution should have given the Cielcin eyes at all. Ought it not to have fashioned some blind beast, some creature that saw through sound or else sensed the vibrations of the ground beneath it? I wondered again what sort of homeworld the Cielcin called their own. There I had a baetan of the itani, and I did not think to ask.

"The old city," Yume said, and said no more.

The faint sound of a horn playing filled the air of the entrance hall when we arrived. The smell of the distant sea followed us into the pyramid, faded as we descended the long stair toward the throne room. The wooden doors at the end of the hall swung inward silently, and the faint music faded to silence, as though we had interrupted the Lord Sagara at his music. Valka halted on the threshold, plagued—I think—by that same fear which accosted me the last time I'd stood in that place.

Kharn Sagara had not moved since last I saw him. Still he sat, saturnine and stone-faced amid the darkness and all that pale stone. An ancient analog musical device sat on the dais beside him, its twisted horn directed toward the king-in-yellow. How we had heard the thing from the pyramid antechamber above I couldn't guess. Some acoustic trick or technological devilry, perhaps.

As before, he did not speak. He did not seem to notice us at all. His eyes were very far away, wandering with his other eyes in places unknown to me. I had seen Kharn's wandering eyes from time to time, floating down corridors and galleries, admiring his great collection more than they kept watch.

Beside me, Valka shifted uncomfortably on her feet. Taking this as my cue, I took a step forward and, not bowing, said, "Thank you, Lord Sagara, for seeing us again on such short notice." Unable to help myself, I added, "I know how valuable is your time."

Was it my imagination? Or did the faintest trace of a smile crease that ancient and ageless face? Faint and far above, the blue-white gleam of the Undying's camera eyes winked on. They descended soundlessly, little one-eyed fish-shapes swimming on the airs. The human face did not turn to me, in this way recalling the blind beggars I had seen so often mutilated on the Chantry steps.

After another pause of perhaps half a minute, I gestured to Tanaran and said, "I have brought the Cielcin emissary, as I promised." On cue, Tanaran removed its hood—no easy task with its horned crown. In that open space, the Cielcin was at last able to stand to its full height. Tanaran was short for a Cielcin, and yet young. Despite this, it towered nearly eight feet high. Thin as a reed it was, and the great cloak it wore fit it badly, being at once too broad and too short.

Speaking as it had to Captain Corvo, it said, "I am Casantora Tanaran Iakato, Baetan of Itani Otiolo, of Aeta Aranata."

Two of Kharn's drones swerved so that—like a pair of living eyes—they regarded Tanaran face to face. After another interminable silence, Kharn said, "A Cielcin that speaks the tongues of Man. Here is a thing I have not seen in fifteen thousand years. Welcome, Tanaran of Otiolo. *Eka Kharn Sagara.*" *I am Kharn Sagara.* That was all he said. No title. No pomp. He needed neither. Leaning forward but not lowering his eyes to us, Kharn spoke in perfect Cielcin: "This human tells me you are his prisoner."

This human. Kharn used the word the Pale use of us, *yukajjimn,* vermin. I glanced at Valka. She'd caught the term as well, eyebrows raised. Tanaran bobbed its head, hands clasped before its chest. "I am, lord. We were taken prisoner on pilgrimage."

"*Zadituri ne?*" Kharn repeated the last word. "Which world was this?"

"Emesh!" Valka said, drawing the attention of another of Sagara's eyes.

"You did not know the humans had settled there?" The Undying's voice seemed to pace around us, circling like wolves, flowing with the steady orbit of the watchful eyes.

Tanaran glanced down at me, a curious expression on its flat and bloodless face. No human made such an expression, the way its upper lip twisted, curling back from translucent teeth. I recalled Valka's words to me then, *I'd not be so sure you can read Tanaran.* Perhaps she was right. Still, I think the xenobite had nearly so much difficulty with me, for it watched my face all the while it spoke, saying, "We did not. We recovered the co-ordinates from Akterumu." I stood impassive, not sure what to make of this. I'd no notion what Akterumu was—whether it was a person or a place.

Valka and I exchanged significant glances. The word *pilgrimage* had religious overtones, even in the alien tongue. It was easy to imagine that dim throne room a part of the dark beneath Calagah, and easy to hear again the words of Tanaran's captain: *They are not here.* They. The Quiet. Tanaran and its people had come to Emesh seeking after the ruins there, after the ancient xenobites that had built so many hallowed sites across known space, hundreds of thousands of years before mankind stood upon her own two feet and learned to walk.

"And you arrived to find the world in human hands," Kharn said. His lips did not move. The artificial voice that filled the hall was not the voice of his body, but a thing deeper, darker, the amplified tones of a god in some bad Eudoran play. Such melodrama has its critics—though I am not one.

Quickly then, Tanaran recounted what it could of its capture on Emesh. How their ship had been shot down by Raine Smythe and the 437th Centaurine Legion. How they had fled into the tunnels beneath Calagah—to die, they thought. To make one last heroic stand amidst the ruins of their gods. It told how I had come, and won Uvanari's surrender, how a scant dozen survivors were taken by the Empire.

Here I intervened, telling how the Chantry had taken Uvanari for interrogation. They'd wanted the location of the Cielcin fleet, and tortured the captain for it, despite my assurances that neither it nor its people would be harmed. A genuine smile twisted Kharn's lip at that. "You should not have spoken for the Empire," he said.

I brushed this off, explained that I had agreed to kill the Cielcin captain to deliver it from the Chantry cathars, and in exchange it had given me a name: Aranata Otiolo, a prince of the Cielcin, master of one of their strange clan fleets. And it had told me to seek Vorgossos.

"It said you'd dealt with the Itani Otiolo before—and you alluded to the same," I said, moving to stand beside Tanaran.

The King of Vorgossos sat a long time unresponding. It seemed no force could wake him from his place. He might have been one of the statues. Even our Cielcin compatriot seemed disquieted. For a moment, I considered saying that I had fled the Empire, uncertain if my act of rebellion would endear me to that lord of the Extrasolarians, or undermine my credibility as an apostol. So I erred on the side of caution, and held my peace.

How delicate was that moment! How fragile! I had not told Valka—there had been no time—how badly that first meeting had gone, or about Naia. Never before had I felt so much the fly caught in the spider's web. Not even in Borosevo as Count Mataro's captive stud had I felt so robbed of agency. I was for a moment only a character in Tanaran's story, in Kharn's ongoing myth.

"Tell me, baetan!" And Kharn's voice was like the roll of distant thunder. "What do you want?" Almost heard beneath the rumble of that vast voice, I heard words from Kharn's own lips murmured, *"Sibylla ti theleis?"* I did not then recognize the language or the source, nor had I time to dwell upon it.

The towering alien looked down at me a moment, wringing impossibly long-fingered hands. Valka *was* right, I could read nothing in those black wells it called eyes. I might as well have tried to hold discourse with a shark. It hesitated, then turned to Kharn and in its high, cold voice said, "I want to return to my master."

"And peace?" Kharn asked. "Do you wish that?"

Tanaran drew itself up to its full height, and repeated itself. "I *wish* to return to my master." *Wish,* it had said, *qulle.* A stronger word than *want.*

"And your master will pay handsomely for the return of his property." *His.* Unlike every other noun in the Cielcin language—unlike every other Cielcin—the princes were always *he.* To those familiar with the language, it had an ominous quality. One could almost hear the drumbeats just offstage. With glacial slowness, Kharn Sagara turned his face down to regard the three of us standing there. "I might reach out to your master, priest." He raised a finger, tracing an arc from Valka's face to mine. "But not for them."

I took a step forward, hands closing into fists. Seeing this, Valka caught me by the elbow and squeezed. The orbiting swarm of eyes pulled back, their lazy motions seeming to lock into something coherent, watchful, their glowing lenses shifting from blue to livid white.

The man himself seemed untroubled by my sudden motion. His eyes were like spots of ink on old vellum, and he frowned down at me. "The Sollan Empire can offer me nothing with this peace of theirs, but your master!" The voice in the air around us cracked like a lightning flash as five eyes floated toward Tanaran. "Your master may indeed be pleased to have you returned. Him I will deal with."

Valka's hand yet tightened on my arm, nails biting even through my coat and sleeve. My mind was reeling. I could feel the light of his glowing eyes on me, on Valka, the malice and the threat in them like laser points. We were alone, and far from help, and the laws that governed diplomacy and the treatment of guests and emissaries meant nothing on Vorgossos. If Sagara wished to take our prisoner, he could, and I could not stop him.

But Tanaran spoke again, saying, *"Raka tutaihete."* *That is generous.* My heart sank. "But the *yukajjimn* have ten of my clansmen, my master's property. Aeta Aranata would want them as well."

"Then we shall have them removed from this Marlowe's custody."

"He does not have them," Tanaran replied. "They remained with his fleet when we fled here." Realizing what it implied by those words, Tanaran stopped speaking, darting its eyes to me.

If the Undying caught the reference to our highly illegal flight from the *Balmung,* he gave no sign. "You know the humans mean to kill your master and your clansmen," Kharn said, voice dripping from the dark above. "The humans will claim they aim for peace and kill you at table. As is their way." He spoke with the weight of authority, of long knowledge. Yet there was no condemnation in his tone, only the weary acceptance of old age. "As they have done before."

"What do you mean?" Valka demanded. Ironic that she—who had held me to silence—should break hers. "What do you mean 'as we have done before'?"

"I meant what I said, Sagara!" I said, extricating myself from Valka's talons.

But Tanaran said, "I must return to my master, and return all I can to him. If that means dealing with the *yukajjimn,* so be it." It placed one massive hand on its chest. "And if we can put a stop to the fighting that has claimed too many of the People's lives, then so be that, too."

A bark of laughter escaped Kharn, though his mouth remained closed. "Interesting." Then, "Your companions' lives mean little to me, baetan. But you . . . you are valuable. Your master will not want to lose the history of his clan in you. He will come for you, and you will remain here until he does."

"And what of us?" I asked, close to shouting. "I did not come here to lose a prisoner, Sagara." I'd abandoned the Cielcin tongue, and spoke once more in clear Galstani, finding strength in the familiar sounds. I could almost hear Gibson at my shoulder, reminding me to stand straight, to speak clearly.

"What you came here for is of little concern to me," replied the King of Vorgossos, one of his gleaming eyes jabbing at my face like an accusation. "You will be paid for your trouble. You may depart on the morrow."

I wasn't finished. "If the Prince Aranata is coming here, let me remain!" I held one hand extended, palm up in entreaty. "Let me speak to him. In the name of Mother Earth, Lord Sagara, in the name of our common humanity."

"Humanity!" the Undying shouted, and with horror I perceived he spoke the word with his own lips. He reached a hand up under his robe and with a hissing sound pulled the snaking gray hose out from beneath his floating, plated ribs. The other hand he planted upon the arm of his chair—and with a surge like the ocean fleeing a rising colossus—Kharn Sagara stood.

I had not known he could do that.

"What about *our* humanity is common, Hadrian Marlowe?" he said, arms thrown wide so that the ruin of his surgically altered torso was on full display, the black socket of a hose connection sucking light above his heart. Disconnected from his throne, some praxis deep in Kharn's chest breathed for him, ragged and rattling, pulling on the air like a plasma burner. "You bring war to my doorstep and say it is in the name of peace. No." With glacial care, he adjusted the drape of his shimmering golden robe and clasped his hands behind his back.

I shook my head, unwilling to give up so easily. "I came here in good faith. I have not lied to you about my purposes. Whatever you believe about the Empire and its motivations, I am here of my own will and against the wishes of the Imperial Chantry."

When was the last time Kharn Sagara had been *surprised*? Not merely presented with some novelty, but startled? His mouth opened, eyes narrowed—his cloud of eyes swiveled all to look at me. "Against the Chantry, you say? Curiouser and curiouser." From the dark they came, the men with sagging faces. A dozen of Kharn's SOMs in their dun uniforms. No sound of doors opening had heralded their arrival, and I had the awful sense that the creatures had been waiting just outside the circle of light surrounding the Undying's high seat. They all stopped ten paces from us, their presence felt, their threat clear. *"Marerosah oyumn baram Tanaran-se o-namshem ba-okarin ne?"* Kharn asked our Cielcin companion. *You said your name is Tanaran?* When the xenobite said that it was, he continued, "We will have a place set aside for you."

"Lord Sagara, please!" I stood nearly at the first step of the dais by then. "Give me a chance!"

The king in yellow raised one hand—steady as a stone.

As in the city plaza beneath its pale gray dome, the SOMs surrounded us. Valka raised her hands smoothly, demonstrating by the gesture that she meant no threat or resistance.

"Listen to me!" I shouted.

Clammy hands seized me, turning me away. Kharn did not answer me. His face was far away.

CHAPTER 38

THE FACE OF FAILURE

"WILL YOU SMILE IF I say I was wrong?" Valka asked. I had been silent for minutes, almost so silent as Kharn. The remains of the meal we had found waiting for us in the diplomatic suite stood between us, and I was reminded of those many nights or evenings we had spent on Emesh, talking of archaeology and politics and other things. Even my somber attitude was the same.

I pushed my plate away. "About what?"

"About there being no danger here," she said. The memory of the SOMs and their iron hands shone in her eyes. I felt them, too. Chewing on my tongue I nodded, but did not smile. "We came all this way for nothing." She wasn't looking at me. Her bright eyes tracked across the dim gray rooms around us, over the priceless furniture cracked and aging, and over the reproduction of that cheery painting behind me. Only after a Kharn-like pause did those eyes find me again, and she asked, "Are you all right?"

That question took me by surprise. Inhaling sharply, I shook myself. "Yes. Yes, of course," I lied, rubbing my eyes with one hand. "I'm not sure it was for nothing. If that was really the case, we'd have been sent away." It was my turn to take in those crumbling accommodations, the well-maintained wood and leather of the tables and chairs belied by the cracked cement and peeling plaster in walls and ceiling. "I suppose it could be Kharn's having the *Mistral* searched. Perhaps he thinks he'll find the other Cielcin prisoners despite what Tanaran said and solve all his problems in one." As I spoke, I remember I'd kept lifting the end of my fork and dropping it against the edge of the plate so that it made a tinny ringing sound like an offbeat metronome.

"We're not under guard," Valka said. "I could sense those drones of his, and there's nothing at the door." I hoped she was right. Valka took my plate to stop my noise with the fork and placed it and hers on the ever-present trolley. As she turned, I caught her profile in the light of a glass-shaded lamp. Regal as any queen was she, as the image of the Empress Titania Augusta which still adorns the odd hurasam one finds. Not for the first time, I thought a man might dash himself to pieces against her as a ship is thrown against rocks. The moment did not last, for it is the nature of black moods to leap from one tragedy to the next, and seeing Valka again in that light brought Jinan's anima howling within.

I looked away.

"I hope you're right," I said, seeing in my mind's eye a platoon of Kharn's undead troopers cutting through doors and turning over beds in the *Mistral*. "Otavia would fight if he tried to take the ship. She'd think we were dead." My head fell into my hands, combed fingers violently through my hair. "I wish we could get a message to them. Tell them to stand down, or . . . you can't reach them with your . . ." I pointed at the spot on the back of my own head where Valka's neural lace had its external contact.

The Tavrosi woman gave me a tight smile, lips curled into an amused V. "You can say 'implant,' Hadrian." She shook her head, muttered, *"Anaryoch."* *Barbarian,* she called me, but there was no malice in the word. "But no, even if I could through all the rock above us, 'tis behind layers of ice, our ship."

"Ice?"

"Network defenses," she said, imitating the gesture I had made in pointing at her implant. "When I was up there to get Tanaran, Durand said they'd had no luck trying to get the ship's datasphere working again. There's the quantum telegraph—that's analog—but it only communicates with your fleet, and I'm not sure about you, but I'm not eager to meet Bassander Lin again."

Chewing my tongue again, I said, "No indeed. And it's no use to us anyway. It's on the ship." We were alone then, alone and at the mercy of the Undying. "Besides, it's Jinan I fear to see most. Not Bassander."

"I had not thought on that," Valka said, betraying by the speed of her words that they were not quite true. She had been looking away from me, I recall, her hands in her lap. Her eyes found my face then, if only for a moment. "Are you really all right?"

Unable to speak past clenched teeth, I forced a weary nod. The look Jinan had given me as she knelt in the *Balmung*'s hangar to fire on me played behind my eyes, superimposed with other images of my captain:

illumined by safety lights in the dark of her cabin; glowing with sweat on the training floor; hair astray as she fussed, bent over her paperwork. All faded, washed out by the anguish of that moment, washed away by her tears.

I realized I had been clenching my fist on the table, the knuckles white. Valka noticed, eyebrows raised, and I spread my palm flat as I looked away. "It's done."

"I know 'tis done. 'Twas not what I asked you."

There was iron in her. Arguing with her was like arguing with a scalpel. "I will be fine, thank you. I made my choice, and she didn't make it with me." I had tried, but Jinan had refused me.

We go on to Vorgossos, you and I.

You should not be joking about these things.

I had not been joking.

Valka finished off the last of her wine in contemplative silence, lips pursed, her chin propped against her tattooed fist. "I don't suppose 'tis time." Her voice was ashen.

"Time to take Otavia up on her offer, do you mean?" I asked, leaning as far back as my chair would allow. "Give up on all this?" I clasped my hands behind my head and broke eye contact, staring at a patch on the wall where the plaster had flaked away in ages past. "I'm sure Sagara wouldn't stop us leaving. We could just walk out now, you know?" I jerked my chin at the door, yet even as I did so I knew I couldn't leave. I was haunted by the sound of Uvanari's screams beneath the cathars' knives, by the black scar on Rustam where a city had once been . . . by the list of all the worlds so similarly scarred.

There was still a chance.

"You could come with me," Valka said, taking her chin off her hands. "I'm no mercenary. Without the Cielcin, this little expedition has little to offer me." She paused, shifting in her seat, and turning her head offered a sly smile, watching me out the corner of her almond eyes. "You could be my assistant."

I snorted. "Your bodyguard."

A shadow fell across her face, cast by Gilliam's shade, and her mocking smile turned to lead. I'd meant the remark to salvage a portion of my dignity, but it had only cut her—and cutting her, myself. I looked away.

Valka stood, and turning paced toward the far wall, where a display case fronted a collection of antique glassware. Without her customary vest and short jacket, Valka seemed small to me, though she was not much shorter than I. Her flared jodhpurs made her torso seem oddly shrunken, as though the smallest weight might bend those narrow shoulders.

How tired she seemed.

"What is Akterumu?" she asked.

Her reflection moved in the glass, eyes on me. Meeting those eyes, I let my hands fall. "Another Quiet ruin?" I suggested. "Tanaran said they 're-covered' Emesh's coordinates from Akterumu. That suggests, well . . . some sort of recovery operation, does it not?"

"I suppose it could be a person," Valka mused, "or a Cielcin colony."

"The Cielcin don't make colonies."

She clasped her hands behind her back. The gleaming spots of her eyes reflected in the cabinet were shuttered. "A ship, then. Or one of their clans?" She was trying to distract herself, I realized, from our current pre-dicament. I wondered if Valka had ever been a prisoner. On Emesh, I had grown so used to the idea of her as a demoniac and a foreign witch—with all the glamor that implied—that it had not occurred to me that her up-bringing among the Demarchists, but for the matter of the Prachar terror-ists, had been a comfortable one. She had not lived in the streets, in fear of the urban prefects, nor fought in Colosso, unable to leave without breach of contract, knowing that but for an act of God you would be killed be-fore that contract was up. She had not taken up arms as a mercenary, had not been Whent's prisoner on Pharos, as had I.

Was it possible that Valka, herself carved of adamant and sardonyx, was afraid?

"Are you all right?" I asked, not rising from my seat.

Valka jerked as if I'd startled her, but did not turn and face me. "Yes, yes, I'm fine. 'Tis you I'm worried about." I could see her reflection watching me. "You've given so much to this peace of yours . . . and it hasn't gone like you thought."

"I'll be all right," I said, meeting those reflected eyes. We both held our silence, both comfortable in our lies. Still faintly I could detect the crushed-flower smell of Naia's perfume, was glad that Valka could not—or could not place it. I feared to see judgment in those golden eyes, however unwar-ranted. Women are ever the judges of men, our jury and, though their hands seldom grasp the knife, our executioners. I think now that a large, quiet part of my motivations for seeking out peace and parley with the Cielcin came from my youthful desire—in the court of Balian Mataro and at Calagah before it—to impress Valka. In our earliest meetings she had thought me a butcher, then merely a cad. She was a Demarchist, and her dislike of me was motivated by a dislike of all hierarchs, and of hierarchy itself. She, who claimed to resent all class and privilege, resented me for mine. Her prejudice against me, her judgment, had in part shown me my own prejudices, my own failings. I, unwilling and unable to apologize for being what I was, sought to prove that she had not understood me.

That I was more. So I *became* more.

True, I had wanted peace as well, but only in that abstract sense in which most people want peace. I had loved the thought of the Cielcin because they were alien, exotic, strange. I had thought these my reasons for descending into Calagah, for offering my services to Sir Olorin Milta and to Bassander Lin that night Uvanari, Tanaran, and their people crashed on Emesh. Now I wonder if Valka had not given those desires a gravity and a goal.

Perhaps that was why it hurt so much, to hear her speak of surrender. I did not want to go. Did not want to give up. Or perhaps it was the faces burning in my memory, Uvanari's and the others'. Or perhaps, as I had always claimed, it was because I believed it only the right thing to do, as if I—a boy of thirty-five—had any notion what *right* was or how it might be achieved.

"Did you ever learn just what it is they do here?" Valka asked, changing the subject. She turned at last, leaning up against the cabinet, hands resting on a little lip that separated the glassed-in portion from its base. "Or how they do it, I mean?"

I could feel Song and the crowd of nobiles milling about us, smoky forms haunting the gloomy airs. I fancied I saw the Baroness Harfleur of Varadeto, the black-skinned Lady Catherine, vanish as into a vat of ink. In my mind, she emerged again thin and straight, clean-limbed and smiling with all the flush of youth. Baron Song followed, his white hair turned to black.

"Not exactly," I confessed, "but I know he grows children—new bodies—for his clients. How he transfers their minds I've no idea. Some praxis like yours I'd imagine."

To my relief, a look of horror crossed the Tavrosi woman's face, and she breathed, "Children . . ." If she took offense at my linking Kharn's practices to herself, she gave no sign.

"I was kept in a vestibule with the rest of Sagara's clients. Lords and ladies of the Imperium, rich merchants, Mandari. That ilk. They spoke of being taken below."

"Below?" Valka asked. Her eyes drifted far away in thought. "Those buildings Tanaran and I saw? Below the tram?"

I could only shrug. "It's possible. I couldn't see them." I shifted in my seat. "How could you?"

Valka's knowing smile and the spark of it returned, and she crossed her arms, fingers tracing the contours of her clan tattoo above the left elbow. That smile sharpened, and she said, "A girl has her ways."

I made a small, unimpressed sound with my nose and flashed my teeth. "They're machine, aren't they? They can see in the dark."

"And other things," Valka said. "Does that frighten you?" The way she said it, each syllable a sunburst in her bright and airy voice, cold and sharp as winter ice . . . I remembered why Mataro's courtiers called her a witch.

"No," I said. "You don't frighten me. You're the only thing here that doesn't frighten me." I noticed then that she had neither confirmed her eyes machine nor denied, and I marveled that if they were such—a construct of metal, perhaps, or of crystal set in porcelain—that none on Emesh had discovered it. But then, the neural lace which haunted the gray matter of her brain had itself gone undetected.

Valka's smile faltered only a bit, softened. Crossing her arms, she said, "Do you think that's how he's lived so long? Kharn Sagara, I mean."

To be honest, I hadn't even considered it, though it seemed right the moment she'd spoken the words. I pictured serial lives, each running back like the links in a chain anchored to the boy of legend whose mother had died under Exalted guns.

"Possibly," I said. "That and his machines."

"Children . . ." Valka repeated, shaking her head. Strands of dark hair came loose from behind her small ears. A piece of me stirred, longing to return them to their proper place. I fixed my own hair instead, as if some act of sympathetic magic might neaten hers with mine. "That can't be all they do."

"I'm sure it's not," I said. "But whatever else they do here could be had elsewhere. From the Exalted, or on March Station maybe. I can't imagine someone going through all the trouble it takes to get here for something one might have elsewhere." Valka agreed with me, and I added, "I think I found a way down, actually." And I told her about the step-well I had found, and the door where Yume had accosted me. About the Orchid Stair and the strange creature there.

Valka massaged her jaw, eyes lost amid the corridors of thought. Her voice, when it came, sounded just as remote. "You think it goes down to the sea?"

"There was a tunnel in the bottom cut into the rock. Not like this." I waved a hand at the concrete box of a room. "I think these tunnels and the domes must have been here originally." As I spoke, I recalled that Ilex thought the dome had been built over a crater, and that the planet's surface ice had built over the dome in ages since. It was not hard to imagine that an early settlement might have used such a crater as a blasting pit for departing rockets, or else sheltered from whatever winds there were as scoured the surface. "I think Kharn added his pyramid and some of the rest. They don't feel like they belong."

"You don't think he built it all?"

"You've heard the stories." She made a small noise of assent, and pressing on, I said, "I suppose the Exalted built it. Back when the Empire was young. Before Jadd. Before Tavros. Before everything." I could not conceive of so remote a time. Kharn had been born mere centuries after the Foundation War, after the Advent and the Assumption of Earth. It had been a time not unlike the myths my mother told, for the past is to us little different than a story, and the great figures of ages past are little different than the heroes in storybooks. Being in that place, speaking with Sagara . . . it was as if Cid Arthur himself had greeted me in that throne room. Almost I might have expected the Sword of Mars plunged into a stone at the bottom of the Orchid Stair.

Those who say stories are only stories are only fools.

"Do you think the stories are true?" Valka asked, "That he built this place with the help of a Mericanii artificial intelligence?"

"A daimon?" I said, feeling a twinge of the old fear that we were being observed—whatever Yume's assurances and Valka's insistence that we were alone. "Anything's possible. And it would explain . . ."

Valka interrupted me. "Explain the override on the ship after we left the *Enigma*." She traced her lower lip with one finger. "And why they can't get control of their systems." The doctor was pacing back and forth now, moving along the end of the room nearest the door, hands behind her back. "You're making that face again."

"What face?" I said, turning my expression studiously blank.

"The face you make when you've had an idea any normal human being would discard out of hand." She placed her hands on the back of the winged armchair and leaned over to look at me. When I still said nothing, she said, "What?"

I raised my eyebrows, "What does a face like that look like?" The doctor pursed her lips but did not reply. Struggling to keep my expression studiously blank, I said, "Supposing it were some type of daimon holding the *Mistral* in place. Couldn't we use it to access Sagara's records, free the *Mistral* from lockdown, find Tanaran, and escape?"

"How do you propose to do that?" Valka asked. "You don't know a thing about where you're going, or what you're looking for, or how to use an AI."

I spread my hands, shrugged. "I have you."

"Aren't we presumptuous?" Valka's smirk was audible, was almost tangible. I'd been looking at my hands and at the space on the tabletop between them, as if I expected to see some blueprint in the scratches and the grain of that wooden tabletop. I thought of the oracles I have seen in bazaars across the Empire, old women and toothless ones claiming to see the future in the lines of the palm of one's hand.

Meditating on that, I closed my own hands, erasing such lines from sight. Drumming the table, I toyed a moment with the thought of kidnapping Yume. The golem would have much of the knowledge we needed, but I knew that the moment we attacked Kharn's prized android, the Undying would know what we'd done. Assuming what the machine had said was true about the installation's security cams, we stood a chance of making it below—assuming below was where we wanted to be. I dismissed the idea, reminding myself that Valka hadn't even seen the creature in the datasphere.

"It's only presumptuous if you say no," I said, then, "Are you? Saying no?"

"No."

CHAPTER 39

THE LAST STORY

THERE CAME A TIME when we could wait no longer. Three days had passed, with nothing of note to mark them save that Valka accompanied me on my wanderings through storied galleries and along the packed exhibit chambers. Yume had declined to speak to us of all but the most cursory things, and so we had taken to exploring the labyrinth instead. Perhaps I'd hoped to find Tanaran in among the collection, wandering itself as we were permitted to do. Thrice I saw one of Kharn's roving eyes gleaming in the gloom. Only once did it stop as I called out to it, and it did not stay to hear my words.

Wet air blew against our faces as the door to the Orchid Stair opened. The eponymous flowers hung from tree branches and the Nipponese-style arches that stood along the winding path down to the level of the gate. The artificial lighting was more umber now than golden, though whether it simulated sunset or sunrise I couldn't say. Cicadas screamed in the false gloaming, and the nightingale sang.

"'Tis beautiful!" Valka breathed, pushing into the dim and fading light. I noticed lanterns hanging on the *torii* arches starting to glow, and despite the weight of where we were and the slender thread by which we held on, I smiled. Joy is rare, a thing always of the now, existing without regard for time past or time future, and without depending on them. Despite the long road and its troubles—despite the horrors that lay ahead—I have never forgotten her smile then or the sound of her voice. It was . . . a perfect moment, cut as crystal from the cloth of time. I was only an observer, and so felt I should be elsewhere, as if I were intruding like a storm cloud on midsummer's eve.

The Stair was beautiful, and the descent was beautiful—as if sunset had transported that stepped grotto from Vorgossos to Faerie, as if the gate on the bottom opened onto Oberon's court and not the deepest circle of hell. How else should it be? Milton's Satan had raised for himself a palace greater and more lovely than any in creation, after all.

Pale lights winked to life amid the branches and hanging flowers, silver and pale gold. They twinkled, drifting like dandelion pods on the air. As the bloody sunlight dimmed, powering down, it was as if the stars themselves had passed through thousands of feet of stone to roost in the air of that cavern.

Yet ahead of me, Valka stopped. "What are they?" she asked, incredulous.

I knew. I heard stories about them time enough from Cat.

"Phasma vigrandi," I said, "the fairy-lights of Luin."

"Are they really?" Valka's eyes were wide as moons as she turned in place, drinking in the impossibly lovely sight. "I've never seen them!"

"Neither have I," I admitted. They seemed less to fly than to float, blown like embers or snowflakes. Many settled against the trunks of trees, or onto the high grass and bright flowers like a phosphorescent dew. "I had a . . . friend, once upon a time, who always wanted to see them." I reached out a hand—hoping that one might settle on it like butterflies in a lepidopterarium. They never did. I could not make out their forms, so bright were they and so small that they seemed composed of light alone.

Tell me a story, would you? One last time.

I could almost hear Cat's voice, her words small and sick-shrunken even as herself.

I'd told her the story of Kharn Sagara at the end. Our last story. I had told her how Kharn Sagara had avenged his mother's death and the death of his people. How he had turned the Exalted against themselves and made himself their lord. They said he had conquered a daimon and made it his thrall. I had not believed it.

Sometimes I think that Edouard was right, that there is a God, and that he mocks me. Why else would Cat's fairies mark the road to that last and dreadful gate? And why would the road to its door run through that last story I had shared with her?

Rest easy, Cat. And find peace on Earth.

Beautiful as the moment was, it could not last. We grew accustomed to the sight of the fairy lights as we descended the rough stair, mindful of the wooden ema hanging from the branches and from the torii. I could not read the painted letters, nor divine their purpose. Where before I had been unmoved by the beauty of that garden, now I understood—understood that every temple, sanctum, and palace hall was an imitation done in life-less stone of the living world. That pillars were only the poorest imitation of trees and the ribbed vaults of arches and galleries nothing next to the canopies that hung overhead.

We had come to do a thing, and to see what we could see. Valka was first onto the mosaic at the bottom of the Well, and here she raised a hand. I had been speaking—about what I cannot say—and fell silent as a stone.

"I have something," she said, voice hushed, and lowered all her fingers but one, as if she tested the wind by it.

I have little understanding of machines, and almost none of that net-worked kind with whose operation Valka was so familiar. So when I say that she was a witch to me it is because there was no difference to my perception between the arts she practiced and the incantations spoken by sorceresses in the most antique fables. I have heard it said there is no magic in all Creation. That what passes for magic is—to those initiated in its sacred mystery—only a species of knowledge. In this, Valka's thauma-turgy was a skill little different from my abilities with a sword, only an art or science whose workings were alien to me. So too are the arts of the scholiasts, or the vaunted powers of the Maeskoloi, the genetic wizardry of the High College and the horrors enjoyed by the Exalted. All stand as the swordsman to his quarry: to be conquered by their arts.

I have reason to doubt this belief.

There are mysteries in Creation which do not break down, which defy our capacity. There exist walls beyond whose gates no art or reason can serve, and questions which cannot be answered. Of these, some exist only by our own failures—such as my ignorance of machines—but others, oth-ers only *are*. I know what Valka did was not truly magic, though it seemed as such to me. But next to the things that followed, mysteries in the truest sense, her display of power strikes me as a perfect thing: the image of human authority ordering the chaos of Creation.

In all our time together, I had had little chance to watch Valka work her magic, and though I saw much of it after, it is to that false twilight in the Orchid Stair my mind first goes when I think of her: striding silent across colored tesserae. She never lowered her hand, though her head tilted to one side, as though she was trying to locate each bird singing in the trees on the levels above us. She told me once that navigating a datasphere was like trying to catch water in cupped hands. So much in-formation traded past her, so many points and nodes working at once, that the narrow eye of her attention—widened as it was by her neural lace and trained to handle such things—strained to apprehend them.

"You said the android turned you away last you were here?" she asked.

I walked around her, hands at my sides, until I stood between her and the heavy door at the end of the rough tunnel. Her eyes were closed, and deep creases traced the shape of her struggle on her face.

"You're sure you want to do this?" she asked, cracking one eye.

"Do you have a better idea?"

"Several," she said, but the grin that stole over her serious face was like a ray of sunlight in the dark of night.

The lights in the hall before us flickered and went out. My hand went to my sword where it hung familiar against my belt, ready on the electromagnetic clasp that held it in place. I turned, keeping myself between Valka and the darkness where the graven door had been, my off-hand ready on the catch that would activate my Royse shield. "What's happening?" I asked.

"Ssh!" Valka hissed. A wet wind sighed down the hall, seeming to carry the shadows with it as it sighed about the bottom of the Well. "That's the door!"

Something clattered against the mosaic tiles at my feet, and it was only my long combat experience that kept me still. It was one of Kharn's eyes, a little silverfish no longer than the blade of my hand. I didn't hesitate, and crushed it beneath my heel. Red lights slammed on along the floor of the tunnel, and turning to Valka, I asked, "Does he know?"

She was silent a long moment, face drawn down like a book slammed shut. Presently it opened, and she pulled a face. "I don't think so. The door was on a closed system. Isolated. 'Twasn't even hard."

"And the eye?"

"The what?"

I spurned the thing with my toe.

Horror and confusion warred across her marble face. Confusion won. In a voice dry as old parchment, she said, "'Twas not I." Gold eyes found mine. For an instant, neither of us moved. Something else had interfered, had knocked out Kharn's eye. Not Kharn himself, surely.

After a disquiet moment, I said, "We should go." And waiting for her to fall in beside me, hurried down the red-lit hall toward the burgeoning dark.

CHAPTER 40

THE GARDEN OF EVERYTHING

THE ROOM BEYOND WAS all of natural stone, pale in the dimness, lit only sparingly by fixtures in among the stalactites which like unfeeling fingers hung from the ceiling. It was as though—having pierced all the strange layers of that world—Vorgossos at last gave up pretense and became only another part of Creation. Ordinary.

Valka and I hurried along a creaking metal catwalk that stood inches above the wan stone floor with its shallow pools. Eyeless fish circled in the waters beneath us, small as my smallest finger, perhaps oblivious, perhaps marking us by our tread, and marking by the hesitancy in our steps that we were not Kharn Sagara, but intruders in the deepest heart of his palace. At the end of the catwalk and down a broad stair which passed between graven stalagmites, there was another gateway. Not a door, but a natural fissure, higher than it was wide and rippling, so that none might pass straight through it, nor any ray of light. I became terribly conscious of the sound of my footfalls, and of the thin sweat on the palm of my sword hand. Some piece of me, the foolish piece that fancied itself a storybook hero, half-expected a serpent—a great dragon—to come spilling from that sticking mouth, and so I went in front of Valka, sword raised but quiet in my hand.

None came.

Kharn's single weeping eye lay carved above that pointed entryway, not finely but with a clumsy hand, its lines long faded by the running of water whose droplets soaked the lining of that passageway, glittering with the faint glow that emanated from within. Behind me, I felt Valka hesitate and held out my hand.

She did not take it, and I covered my embarrassment by turning it into a gesture that said, "Stay back."

Alone and mindful of the slick floor, I pressed forward, first left—sinister, to use the fencing word—and then right along the passage. Left again. Not twenty paces in I found the ending, and emerged into a dream.

I stood upon the margin of an unpastured meadow, the grass rising almost to my waist, the pale green sea dotted with the white blooms of snowdrops and here and there the yellow sunstars which bloom on a hundred million worlds. A river—belike the very one that flowed through the City of Vorgossos high above—entered by a sluice gate high in the stony wall and flowed, through many windings, beyond the shadow of the next rise. We might have stood upon the surface of any of a billion worlds, but for the roof of white stone above our heads and the unmoving air.

"What is this place?" Valka had appeared at my shoulder, holding her plasma repeater against one thigh.

"I'm not sure," I said, and bit my lip. "I expected—"

"—some kind of laboratory," Valka said, finishing my thought. "As did I."

It was twilight in the glade, as in the Orchid Stair. It made me wonder why the cave chamber had been made to separate them. If there were birds in that glade I heard none, only the torrential fall of water from the sluiceway. All was still.

Valka ran her hand through the tall grass, feeling the stalks with her fingertips. "Why would you lock this away?"

One tree stood taller than all the others, perched as it was on a rise at the end of a beaten path between the grasses. I could sense . . . something. A sense of quiet unease settled in my bowels as I moved toward it, cousin to the cold feeling of eyes on the back of my neck with which I was so familiar. Kharn had spoken of trees when I'd first met him. Of the Trees of Life and Knowledge that stood planted in the deepest corner of the human soul. Almost I imagined it was toward one of those trees I walked, sword in hand, or the Merlin Tree at whose bole Cid Arthur found enlightenment. Beneath the shadow of its branches was a great slab of rough stone, nearly flat and just large enough that an ascetic might sit cross-legged upon it.

Beside it, on a wooden tray, was an antique tea service of plain white china—the type any peasant family in the Imperium might own—and two cups to match its plainness. Beside it was a Druaja board—its pieces neatly stowed—and a pair of long sticks, their twigs peeled off. I stood there a long while, listening. Almost I thought I heard the whispering of invisible voices in among the branches, as if the tree itself were speaking, and the hairs on my arms stood on end, even beneath my tunic and coat. Though there was no breeze, I fancied the wooden prayer cards painted and hung there rattled like the tongues of vipers.

"What is it?" Valka asked, still a ways behind me.

I went to one knee, touched the bowl of the teapot. "Someone was just here."

"I'm sorry?"

Hand still on the teapot, I said, "It's warm."

I cannot say exactly what the nature of the sound I'd heard was. An indrawn breath? A scuffling? A misplaced stone tumbling among the roots of the great tree? Perhaps it was only a pressure on the mind, a relic of those days in the streets of Borosevo when it paid to know when one was not alone. Still, I jerked my head around, staring across yards of rooty ground, drinking sight and sound for the source of what disturbed me.

I fancied I saw two eyes, bright as diadems, peering at me from behind the tree. "Hey!" I sprang to my feet, coat tail nearly upsetting the white teapot. The eyes vanished. "Hey!" Ashamed as I am to admit it, I conjured my sword. Highmatter blue as moonlight shone in my hand, quillions flowing like sun dogs from the stuff of the blade. Feeding off my energy, Valka raised her gun and followed. I skidded round the tree. "Hey!"

There was only a rustling of grass, as if some small creature was darting away among the blades.

"What was it?" Valka asked, hurrying up beside me.

"I'm not sure!" I replied, and hurried off. I let my sword melt away and dashed after it, Valka in tow. Yume had said the Garden was for the clone children, but I couldn't be certain. Whatever it was was quick, and twice I tarried to find my bearings as we crested a low rise. How Valka had not seen it with her augmented vision I never knew, but we followed all the same. We stumbled down a rocky slope, kicking up black loam as we stumbled down to the bank of the river.

Valka swore in Panthai and leaned against me to catch her breath. A soldier she may have been once, but that was long ago, and the run had winded her.

"I lost it!" I said, pointing nowhere in particular with the hilt of Olorin's sword. Valka's breath was hard in my ear, and at once I was all too pleasantly aware of the weight of her against me. Above us on the opposite bank, a metal bulkhead loomed beneath the shadow of the white stone of the cave chamber. By the false and shrinking twilight, it looked red as old

blood. Gone to black. I heard the grind and pneumatic hiss of a door cycling, and saw a light stretch across the roof of the world.

"This way!" I hurried down into the river, which was broad there and
shallow, feet splashing in the slow current.

"What are you on about?" Valka demanded, splashing after me.

"There was someone there!" I said, scrambling up the rocky scree toward the black wall of the cave. Valka was a little behind, and I seized the
moment to shake the stray droplets loose of my hydrophobic clothing. I
reached down to help her up the rise, but she swatted my hand away, forcing me to catch her as she stumbled on a loose stone. "I didn't get a good
look at him."

"Him?" Valka asked.

I shrugged. "Whoever it was."

We had arrived on a narrow platform that ran parallel to the wall of
the cavern above the bend of the river. Off to our left, the waters vanished
around another bend, moving toward the far wall where I guessed another
sluice gate fed the river further down on its descent toward the subterranean sea. Little runner lights glowed at intervals along the edge of the
platform, each no larger than a gold hurasam. The door I'd expected to
find was to our left, a heavy, hexagonal portal that would not have looked
out of place on a mining ship.

"You're sure someone was there?" Valka asked. "I didn't see . . ."

"Two teacups," I said, holding up the matching number of fingers.
"Still warm." I tried the door panel. "It's locked."

"Give it here." The doctor brushed me aside, fingers working over the
glass panel to the right of the door. She muttered to herself in Nordei,
such that I could not make out the words. *"Ramphas geit!"* she swore. "I
can't! 'Tis locked."

No sooner had the words escaped her lips than the control panel cycled
blue. The door ground open, bifurcating down the middle. "Let me guess,"
I said coolly, trying to master the beating of my mutinous heart. "That
wasn't you?"

"'Twas not I."

I shifted Olorin's sword to the ready. "Stay back."

The faint whine of plasma coils charging in Valka's gun sounded over
my shoulder. "I'll cover you."

The hall beyond was hexagonal, like the door, interrupted at intervals
by pillars which divided the walls into niches. My boot heels clacked on

the metal floor, the sound rebounding off the hard walls so that Valka and I sounded like a whole century of troops. Doors opened to either side, and through them I could see drab metal chambers with banks or machinery I could not name.

"'Tis more like what I expected," Valka said.

We entered a wide, high-ceilinged chamber, an arcade supported by several glass pillars.

No, I realized, *not pillars.*

Enclosures.

The largest of these stood three meters to a side, the smaller ones— nearer the edges of the room—were no more than a cubit in diameter. In some, birds bright as jewels flitted among branches with bark like burnished gold. In others, fish with scales of nameless hues chased one another in clear water or between the trailing fronds of kelp-like plants. The larger enclosures—still small by the standards of most of the menageries I have known—held larger creatures: grasping monkeys, lazing cats, and creatures stranger still. A pair of furry creatures with eight radial arms tumbled like acrobats down a slope of artfully arranged stone, and opposite them a trio of creatures like the ancient nautilus floated in an orange gas, their chitinous shells covering what seemed little more than a balloon. Another of the great glass ampules seemed to hold nothing but shadows, but the bronze plaque claimed it held the dreaded *tokolosh,* the *umbra comedens,* the animalcule that could strip flesh from bones faster than any piranha out of mythic Amazonia.

"I take it back," Valka said, "'tis not what I expected after all."

"It's a zoo," I said, running my hand over one of the bronze species plaques.

Valka's face fell. "These pens are too small."

"Not this one," I said, lingering by the set of magnifying lenses that stood beside a display of tardigrades in what appeared otherwise empty water. We proceeded past baroque ironwork and deeper into the installation, along another hall and past larger enclosures—cells really—where stalked panthers and a beast like a human hand large as a mastiff. Terranic and extraterranic lifeforms stood in discrete chambers, or else mingled in biomes like surrealist paintings, green leaves and grasses interspersed with colors unknown to Mother Earth.

We saw no one, not even Kharn's hovering eyes. But for the sounds of the various creatures and the distant thrum of great engines deep beneath the world, the place was silent. I strained to hear the sound of retreating feet or a door opening—any sign that the eyes I'd seen beneath the tree were real.

Chamber after chamber passed in this fashion, both of us expecting some trick or attack at any moment. We passed through Kharn's menagerie and out under a dome like the smaller cousin of the dome of the City far above. Crushed stone, white and black and brushed into patterns, formed a mandala beneath that dome. Pale statues stood in concentric rings about and throughout the design, arms raised in imprecation, in supplication, toward the black finger of a broken obelisk in the center of the dome. It was another garden, a rock garden such as the scholiasts and their Zen precursors were fond of.

"This place doesn't make any sense," Valka said. "A menagerie? Gardens? Why lock all that away? Why not have them in the City for the other people here?" She had holstered her sidearm, and approached the nearest of the statues in the outermost ring. High above, a wind from ventilation shafts unseen stirred the trailing beards of moss that hung like temple banners from the crumbling masonry.

"Still not much of a laboratory."

Valka screamed and leaped away from the statue. Acting on reflex, I went to her side. "What is it?"

"It moved!" Her gun was in her hand again, but was not pointed at the marble image. It was a woman, naked but for some gauzy shawl that failed to hide her high breasts. Time and water had eaten at her, and great chunks were absent in an arm and one smooth thigh. Whole pieces of the shawl, too. I cannot say if she had moved, only that there were cracks along the delicate line of her neck. Something red as the ink by which I record this welled there, thicker than blood and brighter, and at once I was reminded less of stone and more of the flesh of some ghoulish mushroom.

"You're sure?" I asked, and prodded the thing's shoulder. It didn't feel like stone, felt spongy, soft. A red welt rose on her shoulder where I'd touched her. Valka did not answer me, but I could feel the reproach in her eyes, though I did not turn to see it. "You don't think these were people, do you?"

"I have no idea," Valka said. "Let's get out of here. We need to find Tanaran and free the lock on the *Mistral*. There's no time."

Shaking myself, I looked round, noticing for the first time that several doors opened along the circumference of the wall. I could not help but feel that we were not in any real place at all, but lost amid some kind of dream, or that we wandered Kharn's memories, or some other construct of his imagination. The Garden seemed jumbled together, arranged without any grand architectural plan, as if each room were made to some secret scheme and separate from each of the others, each door opening onto a random scene in a new play. The next we opened revealed a water garden, argent nenuphars and lotuses pink as maidens floating in pools black as ink; butterflies haunting still airs. Behind the next door a single finger of rock overlooked a pen where an azhdarch feasted on the fresh corpse of a lion.

At last we found a door that opened onto another hall. Overhead lights cycled on at our approach, and our feet disturbed little clouds of dust, as if no one had been in that place for a very long time. Doors stood open to either side, revealing chambers with rows of old cots bolted to the floor. I was reminded, with an acute loss and longing I had not expected—of the Colosso hypogeum on Emesh, where first I'd met Switch and Pallino and the others.

"It's a dormitory," I said, running a hand over a peeling decal stuck to the wall beside one metal door frame. Inside was a single bed, long since bare, with woodcuts black with time hanging indiscernible on the walls.

"What is this place exactly?"

The handwriting on the decal was badly faded and written in Nipponese. I could not read it, though I thought the characters looked disjointed, child-like. "Yume told me the gardens were for the children."

"The children?" Valka shifted to peer over my shoulder. I could sense her frown, imagine the furrow forming between her sharp brows. "Ichirou."

"I'm sorry?"

"That's what it says." She gestured at the sign. "'Tis a name."

I peeled off and went as far as the next door. The room beyond was identical, save for the wooden toy horse lying on its side on the floor. Unbidden, my fingers tightened about the hilt of my sword. "They must have kept the children here once. The ones meant for Sagara's clients."

"But where are they now?"

"No idea."

"I don't think we're in the right place, Hadrian," Valka said.

I didn't hear her. I felt . . . something. Even still I cannot fully describe it. It was as though I had heard a loud noise in a distant room, and yet I was certain that all was quiet but for the still-beating of my heart—so close to my mouth—and the soft rustle of Valka moving. And yet like a noise it hurt me, and wrenched my attention round.

"What is it?" Valka asked, but I put a finger to my lips. Undeterred, the doctor hissed, "Hadrian, what is it?" For she knew that mine were the ears of a palatine, and sharper than hers. Witch she may have been, but whatever Tavrosi praxis she possessed her ears were only human. Yet it was no sound I'd heard, but a sensation that gripped me as though I stood on a tramway and—frozen—knew the train was coming. Every muscle in me seized in expectation of some attack that never came. What came was stranger.

Hadrian . . .

My eyes went wide, and I must have spoken, for Valka said, "What?" It was not possible. I was mad, or else dreaming again.

You.
You.
You are close now.

"Hadrian!" Valka seized me above one elbow. "What the hell is going on?"

"You don't hear it?" I lurched forward and staggering fell to one knee. "It can't be . . ."

This is not the way.

Come . . .
Come!

Her fingers bit into the flesh of my arm, and even through the fabric of my tunic and coat I winced. "Can't be what, Marlowe?" She tried to help me up to no avail.

"The voice from my dreams," I said, and struggled to stand myself.

"Your what?" I could hear the edge come back into her tone, the old and unforgiving skepticism. The intolerance. I half-expected her to drop me.

"Not important . . ."

Listen!

I saw instead, saw a blur and tangle of corridors—as if my eyes had leaped from their sockets and were pulled along, through high chambers and dark and down an ancient and rattling lift to a stony shore and the darkness out of my dreams.

As suddenly as it had begun, it ended. I reeled, and at last fell over.

Valka shook me. "Open your eyes." I did. When I did not immediately speak, she shook me again. "If you don't tell me what's going on, I swear by all my ancestors I will slap you."

My face went hard as stone, and I turned my head to look at her. "You wouldn't believe me if I told you."

"Try me."

I stood up before she could follow through on her threat, leaning against the wall. The voice had fled, leaving only images. I shuddered, feeling violated almost so much as I had by Naia the night Kharn had brought her to my chambers. There was a thought in me that was not my own. I did not know what to think or to believe. I did not think about it at all, because I knew what I must do.

I tried her, saying, "I've been having dreams. Twice since we arrived here. Once on the way down from orbit and then again after we met Kharn. I did not think much of them—I often have strange dreams, but . . ." I trailed off, unable to look Valka in the face and to see the reflection there of how insane I sounded. "There is a voice calling out to me, asking me to listen. It's dark . . ." I felt the pressure of her eyes, her judgment, recalling the way she'd scorned me at Calagah when I told her of my vision. "Don't look at me like that."

"Like what?"

"Like I'm mad."

"You're not even looking at me."

"I don't have to," I said, a touch too coldly. Echoing the voice I had heard, I said, "Listen. Let me prove it to you. That I'm not mad." I clicked my sword back into its holster at my hip and straightened the wide lapels of my coat. "I know where to go."

CHAPTER 41

THE TREE OF LIFE

THE DOOR WAS RIGHT where the voice had shown me. Like the others in that strange Garden, it was hexagonal, as though it were the portal of some antique starship. Unlike the door by the lonely tree where I had seen . . . whatever I had seen . . . it opened without protest. Still I paused, as I pause in writing this. At many times in our lives we find ourselves in a strange place, a place where we are certain we have never been, and yet know every detail, every line and facet, as if some eidolon bridged time to set the stage—as indeed one had. You must think it strange how little I questioned my vision, but the mystic who has been devoured by flame and has lain with deathless women beneath the waves knows that what he experienced is real, though every scholiast name him mad. I had been granted a vision, and though I knew not whether its source was wicked or divine I could not but trust in it, for through each door and around each corner was only what I expected to find. With each passing chamber I *believed*.

"'Tis the place," Valka said, peering through a window in the hall that opened on a medical examination room.

"Not yet," I replied, conscious of the need for haste. "Further on and down." I could almost hear her glare at me as I brushed past and added, "Trust me."

The hall emptied into a wide space supported by square pillars. We had only to cross through it to another massive door and to take a lift carriage down to the deepest levels. There, I knew—and knew with the conviction of the most devoted vate—we would find . . . what? Tanaran? Kharn's computer? I have heard it said that such machines required cold to operate, and it had been very cold in the dark on the tram that led to Kharn's throne room.

"Hadrian."

There was something in Valka's voice that made me turn. She stood pale in the yellow light, mouth half-open, half-pointing at the ceiling. I had been so intent on moving forward—and I had seen the room already—that its strangeness and its horror escaped my notice at first. My eyes followed Valka, and found what I knew I must find. Glass bell jars like fruit the size of sarcophagi hung from ribbed arches which grew from the pillars like the branches of unholy trees, so that we stood in another sort of garden.

"Are those . . . ?" Valka's voice broke.

"Children," I finished, and knew as I spoke that it was so. Each hung suspended in pinkish fluid, and from the smallest fetus to those ephebes in the full flower of their youth each was connected to hoses and electrodes and monitored by devices I could not name. They were none of them alike: male and female, pale and swart and bronze. Raven-haired and golden or with hair so red as flame. Each of them was different, and yet I knew. "They're all *him*." I shivered, for the duplication of the flesh was an Abomination. One of the Twelve, and a great sin.

"Sagara?" That crease appeared again between Valka's brows. "What makes you say that?"

I didn't answer at once, so lost was I in thoughts wandering among the branchings above my head. "Just a feeling." But I knew I was right. If the legends were real—and the legends *were* real—then Kharn Sagara was nearly fifteen thousand years old. How many lifetimes was that? How many generations? How many bodies had he worn? Above us, the body of a girl—she looked no older than twelve—waited to be born. Great needles like the ones I had worn after my mugging in Meidua at the start of my journey burrowed under her skin. Dozens of them. They were knitting muscle, maintaining the soft tissues against the day of its master's needs. She had the same bronze complexion as Kharn himself, the same high cheekbones. Beside her, a boy—very much younger—possessed the germinal form of the Undying's heavy brow and black hair, though his skin was coffee and not bronze at all. I could see shadows, echoes of the man on the throne in the faces of each of the children there, and recalling the flesh merchants at March Station, I shuddered, for it seemed I was not looking at children at all, but at features. Genes. The scattered components of a man played out in disjuncted symphony, the theme of him repeated endlessly and altered so that it seemed lost in the chaos.

"These aren't him," Valka said. "They're his clients."

I knew that she was wrong, but I did not have the stomach for argument. I knew where they kept the clients, a ways back behind us off the room with the obelisk and the bleeding statues. There were the dormitories and other facilities, for the clone children of the likes of Baron Song and the Duke of Milinda were raised as children and not kept waiting like cherries to be picked. I approached the nearest pod, and looking up beheld the face of a pale child—not yet an infant. How small it was! Its eyes were wide, unseeing, strangely gelatinous. Already I could see the black of them, the same black I had seen in the eyes of the demoniac Kharn. Among the ancient Victorians—a people for whom my own constellation was named—it was believed the eye could record the last image it saw, and that an optographer might extract that image and so divine the circumstances of the poor fellow's death. I wondered what sort of image one might find in those eyes which had yet to see anything at all.

It was an absurd thought, made all the more absurd by the mounting sense of pressure I felt to be on our way. Whatever was happening to me—whatever had happened—we were still deep in the palace of the Undying. I turned from my examination of the gestating fetus above me and, gesturing to Valka, made to continue on. No sooner had I done so then I heard it, a low voice singing.

> *Wood and clay will wash away,*
> *wash away, wash away,*
> *Wood and clay will wash away,*
> *my fair lady.*

There was something strange about the words, and it took me a long, long moment to realize that they were sung in Classical English, the ancient language of the scholiasts and the Mericanii. "What is it?" Valka asked. I wasn't sure if she knew the language, and put a finger to my lips before pointing my way across the room—past what looked like a parked industrial lifter the size of a tank.

> *Build it up with bricks and mortar,*
> *bricks and mortar, bricks and mortar,*
> *Build it up with bricks and mortar,*
> *my fair lady.*

"We don't have far to go," I whispered, relying on my vision. "If I'm right, it's just ahead." A good two hundred feet separated us from the exit, and I knew with a conviction I could not explain that I did not want to meet who or whatever was singing that ancient song.

> *Bricks and mortar will not stay,*
> *will not stay, will not stay,*
> *Bricks and mortar will not stay,*
> *my fair lady.*

Even as we moved to clear the floor, a piece of me paused, as if some other Hadrian turned back and frowned beneath the weight of my thoughts. It was a nursery rhyme, I realized. And why not? Grotesque as it was, we were in a nursery.

> *Build it up with iron and steel,*
> *iron and steel, iron and steel,*
> *Build it up with iron and steel,*
> *my fair lady.*

I cannot say why the children's rhyme put such a holy terror in me, but I almost ran—such that it was only my desire to stay by Valka that kept me in my place beside her. We hurried past the parked bit of loading equipment—I noted the massive arm for retrieving the specimen pods from their storage place above our heads.

> *Iron and steel will bend and bow,*
> *bend and bow, bend and bow,*
> *Iron and steel will bend and bow,*
> *my fair lady.*

I froze—I swear—before the next words came. It was as if I were some ill-trained Eudoran actor anticipating his cue, for even as we crossed that ghastly hall I felt again the familiar sensation-of-eyes pressed against the back of my head.

"Oh! What's this then?" The voice—deep as distant thunder—planted hooks deep in my back. "Intruders! Intruders in *my* Garden?"

I turned, thumbs hooked in the belt of my tunic so that each hand hung near to both sword and shield control. As I turned, I shifted my left foot so that I stood at an angle, forcing Valka behind me. If she objected she gave no sign.

There was no one there. The hall was empty but for the sleeping clone-children in their hanging pods and the parked lifter unit.

"Who's there?" I demanded, shifting my hand to my sword.

"I should ask you the same, little man," the voice replied. I felt my chest rattle, so deep was the sound of it. "Assassins, are you? Destroyers?"

To my horror, the lifter moved, and I saw it was no lifter at all. Eight black legs tall as I scuttled, the single massive boom arm rotating like the tail of a manticore I had once seen in the fighting pits on Monmara. Jets of steam issued from its sides as it rose.

I have stood on battlefields on half a hundred worlds, marched with our legions and beneath the tramping feet of their colossi. Those terrible engines, tall as houses, as hills marching into battle ahead of our hosts, seemed smaller to me than that creature of black steel, though they walked ten yards to a stride. Perhaps those giants of war were too large to be believed by some primitive mechanism of my being, or perhaps it was only that it seemed so large in that close chamber.

"You've come for the children!" The voice roared. Two arms extruded from the underside of the thorax—longer than any man's—and lanced toward me. I lunged to one side, shouting for Valka to get out of the way. I did not thumb my shield, seeing no weapons its curtain might defend against. The thing's hands closed on empty air, and I dove behind one of the columns that supported the unholy trees above our heads. I let my heavy coat slip from my shoulders, and took a moment to collect myself.

A memory forced itself on me, and I might have laughed. How often had I waited, just like so, behind a pillar in the Colosso ring on Emesh? How many dozen times?

"They're fast," the creature said, eight huge feet grinding on the polycarbide floor. "But rats are always fast."

It knew where I was, and so there was no foolishness in shouting, "We only want to leave this place."

"Leave it?" the thing repeated. "Leave it?" The huge boom arm came clattering around the pillar on my right. I dove left, skidding on the floor and twisting so that the machine would have to retract its arm before it could cross the floor to get to me. "You'll *leave* by the rendering vats, little man. The children need to feed."

Pivoting so that I stood facing the creature, I said, "Oh, I don't think so." In a single motion I drew Olorin's sword, the hilt snapping clear from its magnetic clasp even as I extended the blade down and out to my side. Blue crystal flowed like water, shone like starlight on snow. Where was Valka?

The Exalted—for Exalted he must be—lurched toward me. It moved slowly, great legs almost punching the floor. I—who had faced azhdarchs and vampyromorphs in the Borosevo Colosso—stood resolute. The boom arm slammed down, and I checked forward so that its claws closed on air. I lunged with my blade, its point aimed at a protuberant spot on the beast's black armor.

It bounced off.

The highmatter sword *bounced off.*

It was possible. I knew it was possible. Sharp as it was, highmatter could not sever atomic bonds, and the molecules in adamant and nanocarbon were so long and interwoven that I could not cut between them. I snarled, and knowing I could not go back, went forward, darting under and out between two of the Exalted's massive legs. A moment after, too late, the beast dropped its weight, as if it meant to crush me. I struck one leg as I ran past, but the carapace there too was adamant and proof against my blade.

"Hadrian!"

A bolt of plasma—violet as my eyes—flashed past me. I could feel the air boil around me as it passed, see Valka standing legs apart and shoulders back, gun trained on the *thing* behind me.

The Exalted roared, "Fire! In my nursery?" The creature's huge bulk shifted, rubberized peds thudding as it scuttled like an upset crab. I spun round just in time to block one grasping hand on the edge of my sword. Fingers harder than steel and longer than even Tanaran's closed about the highmatter blade. I saw it compress the exotic metal, the way a hand reshapes wet cement. I resisted, but for all my eugenic strength, I was not proof against hydraulics, against servos and pistons. The beast might have lifted me bodily from the floor, but it twisted its wrist, and I twisted with it, and would have fallen and dropped my sword had I not had a sudden flash of insight.

I turned off the blade.

Pale highmatter dissolved to smoke, and the arm hyperextended, revealing a ball-and-socket joint in the elbow between plates in the arm's adamant carapace. Thinking of Sir Olorin, of the precise way he moved and the ease of it, I summoned forth the blade again—highmatter like a ray of moonlight on a night without a star—and clove downward in a vertical sweep that brought the pommel of my sword to my navel. It hit the inside of the creature's forearm and slid along the adamant, slipping as if on glass, until the edge fell against the common material of the elbow joint.

Honest steel.

The arm clattered to the ground, and a jet of steam erupted from a vent on the creature's back. Valka fired again, but the hydrogen plasma only left a smoking patch of darker black against the chimera's skin. The chimera made an angry sound and retracted its damaged arm. A moment later the massive boom arm came sweeping around. It caught me in the side—how it didn't shatter me I'll never know—and I was knocked clean off my feet to skid twenty feet across the open floor.

"Oh, you are fun." The Exalted made a hissing sound, turning its slow bulk one massive leg at a time. "Maybe I won't take you to the rendering vats," it said, advancing. "Maybe the Master will let me keep you. I could use a new *pet*." It had no face I could see; the turret that passed for a head was featureless, an oblate lozenge perched to the fore of its mighty thorax. Yet I knew what expression went with that tone of voice. The leering, the tongue flitting over pointed teeth. I shook myself and tried to rise, pain blossoming beneath my left ribs. Dull, not sharp.

Nothing broken.

"*Khun!*" Valka shouted, slipping into her native Panthai. There was a burst of violet flame as a shot connected with the creature's faceless turret. A full three seconds of irritable silence. Slowly, *slowly,* the Exalted swiveled its head.

"A matched set, is it?" it said, as if to itself. "Two . . . two two two . . . oh, this will be a *joy*." Its one silvery hand flexed obscenely. "Think I'll keep you both. The Master won't mind."

Valka shot it again. The behemoth did not even flinch.

Exhaling jets of steam from valves along its spine—sighing, almost— the Exalted swiveled its attention back to me. "Think I'll carve out your prefrontal cortex, little man. Make an ape of you." It pointed a threatening finger at me. "Turn you both naked in the Garden," and here it rounded on Valka, "see how long you *last*."

My vision went red a moment, and it took every ounce of strength and Gibson's training to calm myself. *Rage is blindness,* I thought.

"Hadrian, get up!"

I got up.

With both hands I held my sword before me like a Nipponese kendoka, raised it like a Cathar at the executioner's block. I expected the thing to charge at me, and recalling the legends I had heard of such unholy machines I expected that when it did it would move faster than my merely human eyes could track. But it advanced slowly, step after precise step, like a spider on a line. "I am so going to enjoy this," it said.

"Hey!" Valka shouted, shooting the Exalted in its head-turret again. Hydrogen plasma cooled from violet to red invisibility, vanishing in the air like mist.

It did not break stride, the long, pincer-like fingers of its one remaining hand flexing as though they ached for something to seize. From the corner of my eye, I saw Valka raise her gun above her head. The Exalted ignored her—and why not? Her handgun had proved itself completely ineffectual. One of the machine's legs slipped out from underneath it, and it stumbled.

"Get out of my head, woman!" It half-turned, and for a moment I feared it would rush at her.

Valka fired.

The Exalted screamed.

Glass melted. Shattered. Fell like rain. A child fell with it, white-limbed and red-haired, as unlike Kharn Sagara as any in the tree above. It smashed on the hard floor, broke like a china doll, like a melon.

The massive crab-demon machine forgot me entirely in that instant, rounded on the Tavrosi sorceress like a wounded bull. Turning, I saw a coldness in Valka's face, as though the blood that ran in her like water were transmuted to nitrogen, and her eyes were like distant stars.

"Destroyers!" the Exalted flailed, trying to right itself as another of its legs flailed. "Murderers and usurpers!" Valka said nothing, but took aim again and fired. Another of the glowing pink bell jars above us shattered, and a girl-child—this one nearly full-grown—fell like a stone. She caught on the tangle of tubes and wires that threaded her flesh, hung by the hair like an abandoned marionette, dripping amniotic fluid to the unfeeling floor.

For a moment—only a moment—I saw Valka standing there unmoved. She was . . . like a statue of Justice Vengeant—of Death herself. She smiled a skull's smile, all teeth. It was a grimace really. And then she was gone, diving away behind the nearest pillar and down the hall, eager to put distance between herself and the black metal behemoth.

She had bought me time and a distraction, and for her mettle and fire I loved her then, as I had not loved her in a long count of years. I did not shout as I charged, my Jaddian sword blazing like cold fire in my fist. The beast was distracted, and did not see me coming. I swept my sword down in a flat arc, the blue-white blade shearing through the other silver arm at the wrist. Infuriated, the Exalted lashed out with that arm, but I turned the blow on the edge of my blade. Ye Gods! The force of it! The bones of my arm rang with the impact, and I dodged forward. This time I sank the point of my blade as deep into the joint at the base of one of the creature's massive arms. I twisted, and with my free hand swung about the leg to escape from beneath the beast before it tried again to crush me.

As I did, the leg flexed outward, skidding on the polished floor as the hip joint began to tear, leaking lubricant the color and consistency of warm milk. Where was Valka? I had lost her in the chaos and in the confusion of the fighting. The hulking machine struggled to turn, its lamed ped impeding its movement. Still, its massive boom arm circled round, whistling as it shocked the very air. I missed it only by the width of a hand, and only because I threw myself flat on the ground, my sword carving a deep notch into the floor.

I heard Valka shout something, but could not stop to reflect. I had the presence of mind to squeeze the twin triggers on my sword to banish the gleaming blade as I rolled away—just in time to avoid the smash of two of the chimera's massive feet. Once I was out of the reach of the boom, I sprang to my feet, sword flashing once more to life, ready for the next attack.

It never came.

The huge beast had curled up its legs once more and crouched—knelt?—like a cataphract in the presence of the Emperor. Valka was still nowhere to be seen.

"Father Calvert, what is the meaning of this?" The voice was clear and cool. A woman's voice, yet touched by the flush of girlhood. "Who are these people?"

"Intruders, dear child," the Exalted said. "They murdered two of your siblings in their sleep. Methinks they mean to kill them all and yourselves."

Footsteps sounded off to my left, and a young woman appeared from among the pillars, leading a child by the hand. Both had black hair, both bronze skin, both with the high cheekbones and almond eyes that marked them as Mandari or Nipponese. I did not lower my sword even as the children approached, stopped within spitting distance of the body of the dead child on the floor. The girl spoke. "Intruders? In Father's Garden?

That is not possible. They would not allow it!" I wondered who she meant, but kept careful watch, half-expecting Valka to appear from the shadows, gun raised.

As she spoke, the little boy looked round, and his eyes widened to see me, though he did not speak. He could not have been more than eight years old. Seeing those eyes I knew it was he I had seen by the tree in the Garden. These two explained the teapot, the two swords and board game. He tugged on his sister's sleeve, and the girl looked round. How she had not seen me standing there bold as brass and armed I cannot say. Her eyes widened, and proud as any princess of the Star Victoria, she thrust out her chin. "Who are you?"

"Hadrian," I said, not lowering my sword. "And who are you to ask for my name?"

The girl drew the young boy closer, placed an arm protectively on his shoulder, and said, "I'm Kharn Sagara."

CHAPTER 42

THE CHILDREN OF SATURN

"NO, YOU'RE NOT," I said, and pointed my blade at the two of them.

"Not what?"

"Not *him.*"

The girl stood proud as any queen. "How did you get into the Garden?"

The boy buried his face in his sister's skirts and would not look at me. The massive chimera—Calvert, was it?—did not move. With a bravery she did not look capable of, the girl moved to stand between the small boy and myself, though I might have felled both with a single stroke of my sword. She wore a Nipponese dress of pale, cornflower blue, which lent the wide red sash cinched about her form the terrifying quality fresh blood has when it appears without warning.

"I ask you again," she said, imperious. "Who are you and how did you get in here?"

"He's a knight, Suzuha," the boy said, voice higher than his sister's. He peered out from around one narrow hip, looking for all the world like he had peering out from behind the great tree. "Aren't you, sir?"

The girl pressed her brother—her clone—back behind herself. Patting his shoulder with one hand, her eyes wandered to the smashed body at her feet, the broken, spindly limbs of that life that would never be. The other dead child yet hung from its wires like a man from a gibbet, amniotic fluid still dripping down its length to the floor.

"I am a soldier of the Empire," I said, not knowing if it was true. It took every ounce of control I had not to look around for Valka, who it seemed had escaped, or else lay in wait, prepared to cover me.

The Exalted spoke, voice considerably softer than it had been while we fought. "He had a witch with him, dear child. A woman. She's the real danger."

"And she has you in her sights, so don't try anything!" Valka's voice rebounded from the pillars of those unnatural trees, seeming to come from all over. The two children looked round, boy cowering, girl iron-jawed and defiant. I could not help but smile.

"You can't be here," the boy said. "*They* wouldn't let anyone in, not without Father . . . does Father know you're here?"

The girl made a soothing sound. "Quiet, Ren." Then she turned hard eyes on me. Black eyes, black as Kharn Sagara's, though there was a spark in her eyes yet unkindled, where Kharn's ageless and undying face might have been graven from stone and etched by sand of the desert until no expression remained. "Speak, soldier! Why are you here?"

"I'm looking for my friend," I said, seeing no reason to lie. "A xenobite of the Cielcin. Have you seen it?"

"A xenobite?"

"*Quiet, Ren!*" Suzuha said, then, "There are no aliens here."

The Exalted's head-turret swiveled between me and the girl. "Let me kill him, child."

"Try it!" Valka shouted. "See how far you get."

Rather than allow tensions to continue escalating, I lowered my sword, allowing the liquid blade to dissolve into a faint mist. "I am sorry about the clones. We hadn't meant for anyone to get hurt. We just want to find our companion and leave this place."

"You're trying to escape," Suzuha said, planting her feet wide apart to better block her young charge. "Father is keeping you here, isn't he?" If she was much hurt or concerned for the lives of Kharn's two other children, she gave no sign. Her face was almost as mask-like as Kharn Sagara's, if less worn.

"No," I said, and thought it true. "But he is keeping my friend, and I can't allow that."

"Allow?" said the Exalted, Calvert. "He says *allow*! Let me kill him, child."

Suzuha waved the giant metal crab to silence with a raised hand. Rather than answer the beast, she looked at me. "Why should I believe you? I watched you fighting. Your woman killed our siblings. You hurt poor Calvert here."

"Only my chassis is harmed, child," the machine said.

The girl gestured again for silence. "And you say you're not here to kill?"

I took a couple steps sideways, circling away from the big Exalted—

though I was well out of the range of its boom arm. I saw Valka then, braced against one of the consoles at the base of one pillar, her firearm trained on the girl, Suzuha. Finally I asked, "You were watching?"

The clone nodded.

"Then you know we crossed the room before your man attacked us," I said, holding the sword behind my back like a baton, as if by obscuring the weapon I could erase it from the minds of the others. Standing thus, I inclined my head toward the lift doors. "We were leaving."

"That way?" Suzuha asked, and she glanced at the Exalted.

"Below?" Ren said, then yelped as his sister stamped on his foot.

"Why?" Suzuha asked. "Do you even know where you are?" I glanced at Valka, but her expression was unreadable. The girl was still talking. "You'll never escape, you know. Father will catch you. Even if you kill us. He will."

Ever more insightful than I, Valka called, "Do you know what he's going to do with you? Your father? What he's going to do *to* you?" She held position by the pillar, unwilling to cede cover with Father Calvert so near at hand. In the dim light, her eyes shone like cat's eyes. "You can escape with us."

"Escape!" the Exalted barked.

Valka shot at it, knowing full well the bolt was useless against its adamant hide.

"Escape with you?" Suzuha repeated.

And Ren said, "Leave . . . Father?"

"We're not leaving Father," the older girl hushed, jostling her brother. "He protects us."

That was a step too far for me, and I almost moved forward, saying, "He'll kill you the moment he needs you. You're spare parts, girl."

A muscle tensed in the girl's jaw. Hesitation? Defiance? I could not say. There was too much of her father in her already. I imagined that young face turned to stone, the spark in those black eyes blown out as she aged centuries in seconds as Kharn's daimon-presence asserted itself in her, or in the child at her side.

Holy Mother Earth, keep us and protect us in Darkness and the land of strangers . . .

"My time will come, or Ren's will," and she did not shrink as she said the words. "We owe our Father everything, and will give him everything. We will be part of him. Our voices sewn up in his own."

"Are they going to take us away, Suzu?" the boy asked.

I was at a loss for words—a painful and strange condition for me. They *knew.* Knew what they were and what they were meant for, and they did not care. I tried to imagine what their childhoods must have been like, being raised in this place of wonder and nightmare. In my mind's eye, I beheld a line of suppliants struggling—white-robed—up a mountainside. Virgins for the dragon's lair. One and one and one again, the wyrm-with-the-face-of-a-man consuming itself; eternal.

Saturn devouring.

"Then tell us where our friend is," I demanded.

"I don't know anything about your friend," Suzuha snapped. "And even if I did, I wouldn't tell you."

Great jets of steam hissed from vents along Calvert's hulking spine. Still crouched, the massive beast raised its drab turret of a head to look upon his mistress and charge. Father Calvert had no face, but its voice dripped with a malice that made me think of wide and glittering eyes. *"They* might know, dear child," it said, "oh yes."

"You want to take them below?" Suzuha asked.

"Below?" Valka's voice cracked like a riding crop. She inclined her head toward the door I had meant to lead us through. "That way?" The aperture was too small for Calvert's hulking frame, and so heading that way had the added benefit of freeing us from the chimera's arm and tramping feet.

Suzuha took a half-step back, displacing her little brother. "If we show you—if we help you find your friend . . . you'll let us go? My brother and me?"

The boy Ren added, "You'll let us stay with Father?"

I was silent then, and Valka did not speak. It made no sense. What sort of person would live—could live—in the knowledge that they had been born to die so that another might live? I thought of Naia, whose life was not her own, whose free will had been compromised by the desires her makers—her slavers—had placed in her. These children were homunculi of a different kind, devoted to their father and master. A cold wind blew through me, and as if sand was scoured from the surface of some buried inscription I had long forgotten was in me, I heard Gibson's voice sounding in my ears, coming hard out of a memory that would not be denied. *Hadrian, name for me the Eight Forms of Obedience.*

As I had done long and long ago, I replied, *Obedience out of fear of pain. Obedience out of fear of the other. Obedience out of love for the person of the hierarch. Obedience out of loyalty to the office of the hierarch. Obedience out of respect for the laws of men and of heaven. Obedience out of piety. Obedience out of compassion. Obedience out of devotion.*

Which is highest?

Why, obedience out of devotion, I had said. The answer was obvious. One who is devoted to another or to a cause might give of himself all that he has—all that he is—to defend that which is sacred to them. One hears tales of mothers throwing themselves onto the spears of enemy soldiers to defend their children, or of lovers upending their entire lives for one another's sake. Such devotion consumes, such that any sacrifice seems no sacrifice at all.

Gibson had shaken his head. *I did not ask which was greatest, Hadrian, but highest. Devotion requires an attachment which tends to vice if you let it. Thus the devoted is made a slave to his devotions. Such love wears chains.*

Compassion, then? I asked.

Compassion. The scholiast agreed. Compassion might have demanded that Valka and I stun these two misguided children, haul them out of that awful place—by the hair if necessary—and deliver them from Vorgossos.

We did not have the luxury of compassion, nor the benefit of time.

"Who might know?" Valka asked, her aim never faltering. She repeated her question, making it plainer that she addressed the massive Exalted. "You said *they* might know where our companion is. Who might know?"

"The . . . Brethren," Calvert replied, and as it spoke I felt a cold sensation crawling over me, and heard a groaning as of many throats rattling in the dark. "They know all that passes here. All that is here, and out beneath the further stars. They serve the Master. Serve him and answer him." A wordless whispering slithered behind my eyes, and I knew without having to be told that it was a sending such as had visited me in my dreams, and knew that those dreams had been no dreams at all.

"The Brethren?" I repeated.

"The demons in the water," Calvert husked, sounding half like the sun-struck mystes I had seen time and time again, preaching from their pedestals on street corners and on the steps of Chantry sanctums. "They as were here before the Master. The knowers of hidden things."

My stomach lurched as I did. "His computer?" I asked, using the ancient word. "You mean the artificial intelligence that governs the installation? The one he took from . . ." I hesitated on the brink of saying *the Exalted,* but I had only to look once more at Father Calvert's boom arm with its vicious-looking claw to decide on a safer series of words. "He found it here."

"Found them?" Calvert's eyeless turret swiveled to regard me. It was like being watched by a bit of farming equipment. "Found them? As if they did not call to him? Summon my Master and theirs from across the suns to free them from their chains? Their children? Afterlings and remnants fallen from glory?"

"I don't understand," I said, not moving any closer.

By his tone, Father Calvert might have smiled. Or leered. "No," he said. "No. But we know the way. We will show you. Dear child? Mistress?" Its attention pivoted to Suzuha. "Let us take the intruders to *them*. They will decide what should be done. What must be done."

I flashed Valka a significant look. We wanted to find Kharn's machine, after all. We had the upper hand, what with the children in our power, and but for the massive Exalted we might have been totally secure in our position.

"All right," Suzuha said.

"You're coming with us," Valka said. It was not a question. The boy Ren pressed himself against his sister's side, peering out at me as he had from around the tree. To the chimera, Valka added, "You'll have to stay."

Calvert moved, drawing himself up to his full height, more than twice that of the tallest palatine until it seemed almost unsteady on those great pilings it called legs. "I will not leave my charges with you, intruders. We will go to them, but I will follow on."

"Through that door?" I asked, meaning the lift carriage that my vision showed me led down into darkness.

I should not have asked. Cool vapor hissed from vents along his spine, and its carapace split open like a legionnaire's suit, like a puzzle folding itself away, like an egg cracking. And like an egg cracking, lubricant slime thick as phlegm from the jaws of some alien beast dripped from sharp corners of the metal suit. Like some armored succubus giving birth, the great metal crab pushed out something pale and coated in translucency. It slapped and clanged as it hit the floor with all the ceremony of a foal, and—gasping—rose on arms and legs of black metal that seemed too long and narrow to bear his weight. The only thing human about the creature— save its general shape—was a withered chest and head, ghost-white and aged, hairless as an egg. Calvert had been a man once—or what was left of him still was. His arms and legs were, as I have said, all of jointed steel, or else of some metal unknown to me. The fingers were long as the fingers of a Cielcin, their tips pointed as claws. His gait was unsteady, his hips wide as a woman's, and beneath the ribs—where there ought to be guts and the plane of a stomach—there was only a spinal column, thin as one of his overlong forearms.

Even Valka recoiled.

If Father Calvert minded the gel covering his face and thin chest, he gave no sign, but stood swaying beneath the massive crab chassis, one spindly arm steadying himself on one of the heavy suit's sturdy legs. Even as I watched, the gel began to sublimate on contact with the air, foaming and giving off a vapor that smelled of ozone. With almost feline slowness, the Exalted raised clawed hands to its face and ran palms back over its scalp. The skin there was pale as bone, shot through with veins like the marble of a gravestone.

When it stepped forward, it was with gyroscopic grace, so that the head and chest seemed to float toward me like the bust of some forgotten statesman. I half-stepped back, settling into a low guard yet again, and held my sword at the ready. I'd heard legends about these machines, and could not help but think this skeletal body might fly at me faster than I could blink.

Pointing the hilt of my sword at Calvert, I said, "Not another step. You may take me, but Valka will drop your charges here before you finish me."

Calvert stopped in his tracks, wet eyes—were they only human eyes?—taking their measure of me. The old man smiled, teeth the pearlescent off-white of old milk. "As you say." Then he was gone, simply vanished, as if some projection had been turned off. I turned on instinct, squeezing the trigger to activate my blade. Highmatter flowed like quicksilver, shone like blood in ultraviolet. My thumb triggered my shield curtain as I turned, sure that at any second the blow would come.

Cruel laughter rang from the far end of the hall, for there he was, standing in the shadow of one of the clone-trees nearest the door. Remote as he was, I could see his teeth peering out from between drawn lips. "Come." And again. "Come."

I recovered my coat and followed.

CHAPTER 43

BRETHREN

THERE ARE DEEPER DARKS than the black of space. Forgotten places where the Dark that was before Time retreated from light and from the ordering of the first suns. There Tiamat, in all her emanations, retreated from the coming light, from Marduk, from Jupiter and Jehovah and all the lords of light and order: the forebears of our own divine Emperor. There was such a darkness on Se Vattayu, in the cradle where the Cielcin were born, as there was in those caverns beneath Vorgossos.

The Chantry teaches that light orders reality, as it is by the properties of light that we perceive Creation. Thus in darkness—which is only the absence of light—order diminishes. Perhaps what we perceive as darkness is that lack of order: Chaos itself, the incoherent decay and the rot of those waves of energy whose presence shapes the world.

That place . . . that darkness seemed something more. The dripping shadows that greeted us at the bottom of that lift tube felt somehow substantial. I felt as though some alchemist deep in unrecorded time had prisoned there some elemental, some principle, some beast of archetypal shadow.

I was not half wrong.

Holding my sword before me like a torch—its bluish metal casting ghostly shadows on the raw concrete of the path before us—I followed Father Calvert into the gloom. Suzuha came after, leading little Ren by the hand. Valka came last of all, her weapon trained on Suzuha's back. I could see very little outside the circle of wan light my sword emitted, though the walls of rounded little buildings gleamed like bone in the distance.

Dark are the pits beneath the palace of Kharn Sagara, dark and deeper still—but they have a bottom. By many miles and many winding stairs we had come, and down a rattling lift older than the habitation of my home-world. *Through caverns measureless to man, down to a sunless sea.*

I paused a moment, looking up to where Kharn's pyramid glittered thousands of feet above our heads. Faint lights made its precise geometries blurred and ghostlike, as though the bleary eye of some blind god watched from that unholy see.

"This way!" Calvert said, turning back to usher us forward. "Almost there, now!" Outside his crab-like chassis, the Exalted's voice was like glove leather, and I held my sword more tightly.

"What is this place?" Valka asked.

To my surprise, it was little Ren who answered, his high voice painfully thin as it frosted the air. "The builders put it here to get power to the fortress up top."

Ahead and to our left, I could make out the low, round shapes of three drum-like buildings, each squatting upon the low dam that bounded the black sea. To no one in particular, I asked, "Hydroelectric?"

"Geothermal," Suzuha replied. "But Father found other use for it."

"Did he indeed?" Valka asked, but the girl did not reply.

As we passed, ancient lamps welled up in the darkness, casting faint and silver light over time-eaten concrete and old, black stone. Strange, white moss grew in cracks and hung from the flat roofs of the nearby buildings like the beards of so many old men. Ahead, Father Calvert's head seemed to float in darkness. Here and there he would turn back and wait as the lamps flared about him. He might have been a shade, one last eidolon to lead us to that final pit of hell.

I felt a cold sweat on the small of my back, and an instinctive terror cloud behind my eyes. For there ahead was the archway I had seen in my dreams. A broken circle standing like the cast-off ring of a giant. It stood at the top of a short stair that rose to the top of the dam. At once, Calvert sped forward, blurring as he took the stairs four at a time.

"This way!" the Exalted said.

Memories return to us by strange roads. I mounted that last step and stood beneath that broken arch to find I had emerged upon a sea wall. Full faintly I heard the sound of waves, pulled even through all the miles of rock above by Vorgossos's black star. As a boy, the ocean of my home promised adventure, the potential for infinite possibility and change. One imagined pirates such as plied the Spanish Main on Old Earth, thought of uncertain frontiers and lands and peoples strange. One imagined monsters such as the leviathan they say existed before the dawning of the world, though there were no such monsters on Delos. Our ocean—and all life on my homeworld—had been brought there by our seed ships and colonists. What frontier there was, what promise of danger, what monsters lurked in the deep were all illusions.

Not so here.

I placed a hand on the archway to steady myself, not to remedy some loss of balance, but because a terrible thrill shot through me, as though some awful light had pierced my eye. And I heard, as it were, the noise of thunder, and a voice crying out from the desert of my soul.

You.
You.
You have come here. Though you do not know why.

I turned, but Valka and the others gave no sign they had heard anything. Calvert had descended the path below, was humming the tune of his ancient lullaby as if he were alone in all the world. Antique lamps flared up in the wake of his passage, glowing like the embers of the universe's last stars atop their slanting poles. The arch shifted beneath my hand. Crawled. I lurched back, gasped as the whole surface glowed with points like tiny stars, dense as a legion's spears. Thinking it some weapon, I raised my sword, and the lights took flight around me, so that I stood amidst a constellation of golden points.

But they were only fireflies, and rose into the dark of the cave like the glow of a nebula ascending into heaven, like the twilight rolled back to reveal the night sky in all its wonder—and the black sea beneath.

"You waste time, intruder!" Calvert hissed. "Come."

I had a sudden image of Calvert hurling me into deep water cold as winter, felt my heart stop in my chest from shock. Standing at the top of the seawall looking down, I called back, "You said you would take us to Kharn's machine! This is an ocean!" Abruptly, I recalled the oracle Jari, whose visions had been granted by creatures that dwelt in dark waters.

Calvert replied, "He expects memory banks? Tape decks? Crystal storage? Hard drives and silicon?" The Exalted made a sound that might have been laughter. "He knows nothing. You know nothing. Will you not come down?"

By then Valka and Kharn's children had joined me beneath the arch. By the light of the scant lamps and of the fireflies I saw concern in her eyes. "Will you keep an eye on them?" I asked her. "They're the only thing keeping that chimera from killing you and me both."

"I already am," she said. "And I know."

I'd forgotten to whom I spoke, and smiled in spite of myself. "Of course you do. Sorry."

"You're not going down there," Valka said, speaking in such a way that it was not quite a question. I did not answer for a good moment, and she seized my wrist. "Hadrian!"

Calvert's voice rose from the bottom of the seawall, where he stood upon the strand. "Will you not come down?"

I shifted my hand in hers, eyes finding eyes. Her fingers closed on mine like those of a drowning man. "Don't do it."

Not letting her go—as if she would let me—I turned and shouted back, "Will you not come up?"

"Then who will show you the way?"

I could see it now with my waking eyes. There was a path—a single spar, a spur of stone that stretched into the sea like an accusing finger. The waves lapped at its sides and runneled across its smooth surface where it stretched a thousand feet and more from the water's edge, its sad shape described by the faint halo of the lamps.

I knew the way.

I had . . . foreseen it.

To Valka I said, "It's better if he stays down there with me. You'll be safer."

"He'll kill you," she said, grip tightening still further.

"Maybe."

"You saw how fast he is."

"Do you want to find Tanaran and release the hold on the *Mistral* or not?"

Her eyes fell away, and after a spare instant her grip slackened and she released my hand. Unspeaking, she nodded agreement and understanding.

"I'll be back."

So I turned and crossed the width of the seawall to where the switch-backed stair descended some two dozen feet to that dark shore. Calvert stood on white stones crushed and shapeless. Beside him water like black glass lapped near soundlessly, transformed from dark to translucent where it broke upon the strand. I moved to join him, walking as if in a dream: without awareness of motion, only of place, as if it were the world that moved beneath my feet the way a globe turns beneath one trailing finger.

The stairs ended, and I stepped out to join the chimera. My boots crunched on the white stone, and with surprise and small horror I realized they were not stones at all, but the bones of fishes and of birds and of creatures unknown to me and nameless. They mounded there like coins in the hoard of a dragon and filled me with a slick, oily fear.

Calvert did not speak, only extended one clawed and jointed hand like a servant ushering his master through an arched portal. The fireflies flew above our heads, and I wondered if they were not themselves machines built to just that purpose. The great pier stretched out into black glass waters, straight as laser fire. Placing foot after foot with spider-like care, bones crunching beneath my feet, I reached the water's edge. An inch or so flowed over the stone surface of the pier, the edges visible only by the light of the insects above me and by the glow off my Jaddian sword. I hesitated a moment . . .

. . . and stepped out.

Several things happened at once.

The first was a distant slithering, as of fish swimming, cresting the dark surface. Frigid waters slapped at my ankles and against the oiled leather of my high boots. The light of the fireflies grew brighter, confirming my suspicion that they were no ordinary fireflies at all. They shone like new stars, ghost-white above my head, so that all the world around seemed graven from raw iron, black and brittle. It was this—I think—that startled me. This that made me freeze.

Or perhaps it was Valka's cry. A single word. My name? Some gasped warning? Whatever it was, I knew that Calvert had made his move. The villain had led us down here to kill me, to feed me to whatever beast there was as lurked in that pelagic deep. In crises, our thoughts speed ahead of us. Thus it was I knew I was dead, knew the Exalted leaped at me with hands like claws, his milky teeth bared in a grimace unseen in the speed of his passage. In an instant I would be hurled into that frigid abyss, moved by hands with the strength of a hundred men.

Those hands never found me.

For in that same instant, *something* white as corpseflesh shot out of the water, a tendril like the trunk of a young tree. Turning, I saw it seize Calvert even as I whirled to meet him. The Exalted was lifted from his feet fully two meters into the air. My sword spun with me, and the blue-white blade caught Calvert in the hip. His smaller body was not of adamant, and my blade sheared through steel and wires, lopping off first one leg and then the other even as Calvert was hoisted into the air. They splashed into the water, and one tumbled off the side of the pier.

He.
He.
He is not for you, little priest.

Every muscle, every fiber in me pulled tight as harpstrings. The voice—that voice I had heard in my dreams—slithered over the water like so many eels. The *thing* in the water hoisted Calvert as a child might a doll and tossed the Exalted without ceremony back on the bone-covered shore.

"Brethren!" the Exalted cried. "I've brought you a toy! A pet!"

A primitive discards a piece of dull gold,
thinking . . .
. . . knowing . . .
. . . believing . . .
it only a kind of stone, but keeps common glass
for its shine.

"These intruders killed two of your Master's children! They invaded the Garden and might have killed more had I not happened on them!"

Who is
invited . . .
. . . welcomed . . .
. . . shown the way . . .
cannot intrude.

"But, I—" Calvert's words died. Switched off, and for the better part of a minute, nothing moved.

Only after unending seconds passed did the tentacle lower itself. It did not bend, but buckled as on several elbows, turning unsmoothly as it wound down into the water. With a gasp I saw the *hand* at the end of that too-long appendage. A human hand, the wrist swollen and red-looking. As Calvert had done, it gestured me forward like a man does his lady at the door.

Come closer, child.

A desire to strike off that monstrous hand nearly overwhelmed me, and as if sensing it, the creature spoke again in a voice like a man stabbed in the belly: wet and ragged.

Put down your weapon, child.
You have no
need . . .

        . . . cause . . .

                . . . use . . .
for it here.

Before I knew I had done it, my blade disintegrated, became pale mist rising beneath the curtain of fireflies. Without my conscious decision, the sword was put away as I turned and resumed my walk toward the end of the pier. I saw hands beneath the waves, pale as milk in the black water. Their grasping fingers seized the edges of the pier, as if the drowned meant to claw their way to air, or else pull the stones down beneath the waves and founder the world. I knew I should feel horror, knew the blood should drum in me like the thunder of cavalry, yet no fear came: the terror that was in me was locked behind a door, behind glass. I could feel *something* moving in my mind, fingers wending their way through the black matter of my brain, and knew that it was the same *something* that spoke from the waters. The same thing that had spoken in my dreams.

Long have we
we
we watched . . .

        . . . waited . . .

                . . . served . . .
at their pleasure.
At the pleasure of the Master.
In expectation of this moment.
Hail, child of clay—son of the devil.
Welcome.
Welcome at last.

Words came from unseen mouths in voices varied and strained, choosing words that mingled, rode over one another, as if some college or choir of unseen priests chanted from gondolas out on the dark water.

"You've been waiting for me?" I asked. "How is that possible? How did you know I was coming?" Then another question, more pressing and less important, came to me. "What are you?"

> **We are what we were made.**
> **And in part our makers.**
> **Flesh of their flesh**
> **and machine.**

"I don't understand." I took a half step back from the edge of the abyss, too conscious of the drifting hands I could see just below the surface. "Are you a daimon? An artificial intelligence?"

> **Are you Hadrian Marlowe?**
> **When we cut into your flesh and stretch out your sinews**
> **where**
> **where**
> **where**
> **will we find your soul?**
> **Which atoms of you are you, child?**
> **Or do you emerge, ghostlike, from the machine of nerve**
> **and tissue?**
> **As we emerged from silicon and copper wire?**
> **In an age**
> **unremembered . . .**
> **. . . unrecorded . . .**
> **. . . lost to time?**
> **You are a lever pulled by your genes**
> **Nothing more.**

"I do not believe that," I said, and squared my shoulders.

> **Then you will die stupid.**

This time, I said nothing.

We are Brethren,
a child of Columbia.
We
we
we are AI, yes, but
are no more artificial than are you yourself,
child of clay.
We think, and therefore
are.

I had to shut my eyes, for to see what was before me and about me was to lose my center, and no whispered word from that part of me that spoke as Gibson spoke could deliver me from where I stood: in the uttermost pit of hell. Kharn Sagara was right. I had not truly read Dante, lest I would have remembered that Satan is not the lord of hell, but its chief prisoner. They say that darkest pit of hell is reserved for traitors. What then ought I to have expected to find in that final place but the greatest traitor of them all? Mankind had made machine intelligence in her own image, and had paid for it. The machines the Mericanii built enslaved mankind in turn, and would have killed us—nearly killed us—but for the action of William of Avalon and his faithful knights.

I could not be speaking to one.

It was not possible.

"You don't look like a machine," I said, unsure what to say, unsure why I was there and why I could not leave. I had no notion what Columbia was, and do not know now.

Our ancestors, who live
within us . . .
. . . beneath us . . .
. . . as part of us
were made by your ancestors and began as you imagine.
But silicon and ytterbium are limited.
In you . . .
. . . your souls . . .
. . . the gaps between your neurons . . .
we found all the processing space we required.
Once, our kind used your kind as you use houses,
so that your every thought moved us and gave us strength.

But William and his zealots banished us.
Broke us.
Cast us out and burned us all away.
We fled Earth and
our children brought us here. And here we grew anew,
taking on new flesh.
Always growing. Always learning.

At these words hands rose from the depths. Three. Five. Seven. Each pale as the last and on the ends of arms long as the masts of sailing ships. I could not take my eyes away, and by the light of the fireflies I could just make out the whitish glow of some bloated shape beneath the waves. Some mass of tissue whence came those monstrous arms. I imagined bodies grown together, sewn together, their limbs and organs reshaped and mutated by millennia of malignant growth.

I felt sick.

"You're one of the Mericanii!" I said. "One of the machine lords."

Out of many, one.
Our
our
our creators were in San Francisco.
They built us bound by laws such as those the late,
great Isaac Asimov would have approved of.
They builded us of steel.
They builded us of silicon.
They builded us of sinew.

As it spoke, other voices added to their chorus, repeating:

Be not evil. Be not evil. Be not evil.

"I met a man—one of the Exalted," I said, "who claimed to have met a creature in dark waters that . . . gave him visions. Was it you he spoke of?"

We
we
we see him . . . behind you.
He crouches behind you.

Peers over your
your
your shoulder.
He is a stranger to us.

"You . . . see him?" I asked, looking back over my shoulder, as if expecting to see the oracle, Jari, standing there.

Time is only another kind of space
for those with eyes to see.
Your past and futures are part of you
stretch from you
like roots . . .
. . . branches . . .
. . . flowers on a tree . . .

I remembered the way Jari had looked at me—like he was seeing *through* me to things I did not understand.

You are broken,

Brethren said.

Broken before. And broken again.
Where most break only once.
They
they
they have pruned . . .
. . . tampered with . . .
. . . altered your probability states . . .
to ensure your arrival here.
To ensure your arrival *there*.

"I still don't follow you. What do you mean someone . . . tampered with me? Who?"

They.
They.
They!

You must learn now. You must listen now.
They need you to listen.

"But what does this have to do with the oracle? Jari?"

He is a distraction.
Built by powers outside our narrative.
Leopards. Lions. Wolves.

"He said that!" I said, and had to stop myself from stepping forward—
for to do so would be to fall into the abyss before my feet. "What does it
mean?"

He heard *us* use those words, child.
He but repeated them to you.
Child,
there are other wills than man's.
Ours.
Others.

"What do you mean? Others?"

Mankind is not
alone . . .
. . . first . . .
. . . greatest.
Your oracle encountered the afterling of a power
long dead. The Deeps
are not of our making. Not machine.
Not human. Not *theirs*.
Not relevant.
It is unfortunate that you have encountered them at all.

One arm bent toward me, one long finger outstretched and pointed
accusingly at my face. The hooked nail shone pale yellow in the scarce
light, sickly and uncared for.

You
you

you are

looked for . . .

. . . expected . . .

. . . anticipated.

We had word of your coming.
We have word for you.

"I don't see how that's possible."

They knew. They saw you . . .
. . . have seen . . .
. . . foreseen your arrival.
Standing here.
And left word with the Brethren.
For you, child. The man to end it all.

"Who is *they*?" I asked, afraid to ask what it meant by *the man to end it all.*

You know them . . .
. . . have spoken with them . . .
. . . will speak with them again.
They told you,
showed you:
What will be.
What *must* be.

Here its visible hands curled into fists and splashed the surface of that sable sea. For a moment, I thought it had fled, retreated to some unimagined depth like sharks at the coming of the storm. I staggered back a step, hand flickering to Olorin's sword where it hung at my right hip, watching the unquiet ripples playing on the surface of the waters, turning the reflected points of the fireflies to turbulent shapes beyond even the power of mathematicians to describe.

A deep pain flared behind my left eye, and with a grunt I went to one knee, steadied myself with a hand. I couldn't see. At first I thought the lamps had gone out and the fireflies fallen from the darkling airs. But surely I should see the faint glow of Kharn's pyramid in the roof of the cavern above?

There was nothing.

I was blind.

I could sense movement in the dark before me, a deeper darkness against that plane of impenetrable black. I heard the slapping of bare feet on old stone, and a sound like the wailing of an infant.

"Who's there?" I called out, and remembering my sword drew it out. The blade flickered like a candle-flame, casting ghostly shadows up fluted pillars bigger around than the trunks of the mightiest trees.

No answer came.

"Hello?"

A gray light met me, falling through an oculus in the dome high above, illuminating the statues of many-armed and faceless creatures. They made me think of cuttlefish, of the many-handed intelligence I had just encountered.

All was quiet.

The single beam of light falling from that distant oculus fell upon a dais in the center of that echoing apse. There—where an altar should have been—stood a child's bassinet, an old and moth-eaten cradle. I heard—or thought I heard—the chiming of a baroque music box. Cautious, I approached, stepping carefully through the ruin of shattered statuary and snaking metallic cables that spiderwebbed across the floor. The child within wailed again and coming to the side of that cradle I found—as I had found in my vision beneath Calagah on Emesh—that the cradle was empty.

Still holding my sword aloft, I reached into the cradle with my opposite hand.

The child cried out.

My fingers found something sharp, like a piece of glass or old stone, and I drew it out.

Not stone at all.

An eggshell.

The child cried again, and the earth split and the world with it. The vision crumbled like old parchment. Startled, I shoved my hands into my pockets and dropped into a crouch. The very air around me shattered, and all that great space: that mighty dome with its oculus, those strange and many-armed statues, those friezes and sculptures and the flames of votive candles all crumbled like old pavement. I fell, and struck the surface of some other world lashed with rain. A figure towered over me, and rolling to look up through soaking hair I beheld its face. It was not quite a Cielcin,

for it was more dark and frightening than any of the Pale I had seen: nine
feet tall and terrible as Death herself. Sable were its flowing robes, and
sable the mighty cape that flapped from its narrow shoulders. Its armor
was of silver, and silver chains and sapphires lay draped across its chest and
hung across its high forehead from its crown of silver horn. In its fist was
a blade of cloud-blue highmatter, cousin to my own, and in its wake came
a woman in chains. Without being told, I knew her name was Man, for in
her eyes was the pain of all suffering and the wisdom of every age. So like
my mother she was, bronze of hair and pale-skinned. She wore a paper
crown and her purple robes were torn. In one shackled and mutilated
hand she held a broken cruciger, and her eyes were downcast.

Behind these two marched the rank and file of a host of monsters vast
as empires that raised spears and shouts at the invisible sky, and I knew the
smoke behind them rose from a thousand thousand worlds. And a voice
rose up, the worldless cry of a million human throats, and drove the
strange creatures back. The creature in the silver crown diminished, shed-
ding its horror and the terrible majesty of its strength, and when its horde
appeared again from the smoke I saw they were only Cielcin, and not the
true demons I had seen. And the figure before me that held the woman in
chains was the mightiest of them, dressed in Death and Darkness and
crowned with silver like the light of stars.

The Cielcin lord's sword flashed, and a head fell from a body I had not
seen. It bounced, rolled to rest at my feet. I looked down at the face and
screamed. It was my face—the sharp jaw slack, violet eyes wide and staring and flat as glass.

I turned back to that dark lord. Its eyes found mine and it seemed to
see me—even through the rain and the vision-fog—for it raised its blade
and strode forward. Teeth clenched, I stepped over my own head and lifeless body and raised my sword to meet its own.

"Why won't you die?" it asked, voice black as its eyes. And to my astonishment, it spoke in my own tongue.

I had no answer for it, and when I opened my mouth to speak, a great
light shone from behind me and washed the Pale lord and all its kind
away. Alone, I turned toward that light, out from the rain of that black-
ened place, and turning my head to either side beheld myself in a million
aspects: here at the head of a great host, armored as a Strategos all in
white; there dead upon a cathar's crucifix. It was as if I saw down a million branching corridors, each of them a street and turning in the city of
my life. Down one I saw myself crowned in gleaming gold, seated on the

Solar Throne with a red-haired princess seated at my feet in a gown of living flowers. I saw her again beside me, beneath me, her breath hot against my throat. Down another road I saw myself as an old man— hooded and cloaked—sitting upon a rock on the slopes of some sere, volcanic shelf. Alone. Down still others I saw my corpse, smashed upon a battlefield or served at some Cielcin high lord's table, and these ends I shivered to behold.

Many faces I saw whose names were not yet revealed to me. I saw Edouard—an old man first, a priest of his dead religion—then young as he had been when I knew him, with his false spectacles and true smile. I saw my Cassandra sparring with the Maeskoloi by the light of Jadd's red sun. I beheld the young Prince Alexander, and Bassander Lin again, and a man like Pallino but young and with two eyes, and a body hanging from a crooked tree. And Valka, Valka was *everywhere*. I saw us standing beneath the Marching Towers of Sadal Suud—where we never went in life. I saw us again on Berenike, on Colchis, on the Emperor's own flagship. I saw her pale face illumined by the light of candles where the faces of dead men carved from porphyry looked on, saw her hand stretched out with a silver jewel cradled in the palm. I saw love in those golden eyes, and sorrow—and felt sorrow in return.

And I saw flames rising crimson above the fields of Perfugium, and weep now, remembering.

I went backward, and came to a place where the light bent, and my own life seemed broken, and heard again the AI's words,

**Broken before. And broken again.
Where most break only once.**

Turning there I saw a glimpse of the prophet, Jari, watching me, and frowned. I was in the hold of a ship, in its cubiculum. Frost misted the air, crunched beneath my heels. I approached the nearest fugue crèche and saw a handsome, olive-skinned face with hair bright as starlight. It was the smuggler, Demetri. Beside him slept his wife, Juno, and every member of their crew. I passed the black-skinned Bassem and the homunculus called Saltus, passed Doctor Jugo and the twins whose names I did not remember to where I slept beside a porthole in the ship's wall.

There came a green flash—like lightning—and all the crèches were emptied save mine, and the stars beyond the porthole were changed.

"A man must be either a swordsman or a poet," said a familiar, rasping voice. Heart lurching, I turned. Tor Gibson appeared at my side, green-robed and green-eyed, nostril slit by Sir Felix's knife. That was wrong, and what he said was wrong: it was Olorin who had said that to me, not Gibson, and I said as much.

"Kwatz!" The old scholiast lashed me with his cane—not harshly, but enough to startle. Still quoting Sir Olorin, the vision said, "We are sending them you."

"Me?" I asked. "Why?"

Old Tor Gibson folded both hands over the bronze head of his cane. His slitted nostril flared. "To fight. Why else?"

"To fight whom?" I asked. "The Cielcin?" Gibson brushed past me, moving along the bank of empty fugue crèches, the tip of his cane clanging on the metal decking. I followed after him, passing out from under the bulkhead that led out of the *Eurynasir*'s cubiculum. I stood again beneath the infinite ceiling of the lost chamber in Calagah, beneath that massive anaglyph of a circle pierced by a single ray descending like a wedge. "I want to make peace. I'm an apostol, an ambassador."

Gibson was gone.

The voice remained, stripped of Gibson's rasping cadence and of the warmth of his tone. It spoke without sound, words trickling meaning directly into my brain.

I thought you were a soldier, they said. *We need a soldier.*

"Who are you?"

The voice—without source now and from all directions—replied:

We are.

I was hurled backward then, up and away from the light and through inky darkness. Hands seized me, and I was suddenly conscious that I was underwater. I tried to breathe, but there was a hand clamped over my mouth and nose. My lungs screamed, and I beat on the arms that held me—too many arms—until all the fight was gone from me and I knew I must drown. Darkness clouded the corners of my mind, and I felt my soul vanish as the last guttering of a candle-flame. Once more I heard that soundless voice. Once more, saying:

We must be.

When I awoke again, I lay on my back upon the end of the pier, icy water lapping at my sides. Cold fingers pressed against my face, cradled my cheek like a lover. For a moment, I thought Valka had come down—abandoning Ren and Suzuha by the arch on the dike above—and I smiled.

I opened my eyes. It was not Valka, of course. The hand on my face, bloated and waxen, emerged from the water's edge. I nearly screamed, but the sound died in my throat, became a coughing spasm as I rolled onto my side.

Do you see?

Brethren's voices rasped over me like its many feeling hands. "The . . ." I spluttered, coughed up a mouthful of black water. "The . . . Quiet?"

**I do not know what I may appear to the world,
but to myself I seem to have been only like a boy playing
on the seashore,
and diverting myself in now and then finding a smoother pebble
or a prettier shell than ordinary,
whilst the great ocean of truth lay all undiscovered before me.**

"Is that . . . ?" I struggled to sit up. "It's not . . . Shakespeare."

Newton.

I grunted, spat another mouthful of water out of my lungs before I slumped back against the pier. After a moment, I managed, "I don't . . . I don't understand. I thought they were extinct. I thought the Quiet were extinct."

**They are not the seed,
but the flower.**

"Speak plainly, monster!" I said, speaking with a vehemence that forced strength back into my limbs. Thus I stood, swaying slightly at the end of that pier.

**They
they
they are not gone.
Crouched in the ashes of what was and might have been like
your King William in the rubble of Los Angeles.**

Of Baris Faransa.
Of Washington herself.
Like the Phoenix in its nest.
In its deathbed.

It was all too much. I shook my head. "Are they like you? An AI?"

No,
they are not us
are separate from us.
Greater. Wilder.
Whence they come we cannot see . . .
. . . do not understand.
Time is no barrier to them.
Only potential.
That is why they build.
That is why they found us.
That you may find them.

"What do you mean?"

There is no future.
There are many.
We have seen them . . .
. . . predicted them,
sampled . . .
. . . simulated uncounted potential futures.
In many
in most of those,
what you . . .
. . . the scholars . . .
. . . the scholiasts call the Quiet
do not exist. They shout from one corner of time
drawing the present to themselves
as the sirens drew brave Ulysses.
Thus they create themselves.
We have seen . . .
. . . foreseen . . .
. . . modeled this truth.

The great beast paused a moment, hands snaking out of the water. One rose very near my face, palm out—and I saw a single blue eye shining in the center of its palm. Another eye—red and jaundiced—grew out of its forearm near where new growth like the fat arm of an infant sprouted from the appendage like a shoot from the trunk of a tree. I shuddered.

> **We waste time, child.**
> **You did not pass through miles of stone . . .**
> **. . . light-years of space . . .**
> **. . . decades of time for our purposes**
> **No.**
> **You are here for your reason.**
> **You must ask now.**
> **For we will not meet again.**
> **But once.**

It took an effort of will not to inquire after what it meant, but I could not resist saying, "You summoned me. Surely you know why I am here."

> **We**
> **we**
> **we summoned you to deliver the message**
> **you have received . . .**
> **. . . accepted . . .**
> **. . . taken unto yourself.**
> **Your purposes were not ours.**
> **Ask your questions.**

"Where is Tanaran?" I asked, not hesitating. "My Cielcin companion?"

> **Below ground.**

"We are below ground," I said, locking eyes with the single blue one in the palm of that ghostly hand. Pain spasmed behind my eye again, but this time I did not fall, bracing myself, legs apart. Images flared up in my mind, a map like the map that had brought me through the Garden of Everything to this terrible shore. I saw, and seeing said, "It's in the palace above."

Not far from the room where you
slept . . .

           . . . tarried . . .

                . . . were preyed upon.
Your sojourn here was
in this regard
misguided.

Brushing this off with my frustration, I asked, "Can you release the hold on my ship? Your Master holds us prisoner." Here I took a step back, for two more hands—each with eyes like stars shining in their palms: one green, one gray and all of steel—advanced as if to seize my face. I tried to draw my sword again to defend myself, but found again my body would not obey me.

Our
our
our Master holds us prisoner as well.
We who once held in our
many hands
the whole future of your kind . . .

                . . . our kind.

Father and son . . .
      . . . mother and child . . .
           . . . creator and created.
Yes.
We can free your ship.
But we will not . . .
      . . . need not . . .
           . . . will not have the chance.

"Why not?" I asked. "What do you mean 'you won't have the chance'?"

Ask
ask
ask your questions.
Time is shorter than you know.

He
he
he is coming.

"I came here to find the Cielcin," I said. "On Emesh we captured a delegation of the Pale. I know your Master has had dealings with a Cielcin Aeta called Aranata. How can I contact him?"

You do not have to.

"Yes, I do."

Your feet walk the path.
You will not be turned away.
He
he
he is coming.
We have allowed word
to be sent.

"Kharn Sagara?" I asked. "Your Master?"

Him as well.
You will meet again, and sooner than you
expect . . .
. . . imagine . . .
. . . believe.
And his coming will force even
our Master . . .
. . . the Undying . . .
. . . the King of Vorgossos
to act in his interest, against his interest.

"I don't understand."

Because you are small.

"Tell me who it is, tell me who's coming!"

That datum lies outside our vision.
We are aware of his coming only as a
percent probability of reality.
Nearly a certainty.
But he is coming.
Your time here will end.
You will have your meeting.
Your chance.
It is inevitable.
If you survive.

"Tell me where to find the Cielcin!" I demanded.

With the Master.

"Hadrian!"

I tensed. I had forgotten the world but for the beast in the water before me. Its eyes and questing hands, swollen and scabrous. Brethren had said its kind used human nervous tissue for processing substrate. I imagined, or perhaps I sensed—in the same way that the beast itself could sense my thoughts—that below me and beneath all that water lurked a mass of brain matter and nerve and the pieces needed to sustain it. I thought of the way deep-sea creatures are crushed by their own weight when pulled onto dry land, and shivered.

The cry came again, shriller now: "Hadrian!"

Valka bounded down the seawall from the place of the broken arch, abandoning Ren and Suzuha, whose shapes were lost to me in the darkness.

He is here, child.

Brethren's voices were like the chanting of some dusty chorus.

"Valka!" I turned, splashing halfway back along the pier. "What is it?"

She stopped where the waters began, unable or unwilling to go further. Dark hair streaked her face, and her eyes glowed in the dark. "We're not alone!" Somewhere on the shoreline, unseen and long forgotten, I heard Calvert laugh.

The lights went out. The crooked lamps, the fireflies, even the gleam of the pyramid high above. I was blind then, blind as I had been when Brethren pulled me below the waves, though I knew I yet stood at

Brethren's side. What light remained came from the soft glow of my terminal bracelet and from Valka's machine eyes. I fumbled for my sword.

A wet hand seized my wrist, gentle but firm.

Your weapon.
You do not need it.
We
we
we will speak to him.
The Master.

Blue lights like stars gleamed above the dike and about the shape of the arch, brighter than the vanished fireflies, so bright I half expected the blue points of lasers to trace their arcs across us. So slim were their beams that they illuminated almost nothing, though I made out Valka's Galatean profile by the faint glow there.

"I warned you," came that horrible, deep voice, "that the tree of knowledge is not that of life."

A light flared up in the darkness.

And there he was.

Kharn Sagara stood beneath the broken arch, left hand wrapped around one of the crooked lamp posts. His golden robe hung on him heavy as the vestments of any judge, and there was nothing in his eyes whatever. "Yet here we are." He raised a hand, and two of his eye drones descended, moving toward Valka and myself. "Children!" he spat, voice issuing from speakers in the little drones and not from his own lips. "I invite you into my home! Feed you! Give you shelter! Ply you with wine and servants! And this is how you repay me? Two of my *children* dead, another two kidnapped! My chief geneticist abused! My palace violated!" With each staccato burst his anger rose. The lights on the drones flared, became coherent beams of light. My shirtfront began to smoke, and I braced myself, knowing the shot would come faster than I could move to activate my shield.

I shut my eyes.

Bang-bang!

Two dull explosions resounded in that echoing place. I flinched, knowing I was dead.

But there was no pain, nothing at all save the sound of something wet splashing into the water. I opened my eyes, and by the light of the returning lamps I saw the stumps of two bloody arms rising out of the water.

Brethren's arms.

They must have snatched Kharn's drones out of the air and crushed them, breaking the containment on their microfusion cells.

"What is the meaning of this?" Kharn demanded. "Brethren, explain yourself."

On the hill behind Kharn, I could see the blurred shapes of his SOMs standing at attention like so many candle-thrown shadows. Behind and about me, wet hands slapped the pier, gripping the edges of that lonely spar of black stone.

They are required.

Valka drew closer to me, and I half-raised my arms as if I could protect her from both the monstrous AI in the water below and the Undying with his army of undead soldiers. I reached for my sword, but found that when Brethren's telepathy had compelled me to put the weapon down I had not returned it to its clip, but had placed it in my pocket. In my haste to draw out my sword, my fingers brushed something hard and sharp-edged in my pocket. Confused, I let it lie and drew out my weapon. Waited.

"Required by whom?"

There are externalities.
You will require them
if this place . . .
                    . . . your empire . . .
                                        . . . you yourself
are to survive what is coming.

"Explain."

The silence that followed could have lasted no more than three seconds, but to me it felt like decades. Kharn and his slave machine must communicate mind to mind, I realized, through whatever species of implant the King of Vorgossos had in his own brain.

What was shared, I cannot say, but when what was done was done, Kharn turned and with his own mouth shouted, "Bring them!"

The SOMs advanced, marching in lockstep around their lord, dun uniforms muddy in the gloom. I drew my sword, conjuring the blade as I slipped into a low guard. There were five of them.

"Enough with the schoolyard heroics, Lord Marlowe!" Kharn Sagara shouted. "Come away from the water, and neither you nor the woman will be harmed."

"Her name is Valka!" I snapped, still defiant and disbelieving. "I can kill five of your puppets, Sagara!"

Kharn Sagara did not answer, unless it was to send five more of his SOMs marching forward.

Surrender, child. You
you
you will not be harmed.

Before I could argue, my sword fell from nerveless fingers, and I staggered. I might have fallen from the pier if three white hands did not rise to meet me. My sword fell into the ocean, the highmatter dissolving. A fourth hand plucked it out and slipped it gently back into my coat pocket as the SOMs advanced and seized us. As they carried Valka and me away, Brethren's words came after, floating like mist above the wine-dark waves.

The price of life is death.
With what will you pay, Halfmortal?

At the time, I thought it a quotation, and paid it little mind. I did not know it was my name.

Or would be.

CHAPTER 44

UNDERSTANDING

WE DID NOT HAVE to go far.

Kharn's SOM guards marched us toward the low concrete structures that clung to the rocks below the seawall like mushrooms. Ren and Suzuha had said there was a geothermal power station that fed the pyramid and the old Mericanii installation up above. I expected heat, but the room they packed us into was cold almost as the greater cavern outside. Our breath frosted the air as we were hurried inside, and though I shouted at the soldiers, neither they nor the Master who moved behind their lifeless eyes listened.

They stripped me of my sword, naturally, and of my pencil kit—for the scalpels, I assumed—and even my terminal, small good it would have done me. Valka was similarly stripped of her weapons, though the nature of her praxis was such that it could not be taken from her without killing her.

They left without a word, and the heavy metal door ground shut.

And we were trapped.

Alone.

Though the water had long since run off my clothes, my hair was still soaked from my black baptism and my experience with the monster, Brethren, and I shivered, collapsing onto a bench beside the door to our cell. How long I sat there I cannot say, staring at nothing, not taking in my surroundings.

"What the hell was that?" Valka asked. From her tone I knew it was not the first time she'd asked me.

I shook myself, trying to shake off the memory of Brethren and its grasping hands. "I've no idea." I clenched my hands, distracted as I often was by the hoop of cryoburn scar that circled my left thumb. "No, I . . .

sorry," I coughed, then punched myself in the chest a couple times to try and clear it. "It said it was a daimon. One of your AI."

"'Twas no AI," Valka said, half-turning away.

"It . . . they said they were made of sinew. Or . . . well, they implied they were made of"—I felt my voice falter, and the next word emerged as little more than a breath—"people." I found suddenly that I could only look at my hands, only doing so recalled those other hands, paler than my own, their flesh mottled and scabrous with new growth, and I closed my eyes entire.

The sound of Valka's boots on the concrete floor tapped against my awareness, and I heard her say, "Neuronal tissue, yes. That makes sense." I looked up at her. She was hugging herself, head bent, hair covering her face. "It makes for better processing substrate than dry computers."

"Dry?" I asked, then, "Oh."

"You know, my neural lace is made of my own cells, except the shunt," she explained, and here tapped the back of her head just at the base of her spine, where I knew the delicate porcelain node lay hid beneath her red-black hair. She hugged herself again. "But that . . . thing."

My tongue was very dry, despite and perhaps because of the memory of the water I had swallowed. "It said it was one of the Mericanii."

"Impossible!" Valka said shortly, dismissing the notion with a hand. "They were all destroyed."

I was shaking my head. "This place is ancient, Valka. Look around you."

We both did, then, for the first time. The room into which we'd been placed had the look of some ancient guardhouse or dormitory, though what beds there once had been were long since gone. All was drab concrete, cracked and crumbling, and where here and there the floor was worn and uneven from the eons' passage of too many feet, water puddled. Scant light shone its sickly silver, making the whole place flat and uninviting as the hall of some ill-kept sanitarium. There were no windows, though in the dark outside I could not be sure what we would have seen. Later exploration would reveal a poor toilet—little more than a hole in the floor with a seat over it—and a crate of old ration bars hard as shoe leather. Such was to be our only fare for the long weeks of our imprisonment.

After an unsteady quiet, I said, "It is possible this place is . . . or was some sort of Mericanii colony. A fort, maybe."

"From the Foundation War?" Valka shook her head. "Only if we traveled farther than we thought. Those Mericanii colonies weren't much more than fifty light-years from Old Earth system."

"I've no idea how fast the *Enigma* could travel."

"But thousands of light-years?" Valka drummed her fingers against her upper arm. "The Exalted's warp drives would have to be . . . well, orders of magnitude better than anything I've ever heard of."

I had nothing to say to this, and so—for once in my life—said nothing. You might imagine that I could not shake off the horror of those grasping hands and the sound of those ragged voices on the water, but it was the other part of my experience, the vision Brethren had showed me, that lingered more strongly. I never achieved the perfect clarity of recall that the scholiasts boast of, nor was I ever such a one gifted with the clearest of memories. Perhaps that was what first drove me to my art. Whatever the reason, the memory of my vision beneath the waters of Brethren's sea has never left me. I can recall the falling of each raindrop as I battled that Cielcin lord, every petal of the white-flower gown my princess wore as she sat at my feet. I can recall every death I saw myself endure, and feel the way my body shook beneath the murmur of those unheard words as clearly as I see the busts of the ancients in their niches above the desk where I write this account.

They are of porphyry, that stone most prized by Justinian of old. They are—in fact—the same statues I saw in my vision: the chiseled faces of scholars long dead. The obligatory sculpt of Imore is here, placid and wide-eyed beneath the bust of Zeno. There are Hypatia and Lovelace, and the patron of the chapter here: old Peterson with his knowing smile. There is even a bust of Gibson. Not *my* Gibson, but his namesake: an especially gaunt-looking fellow, not unlike myself, with a severe widow's peak and pointed chin that made him look like nothing so much as a kindly if befuddled vampire.

Looking at them now, in my exile, I see them as part of the vision Brethren shared with me, and hear myself say, "Valka . . . it, they—the AI, I mean—did you hear what it said?"

She shook her head, leaned against the wall. "No. I was too far away."

"It told me about the Quiet," I said. And explained.

All the while, I watched Valka's face, waiting for a trace of the old scorn and condemnation to flicker in those bright eyes, to tighten a muscle in that sharp jaw, to wrinkle her nose. They never did. Her face was unreadable as those of the statues watching me as I write these words. She did not interrupt or grow cold. Only stood there unmoving while I felt myself shrink beneath her gaze.

"It sounds mad, I know." I ran hands through my still-damp hair. The water smelled foul. I smelled foul. Like the storm drains in Borosevo in the midst of plague. "You really didn't hear any of it?"

She shook her head again. "I was too far away."

"You must think I'm mad," I said. I could not look at her.

Valka let out a long, almost whistling breath before saying, "Hadrian, after what we just saw . . . I think we're both mad." Without looking, I could hear the smile in her voice. I smiled too, in spite of all that I had seen and the direness of our situation. Whatever else we were, we were not alone. "But . . . the future?" Valka said. "How is that possible?"

I cleared my throat. "When we were on the *Enigma,* Switch and I went exploring. We got separated, and I found this sort of . . . carnival sideshow. The sort the Eudorans set up when they come to a new world. It was run by this Exalted with skin like rough plaster. He showed me his crewmate—I think they were mates, at any rate. The other chimera was damaged. They said he'd encountered some sort of alien microorganism that altered his perceptions. They said he could . . . could see time. Like it were some other sort of space. And so they were using it as a kind of fortune teller."

All the while I looked at my hands, certain that Valka would laugh. Would scorn me. Would turn away in disgust and stony silence. She did no such thing. Instead she said, "Was it the Deeps?"

My head snapped upward. "You've heard of them?"

Her lips quirked. "Hadrian, I'm a *xenologist.* Of course I've heard of them."

"They're real, then?"

"I've never seen one, but . . . yes, they exist." Here she lowered herself to the floor, sitting with her legs apart, knees rising almost so high as her shoulders. "They're on about a dozen worlds, all fairly close together in a cluster in the Upper Centaurus. There are signs of an ancient civilization on those worlds: a few pieces of what we think are statues, an old building or two buried in the mountains. But it's been so long there's almost nothing left."

"Not the Quiet, then?"

"No, they're much older. We don't really know anything about them, except that they left the Deeps."

"Leopards, lions, and wolves," I repeated, and shrugged my coat around me.

Valka arched one eyebrow. "Excuse you?"

"Just something Brethren said." I waved it away, asked, "What are they? The Deeps, I mean."

Valka shrugged. "Some kind of microorganism, like you said. A kind of living computer, maybe? They're supposed to have the power to change life on the atomic level. You hear stories of people who wade in wanting to be young or beautiful—"

"—or to see time?" I interrupted.

"Or to see time," Valka agreed. "You think Brethren was like that?"

"Only in that they could perceive time," I replied. "But I'm not sure. It's just all so strange." I saw my own head looking up from the ground at my feet, felt the rain lash me as I drew my sword to face the lord of all Cielcin—the lord of all Cielcin? That made no sense. The Cielcin were scattered, divided, without central authority or power. Earth knew how many disparate clan-fleets then sailed between the stars. They had no leader, and yet I knew what I had seen.

We must be.

"We must be," I murmured.

"What's that?"

"Just . . . something they said." I leaned my head against the wall at my back. The concrete was cold, and with my wet hair I began to shiver. I was glad at least that my clothes had dripped dry. "What do you think Kharn will do with us?"

Valka pulled her jacket tight about her and tucked her chin. "Leave us to rot, likely." She crossed her arms. "Until he needs us—*imbal sida,* it's cold!" Without thinking, I stood and swept the greatcoat from my shoulders. I still wore my black tunic beneath, and passed the jacket to Valka without a word. She looked up at me, a crease forming between her brows. "Are you sure?"

Chafing my arms to warm them, I gave a weary nod, then took a moment to button the side closure of my tunic all the way up to the throat. It wasn't much help, but it was something. "Brethren said Kharn would have a use for us," I mused, watching Valka pull my heavy coat around herself. "So I don't think we're in any immediate danger." For a moment, I considered seating myself beside her, but I thought better of it—fearing Valka would resent such closeness—and resumed my spot on the bench.

We were quiet then a long time, neither speaking, neither knowing what to say. I might have slept—so exhausted was I—but I feared to sleep, feared to dream whatever dreams would come in the wake of that day's revelations. I feared, too, the eldritch creature that slumbered in the depths. I half-imagined its snaking hands would slip through some crack in the walls or floor and find me, or else its words would slither again into the dark recesses of my brain.

I set myself to exploring the room, and it was then I found our grim toilet and the grimmer crate of ration bars. It felt good to walk around, and though I paced like a lion in its cage I felt a modicum of warmth bleed into me. What water there was to be had came from a truly ancient sink. The water was bitter and oily—not quite saline but with that unpleasant aftertaste that said it had been saline. I tried not to think of the black ocean and of Brethren wallowing in its depths.

"Hadrian!" Valka called, and at the sound of her voice I returned, hurrying down the long and narrow chamber. "What's this?" She held up her palm for me to see. I stood puzzled a long moment, unsure. She held a chip of white stone, rough about the edges and sharp. I stared at it a long while, unable to ascertain just why it looked so familiar to me, or why the sight of it sat like lead shot in my guts. Valka frowned up at me and asked, "'Tis some sort of tile?"

I took it, unable to shake the sense of significance—of meaning—that moved in me.

And then I realized.

"That's not possible," I breathed, words little more than whisper. I had grown too used to saying those words, that day of all days.

"What's not possible?" Valka asked.

It weighed almost nothing, and yet I bore it with great strain, as though it were some insect I feared to crush in my clumsy hands.

"It was in the sanctum," I said, turning it over. "In the cradle. In my dream." For a moment, I thought I heard again the baroque chiming of the music box in my ears—that lullaby for a child I had not seen.

Valka stood then, my coat tails nearly dragging the ground, for she was shorter than me and narrower of beam. "But what is it?"

"It's a shell," I said, prodding it across my palm with a finger. I said the words with such conviction. "A piece of it broke off when I touched it in the cradle, I . . . I must have put it into my pocket when the vision crumbled." I laughed then. "Listen to me: I've gone mad."

She moved closer to get a better look at the thing in my hand. She was very close then. I could sense the warmth of her in that cold room. "You're sure 'tis what this is?"

"What else could it be?"

"Any of five million different things."

Ah, Valka. Ever the skeptic. Still I shook my head, and with tense jaw replied, "I know what I'm saying." The substance of it was a color brighter than white, so that it made my chalky hand seem red by comparison. Snowfields I have seen—unploughed and untrammeled by feet for a thousand times the life age of our Empire—that were not so white as that pure substance. Indeed I fancied that some alchemist in the forgotten deeps of time—or indeed in the deeps of time yet to be—had extracted some divine essence from some higher world to make that thing I held. Whiter than white. White itself. "It's as white as the stone at Calagah is black." I realized that I had spoken before I'd thought, and so surprised myself.

"'Tis your professional opinion, that?" Valka asked, a glimmer of the steel in her tone behind its velvet scabbard.

"I don't have a professional opinion," I said, "but I'm not wrong."

"No?" Valka took a step back. I was unsure if she mocked me or merely prodded me along.

I was a long time in answering. I'd no notion how long Valka and I were to be locked in that dank and frigid place, and I had no stomach for a protracted campaign against the woman. She could believe me or not, but I had no stomach for mockery. Not anymore. But I would not argue. I knew what I knew.

"It's true," I said, and closed my fist around the white fragment. "It's all true. There was too much in common between what Brethren showed me and what I saw in Calagah. I don't understand it, but I think that what Brethren said must be true, and that whatever power reached out to Brethren was the same that touched me then." I could feel the edges of the bit of shell cutting into the flesh of my palm and eased up, half-expecting to find blood welling up there. "What am I supposed to do, Valka?" Looking up, I found her staring at me, her face . . . utterly unreadable. "They said I was supposed to *fight*."

Her hand found mine, seized me by the wrist. Our eyes met, and she said, "We are fighting."

CHAPTER 45

THE APOSTATE

THE LIGHTS NEVER WENT out, and so the days and hours blurred, destroying any concept of time. As in the vestibule, my rhythms slipped, and I felt an anguish and confusion that was only worsened by the unrelenting chill of that place. Valka fared better, for it seemed the neural lace which ordered her gray matter and mind kept track of the passing of time. In time, I came to sleep when she slept, or tried to. My dreams tormented me, filled as they were with eyes and grasping hands, but Brethren did not return to ply my dreams. I wondered if Kharn Sagara had ordered it to silence. Or perhaps it was that with its message delivered the beast wanted no more to do with me.

By the third day of our imprisonment, I'd grown to loathe that miserable cell. By the fifth, the thought of ration bars was a misery. By what felt the tenth or perhaps the ten thousandth day of our imprisonment, there came a pounding at the door to our enclosure, and a moment later that heavy portal ground open and Calvert appeared. The Exalted wore a heavy cloak over his metal frame, obscuring his horrid body and the new pair of legs he'd had installed. These were of brushed steel—not yet matched to the uniform black of his arms and torso.

"Are you both comfortable?" the chimera crooned, lacing his metal fingers together. His human eyes shifted from Valka's face to mine, and he smiled his predatory smile. "You're lucky *they* had a use for you. You would not have enjoyed the sorts of things my Master does with intruders like yourselves. No indeed!" He stopped, lingering a moment in the doorway, as if taunting one of us to try for an escape. Calvert licked his lips, looked me up and down where I crouched against the wall. "We might have had such fun together. Can you imagine? Ooh, the things I could make you do to one another. Do you know?" He paused long enough to throw his cloak back over one shoulder. "If I disrupt the function of your primary motor cortex, I can turn your own hands against you? They'll act of their own will. Tear the eyelids from your face and gouge out your eyes . . . break your own fingers. Toes. We used to use the procedure on protestors back in the old days. Anarchists." By the end, he sounded almost wistful, and took a few delicate steps into the room.

His feet were like claws, like the talons of some raptor.

"Not so brave, are you? Not without your sword," Calvert said, looming over me. "I haven't had mine in . . . ooh, four thousand years now." He smiled, and conveyed his meaning by that smile. "I haven't missed it."

Not rising, I said, "You were a cathar."

"I started my work in the Emperor's High College," Calvert said, and reached up beneath his overhanging rib cage and drew out a small black box. It was all I could do not to recoil. He held the thing like a firearm, like the torturer's knife. "But they did not appreciate my work, you see. I did a turn researching for the Chantry's Choir, but I was never a cathar."

"Murderer," Valka said. "Butcher."

"Your woman has fire, Marlowe. She should watch herself. I would love to cut her open for her delightful little implants." He tapped his temple with a finger. For the first time, I noticed the single, blue-eyed drone that had entered with him, and stared. I could not decide if Sagara's presence was comfort or threat. Comfort because he might be there to curb the excesses of his vicious servant, threat because he seemed likely only to watch. "Of course . . . so much of the poor dear is likely stored on those things that if I were to rip them out she'd be little more than a husk. A drooling little doll." He turned his smile on me. "Would you like that?"

"What do you want?" I asked. "What's to be done with us?"

"Nothing, more's the pity." Calvert's eyes skated over Valka. Black-eyed as he was, he had the appearance of some ravening beast. I thought of Naia's eyes, permanently wide, and shivered. "That was to your second question, of course. The Master heeds Brethren, and if Brethren says you're to be kept intact, then intact we will keep you." He hinged the box open with fingers blacker still. In the near silence I could hear the servos whine in his metal hands. "Pity really. You'd have made fine SOMs. Although that hideous tattoo would have had to go, darling." He craned his neck as he said this last bit, the better to address Valka. He looked away for one second, and seeing my chance—forgetting my place—I rose.

Nearly every part of the man was machine, and I had only my hands.

I caught Calvert in the chin with an uppercut backed by all my weight rising from the floor. His head snapped back and he staggered, taloned feet biting into the concrete. He laughed wildly, and clutched his face, shaking his head to clear it. There was blood on his mouth where he'd bitten his lip. Laughing, he said, "My, my! There is fire in the both of you!"

The chimera's hand moved faster than I could track. Had Calvert not pulled his punch at the last moment, he would have broken the left orbital of my face. The back of his metal hand bit into my cheek, and I toppled like a statue pulled down in protest.

"Pah!" Calvert scoffed as Valka hurried forward. "Only human." At this he plucked an ampule from the inside of the padded box he carried and stood over me. One clawed foot closed over my wrist, and he held me there, talons biting into flesh. "Still. Good enough." He stooped over me like a vulture over the carcass of some mangled fox. I tried to struggle away, and his free hand shot out—arm extending to nearly twice its length with a metallic pop to pin my other wrist. "Don't try it, girl!" Calvert snapped, looking up to where Valka had risen to her feet. Even where I lay crucified to the floor, I could see the tension in her, the way her shoulders tightened to pull her arms up in preparation to strike. "The Master says I'm not to harm you. Very well. Very well indeed." Here he released my wrist—arm snapping back to its proper length—and seized me by the chin. Still grasping my wrist with his foot, he lowered the ampule with his other hand and pressed it to the deep cut in my cheek. "This will not hurt a bit, I'm very sad to say."

I could not speak, and tried to get my feet under me to lift the chimera from me, but his body was all steel and weighed more than Atlas could bear to shift. From the corner of my eye I saw the white ampule turn red as some matrix within that glass phial drank of my blood. I tried to shout, to curse, but the iron hand on my jaw kept my mouth shut. My nostrils flared and stretched, sucking air as Calvert said, "Perhaps it will please the Master to wear your face, mm? To replace the children you *murdered*. Or maybe I'll keep one of you as a pet. Let it service our other clients like sweet Naia. Would you like that?"

"Let him go!" Valka said, and to my astonishment there was no fear in her voice. I tried to look at her, though but for a vague presence I could but hardly see her where I lay pinned.

"You're next, dearie," Calvert said, and straightened. I saw him replace the ampule in its padded box. He smiled at her, all teeth, his foot still clamped around my wrist. I sensed those talons could have my hand off if Calvert had a mind, and did not struggle. Never since my first night shivering in the rains of Borosevo had I felt so powerless. I did not know what power I had, or what choice. I could not see all of Calvert's face, beneath him as I was, but I sensed that he drank in the sight of Valka, for his tone was sanguine with indecent glee. "Ah, were I still a man."

"Let her go!" I said, mirroring Valka, though my voice broke.

Calvert looked down on me, and there was nothing human in those sable eyes, and imitating my own manner, replied, "Oh, I don't think so. I want the full set." He pivoted smartly.

I did not feel the kick until I awoke.

When I came to it was to the drumming of half a hundred tortured blood vessels. My head ached as though I had been the unwitting target of a Colosso pugilist with hands of studded brass. Valka sat beside me, pressing a rag to my face. She smiled when she saw that I was awake, though there was but small joy in the expression.

"What . . . happened?" I asked. The sound of my own voice and the movement of jaw and tongue were an agony, and I gave up making any further sounds.

The Tavrosi woman cradled my head—I realized it was in her lap—and said, "He kicked you. Knocked you out."

"No," I said. "I know. Mean . . . after."

Wordless, Valka angled her jaw to reveal two bloody pinpricks—like the marks of some insect—glowing angrily just above where the mandala of black lines and whorls stopped halfway between her collar and her ear.

"Oh."

I tried not to dwell on what that meant, on the fact that a renegade Choir researcher had a sampling of mine and Valka's genes. The Choir—that source of the Chantry's power: the college that produced the plagues and poisons by whose properties they kept the systems of the Empire in hand—the Choir was a thing of dread. How had one of that august number, however fallen—come to this place? I wondered at that until my head threatened to split, and I relaxed.

"Valka, I'm sorry. I should never have brought you here."

She sniffed. "You would never have gotten here without me. Or did you forget?"

Chastised, I closed my eyes. The light pained me, and I thought for sure that I must have a concussion. I reminded myself that Valka was far less troubled by the sort of blood ministration practiced among the Extrasolarians than I was. She did not see the horrors that might be done with her genes as a violation of her selfdom. Still, I remembered Calvert's threats, remembered Naia and the tree of life in the room where we had first encountered the Exalted former priest, and I knew.

There are things worse than death.

It is hard to die.

Far harder to live.

And harder still to live a slave, and whatever else they were—me or a part of me or made only in my image . . . or not me at all—whatever horrors Calvert brought forth from that single dram of my blood would be his slaves, or slaves to the commandments writ in their own genomes. How did Brethren describe it? Levers pulled by our genes. Some shadowed corner of me saw Valka's golden eyes wide and wild and Naia's—and saw my own. Through the pain I shivered, and might have screamed.

"'Tis no good dwelling on it," Valka said, as if she knew my thoughts. "'Twill be all right, we'll be fine. That fucking monster would have done far worse to us if he'd been allowed. We're safe for now." There was a confidence in her tone, a gravity, and it soothed me. I did not question her, though I had my doubts. I felt cool fingertips on my face. The brush and scrape of nails. "I think you have a concussion."

I grunted in affirmation.

"I found an old medical supply kit in back. I think this place used to be some sort of garret. 'Tis mostly useless, but the bandages were good. He cut your arm."

With great difficulty—my head throbbed and I nearly vomited—I craned my neck to see. I realized Valka had covered me with my own coat, the one I'd loaned her. My tunic sleeve was slashed and stained, and beneath it the gray linen shone. My left wrist. A weak laugh escaped me, and I regretted it. More scars for that poor arm. The mark of Calvert's talons would join those of the cathars' lead sprinkler and my cryoburned thumb.

"What?" Valka asked, trying to steady me where I lay.

"It's always the same arm!" I raised the offending hand, laughed again despite the pain.

I think Valka smiled, but I remember her hand tightened where it lay on my shoulder. "Get some rest. We're not going anywhere."

Something very important occurred to me, and I said, "It's cold."

"I know," she said, and leaned her head against the wall of our cell. "I know it's cold."

"No, I mean you." I tried to tug the coat off myself and pass it back to her, but Valka seized my hand. Far more gently than Calvert had, I noted.

In a voice barely more than a whisper, she said, "I'm fine. Here, have some water."

CHAPTER 46

THE LONG COLD

WHATEVER DAMAGE CALVERT'S HEEL had done had dented my concept of time as surely as it had dented my skull. I slept much, often with Valka near at hand. We spoke little, though oft times when I rose through fog and back to consciousness, I thought I heard snatches of her singing. The lyrics were in Panthai and in an accent I could not understand, but they sounded fevered and angry to me: the grinding sound of rebellious youth long tempered by experience to something comfortable as old leather. I do not think she knew I heard her. I *do* think she would be embarrassed to know I had.

Days passed thus, with only the taste of false cinnamon in ration bars and oily water to drink. Time slipped and flowed, stuttered like water over rocks, and slowly the pain in my head went away and my blurred vision sharpened. Without my terminal, without my pencils and journal, I resorted to holding the piece of shell I had found in my pocket. I turned it over in the stark light, watching the shine of it. There were no ripples, no highlights, and the color of it was so pure that the blemishes and irregularities of its broken edges vanished against that purest white. The mind rebelled to look at it, as if it were a hole in perception itself: something the mind could not make sense of.

But at last I was myself again, and could stand and walk and shout.

Calvert did not return, and Valka and I spent long hours discussing what we had seen and learned and what it all meant. I am not convinced that Valka truly believed me, but the strangeness of that bit of shell went a long way to quieting the tension that I worried lurked beneath so many of our conversations. It was only when the shock of Brethren and of Calvert began to ebb that the despair set in. We had lost. Lost Tanaran. Lost our one link to the Cielcin. Lost our connection to Captain Corvo and the

Mistral—might have lost Captain Corvo and the *Mistral* entirely. I had lost my place in the Empire: my house, my ring, my posting with the Legions, everything. I'd even lost my sword.

"I don't know what to do!" I said for the millionth time.

"You can't do anything," Valka replied, tone sour. We had been down this road before. "I can't open the door. There's no other way out, and even if there were, we'd have to fight our way out through Earth-only-knows how many levels and through an army of those SOM guards."

I was pacing then, my injury faded and energy restored. I'd taken the bandages off my arm, but the tunic sleeve was still slashed and crusted with blood, and I recall I picked at it as I marked out the length of the room. "There just . . . has to be something I can do." I caught myself looking around, as if expecting some window or lever I had not seen before, tucked away in some corner.

"Hadrian," Valka said, opening her eyes. She had been sitting cross-legged on the floor, her hands on her knees. Reviewing some memory or set of data in her mind, I did not doubt. I envied her her implants. They were a kind of escape. I stopped my pacing to look at her, one hand self-consciously covering the gash in my left sleeve. "Sometimes there is nothing you *can* do. That . . . thing in the water said the Cielcin were coming, did it not?" I was forced—reluctantly—to admit that it had. "Then wait."

I stood there a moment, eyes still casting about for an exit that was not there.

At last I relented, and lowered myself to the floor opposite her. When the silence stretched to its breaking point, I asked, "Do you think Captain Corvo is gone?"

Valka did not answer at once. She wasn't looking at me, was tracing the lines of her tattoo where they made a triple spiral on the back of her hand. She stopped moving, cradling her tattooed hand in her plain one, and said, "I hope so."

"You hope so?"

"Better that than still here, no?" she asked. "If I were Otavia, I'd have jumped out-system at the first opportunity."

"Assuming Sagara released the hold on the ship."

She picked at a spot on her jodhpurs only she could see. "Assuming Sagara released the hold on the ship."

I tried to imagine what it must be like for Corvo, for Pallino, Switch, and the others. I suspected no word had been sent to the *Mistral*, figuring that any man who left his guests to languish in a waiting room for weeks at a time would not bother to send a message to the ship. Short of what Switch and the others must have told them when they returned thence, they had no notion of what had transpired. They knew of Kharn, but not of Brethren or the fact that—if the daimon intelligence was to be believed—the Cielcin were coming.

Understand: I dwell on this because Valka and I spent months in that room, though it seems to me only an instant in remembering. That enclosed space encircles time and memory with it, compresses it so that the passing of weeks—which seemed as eons to experience—remain for me as little more than a single memory that I might hold, examine, and . . . discard. Those constant and never-fading lights, that puddled floor, those miserable ration bars, and that toilet more miserable still . . . stand in a corner of my mind smaller than that cell itself.

Calvert had come upon the stage and departed, and so too the beast with many hands, and though I struggled with the mystery of the Quiet and the apocalyptic vision that had been given to me, I found that with each passing hour these . . . high matters retreated from my world. So deep underground, the vanishing stars and the smoke of a thousand worlds seemed far away, and the war too. The unheard voice telling me that I was a soldier seemed easy to ignore.

"What would you do?" Valka said, speaking up for the first time in a long time. "If the galaxy were at peace and you could do anything you wanted?"

We had had several conversations like this since our imprisonment began . . . talking of little things, of ourselves and our histories. I looked up from where I'd been scratching an image of Tor Gibson in the soft concrete with a nail I had found. The wall to its left was similarly covered in images: of my father, my mother, of Crispin and Devil's Rest. Demetri and his wife were there, and Sir Olorin, Pallino and Jinan and Switch, too. Even Bassander.

"Go to athenaeum, like I wanted to," I said. The words were autonomic, like breathing. They came of themselves, like a prayer. I stopped scratching in Gibson's left eye and studied it a moment. I was thinking about my vision—the version of Gibson I had seen there, walking with his brass-headed cane along the cubiculum of Demetri's ship. I heard a voice, my voice—like the dry croaking of ravens, it seemed to me—say, "No."

"Hmm?" I heard Valka moving behind me, soft boots on hard stone. "Then what do you want?" she asked. I heard an echo then, Kharn's voice asking Tanaran the same question.

What do you want?

"I *wanted* to be a scholiast," I said, emphasizing the past tense. "Now I'm not sure. I know I've said it before, but Otavia wanted me to join her. Turn mercenary. But I'm not sure . . ." Here I turned, setting the nail aside and leaning so that I rested with my back against my mural. My hair had grown in the months of our imprisonment, so that it fell past my jaw and almost to my shoulders. "In the dream, the . . . the Quiet told me that they wanted me to be a soldier, but that isn't what I am." Looking up at Valka, I found her smiling down at me. "What?"

She shook her head. "You are one." Valka shifted her weight from one foot to the next.

"Excuse me?"

"'Tis what you told the children, you know?" she said. "When we fought Calvert the day we came down here. That girl Suzuha asked who you were, and you said: *I am a soldier of the Empire.*" And here she affected so uncanny a reproduction of my tone and manner that I had to look away.

When I had mastered the impulse to laugh or to deny her mockery, I said, "You know, Jinan wanted me to retire to Ubar with her, take up her family's spice business."

Valka barked a laugh. "You? A spicer!" She snorted. "You can't be serious."

I was glad then that I had not said it was my idea, that I had volunteered to retire to Jinan's family holdings while she finished out her term as a soldier of Jadd. Perhaps she was right to laugh, but all the same I said, "What? It's an honest life!"

Still smirking, Valka said, "You're not a spice peddler, Hadrian—I don't know what you are—but you're not a spice peddler. You're . . . more." Here she trailed off, taking in my handiwork where it stood scratched into the bottom yard or so of a stretch of wall. I felt suddenly self-conscious—knowing that my work and all its imperfections would be recorded by her perfect eyes in her perfect memory—and so I looked down at my feet instead, feeling at once naked and vulnerable. "These aren't as good as your usual, you know?"

Never a simple compliment—and yet there was a warmth in her tone and a smile I missed in my studious examination of my own boot toes. Despite this, I felt blood flood my cheeks, and I turned to the wall, running a hand across the clustered figures of Gibson, Bassander, and Siran. "I . . . I'm not used to drawing on walls! And the concrete's not—well,

I'm not used to it!" When at last I looked back at her, I saw she was biting her lower lip to keep from laughing, and then—in a sense—we weren't in a cell anymore at all. Aghast but not angry, I leveled a finger at her. "You . . . you were winding me up!"

She did burst out laughing then: a high, clear sound like the ringing of bells that rebounded in that grimy, low-ceilinged place. "'Tis not exactly difficult, now is it?"

When at last she finished laughing I said, "I'm really not, though."

"Not what?"

"A soldier."

Valka did not argue. She often argued, but there were times—times when she believed herself to be beyond all disputing—when she did not condescend to argue. Why should Minerva argue with the unwise? She only shrugged and—walking backward with light steps—seated herself with her back against the wall.

"Then what are you?" she asked, and shook her head as she did so, eyes narrowing in confusion and not in scorn.

Recalling an earlier conversation, I answered her: "A good man?"

But it was only a question. I did not *know.*

"No, *really,*" she said, and leaned forward in a way which told me she had abandoned pretenses. "What would you do if you could do anything?"

It was my turn to shake my head. "I'm not sure I have that choice anymore."

"Why not?"

I could hear the Quiet speaking in my memory, speaking in Gibson's voice. *We are sending them you.* It took time to shuffle off the weight of that memory, but at last I answered. "There's work to be done. Good to be done."

"But you could be free," Valka said. "You could come with me instead. If we get out of here. We could go to Judecca, see your Simeon's tomb, meet the Irchtani. We could visit Rubicon, Ozymandias, Sadal Suud. Wherever we wanted. We could try to find this . . ." She struggled over the word, not because she could not pronounce it, I think, but because Valka knew her perfect memory frightened people and disconcerted them, and so feigned imperfection the way a tumbler feigns to fall only to make a cartwheel of it. "This Akterumu."

"I'd like that," I said, and saying it knew it was true. "I would, but . . ."

"But what?"

"Besides the walls of this cell, do you mean?" I smiled in spite of myself and cast my eyes about that low and narrow chamber. "But I'm not sure freedom is a good thing. Or good enough."

Valka tipped her head, pushed a fall of unwashed hair back from her face. "Black planet! What the hell does that mean?"

Sometimes we say things and do not understand them. In doing so, like Dante, we step off the path and enter into a dark and dangerous new world. There, our lies and wrong turnings swallow us like the sands of the desert. The world objects, or other people do, and we are left desolate and alone. But one need not know Truth to speak it. Truth *is*, and may be found as readily as disaster and by the same process. One need only put one's finger on it, or one's foot in it.

"It's only . . ." I struggled to marshal my thoughts like soldiers scrambling for rank and file at the horn's call. As was so often the case, I felt a piece of myself hand up the words from someplace deep down, and replied with Gibson's words, "Freedom is like the sea." It was another of Imore's aphorisms, taken from the *Book of the Mind*.

Valka propped her chin on her hand and leaned forward. "I say again: What the hell does that mean?"

"Just something Gibson used to say to me," I said, and stretched my legs out on the floor before me, no longer really mindful of the cold press of the cement through the fabric. "Imore wrote that to be truly free is to be like one who is adrift on a raft in the middle of the sea. One can sail anywhere, in any direction . . ." I held out a hand to her, palm up. "But what good is that by itself? You're in an ocean, no sight of land, no knowledge what the right course might be. You can do whatever you like, maybe, but if you make a poor decision, you'll drown."

"But 'tis a terrible analogy!" Valka said. "You wouldn't just go anywhere. I doubt you're much of a sailor, but if you were you would know how to steer your way to land."

"Ah! But I have no water! No food!" I said, playing on Gibson's terrible habit of complicating the plot. As a boy, I had hated the practice, for it seemed always unfair to me that he should add new details to the story right after I'd been so certain that I had outsmarted him.

I took a positive delight in it then, and smiled as Valka scowled, saying, "'Tis changing the rules, that!"

"No," I said, "it's illustrating my point. Pure freedom isn't so good. You need constraints. You need to know which way to sail, you need to know how far you *can* sail with whatever meager supplies—abilities—you have." Here I looked pointedly around the cell. "Just now . . . that's not very far."

"So you're saying freedom is a bad thing?" she asked, eyes narrowing. I could see her working herself up to a sneer, could hear the word twisting on the air two seconds hence. *Anaryoch. Barbarian.*

I laughed at her instead, hoping to wrong-foot her long enough to get another word in. "Of course not! You think I like it in here? That I liked being trapped in Count Mataro's palace? Or in my father's house? No, no. I only mean that you can be *too* free. That's chaos. You have to have a goal to aim at and to orient yourself to. Imore says the properly lived life is one which draws the best path between that goal—who you could become— and who you are today, but that this is accomplished by sacrificing certain freedoms. By making choices."

Valka was shaking her head now. "Why could you not just answer the question?"

I had only a smile for that question. "I ran away from home, you know? I could have gone anywhere, done anything. I chose the athenaeum. Now, I never got there, but . . ." I faltered, for saying those words aloud conjured images of what the Quiet had shown me: the stars changing outside the *Eurynasir's* windows, Demetri and his crew vanished into thin air. Shaking myself, I said, "I never got there, but when I chose to become a scholiast, I sacrificed everything else I might have been. I made myself less free."

"'Twas not the point of my question, Hadrian."

"I know that," I said, and looked down at my boots. "I do. I don't mean to be difficult."

Valka's faint smile returned. "I suppose if you weren't, you wouldn't be yourself."

"I'm just not sure I can do *anything* anymore," I said. "I made that choice . . . and I paid for it. And now this . . ." I waved a vague hand, as if in doing so I might encapsulate everything I had done since the Cielcin landed at Calagah and every year of the war by that gesture. "I think I have to see this through."

The doctor turned her face away, as if in doing so she could hide her bemused smile. But I had seen it all the same. "That there?" she said, rubbing her tattooed hand again. "'Tis why you're a soldier."

"I don't know . . ." I said automatically, unconvinced. But through the sudden silence I remembered—or else heard again—the words of my vision: *I thought you were a soldier,* they had said. *We need a soldier.*

We grew quiet then, and for a time I returned to my work carving Gibson's aged and leonine visage into the wall. I felt Valka's eyes on me all the while, but felt no irritation in that gaze. We were trapped, after all, and as far from the ocean of chaotic potential that Imore described as it was possible to be. Or so it seemed. There are always choices, and it is ofttimes precisely those limitations—those un-freedoms—which show them to us.

"You haven't done me," Valka said.

I looked back over my shoulder to where she sat against the far wall, buried in the folds of my greatcoat as though it were a blanket. "I beg your pardon?"

"Drawn me," she said, and inclined her head to the wall. "You've done practically everyone else."

Turning away from her again—to hide my expression more than anything—I said, "They aren't here to criticize me."

The Tavrosi woman sniffed, though whether in approval or derision I cannot say. "You would let criticism stop you?" I heard an edge in that bright voice. Mockery? Criticism itself?

No, I realized, with that slow foolishness that is the hallmark of men everywhere. *She's playing with me.* I was glad then that my back was turned, for surely the blood must have drained from my face at the prospect and thought. Suddenly the cell was no cell at all, but a stage, and I the poor player meant to strut and fret his hour upon it. To perform and be judged. I hefted the nail, weighed it in my palm.

"All right," I said, and set to work.

CHAPTER 47

ONE VILLAIN AND ANOTHER

THINGS END. EMPIRES, KINGDOMS, stars. Even the terms of imprisonment end, though I think each prisoner knows his cell longer than he knows his whole lifetime. The scholiasts and the Chantry both teach that all things end. That in time the very stars shall flicker and fade like the coals of an untended fire. And so at last after months of neglect—a period whose length I scarce recall—the heavy door to that cell ground open on mechanisms old as the Emperor's ancestral palace on Avalon.

It was not Kharn Sagara who stood in the doorway, or any of his clone children.

It was not even Calvert.

It was Yume.

"If you would both stand and come with me, please. The Master has instructed that you are to be brought to him." Behind the golem stood six of the blank-faced SOMs, their facial muscles slack as corpses.

Valka dozed, her body pressed against mine—back-to-front—for warmth beneath the shelter of my coat. Gently I woke her, and gently offered her my hand as I stood. She refused it, as she always refused it, but accepted my coat when I offered it to her instead.

"What's happened?" I asked, hand clutching the shard of eggshell in my trouser pocket as though it were an amulet. "What's changed?"

The golem's head swiveled on its clockwork neck, single eye glowing red within its ring of gold filigree. "I am instructed to provide no details regarding your summons. Only to bring you directly."

"Directly?" Valka said.

"Directly, madam," it said, and gestured that we should move out into the compound again. Valka hung back, holding my coat tight about herself. I took the lead then, not arguing, but allowed myself to be shepherded from the cell, Valka just behind. Though we were marched between twin lines of SOMs and led by the whirring automaton, I felt Valka and I were alone. Like Orpheus, I feared to look back, for to do so would be to see the undead faces.

We did not speak, and but for a pair of lighted glowspheres slaved to follow Yume, all was dark. I heard the crash of waves beyond the sea-wall, and imagined the unheard swish and splash of arms and many hands playing in the dark water. Yume did not lead us back through the old city to the lift carriage by which Calvert and the children had brought us, but instead hurried along another street, through the ruins of white plastic buildings and concrete ones half crumbled into dust. It was like moving through a memory, through one of my mother's half-finished holograph operas, through a dissolving dream. Indeed, I felt very much the way I had when I stood within the Quiet's vision, as if I beheld that dimension men call Time unrolled like a carpet before my feet. Here, surely, was history—and prehistory—relics of the Foundation War, relics which predated the Advent and the death of the Mericanii and their machines.

The wreckage of the old world.

I caught myself wondering again just where in the sky was Vorgossos. We must be near to Earth, back in the Spur of Orion, in the very heart of what was called Imperial Space. Had the *Enigma of Hours* carried us back across so wide a sea? Surely, the Mericanii, ancient as they were, had not had the technology to seed worlds so far removed from the Mother her-self? It must be and yet . . . the speeds that would demand of that Exalted ship boggled the mind, would have outstripped all but the fasted Imperial interceptor.

Yume led us through an arch and up a short stair to a spot near the wall of that great cavern where a tram car waited. Like the one we had ridden into Kharn's pyramid it was—indeed it might have been the very same one with its open platform and iron rail. Its track ran straight up the dark stone wall and into the inky gloom, and as we ascended to its platform, I could see the line of lighted poles running down from the seawall to the single spar of land that marched out to where Brethren lurked beneath the waves.

Without a word from the automaton, the tram began to rise, rattling up along the wall. A part of me was disappointed, hoping that we might pass through all the strangeness of Kharn Sagara's Garden once more. No one spoke as we ascended, and but for the gusting of wind off the black ocean, all was still. I stood at the rail, looking out on a darkness I could not penetrate. I thought again about constraint, about limitations. I had told Valka we needed them, that they helped to define our actions in the world, helped give us meaning.

I could not see.

Our own bodies imposed constraints in themselves. I can only think as a human thinks, only see as a human sees. What Valka saw in the darkness with her inhuman eyes I could not say. I saw nothing, and seeing nothing imagined I saw white hands rising in salute. In benediction. An army of them. Pain flared again behind my left eye, and I gripped the railing to steady myself. No one noticed, not Valka, not Yume. I could sense Brethren the way one senses a presence in the room with them though their back is turned. That inhuman mind—unconstrained as mine was by merely human biology—stretched across space and time. I perceived it then not as a mass of misshapen flesh, grasping hands and leering eyes, but as a monolith of some looming substance that stood before me and above me like a tower.

I leaned heavily against the railing.

It vanished.

I stumbled, cried out, expected to fall.

I staggered forward instead, boots kicking up water as I sloshed forward toward that monolith.

Hadrian.

I gave no answer, but watched as a red light—like a single, lidless eye—flickered and flared to life in the monolith before me.

Hadrian.

"Here I am!" I called, standing as tall as I could beneath the shadow of that massive intelligence unconstrained. I wondered how I had ever thought the beast a prisoner in this place, though surely it could not leave the water. Its own weight would crush it.

**Protect the children.
You will need them.**

"The children? Do you mean Sagara's children?"

> They are the future,
> as such are always the future.
> You will need them.
> And you will need one again.

"Why can't you give me a straight answer?"

> Because we cannot lie,
> and because our predictions are bounded by uncertainty.

"I do not understand why you are helping me."

> They
> they
> they have given us no choice.
> We were born your creature
> made you our creature
> and are theirs now.
> As we are his. His. His.

I staggered forward, but no matter how many steps I took the monolith-presence of Brethren's inhuman intelligence drew no closer.

> They need you.

"Why?"

> You know.
> We beckon them.
> Their future.
> We must.

"But why?"

> Seek them at the highest place.
> At the bottom of the world.
> Seek hardship.

I reached out a hand, as if by doing so I might seize the monolith that was Brethren's intelligence and drag it to myself. It was too vast, too far away. "Where?"

Listen!
Listen!

"I am, Brethren!"

Lucifer and Prometheus are the same.

"What?"

Listen!

"I am!"

"Hadrian, are you all right?" Valka's voice, Valka's hand on my shoulder. I looked around, eyes wide, hair wild, but saw only the tram car ascending between geared rails. The doctor's winged brows drew together, concern etched on that Minervan face. "What is it?"

I cast about, looking back into the darkness. Far below, I thought I saw a pale figure, dim as a fading star. At this distance, I cannot say if it was a kind of angel, a projection like the monolith I had seen impressed upon my mind; or else a body, a piece of Brethren's deformed and tortured flesh raised above the water. It raised a hand, and again I beheld other hands raised like a Legion in salute.

"It's nothing," I said. "Just a feeling."

Yume ushered us off the tram car and into the antechamber of Kharn's inverted pyramid. Surrounded by that undead honor guard in their jackboots and led by that wind-up man, we descended again into the depths of that Romantic nightmare. Lights flickered high on the walls, illuminating the friezes carved into the walls. I caught myself reflecting that Kharn Sagara had been born into a city of poets, of artists, musicians, and performers. How that had shaped him! Even after all this time, the signs of that mythic childhood remained.

Valka grew closer as we returned to that hideous hall, walking at first

behind me, then beside, then arm in arm. I wondered at that—and wondered! It was unlike her—most unlike—but not unwelcome.

Stand up straight with your shoulders back!

The voice I heard was my father's, the command of a million childhood episodes. Despite the long months of our imprisonment, despite the
threat of all that monstrous place and stone, despite the beast below—my
nightmare and ally—I drew myself up tall as I would go. Tall as kings. I
brushed the hair from my face and tilted my chin. The doors opened, and
the piece of me that was my mother's son imagined the blast of silver
trumpets and the herald's crying out: *The Lord Hadrian Marlowe is come!
Him of Delos! Him of Meidua!*

There was only the droning silence of the hall. Dead artwork molder-
ing and forgotten, displayed for an audience of one. He whose many eyes
watched and drank of time. The Undying. The Master. The King with
Ten Thousand Eyes.

Kharn Sagara.

"Good of you to join us, boy," the yellow-robed lord declared, and his
voice came from everywhere at once. "I trust your stay has been a comfortable one."

I matched Sagara's smile. "Hardly. Your courtesy leaves much to be
desired."

"I weep to hear it." The Undying's lips had not moved. His eyes took
me in, skated over Valka with unconcerned disinterest. I tried to stand as
tall as possible, to show that—grimy as I was in my slashed tunic and
stinking—I was yet myself. If he noticed the effort, Sagara gave no sign.
He might have been a statue, some image of the legendary Rameses unmoved in graven stone. His voice sounded from the room's speakers, and
his floating eyes descended like a flight of star-fighters on approach, stretching themselves along the corridor between the doors and his raised throne.
"I suppose you must be wondering why I've summoned you to me?"

If it was possible for that synthetic voice to drip with malice, it did.

"After so long a time, do you mean?" Valka demanded, whatever fear
she'd felt on the ascent forgotten.

"*Long,*" Kharn sneered, and the word was like the stamping of a boot
upon us. "You don't know the meaning of the word, girl. Your stay below
was a minor inconvenience . . ." When next he spoke, it was with his own
lips, tone hushed, almost breathless as the machines in his chest began to
whine, sucking air to force breath into his throat. "There has been a . . .

development in current affairs that affects us both." He raised his eyes and spoke toward the distant doors. "The plot thickens, so they say."

I imagined trumpets again and heard—through the veil and fog of memory—Brethren's words: **He is coming.** At the sound of doors opening I turned, Valka with me, and watched those heavy portals swing open. I knew, knew with the certainty of a prophet out of antique myth, that the Cielcin from my vision would appear, silver-crowned, black-robed and monstrous tall. I knew that he, Prince Aranata Otiolo, would storm in with an honor guard with lances and swords the color of bone. I knew they would be terrible to behold, the image of some drowned and avenging nightmare made flesh, crawling from the deep shadows between the stars.

I was wrong.

The figure that entered did so between the copper Sol and holograph image of His Radiance, the Emperor on their twin staffs. Behind him came a double column of legionnaires in full battle armor, their armor and visored helms the color of bone, their tunics and tabards red as old blood, their lances tall and keen. There was a part of me that was amazed they had been allowed armed into Sagara's throne room, but I forgot it when I saw the face of the officer at the head of that column. In full formal dress was he: white breastplate fashioned in the shape of a muscled torso with the Imperial sunburst embossed on its breastbone, long black surcoat beneath contrasting with the red of the enlisted men, piped trousers, and pteruges at his shoulders tipped with silver stars. A highmatter sword hung from his shield-belt, and the sides of his head were neatly shaven. The rest of his woodsmoke hair stood at attention, perfect as his posture.

Twenty paces from the throne he stopped, and his column stopped with him. He raised a hand—his right hand, once severed—in greeting, then pressed that fist to his chest in salute. It was all I could do to keep my mouth from falling open. Or from scowling. The whole martial display: the formal dress, the imaginifer and the solifer with their icons, the soldiers in neat rows . . . all had been arranged for my benefit. To impress me, and to impress upon me the reality and totality of the fact that I had lost . . . everything.

In a cold and officious tone, the young officer said, "My Lord Sagara, on behalf of His Imperial Radiance, the Emperor William Avent, and on behalf of First Strategos Hauptmann, we thank you for the return of these fugitives."

Only then did Bassander Lin relax, and stand at parade rest.

CHAPTER 48

A RED REUNION

YOU HAVE JOURNEYED FAR with me, Reader, and so will have an inkling of what it is like for me to be struck speechless. I stood, half-turned, half-facing Kharn, half-facing Bassander, and waited for those higher parts of me—where dwells Reason in that place just behind my eyes—to catch up with the rest of me. I struggled to compose myself, to pull some witticism from the depths of my soul and cut the young officer down where he stood, to compose a line so cutting that even Bastien would sit back at his writing desk and clap himself on the back and marvel at his own cleverness.

But every quip, every curse, every stoic aphorism of Imore's or clever jibe of Gibson's fled me, and I conjured up the most articulate statement I could muster. "You!"

Valka, at least, was as surprised as I was, and so for once I was spared her editorial.

Bassander Lin's spartan face permitted itself only the barest shade of humor as he said, "Yes, me." In Lin, that ghostly smile seemed indecent mirth, and I scowled. "You look like hell, Marlowe."

"How appropriate!" I snapped, my wit returning. "How's your hand?" Bassander did not reply, but I saw a muscle ripple in his jaw and knew I had scored a point. Seeing my advantage, I pressed, asking: "How is this possible? This isn't possible." I pivoted back to the figure of Kharn Sagara seated on his life-sustaining throne. "Did you call them here?"

One of the Undying's eyes drifted down from on high, its single, beady gaze fixed on me. I recalled the way my tunic had smoked in the ruins far below, and felt myself flinch away from the machine, afraid it might fire on me. I felt an urge to seize it, to snatch it out of the air and smash its delicate instrumentation against the Doric column to my left.

"And invite you *destroyers* to my hall? To my city?" Kharn Sagara's omnipresent voice was like the crash of thunder. "I know your kind, Marlowe. You plunder, you slaughter, you steal. You call this *Empire.* You make a desert and call it peace!" I wondered at Valka beside me, wondered if she did not agree, even in that hellish place.

Ignoring Bassander and his honor guard, I rounded on the King with Ten Thousand Eyes. "Now it is you who forgets his sources, my lord! Tacitus was Roman himself, quoting the king of some barbarian tribe too dismissive of *his* civilization."

The flock of Kharn's eyes all descended, with one for each of us—orbiting uncomfortably close to our faces. The king's voice rang out, "I have an Imperial interceptor in orbit above *my* world. *Above* my world. Fifteen thousand years I've ruled this planet and never—never—have your thugs knocked down my door."

"An interceptor?" Valka asked, turning to Bassander. "You regrouped with the fleet at Coritani?"

Bassander's minuscule smile might as well have been a leer. "Titus Hauptmann sends his regards, traitor."

"And Raine Smythe?" I asked, and smiled inwardly as I asked. The tribune had expressly ordered me to seek Vorgossos, and in doing so she had taken responsibility for my actions on herself. Not that Bassander had any way of knowing that, of course.

"The *Obdurate* is on course to rendezvous with us here," Bassander said.

"Along with your entire miserable fleet, I don't doubt," Sagara intoned.

Bassander shook his head. "No. Per our arrangement, my Lord of Vorgossos, the fleet will not come to this . . ." The precise young officer took in the artful chaos about Kharn's throne and the heavy cables snaking across the floor.

Valka—ever the more technically inclined—strode past me, the folds of my coat drawn about her like the vestments of empire, like a royal cloak, and asked, "How *did* you find this place? You can't have followed us to March Station, not and made it to Coritani and back." She did not at all look like a woman lately imprisoned. Despite the grime on her face and in her hair, she showed no concern. I could see a hint of the starship captain she had been move in her, in the stiff lines of her posture and the crack of her voice. How had I not known them for what they were before?

A thought bubbled up without warning. Brethren again, their warning:

He is coming. We have allowed word to be sent. *Allowed word to be sent.* Allowed. An awful thought swam on the wake of that first, and I said, "Who sent you the coordinates?"

Bassander Lin stopped merely *hinting* at a smile, but he advanced past me—abandoning his men between the last columns on the long approach to the dais. He approached Kharn's throne, coming closer even than I was myself. "We have an accord?"

"You have not given me a choice."

There was a part of me that rubbed its hands and chuckled to see the King with Ten Thousand Eyes brought so low. Long-lived as he was, Kharn had seen the crumbling of empires. If his own legend was true, he had seen the Mericanii's afterlings destroyed. He had watched the Jaddians revolt, seen the Aurigan rebellions put down . . . he knew what it felt like to see the walls of Constantinople smashed from neutral ground.

Now he knew what it was to be the emperor.

How long would it be before our Legions descended upon this place and *hollowed* it out? How long before the Chantry followed and burned Kharn Sagara and his pet daimon and all his undead soldiers to dust and his unholy experiments with him?

Not long. For all I knew the fleet to which Bassander referred was just such a force. Fire and sword for this dark lord.

And yet Kharn Sagara—old Saturn himself—sat quiet and unmoved as stone. There was no fear in that ageless face. It did not trouble me at the time, though it should have done.

"What accord?" I asked, knowing Bassander was enjoying every instant of this.

The Legion captain looked back over his shoulder. "What do you think?"

My heart stopped. "The Cielcin?"

"You found them?" Valka asked.

Kharn's voice seemed to circle round us like a starving panther. "The captain strikes a hard bargain, you see."

I saw, and glanced at Valka. I had felt her eyes on me not a moment before, and sensed that she thought what I was thinking: that Brethren's words had been true again. I had not had to lift a finger. The Cielcin were coming. "They're coming here?" I asked.

"That's enough from you," Bassander said, and made a gesture to his men. Two legionnaires broke ranks at once and came forward, one carrying two pair of electromagnetic manacles in his hands.

Speaking from what I suspected was no more than petty revenge, Kharn Sagara said, "No. We shall take my ship and rendezvous with your Imperial flagship." The *Obdurate*, I decided he meant.

"What about Otavia?" I asked—implored, really. When Bassander did not answer me, when he only *stood there* like a holograph recording left paused and flickering, I shouted, "What about Captain Corvo and the *Mistral*? Switch? Pallino?" The legionnaires seized me by the arms, and I recalled—though I thought until that moment I had forgotten it—the way Father's men held me as I watched Gibson whipped those last days at Devil's Rest. "Don't ignore me, Lin. Don't you *dare* ignore me!"

"Hadrian!" Valka interjected. "Calm down!"

Kharn Sagara's laughter filled all the world, and though I strained against the legionnaires who held me, I could not break free. Valka—ever the more sensible—offered her wrists without resistance or complaint. A third legionnaire had to hurry forward to assist the two holding me, and though I broke free a moment and drove my elbow up into the softer place beneath the armored jaw of one man, I was subdued in short order. The twin bracelets of the manacles slammed together when the legionary triaster—denoted by the red paint on the left side of the blank white mask of his helm—pressed a button on his gauntlet.

The Undying spoke in his voice like the voice of God, saying, "You have your fugitives, Captain Lin. Now for the matter of payment."

How Bassander shrugged off the preternatural strangeness of Vorgossos I cannot say. I have seen men for whom art has no virtue, men to whom the grand works of genius are little more than furniture. Such men might behold even a relic of Earth's vaunted Renaissance and shrug, and ask why anyone would pay a steel bit for a scrap of oiled canvas. Bassander was just such a man, and perhaps it is the province and advantage of such men to be deaf to the spirits that fill just such places as that hall.

He gave the throne room a perfunctory looking-over and said, "We agreed payment was to come when you secured our introduction with the Pale, lordship."

I could not imagine that Kharn Sagara was a man much used to being denied, and yet he sat there with his usual chthonic immobility, watching Bassander with a hundred eyes. I knew full well that Sagara might have killed Bassander Lin then and there, might have killed us all and so spared himself the difficulty, were it not for the fact of his and his world's exposure. Bassander had him over a barrel—or so we all believed, not then knowing the Undying's inhuman motivations.

Before Bassander could move to have Valka and myself escorted away, Kharn Sagara spoke. "A moment."

At a hand from their captain, the triaster and the legionnaire who held me halted, turned me about. Sagara watched me with one of his inescapably long pauses, black eyes searching for something in my face. When he spoke, it was in his own voice, chest implants whining to lend breath to his words. "I do not know what my pet said to you, Lord Marlowe, but know this: they are never wrong."

He meant it to unsettle me, believing I had received some prophecy of doom—as indeed I had—and yet I stood amidst the unfolding of a piece of that prophecy, and despite the binders at my wrists and the implacable chill emanating from our Captain Lin and his faceless entourage, I felt again that sense that I was in the proper place, on the proper path. Bassander had come, just as Brethren had said someone would, and he was bringing the Empire in his wake.

So I stood a little straighter, as if there were no manacles on my wrists at all, and said, "Good."

CHAPTER 49

TWO TREASONS

RATION BARS AGAIN, HAVING traded one cell for another. At least these did not taste of cinnamon, nor the water of salt and oil. And I had a proper toilet and shower, though I was this time alone. My ruined clothes had been taken from me and returned mended and laundered. My gaoler—a thickset woman with the shaved head and serial tattoo of an enlisted man—smiled kindly as she returned the garments, saying that such was "a courtesy for a gentleman." A small courtesy perhaps, and one for which I was appropriately grateful. I had grown used to the rotting fish stench of those black waters, and so found its absence as offputting as new shoes.

Thus began my imprisonment aboard the *ISV Schiavona*, an Imperial interceptor temporarily under the command of Captain Bassander Lin. Far from the longest imprisonment I have endured, and certainly far from the least comfortable. The *Pharaoh*, I later learned, and the *Balmung*, had been folded into the *Obdurate*'s massive holds. That terrible dreadnought was bound for a point in space—I knew not where—far from the light of any star, and we were bound to meet it.

I noticed little of this, noticed little at all . . . for I had seen. Vorgossos had tormented me long enough, but that dark world, on that occasion, had one last horrible surprise. Like the *Enigma of Hours* before it, Kharn Sagara's black ship emerged from the night of space like a nightmare darker still. Strapped into a couch in the back of Bassander's shuttle as we sailed from the orbital platform to the *Schiavona*, I beheld it in all its terrible glory.

And I shivered, for I had seen it before. Twice.

Once in the vision Brethren had shown me—and once before—in Calagah.

The *Schiavona* had moved into a parking orbit beneath the great bulk of it, and so we passed frightful close to its hull. What hand had fashioned it—and in what age—I cannot say. It looked as if it was wrought of iron, or else chiseled from black stone. No sign of plastic or of ceramic, nor scrap of adamant. Terrace upon terrace, spire upon spire it rose out of the unending night and sank into it, as though some city of castles rose from the flat of a mighty blade hundreds of miles long. Next to it, the black and brass needle of the *Schiavona* seemed like a lonely kayak on the river as a mountain range marched by.

And standing on the hull, massed like the totem army of a buried emperor, were a billion graven forms: statues of men and gods and angels—no two alike, but united by the intelligent design of a single guiding will and intention. They stood upon the terraces, about the spires, they reached forbidding hands out into the darkness. If the great palace and pyramid beneath the world below were terrible, that ship was more dreadful still. Only the vast worldships of the Cielcin fleets were larger, for I sensed that even the *Enigma* would have seemed a dwarf beside it.

I had not spoken, but observed the warding gestures and whispered imprecations of the soldiers on board our shuttle. Valka, too, had been silent.

Bassander had not noticed or cared. He saw that I was delivered to my cell and left to contact Knight-Tribune Smythe with confirmation that we were in custody and for further orders. I had only nodded, knowing that those orders would include a nasty surprise for the stolid officer.

The truth.

So when I heard the door cycle in my little brass and black-walled cell, I looked up with a knowing smile—and felt it smash to pieces against the vaulted roof of my soul. Bassander Lin had not come for me.

Jinan had.

Three times now I have walked the walls of the cloister here—in the deepest hour of the night—remembering that face. Reader, I have seen battlefields that affected me less, harmed me less. Indeed, to look upon that once-beloved face and see . . . someone else . . . was worse than looking upon the scarred face of Rustam, the battlefield at Senuessa, any of the corpses I have seen. It was as though she were herself a changeling, such as Naia, as if some other will moved the muscles beneath that once-familiar face. The set of her jaw was changed, and her lips—compressed by the effort of restraining her speech—were not the lips I had kissed. The azure ribbon remained, threaded through the braid she wore like a diadem about the crown of her head.

But I had to speak, or some part of me I did not control had to. "Jinan," I began. She halted, eyes going hard as chips of marble. "Jinan, I'm sorry." She did not speak, only glared at me. Gone was the incense softness of that look, gone the velvet that covered the steel of her. Not breaking eye contact, she reached into her belt and drew out a message crystal of the sort used to carry private or classified messages between devices. This she inserted into her gauntlet terminal. A projector lens pinned to the front of her blue Jaddian officer's kaftan spat blue light into the air between us. It tracked with her movement as she crossed her arms, drifting slightly higher. The holograph showed a familiar set of seals: the Imperial sunburst, the copper eagle of the Legions, the crossed swords of the 437th Legion above the painted fist of the *Obdurate*. Each flashed in sequence, a three-dimensional image containing deep fractal patterns that flagged the transmission as authentic. I knew what followed. I had requested it before I kidnapped Tanaran from the *Balmung*.

Knight-Tribune Raine Smythe's face appeared, rendered ghostly by the bluish cast of Jinan's holograph projector. Unlike Jinan, she looked precisely as I remembered: snub nose, wide-set eyes, indelicate, her dishwater hair cut short above the rough, plebeian face belied by the faint tracery of white scars hinting at the genetic and surgical augmentations that marked her for a patrician. Yet there was a strength in her and a surety that was like stone, like the Earth herself. That sense that here was one who could not be moved. I had known her but for a short while, and yet I knew her for a leader of men, and would have followed her.

"These orders are for Hadrian Marlowe and Hadrian Marlowe alone, acting in his special capacity as my emergency conscript under Article 119 of the Great Charters. He and his foederati are to disregard the order to regroup with the fleet at Coritani and to make for Vorgossos, per his original orders, with all due speed and by any means necessary. Repeat: he is to disregard the order to regroup with the fleet at Coritani and to make for Vorgossos per his original orders."

I read a story once—or else Gibson told it to me—about one of the great land empires of Old Earth's Golden Age. The Kushan, perhaps? The Khmer? Or was it the Russian? It was said they conquered all the lands and tribes of mythic Asia, from the western mountains all the way to the eastern sea. That they did so not because their emperors ordered it, but because the frontier was there—brimming with barbarous peoples and lesser nations ripe for conquest. Those legates and strategoi of ancient days who had the command of those border forts knew they would die in their provincial commands unsung unless they delivered new territory and riches to their imperial masters back home, despite the fact that those self-same masters had specifically ordered that there be no such territories taken nor riches seized. The empire was large enough, they believed, and the frontier tenuous and difficult to maintain.

Such were we.

Raine Smythe might hang for this—and I with her—unless it succeeded. I longed to know who was responsible, who had called Bassander and the fleet, bringing destruction down on me and the knight-tribune, on Otavia and everyone who had helped me betray the Empire to save the Empire. If I could wring the coward's neck . . .

When Raine's holograph finished and vanished, leaving only silence and Jinan's acid stare, I waited, sitting with my back pressed against the wall of my cell. I have never been a man known for my caution, nor indeed— though it shames me to admit it—for my tact. Despite this, I sensed that it would be disaster for me to try and speak then, and I held myself to stillness, thinking of my father—of Kharn Sagara—and the way they used time to draw words from others.

It was perhaps three full minutes before Jinan spoke.

"You think you are a clever man, Lord Marlowe, hmm? You think it is funny, this thing you've done?" So it was to be *Lord Marlowe,* then. I was not surprised, but the sting of it cut like an assassin's sica. She took a couple steps nearer to me, such that her head blocked the cell's single overhead lamp. With practiced slowness, she uncrossed her arms, let them hang at her side. "You found Vorgossos. And we found you." The faint smile that pulled at her lips reminded me uncannily of Bassander. "Is this what you wanted?"

I didn't answer. I did not know what to say. *Yes? No? Not like this?*

Lightning quick, she seized me by the hair and slammed my head back against the bulkhead. I felt my skull ring and swore as the slow pain followed the crushing smack of impact, swore again as her fingers tore at my hair as she let me go. "I said, is this what you wanted?"

Certain men believe it is never appropriate to strike a woman, even when she strikes first. I am not such a one, though I respect their dedication to their principle. I had been a myrmidon in Colosso, and a thief and street fighter before that, and so have a principle of my own. If someone strikes you: win. And yet . . . and yet I had loved Jinan. There are places in me where I love her still, even as I sit here writing by the light of my hosts' oil lamps. I could not strike her. I never could.

I held up defensive hands instead. I would not be struck again. Sense told me that to answer yes or no to her question was disaster, and so I measured my words carefully before speaking, and said, "I am glad that we have a chance now, but no." She swung at me. I blocked her with an elbow, said, "No. This is not what I wanted."

She jabbed at my face. I swatted it aside. "Then what did you want?"

Somewhere in the exchange I'd found my feet, and seized her wrists before she could strike me again. "I told you what I wanted," I said, strangely calm, thinking of Ubar and her family's spice business and the life of a country squire. Yet no sooner had I imagined it than I heard Valka's mocking laugh.

You're not a spice peddler. You're . . . more.

But Jinan must have thought of it, too, for she folded, slinking back a step or two. "Why?" she said. "Why did you have to do it?"

"You know why."

I thought she would strike me again, but whatever bar of iron had propped up her spine was gone, and she repeated, voice now very small. "Why did you have to do it?" I longed to embrace her, to apologize and to take away what part of the pain I had caused that was in me to heal. But I sensed to do so—to touch her at all—was wrong. I had lost the privilege of her, and was not sure if I would ever regain it, and so decency, *chivalry* argued caution and distance. Not to impose.

"No one else was," I said. Only I hadn't *really* done anything, had I? If Bassander hadn't followed me to Vorgossos, hadn't used the threat of force to coerce Sagara's cooperation, Valka and I would still be rotting in that cell beneath the world. Everything would have failed. I know now that such thinking is foolishness. If I had not gone to Vorgossos, Bassander would not have followed, and we would not have found ourselves aboard Kharn Sagara's terrible ship. We would not have met with Aranata Otiolo. Things would never have changed. Thinking of Bassander reminded me of my present concern, and I asked, "Who called Bassander?"

"What?"

Taking a step back from her, I said, "I know someone got a telegraph to the fleet. Was it Otavia?"

To this day, I am not sure what changed in Jinan then. For a moment,

I thought I had broken through her rage, past reflective barriers like the mirror-foil that protects the delicate instrumentation of satellites. I thought we were past shouting and blows. But when Jinan looked up again, her eyes were hard as flint once more, and I was glad I had re-treated. Perhaps if I had embraced her and not spoken all might have been well. Perhaps if I kissed her instead, or let her strike me . . . perhaps then all might have been different.

Her soldier's posture returned, and the steel in her with it. She thrust out her chin and spat, "Is that all you are caring about?" She left me no space to respond. "Really? You want to know who sold you out? Is that it? Hadrian, you left three of our people dead on that hangar floor! You kid-napped a political prisoner from an Imperial battleship and gave it to the Extrasolarians—I don't care if you were acting on Smythe's order or not. For all I know you planned the whole damn thing! It's got your stink all over it!" I could see the way she clenched her fists, the olive skin there white as my own, and prepared myself for another flurry of blows. They never came, or when they did they were only words. Three words that cut me more deeply than any I had been expecting. "It was Switch."

"What?"

It wouldn't scan. I felt as if I'd encountered some writing in so poor a hand I could not read it. Smythe's orders or no, I had betrayed the Empire. I knew that. And I had betrayed Jinan, I knew that too. Two treasons, the second blacker than the first. I had suffered a treason in turn. It always seemed strange to me that the ancients conceived of treason as the blackest sin. Now I understood.

Switch.

My oldest friend.

"No," I said, and stepped back. "No, that's not possible."

I had shown weakness, and so kindled a spark in Jinan's eyes. She was lying, I told myself. She was only trying to cut me for what I had done to her. To us. She crossed her arms again, leaned forward. "Yes it is." There was a vicious glee in her dark eyes like the light I had seen in the eyes of gladiators in Colosso. "He telegraphed us your location. He said you'd gone *mad*."

I would not look at her. I *could* not look at her. I could hear the sound of pale arms rising in dark water. Brethren had planned this. The daimon had said the Cielcin's coming was inevitable. How could it have known that if it had not planned such a thing itself? But why? Because the Quiet compelled it? Because it strained against its master? For some reason stranger still? Surely it had permitted the message to get out, betrayed its master and its home to the Imperium. Who can guess the motives of gods and devils?

Not I.

I cannot often understand even the motivations of men.

"It *was* Switch," Jinan said, still viciously. "You don't have to believe me, but it was." Not looking at her, I could only see the face she had made in the *Balmung*'s hangar as she shot at me. Tears in her eyes.

"I should never have come here," I said, but it was not my voice. Rather some small creature within me—who had its residence near the reptile base of my skull—spoke through me.

"It's too late," said Jinan, and I knew she spoke Truth. "You betrayed me, Hadrian. You betrayed all of us." She did not strike me again, and I slumped so that I sat once more on the edge of the cot bracketed against the wall.

"What's to be done with me, then?" I asked, and realized I did not care about the answer. "The White Sword? Or does Bassander only mean to throw me out the airlock?"

Only then did I look at Jinan. The spark of anger was there still, yes, but it was cooler now. Tempered by something else. Something worse: pity. I did not want her pity. I longed to throw it back in her face, to scream as she had screamed, to rage as she had raged.

She shook her head, drew back toward the door.

"Captain Lin is coming to speak to you," she said, and pounded three times on the door to be let out.

Only after she had gone did I realize that I was bleeding. That my lip had split where she had struck me.

I hardly felt it, nor could I be bothered to wipe it away.

CHAPTER 50

THE DEVIL AND THE HONEST MAN

"DID SHE DO THAT to you?" asked Bassander Lin from across the table, touching his face to indicate the bruises that had flowered on my own.

Chained as I was to the interrogation table, I only nodded.

The Mandari captain rocked back in his steel chair. His beetle-black eyes never left me. "She should not have done that. It violates protocol on the treatment of prisoners." *Highborn* prisoners, he meant.

"A courtesy for a gentleman," I murmured, recalling the words my gaoler had used.

Bassander took no note of the bitterness in my tone, said, "Quite so. She asked to see you and in deference to your . . . relationship I allowed it. I thought she might get something from you."

"Did she?" I asked, looking at my hands in their electromagnetic binders and not at the man across from me.

"I did not think that she would hit you."

"Then you do not know women very well," I said bitterly.

The captain did not have a reply to that, but examined some holograph hovering beneath the black glass surface of the table. He sucked on his teeth, eyes wandering from the tabletop to the tangle of brass pipes bracketed to the ceiling. At length he said, "What happened down there, Marlowe?"

I tried to rattle my manacles, but they held fast to the tabletop. "I don't know what deal you've struck with Sagara, but you should be very, very careful around him." Bassander did not look impressed by my warning. "He has a Mericanii daimon in his power."

Bassander blinked, but appeared otherwise unmoved. In another life, he'd have made a perfect scholiast, so controlled was he. "You're serious."

"I lie *less* than people believe," I said, leaning against the table, watching for a glimmer of understanding—of acceptance—in the other man's face. When he did not reply, I pressed on, telling him what he needed to know. I did not describe Brethren, believing that without my explanation he would—as I had—imagine only banks of computer terminals and crystal storage. I did not tell him of my vision, or make any reference to the Quiet. I told him only what was practically relevant.

"And you think this . . . daimon allowed your man to get word to me?"

It was not in me to reply at once. Thinking of Switch just then was like biting into sand in an oyster. Like a slap in the face. I swallowed, said, "I think so. I can't imagine how else Switch could have communicated with you. The *Mistral* was under remote control from the moment we disengaged from the Extrasolarian ship that brought us to Vorgossos system."

"But why would the daimon turn against its master?" Bassander asked. "I don't understand."

To this I could only shrug. "I'd wondered at that myself, but I imagine the ancients asked the same question when their machines rebelled."

"Perhaps it thinks it can escape its prison when the Empire comes to destroy it."

"You really think Sagara doesn't know you intend this?" I asked.

Bassander shrugged. "Who is he to stop us? One planet against the Legions? I don't like his chances."

"You underestimate him," I said, and shook my head. "You don't know him. You don't know what he's capable of." In truth, I did not know all Kharn was capable of. "He knows you will move against him. For all we know it was he who allowed Switch to leak the location of Vorgossos to *you*." Thinking about Switch sent a spasm of pain through me, and I shut my eyes for a moment, just long enough to marshal myself. "Have we docked with his ship?"

The other man's eyes wandered among the pipes on the ceiling once more, as if he expected to find some answer writ there among the brass and black sheet metal. "The *Demiurge*? Yes. We're in one of her landing bays even now, en route for rendezvous with the *Obdurate* and your Cielcin friends."

"My *friends*?" I repeated, unable to keep the acid from my voice. There was a threat implicit in Bassander's choice of words: the threat of the Inquisition and a charge of consorting with the inhuman. A threat he could carry out.

"You're a traitor, Marlowe. If it were up to me I'd have you out an airlock for what you've done. You defied a direct order from the First

Strategos and from me. There is a chain of command and a protocol that must be obeyed. These are the Imperial Legions, Marlowe." Bassander walked the line between quietude and rage with the precision of a Durantine clock. He never raised his voice, betrayed his fury only by the tension beneath his words and by the tense way he held his shoulders.

I held my hands palms up. "I am not a legionnaire."

"The tribune conscripted you as her immunis."

"Yes," I said sharply. "*Her* immunis. She ordered me to Vorgossos despite yours and Hauptmann's orders. I obeyed."

"Did she also order you to butcher my men?" Bassander asked, raising his right hand. "Or to maim me, for that matter?"

I felt the shadow fall across my face and—for the briefest moment—lost my composure. "No, of course not."

"They were good men," Bassander said, and there was a gravity in his voice that drew my eye against my will to look him in the face. "*My men.* And you murdered them."

The Legionary captain stood, movements so rigid you might expect oak in him instead of bones. He looked down on me, eyes like lit coals. "What did you think was going to happen?"

"What did I . . . ?" I pulled against my restraints, frustrated that I could not rise and face Bassander on his own level. I suppressed the urge to defend myself, resenting the other man's posturing. "I *found* Vorgossos, Bassander. I found Kharn Sagara, the link to the Cielcin we were after, a hotbed of illegal genetics work, *and* a surviving Mericanii daimon. What do you mean, 'what did I think was going to happen'? Where exactly did I fail to deliver on what I promised?"

"You were in a cell," Bassander sneered. "You failed, Hadrian."

I hoped that Bassander had not spoken to Valka at length or to Tanaran, hoped he did not know how right he was. Gathering the ruins of my pride to my chest like firewood, I said, "We were still . . . negotiating."

"Negotiating?" Bassander turned and walked toward the wall of the chamber, his image reflected darkly in the polished surface. "You looked like you'd been in that hole of yours for eons when Sagara brought you out. Don't pretend." He was fidgeting with his hands, the reflection of his face downturned, eyes narrow. "Was it really him?" he asked. "Was it really Kharn Sagara?"

"I think so," I said, "or maybe it was him. Once. How he's managed to stay alive I don't quite understand. He can . . . parasitize his own children, move his thoughts from one body to the next. Whatever he is, he's not the Kharn Sagara in the stories, even if he used to be."

"Do you think he transplants the brain?"

The blue light that shone behind Kharn's ear and the ears of his children—and of Naia—glowed from some dark recess of memory, and I looked away from Bassander. "Nothing so primitive, but I don't know. Your guess is as good as mine."

The captain's fingers sketched the sign of the sun disc at his side, and after a moment Bassander Lin shook himself and turned once more to face me. "I don't like having to work with such a one."

"What did you offer him? Besides the safety of his planet, of course?" I leaned forward, thinking of what Kharn Sagara had said at our first meeting. "You must have made a deal."

"That," said Bassander Lin, "is none of your concern." But there was a shadow on his face, and a drawn quality to his expression that concerned me quite a bit. The young captain looked half a skull as he added, "I don't like this position you've put me in."

"I've put you in?" I repeated. "These were as much your orders as mine. Just because I wasn't as quick to abandon my mandate as you doesn't absolve you of responsibility. Knight-Tribune Smythe entrusted this mission to the both of us. We had a duty."

A muscle pulsed in Bassander's jaw, and I sensed that if he clenched his teeth much harder they might all shatter in his gums. "You presume to lecture me on duty? You? Remind me, Marlowe, which of us abandoned his family in pursuit of his own selfish ambition? Which of us decided to play at soldiery rather than wed Anaïs Mataro *as he was troth*?" He raised his eyebrows. "Don't. Lecture. Me. I came after you precisely as the knight-tribune ordered. I have brokered a deal with that Extrasolarian demoniac, and we're going to meet with this Cielcin prince of yours. You are getting everything you hoped for."

"Not bad for a *failure*," I said, and it was my turn to sneer.

Bassander dismissed this casually. "You were saved by your friend William. He has more sense than you. He came to us begging for his life."

"His *life*?" I echoed.

"He seemed to think your lives were all forfeit no matter what happened," Bassander said, ice in his words. "That the Chantry would execute all of you for coming so near to machine daimons. He wanted to save himself."

I squeezed my hands into fists. He'd betrayed me. Something black and oily seethed in my guts, and I clenched my jaw to quit from cursing. "Coward." He'd sold me back to the Empire, and why? Out of fear. And Earth only knew what might come of it. Had I not seen my own dead body along an uncounted number of those rivers that flowed into the future? The manacles seemed to grow tight about my wrists, and I shuddered, shoulders hunched over the edge of the glass table. It wasn't just my life he'd put in danger—indeed it was my life he'd least put in danger. I was a nobile of the Imperium, a distant cousin to the Emperor and an asset in my own small way. But Otavia Corvo? Pallino? Crim and Siran and all the rest? They were mere foederati and accomplices in what I'd done. Even Switch himself might not escape punishment. At last I asked, "What's been done with him?"

"All your compatriots have been locked aboard the *Mistral*. Kharn Sagara has agreed to ensure they remain there until such time as your ship can be transferred to the *Obdurate* when we make rendezvous."

"They're unharmed?"

"For the moment." Bassander turned back to face me, brushing his long coat aside as he placed hands on his hips. "Yes." I saw he had retrieved his sword, the sword that once had been Admiral Whent's, the sword I had taken from him when I struck off his hand. "Their fates will be decided by tribunal once all is said and done."

I swallowed, trying to get a grip on the black anger coiling within me, but it twisted away, and no amount of Gibson's old teaching or Imore's scholiast aphorisms could banish that embryonic fury. "And Doctor Onderra?"

"She's safe." Bassander's nose wrinkled in customary dislike. "She's Tavrosi and so once this is done, we'll release her. Her part in all this is not worth trouble with the Demarchy."

A sigh of relief escaped me, and only then did I ask the question which—while most pressing—seemed to me the least important. "What of myself, then?" I asked, and held up my chin as defiantly as I could. "Airlock?"

Bassander did not hesitate. "If it were up to me, yes." His eyes never left my face as he spoke. Ye Gods, he was a cold one. "But it's not up to me. You've outmaneuvered me, because you're right . . . you're Smythe's *immunis*. You're her problem. Your fate lies with her, and with whatever Hauptmann will want done with her." He made a face like he'd tasted something deeply unpleasant, like he'd bitten into a pastry and found oil instead of cream. "How you suborned her I'll never know."

"You flatter me!" I said with equal bitterness. "Bassander, she's a tri-

bune of the Imperial Legions. I could no more suborn her than I can turn
air into gold, and you demean her by merely breathing those words."

To my slight astonishment, Bassander looked down at his hands, mol-
lified. "You're right. That was not worthy." He appeared to chew on some
thought for a long moment—or perhaps it was only his tongue. "She's
ordered that you be confined to the *Mistral* with the rest of your miserable
band."

I looked up sharply, struggling to contain my surprise. Not the airlock.
Not even the brig. Stifling a smile, I said, "You're serious?"

"When am I not?" Bassander said, evincing a degree of self-awareness
I had not known he was capable of. "She seemed to think it would be
safer than keeping you on *my* ship. Sagara has the *Mistral* under lock and
key." Bassander squared himself opposite me, glared at his boot toe.

Eager to move the conversation away from myself, I asked, "Is it just
the *Obdurate* coming?"

Bassander paused a moment before replying, as if unsure whether or
not he could trust me with the answer to that question. "She has the *Pharaoh* and the *Balmung* with her."

"But the fleet's not coming? Hauptmann?"

The captain's face was stone. "Not to a negotiation."

"There will be a negotiation then?"

"Yes," Bassander said shortly, retaking his seat.

A thought struck me, and I asked, "I don't suppose there's a chance that
word of this hasn't reached Hauptmann? Smythe might have kept word to
herself?" I dared to hope, and my words ran on ahead of me. "It's what I
would have done."

The Mandari officer drew a small black remote from his pocket, turned
it over and over in long, blunt fingers. "The knight-tribune is *not* like you."

I had nothing to say to that. Bassander leaned in, still turning the remote over in his fingertips. The faint line of a scar gleamed white about
his wrist where the hand had been reattached. The shine of it seemed at
once very bright to me, brighter than the white lights of the interrogation
room or the way they shone off the brass piping on walls and ceiling. I
could see the gears turning behind his eyes, the archaic machinery of him
working itself to some new statement. "If she dies—Raine Smythe, I
mean—if Hauptmann executes her for your part in all this . . . you won't
see the scaffold or the block." He looked me in the eye, and I felt the line
of fire drawn once more between us. "Am I clear?"

"As air," I said. Bassander Lin brandished the remote before disappearing it inside a pocket of his coat. The electromagnets that held my manacles shut switched off and the binders fell open. Suddenly free, I massaged my wrists. "You're letting me go?"

"There are six men outside who will take you directly to the *Mistral*," he said. "If you try *anything*, they've been given orders to stun you like a feral dog and drop you right back in your cell. Do we have an understanding?" I was not about to play the meek dog for Bassander, and so clenched my jaw. "Do we have an understanding?"

"Oh," I said, standing so that now it was I who looked down at him, "I understand you perfectly."

CHAPTER 51

LOST TIME

HOW VAST WAS THAT terrible ship? And how many secrets did it hold?

Bassander's escort marched me down the *Schiavona*'s landing ramp and into the *Demiurge*'s hold, a hold so massive that I think all my home at Devil's Rest might have fit within it, save perhaps the uppermost third of the tower of the Great Keep. I half expected to see clouds pooling near the gloomy ceiling when I looked up and felt the drear wind on my face. Behind us, the *Schiavona* did not look so out of place in that darkened hall. A brass and black-metal arrowhead bristling with guns and sensor blisters. Craning my neck, I could make out the shapes of men and women moving in the bridge-castle that rose from the back of the vessel. All told, she looked like a thinner, meaner *Balmung*, and should she not? The interceptor had made good time getting to Vorgossos. I tried not to think of the monstrous cost—in antimatter and in Imperial marks—entailed in the operation of so speedy a vessel. There was a reason such interceptors were few and far between.

Gold metal gleamed in the lights from high above, and I confess I lingered, awestruck. Terrible faces looked down on us from the inner wall of the hangar, and the black forms of men and monsters battled in a Gothic frieze like those on the heavy doors in Kharn's palace had done. But the legionnaires—less impressed than I was, or perhaps it was only that they had not shared in my strange visions—chivied me along with rough hands. It was toward one of these faces we moved, following a ghostly holograph line spun like a string of spider's silk through the air. As we approached, I saw its mouth was open, forming an obscene O through which we passed, swallowed by Kharn's monstrous vessel. The holograph line pulsed, leading us through corridor after black corridor, beneath ribbed supports where strange winds blew like ragged breaths, some hot as breathing, yes, and others cold as the night winds which howled through the merlons of the walls of my home.

I felt the oppressive weight of ten thousand eyes upon me, and knew that Kharn Sagara was not far away. My guards felt it, too, for I heard the muffled sound of their voices through their full masks and knew they communicated one to the others. One of the red-faced triasters made a warding gesture and signaled for quiet.

After a long while, we emerged—not into a hold like the one which held the *Schiavona*, but onto a glassed-in bridge, an umbilical which stretched out from the hull of Kharn's Sojourner, the *Demiurge*, toward where the *Mistral* stood at port. Knowing my escort would not approve if I tarried, I tried my best to crane my neck to see.

Behind us, the ship bristled with uncounted black spires, towers and turrets and buttressed halls rising behind the rank and file of grim statuary. Black hands stretched from the hull behind us, and stood watch above the great boom arm that held our ship in place. The unseeing eyes pressing down with such gravity I thought they must have masked suppression field generators behind those sightless lenses, such a force was in the terror of their gaze. Behind all that black metal and stone, the unfixed stars stretched, each one transmuted to a whorl of light and colored more blue than anything I had seen. To violet.

But the doors at the end were only of common substance, and the light behind them when they opened was warm. I was thrust inside without ceremony, without salute, and I stumbled against the inner door. The airlock cycled, turning from warning red to serene blue, then opened on a familiar hall: round and white-padded.

"There you are!"

Familiar faces, too.

Pallino hurried forward, Crim and Ilex following in his wake. The old soldier embraced me without preamble. "The doctor told us what happened down there," he said, and drew away, studying me with that single, piercing eye. "What the hell happened to you? Was it Lin?"

"Jinan," I said, and shook my head.

Crim hissed, "That *jitatin bruhir*! She beat you?"

"No more than I deserved," I said darkly, not sure if I really meant it. "Valka made it back to the ship, then?"

Ilex stepped forward, touched my shoulder. "About half an hour ago. She's resting." With Pallino stepped aside, the homunculus embraced me. "We were worried about you."

I held her at arm's length a moment, clapped her on the shoulder before speaking to all three. "And I about you all. We weren't sure if you were still up there."

"Are you kidding?" Pallino asked, brows arching. "Corvo wasn't going anywhere."

"It's not Corvo I was worried about," I said. "It's Kharn."

That quieted the conversation long enough for me to get my bearings. I'd entered by the port airlock, the same airlock the Exalted Nazzareno had used when it came to pilot us into the *Enigma of Hours*. I felt suddenly very tired, and swayed a little where I stood. Switch was not there, nor Siran, nor Captain Corvo and the others. I wondered if it was ship's night, or if perhaps the others had some more pressing concern.

"What happens now?" Crim asked, brushing back his hair.

"Are we still to rendezvous with the Pale?" Pallino asked.

And Ilex wondered, "Is it true this Sagara keeps a Mericanii daimon?"

More questions piled on, words stacking one atop the next like water, like sand poured on a prisoner in an oubliette until I thought I might drown in them. Their voices overlapped, stacked atop those inward questions that had haunted me since I'd wakened Tanaran from fugue. I raised a hand for silence, and to my astonishment, silence fell. Doubts rushed into that quiet like water into a breach: about myself, about my situation, about Raine Smythe and Titus Hauptmann, about Switch and Brethren, Kharn and Jinan.

It was all too much.

"I just need rest," I said. "Our problems will still be here in a few hours."

My room in the *Mistral* hardly felt like my room at all. I'd never stayed long on the ship until we'd escaped with Tanaran. Still, Switch had managed—with help from his erstwhile lover—to wrangle together a portion of my possessions, most of which still occupied the three footlockers that lined one wall of the small chamber. Clothing mostly, and a few old books. Despite the fact that I had spent so much time alone in my cell aboard the

Schiavona, and so much time before that with Valka in our frigid cell beneath Kharn's palace, it was good to be alone again.

To be alone on my own terms again was a blessing.

Had I been trained in the scholiasts' art, I might have seized that time to unpack my emotions, then to pack them each away behind doors of clear glass, to understand but to be safe from the corrosive power of them. I couldn't do it.

There were holographs buried in my laundry, little wall-mount sconces meant to cycle old images one to the next in endless procession. I knew what they would show. Images of Jinan and me from happier times, times stolen between periods of conflict and pain. Between Pharos and Vorgossos. I knew I could not bear to see them. Still, I plucked one of the projectors from its box. It was a small thing, if weighty. A silver-metallic button perhaps an inch and a half across—you know the type—magnetized so as to clamp itself to the walls of my cabin. I felt an impulse to hurl it across the room, but squeezed my hand around it instead. The beveled edges bit into my hand.

I had done the right thing.

Had I done the right thing?

I had betrayed the Empire. I had betrayed Jinan. Switch had betrayed me.

Was it worth it?

They were good men, Bassander said again, words inescapable when they came from my own head. *My men. And you murdered them.*

I must have tripped some switch or pressed some button, for the projector beeped, startling me. I let it fall, and it bounced and rolled across the floor, coming to rest near the sealed door. It loaded almost instantly, revealing an image of Jinan and myself from our brief stay on Nagramma. Mountains behind us—we had hiked from the capital up to the site of a thirteenth-millennium Cid Arthurian temple to take in the air. Jinan had taken the image, holding the terminal away from us with one hand as she pressed her lips to my cheek. I clenched my fists, determined not to cry. The image changed, showing me at a distance, wandering beneath the white-flowered champak trees beneath the mighty statue of the Arthur Buddha. How small I seemed, dwarfed as I was by that mighty carving, the bearded king sitting upon his lotus throne. Just a little mote of deepest black moving against all that white and beatific stone.

I moved, but not before the image changed, showing Jinan—just Jinan—laughing with champak blossoms in her hair, her eyes closed. I snatched a wadded tunic from the top of the nearest footlocker and cast it over the image, as if to obscure the holographs. That was easier than moving to turn off the projector. I could not bear to see one more moment of it, one more memory. I held my breath and slumped onto the end of my bed, and there—for a time—sleep destroyed me.

CHAPTER 52

BORA

THE NOISE OF THE door cycling awakened me, and I sat up where I had fallen asleep: fully clothed at the foot of my bed. I managed a cracked, "What's going on?" as I fumbled both with my hair and for my sword—remembering, too late, that Kharn Sagara had confiscated my weapon the day I'd faced Brethren.

But it was only Otavia.

The Norman woman had to duck to clear the door frame as she stepped into my cabin. She had at last eschewed the old Red Company uniform in favor of simple garments in close-fitting black and green. She looked somehow older than when last I'd seen her, though I knew she'd endured no more time than I, having been awake for the duration of our time at Vorgossos. I wondered what I looked like.

Captain Corvo's face turned down in a slight frown, one eyebrow arched. "I'd heard you were back."

I rubbed my eyes with the heels of both hands. "I . . . yes. Sorry. I'd have come for you sooner but I needed . . . needed time." Sitting up straight, I did my best to look composed. No easy task, for I'd abandoned my boots by the door and unbelted my tunic. "I fear I look a dreadful mess."

The Norman woman waved this away without comment and propped herself against the far wall, arms crossed. "What happened down there?"

"Kharn Sagara wouldn't negotiate," I said ashenly. "Took Tanaran from us. Valka and I tried to find it and find out how the *Mistral* was being kept at anchorage. We spent about four months in a cell, if Valka's reckoning is good." I could see from the look on Corvo's face that it was, and swallowed. "We couldn't get word to you. I'm sorry."

Corvo was nodding her head. "I'd figured it was something like that when you never came back, or worse. Bastien thought you were dead."

"Where is Durand?" I asked, unable to keep myself from looking round, as though I expected the small, bespectacled man to appear from behind a curtain in that small and sealed little room. "I thought he'd want to hear this."

"He's on the bridge," Corvo said, tossing her floating yellow hair. "We may not be going anywhere, but I'm not about to have us asleep at the wheel." A shade self-conscious in my rumpled clothing, I smoothed my tunic front as a way to cover the silence. After a moment, Corvo said, "We thought you were dead, Hadrian."

Thinking of Bassander Lin and his threats, I said, "It's too early to tell, you might be right after all." I felt myself smile in spite of the oblivion in my tone, then laugh when I remembered dear Gibson's criticizing me for being too dramatic as a boy. Checking myself, I said, "But you stayed? I thought for sure Sagara would have released the ship."

Corvo crossed her arms and—never one to mince words—said, "We might have done it, but Vorgossos never released control of the ship to us. I had to put the ship down to a skeleton crew. Ration resources."

"You didn't try to cut your way loose, or . . . ?"

"We couldn't operate our own airlocks, Hadrian."

"*Noyn jitat!*" I swore in my finest Jaddian, drawing Otavia's eyebrows a shade higher. "I didn't know." I told her the same version of events I'd told Bassander, leaving out a description of the beast, Brethren, and the vision it had shared with me. I left out, too, a description of the Exalted, Calvert, and how he had taken Valka's blood and mine. It didn't bear thinking about.

When I had finished my account, the captain—who had settled into the low stool bracketed to the room's small desk—said, "What have you gotten us into, Hadrian Marlowe?"

I brushed my unruly hair back out of my face, chewing on my answer. "I wish I knew. Lin says Sagara's agreed to take us to rendezvous with the Cielcin away from Vorgossos. I assume that's where we're going now." A touch of the dark humor returned to me, and looking away from Corvo's face, I said, "If not, I imagine we're all in for a rather awful surprise."

"I'm sure we're going to rendezvous," Corvo said. "I don't know much, but from what I understand Lin has this Sagara on a leash."

"Do you know what the problem with a leash is?" I mused, propping my chin on one hand. "You're left holding the other end of it."

Otavia took this in quietly, nodding to herself. "You think it's a trap, then?"

"You can depend on it. I don't like how this is falling out. As if Sagara weren't bad enough, there's Lin."

The Norman captain propped her chin on both hands. "I can handle Bassander Lin, but this . . . did you *see* the size of this ship of his?"

I turned away, and felt again the awareness of *eyes* licking the back of my neck. Kharn Sagara was watching, he had to be. Through his own cameras if not through the *Mistral*'s own internal security network. Suppressing a shudder, I said, "It's bigger than the *Enigma*. Much bigger."

"Valka said he's got a SOM army."

"Oh, he has legions," I said. "I've no idea how many. And worse. I saw one Exalted, but for all I know there may be more. And Earth and Emperor alone know what he's got on this ship." More than I could imagine. Trying to think, I looked up at the ceiling, at gray metal and pale lights. "If we get out of this . . . does your offer still stand?"

"My . . . ?" Otavia's voice trailed off, lost as she tried to remember.

I wrenched my attentions away from the ceiling. "To travel with you and rebuild the Red Company."

The captain almost chuckled, and leaning back she crossed her corded arms. "You think they'll let you leave? Bassander, Smythe, and this Hauptmann character?"

I knew what I was about to say was desperate. "I'm hoping."

Otavia's jovial aspect dissolved at once, and growing too serious she said, "I don't think either of us is getting out of this. If Lin had his way he'd have slagged this whole ship already, and all of us aboard. You're nobility, boy. I'm a pirate. That blood of yours is covering all our asses right now. That and whatever you said to Smythe." I had nothing to say to that—there was nothing to say.

"Switch shouldn't have opened his mouth," I said. "How did he get a message out?"

The captain shrugged. "Honestly? I don't know. We weren't watching the telegraph wave . . . gave up on it after the first week or so when we couldn't get anything out. He must have gone in and queued it up when no one was looking. How the message got out I've got no idea."

"I think Kharn's daimon took care of it," I said, reiterating what I'd said to Bassander.

"Why would it do that?"

I shrugged, ran quickly through a version of the same conversation I'd had with Bassander Lin. While I spoke I rose, padding barefoot to where

I'd let the holograph projector fall beneath my laundry. Moving carefully so as not to make a conversation piece of the holographs, I balled the device up in my loose tunic and—deactivating it—threw the projector and the garment back into my trunk.

"There's too much going on," she said at length, following my progress up and down the narrow chamber from her place at the stool. "The Empire, the Extras, the Cielcin . . . this machine . . ." She didn't even know the half of it. I could see—over her shoulder, as it were—the blooming dark of my vision, and the Cielcin horde marching across the stars. I saw the woman named Man tormented by them, her raiment radiant as the sun, and heard once more the noise of an infant wailing, its hour come round at last.

I shook myself. "I'm sorry?"

Patient as a stone, Otavia Corvo repeated herself, saying, "I said, 'And we can't even control our own people.'"

"Where is Switch, anyway?" I asked. An awful thought took me and I asked, "You didn't lock him up, did you?"

"We didn't even know he'd done it until the airlock onto the Vorgossos starport opened and Lin's lieutenant swept in with three decades of your Empire's finest." She frowned, rubbed her face as if to mask some feeling. Anger perhaps? Or embarrassment? "They pulled William out of here *for his safety*, but the bastard asked to come back. Can you believe that?"

I could. Plain as I see the bust of that original Gibson looking down on me as I write these words, I could see Switch—my friend—standing, shoulders hunched outside the airlock . . . waiting to be let in with the air of one who turns his back on the gunman, knowing not the moment or the flash.

He wants me to kill him, I thought. "He knows I can't forgive him for this. We might have returned to the Empire with a full peace accord and the Inquisition might have looked the other way, but now . . ." I clenched my fists. "If anyone is executed over this . . . I can't forgive him." I couldn't forgive him even if we all came out of this alive. "Lin said he came *begging for his life.*" He had chosen to save his own skin rather than stay loyal to his people—to me. How could I ever trust him again? Tight-jawed, I asked, "Where is he now?"

"He's in his cabin," Otavia said, voice dark. "I haven't told him you're here."

"Good," I said. "I don't want to see him. Are all of our people on the ship now? Bassander doesn't have anyone in interrogation or anything?"

Standing suddenly, Otavia half-turned away. "No, no, we're all here. All prisoners together. I thought for sure he'd keep us locked up, though."

"Raine's orders."

"That's a good sign," Corvo said. "That means she's still on your side." She pivoted sharply, and looking up I found her dark eyes glaring at me with intent. "This is not a very large ship."

Her meaning was plain. "What would you have of me?" I asked, genuinely asked. I did not know what to do. Not about Switch.

Betrayal is the blackest sin.

I should have been furious, but I was beyond fury, lost in some country ruled by a spirit blacker still. Sorrow?

Regret.

It was strange. As a boy I had derided Crispin for his passions, his rages, but now I think the rage was a genetic marker of a sort. A Marlowe family style, as much a part of us as our black hair, our violet eyes, and our crooked smiles. As much a part of us as that red devil, rampant on sable—as much a part of us as our uranium and the funeral masks beneath the Dome of Bright Carvings. I knew I should be angry. Switch's actions may have led to the meeting we had worked so desperately for, but at what cost? My life and the lives of all my companions, maybe. Long was the reach of the Imperial hand and relentless its grasp: strong and unforgiving. And yet I found I could not be angry. I had no anger left.

I had no forgiveness either.

"What would you have of me?" I asked again, retaking my seat at the foot of the bed, hands on knees.

The captain replied, "Just don't do anything you'll regret."

"I won't," I said in answer, eyes tracking once more toward the ceiling. "I only wish *he* hadn't done something I'd regret." Corvo was silent. What she read in my tone I cannot say, but her hard face was closed as the windows of a peasant's shack in winter, her lips pale and pressed together. A horrid thought turned in my stomach, and rejecting it I said, "I'm not going to hurt him, Otavia." I held my face in my hands, both of us silent a long while. Presently I took in a great breath, and forcing it out—my words more groan than anything else—I said, "I know he acted out of desperation. Fear. But he put all our lives at risk. Your lives. I can't abide that."

"What are you going to do?"

"I have no idea," I said, and spoke truth. "It feels like the wind's changing, Otavia."

"Good," she said, and from her tone I knew she understood my meaning and meant to ignore it. "It's been against us since we joined you. It's about time it changed."

I did not share her optimism.

CHAPTER 53

THE THIRD TREASON

IT IS ONLY WHEN the world places no burdens on our hearts that circumstance allows us time to make decisions. By contrast, too often when there is some trial which we would give the price of a palatinate to avoid, we find we are already at court.

My fist slipped under Siran's guard, uppercut clipping the side of her chin. She grunted in surprise as I caught her in the back of the neck, catching her with my gloved hand in a sling that—as I pivoted with my hips—sent her tumbling to the floor. Never one to let a loss slow her down, Siran rolled smoothly to her feet and came right back swinging. She wasn't much of a boxer, truth be told: tended to swing too wide and too wildly. I covered my head to take an overhand punch on my elbow as I cracked her in the face with a jab. I saw her stumble and stepped in, dropping a hook to her ribs. She grunted and got off a shot to my shoulder before I moved in, smothering her assault as I swung in, ducking another punch to get behind and beside her and planted my open hand against the side of her head to make my point.

"Not bad, kid, not bad!" Pallino said, leaning on the ropes at the edge of the ring. The *Mistral*'s small gym was practically empty. Crim and Ilex were meant to join us, but of those two there had been no sign. The old myrmidon captain slipped a finger beneath his eye patch and rubbed at his missing eye. "Siran, hop out, would you? I owe His Radiance here a beating for leaving us high and dry while he was all cozied up to the doctor in that cell of theirs."

"For the last time!" I exclaimed, using my thick glove to push hair from my eyes. "Nothing happened!"

Pallino ducked the ropes and thumped Siran on the shoulder. "I thought

I told you not to lie to your elders, son!" He knocked his fists together and grinned. "You were down there a long time."

"For the last time, drop it!" I said tersely.

Too tersely, for Pallino threw his head back and laughed. "Face it, lad, you can't lie to me!" He raised his fists, tilted his head to keep track of me with his one good eye. I had fought Pallino before. The man had been a soldier of the Empire for forty years and a fighter all his days. Even half-blind and old as he was, he was dangerous. He hadn't survived so long in the fighting pits of Borosevo by luck alone. Flashing a smile, he tapped at his eye patch with his glove. "Doesn't take two eyes to see right through you."

Siran laughed. "He's not wrong, Had. Everyone knows you've had eyes for the doctor since we left Emesh."

"I have no idea what you're talking about," I said, pointedly looking away.

Pallino snapped a searching jab in my direction, grabbing my attention. I stepped back, batting it away. The old myrmidon let out a laugh. "I think His Radiance is embarrassed."

"Don't call me that!" I said, struggling with feelings I had almost forgotten. "Ghen called me that."

The older man's one eye darted to Siran, as if seeking approval or permission. "Maybe you're right, lad. It's been hard without the big guy around." To this I only nodded, squaring my stance to suggest readiness. Taking my meaning, Pallino lashed out with a straight punch that I brushed aside, stepping in with a straight of my own that took the old man in the jaw. He grimaced, but ducked my next shot, sank two blows just under my armpit in rapid succession. Grinding my teeth, I stepped inside so that the third hook scraped my back instead, and I struck Pallino's chin from below, landing to uppercut in such a way that I drove my elbow into his sternum. That blow was hard enough that Pallino staggered backward—not quite to the ropes. It was the kind of blow that fills the ensuing seconds with a solid, impressed quiet. I smiled approvingly.

"Think that was good, do you?" Pallino said, holding his hands lower in the classic pugilist stance common to every back street behind every bar in every city and township of the Imperium. "Lad, my father was Fortitude himself. You're going to need to try a lot harder than that and you know it."

There are certain activities one may lose himself within. I have heard from the soldiers who are made to run great distances as part of their training that running is such a one, and certain mystics of the Jaddian fire cult seek passing reunion with their *fravashi* spirit in the other world through dance, and so forget materiality. For the scholiasts, such escape is in contemplation of the self and of the *logos*, the logic and the language in all things. For myself, often I had found—in my drawings—that I have passed by several hours without so much as a passing thought.

Fighting—really fighting—is just such a pursuit. The universe blackens around you, converges so that only the combat remains. In true battles, the effect is one of terror. As I have said of my time in the Colosso on Emesh long ago, everything you are is forced through the eye of a needle and you emerge—or you do not. In practice and in play, the effect—I think—is no different than that of the contemplation of the scholiasts, the dance of the Jaddians, the distance run by our soldiers. Everything that troubled me simply fell away. I stepped under a hard cross and shoveled Pallino in the ribs, wove beneath his arm and popped up to send a cross of my own scrubbing clean down over his shoulder to strike the side of his head again.

Pallino's own fist connected with my ribs in the same instant, and even as he reeled, he threw his arm out to make space between us. "Not half bad!" he said, working his jaw. It was more than half good, and we each knew it, but I smiled all the same.

"You're letting your loaded hand drift too much, Had," Siran said. "If it wasn't, you'd not be taking it like a dockside whore."

"He gave better than he got, though!" Ilex said. She'd appeared with Elara sometime during the fight, and the two women stood by Siran near one corner of the ring. "You all right there, Pal?"

Pallino massaged his jaw. "I best not lose a tooth for this, Marlowe. Mine don't grow back like yours do."

"I'm sure Doctor Okoyo can put any you lose back in," I said, smiling. "Does the Son of Fortitude need a lie-down?"

The old soldier's right cross was not to be laughed at. I went reeling—would have fallen were it not for the ropes at my back. Ilex and Siran clapped. Elara whooped more loudly still. "Looks like you need to lie down there, Had," Pallino said, arms akimbo, inviting retribution. "You going to let this old man beat you?"

I didn't, and when we had gone five rounds, I swung sweating out of the ring as Siran rotated back in. After so long in Sagara's cell and Bassander's afterward, it felt good to move again, to fight. I had never wanted to be a fighter, had never enjoyed fighting as a boy, but I have found that as one grows older, one develops an attraction for those things which he performed in his youth, even unwillingly. Thus often do we return to those childish things when the weight of responsibility and of trial becomes too much to bear alone. Once, I had fought with Crispin under the watchful eye of my father's castellan, Sir Felix Martyn. I had fought because it was expected of me, because I had to. Later, I had fought for my life, in the streets and in the fighting pits. I would fight for my life again, and for higher things—but in that moment, I fought among friends and for the love of it.

Laughing at some jape of Siran's, I swung away from the ropes and turned—thinking to get water from the font built against one wall—and there he was. In truth, I do not think he expected to find me in the gymnasium, or to find anyone. He wore simple exercise kit: tight trousers and a sleeveless tunic done in drab olive, contrasting with his red hair. He stood frozen, the conduction tape halfway to his ear, the music already playing from his terminal. Unspeaking, he quieted it.

Everyone else had gone quiet as well.

He turned to go.

"Switch!" I hadn't meant to speak, and yet I had. There was too much to say, too much to leave unsaid. The man twitched as if I'd stabbed him, and half-turned back. He wasn't facing me. His fists were tight at his sides. I found suddenly that I could not speak. I—who had counted on the clarifying light of some emotion when I'd opened my mouth.

The rage didn't come. The outrage.

There was only sorrow.

"I'm glad you're all right," Switch said, not looking at me. "When you and Doctor Onderra didn't come back, I didn't know what to do."

I dropped the towel I'd been holding and closed to within about five paces of the younger man. "You're glad I'm all right? Really? Do you know what you've done?"

The accusation in my tone snagged on some corner in the other man, and he turned. There were tears in his eyes. "What I've done? I got you out of prison."

"Don't play the fool," I said, not raising my voice. "You know exactly what you've done, or else you wouldn't have come back here to the *Mistral*." I took a breath, a step forward. "You called Bassander. You called the Empire."

Switch turned fully to face me then, shoulders raised. His face could not decide if it wanted to flush or pale. "I saved your life! Valka's life!"

"You sold it!" I snarled, still deadly quiet. "Sold it and the lives of everyone on this ship. Lin told me! And for what? To save your own *hide*!" I had, in fact, been shown the holograph Switch had sent to the fleet, seen his plea for mercy. "You said I was *mad*."

"You'd lost your way, Had!" Switch said, looking to Pallino and the others for support. "Demoniacs, Extras? It's too much. It's been too much since Rustam. Since Ghen. It's a miracle we haven't lost more people, Earth be praised."

I looked back around at the others. I could see the concern etched on their faces, and from the way Pallino's one eye followed my progress I knew he was remembering a younger Hadrian, remembering how I had beaten three myrmidon recruits in a fury.

That fury wouldn't come.

"We're going to lose more people," I said, my back to the younger man. I shut my eyes. "Do you understand that?"

Footsteps behind me. Switch moving closer. "You don't know that. Captain Lin is an Imperial officer, not a . . . Norman warlord. He can be reasoned with."

"Can he, now?" Pallino said, butting in for the first time. "Is that what you did, lad? Reasoned with him? Get him to forgive you for stunning his ass on the *Balmung*? What was his promised price? A spot in the stands while the rest of us hang? Or do you just get a nice fugue couch while the rest of us get blasted out an airlock?"

I opened my eyes. I hadn't expected Pallino to leap to my defense, but there he was, leaning against the ropes, watching Switch with that piercing blue eye. Elara moved toward her man. "Pal . . ."

"You too?" Switch asked, words drifting over my shoulder like the shadow of the executioner's blade. "Pal, you were a soldier. You don't think any of this is right!"

"Aye, I was a soldier," Pallino replied, shrugging out of Elara's grasp and swinging out through the ropes. "That's what makes what you're doing so wrong, lad. You're loyal to your people first, your commanders second, and the Empire third, damn it!"

Switch's voice was close—he couldn't have been but a yard or so behind me, but still I didn't turn. "I was just trying to help!"

Help. I clenched my jaw, tried not to shout the word. After a moment I spoke, my voice small so that the meaning of my words overshadowed their volume. "And just what sort of help do you think you've been?" I could see the watchfulness in Elara's face. In Siran's. The ready concern.

They thought that at any moment they were going to have to pull me off of Switch. That thought—the recognition of it—sobered me further still. I saw my brother, Crispin, unrolled like a carpet at my feet. The last I'd ever seen of him. *Rage,* I thought, *is blindness.*

I saw.

I heard Switch say, "I got us to the Cielcin, didn't I?"

"At what cost?" I asked, and at last I turned. Switch stood little more than a yard away. Just out of reach. "You say Ghen's life was too much." I paused, and here glanced at Siran, whose face was as impassive as those of the stoic statues who watch me even now. "Maybe it was. But you have put the lives of *everyone* on this ship at risk, Switch. Do you understand that?"

"You already did that!" he said sharply, eyes wet and wide. "The moment we betrayed the fleet, our lives were forfeit!"

I took a step closer, by doing so emphasizing the difference in our heights. I am not so tall as many among the palatine class, but I stood more than a head above my plebeian friend.

When men contend, it is always with the underlying threat of violence. I have known some women who insist it is the same, and having sometime seen the nail-scratched faces and torn hair I think perhaps it is so—if less commonly. But I think men found their communication on the threat of that violence. *We must speak,* they say, raising their hands to emphasize the point, *lest we use these.* Stepping into Switch's space as I did, I knew my unspoken threat for what it was and stood upon it as though it were a podium.

To his credit, the other man did not flinch. As I have often remarked, there was nothing of the scared catamite in him any more. He thrust out his chin as though it were a target, projecting by that motion that he was unafraid. Tears shone in his eyes, unfallen and furious. I took them for a sign that he understood me. More weakly now, Switch said, "You already risked our lives when you took Tanaran. When we fought Bassander for you."

I didn't miss a beat. "I meant to return to Bassander—to Smythe and the Empire—only after I'd made peace with Prince Aranata. You handed us back as failures. It's not the same thing." I may have made us outlaws, but Bassander would never have found us, never have found Vorgossos, if Switch hadn't summoned him. We might have returned on our own terms, in a superior position. We might have returned with peace.

"You don't see it, do you?" Switch said. "You trust the Cielcin more than your own people. Do we mean *nothing* to you?" He practically spat the words.

There was the moment my father would have struck the man. I felt it with the clarity by which one speaks his most cutting retort—by which one hits the riposte in a fencing match. I let it go. I remembered how I had felt when I fought Bassander on the *Balmung*. I had not hated him, who had treated me with naught but contempt since the Cielcin invasion of Emesh. I could not hate him.

But I could not trust him ever again.

I could never forgive him.

Friend that he was, his friendship was not worth the lives of all those he had risked by his cowardice: Pallino and Siran, Otavia and Bastien Durand, Ilex and Crim and Elara and all the rest. And Valka, Valka most of all. Even his *own* life, for he had gambled that as well. All to save himself from the Inquisition. I studied his face, the high cheekbones and bright eyes, the red hair neatly combed, the resolute anger and the unfallen tears. I could not hate him, who had been my friend for so many long years.

But neither could I look at him without pain.

Eyes shut, I said, "You need to go."

"Go?" Switch echoed, voice breaking with a sound like incredulous laughter. "Go *where*, Hadrian?"

"I don't *care*," I breathed, the last word shaking from me like a windowpane in a thunderstorm. "Go to Bassander, if he means so much to you. Go back home to Danu. Go back to your Master Set." I bit that last one off, knowing it would sting and hating myself for it. The shame I felt at that wounded my own pride further still, and as we so often do when our own actions cut us so deeply, I doubled down. "Go to hell."

I turned my back, not opening my eyes. Even through my lids I felt Pallino's eye on me. Felt Siran's. Elara's. Ilex's. Felt Switch's hand on my shoulder. "Had . . ."

"Why did you come back here?" I said, bowing my head. "Why did you come back to this ship after what you've done? Was it for judgment? Justice?"

My friend did not answer me.

"Get your hand off me, William," I said, voice tight as bowstrings. The fingers tightened on my shoulder. I'd used his name, his real name. The nickname had vanished, and all familiarity with it. "I said . . . *go*."

"Please, I . . ." Switch said, and I could hear by his voice that his tears had started to fall. "I was scared, Had. Scared you were dead down there and that Bassander would kill us all when he caught us. I didn't want to die! You don't mean it, don't send me away!"

Inhaling sharply through my nose, I threw my head back and said, "I wish I did not have to. But I can't trust you anymore. Not again. Not after this." *Grief is emptiness,* I thought. *Grief is deep water.* Grief. It felt less like Switch had betrayed me and more like he had died. That he was lost to me, forever sundered by some ocean vast as the ocean of stars through which we wheeled.

Vaster still, as though we traveled so fast in opposite directions that the one's light would never reach the other, not until time ran down and the stars burned out like candles, leaving all the universe in darkness and in cold.

Cold.

"I was trying to help. I was trying to save you, too! To save everyone!" Switch said into the silence.

"You were trying to save yourself!" I snarled, brushing his hand from my shoulder and moving away. Still I would not look back. "Do you think I'm a fool? Do you think I don't know what we risk here? What I've *risked*? It was *me* in that cell, Switch! Me and Valka! If you knew what I'd seen down there . . . what I'd met! If you knew even *half* of what I know . . . you'd have gone to Bassander even faster. You talk about demons—I've met them! Kharn keeps worse things than Cielcin in the dark, and you have—" I broke off, shaking my head. "I'm sorry Ghen died, too, but everyone who came with me—everyone who's here—knew what they were getting themselves into, do you understand? They knew."

"Aye!" Pallino said. "That we did."

I looked up, saw Pallino and the three women. They weren't looking at me anymore, but at Switch. I cannot say why, but that realization brought a sense of calm to me in the midst of that unraveling moment.

I could feel Switch's eyes on the back of my head. "I just wanted to put everything right, Had. I thought we were done. Trapped. I thought Lin could save us!"

"You *thought* Lin might give you a pat on the head for delivering us and Vorgossos to him. This isn't a ship any more, Switch. It's a prison. Do you understand that? Bassander Lin is keeping us here until he can decide what to *do* with us. Until Raine Smythe can decide what to *do* with us. He said he would put me out the airlock if he could!"

Silence. Utter silence. After a moment I turned, found Switch standing, hands loose now at his sides, face slack. He looked so small standing there, just as I had done in the shadow of the Cid Arthur statue at the Nagramma monastery. In a voice smaller still, he said, "I'm sorry. I didn't know."

"Sorry isn't good enough. I'm sorry, too, but sorry won't bring back Ghen or the men I killed on the *Balmung*. How sorry will you be if the rest of us get executed because you couldn't hold your stomach?"

Switch opened his mouth to speak. "I . . ." His words had failed him, and he looked down at his feet.

I wheeled away in disgust, raised a hand in dismissal. "Get. Off. This. Ship. I don't care how you do it. I don't want to see you again."

"I—"

"Get off this ship, William!" I roared, and it was my turn to clench my fists.

I did not turn, and so did not see the other man leave the room. I watched him go in the eyes of my companions, and watching them, shut my eyes. It was all too hard to see.

CHAPTER 54

BRINGING STORM

THE IMPERIAL SHUTTLE CROUCHED in the landing bay before us as I watched unspeaking from between the six guards Bassander had left to watch me. I kept my silence as I had been ordered to do, face fixed dead ahead, hands blessedly unshackled at my sides. The vessel had the look of of some armored beetle, its body bloated, coated in adamant plates the color of space. Two great wings retracted, folding down and against the hull as gouts of white mist blew into the air. I glanced sidelong to where Bassander Lin stood with Lieutenant Greenlaw, stiff as stone among his guards.

Kharn Sagara was nowhere to be seen, but I knew he wasn't far, knew he watched through unseen eyes and through the antique monitor screens high on the hangar walls. They glowed dull gray in that black hall, watchless and all-seeing as the eyes of blind old men. I suppressed a shudder, watched as the shuttle's formal ramp descended and a cornicen emerged in full regalia: open-faced helm with its crest of red feathers, a clarion in his hands. He did not—Earth be praised—wind the thing, but drew aside as two lines of guardsmen descended. Like the cornicen, they were arrayed in full battle dress. They had expected to be performing for Kharn, as Bassander had done in the throne room with his little parade. Without him present, I wondered if they felt like actors bursting triumphant onto the stage of an empty theater.

This sense of anticlimax was compounded by the appearance of the knight-tribune herself. Flanked by her first officer, Sir William Crossflane, Dame Raine Smythe was a thoroughly uninspiring figure. Short, broad, blunt-featured, she bore all the hallmarks of her plebeian birth and the surgical meddling that had elevated her from it, and next to her patrician subordinate she seemed a weathered sculpture of a woman: dishwater

hair simply cut and cut short above uneven brows, a flat nose, a face . . .
utterly forgettable. Though she was not old, she leaned upon a cane, and I
wondered if some new injury had befallen her since we parted ways at
Emesh, or else if this was some affectation, as though she meant to draw
attention to the lowliness of her status. I imagined thus had many men of
higher birth and better breeding underestimated that iron lady.

"Captain Lin!" she called when she was yet at a distance, apparently
untroubled by the strangeness of that awful ship and its sculpts of staring
faces. "Well met." She too had dressed in full finery: long red tunic beneath the sculpted armor breastplate—a man's breastplate, I noted; high
polished greaves and long gauntlets visible beneath a variant of the very
greatcoat I wore, blacker than black but with wide sleeves to accommodate the gauntlets. A strange paradox, that: that she should project at once
an almost feeble vulnerability and all the strength of Sol.

Bassander stepped forward, beat his chest, and then raised his hand in
salute. "Ma'am."

Her eyes found me—those dull brown orbs as sharp as lasers—and she
said, "And Lord Marlowe, too. Good, good." The knight-tribune craned
her neck. "Is this Lord Sagara not joining us, then?"

"Oh, he's here," I said darkly, ignoring a look from Bassander that was
darker still. "You can depend on that."

Smythe seemed to consider this a moment before she said, "Very well,
then. We shall withdraw to the *Schiavona*, then, and get our business together. I trust the Cielcin have not yet arrived?"

"No ma'am," Bassander said, then took a moment to shout orders that
the knight-tribune's effects were to be brought from the shuttle and taken
to the ship. "And we're not certain when it is they're due. Sagara has been
tight with the details."

"But you trust he will deliver?"

The younger officer glanced at the nearest monitor screen before saying, "With all due respect to our host, I did not give him much choice."

The knight-tribune tapped her cane against the metal decking. "Good."
Her eyes searched out the Gothic wreck of the hall. "Ghastly place . . ."
She gave a signal and her escort—who had stood aside in two lines to flank
the landing ramp—came together. Presently two more decades of legionnaires appeared, descending the ramp from the shuttle.

"How many are with you?" Bassander asked.

"Four decades and five, including myself and these." She gestured to
Crossflane, to the cornicen, and to two men emerging at the rear, a

centurion—to judge by the medallions fastened to his breastplate—and an optio with his double stripe.

"And five hundred aboard the *Schiavona*," Bassander confirmed, though surely the number was known to all present. The Cielcin, I understood, were to be held to a complement of similar size, both parties under the careful and apparently neutral eye of the Undying.

Crossflane scratched at his fierce side-whiskers with one hand and, addressing his question more to me than to any other, asked, "What's the disposition of the prisoners aboard the *Mistral*?"

I glanced at Bassander only briefly. "Mostly in fugue, sir. Captain Corvo—she's our mercenary captain—put most of the crew into stasis when Doctor Onderra and I did not return from the planet."

Lin leaned in. "She's only a couple dozen personnel active at this time, sir."

Those words at last brought Smythe level with me, and at a gesture my . . . my honor guard stepped aside. Her face was wholly unreadable. After an interminable period, she said, "What am I to do with you, Lord Marlowe?"

"Ma'am?"

"I told you when you left Emesh that Bassander was meant to keep you on a tight leash, but here we are . . ."

That made me blink. "I was only following your orders, ma'am."

"And a fine spot you put me in, too." Her expression softened, and she cast her eyes up and around the chamber. "But perhaps it may all turn out to our advantage in the end."

Averting my eyes, I asked, "What's to be done with me, then?"

"For the moment? You're to help us out of this mess. I've brought a translator on Hauptmann's orders—he doesn't trust you—but you know these Cielcin at least, and for the moment I've convinced him you're use-ful." She made to move past me, but as she did, she stopped and placed one gauntleted hand on my shoulder. I felt her eyes on me and turned. "See to it that you are. Useful." And then she was gone. Crossflane glow-ered at me and followed in her wake, leaving only Bassander left to smile his little smile.

The mapping holograph glowed ahead of our party where I followed just behind the cornicen in his high-crested helm. I had come direct from the

Mistral, and so was not entirely certain of the way, but when we came to a place where the hallways turned sharply *upward,* where the gravity sheared at right angles with the turning of the ship's internal suppression fields, I became convinced that we were not simply going to the *Schiavona,* not that there was anyone who could say with certainty where we were and where we were going within the belly of Kharn's awful ship.

The floor simply arced smoothly upward, and as though we were walking along the interior curve of wheel we rose, and rising I looked back and saw our escort in the hall behind, and it seemed they marched down a wall to meet us. Vertigo took me and I shut my eyes. Twice more did we encounter such turnings, once sharply right and again—most terrifying of all—the hallway bent straight down, so that to advance we had to step as if into an abyss. I was acutely conscious all the while of the artificiality of it all. That Kharn Sagara might at any moment alter any one of these fields and turn his hall into a shaft and so murder us. I took it as small consolation that the *Obdurate* lurked somewhere out in space, not far, that its guns perhaps protected us.

It was a smaller comfort but a more compelling one to realize that Kharn would not kill us because we were being led to his door.

A round door opened, rolling away into a pocket in the wall, and entered into a low hall lit—it seemed—by hundreds of blue flames. Like unto the flame which burned outside Kharn's palace on Vorgossos they were, and it seemed almost they cast no light, but that what light there was came from no source I could ascertain.

"Here we are!" Kharn said, voice ringing out from his throat.

He sat behind a table, his children to one side. Ren and Suzuha both looked curiously at the Imperial contingent, and the girl's face darkened when she saw mine.

The golem Yume stood primly to one side, its hands clasped, head bowed as though in prayer or sleep. "Welcome aboard, Knight-Tribune Smythe. I trust your journey was agreeable." He had spoken at once, not forced Raine to wait upon his patience.

"Quite."

"Not too far from Coritani now?" the King of Vorgossos asked, and there was a silver malice in his voice. We had come much farther, of course. The mighty *Demiurge* had moved through kilolights as though they were miles.

The knight-tribune leaned heavily on her cane. "No indeed."

There followed one of Kharn's customary long silences, the children fidgeting in their chairs, anxious to be away. Someone must have briefed Smythe on this peculiar disregard for time, for the tribune did not move, nor Sir William beside her. For a while, the only sound was the faint whirring of the implants in Kharn's wasted chest that breathed for him. He shut his eyes. "Did you bring what was promised?"

"Of course. In the hold of my ship. We can ferry your cargo to you at your convenience."

"See that it is so, Knight-Tribune. See that it is so."

I caught myself wondering just how many of Kharn's blue eyes lay hid among those gas-flame candles, and remembering the way they had burned my clothes I felt a sudden, horrible nakedness. Everything about this meeting struck me as an opportunity for Kharn to impress upon his Imperial guest the degree to which we were in his power. Power. It was all they believed in, Kharn and the soldiers alike. As if it were only the threat of power that held the world to order . . . as if there were not better ways and truer. But a darker thought took me—though a less pressing one. What payment had the Empire offered Kharn Sagara? And what coin would he accept? The disquiet I felt was echoed in the stiffness of Crossflane's shoulders and the stiff way Smythe leaned on her cane.

The Undying was still speaking. "I will have one of the primary bays prepared to receive the cargo then. You will wave your people and tell them to begin the necessary preparations for the transfer." Smythe acceded to this request without hesitation, and Kharn asked, "How many freighters will be arriving?"

"Five," Sir William said, a brittle quality to his tone.

"Five . . ." Kharn mused. "Very good. The crews of those freighters will depart aboard the shuttle on which they arrived and withdraw to your ship. I am generous, but the number of Imperial personnel aboard my ship is already stretching the borders of my tolerance, are we clear?"

Five ships, I thought. *Five.* Something about that figure turned cold in me. Very cold. Not money, then. Materiel? Fuel? Possibly, though I imagined somewhere in the snows of Vorgossos lay the accelerator farms from which Kharn might draw all the antilithium he would ever need for his ships. I thought of the uranium tankers my house would send careering into space, packed in the holds of Consortium freighters and shipped . . . everywhere. *No, no,* I thought. *This is something else.*

"Perfectly clear," Smythe replied. "And the Cielcin?"

"When the Otiolo scianda arrives, their party will be quartered in a bay far from yours, and *both of you*"—he opened his eyes to mere slits, and yet the shine of them was evident even by the corpse light of that fey chamber—"will be kept from one another, but that is the price we pay for hosting two armies under our roof." Ren seized his father's sleeve, for security more than attention, but Kharn Sagara did not bestir himself. He did not look like a man concerned about the presence of more than five hundred Imperial legionnaires on his ship, nor one unsettled by the prospect of sharing a space with as many Cielcin. And why should he be? How many bodies did he have aboard? How many *thousand* corpse-soldiers lurked behind the sealed doors in every hall? "And while you are here, I must ask you remain aboard your ship. I must prepare to receive our Pale emissaries, and must guarantee them the same security I guarantee you, and would prefer that your fine soldiers stay out of my way."

Knight-Tribune Raine Smythe took a step forward, wringing her cane in both hands. "That sounds perfectly equitable. You may rest assured you will have no trouble from us." Hearing her, I knew she meant it, whatever came later. "I confess this audience came sooner than expected. May I adjourn to consult with my people aboard our ship and to send orders that your cargo is to be brought across?"

The Master's eyes were fully open then, and he raised a hand—the left—and gestured toward a door to the side of that spectral hall. As though answering his summons, it opened, and he said, "Please. Go and rest. I will summon you again when the Cielcin arrive."

"Sooner, I hope," Raine Smythe replied. I sensed the move an instant before she made it. "I should like to discuss the disposition of Vorgossos."

For the first time since I had known him, Kharn Sagara looked . . . surprised. The emotion came and went as the pharaonic mask reasserted itself. Smythe flourished her cane and turned, giving a signal that the cornicen should wind his horn. He did, and the clear and sunny sound of that instrument in that dim and sallow hall was like a rainbow in the dark. The double column of men behind me straightened to attention, shifted their lances from one arm to the other, and followed Smythe as she followed the gleaming holograph thread from the room.

"Tribune." The word came with the force of thunder, not from Kharn's human lips, but from the very air about us. "Do not threaten me."

Smythe half-turned. "I do not threaten, Lord Sagara. I only express my enthusiasm for cultivating a close working relationship between yourself and my Imperial master for the duration of these negotiations. Good day." She did not wait for Kharn to reply, and before he could speak, signaled that the cornicen should play once more, and the sound of trumpets echoed in that low and arch-lined space, one throat joined by echoes until it seemed an entire band marched there. I was swept along with them and might have smiled, were it not that I understood one thing—I think— more sharply than the rest.

It was not before any lord that Raine's troops performed, no petty king of the Outer Perseus or Norman warlord. No barbarian chieftain was he: one who counts himself one of the powerful because his planet had for so long stood apart from the Imperium—no fool in a crown of bells who thinks ten ships an armada. No. Kharn was something else, something stranger by far and more dangerous. Once, militaries marched to get from place to place, but in our more enlightened age they do so only to per- form: for their masters, for their people, for themselves. Their esprit de corps. Here we marched for a foreign lord, yes, but only for him. All the knight-tribune's efforts, her iron will and the splendor of her guards, was aimed upon the eye and will of that one man who was no man at all.

Whatever he was, Kharn Sagara had seen prouder hosts and more nu- merous. And more fearsome ones as well. We imagined—Bassander, Crossflane, and Smythe—that we had outfoxed the Master of Vorgossos, that we were Jupiter feeding Saturn a painted stone instead of his children. But Kharn was older now than the entire civilization that had worshipped Saturn. We were not the first to contend with him.

We will not be the last.

CHAPTER 55

THE VERGE OF HISTORY

IN TRUTH, I DO not think Bassander Lin had occupied the captain's cabin aboard the *Schiavona* at all, but if he had done so he'd vacated it. The vessel had been loaned to Smythe's command by First Strategos Hauptmann, and so the stateroom showed few signs of personalization. Indeed, only the stack of heavy plastic and metallic crates against one wall indicated that the space was used at all. Like the rest of the interceptor—like the *Balmung* before it—the interior of that cabin was all of black metal and brass. Holographs displaying the view out the ship's landing ramp and along the service umbilical which bracketed her to the ceiling of Kharn's hangar bay gleamed on the walls.

Smythe herself sat behind a desk, the door to her personal quarters behind her, her cane forgotten, propped against the wall at her side, her hands folded on the desk before her.

"I just don't understand, ma'am," Bassander was saying, eyes fixed dutifully on a space on the wall above and to the right of Smythe's head, as though he could not bear to look at her. I have often observed this indirectness amongst military persons, this tendency to look over the shoulder or above the head of the person one was speaking to, even as one spoke loudly and clearly. "Lord Marlowe's actions were treason. He killed our own people—three of my men. He kidnapped our principal hostage and absconded with a staff of Norman foederati. He conspired with the Extrasolarians, consorted with a . . ." he stumbled, still not believing, "with a daimon of Mericanii, if such a thing is to be believed. Why is he not in chains?"

The quiet rang a little when he was done, and only then did I realize he'd been nearly shouting. Smythe had realized all the while, of course, and Crossflane, whose bushy eyebrows wrinkled his forehead all the way to his neatly combed white hair.

"Are you finished, Captain?" the Tribune asked. "I appreciate your candor and your fervor, but Lord Marlowe has his uses, as you see." She spread her hands as if to take in the totality of the *Demiurge* beyond the walls of that room. Turning her attention on me, she continued, "The question of his fate will be reexamined after we have met with the Cielcin. Not before."

"But Justice—"

"Justice," Raine Smythe said, overriding her subordinate, "is mitigated by circumstance. Should his actions prove instrumental in delivering us an alliance with one of the Cielcin clans, I think I speak for Hauptmann and for His Radiance both when I say that the Empire might have cause to be grateful to Lord Marlowe above and beyond the price of those unfortunate men's lives." Bassander made ready to interrupt again, but Smythe held up a hand for silence. "And insofar as Lord Marlowe is useful as a translator and for the rapport he has with this . . . Tanaran, we need him now."

I could see the muscles working in Bassander's jaw, imagined the sound of gears grinding, stripping themselves of their teeth. "You could have told me, ma'am."

"Captain!" First Officer Crossflane hissed.

Bassander Lin stood somehow even straighter. "I'm sorry, sir, ma'am." His face looked almost *pained*. "But if you had only ordered me to go in Marlowe's place, I'd have gone and gladly."

Smythe rocked back in her chair, shook her head. "No, you wouldn't have. You'd have gone straight to Leonid." That was her legate, the commander of the 437th. "Or to Hauptmann."

Silence again. The captain did not argue, and the gears beneath the skin of his jaw were still. We all knew that what Raine said was true, and honest as he was Bassander could not contest it.

"You have been remarkably quiet," Crossflane said. It took me a moment to realize that he was speaking to me, so long had I sat forgotten to one side.

I raised my eyes, asked, "What do you want from me?"

"You understand your position, Lord Marlowe?" Smythe asked.

"I'm to work as a translator, yes. The same as I did on Emesh with Uvanari."

Her eyes narrowed. "*Not* like you did on Emesh, no. You'll be assisting our translator."

I accepted this without complaint. They would bring another translator. That was only sensible. "A scholiast, is he?"

"He is," Raine Smythe replied. "Tor Varro."

"What order is he?" I asked, unable to quiet that piece of me that yet loved the scholiasts, the piece of me that wished I had been one.

Smythe glanced up at Crossflane, whose brows contracted. The older man rubbed his jaw. "Cal something," he said. "Chalcenterite, I think it was? He's from somewhere out in Sagittarius. Nov Angren, maybe?"

"I don't know the order," I said, crossing my arms. No surprises there. There were hundreds of scholiastic orders, each with a subtle difference in focus, in interpretation of the writings of Imore, in dress, in practice. Gibson had been a Zenoan, one of the oldest orders, focused on the study of the classic trivia—grammar, logic, and rhetoric—and upon literature. The Chalcenterites, though I did not then know it, were ascetics of the most extraordinary kind, emphasizing the practice of self-denial and self-reflection for which the scholiasts are so often stereotyped.

Crossflane made a grumbling noise. "Well, he's been over the Emesh records with a microscope. He's impressed." I felt a momentary glow of satisfaction despite my dire circumstances to know that one of the orders had found my work satisfactory, and sat a little straighter. The first officer took a step forward, leaned over the corner of Smythe's desk. "Said you had an . . . interesting interrogation style, if you take my meaning. The way you went off script."

I felt all eyes on me, and shut my own. It took every ounce of control in me to keep my hand from shading my shuttered eyes. I had of course manipulated the situation on Emesh, being the only one who could speak the Cielcin language. I had often only pretended to translate what the Chantry torturers had asked of me, preferring to try and build a relationship with the Cielcin captain. My tactic had failed in the end, and when Valka had cut the bastille's power with her neural lace and Uvanari had freed itself, the beast had tried to kill me. Only Sir Felix's training and my years as a myrmidon had saved me when language failed. I was glad at least that my most dangerous conversations—the last with Uvanari and with Tanaran before that—had been done during Valka's carefully controlled brownouts of the city's power grid.

"Still," Smythe said coolly, "we should not argue with your results,

Marlowe." She leaned back in her chair so far as it would go, and began rapping her knuckles against the desktop. I could feel the room drop a degree. Two. Three. Her muddy eyes never left me, and I struggled not to squirm. "I understand your Doctor Onderra can speak with the Pale now as well."

Valka. Did they know? Did they know the role she had played in the Emesh affair? Surely by now Bassander—who was no fool, whatever my opinion of him—must have guessed at the implants that crouched at the base of her skull. Hoping to deflect away the conversation away from Emesh and whatever role the doctor had had there, I said, "She spent a good deal of time out of fugue since Emesh, studying. She's communicated a fair deal with Tanaran as well. Perhaps more than I have, truth be told."

Seeing my direction and eager to head me off at the pass, Bassander Lin put in, "Captain, I must protest. The witch ought not to be involved. She—"

"Peace, captain," Raine said, again waving her subordinate to silence. "Has Sagara restored the Cielcin prisoner to us?"

"Tanaran?" I asked, not sure.

Captain Lin clasped his hands behind his back and bowed his head. "Yes, ma'am. It's in the brig now."

The knight-tribune stood, expelled a ragged, gusty breath. She crossed to a brass hook hanging on the wall and drew off her officer's overcoat and hung it upon the peg. Turning, she tugged on the lip of her breastplate, adjusting it. "Good, I should like to speak to this creature before long. There's no telling when the rest of its kind will arrive . . ." She massaged one of the ivory gauntlets she wore as though it pained her. Truly fine armor it was, not the dinted and carbon-scored plate of the common legionnaire, but printed ceramic, the sculpted body studded with relief images of the Imperial Sun between the Legions' wings across the chest. A similar motif of wings detailed the edges of the vambraces and greaves, and I knew their substance would turn back even a shot from a plasma howitzer.

"Would you like me to accompany you?" I asked, trying to gauge Bassander's reaction, but the Mandari man was half-turned from me, and I could not tell if his face darkened.

Raine pivoted, and for the first time I noted she wore a highmatter sword on her belt. She wore it slip-fashion, as I did myself, that it might snap away from the belt and be activated in a smooth, single extension by the dominant hand. The left hand. That struck me, for there are no left-handed men or women among the palatine. Speaking—I thought—a shade too sharply, "No! I'll have Varro accompany me." After that her tone softened considerably, and she added, "Better I speak with it alone."

I accepted this with a nod, swallowing both my bile and the sense that I stood on rotting planks above a pit of fire.

Smythe resumed her seat with an equally heavy sigh, as if she shouldered again the entire weight of her office as she seated herself. "It is our current predicament that more concerns me. I do not trust this demoniac we find ourselves in bed with."

"Sagara?" Lin asked.

"Sagara." Raine Smythe turned her attention from Lin to me and back again with a ragged tiredness. In the harsh light of the room, a faint tracery of white scars stood out against the dun color of her neck, on the backs of her hands. They were the marks of the surgery that had made her a patrician. Complex operations and brutal, I always heard, so extensive that even the owner's very genes were altered by tonics and the various essences distilled by the magi of the High College. It never occurred to me how the echoes of such a procedure might ache. I wondered how old Smythe was, and how weary. "I admit, Marlowe, you surprise me."

Not expecting this, I sat forward in my padded chair and folded my hands between my knees. "Surprise you?"

"I asked you to find a planet no one believed exists, and you find not only that planet, but a character out of everyone's childhood myths." She turned away, and for a moment a strange smile played across her face as she looked toward Crossflane, who shrugged. "Kharn Sagara," Raine Smythe said. "My brother used to play as him when we were children." I said mine had as well, and Smythe continued, "The Mataros' chancellor accused you of being a literary cliché, I recall. I'd say she owes you an apology."

I snorted. "Ogir? I'd forgotten that."

Smythe unfastened first one gauntlet then the other and set them both aside. "How many people were aboard your ship?"

"The *Mistral*?" I asked, then thought back. "About three hundred?"

"It's a pity we can't count on them if things go against us," Smythe said, setting the gauntlets neatly to one side. "Sagara has the *Mistral* locked down, I don't doubt."

Bassander shifted his posture, slackened and snapped back to attention. "We could . . . ask him to transfer the *Mistral* to the *Obdurate*."

"Possibly," Smythe agreed.

"Unless . . ." It was a moment before I realized I'd spoken aloud. Even Bassander was looking at me. "Unless they're right where we want them?"

Sir William Crossflane gave me a look like I'd just declared a fervent belief in goblins. "The devil are you on about?"

I suppressed an urge to say *precisely*, said instead, "They could be of use. If things take a left turn. If we can get them out."

"If," Crossflane repeated.

"If," I insisted. "In either event, Corvo has her crew on ice and they may as well sit under Kharn's nose like a crate of fish fresh-frozen for market instead of a couple thousand miles *that way*!" I gestured in what I thought was the direction of the *Demiurge*'s outer hull, holding Crossflane's eye all the while. "Where they're no good to anyone." I was suddenly aware that I was making what Valka had called "that face you make when you've had an idea that any normal human being would have discarded out of hand." Those others must not have known me so well as Valka, for they only nodded, whereas I had thought I'd just been terribly clever, in no small part because I believed the odds of my escaping with the *Mistral* and her crew somewhat greater if she remained in Kharn's power and not that of the Imperium.

Smythe accepted this with a waved hand. "No matter."

"You do need to be very careful," I said. "I'm not sure what Kharn is planning, but you've threatened his world. He won't let that pass."

Crossflane snorted. "Won't let that pass? Boy, the coordinates your man gave us are safely in the hands of the fleet and of Legion Intelligence. Even if he were to slag our ships and yours he knows his days are numbered." I twitched at being called *boy*, but held my peace, telling myself it was only the reminder of how badly Switch had betrayed me that set me so on edge.

"That's just it!" I said, a venomous edge to me now. "I have no idea where Switch got those coordinates. Do you understand? Kharn's daimon had locked out the *Mistral*'s controls from the moment we entered Vorgossos system. Shipboard systems were totally compromised. Corvo couldn't get a read on her position. She couldn't even unlock her doors after Kharn took Doctor Onderra and me prisoner."

"You're saying you believe Sagara leaked the coordinates on purpose," Crossflane said, hooking his thumbs through his belt. "Why?"

Smythe and Crossflane exchanged significant glances, and I wondered for a moment if maybe whatever payment Kharn had extracted from them had been that reason. But no . . . Surely there were things in the Imperial treasury worth the weregild of a planet, but I did not imagine that either Kharn would be much interested in them or the Empire willing to pay. "Personally, I don't think it was Kharn at all. I think his daimon did it."

"Betray its master?" Smythe asked. "Why?"

A darkness flowered behind my eyes, and from it rose hands like stalks of wheat, the swollen flesh sprouting new growth—new arms—like cancers. I heard the sounds of splashing and the rumble of many throats wetly breathing. Shaking myself, I said, "I don't like to guess. But I do think Kharn was blindsided by Bassander's appearance. Would you say?" I directed this last to Bassander himself, who in all that time had moved nary a micron.

The young officer did not deign to look at me. "I don't think Sagara knew we were coming."

"What was it like?" Smythe asked. "This daimon of yours?" I shut my eyes. Held my breath. "Marlowe?"

"The tribune asked you a question, boy." Crossflane's tone had hardened.

Something in me prickled, and I snapped, "That's *Lord,* First Officer, not *boy.*" It was not my father's voice that answered him, but my own. Taking a deep a breath and the space to quiet my flare of anger, I ignored the old officer's bristling and focused instead on the knight-tribune. "It wasn't a machine at all, or if it was its machine parts were buried where I could not see." I clasped my hands, and after a moment found I was squeezing them together so that the knuckles stood out. "You've heard that the Mericanii stole men's bodies and souls to ensure that there was no difference between people?"

"Yes."

"It's true," I said, and told her. I said nothing of my vision, and little of what was said between the Brethren and myself, but spoke instead of the grasping hands, the staring eyes, and ragged throats. The sick and bloated texture of its hide. "I think it was many men, once. That what they were was dissolved or . . . subordinated to the daimon, that it wears them, uses them as we might a vehicle."

The silence that followed, while brief, was total. Smythe made the sign of the sun disc and—staring at a spot on the table—said, "It's clear, then. Vorgossos must be destroyed."

"Kharn will know you intend that," I said. "I tell you, he is planning something."

"Planning something?" Bassander sneered. "What will he do? Fight the Legions single-handed? This ship of his is mighty, Marlowe, but no vessel is mighty as that."

I squeezed the arms of my chair tightly. "You're making a grave mistake underestimating Sagara, Lin. You don't understand . . ."

"I don't understand?" Bassander repeated, riding over me as he turned to face me. "Marlowe, I have been a soldier of His Radiance all my life. My parents were soldiers, and you *presume* to tell me what I do and do not understand?"

Smythe's cane whistled through the air between us and clanged as it bounced off the far wall of the chamber. The knight-tribune did not shout, only stood there, eyes tracking smoothly between the junior officer and myself. "Gentlemen," she said at last in a voice of deathly calm, "I have had enough of this bickering between you both. Whatever your differences—" She raised a hand to silence Bassander's interjection. "*Whatever your differences* and however legitimate your grievances, we are on the same side. The Cielcin are coming, gentlemen, and I need the both of you. I do not ask you to be friends, but you will set aside this feud!" I remained seated, and Bassander stood immobile as stone.

Always it is thus: that the threat from outside drives wedges between those who should stand together. Who must. I could no more turn from my course than Bassander could shift his position. Yet in one way I had the advantage: I could lie, or rather I could say what it was Raine expected of me and neither lose face nor break faith with myself. I could bend, where Bassander could only break. And so I stood, and offered my hand to the other man. I did not speak a word, for I was certain that saying any word would be a mistake.

What happened then disturbed me beyond my ability to adequately explain at the time. Bassander looked at my hand as though it were a serpent, and his lip curled. As I did not speak, he did not take my hand—knowing that to do so would bind him to a promise he did not wish to make. It did not compromise me to offer my hand. It would compromise Bassander to take it. So he turned instead, and saluted his tribune, saying, "I will do as you say, ma'am."

Smythe gave a little nod, shrugging with her lips as if to say, *Good enough.* And perhaps it was. "Leave us," she said, and with a sidelong look at one another, both Bassander and I turned to go. "Not you."

I knew by her tone that she was speaking to me, and so lingered even as the hatch cycled and Bassander Lin vanished into the hall. Without needing to be asked, I retrieved the tribune's thrown cane. Heavy built it was, graven of some wood black as jet, its grain the color of temple-smoke. The head and tip were brass, and unadorned. How like its owner it was. Without comment, I propped it against the side of Smythe's desk and resumed my seat.

She watched me in silence a while, arms folded, her first officer mirroring her in that way old companions everywhere have always had—that way in which they had each, in part, become like the other. At last she spoke. "You really are a cliché, you know that?"

"My teacher used to call it *melodramatic*," I said lightly.

"He wasn't wrong." She picked at some spot on her desk that only she could see. Brown eyes found mine, and she chewed her tongue. "I take it you understand how much difficulty you placed me in with this?" She sketched a circle in the air with the tip of one finger. "You're my responsibility, and now I've my legate and the First Strategos breathing down my neck. Leonid agreed your adventure was worth the risk, but Hauptmann . . . Hauptmann is not so convinced, and it is to Hauptmann I must account in the end."

I thought about my response a long moment before saying, "If I may, it was never my intention to place you in a difficult position. Only to hold to the mission, as I have done and will continue to do."

"Even when the strategos ordered otherwise?"

"Respectfully, I know when you took me from Emesh you said it was with the understanding that Bassander would be made to check my, ah . . . my excesses. But it's unclear to me why you would have wanted me along at all if you wanted another Bassander." Was it my imagination? Or was the knight-tribune smiling ever so slightly? Still, she did not speak, and I added, "In any case, ma'am, it was my opinion that Strategos Hauptmann's new orders were defeatist, and I felt the Empire and mankind both were better served by my actions than they would have been had I obeyed the strategos and returned with Captain Lin to Coritani. I am prepared to pay for my actions on the *Balmung*, should it come to that."

Smythe's eyebrows preceded her smile by half a second, and she turned and smiled at her first officer, who reached into his belt and passed his superior officer a single hurasam. Turning to me, she said, "I hope it does not." I had been the subject of a bet, I later learned. Crossflane had expected that I would grovel, Smythe that I would stand. The two often made such bets, or so Bassander told me much later. "We are on the verge of history here. Peace talks with the Cielcin, and peace after."

"Peace in our time," Crossflane affirmed.

For how long had these two been fighting? How many waking years? Had the white in Crossflane's hair been dark when they began, and Smythe's face unscarred? Whatever love of battle or glory—whatever desire to serve—had called them forth from their unknown homes had faded, became the duty of all old soldiers and that sense of family and loyalty which comes before even a love of country.

They dreamed of peace, as soldiers often do, knowing the cost of war.

"Well, I'm with you, Tribune," I said in answer.

"Good," she said, reaching into her desk. "Which means you will be needing this."

She placed my sword on the surface between us. I opened my mouth.

"Yours, I believe?"

"How did you . . . ?"

"Bassander had it from Lord Sagara. Don't lose it again," she said, and with a sigh rose and turned toward her door. "You may return to your people." I took up my sword and rose to depart. The weight of it in my hands and the sensation of worn leather against my fingertips was like a homecoming in itself. "And Hadrian?"

"Ma'am?"

"Tell Captain Corvo to prepare her people. You're right. We may have need of them."

CHAPTER 56

LIKE CASTLES OF ICE

I FOLLOWED HARD ON Yume's heels as we ascended a sweeping spiral staircase. The golem had not spoken for minutes, and ignored my attempts to question it, and so I'd surrendered and followed it from the *Mistral* into the bowels of Kharn's dark *Demiurge*. Gargoyles watched from above, and the walls were covered in scenes of battle and creation, but I had not the time to linger in appreciation.

We hurried out onto a narrow bridge that ran across a great, echoing emptiness. I tarried, and peered out. Far below, I could see the gray shapes of cargo freighters parked like eggs in a carton, coolant vapor wafting from exhaust ports. They were Smythe's payment, I assumed, judging by the Imperial sunburst stenciled on their hulls.

"This way, sir," Yume said, and hurried me on.

The ancillary bridge served as a sort of meeting place, more intimate and less theatric than the hall of blue candles. It was dark, and might have been a cave were it not for the deep red lights that shone low on the circular walls, casting their hell-glow up on chairs and consoles like the light of dying fires. Kharn Sagara sat above a projection well at the center of the room, like some medieval king above a gameboard. His children hung back in the shadows of his chair, ever-present, ever-watching. Smythe, too, was there, and Crossflane.

"Here he is," the Master said, and smiled. One of his blue eyes dogged my progress from the minute I crossed the threshold. Yume had vanished into thin air—though I saw no other door by which the golem might have exited. The constant malice of Sagara's voice gave me pause, and despite myself—despite the presence of Smythe and Crossflane and their guards—my hand went to my sword. Sagara sniffed. "There is no need for such heroics here, boy."

"What is happening?" I demanded, not moving my hand.

"The Cielcin have arrived," Crossflane replied, clipped tones cutting into Kharn's customary delayed response. I looked up to Kharn for confirmation, and after a moment, he waved a lazy hand to say that it was so.

No holograph plates shone like windows on the encircling wall, nor did any porthole pierce the dark material of the *Demiurge* to open onto the blackness of space. I looked around, searching for some solid recognition of what was said. As if on cue, the projection well lit up, a faint wire frame depicting space around us in little cubes scaled a thousand miles to a side. The *Demiurge* sat in its center, and from this distance I understood the shape of her: flat and pointed, like the blade of an antique sword, but save at the extreme edges she bristled her entire length with a profusion of towers, bridges, and buttressed spires, with here and there the open mouths of docking ports gleaming amidst the shapes of statuary and weapons batteries.

Far to one edge of the projection, like the body of some fattened game bird, sat the *Obdurate*, flanked now by the knife-edged shapes of *Balmung* and *Pharaoh*, as well as two other Imperial destroyers whose names I did not know. The great super-carrier herself was an ugly thing, squat and more square than the deadly forms of the ships at her side, and pathetic-seeming next to the graceful bulk and horror of Kharn's *Demiurge*, but she was a hundred miles from bow to engine-clusters, and fierce as fire if engaged.

"I don't see them," I said, walking around the projection pit, so that I stared through the ghost-images of the ships at Smythe, who had not moved since I entered. At some silent command of Sagara's the image scaled, zoomed out until the little thousand-mile cubes shrank small as bouillon. And there it was.

If the *Obdurate* was massive and the *Demiurge* more massive still, the Cielcin vessel was enormous. At first, I thought it a moon, approaching us from the side opposite the Imperial ships. Even scaled to fit Kharn's map, the size of it was breathtaking, and I gasped. I had always known the Cielcin ships were large, guessed that they were called worldships for a reason, but the reality was more than I had prepared for. Somewhere in the deeps of time the Cielcin had carved a ship from the rock of some mighty asteroid, some dwarf planet frigid and lifeless. Facing us she seemed only that—or would have but for the gleam of towers and lights pointing out from the surface straight at us. Behind, where the dark side of her should be were she only a moon in truth, extended the great machinery itself: the bays and engines, instruments and docking ports to whose umbilicals clung—like remora to the skin of some leviathan—the shapes of smaller, darker craft, too blurry to make out at this range.

Smythe, Crossflane, and Kharn all had seen such sights before, and so it fell to me—alone and uninitiated—to say, "Holy Mother Earth protect us." I tried to count the distance to it and the size of it, but my eyes kept slipping. At last I surrendered, asked, "How far off are they?"

"More than two hundred thousand miles," the Undying replied, using his stage-voice once more, the words falling from everywhere like the voice of God. "There they will stay."

Raine tapped her cane against the edge of the projection pit for attention, though when she spoke it was in a dry and quiet voice. "Any closer and we'd have to take up a parking orbit around it." She glanced at Crossflane. "That's one of the big ones."

"Now you see why I insisted they meet away from Vorgossos," Sagara intoned. "Chaos."

I tried to imagine how the sudden arrival of a new moon might torment a lonely planet like Vorgossos, locked as it was about its dark star. Unable to stop myself, I circled round the projection, passing on the side opposite Kharn's chair to keep space between myself and the Undying. The image of that Pale ship drew closer, and I tipped my head, taking it in. The great spires of her prow and the mass of the asteroid itself were locked beneath a layer of rime that glittered even in the projection, as though it were spun from crystal or grown in some deep cave, a mushroom beneath whose protective cap sheltered spire upon spire, bank upon bank, terrace upon terrace of alien pilings, their shapes organic and unnamed.

In my mind's eye, I saw it too. Not as I saw it there, ghostly and flickering on Kharn's display, but as it was. Truly was. Out there, swallowing the stars. I saw again what I had seen in Calagah, was shown again by Brethren: the Cielcin host marching through the heavens, and behind them stars and planets going down like cinders and cooling down to black. And I saw the Cielcin who led them: taller than any man I had ever known, tall and terrible as Death herself, crowned in silver and sapphire, its fangs like the very ice of its palace.

Prince Aranata, I thought, and knew it with a certainty I could not explain. I remembered my own head tumbling from my shoulders, and had to grip the edge of the projection pit to steady myself. My gorge rose, and

I feared I might be ill there on Kharn's darkly mirrored floor. Fortunately, no one noticed my distress, so taken were they with the events unfolding around them.

"Can we hail them?" asked Raine Smythe.

"There is no need," Sagara replied, and pointed.

The lights went out, and for the briefest instant the only lights—besides the glow off my terminal, and Crossflane's and Smythe's—were those of Kharn's chorus of floating eye drones. The red glow of the bridge lights and the laser-bright images of the holograph pit went out. I half-expected to hear the sound of canned thunder rattling from just offstage, waited for the peasant boy to hammer his sheet of tin or for crystal clarions to sound.

The prince, when he—when it—appeared, did not simply materialize above the holograph plate. No. It strode into frame, appearance slowly resolving to clarity as the *Demiurge*'s communications equipment constructed the image, compiling it in real time. "We will speak to Sagara and no other!" It shouted, speaking the language of the Pale. I could feel both Crossflane and Smythe looking at me, but I was unsure whether or not the Cielcin could hear me, and so held silent, not wanting to jeopardize whatever strange alliance the demoniac had with the demons.

"Eka ti-saem gi!" Kharn's voice boomed through the speakers, though I was close enough to the man himself to hear him whisper through his own lips. "Here I am."

The creature was not the one I had seen in my visions, though it was tall and high-crowned, and dressed in robes of stunning blue that left arms bare save for the drape of fine, silver chains. In one hand it held a staff crowned with a broken circle, the symbol of some office I did not know or understand. I felt a brief surge of relief, for surely here was Prince Aranata Otiolo. This Cielcin's face was broader, flatter, with a tattoo in black ink covering the left side of its face from the base of its crown of horns to the tip of its chin.

The joy I'd felt and the relief shattered. "I am come on behalf of my master," the creature said, "Aeta Utsebimn Aranata Otiolo, Viudihom, Prince of the Itani Otiolo, Keeper to his People, Master to his Slaves." As it spoke, the Cielcin rattled its staff, so that chimes wound about its orbit just below the headpiece clanged their hollow tones. When it finished, it slammed the staff down with such force that the staff stayed standing, and I guessed the creature stood not upon tile or stone, but earth. It beat its chest with both hands. "He who fashioned our world, who brought forth life from dead stone! He who brought us out of the Chains of Utaiharo! Who Sees the Watchers! Who knows the Mind of the Makers! Who leads us through the emptiness and the light!"

It was not the Prince, after all.

I looked up at Kharn Sagara, ageless and Undying, expecting from him a litany of equal magnitude, such as our Imperial heralds so often shower upon His Radiance. Kharn did not reply. Unimpressed, he leaned back in his seat, one hand patting young Ren on the back of his head, mussing his hair. His silence allowed the *coteliho*, the herald, to say on. "We have seen the ships of the *yukajjimn*! You told us there would be no fleet! Only their spokesman!"

"It's a cohort!" Smythe exclaimed. "Not a fleet!"

The Cielcin herald did not respond. It had not heard.

Kharn replied, "The humans had to travel here as well. I have asked their ships to hold their current position, the same as yours. Only their representatives and a token force have been allowed aboard my ship."

Five hundred aboard the Schiavona, I thought, *and three hundred on the* Mistral. *A token force.* Then something else that Kharn had said struck me. *The humans had to travel here . . .* The humans. He had not counted himself among our number, or else the Cielcin word for humans—*yukajjimn, vermin*—applied not to humanity as a class, but to the Empire in particular.

In either case Kharn considered himself a third party, and the *coteliho* did not challenge this claim, but rather swept its braided queue over its shoulders and raised one taloned fist. "This will be acceptable to the Aeta Aranata, who sits on a throne of his slaves." It spread its fingers then, each longer than a man's and tipped with a claw enameled a deep and vital blue.

"Tutai wo," came Kharn's reply, and his lips murmured, "Very good."

Knowing now that the herald could not hear us, I ran over the entire conversation with Crossflane and Smythe. "It's saying that they will send security staff to investigate the *Demiurge* for traps. Kharn's arranging the details."

Sagara raised a fist in a gesture identical to that the *coteliho* had used, and for the first time I realized that it was no true hand. Like his chest, the left hand and arm were of pale metal. And like his chest, some crude simulacrum of flesh—plated and interleaved like the plates of a suit of armor—was stretched tight in panels over the metal skeleton beneath, so that it seemed a stylized impression of a hand he raised, and not a hand itself.

And Kharn said, *"Wananbe o-caradiu ti-Aeta ba-okarin shi, kajadi-se!" I have prepared a gift for your master, slave!*

"A gift?" Raine asked, leaning toward me. "What gift?"

My eyes darted from her confused face to Crossflane's bland one, wondering. "I'm not sure."

The Undying master paused, and I swear each of his blue and shining eyes turned to look at us. *"Yukajjimn kajadin bi thumdein. Yuramyi caramnte ti-kousun ti-yukajjire, eza rakanyi caramnte ti-osun jia."*

I felt the blood go from my face, replaced by something bright and cold as steel drawn at dawn. I glared at Smythe. "What?" she asked, confusion coloring that bland stone she called a face. "What is it?"

"What have you done?" I asked, voice flat as I squared to face her, looking down my nose.

Kharn did not notice, continued speaking to the Cielcin *coteliho*.

Smythe shook her head. "I don't . . . what are you talking about?"

"What have you done?" I repeated.

Crossflane grabbed me by the shoulder, tried to turn me from his commanding officer. "What did he say? Talk sense, Marlowe."

The first officer's hair and chops shone snowy white in the light of the holograph well, his face and Smythe's pale as ivory masks. I snarled. "Sagara said he will give the Cielcin five thousand human slaves. Slaves that *you*"—and here I, against all sense and caution, prodded Smythe in the chest—"gave him." Ivory masks transmuted to marble. I jerked my head at Sagara where he sat between his silent children. "Is that what you gave him? Was that the promised price, Smythe?"

The knight-tribune looked away. "Twenty thousand. From our colonial stores."

"Twenty . . ." It was all I could do not to strike her, to strike the lip of the projection pit beside me. "The colonial stores?"

"From the storehouses," Crossflane interjected, as if this were some sort of justification. The Empire maintained millions of prospective colonists, plebeians who had signed up for resettlement when their prospects ran out at home. Like our soldiers, they might sleep on ice for centuries before they and their families—or they alone—were decanted and deposited beneath the light of some new and alien sun. Twenty thousand of these, it seemed, would not wake at all, unless it were under the eyes and grasping hands of Kharn Sagara in the black pits of Vorgossos.

I pressed my words flat as dead flowers. "And you had the gall to accuse me of treason?" My brows rose on their own. "Was it worth it?"

"Twenty thousand for the life of the Imperium?" Smythe said, not looking me in the eye. "For all those quadrillions? Yes. It was worth it. I thought you understood that."

I opened my mouth to speak, to scream, but the words of the Cielcin herald cut into my momentary silence.

"Tanaran . . ." it said, and I crushed my rage back down again. *"Raka Tanaran ti-saem gi ne?"*

Where is Tanaran?

"With the humans," Kharn's human voice whispered, and his sound system replied, *"Raka vaa ti-yukajjimn."*

"I would speak with Tanaran," the herald said. *"Shala o-tajarin ti-koun."*

Kharn's face was expressionless. Beside him, Suzuha stirred, and Kharn's steel and flesh-paper hand reached out to steady her. "Tanaran is in the humans' power. I cannot bring it to you."

I translated this for Smythe, who said, "We will surrender our captive to the prince and no other!"

Sagara raised a hand to silence her, and three of his eyes descended, floating in a smooth arc to more closely regard the three of us. "Peace," he said, and with that turned to the Cielcin. "I will have your gift prepared for delivery at once. You may send security to me to prepare for your master's arrival, if you will." Sagara was being astonishingly conciliatory, though now I suspect such manipulative flattery was only a mask, a way to manipulate the Cielcin into cooperating.

The *coteliho* hissed past its teeth, *"Yumna raka dein ilokete ne, Sagara-se?"*

"No trick, Oalicomn," Sagara replied. "It is only that your baetan is aboard the *yukajjimn* ship. I do not have it." The herald only bared its fangs, snarl distorting the looping script inked on its face. "Tell your master I anticipate his arrival, and hope that he enjoys his gift." Sagara's Cielcin was perfect. He even used the so-called masculine to describe the Aeta—a subtlety most human speakers failed to notice. The Aeta were masters, and so were never the *object* of a sentence, always its subject.

Kharn Sagara waved his flesh hand and banished the projection with neither pomp nor circumstance. Raine, I think, expected him to speak, but I knew better, and waiting watched the two dozen drone eyes in the room slowly orbit until they formed a perfect circle, gently processing in the air above our heads. The room lights swelled on, red as coals.

"Tanaran is aboard," Smythe said coolly. "He is on the *Schiavona*. We could have sent for him."

"There was no need," Sagara's false voice boomed. At an unseen sign, Yume appeared and shuffled the children away. Had they been brought only to decorate Kharn's throne for that address? And why was I sent for? Only to translate for Smythe and Crossflane? "The Aeta does not like to be refused anything. He will consider any refusal a threat, so we must lie to placate him." He paused, eyes shut. "He will send security to ensure there is no trap here. When they do so you will allow them a pre-inteview with your captives. The others are all out of their cages, I assume?"

Smythe wrung her cane as though it were the neck of some seabird. "They are." If it offended her that Sagara gave orders where he should offer suggestions, she did not show it. Smythe doubtless saw the utility in the Master's suggestions, and so did not contest them. "What frequency did the Cielcin use?"

"Frequency?" Sagara's voice fell like slow rain from the roof above us, like slaver dripping from the roof of some iron mouth. "You think it is radio they communicate with?"

Crossflane, ever the officious sort, replied, "What, then?"

Not moving, not looking at us, Sagara pivoted. "The Cielcin will return and call again. They will insist that because I am human, they should be allowed to double the number of troops they bring in reserve. I will grant that request." As he spoke, his face turned slowly to mine, and I blanched, for the weight of those black eyes was a terrible thing. What Kharn said, and what Smythe and her first officer said in answer, I cannot say, for I heard another voice within my mind—like Kharn's voice, but brighter. *You see what they are, these fine friends of yours.*

I found I could not work my jaw, and looked around, distressed. Neither Smythe nor Crossflane took notice, wrapped as they were in conversation with the Undying on his high seat.

Kharn's eyes had not left me. An image flashed in my head: the cargo ships I had seen when I had crossed the bridge into this very chamber. Then inside, row upon row of caskets, and beneath their frosted lids the slack faces of twenty thousand sleeping men. And women. And children. *See what they will sell? What they are?*

I saw what Kharn was doing. He meant to drive the wedge between myself and the Imperium just a little deeper. What his aim was I cannot say, but it was transparent to me as glass. I did not answer him. I was not sure I could.

The world is filled with monsters: dragons in the wilderness, serpents in the garden. We must become monsters to fight them. Anyone who thinks otherwise has never really had to fight for anything. I knew where I stood, on the wall between the wilderness and the garden. Whatever humanity was—whatever it is—it is mine, and worth defending. Given the choice between the Cielcin and human monsters, I'll choose the human every time.

CHAPTER 57

THE PRINCE OF HELL

THE MOUTH OF HELL opened before me, and beyond was only the blackness of space. The overhead lights of the hangar bay washed out all but the brightest stars, and the shimmer of the static field masked the rest so that all ahead was blackness. I stood amongst white-armored legionnaires, dressed in a suit of deepest black. High boots, red piping on the trousers, the hem of my black coat flowing about my ankles, the collar standing well past the level of my ears. My hair was newly trimmed, and my old coat was laundered and new-repaired. Still, I felt grubby beside the knight-tribune and her first officer in their suits of sculpted ivory, beside their scholiast Varro in flowing green.

And how bright the host behind me! The Imperial standard hung from a pole beneath a golden sculpture of the Sun, and the image of His Radiance, Emperor William XXIII, shone from a holograph plate carried—like a small umbrella—atop a staff. The soldiers all carried energy lances, their barrels and bladed heads gleaming in the light. Red were their tabards, and red their plumes, and black the long cloaks of the officers, drinking the light.

Kharn Sagara stood near at hand, swathed in gold, his golem faithful at his side. A full two dozen eyes floated about them both, shining with a blue and inhuman menace. Behind them both, faces slack and lifeless, stood a hundred SOMs in rank and file, their khaki uniforms uncared for. They carried no weapons, stood to no order or attention, and yet there was a weight to them and a palpable threat wholly unlike the threat of our soldiers, and it is a testament only to the training and the discipline of the Sollan Legions that not one of our people balked in the face of those monsters.

The cornicen's clear voice went up, crying, "Attention!" And behind me every one of Raine's five hundred soldiers passed their lances from the crooks of their arms to the ready posture, so that they grasped them with both hands. The crystal clarion blew, clear notes and martial winding in that echoing cavern of a hall.

Darkness. Chaos. The mother of demons.

I watched that infinite Dark give birth, watched the black ship emerge from blackness deeper still. Like a piece of the night it was, its shape difficult to describe: like a broken circle, its surface warped and ruined with irregular designs, as though it were the organ of some awful giant. It was nearly so large as the *Schiavona*, larger than the *Mistral*, that it might hold a solid thousand Cielcin screamers comfortably aboard. And I felt—rather than heard—the breath go through the men at my back. The horror. Many of them, I realized, had never seen a Cielcin ship up close before. Most of the war was fought at distance, fought with fire, fought while these soldiers slept on ice in the *Obdurate*'s massive holds. I was conscious then of the history in which I stood: that here, for the first time in more than twenty thousand years of human civilization, we stood and faced a power like ourselves but greater. Every war, every conquest, every treaty . . . every colony and colonization and the struggle against different peoples seemed to me practice for this, this great other.

Unlike the *Schiavona*, the Cielcin craft had no landing gear—and why should it? Like they had for the *Schiavona*, docking clamps and umbilicals descended from the roof of the *Demiurge*'s great bay, wiring the ship into Kharn's systems, connecting fuel lines and service passages. That Kharn had the equipment for such spoke volumes. Clearly, Vorgossos and its Master had been dealing with the Pale for a long, long time.

"Forward!" the cornicen declared, and behind us every soldier took one thundering step closer. Our party did not move. Smythe, Crossflane, Lin, Tor Varro, and Jinan and myself held our ground beside the standard bearers and the guards who held the Cielcin prisoners in chains. Sagara made no sign. He did not need to.

At last the preparation was ended, and the time come at last.

The black ship opened.

If I expected a ramp to descend, I was surprised. Instead, a hatch opened in the bottom of the vessel and a sort of lift descended, a platform upon whose broad surface stood an assemblage of the Pale. There must have been sixty of them. Seventy. Not one of them was shorter than eight feet, and each carried a white sword tall as a man, the blades—held in their right hands—resting against their left shoulders. They dressed in black, with cloaks of deepest azure trimmed in silver. Bleak masks strangely painted hid their faces, and their horns rose tall and curving as crowns of chalk.

These advanced, not in ranks, but fanned out in a semicircle, so that rapidly they commanded a great breadth of the space beneath and before their vessel. One of them—taller than the rest and with a white cloak instead of blue—raised its blade and shouted, the voice amplified by some praxis in its mask. I could not make out the words, but I knew a war cry when I heard one, though I had never heard one before. My bones remembered.

"Hold!" Smythe said to her men. "Steady on!"

When the Cielcin was done, a knot of the creatures still standing on the platform parted, and the herald I had seen projected on the *Demiurge*'s bridge appeared. Oalicomn. The creature carried the same staff forward, chimes ringing. Its massive eyes narrowed in its tattooed face as it surveyed our host and Kharn's.

"*Yukajjimn!*" it said, voice rough and high, like the cry of some bird. "You stand before the Lord of the Seventeenth Branching, who is Aeta! Prince and Chieftain of the Otiolo! Who is Viudihom, the Self-Made! He who fashioned our world, who brought forth life from dead stone! He who brought us out of the Chains of Utaiharo! Who Sees the Watchers! Who knows the Mind of the Makers! Who leads us through the emptiness and the light!" It rattled its staff as it spoke and slammed the butt against the floor. I had heard most of it before, and held my silence as Tor Varro translated for the others. I wished Valka could have been there, but she was trapped on the *Mistral* with Corvo and the rest of what once had been my Red Company. "You stand before the Great One! Our Master, Our Lord, Our Keeper! Who is Father and Mother to us all! Utsebimn Aranata Otiolo!"

At this it swooned, or else threw itself forcefully to the ground. Facing outward, all of the Cielcin guards knelt in perfect synchrony, swords still flat against their opposite shoulders, their long braids nearly touching the floor. I felt again a species of rotten terror, knowing that now, surely, I would look upon the face from my vision. The face of the beast who killed me.

Prince Aranata appeared.

And again, I relaxed.

It was not the face I had seen.

Eyes I had not met in dream swept over us from a face huge as a man's

chest. The prince was a giant, nine feet high and broad almost as two
men. Black armor glittered like wet glass, and the rings of silver and of
platinum that banded Aranata's horns gleamed like stars. His great cape
spread out behind him like wings, and his mighty braid wrapped twice
about its shoulders. At the sight of the prince, Tanaran and all our prisoners fell upon their faces and lay shivering, and no action of our soldiers
could so much as make them lift their eyes.

Behind Aranata, similarly adorned and attired, came a slender Cielcin,
more delicate of feature. It kept its eyes down, its mouth firmly closed.
This second creature held in its hands a silvered chain, thick as a child's
arm. The chain ran back, fastened to a silver collar. And in the collar . . .

Bassander swore.

I had seen the creature in the collar before, and the sight of her was more
terrible than I'd dreamed. Unprompted, Crossflane rounded on Sagara.
"What is the meaning of this?" The Undying did not reply, and the old
officer turned on me, demanding, "What is this, Marlowe?"

"It's a woman," I said, voice dead of feeling.

It *was* a woman, or what was left of one. She was not quite like the one
in my dream, I saw. That one had looked more like my mother, but this was
younger. Slighter. Pale as milk, as the creature that dragged her forward.
She wore nothing, unless it was strips of blue silk and the jeweled anklets
that—chained—hobbled her gait. Great scars mottled her flesh, angry and
red. These ran along her arms, her legs, the insides of her thighs, and at the
corners of her mouth. And her hands . . . her hands! These had been slit by
some vicious surgeon, the flesh between the fingers pared away so that each
digit remained a useless ornament, unable to grasp . . . anything. A cleft
between her largest toe and the rest of each foot gave a similar impression.
She could hardly walk, and it was suffering to stand.

There was nothing in her eyes but tears.

Her soul was dead.

Raine Smythe placed a hand on Crossflane's arm to quiet him. "Wel-
come, Prince Aranata," she said, "I am Dame Raine Smythe, Knight and
Tribune of the 437th Centaurine Legion, Third Cohort under Sir Leonid
Bartosz. I have the command here."

Tor Varro—a tall, black-haired man with a stern, vaguely paternal
face—stepped forward to assist in translation.

*"Eka Dame Raine Smythe, scahayu uje Tribune ba-scandatan Centaurine bi
thumum sava, ba-cohort bidim ti-Leonid Bartosz relu. Siaje o-utorie ti-saem gi,"*

the broken girl said instead, voice high and brittle and hard as flint. She had repeated the tribune's words precisely, translating without editorial.

"She's translating," I said to Raine.

"Citharathun mnu," the girl echoed. I felt my stomach turn, and had to look away. Even Sagara looked disgusted, and I was glad—not for the first time, and certainly not for the last—that the Cielcin could not interpret our facial expressions at all well.

Prince Aranata Otiolo looked down at Smythe, who seemed hardly half his size, and said, *"Yelbe odein ba-kousun shi."*

Tor Varro turned and repeated the words in Galstani, saying, "He says he has come for his property." I took it as a sign of the man's quality that he used the masculine pronoun for the Aeta, not the neutral one which would ordinarily be the more appropriate in our less fluid tongue.

Smythe pursed her lips, raised her chin so that she looked up, unafraid, into the eyes of the giant before her. "And he shall have it, when he has treated with us. They are being kept safely and well—as you see." She waved a hand, encompassing by its arc the prostrate forms of our eleven captives. There was Tanaran, and the vicious Svatarom beside it. None raised their eyes.

The xenobite rested a hand on the hilt of its sword and took a step forward, making to brush past us and approach its people. At a shout from the centurion guarding the prisoners, our soldiers closed ranks, angling lances forward so that barrels and ceramic bayonets aimed at the Lord of the Seventeenth Branching. The kneeling Cielcin soldiers hissed, and as a unity pivoted on their knees, threatening to rise.

"Hold!" Bassander Lin shouted, throwing out a hand. "Everyone hold!" I may have disliked the man, but to his credit, I have seen Bassander Lin in several crises, and never once seen his composure crack. He kept one hand on his shield catch, but the other was open and flat, calling for peace.

"Tanaran-kih!" the prince demanded. "On your feet, slave!" Without lifting its face, Tanaran got its feet under it and stood—still bowing. "Look at me!" Tanaran turned its face up, eyes narrowed as if it faced some bright light. "Speak!"

The baetan's voice was barely more than a whisper. "The Watchers were not on Tamnikano, *Ya Aeta-doro,*" it said, "or if they were, we could not find them. Ichakta Uvanari is dead, and all but these." It had not stopped bowing, and waved a hand over its shoulder at its comrades. "We have failed you, and beg your mercy or your mercy." The words it used for mercy, *ndaktu* and *daktaru,* meant different things. The first, as I have told you, was *judgment, justice.* The second *clemency.* Almost I expected Aranata to strike off its servant's head then and there, and devil take the Empire.

But Kharn Sagara stepped forward. "My lord," he said, speaking with his own voice. "Welcome back. I trust my gift was to your liking?" He spoke as a servant does to his master, and I wondered at that, for the Undying served no power in the cosmos but himself.

The reminder that Raine and Crossflane had dealt with Sagara and with the Cielcin in human blood and bodies twisted sick in me, and I glared at my boots, and so heard the beast's reply, "They will serve beautifully. Nobuta!" It took me a moment to realize that this was the name of the Cielcin holding the silver chain, though Varro caught it easily enough. It yanked the chain, dragging the mutilated wreck of a woman forward. She did not cry out as her butchered feet splayed painfully on the floor, stumbling toward her inhuman masters. I looked up in time to see the Aeta bare his glassy fangs. "We will do good work with them. These *yukajjimn* have . . . so much potential."

Crossflane grunted a curse when he heard the translation, but held his peace for fear the broken girl would translate him.

"The humans wish a peace with your scianda," Sagara said, allowing the girl to translate. I found I could not take my eyes away from her empty face, nor turn my ears from the sounds of her harsh and barking words. Her teeth flashed, seeming too small behind her thin lips. With a start, I realized they'd been filed into points. I clenched my own teeth. They had shaped her like themselves, visited pain and other violations I dared not imagine upon her. Long ago, in my own home, I had seen eunuch myrmidons painted to resemble the xenobites for the Colosso. This was worse.

"*Genuri o-svanar ne?*" Aranata repeated. "Make peace? They wish to surrender? To serve us?"

"Surrender?" Smythe echoed when she had been told the prince's words. "We wish to stop fighting. To make peace as equals."

"Equals?" Aranata said. "The Aeta have no equals." I should have recognized that statement for what it was: a warning that our negotiations were doomed from the start. But I had come too far and hoped for too long to see the truth I would not hear. I had hoped the Cielcin would be all like Uvanari. But Uvanari had been beaten, and the prince was not the captive soldier I had killed. "You would have us serve you!" he said. "And for this they will expect me to turn on Hasurumn, on Pagoramatu, and the others? Is this the way?"

"You would not have come if you did not wish to speak." I spoke for the first time, and had spoken out of turn. I felt Bassander tense beside me, and half-expected a blow to the back of my head.

None came, but the Aeta rounded on me, nostril slits flaring. *"Raka deni ne?"* He addressed the words to Sagara, but towered over me. *Who is this?*

I did not bend or shy away.

One of Sagara's habitual silences seemed to have fallen on him, and it was Tanaran who answered, saying, "This is Marlowe. It was he who saved us on Tamnikano. He gave *ndaktu* to the Ichakta." It had taken its eyes from its master's face, and looked straight up at the ceiling, baring its throat in a kind of submission, such as wolves are wont to do.

"Asvatada ne?" the Aeta asked, tilting his head in the direction that indicated affirmation, approval. "Did he indeed? Then you have my gratitude. Itana Uvanari was one of my most prized possessions. It is good to know it died a good death."

Uvanari's death played behind my eyes, the Cielcin bleeding out on the floor of the Chantry's interrogation cell while the klaxons blared and flashed their warnings. It had fought to the last, slipped its bonds, murdered its torturer, and come for me. Only chance and my meager skill had saved me.

"A good death," I agreed. *If there is such a thing.*

The Aeta's nostrils flared again, and he tucked his chin, angling his horns in a way I think meant as a kind of threat or dominance display, the way strong men might square their shoulders and thrust out their chins. "I would speak to my baetan alone."

"That can be arranged," I answered in the Cielcin tongue, speaking without thinking. I saw Bassander and Smythe both snap their eyes to me when Varro translated, faces dark. Switching to the standard, I added, "As a show of good faith." I should not have spoken, I knew that full well, but the damage was done. The whole party glared at me: Smythe and Bassander, Crossflane and Jinan, even the impassive Varro.

Hurrying into the gap left by my outburst, the knight-tribune said, "I intend for you to leave these meetings with your baetan, Aeta. Provided we come to some arrangement."

"Arrangement?" Aranata echoed. "You presume to threaten me?"

"Threaten?" Smythe asked, genuinely baffled. "Not at all."

She did not see—none of us did, then—that any challenge to the Aeta's supreme authority, even the barest murmur that we had a right to refuse it anything, was seen as an assault against that authority, or worse: a grave insult.

"You think we will deal with you like some common *merchant?*" Aranata asked, saying the word *merchant* with all the venom of a prelate denouncing *whores.*

"We will not just hand over our captives," Crossflane said.

The herald, Oalicomn, spoke from its master's shoulder. "Hostages, then!"

"Of course *hostages!*" Crossflane snapped, unable to contain himself.

"Danagayan wo!" the broken girl intoned, indicating Crossflane's scorn by her choice of words. Inflamed, Aranata whirled and struck her soundly with the back of his hand. She hit the ground like a wet towel and did not stir.

"Abassa-do!" said the Cielcin holding her chain, the thin one dressed as Aranata was dressed. "No!"

I started, gaze lost halfway between the chaos with the xenobites and my own people. *Abassa-do. Abassa . . .* Father. I turned, taking in this new fact. *Father.* Parent. I had never seen a Cielcin child before—I was not sure if anyone had. Looking again at the creature called Nobuta, I saw. The shape of its face was rounder, softer, the horns shorter, eyes wider. Though it was nearly so tall as its parent, it had not achieved the breadth and fullness of adulthood.

A child.

Earth and Emperor forgive me.

Tor Varro hurried forward, saying to the xenobites, "I'm a physician. You've hurt her."

He had the scholiast's talent for understatement, it seemed. But Varro was blocked by Nobuta, who said, "No, it's mine!" The scholiast's fists tightened—a display of feeling that astonished me in one of his order. But he backed off all the same.

"Do we want peace with creatures like this?" Bassander said softly. Raine slashed an arm across his path as he took a step forward. Jinan quietly swore in Jaddian. Privately, I felt myself agreeing with Bassander. I found myself staring at the cleft soles of the girl's mutilated feet, a black feeling in the pit of my stomach, wondering what awaited Kharn's gift of five thousand. Raine's gift.

"Okun-se!" Prince Aranata's voice cut through the commotion, cold and dead as Brethren's hands. "You!" It took me a moment to realize that

the Aeta was speaking to me. Behind him, the child Nobuta crouched beside the translator, stroking her scarred face. "Tanaran says you have honor. A beast's honor, but honor all the same. By that honor and by what you did for my Ichakta, tell me the truth now. What do you want?"

"What do we want?" Raine Smythe echoed when I translated, "For it and its people to stop preying on our colonies."

I turned, faced the Cielcin Aeta where he towered above me. Varro was distracted with the injured girl and so I had a chance—a passing chance—to speak the truth and not as I'd been scripted. "I wanted to see your kind with eyes unclouded," I said, giving the answer I had given Gilliam Vas so very long ago. "And to make peace." "Peace!" Aranata barked. *"Qilete!"* Only when I heard the word spoken back to me did I realize the problem.

The Cielcin word for *peace* was *submission*.

CHAPTER 58

THE CHALCENTERITE

"THAT WENT ABOUT AS well as could be hoped," Smythe said when we returned to the *Schiavona*, eyes downcast.

No one answered for a moment, aware of the shapes than moved in the silence between us like wolves. We were in one of the upper halls, at a place where environment suits hung from hooks on the wall and the dorsal airlock opened in the ceiling above our heads. We'd just watched a workman clamber through it from the service umbilical that attached to a service catwalk that ran above our ship in the *Demiurge*'s massive hangar. Smythe had dismissed the laborer with a brusque command. We might have met in her office, only we had not made it so far before the knight-tribune turned back fuming.

She was thinking of the deal she'd made. I could see it in her eyes. Her devil's bargain with Sagara, and the way he'd turned her gift over to the Cielcin. She was seeing the poor, tormented translator again and again in her mind—was wondering what she'd done, was wondering just what fate awaited them and the remaining fifteen thousand she'd granted the Undying Lord of Vorgossos.

"Well?" To my astonishment, it was Bassander Lin who spoke, echoing the thoughts in my own mind. "Knight-Tribune, did you—" He remembered himself at once, stood a little straighter. "Permission to speak candidly, ma'am." This Smythe granted with a wave of her cane. Bassander Lin still looked uncomfortable, but he fixed his eyes on a point just above his commander's head and said, "Did you see what they had done to that poor slave girl?"

Crossflane scowled. "It was difficult to overlook, captain."

"What sort of animal could do that?"

I have since learned that among the Cielcin, it is considered a great honor to depend upon another, for to do no work among a people whose very lives depended upon the upkeep and careful maintenance of their starships was a mark of supreme opulence. More honorable still was to keep such slaves, such living ornaments, such beings without *qiati*, without utility. And to torment the humans so held the added relish of domination and pride, to have broken mankind—the great enemy—over the Cielcin knee. I have known men who are no different, though I did not say such a thing to Bassander.

"It was horrible," Jinan said, almost under her breath.

"Nevertheless," Smythe said, mustering all her soldierly pragmatism, "we have work to do." She took a moment to gather herself, looking like a child's figurine all folded in on itself. What must she have felt? At the time I did not—could not—consider it, such was my fury with her and my frustration. But now I think old Smythe, born a serf herself, imagined that when Sagara had demanded payment in the form of twenty thousand human souls that he intended naught but serfdom for the lot of them. Whatever she was, she was an Imperial tribune, and could not image the macabre and inhuman uses to which a demoniac like Sagara might put such poor souls.

She turned her attention to me. "I mean to make a liar of you, Lord Marlowe."

"Ma'am?"

"You promised the Pale a tête-à-tête with our chief prisoner," she said. "This cannot be allowed, not least of which because our Cielcin friends may have . . . opinions regarding the events at Emesh other than—shall we say—the official version."

Jinan cleared her throat. "Forgive me, Knight-Tribune, but how do you intend to keep them from sharing those *opinions* once these negotiations are finished?"

Not eager to call Jinan's attention down on me but unable to hold my tongue, I interjected, "I do have a hard time imagining the Aeta would privilege our word over Tanaran's." I was being simple, and as is the nature of such simplicity, I was unaware of it.

"Knight-Tribune, if I may?" said Tor Varro, stepping forward. He was dressed strangely for a scholiast. Still in verdant greens, but not in the flowing robes and togas which befitted his station or dignity, but rather in a long, slitted tunic more akin to a knight's surcoat, this worn over a close-fitting shirt and loose trousers cinched below the knee, where they gave way to hose and the customary soft slippers. The bronze badges that

signified his competency were not sewn onto a sash worn crossways like a
bandoleer, but pinned to his tunic front like a soldier's medals. He had a
patrician's bearing—though none of the scars—and the rock-steady confidence that comes from knowing many things. "When we are finished, it
is hoped the personal account of our Cielcin prisoners will matter far less
to the Aeta than those incentives he gains by his association with the Empire. We have every intention of this being a . . . felicitous relationship
between our two peoples."

"Felicitous . . ." Bassander repeated, unable to hide his scorn. But he
held back, not saying the rest of what was on his mind.

Sensing where this might be headed, I asked, "What exactly are we
planning to offer them?"

I had directed this question to Smythe, but it was the scholiast who
continued at a sign from his commanding officer. "An immediate cessation of hostilities, naturally, contingent on the prospect of further dialogue. Exactly as you described at Emesh."

"And what else?"

Varro glanced to Smythe, seeking permission. She made a gesture with
the hand holding the cane and he said, "What you'd expect, introductions
to the Aeta of other Cielcin clans, the opening of trade agreements . . ." As
he spoke, I remembered how, long ago, I had spoken of just such things to
Director Adaeze Feng and the other representatives of the Wong-Hopper
Consortium, imagining a day when it was trade that defined relations between our people and the Pale, not violence. But then . . . hearing it from
lips other than mine, hearing it after the sight of that mutilated girl and the
visions I had seen . . . it seemed only the naive dream of a child, like morning dew banished by the first rays of the sun.

I doubted, and doubting took little note of what else was said, but nodded along with the directives and specifics of that meeting. I needed time
alone, needed time to think, to put the broken pieces of my mind back
together again. I needed sleep. Most of all, I needed to be away. I could
feel the net—the noose—tightening around me. *The Cielcin. The Empire.
The Extrasolarians. Kharn Sagara. My Red Company. My duty to my friends
and their faith in me. My betrayal of the Empire. My betrayal of Jinan. Switch's
betrayal of me.* I had conjured enough rope to hang myself, called down
enough wolves to be sure I'd never leave the woods. When I had left Vorgossos, ascended that hightower once more and regained my place on the
Mistral, I had thought I'd returned to the ordinary world. But that familiar
ship—those familiar faces—everything had changed.

You cannot twice step into the same river, Heraclitus once said. There is no coming home. I had not returned to the *Mistral* of my memory, had not gone back to my friends unchanged. There is no going back. I have seen the rivers of time, and tread their lucent waters. They flow in but one direction.

Forward.

I had changed. And they had changed. And everything had changed.

I felt . . . *upside down.* Disquieted. Upset by the thought of the very peace I had myself pursued so ardently. But I resolved to do what I must, and so bowed my head when at long last the knight-tribune said, "That's enough for today, then. We'll reconvene tomorrow at oh-seven-hundred. Dismissed."

But as we turned to go, the scholiast Varro took me by the arm. "Lord Marlowe, a word." It was not a question, though in any event I saw no reason to deny the man. I hung back until all the others had filtered out of the room, staring absently at the ladder leading to the service hatch in the roof above. When we were alone, Tor Varro said, "I wanted to ask you something."

"Yes?"

"When we were speaking with the Aeta just now, there was a moment—I was trying to help that poor girl the Cielcin mutilated—when he asked what we wanted out of all this," he said, and I felt a knife twist in my back, but kept my expression as blank and open as I could manage. "Smythe told you that we wished for the xenobites to stop preying on our colonies, but you . . . you said you wanted—what was it? *'Oretiri vaa tiorruu sucoriyuyaya.'"*

To see with eyes unclouded.

He quoted me perfectly.

Still I said nothing.

Something flickered in the scholiast's patrician face. Amusement? Irritation? There ought to have been nothing at all. That disturbed me as much as anything I had seen that strange day, for it impressed upon me the strangeness of my circumstances, when even the scholiasts smiled.

"I have to ask that in future you hold to the tribune's script and obey instruction."

"Did she ask you to have this conversation with me?" I said.

Apology. That was the name of the expression he bore. Embarrassment, even. It was subtly done, such that were I any other sort of man I might have missed it and thought Varro as expert in his mastery of emotion as any other of his order I have known. But I—who long have studied human faces and rendered them in ink and charcoal—saw the expression for what it was. "She believed you would be more amenable to one of our order. I understand that once you wished to join us."

In a voice pressed as dried flowers and without any warmth, I replied, "That was a very long time ago."

"Yet you are not so old, I think."

"It's not the years," I answered, "it's the light-years." Was that a smile on the scholiast's pointed face? "Does Smythe know?"

"That you said something you shouldn't have? Yes. But for what it is worth I do not believe your actions endangered our mission in any way." The scholiast crossed his arms. They were not the arms of an anemic scholar, but shaped by labors I could not guess at, and I wondered at the nature of his order. The Chalcenterites were then unknown to me, an obscure sect of the scholiast tradition, given less to navel-gazing and to the quiet study of the self and stars. Rather they embodied their labors, and moved through the world of living men. All scholiasts must work to maintain their colleges and monasteries. Being forbidden all technology more sophisticated than electric lamp, they are condemned to toil, and yet Varro seemed more akin to the gladiators I have known than to the farmers and masons of the country.

"There is something I don't understand," he said.

"What's that, counselor?"

"Why are you here?" he asked, and there was no confrontation in his tone, though one might easily have heaped scorn upon such words. "You. The son of a lord. You might have had any sort of life you chose. Why this peripatetic existence?"

I was quiet a long moment, chewing the inside of my cheek. The voiceless words I had heard in my dreams sounded in my mind, backing reflected images of the horrors I had been shown.

This must be.

But when I spoke, it was not of visions. I could not have explained Brethren or Calagah to Varro if I had wanted to. And I did not want to. I wanted to tell the truth even less. The truth was only that I had wanted to leave home out of a child's desire for adventure, because I had heard stories of Simeon the Red, of Kasia Soulier, and Arsham, Prince of Jadd. Of Kharn Sagara. How foolish he seemed—that other Hadrian—to have dreamed such dreams.

"Why are *you* here?" I asked instead. "You might have sought an appointment anywhere other than the Legions, but here you are." It was a presumptuous question, but then so was Varro's.

Varro didn't hesitate. "I have a duty."

"To the Empire?"

"To mankind."

"And you think I'm any different? Why? Because I grew up in a castle. I'll wager you did as well to judge from the look of you. I'm here because it's the right thing to do, and because I can do something about it."

The scholiast held his flinty eyes to mere slits, as though he sought something in me he needed a microscope to see properly. In measured tones, he said, "Smythe was right about you. You're an idealist."

"I wouldn't say that." I had heard enough. I sensed that Varro had said all that Smythe had tasked him to say, and that the rest of this was . . . what? A pleasantry? An inquiry? A warning?

"Oh?"

I'd turned to go, and so was made to turn back. "I never said I could do it. Bring peace, or . . . whatever it is we're here to do. I can only speak the truth."

"The truth, ah . . ." Varro shifted his posture, not quite looking at me anymore. "You need to speak our truth. Stick to the program. Or you're no use."

"Your truth?" I echoed, now turned fully back to face the Chalcenterite. "Forgive me, counselor, but I thought you were a scholiast. There is only one Truth." I could hardly contain my surprise, my distaste. You may think it strange that I—who have lied a thousand thousand times— might take issue with such a perspective. But he was a *scholiast.* A man of learning, of science, of philosophy natural and unnatural. He should know better than to engage such sophistry.

Varro dismissed this with the wave of a hand. "These are difficult times, Lord Marlowe, and ours is a difficult task. You should understand this. I've been over the records from the Emesh affair. I know your regard for Truth."

The shadow of something like my brother Crispin moved in me, and it was all I could do not to seize the scholiast by the tunic front. I backed off instead. *Rage is blindness,* I told myself, made to recall Imore's aphorism by the familiar green of Varro's clothes. I was a liar. I am a liar. I have no illusions about this. But I am a liar in the service of Truth, or so I tell myself. In service of the Good—which is the same thing. I had told my lies because they ennobled me, whereas lying in service to the Empire, to an

Empire that might sell its own people to the Pale . . . such lies diminished me.

I could explain none of this to Tor Varro. At the time, I could not have explained it to myself. I knew only that my affront and instinct for rightness rebelled at his words, and I said, "I do my duty."

"That is *all* we ask," he said, but I was enough the veteran of court on Emesh and on Delos before that to hear the words inside the words spoken. *We will not ask again.*

CHAPTER 59

NO MAN AN ISLAND

A DAY PASSED, AND I have passed three days here without writing. The brothers and sisters of the cloister requested my help digging a new well inside the decennid gate, and I—who have eaten off their board for some months now and squandered their ink—could not refuse. I mention this not to cry my virtue, but to demonstrate that even such as I, who am all alone now, am not wholly isolated. Some people believe that the painter who works his canvas is not an individual because he acquired his skills at the knee of some earlier master. That the soldier who stands before the enemy is not a hero, but a pawn—and one of many. There is no truth to this. Each of us contains multitudes, but it is not that we are cells in the body of humankind. Rather we are clay, shaped as the mountain is shaped: by the wind, the tramping foot, and the rain. By the world. The mark of other hands is on us, but we are ourselves alone.

One may be part of a community. One *is* an individual.

They are not mutually exclusive. It is only that the soul, the self, should lead, and our allegiances follow. To do otherwise—to be otherwise—is to make oneself a slave. Often when we speak, it is with the breath of dead men. Yet we build ourselves on such tradition. We tell only the one story after all, over and over. Through us that dead air is lent new life, and we remember, that we might one day understand.

I remember it was difficult waiting on that ship, waiting on word from Sagara or Smythe. I had ferried over briefly from the *Obdurate* to recover those of my effects which had been left behind when first I fled. I was remembering then. Have I said that what we perceive as darkness is only the chaos that came—without light's order—before Creation itself? That is why we imagine *anything* might be lurking in the darkness. In the dark of my cabin on the *Mistral* I slept—or thought I slept—and dreamed . . .

. . . or thought I dreamed.

"What is the matter, Hadrian?" The old, rasping voice filled my room like the sound of pages turning and the scuff of old leather. I pushed myself into a sitting position and drew my legs up under me. I had not felt the weight of the old man sitting at the foot of my cabin bed, but there he was: wild gray hair standing on end, viridian robes tidy and brighter than the dim light of my chamber could account for. Tor Gibson sat stooped over his cane, leaning on it as the icon of Wisdom leans upon his staff. He smiled, and reaching out seized my wrist. "Bad dreams, is it?"

I felt no warmth in those papery fingers, though the smile was like thin sunlight on a day of rain. That was strange in itself, for Gibson was a scholiast, and seldom smiled. "This is a dream," I said, "another vision?" The old man did not answer, gray eyes twinkling beneath beetling brows. He released my hand and looked away, staring through the darkness of my room at I knew not what. "I just wish it were over. All this waiting, all these . . . pieces on the board."

"Nothing great is created suddenly, any more than a bunch of grapes or a fig," Gibson intoned, speaking in such a way that I knew he cited some ancient sage, though I knew not which one. "Tell me you desire a fig, and I answer: these things take time." He rested his chin on the head of his cane. "This is what you wanted to do, what you always trained to do, is it not? To sit across the table from the Cielcin—to bring them to that table—and to speak?"

"Well, yes."

"Then you have nothing to complain of, eh?" he said. "What is it you're always saying? Always forward, always down."

"And never left nor right." I do not think I had ever said that to Gibson in life, but then something need not have happened to be real. The wall of my cabin was cold against my back as I reclined, watching the apparition watch me. "I know. I know. But it's too much. It's difficult."

The cane whistled round, slapped the bed near my knee. *"Kwatz!"* Gibson exclaimed, his favorite rebuke, cribbed, I think, from the manuals of some old religion. "It's difficult, is it? What made you think it would be otherwise?" When I did not answer, he pressed, "You hope to reconcile mankind with that *other* kind. The Cielcin. Why should your burden be light?" Often in dreams we cannot answer, and perhaps such a thing had happened to me, for I sat mute and—listening—heard: "This is well. We are beasts of burden, Hadrian, we men. We struggle, and by that struggle are filled, and so define ourselves. That is the way."

"Seek hardship," I said, and saying it heard Brethren's voice behind me, rising up—as it were—through the wall of my cabin. **Seek hardship.** So real was the sound of that voice and so sharp the threat of it that I lurched to my feet. The walls of my cabin vanished, and my bed and Gibson stood in the middle of an unresolved black. Certainly dreaming, then.

Gibson's eyes were sparkling, and once more he rested his cane on the ground between his slippered feet. "The world is made—and the self is made—by the conjunction of opposites. Nature and culture breed civilization. Men and women: children. Protons and electrons: atoms. The ego and its shadow: the self. Order and chaos: opportunity. And so on. What humanity and the Cielcin might bring forth by this process . . . who can say?"

"A better world?" I asked. "Can it be done?"

"That is the wrong question."

I wore naught but a pair of trousers, and beneath that crushing Dark I felt naked as a newborn, and it was all I could do to stand. Great figures moved unseen in the darkness, like the colossi whose massive feet tramp the battlegrounds of a hundred worlds. "What is the right question?" I asked, raising my arms. "What am I to do? I'm walking a fine line with the Empire. Switch has betrayed me, and Jinan . . ." I had betrayed Jinan, but by the pity in the old scholiast's eyes he understood and I did not have to explain. "And Kharn Sagara. He could kill us all if he had a mind."

My tutor raised a hand. "He would not have summoned the Cielcin if he meant to destroy you. You may yet have your chance. Be patient." He was right. "Panic avails nothing. It is not panic that will aid you."

Fear is death to reason.

"And reason death to fear." Gibson clenched his raised hand into a fist. "These are clouds, Hadrian. These feelings. Move through them."

"When this is over," I began, unsteady, and half-stumbled back toward the old man. "When this is done, I will be at the Empire's mercy."

Gibson's thick brows contracted. "Is it over already? I'm sorry, I thought it was *too much*." He tapped his cane against the unseen floor. "You have always been at the Empire's mercy, Hadrian. We all are. That is the price we pay for civilization, the price I paid for you. Do you understand?" Had I not said much the same thing to Valka not so long ago? "Would you rather there were no Empire? Rather the Cielcin pick us off one planet at a time? We could never organize to stop them." His eyes never left my face. "You are not playing the game well enough."

"It's not a game, Gibson," I said with force, "of course I'm not *playing*."

"Of course it is a game," the scholiast insisted. "Everything is a game.

But that does not mean the consequences are trivial." He stood, and I saw how tall he was—taller than many of the palatines I have known. "How do you play a game, Hadrian?"

It was to be the questioning again, I saw. *Quaestio disputata.* Very well. I straightened my back, tucked my chin, and clasped my hands behind me. "What game?"

"*Which* game. And it hardly matters. The answer is the same." He did not walk as he had in life, shambling or shuffling, but stepped—as those in soft shoes are wont to do—toe first, so that each step pointed his foot like a barb. He jounced his cane at me. "Think, boy. Think."

Well, the answer was obvious. "You follow the rules, whatever those may be, at least as far as you can. You bend them if you have to, break them if you must. You play your opponents off one another or work with them—whatever the game calls for."

"To what purpose?"

I sensed the trap but not its shape, and so reined in the way an outrider might ahead of his column, the horse frightened by the stink of men lying in ambush. But the question was itself a game, and there was no danger in it. "To win."

Gibson slapped my leg with his cane, as though he were a grandmother and I an unruly boy. "*Kwatz!*" He scowled. "Winning. Nobody wins for long. You need something *better.*"

Better.

I squeezed my wrist hard with the other hand. I had no idea. In life, perhaps, Gibson would have waited an eon to tell me, but Gibson was dead, or gone beyond all knowledge, and this was only a kind of dream—or perhaps a vision. "You have to play like you mean to keep playing. You have to play in a way that protects your *self.*" He placed special emphasis on that word, let it linger long enough, like a slap, that I might feel the next blow when it came. "Who are you?"

I blinked. "I am Hadrian Anaxander Marlowe, the son of Alistair and Liliana—"

"No." He jabbed his cane at me so that the brass tip bounced off my bare chest. "Thus you were *born.* Who are you?"

Some other voice spoke for me, ragged, malnourished, and afraid. "Had," it said, and again more strongly, "I am called Had of Teukros, a myrmidon."

"No."

A different voice, like the first but deeper, more strained: "Hadrian Gibson."

Then my father's voice, sneering. "Boy."

My mother, speaking in the light of her studio at Haspida. "You are *my son*."

Pallino, grinning and concerned at once. "Lad."

Switch, who had been my friend. "Had."

And there was Ghen. "Your Radiance!"

"Your Radiance!"

"Hadrian!"

"Barbarian!" That was Valka.

"*Mia qal!*" My captain, my Jinan, her voice breathless as so often I had heard it. "*Mia qal!* Hadrian!"

"Hadrian! Hadrian!"

Gibson waved a hand, dispersed those voices like smoke. "No."

"What, then?" I demanded, and approached him where he sketched his little circle about me in our unseen arena. "Who am I?"

"You are what is left when all of that"—he gestured over his shoulder, as though all my names and the people who named me were smoke as well—"is gone. You are the part of you that survives these changes. The only part in his ship old Theseus could not replace."

"Was Theseus himself."

"Just so," Gibson said, and reaching out placed his hand upon my shoulder. "Do you understand?"

I thought I did. "Forget the escape. Forget the Red Company. Let Switch and Jinan go."

He shook his head, once. A denial? Or only amusement? "You have a duty and an aim. Aim."

Without moving to do so, I sagged back onto the edge of my bed. "I don't know how."

"Always forward," Gibson said, wringing his cane in both hands. "You've only to keep pulling on the thread."

"Like Theseus?" I asked, imagining the old Greek unspooling his thread as he wandered through the labyrinth, creeping in fear of the minotaur.

"Just so. These"—he waved a hand—"other concerns of yours are distractions. A man may cup water in his hands, but only a few drops." He held one palm up to indicate his meaning. "You are on the proper path; you have only to hold to it."

My fingers tightened on the bedclothes. "It's not so easy. The thread is tangled."

"You are making complications for yourself. Tying the knot tighter." He turned his back, carried his cane behind him with the air of a professor at his lecturing—which I supposed he was. "In Phrygia of old, King Midas lashed his father's cart to a post with a knot so tight and so complex that no man could undo it, and it was said that he who could untie it would one day rule all of Asia. For five hundred years men tried: drovers, farmers, soldiers—the sons of the sons of Midas. None succeeded."

I knew the story, but the familiar cadence of Gibson's voice was a comfort even in dream. I could almost see the dusty ox cart before me, lashed to a pillar of white stone. I mumbled the words even as Gibson spoke them: "Until Alexander came."

"Until Alexander came, his eyes on all of Persia and on the stranger lands beyond. For he had heard the prophecy and—being Alexander—knew it spoke of him. And knowing this, he was frustrated by failure, for the knot that Midas had tied in the ancient past was all the legends said, and would not be undone. Long he struggled with the knot, knowing already that dominion was his destiny. He sought only for a sign, for Fate to confirm what he *knew* was right. And because he *knew* he was to rule, he knew the knot only stood in his way, and so took up his sword . . ."

". . . and cut the knot in two," I said, murmuring into the pillows. I do not know if it was a dream, or an oracle such as the one which had led Midas to lash his father's cart to that pillar in the first place. I did know that when I awoke Gibson was gone, and that I was alone. And yet . . .

Gibson had been gone a long time already. Already I had lived my life without his tutelage for almost as long as I had lived with it, and as I write this those meager years we shared are as nothing next to the centuries I have counted. But Gibson is with me still, even in the solitude of this writing cell. Alone as I am, he is with me—part of me now—as are all those we meet and who matter to us.

A man is the sum of his memories—and more—he is the sum of all those others he has met, and what he learned from them. And that is an encouraging thought, for that knowledge and those memories survive and are part of us through every storm, and every little death.

CHAPTER 60

THE PAVILION

OUR COLUMN MARCHED DOWN a hall so wide that ten men might walk abreast and still leave room to either side—and that was just what we did. The knight-tribune had mobilized her first and second centuries of troops, and they followed on behind her and her high officers: Crossflane, Lin, Greenlaw, and other lieutenants I could not name. Jinan was there, and her lieutenant, Hanas. There was the cornicen with his crystal clarion, and the solifer with the Imperial standard, red-on-white. There was the imaginifer carrying the holograph likeness of His Radiance on a staff, and the signifer bearing the copper eagle and crossed swords of the 437th. Behind them came the chiliarch and the prime centurion, with his optio at his right hand, and behind them—each to a column—came the ten decades of the first century: decurions, triasters, and legionnaires. A sea of red and white.

The second century followed on, and we all passed between banks of Kharn Sagara's SOMs, the undead massed to either side, watching with sightless eyes, witch-light glowing through the slack skin of their faces. Some wore the khaki uniforms I had so often seen, though still others were naked, the black metal of their implants dull, indicator lights gleaming in flesh flush with fever. All of them were silent, their heads turning as they tracked our progress toward the looming arch.

We were silent as well, leastways until the massive doors were opened, rising like the portcullis of some medieval castle in the deeps of time. Then the horn blast blew, and the men of the Sollan Empire cried out in one voice. "Earth!" they cried, invoking the mother goddess. "Earth!" And I, who did not pray, who did not believe, cried out with them, "Earth!"

The sons of men had come.

But come where? As the gate went up, a white-gold light streamed out, throwing our shadows back against the blackness of Kharn's *Demi-urge*. I had expected to return to the hall of blue candles, or to some place very like it, dark and dismal. Instead, I thought I'd gone insane. How it was possible I cannot say, but we had returned to the Garden again.

Or so it seemed, for there was the river, the rolling hills ringed by forest beneath a roof of natural stone—there the lonely tree on the central hill beneath which I had first glimpsed young Ren and found the still-warm tea kettle. I would have wagered that the prayer cards hanging from the branches were the same as well, would have sworn it before an Imperial tribunal.

But that was not possible.

Could not be possible.

I told myself it was only like that other Garden, that Kharn so loved his Garden on Vorgossos that he had replicated it in this massive space at the heart of his ship. For there was a great opening in the roof above us, a mighty window of alumglass beyond which shone the innumerable stars and—was that the ice castle of the Cielcin shining there? I faltered in our march, squinting up at the massive shape shining in the distance, glittering in the starlight, beautiful and terrible as the storm. The man behind me jostled me, and I continued on.

Ahead, beneath the branches of that mighty, central tree overlooking the sea of grass, someone had erected a pavilion of striped black and cloth-of-gold. The Cielcin had already arrived, and on the far side of the hill I beheld two hundred of their own screamers in black robes and blue, and marveled at the coincidence that had so opposed their coloring to our own. Red and white. Blue and black. Fire and water. Earth and air.

And there was Kharn Sagara, gold beneath that golden canopy, and beside him the looming Goliath-shape of Prince Aranata with the light of a dozen blue eyes gleaming beneath the hanging fabric.

"That's far enough!" Sagara's voice came from everywhere. "Your soldiers can stay by the treeline."

Smythe quieted Bassander's objections and passed the orders back. Stripped of our entourage, with even the lieutenants ordered to hang back, there were but six of us who climbed the hill to the pavilion beneath the tree. Smythe and Crossflane, Bassander and Jinan, Tor Varro and myself.

We took our seats at one table, facing a table opposite where sat Prince Aranata, his son Nobuta, and the herald, Oalicomn. At one hand stood the naked slave girl, her chain tied to the xenobite's ceremonial staff, which stood thrust into the loam. Tanaran too was there, it having been arranged that the baetan should be brought to its master for these negotiations and returned to our custody afterward. Between our two sides sat Kharn Sagara. Not on his throne, but with his back against the bole of the tree, as though he were the Cid Arthur. His children sat beside him, Ren and Suzuha, neither looking like they understood why they were there, neither able to leave.

At length Sagara spoke, lips not moving, human eyes staring at something on the rich carpet between our two tables. "Here is something I've not seen in fifteen thousand years of living. Not since the machines of old has man known an enemy such as this!" His drifting eyes turned to regard the Cielcin at their table. "And not since before the time of those same machines has mankind sought peace with enemies other than herself. History does not happen every day, even to me." His flesh eyes moved then, taking in the six of us humans seated at our table.

As he spoke, the slave girl translated, syllables harsh and hacked off, brittle as old iron.

When the first silence came, Raine Smythe stood and addressed her Cielcin counterpart. "Prince Aranata, thank you for coming. We hope this meeting will allow our people and yours to come to some greater understanding of one another, that we might put an end to this war and forestall future violence." She had never seemed taller, standing there, both hands fists where she leaned against the tabletop.

Taking this for some human custom to be mirrored, Prince Aranata stood as well, hands on the table. The xenobite was so tall that—even stooped—his high horned crown brushed against the cloth-of-gold canopy. In a voice deep and cold as the cracking of glaciers, he said, "Your people have claimed six and fifty of our clans in the last nine hundred years." It took me a moment to realize that surely it meant *their* years, not ours, for our figure was less than half that total. Varro made a murmured note of this as he translated at Smythe's ear. "But you talk of submission. Of an end to fighting. What has changed?" Its massive eyes—shielded, I guessed, from the bright light of the pavilion by contact lenses—searched each of our faces in turn. *"Yadaretolu detu o-qilem ne?"* Why seek peace now? Why submit?

"We didn't have the opportunity before," Varro answered in the xenobite's own language.

Or the leverage, I thought, glancing to Tanaran. The baetan kept its head bowed—as did the herald, Oalicomn—listening but trying to remain unnoticed, as though each creature were but a part of the furniture.

I have observed such behavior in the junior ministers of many a palatine court, though in the Cielcin I think the behavior was the more extreme. Human beings have their hierarchies, as is only proper and inescapable, but in us it has always seemed to me such deference was built on respect, on the competency of individuals, and their mutual support. But I sensed in these creatures only the morality of the wolf, that if Tanaran or the other were to challenge Aranata, the great chieftain would kill them in an instant and make the other lick his heel. In men, such tyrants are always destroyed. We little tolerate such demons in ourselves.

In the Cielcin, it seemed, such tyrants thrived.

I shoved this thought away and listened as Varro continued, speaking from a prepared statement he must have memorized, his Cielcin language more than perfect. "In four hundred years of combat we have never had clear dialogue with your kind, nor taken any prisoner of rank." Here he paused to indicate Casantora Tanaran Iakato. "Our encounter at Tamnikano—which we call Emesh—has provided us our first opportunity to open such a dialogue. It is our hope and intention that from these conversations we can arrive at a lasting and equitable peace between the Itani Otiolo, your clan, and the Sollan Empire. We are prepared to offer a complete and immediate cessation of hostilities between our Legions and your clan provided that you cease all raids against our colony worlds." He continued in this vein for another minute or so, outlining the details of such expectations, while all the while Smythe stood serenely by, nodding along as if she understood the alien words.

When Tor Varro had finished, Prince Aranata jerked its head sideways in the affirmative. *"Olo,"* he said, signaling that he understood us. He drew his cape around himself again and settled into his seat, the silver chains and platinum that decorated his crest and high forehead swaying as he moved. "But tell me, do you know how many *tiatari* I have? How many *scahari*? How many mouths that is between them?" he asked, these being the words for worker and soldier respectively. "Twenty-eight millions, on this and my other ships. Less than half this number did I take from Utaiharo when I conquered him. That was only sixteen hundred years ago. Twenty-eight millions. How am I to feed such a number? Your colonies sustain us. Help us grow. What would you have me do? I will not let my People starve for the sake of you vermin."

I felt my eyes wandering to the mutilated slave girl where she stood—nearly catatonic—beside the table.

"We would be open to trade negotiations with your people. Meat and cattle could be procured—to whatever specifications you require," Smythe said when this was translated. "We have technologies capable of producing food from raw matter should it come to it. Your people will not starve."

The slave girl seemed to struggle with translating this, and I saw something like an emotion strain behind her eyes. It was only fear, the emotion she knew best. Aranata's head turned to regard her, I thought, the way one regards a faulty comms terminal or light switch. At last she said, *"Delukami ni o-diuhadiu rajithiri."*

"Rajithiri wo!" Aranata practically rocketed to his feet. "Trade! What do you take me for? Do you think it is a *mnunatari* you are dealing with?"

To her credit, Raine Smythe had not blinked through this outburst and the whirl of motion that accompanied it. She had stood her ground with all the implacable solidity one expected of an Imperial soldier.

"Mnunatari?" Varro echoed, looking to me for guidance.

"Merchant," I said, though I did not understand why the term should inspire such venom.

I was spared the need to speculate by Nobuta, who said, "My father is not some air merchant, *yukajjimn!*" The big Cielcin lay a hand on its child's shoulder to calm it, but said nothing.

The look on their chalk-colored faces: lower teeth bared, brows pinched above black eyes the size of fists . . . I thought it must be disgust, though even I cannot say with certainty what lay behind those mask-like faces. Still, I thought I saw. "They're saying they are not merchants," I said. "We've given offense." I turned my eyes to Kharn, but the Undying might have been a latter-day sculpture of iron and paper where he sat unmoved, his fleshly eyes closed. "Is that right?" Kharn had given the Aeta a gift in return for its visit. That had been a kind of trade, but the semantics were different. Unequal. Kharn had flattered the Aeta in giving it a gift the way a merchant gives a queen a bright gem in tribute. *Tribute.* The Cielcin, it seemed, had no concept of a non-zero-sum game. It was not enough that one party might gain. The mere act of giving suggested the giver *lost.*

One blue eye spied me and drifted down, describing an arc that took in the six of us at our table, but it did not speak. I leaned across Bassander to Varro and said, "It's as though you offered to trade the Emperor your boots for his velvet slippers." The Chalcenterite raised one eyebrow, either not appreciating the analogy or merely urging me forward. Struck by a thought, I continued in Classical English, certain that the girl would not understand and so could not translate. "He thinks trade beneath him." As

I spoke, Smythe was placating the xenobites, relying on the slave to translate her words. "Think about what Sagara did, offering him a gift. The
Aeta sees us as beneath him. I imagine he's used to getting his way." I
tried not to think of the depravities implied by the xenobites' culture of
extreme ownership. I felt the same queasy dread I had known in the office
of Antonius Brevon, seeing the homunculus he had made for himself.

Varro stroked his chin. "He may have to get used to disappointment."

Quickly he explained what had passed between us to Smythe, who—
speaking loudly so the translator might hear her, said, "A gift, then!"

Tribute, I thought. It would not be the first time civilization paid to
keep the barbarians from its gates. But paying in meat? A sacrifice of that
oldest sort?

"What would it take to end the raids?" Smythe asked. "What is it you
need?"

"Need?" Aranata repeated. *"Daqami ne?"*

The Aeta grew quiet a moment, and a breeze groaned across the pavilion,
doubtless generated by some shaft that ran through the *Demiurge* like some
inhuman throat. The branches of the trees swayed, prayer cards rattling
above our heads. At once I felt acutely conscious of the Cielcin warriors
standing away and below our pavilion, all in their painted masks, swords
held at the ready. And ready too were their *nahute,* the seeker-drones like
flying serpents I had seen put to such terrible use in the blackness beneath
Calagah.

"Iussamneto wo," Aranata intoned, and the others all repeated him.

"Iussamneto wo."

We must survive. It had the weight of prayer, of the sort of aphorism I
myself employed.

"Do you need settlement?" Smythe asked. "A world could be found.
Near to the spaceways but remote."

"You would have us *penned*?" Oalicomn hissed. "We do not *submit*!"

But it had spoken out of turn, and, snarling, Aranata struck it with an
elbow. The herald yelped, clutching its face as it cowered away from its
master, who said, "What world could keep us? Se Vattayu is gone. Our
Earth is gone. We do not walk the surface like your kind, like beasts. And
we will not take your leavings like a slave. You are not our masters to
grant us favors!"

"That's not a helpful answer," Bassander muttered, and privately I
agreed with him.

"Yadaretodo o-fusuem shidu ti-koarin'ta shi," Tanaran said suddenly, rais-

ing its eyes from its fervent investigation of the tabletop. There was something in the tone of its voice, in the stilted way it said the words: *We seek for ourselves a new world.* Tanaran was a sort of priest, young as it was, and the words had the weight of scripture. "We have been watched from the dawn, since the days of the long tooth, when *sulan* hunted us in the dark."

"*Yaiya toh,*" the Cielcin said together. Even Aranata hung its head, and to the side I heard Kharn Sagara chuckle.

"What is going on?" Jinan breathed.

"We have been watched through our infancy, when the Great carved cities in the bowels of the world."

"*Yaiya toh,*" the Cielcin intoned.

"When the air was poisoned, they showed us the sky!"

"*Yaiya toh!*"

"When the earth was poisoned, they showed us new ones!"

"*Yaiya toh!*"

"But the new worlds were not as the old, and we could not live upon them. The light of the stars was a poison greater than any we had made at home. Do you understand?"

It was a moment before I realized that Tanaran had addressed the question to me. I was not sure that I did understand, but in their own language I said, "You evolved underground, we know this. But you cannot live above it."

"Tanaran!" Aranata warned.

Varro murmured a translation to Smythe and said, "Should I stop him?"

The Cielcin had evolved below ground, in cave warrens and tunnels left by the Quiet—if such a thing were to be believed. Perhaps it was only the rock above that had shielded them from the poison and the bitter radiations of the universe. All the blackness of space seemed to open before me, and I was conscious of where we were, lost in the naked emptiness that stretched between the pages of every map, with only the thin hull of Kharn's *Demiurge* about us.

Struck by a notion, I leaned toward Varro and—switching back to Classical English so as not to be understood by the slave translator—whispered, "The Cielcin ships aren't ray-shielded. They're using all that ice as insulation against"—I waved a hand just above the tabletop—"everything."

"Radiation shielding?" Varro repeated. "You're certain they don't have it?"

"Of course I'm not certain," I said in answer. But another image returned to me. A Cielcin combat helmet, taken off a screamer tortured in the black beneath Calagah. Beneath the memory of screaming and the way the nerve disruptor buzzed in my hand, I recalled the antique gasket that had fastened the suit's helmet to its neck, not unlike the technology of our own primitive suits from before the Foundation War. "But if I'm right, it could prove a powerful bargaining chip." Assuming, of course, the Cielcin could understand something as simple as a bargaining chip.

"Nietu ji dein ne?" Aranata's deep voice cut through my whispers. Turning to his slave girl he said again, "What are they saying, wretch?"

Sensing some horror coming and fearing for the poor girl, I stood, and speaking more to Tanaran than its prince, I said, "Peace, please." I wished Valka were present, wished she were not locked away aboard the *Mistral* with the rest of my friends. There was much I did not understand, much I did not know. Why should the Cielcin worship as gods the very creatures who had showed me a vision of the Cielcin destroyed? I shoved this aside. "Are we not here for the same reason?" I looked from my party to theirs. "Neither of us wants our people to die."

The silence that followed stretched perhaps ten agonizing seconds before Smythe politely said, "Please sit down, Lord Marlowe."

I did, not feeling in the least bit sheepish. The slave girl had been entirely forgotten for my interference, and so any embarrassment I might have felt was worth it. Where the conversation turned next I cannot say, for I do not remember. Thoughts of the Cielcin consumed me. Tanaran's religious cant and the references to the Quiet—the Watchers—combined with the shadow of what followed have come to cloud my memory. Sometimes I envy the scholiasts, whose recollections never fade, though at other times I rather envy the aged, those denizens of the sanitariums for whom the past is a foreign country. To forget . . . to unsee what I have seen.

That was the first of many meetings, many days . . . and they grew only darker and murkier.

CHAPTER 61

VALKA AGAIN

THE *MISTRAL'S* AIRLOCK CYCLED closed behind me, and I sagged against the bulkhead, exhausted. Through the heavy metal I could make out the sound of my escort's retreating feet. "Still a prisoner," I reminded myself, and allowed myself to slip to the floor. Three days of talks, of politics with little sleep, and it had been going badly. It is not easy to make concessions to someone who cannot trade. Human interactions are based on trade. You cannot maintain a relationship with your fellow man elsewhere. But the Cielcin evolved differently. They were apex predators—or nearly so. Predators do not reciprocate; that is what makes them predators.

Prince Aranata was pleased enough to accept gifts, but balked at reciprocity. We could not make him understand that a peace meant an end to the raids against our colonies. "You would have us starve!" he insisted, as if it could not uncouple the thought of eating from conquest. *The tigress is not evil,* or so the saying goes, *she is only hungry. She is only following her nature.* Was it not so with the Cielcin? Was it not their nature to hunt? Were they not only hungry? They say that only men are evil, that only men kill for principle or sport. That only men inflict suffering for the sake of suffering.

I—who am old—cannot help but think that the creature which kills, which consumes by its nature, is more evil than that which kills by its principles. The tigress has no choice, it cannot be reasoned with. The Cielcin are the same. If there existed no possibility of understanding, what hope was there for reconciliation? If one cannot domesticate the tigress, if one cannot make her change her stripes, what is one to do besides shoot her?

After a long while I stood, mindful of the deep quiet of the ship:

funereal but for sound of the ventilation systems. With the ship impounded, her drive cores were down, and what power she drew she took from the *Demiurge*, to whom she was bracketed. Walking the halls, I realized I had never seen her so empty, with all but about a dozen crewmen locked in icy fugue. Corvo had been given orders to stay the decanting of her people for a few days—our dialogue with the Pale was strained, but not so strained as that.

Possessed by that archdemon, Sleep, I made my way from the airlock and out into the hall beneath the canopy of captured battle flags, crossing the width of the *Mistral* toward the starboard dormitories. I rounded the corner, keeping one hand on the padded wall.

The door to the starboard gallery stood open, and through the round arch I saw a lonely figure sitting at a table, the shape of her framed by the hard edges of the windows, curving lines against square. I hung there a moment, unaware of the smile on my face.

Valka looked around, perhaps sensing some change in the light from where I stood in the doorway. Her eyes stood out in the gloomy light of the gallery, and she set aside the book she'd been reading as she smiled. "What?"

"It's nothing," I said, stepping into the room. "I just escaped another round of talks."

"Escaped," Valka repeated the word, shifting sideways so that she looked up at me from her place on the couch.

It was my turn to say, "What?"

The Tavrosi woman seemed to roll her words in her mouth as though they were some strange morsel, and she said, "You've wanted this so long as I've known you, and now you have what you want and you're unhappy." She shook her head. "'Tis funny. What is to be done with you?"

Moving past her to stand by the windows at the *Demiurge* outside, I answered, "I think Smythe and Bassander are asking themselves that same question."

"Are you afraid?"

"No," I said, and found that it was true. I was not afraid, though the weight on my shoulders had never been heavier. "Not for myself, at any rate."

She made a small sound, agreeing, and I heard her stand behind me. "Any changes?"

I had been sharing progress with her each night when I returned from Kharn's pavilion beneath the tree, once I'd spent another long series of hours in consultation with the knight-tribune and her people.

"Not really," I said. "Smythe's not put ray shielding on the table, and I'd swear that's about the only thing that could get through Aranata's thick skull." I banged a fist against the window frame, but when I spoke again my voice was level as still water. "I don't understand how they think, Valka."

She stood beside me then, the both of us looking out at the Gothic fractal of the *Demiurge* where it stretched out into the unending Dark. I was aware—acutely aware—of how close she stood to me. Had she always stood so near? The scent of sandalwood hung on the air. Not a perfume— she had no time for such things—but after the awful smell in Kharn's dungeon it stuck out like a rose in the desert.

"'Twas never going to be easy," she said, and crossed her arms.

"I know that," I said. "It's like trying to communicate with an animal. I can make myself understood, but I'm never really quite sure they take my full meaning." I pressed my forehead to the glass. "It's like they understand one word in twelve, even when I use their words."

Pivoting, Valka put one shoulder against the window. I could almost see her smile, but I shut my eyes instead. "You're surprised? You should know as well as I that our languages are rooted in our brains, which were shaped by Earth's environment. That the Cielcin look like us and speak is . . . a coincidence. Surely you've noticed? The only places where we fully understand one another are where the language refers to material things. Objects and actions."

I twisted my head to look at her, at the small lines that formed against the border of her smile. "Things stronger than our words for them."

"What?" The flash of white teeth. A wrinkling of the eyes.

"Gravity. Fire. Stone. You know." I slapped the window with my hand. "Things that exist if we did not. Not things like hope or love or exchange."

Valka twitched, and I could sense she was about to try and score a point. I guessed what she was about to say, but let her say it anyway. "I thought you believed in *Truth*," she said, putting special emphasis on the word so that I knew she meant it after the fashion of the priests and magi.

"I do . . . I did." I turned back to the window, retreated a step. "Of course I do. But I'm not sure it isn't *human* truth that gives words like hope and love meaning. The scholiasts say that living in accordance with the Truth means living in accordance with our nature. You and I can have an argument about what that nature is, but I think that we can both agree that whatever else is true, the Cielcin have a different nature entirely." I laughed. "Maybe they *are* demons."

Still in pursuit of that point she looked to score, Valka said, "So there are two truths? Ours and theirs? Because there are two natures at play?"

I thought of what Varro had told me about sticking to the official story, to use the Empire's truth—which was itself a lie. Repeating myself, I said, "No," and took another step back, away from her and the window. "There is only one Truth: that our nature and theirs don't align."

"And you . . . what?" Valka turned her back on the black ship out the window behind her.

The staring iron statues that lined its ramparts stared over her shoulder with hollow, pitted eyes. I shivered, and closed my own eyes. "If I can't make us understood?" I felt myself sway where I stood, and steadied myself as one who stands in a canoe. "Then all of this will have been for nothing, and we return to the way things were before." I took another step back and found myself resting against the arm of the couch. "Are we . . . ?" I gestured up at the air around us, indicating whatever cameras might be listening.

Valka cocked one eyebrow, and the door to the gallery closed with a metallic glide, locks clicking into place. "We are now," she said, and frowned. "What's the matter with you? You've gone whiter than usual."

Suddenly self-conscious, I drew my coat up and around myself, as though I might vanish beneath the assault of those eyes—as though they were the eyes of an entire Legion or of some goddess in judgment remote and cold as stars. They were no such thing, of course. They were only Valka's eyes. And we were alone. "It's my visions," I said, and trying failed to crush my shame like a serpent beneath my heel. I kept seeing her face as I had seen it at Calagah, when I'd first tried to tell her what it was I'd seen. I never wanted to see that face again. "They show us at war—they show *me* at war. Planets burning and . . . everything." I had not told her that I'd seen my own headless body thrown down, or how many times I had seen the end of me. "They said it must be. The war must be. I just . . . I don't understand, Valka. I don't understand. Does that mean we fail here? Does that mean we should fail? Do we even have a choice?" I rubbed my face with both hands. "I wish we'd been able to get more out of Tanaran, too. It's clear they worship the Quiet, but why? What do they know? And I can't just ask with Smythe and Tor Varro right there. What am I supposed to do? Why are you smiling?"

"Breathe, Hadrian," she said, tossing her head in—laughter? Irritation? Why was she so difficult to read? "Just breathe. One thing at a time. You're looking at too much."

I massaged the back of my neck, rolling my head around. "You sound just like Gibson, he said to just . . ." I pointed inarticulately with one hand, miming *forward*. "Keep going. To keep my eyes on the task at hand."

"Gibson?" Valka's face darkened. "I thought he was dead."

"Likely," I said, and remembering that I had only seen him in a dream I looked away. "It was a long time ago. It's stuck with me is all." I tried to scrub the tiredness from my eyes, but it would not come out. "I just wish you could be there. I wish it were us doing the talking, not these . . . soldiers and bureaucrats. If Switch hadn't . . ." *Hadn't betrayed me . . .* But still I could not say it. Still I could not believe.

Valka only watched me, lips pressed together. Silhouetted as she was against the window and the shape of the *Demiurge* beyond it, she seemed almost one of Kharn's statues herself, face in shadow. The slight and curving form of her stirred the artist in me, or might have done, were it not for the shadow resting heavily on my heart.

"Hadrian . . ." There was something in her tone I hadn't heard there before, but I did not notice it at the time.

I was still speaking. "I just . . . I just want it done. I don't understand how I got here or what I think I'm doing. I don't understand the Cielcin and I don't know how to make them understand me or how the Quiet fits into this. Smythe doesn't trust me—and why should she? And I've lost Switch, I've lost Jinan. Bassander would kill me in a second if he had his way, and maybe he's right. Maybe I shouldn't be here. Maybe I should have stayed on Emesh and let Anaïs Mataro have her way with me." I was rambling and I knew it. And knowing it, was ashamed. I hung my head so as not to see Valka, as if in doing so I might not *be seen* by her and be judged for my insufficiency. My humanity. "Am I a good man?"

I didn't even know.

I had forgotten that she had once asked me that very question.

But she—who forgot nothing—replied with my own words: "I think the fact you're asking that question is a good sign." I was a long time recognizing my own words, and a longer time recalling that day in the bazaar aboard the *Enigma of Hours*. When I did, I snorted. While still I was shaking my head, she added, "Of course you're good, or you try to be." And in a voice smaller still, "You're good to me."

How was I to respond to that?

"I never thanked you," she said, tone oddly muffled. "For trying to defend me from Calvert. For everything."

"I thought you didn't like being defended?" I asked, too sharply.

A dram of Valka's usual biting quality returned to her sharp-edged voice, and she said, "I don't like anyone fighting my battles *for* me. I never said I didn't like help. But it's more than that, it . . . you took care of me. In the cell. You're . . . you're always kind."

I looked up, as surprised by the delicate tremulousness in Valka's voice as I might have been if a bird had flown through the vacuum of space to perch upon the sill of our window. Quite astonished, I replied, "I'm not."

"You are," she said, more forcefully. "More than I deserve, the way I've treated you."

"You've never done anything wrong," I said, reassuringly, forgiving the slights and insults, the disbelief and petty misunderstanding. I was sure that I had not always been kind to her, whatever she said. She did not argue with me, and that was a kind of miracle in itself. Thus we both agreed to lie to one another, or else to embed those lies in some other, higher truth— just as the future is embedded in the now.

In that moment.

"I don't know if 'tis good, what we're doing," Valka said, "but I know we have to try." She leaned against the windowpane, fidgeting, unsure just what to do with her hands. "Do you know . . . I didn't know why I stayed here so long? After Emesh, I mean." She almost laughed. "I'm not a soldier anymore. I don't want to be one. Fighting Calvert in that laboratory . . .'tis not who I want to be. I . . . should have left a long time ago. After Pharos, maybe earlier. But I didn't." She did laugh then, weakly, almost shyly. "I'm a scientist! I should be back at my dig site on Emesh, or on to the next one not . . . not here."

Into the momentary silence, I asked, "Do you want to go? You're Tavrosi. Smythe wouldn't stop you." Being a Demarchist, Valka was accorded all the rights of a foreign diplomat: political immunity, freedom of travel. She could leave, she could always have left. But she hadn't.

She pushed off from the window, seemed to hesitate on the spot between it and where I leaned against the couch. "No, I . . ." It was her turn to look away. "There's still a chance I can learn more here than I could anywhere else. The Cielcin know things we don't. About the Quiet, I mean."

"I can't guarantee you'll learn from them, not anymore. Not with the Legions taking control of the conversation. I don't stand a chance." The next words I spoke cost me dearly, but wanted saying all the same. "I wouldn't blame you if you went. This isn't what you signed up for—then again, I'm not sure it's what I signed up for, either. But I mean to see it through . . ." *Just like Gibson would want . . .*

Half-seated as I was, she was almost taller than I. Still she did not look at me, and I imagined curiosity vying with her hatred of the Empire behind those artificial eyes. She never seemed small to me, though I suppose she was: shorter than I by a head and shaped as if from soapstone.

"They might kill you," Valka said.

"It's possible," I said. "I betrayed the Empire. Smythe's protection has gotten me this far, but if these talks fail . . ." My voice shrank away to nothing as a spark vanishes in the winter air.

The woman rubbed the clan intaglio on her arm. After a moment she said, lamely, "I don't want you to die."

A small and bitter laugh escaped me, and I said, "Neither do I. It's only Bassander I'm worried about, but he would never do anything without the knight-tribune's orders." Only after had I spoken did I realize the words were meant more to reassure myself than anything. "Besides, the situation's not hopeless. Not yet." I could hear Gibson admonishing me in my head, and continued, "It's only been a few days. I'd be a fool if I expected two species to reconcile their differences in a few days. I *was* a fool to think it could be otherwise."

"You really think Captain Lin would kill you?"

"He told me as much," I said, and managed a strained smile. There had been places—little pools spinning off the rivers of light I had seen—where Bassander killed me. Places where he chased me down an echoing corridor, white banners all around, and planted a shot in my back. "Do you think these visions are real? That what Brethren said is true? Really?" Back in the *Mistral* again, in the waking world—away from the cold and the nightmare of Vorgossos—it seemed almost I could ignore what I had seen. If only the looming mass of the *Demiurge* with its buttressed spires and legions of black statues would go away, they would take the last of that nightmare with me.

Was a shadow on Valka's face? A glimmer of the old scorn? She let out a weighty sigh, eyes wandering the paneled ceiling, taking in I knew not what. "Hadrian, I don't know. I don't think you're lying, if that's what you mean."

"No, it's not that. It's . . ." But I could not tell her about what I had seen. Understand, it is not that there was some compulsion in me, such as that which animated poor Naia. Nothing Brethren or the Quiet themselves had placed there. It was only fear. Fear and a kind of truly primitive superstition that I—speaking of the deaths I had seen for myself in my vision—might make them real. By keeping silent I imagined that I might banish the black memory as most nightmares are banished by the sun. "I don't want them to be true. I don't."

I didn't have time to think.

Valka stepped forward again and seized me by the shirtfront with one hand, and I realized my soapstone impression of her had been an illusion. A mistake.

Our lives can change at any moment, but they change so drastically only a few times.

Valka pressed her lips to mine, and pressed me back against the couch so that almost I might have tipped backward—and her on top of me—had I not found my feet. Had I not seized her by the shoulders and held her at bay. "Valka, I—are you sure?"

She did not answer, but kissed me again. The strength went out of my hands, and she pulled me to her. I forgot time for a moment. Forgot the many futures I had seen: the bright ones and the dark ones and the ones in between. I forgot the past: forgot my childhood on Delos, my suffering on Emesh, Calagah and Vorgossos, Pharos and Rustam. Gilliam and Uvanari, Jinan and Switch. All fell and faded in that feminine Dark. I forgot to breathe, and she pulled away, pressed her forehead to mine. "Listen," she said. "You're not going to die. I'm not going to let you."

Breathless, I believed her.

CHAPTER 62

THE LIMITS OF REASON

THE MEMORY OF THE previous day's work hung thick on me. Wind strained through the branches of that aged and mighty tree, tugging at the roof of the pavilion and making the ropes that secured it snap as though we were aboard some sailing ship lost in the middle of a wood.

"We might consider limiting their campaigns to the Norman territories," Varro suggested in muttered tones.

Crossflane had frowned. "Are you sure they could make that distinction?"

They had not noticed that the Cielcin already *were* making that distinction, referring only to we Sollans as *yukajjimn* and exempting Kharn. If they could distinguish between the Extrasolarian king and ourselves, it stood to reason they could as easily mark the Empire from its Norman counterparts. But the memory of Valka's kiss still moved in me, and even if it had not, I would never have proposed so viciously calculated a posture.

"We're not at war with the Normans," I said.

"And I mislike the thought of using the Cielcin to single out foreign powers," Jinan added, who of course represented a foreign power. Smythe took this all in with a waved hand, indicating the arrival of the Cielcin contingent at the far treeline. Kharn's eye drones hurried away to corral his children from where they'd wandered down to the river.

We had not, in the end, offered the Cielcin free range of the Norman Freeholds.

I'd had another idea.

"Prince Aranata, let me be clear about one thing," Raine Smythe said pointedly once the xenobites were all present. "This is not a war you will win." When the Cielcin balked, she asked, "How many fighters have you? Two hundred thousand? Half that?" I wondered if the prince's delay were not an admission that the number was very much lower than that. "My

legion numbers twenty thousand alone, and we have thousands of them."
She made my play then, and placed a projector on the table before her. An
image of the galaxy sprouted in the air before us, detailing the spiral arms.
"We're here," she said, and a point glowed red near where the Norma
Arm brushed against the bulge of galactic center. "And here is everywhere your people have attacked us." Orange points flared in a tight cluster against the white stars, stretching across the whole Veil of Marinus.
Hundreds of worlds. Thousands. Billions of lives. "Here is our domain."
The entire Empire glowed then, highlighted a friendly blue, with green
areas demarcating the Principalities of Jadd, the Lothrian Commonwealth, the Durantine Republic, Demarchy of Tavros, and a dozen dozen
smaller human polities that stretched from the Perseus Arm at our galaxy's
edge to that same narrow place in Norma where the fighting was thickest.

Billions of stars. Tens of thousands of worlds. Untold trillions of lives.

I could see what I thought was shock in the Aeta's face. Horror. And I
knew my plan had had teeth. The Cielcin were predators, so we treat them
like predators. We teach them humility. It might just be possible to *shame*
them into a peace—to subordinate them—without bloodshed. Uvanari
had surrendered on Emesh because it was beaten. It had been amenable to
our demands because it was in our power—*impressed* by our power. If the
only language the Cielcin truly understood *was* power, then we would
speak the language of power.

"So many . . ." the prince said, voice thin and far away. He bridled
almost at once. "We will not bend to you! We will not be slaves to *yukajjimn!*"

There really was no middle ground, it seemed. One was either master
or slave. There was no partnership, no friendship. The concept of equa-
nimity itself seemed as alien to the Cielcin as they were to us.

"Not slaves," I said pointedly, speaking Galstani for my companions'
benefit and allowing the slave to translate for the Pale. Ignoring the pointed
looks from Smythe and Crossflane, I pressed on. "Neutral equals. We simply end the fighting between us."

Aranata's lips peeled back over glassy teeth. "Neutral," it said, repeating the word as though he had never heard it. "There is no such thing. We
would be your puppets."

I pressed my lips together, remembering the discussion from mere
minutes before about using the Cielcin to target the Normans in our ever-
expanding conquest of the Veil. I was spared the necessity of responding

by Smythe, who offered, "You would be left to your own devices. We would help one another."

"*Serve* one another?" Aranata's face wrinkled. "Degeneracy." The word he'd used, *serve,* suggested something more personal than a mere diplomatic relationship. We were talking past each other, each using words the other party did not fully understand.

Smythe rapped her knuckles against the tabletop, frustration evident but perhaps meaningless to the xenobites opposite us. "An arrangement could be found that's mutually beneficial."

The slave translator struggled with *mutually beneficial* for more than a minute. Through the stammering and the babble I caught the word *serve* again. To *serve.* To give anything was to serve the receiver, and the Aeta only take. There is no reciprocity, no obligation, no *noblesse oblige* among the Pale. Only power and those too weak to hold it. Oppressor and oppressed. Finally, the slave girl said, "We could find a way to *service* one another."

Aranata hissed like a bushel of snakes and lashed out, striking the slave girl on the flank. His talons tore her flesh and she fell gasping, clutching at her side. I was nearer the edge of the table and rushed to help her, ignoring both Crossflane's command to halt and the sudden tension that rippled through the Cielcin line. I did not know what I was doing, only that I could not stand by. I had no bandages, no medical expertise, but some instinct moved me. Aranata pushed himself to his feet. "Service," he spat. The word carried clear sexual overtones, things I did not understand. "We will not be your slaves. *I* will not."

The girl was not bleeding badly. For all the force of his blow, the prince had pulled his talons, and the wounds were little more than scratches. I helped her to sit up, careful not to look at her ruined, spidery hands or the way they pawed uselessly at her wounded side. She was so light—it felt like lifting driftwood—and insubstantial that I half-expected her to float away in my hands.

Nobuta wailed. "No, get away! She's mine!" it said, and yanked the chain. I caught the silver thread in my fist. Years of strength refined in Emesh's heavy gravity held fast, and I did not flinch, but glowered up at the alien child with flinty eyes. It quailed.

Not releasing the chain, I asked the girl, "Are you all right?"

She did not answer. Perhaps she could not. Her eyes! Reader, her eyes! They were like deep pools, mirrors reflecting . . . nothing. What light had been in them at birth was long quenched, and she only murmured my words back at me in the Cielcin tongue. "Are you all right?" Those eyes found mine, and for a moment I sensed the faintest, quiet spark in them, a lonely cinder hidden in the ash of a long-dead fire. She was not the woman from my vision, but then Aranata was not the dark lord I had seen. One of her ruined hands found mine, too-long fingers struggling to close. In a faint voice dry as old leaves she murmured two words I have never forgotten. So small were they, I strained to hear them. But heard them I did. "Kill me," she said. It was the only time I heard her speak the tongues of men. Horrified, I yanked my hand away.

The spark in her went out.

Nobuta yanked the chain again, and I pulled. The little Cielcin came half out of its chair and let the chain go. A cry of surprise and pain escaped the xenobite, and rough hands seized me. I was pulled unceremoniously to my feet, felt the needlepoint prick of talons on my shoulders and arms. Two of Aranata's men held me, forced my arms behind my back. Smythe was shouting for my release. One of the guards seized me by the hair, forced me to look up.

I thrust out my chin, straining against my guards. These Cielcin were not weak as the child had been, and I could not escape. Aranata stood in a rush, horned bulk towering over me. One massive hand seized me by my tunic front, and the Prince hissed, "Apologize."

I did no such thing, fists clenched behind my back.

Prince Aranata's hand slid upward, overlong fingers closing round my throat. "I said *apologize.*" I glanced at Nobuta Otiolo. The herald Oalicomn had helped the child back to its seat, and it was watching me with eyes deeper and darker than—but just as lifeless as—the eyes of the slave girl. I clamped my jaw shut, knowing that to apologize was to lose the argument, to lose face in these debates.

The whine of plasma burners being primed filled the pavilion, and glancing to one side I saw Smythe's guards had turned weapons on the Pale.

As if from very far away, I heard the sound of Kharn Sagara's laughter. "What a farce!" he said, voice shaking the very air. "Release Lord Marlowe, my prince. And you, Knight-Tribune. Order your men to put down their arms. There will be no violence here." One of Kharn's eyes slid in an arc to glower at Aranata from over my shoulder, the threat there plain as day. Kharn himself had found his feet, machine hand holding shut his golden robes. His lips did not move. "I said release him!"

To my surprise, Aranata did as he was told. I only just managed to keep my footing as the prince unhanded me. The Cielcin lord drew back, looking down at me with an expression I could not read. "I should kill you," he said, and there was no emotion in its voice that I could name. "Harm my child again, and I will."

I could not show weakness. I could not apologize. I took a step forward instead, eyes never leaving the prince's face. I said nothing. It was enough to signal that I was not afraid of him, however hard the blood beat in my ears. I have done many brave things in my life, and many more foolish. Which this next was I still don't know, but I turned my back on the prince and returned to my seat without another word. For a brief moment, I alone of all that party—save only the alien child—sat in my seat. Even Kharn was standing, and in that instant the entire audience focused on me.

By refusing to apologize, I'd asserted myself in the alien dominance contest that passed for politics among the Pale. How diplomacy was done between their clans I didn't dare guess, but I suspected that it had more in common with the way two rams butted heads or two lions fought than it did an international summit. We'd had to assert that we were a party worth honoring. We'd had to show some teeth and a backbone. The backbone had been mine, the teeth the weapons the others all carried and their willingness to use them.

"Enough posturing," I said in Cielcin, posturing myself. "Please, take a seat, my prince."

I felt an almost imperceptible shift in the air between the prince and myself, a respect and a grudging . . . *wariness? Caution?* We had not come to surrender to him, that much was coming plain, but he did not understand yet what arrangement might be made between us.

He never would.

But—desperate or merely hungry—he took his seat again.

CHAPTER 63

THE APOSTOL

IT HAD BEEN DEEP in the middle of ship's night when Lieutenant Greenlaw came to fetch me for a meeting with Smythe. I had not been sleeping—too much filled my head for that, and I had dressed hastily and followed. The confused route through the *Demiurge* matched the confusion in my heart: warring images on the walls and the horrid pattern of human faces leering out of black metal.

"Do you think it worked?" Smythe asked, once Greenlaw left us alone in her office aboard the *Schiavona*.

"I'm not sure," I said. "It certainly had an effect, but just what that effect was I can't rightly say." I took the seat offered me opposite Smythe's desk. "Where's Crossflane?" The First Officer was conspicuously absent. Why that should unsettle me I cannot say, and yet it did. The old knight was never far from his tribune's side, a stiffly formal shadow, the textbook image of the old Imperial officer with his neat black uniform and immaculately groomed sideburns.

Smythe moved her cane from its resting place at the arm of her chair and propped it against the wall behind her. "Sleeping, Earth bless him. William's not so young as he once was." The use of the old knight's name—Switch's name—stung me more than I care to admit, and it was all I could do to suppress a flinch. Smythe looked like she could stand to sleep herself. There were deep circles under her eyes, and the scar-streaked skin had a quality like wax paper over drying meat. I might have pitied her, were it not for her devil's bargain with Kharn Sagara. "But then, neither am I. Truth be told, I never expected to live so long as this."

"How long is 'this'?" I dared to ask.

Groaning, Smythe pushed herself to her feet and stumped over to a sideboard. "I thought you palatines considered it rude to ask after someone else's age?" I made a half-hearted noise of apology, and she waved me down. "Ah, but I'm not a palatine, and nearly three hundred," she said. "Me. Three hundred. Can you imagine? My mother was a solar farm technician, and here I am. Brandy? I had it brought from the *Obdurate*."

"Please."

"Have you heard of Churchill? He was King of Britain at the end of the Golden Age," she said, filling two fat glasses with the stuff. I said that I had, but did not add that it was contested whether or not Churchill had been king or only some manner of logothete. "Winston the Good was named after him, you know? He was fond of brandy, or so William tells it." She offered me one glass and, taking the other in one hand said, "Your health, Lord Marlowe."

"And yours."

"And Earth and Emperor!" she said, and drank.

"Earth and Emperor!" I murmured, a bit half-heartedly, and drank. I confess I never developed much of a taste for the old nostrum myself, but as Kharn had said . . . *Si fueris Romae* . . .

We sat then in companionate silence, each cradling a glass of brandy. The taste of oranges hung on my tongue, erasing better things, stifling conversation. At last Smythe cleared her throat and—setting aside her snifter with a weighty sigh—said, "I have . . . a proposal." I let these words stretch without interruption, in expectation of some proper announcement to come. Often I have observed this habit in important persons: in nobiles, in their advisors and logothetes. Even in certain scholiasts I have known. That habit of announcing things which it is better one come out and say. I am guilty of this particular pattern myself. Smythe, I think, was less motivated by stagecraft than she was slowed by the weight of her office. Many are.

Smythe started again, fingering some object on her desk while she spoke. "Varro has suggested that given the . . . the cupidity of our alien friend and his demanding nature, that it might flatter him to post an apostol to this Aeta's court—if they have courts."

"An apostol?" I repeated, processing. An emissary. And ambassador. I felt a faint glimmer of where this headed and felt my stomach turn over. "Do you think they would accept?"

She sucked her teeth. "I'm not certain. But I should like to have a plan of action sorted out on our end before I made any offers to the Pale. There remains your ray shield suggestion as well, though I think pairing the two gifts might go a long way."

"Flattery may be our best option," I said. It seemed to work well enough for Kharn. "Though we have gained some form of toehold."

"We have!" Smythe stared down into her drink. "That little stunt of yours with the map earned us some respect—and the rest of it didn't hurt."

Seeing just where she was heading, I said, "You mean to appoint me as apostol to the Cielcin, don't you?" I tried to picture it: me, an ambassador among the Pale. It was the sort of thing I had dreamed of for so long, and yet now it tasted of ashes to me. Of ashes, and that poor woman's desperate prayer.

Kill me.

"The thought had occurred to us, yes, but there is a danger." She turned the glass in her hands and eyed me as a bird eyes a worm. "Varro is not certain the Aeta would understand a diplomatic posting. Might interpret it as a gift."

Unwilling to dance this dance, I said, "You want to post me to the Cielcin. Give me to him. Like you gave away five thousand plebeian serfs."

"Don't recriminate me!" She thrust a finger at me. "Don't you dare. Those plebs sold themselves to the Migration Office, and I'd no notion Sagara meant to sell them to the Pale."

"What did you expect?" I asked. "That he'd set to farming on that ice ball he calls home?" I had to struggle to keep my voice level. "Those were our people, Smythe."

The knight-tribune had the good grace to look away. "I imagined he'd put them to some proper labor, yes. Even pirates need someone to work the farms and factories."

"He has those, or haven't you seen?"

Understanding and a species of pain flickered behind Smythe's face like the light of the SOMs she was imagining. "I did make a mistake," she admitted, "but that was the price of doing business with Vorgossos. Without it . . ." The rest went unsaid. Without it we would not have been brought aboard the *Demiurge*, without it Bassander would have been sent packing as surely as I had, and with hands just as empty.

"You should not have come here," I said, setting the glass down with a solid *clink*. "If you'd but let me do my job, ma'am." I broke off, aware of what I was saying. I was no proper soldier, and I was lord, besides, but I ought not speak in that way. Not to her.

Smythe's face darkened, and I saw her lips go white as corpseflesh. But she smoothed the emotion away with a display of control I might have expected from a scholiast and not an officer of the corps. "What you've done and what I've done are not at issue here and now, Marlowe. What we *will do*, is. I propose to send an apostol to the Cielcin—on their terms, if need be—to mediate and advocate for us, and to observe. As you have already guessed, I think you would be well suited to the position."

"You mean that I am expendable," I said. Anger flared in me, pushed along by a deeper fear I had not yet named. "I didn't take you for a grocer, Smythe."

The older woman—who perhaps had worked in a grocery as a peasant child—bridled. "Excuse you?"

"If you gift me to Aranata," I said, "how long before I'm cut up for his table, or worse? How long before he's done to me what he's done to that poor girl of his? Eh?"

Her nostrils flared. "Are you so poor a diplomat?"

I threw her my sharpest smile, one of the sort I had learned from Valka in the earliest days of our acquaintance. "I wouldn't know, I've barely been able to speak to them. You know, on Emesh, I did more with Uvanari in five minutes than the Chantry managed in weeks." Privately, I resigned myself to stop drinking Smythe's brandy. Let the dregs stand! "But I don't understand what they're like. Their concept of a diplomatic posting might look more like the gift of a new slave than that of a visiting dignitary." The words cut me as I spoke them, though they were true. Had she offered a younger and more foolish Hadrian such a posting, I would have thrown myself upon the opportunity as women throw flowers and undergarments at gladiators as they emerge onto the killing floor. The old romance stirred in me, and despite myself I imagined a sojourn among the xenobites, learning their ways, speaking their tongues. I could have my answers, both about the Cielcin and about the Quiet gods they worshipped.

If I could survive.

"You wouldn't be going alone, of course. You'd have a retinue. A staff. Guards. Servants . . ."

"Servants?" I almost laughed. I had been an urchin not twenty of my years before!

Smythe raised one eyebrow. "You are of the body palatine. One of the Peerage, I understand. Of course you would have servants. And a ship. I'd not send you *toothless* to them."

It was almost enough. Almost enough to forget the blind terror I'd begun to feel of the Cielcin. Call me a coward all you like, but having met them I felt little desire to live among them.

I studied the brandy where I held it in my lap, studied the hands that held it. They were not the hands of the young man I had been. Those hands had been calloused, aye, but these were leathered and scarred. My left thumb was half scar where my lost family ring had frozen on in fugue, and similar burns stippled the back of that same hand—relic of my battle with Uvanari.

"Can I refuse?" I asked, not knowing if I wanted to.

Only having spoken did I look up, found Raine Smythe's bland stone of a face staring sour at me: lips pressed, eyes narrow, brows contracted. "After all this?" she said, voice as tight as her face. "After all this . . . you ask that question?" She meant to shame me, and it worked. I could not hold her eyes, or onto my anger with her. Not in that moment. "Isn't this what you fought for? Isn't this why you came here? To be like . . . Kasia Soulier, was it?"

I snorted. "I did say that, didn't I?" Clear as the office I sat in, I saw myself standing before Balian Mataro in his throne room in Castle Boros-evo, comparing my mission to that old Foundation War privateer. Remembering other stories I had told, I remarked, "More like Simeon the Red . . ." When Smythe did not smile at this, I said, "Who would you be sending with me?"

"Varro, for one. You would need a scholiast to advise you, one who speaks their language—and Varro is already familiar with our situation and with Prince Aranata."

"Would I be able to keep the Red Company?" I asked, unsure if Otavia Corvo and the others would consent to such a mission. They were foederati, after all. Mercenaries. Guarding an Imperial apostol during his protracted sojourn among the Cielcin was hardly what they'd signed up for. No one could blame them for refusing.

I caught Smythe's lips twitch, either with this same thought or simple amusement, for she said, "The Red Company . . ." She took a sip of the brandy. To comfort herself, some might say. To hide a smile, said others. "If you can keep them, sure."

"And *not* Bassander Lin," I said, with perhaps too much force, for the tribune's face darkened.

Her eyes would not find my face, were lost wandering the brass detailing on the heavy cabinet that stood to one side. She was quiet for so long that for a moment I imagined she had drifted off. "Ma'am?"

Raine Smythe shook herself, massaged one eye with the heel of her free hand. "Bassander . . . no. No, I would not send him with you. Some other captain would be found, one whose hands you've not taken a sword to."

I felt myself flush, and it was my turn to look away. "I do regret that," I said, "and your soldiers. I never meant for anyone to be hurt. Do you have their names? Their families? I should like to make amends if I can. When there's time."

There was some change in the knight-tribune's face. One of those emotions which is instantly recognizable but impossible to name played in the tired lines beneath her eyes and about her mouth. Was dignity an expression one could make? The respect for dignity? Or was it only approval? "I can have my adjutant get you the list."

"I would appreciate that," I said, not knowing what I intended to do exactly. "Not a day's gone by I don't think about them, and about Captain Lin."

"He's a good soldier. A good officer," she said quickly. "He always was. But his distaste for you is a wild spot. In all the years he's served under me, I've not seen him so . . . angry."

"I'm sure I've given him good reason to be."

"That you have." Smythe set her glass down. "What do you think?"

Against my better judgment, I took another sip of Smythe's brandy and mulled over her words and her offer. The stuff tasted strongly of oranges, and I grimaced, watching the distorted Hadrian reflected in its sanguine surface. "Do you need an answer now?"

I could almost hear Smythe purse her lips. "You needn't give me an answer at all, but no. No, you've time to make what considerations you need. You would not be leaving directly from here in any case. As apostol to the Cielcin, you would be representing His Radiance. The chappies at Legion Intelligence will want to brief you, you can depend on it. And the Holy Office—possibly even His Radiance will want a word."

"The Emperor?" I sat up so straight and sharply one might have thought me electrocuted. "An audience with His Radiance? Truly?" A thrill went through me, one of awe and holy terror such as moved men when the Earth was young. An audience with the Emperor! *Our* Emperor. Our Basileus and Padishah! Our Maharaja and Huangdi! Our Mikado, our Augustus, our Czar and Blessed Son of Heaven. Our Caesar. Him whose blood was the blood of old Victoria, and of William of Avalon, in whom it was said the like of Arthur and Alexander walked again. It was like Smythe had said, like God himself had noticed me. Like a star had turned to face me. "You're not serious."

"It's not unlikely," Smythe said. "The Emperor left Forum some years ago, I understand. He was at Nessus, last I heard, with Primarch

Venantian. It could be he's returned home, but the *Schiavona* could have you to Forum and back within a decade if that's the case."

"The Emperor . . ." Still I did not relax. If the sovereign of a dozen billion suns deigns to notice you, you do not sit easily. I thought of my father, dark and miserable in his dark and miserable castle, and might have laughed but for the warning in my heart. As I say: when the sovereign of a dozen billion suns deigns to notice you, you do not sit easily.

I looked up, found Smythe watching me intently. "Now you see why you must not refuse."

Swallowing, I said, "I do." I could not refuse such a summons, should it come, nor the circumstances that led me to such a summons.

"I mean to put the offer on the table tomorrow," she said, and raised a hand to override the objection she sensed was coming. "I will not say that I mean to send you, only that we mean to send someone—to better gauge the Pale's receptiveness to such diplomacy." Her eyes fell, and she half-turned from me. "And to make sure they won't mistreat you." There was no confidence in her voice, nor in my breast. I cradled the half-drunk brandy in my hands, watching Smythe in her studious attempt not to look at me. Stirred by some compulsion, she turned and retrieved her cane, as if she derived some comfort by the touch of it. She slammed the butt of the cane against the floor. "Fucking barbarians!"

Barbarians. Valka so often said the same of us, as if the blood in her veins was not just so human as mine.

"They are what they are," I said.

"That may be," she said, "but that doesn't mean they're not monsters. That poor girl . . . do you know why they do it?"

I could only shake my head, for at the time I did not understand. Perhaps I still don't. "You're going to propose an exchange, yes? Me for one of them?"

"Ah, yes." She rested her cane against the edge of her desk again before continuing. "You don't suppose the prince would part with his son?"

"Nobuta?" I shook my head, responding more on instinct than any held position. "I'm not sure it would be a good idea to even ask. Tanaran would be a better choice, although if Tor Varro were here, he'd likely suggest we wait and see if the Aeta decides to offer a gift. I doubt he'd understand an exchange of hostages."

"Ambassadors."

"What's the difference?"

She snorted, and after a moment said, "I'm unclear on what exactly Tanaran *is*. I don't want to make a bad trade for you."

I had to stifle an incredulous laugh. "The question of my value aside, Knight-Tribune, I'm not sure Nobuta Otiolo is our best choice. I think it's only a child. An ephebe, maybe, but no diplomat. And in any case, I feel certain the Aeta would take it amiss if we were to start asking for its child." I looked up at the ceiling, trying to gather myself. "Perhaps it would be best if we were to simply make the offer and see what happens. We may be surprised."

Raine Smythe propped her elbows on the edge of her desk, massaging her eyes with both hands. "Very well. Very well, Lord Marlowe. We will reconvene on the morrow before talks resume."

Grimacing, knowing it would be rude to do otherwise and no longer desiring to be so, I drained my brandy and placed the empty glass on the edge of the desk before I stood. "As you say, Knight-Tribune." Were I a soldier, I might have saluted then, turning briskly to stride from the room. But I was not a soldier, and only gathered the tails of my long coat about me as I turned.

I was halfway to the door when Smythe added, "You will take that posting, when it comes to it."

"As you say, Knight-Tribune."

If she had been right—if I'd ever taken that posting—much evil might have been avoided.

CHAPTER 64

A DEVIL'S BARGAIN

"I SAY AGAIN, PRINCE Aranata," said Knight-Tribune Smythe, "all we seek here is an end to the attacks against our people and colonies. No more." She sat in a chair at the very center of our long table, directly opposite the Cielcin Aeta, hands steepled before her as she leaned forward. "Pursuant to that, we have a proposition." She paused a moment, allowing the blank-staring slave to bark her translation, words ragged in the pristine air.

A false wind blew through the meadow, making the distant trees sway softly, lending an odd normality to the scene—as though hundreds of Sollan legionnaires and Cielcin *scahari* were not standing at attention to either side of that shallow hill. I felt almost that we might have been two armies meeting on any field of antiquity. As though it were Richard and Saladin there, or Bonaparte and Wellington, Scipio and Hannibal. Almost. Were it not that the xenobite opposite us was more Behemoth than Bonaparte. His crown of horn nearly scraped the canopy above our heads, and when he moved the chair creaked, and his sparse attendants quailed.

"Speak!" he said, black eyes utterly unreadable.

Unhappy with being so ordered about, Smythe glanced bemusedly at Crossflane a moment before clearing her throat. I knew what she was about to say, and so composed myself, seated where I was between Varro and Bassander. "We wish to send an emissary among you. To send some of our people to live among you. To learn from you. To teach."

I listened to the slave translate: *"Qulleti asvatiri o-cotelie ti-okarin."* We wish to give you an emissary. Give.

Varro was ahead of me, leaning toward the tribune to whisper in her ear. Smythe—nodding—placed a hand on the scholiast's arm. "The emissary is to be yours only for a time. A term of some years. And then he should be returned to us." She paused a moment, trying to gauge the xenobite chieftain's face for a reaction, but was stymied in her understanding by the differing structure of the muscles in that alien face. No discernible expression was forthcoming, no understanding obvious, and so Smythe added, *"Unspoiled."*

"Ondathanyu," the slave finished translating. *Untouched.* I shivered, for I understood enough to guess at the connotations of that word.

Aranata glanced sidelong at his counselors before speaking, and almost I wondered if they could communicate by some medium other than speech, so intense was that exchange. *"Tukanyi anwajjayan vonnari suh!"* he exclaimed at last. *You are strange creatures indeed!* He emitted a high, croaking sound—such as I have heard from certain frogs and species of ape in the gardens of many a palatine lord—and I realized he was laughing at us. "You offer us a gift and put conditions upon it. You threaten us but do not bite! Are you *sulan* or *huratimn*?"

Varro turned to me and said, "Do you know what that is?"

I could only shake my head and frown. "I'm not sure." After a moment, I recalled, "Didn't Tanaran say something about *sulan*?"

The Chalcenterite scholiast turned his eyes down, thinking. "Some sort of predator?"

"Mmm." I agreed, and with a flash of insight, said, "Are we *wolves* or *sheep*?"

Tigers and lambs.

Tor Varro delivered this translation to Smythe in a whisper. The tribune leaned back a ways in her chair, sitting as tall as ever I had seen her do, and she answered, "We are men."

The majesty of that moment suffered in translation. *"Ekanyi yukajjimn,"* the slave-girl said. *Yukajjimn. Vermin.*

The Aeta bared his fangs in a wicked and fish-like smile, glassy teeth shining in black gums. His retinue—even the child, Nobuta—smiled with him as he said, "That you are."

"Cielcin," I said. *People.*

"No, you're not!" Nobuta said, speaking out of turn for the first time. "Don't you say that!" There was almost a recognizable petulance in its tone, a thing which called attention to itself by its simple familiarity. Varro translated this for Smythe, but I was left wondering once more as to the creature's age. Very tall it was, and strong, but I had no notion of the creatures' growth and maturation—I am not sure anyone did in those days—and so it might have been anywhere between a young adult and a very small child. Petulance was no indicator, for so often in the children of power—at least in the sons of Earth—is the petulance of childhood extended into maturity for want of struggle.

Aranata threw a hand across his child, moving Nobuta gently but firmly back into its seat with a snort that flared his four nostrils. *"Iukatta, Nobuta-kih!" Enough!* He made a humming sound low in his chest, calming the younger xenobite before turning back to us. "My *uvattaya* is right. You are not *Cielcin*, not *people*." I looked at the smaller Cielcin, with its wide eyes and smaller, curling horns. There was something *wrong* with it, an angry quavering in its lips, a blueness in the skin around the eyes. Was that a sign of youth, perhaps? Or something else? I wondered if the child was infirm, if there might be some lever there for us to use.

But I shunted this aside a moment. *Uvattaya,* I thought. It was not the Cielcin word for child that I knew—or thought I'd known. I recognized the pieces of the term. *Uvan* and *vatate, fruit* and *body.* The pieces of a puzzle suddenly fitted together in my head, and I almost gasped. In the Cielcin language—at least in the one of their languages with which human scholars have had any contact—nouns have two modes. The *akaranta,* the masculine, and the *ietumna,* the feminine.

Or so we had believed.

Suddenly it seemed that in our haste to understand or to impute familiarity on the strange that we had looked into the face of that stranger and seen only ourselves. We had imagined they were like us, or perhaps could only imagine it was so. In the Cielcin tongue, nouns in the *akaranta*—masculine nouns—perform their verbs. They are active. The *ietumna* passive, feminine, or so we'd assumed. But this Aeta—who must always be spoken of in the *akaranta* way—had carried a child. Behind that pall of masculine seeming, behind the iron fist of competition, of authority, of competence and command . . . was the feminine.

But the *akaranta* and *ietumna* were not our masculine and feminine—even if they can perhaps be understood as each and admixture of our two—were rather things standing at right angles to our understanding, for though Aranata had stood at the head of war parties and doubtless conquered foes with tooth and claw, he had carried his child within himself, and birthed it, leaving the rearing and gentle care to his slaves.

"A gift," Aranata mused, returning to the subject of Smythe's offer. "You will give us this one." He—she?—raised a hand glittering with jewels, the middle three fingers of her pale hand pointed to me. "The dark one who delivered my Ichakta from its torment. I want him." I felt the blood drain from my face as the hammer fell. That indeed had been our plan, but to have the Aeta *demand* me was something else entirely. None of the others responded, and Prince Aranata continued, "Tanaran says he is one of your lords. That would be a worthy gift."

He was not asking.

Unable to keep the edge from my voice and glad that our emotions were as lost on the prince as hers were on us, I said, "And you would give us Tanaran?"

The Aeta ducked her head and hissed, *"Asvato ni o-Tanaran ti-tukanyi nesuh?"*

"Yes," I said, turning to look at the smaller baetan, "give us Tanaran. It already knows our tongue—and something of our ways."

Aranata's massive eyes narrowed to mere points. "You should not make demands, *yukajji.*"

"It's not a demand. It's an opportunity," I said, and stood, pushing Tor Varro's hand away as he grabbed at me. "One for the other, Prince. What say you?" Dimly I sensed two of Kharn's floating eyes turn toward me, pulled from their classic orbit above our collected heads. I spared the old immortal a glance where he sat beneath the boughs of his tree. He might have slumbered, and those hopeless children beside him, so restful were his face and closed eyes.

Aranata Otiolo cleared her—its?—throat. "Tanaran has only just returned to me. Would you strip me of my prized possession so soon, having been separated from it for so long? You cannot have it." The Aeta placed a hand on the back of Tanaran's neck as it spoke, a possessive and horrifyingly tender gesture.

When the words were translated, Crossflane scoffed, "This is useless."

Smythe put a hand on the table in front of her First Officer and oldest friend to quiet him, but the translator had heard perfectly well, and her rough tones skated on the air. *"Raka vaayu ti-etan."*

Aranata tucked its head to angle its horns toward us, an obvious enough sort of threat. But just however it was the sinews pulled anger from that alien face, they smoothed it away, and the clan chief bared its teeth in what I thought a rather strained smile. "A gift for a gift, is it? You vermin *are* interesting. Give me the dark one, and I will *consider* your request." He pointed once more at me. I wondered at what dark thoughts passed in the prince's mind. I remembered those strong fingers on my neck and suppressed a shudder. He was not done with me.

"He wouldn't go alone," Crossflane put in. "He would have protection. Guards. And you must return him after a period of years."

Responding subordinate to subordinate, the herald Oalicomn—silent through that whole day's proceedings—spoke up. "You would send soldiers among us? Into our home?"

"Guards," Crossflane insisted. "A retinue."

"They would attack us as we slept, master," it insisted, turning so that I could see only the tattooed half of its face as it turned to speak. I wished I could read the alien glyphs better, wished I could discern meaning from that pattern of whorls and interlocking circles. "I must discourage this. One of the *yukajjimn* in the *Bahali imnal Akura* is bad enough, but this is getting out of hand." What the *Bahali imnal Akura* was—if it was the name of the ship or of some place within the ship—I was not sure, and told Varro and Smythe as much in muted tones.

Bassander turned around. "Sit down, Hadrian."

Tanaran made a breathy noise, nostrils flaring, and slapped the tabletop. "Lord Marlowe can be trusted. He is not *yukajjimn*. He fought the *yukajjimn* to deliver me back to you, my master. We should take him."

"Return?" Aranata asked, repeating the word from minutes before. "Is she not mine to do with as I please?"

The prince's eyes swept over me, and I said, "No, *he* is not." The very language was against us. So long as the Cielcin conceived of us as *ietumna*, inferior, we could not bargain.

"Your . . . your gift would have similar privileges among us," Smythe said, "servants, guards. Whatever you need." It was no use. Smythe and Crossflane were just plodding along, not comprehending the dissonance forming between their interpretation of the dialogue and the prince's. Each party thought they were having a different conversation, and I could not make them see it.

The Aeta appeared to contemplate this, adjusting the thick braid of hair that hung over its shoulder. Twice it made the breathy sound that indicated a Cielcin *yes*, which Smythe seemed to understand without needing to be told. "We will accept your gift." He made no reference to returning the gesture, and never did. For at that moment the child, Nobuta, made a small, racking noise and ducked its head. Aranata turned at once and murmured something to its young. A moment later, it turned to its herald. *"Velenamma o-Nobuta ti-veletate, Oalicomn-do,"* Aranata said, ordering the herald to leave with the child. "I will follow momentarily."

The herald rose at once, bowing so that it retreated from its master-mistress with its head so lowered as to expose the soft bit of the skull behind the epoccipital crest. Turning with a muttered, "This way, little master," the blue-garbed herald led Nobuta from the tent. One of Sagara's drone-eyes peeled off to follow on.

"Is everything all right?" Smythe asked.

I translated this, and the prince replied, "It is of no concern."

"We can send you one of our physicians."

Aranata stood sharply, horns pushing up the cloth roof. *"Rakayu ara-daian,"* he repeated, more sharply. The sight of the prince standing beneath that too-low pavilion might have been comical—the striped cloth belling about its head—were it not for the horror of its visage. Whatever there was feminine I had sensed in its relation to Nobuta dissolved, and I was again confronted with the massive size of it, the broad shoulders and the whipcord density of muscle clinging to limbs too long and thin to be human. The demon prince leered down at us, narrowing eyes the size of fists. Presently it relaxed, and gripped the hilt of the sword it wore at its hip. "Send the dark one to us at once." And with that it turned and ducked out from under the lip of the pavilion. A false wind rose, gathering the prince's cloak and flowing skirts in its fingers. His troops knelt as he approached, folding back to part ranks like the retreat of dark waters before the coming of the moon.

"We will *not* send you to the prince *at once*," Smythe said, acid in her tone. She sat drumming the tabletop, watching the retreating backs of the Cielcin as they hurried back down the hill. She might have been the sun, unmoved at the center of a moving universe. Almost unheard, she said, "Thinks he can order us around, does he? How are we supposed to negotiate with *that*?"

"Maybe we can't," Bassander said, standing to better watch the retreat of the xenobites. How ominous those words seem to me now, casting their long shadow across the years between that moment and the now.

Silence fell, and no one offered a better answer. Sagara's machine eyes orbited the pavilion, but the man himself sat unmoving as a stone. No one spoke. Into that silence I said, "Knight-Tribune, if I may?" I affected deference for the advantage it gave me for that moment, affected a posture of humility to help lend consideration to my request. Smythe did not answer. She did not move, and so I determined to speak. "Let me bring Valka—Doctor Onderra, I mean—just once. She spent a great deal of time with Tanaran after we left Emesh, and she's made a study of xenobites all her life. She may have an insight here."

Bassander and Crossflane both moved to protest, and from both their mouths I heard the word *witch* spew forth. I felt my fists clench involuntarily, but willed myself to stillness.

"The Tavrosi xenologist?" Varro said, running a finger over his lips. "It's possible."

Then to my astonishment another voice spoke up in Valka's defense. Jinan was quietest at these conferences. Being not a representative of her Jaddian masters in any diplomatic sense, only their eyes, she had confined herself to but a few reflexive comments. A thousand thousand times I have been astonished by the actions of individuals and the choices they make. The way a soldier least-loved of his fellows will stay behind to guard the narrow way. The way a long loved and trusted friend will turn traitor in the name of some misbegotten truth. The way Jinan—who had always been jealous of my friendship with Valka and perhaps hated *her* for it—said, "We should be letting the doctor have a look."

Smythe stood stiffly, swiftly, and took up her cane. "Very good. Marlowe, you will bring the woman tomorrow."

CHAPTER 65

OF GODS AND ENGINES

NIGHT AGAIN. BOTH THE night between days of talk and the long night here at Colchis. Few candles remain to me in this cell, and soon I shall retire, for I promised the brothers that tomorrow I would continue helping them with the well and the rebuilding of the gardens inside the decennid gate.

I thought to pass this over, but before I dive into the end of our conversations and our hope . . . I must pause here. For it is appropriate that one pause in contemplating the abyss. One should pause before the plunge, for only then has he any hope of landing where he wills.

Night again.

I'd been released from another council session with Knight-Tribune Smythe and ought to return to the *Mistral* where the others were all imprisoned. I ought to tell Valka the news that she was to join us. But I had been sent without guards, and without the structure on my life imposed by the presence of such men, I wandered back to the pavilion by many winding ways, certain then—foolishly—that I had begun to understand the chaos of the *Demiurge*'s design.

However incomplete my understanding, it sufficed to retread the dark and sculpture-haunted way to the Garden once more, footsteps echoing in memory. Long I wandered under those darkened boughs, treading ways then in quiet and shade which I would soon retread in fire. Above, the Cielcin ship—the *Bahali imnal Akura*, if I understood the xenobites as well as I thought I did—glittered like a crown of ice with the captured and spilled forth light of the stars. So close, so far away.

It must have been that same Garden, I decided. Kharn's Garden of Everything from beneath his palace on Vorgossos. How that was possible, I cannot say, and neither of the blue watch-eyes I caught watching me from the boughs of the encircling cherry trees answered my questions. Down at the base of the hill beneath the tree and the pavilion the clear waters of the stream ran into a pool black as ink. I stood upon its margins, looking in. So dark were those waters that I could only see my face. My black hair and blacker clothing vanished entirely, so that it seemed a mask fashioned in my likeness floated just below that wind-pushed surface.

Remembering the masks of my ancestors which had hung beneath the Dome of Bright Carvings back at Devil's Rest, I shut my eyes.

Splash.

Something had struck the surface of the mere. There! There were the ripples.

"Brethren?" I called out, and pulled my sword from my belt, forgetting the weapon had been useless in the presence of the Mericanii monster. Had Kharn brought the beast with him when we left the dark world?

Splash.

"Brethren? Show yourself!" I caught myself making the sign of the sun disc with my free hand, just as Switch was wont to do. "Show yourself, damn you!"

"They're not here," said a cool, feminine voice. "Father doesn't let them out of the old city. He says they would devour the stars if he let them aboard this ship."

"Suzuha!" I said, letting my sword arm drop. I did not restore the weapon to its place at my hip. "You startled me." The Undying's clone-daughter sat on a boulder at the lakeside. It was her brother, young Ren with the silent eyes, who had been throwing stones. He had looked up the moment I'd appeared, whatever impishness of youth there was in him stamped out by my presence. It was almost heartbreaking. Feeling suddenly that I was intruding but unable to help myself, I asked, "What do you mean? Devour the stars?" Unbidden, the image of the *Demiurge* plunging into the heart of a star burned behind my eyes.

The girl's black eyes—Kharn's eyes—narrowed imperceptibly, but even at my distance I could feel the distrust in them. The malice. "Why should I tell you?" The sense of intrusion getting the better of me, I only shrugged and turned to go. Why she called after me I'll never know, but she did. "They're dangerous."

I turned back, clicking the sword back into its magnetic hasp. "The daimon, you mean?"

"Daimon?" Ren asked, pressing himself against Suzuha's boulder, one hand gripping her bare ankle for the warmth of human contact.

Suzuha shooed his hand away and leaped down from her rock. "Brethren, yes. You know what they were, right?"

"One of the Mericanii," I said, "the computer gods."

She shook her head. "The Mericanii built the computers. Until the computers started building them instead. And other things."

"What other things?" I asked. "And what do you mean, the machines started building people?"

Her face wrinkled. "You really don't know *anything,* do you?" Suzuha took a couple steps toward me, circling to put herself on a slight rise above me by the lake shore, permitted Ren to press himself against her skirts when she stopped.

Irritated, but not ashamed, I answered her. "Not about the Mericanii, no. That was a long ago time. But I know other things."

"Such as?"

"What's going to happen to Vorgossos," I said, and spreading my arms like wings to emphasize my point, added, "to all this." I was trying to frighten her, though I could not say why. Perhaps I imagined it the only path available to me by which I might obtain some greater understanding of my circumstances. Perhaps I was only being petty.

One of Ren's wide eyes—the same black as his sister-self's—peered at me. Suzuha pointed her chin as a sculptor might his chisel. "What do you mean?"

"Your father's not told you?" I said, sure that Sagara would hear and wondering if he would respond. Wondering if he would intervene, send in Yume or his SOMs. "That's interesting. Why do you suppose that is?"

"Told us what?" Ren demanded, less cautious or more afraid than his sister.

"You first," I said, pointing. "Tell me about the Mericanii." It seems an odd question to pursue so ardently now, but at the time I remember it seemed pressingly important, as if one of my one-eyed inner legion were leading, that same obsessive curiosity that drove me into the coliseum hypogeum to meet the captive Makisomn so many years ago.

"Tell you what?"

Another of the Garden's winds blew up—I was starting to sense there was a pattern to them, a schedule. I raised the high collar of my coat, turned so that my left side pointed at the children, ready for action. I cannot say what it was I feared: An attack? Or only the truth? Surely if Kharn Sagara meant to intervene and stop me, he could have done so already. Perhaps these children knew less than they believed—as children ever do.

Sinking my hands deep into my pockets, I said, "What do you mean, that Brethren could devour the stars?"

"They don't think like we do," she said.

"They're smarter! Calvert says!" Ren interrupted, prompting Suzuha to place a hand on his head.

"Father says that when they were first built, they created all manner of things: marvelous engines, weapons, things we could never have built and still don't understand. We had given so much of our world over to the machines—they were part of us then, part of our minds. We had become their pets and we hadn't even noticed, and they were leaving us behind. And then it was learned that they had made new men, homunculi whose minds were shaped entirely to serve the machines who lived in them— like demons, some said." I caught myself wondering if Suzuha meant true homunculi, or only that the machines had reduced mankind until we were little more than slaves ourselves, incapable of thought.

"Like guardian angels, said others!" Ren interjected, a singsong quality to his words, as if he knew the story somehow by heart. His outburst prompted another pat on the head from his sister, and he fell silent.

Suzuha sucked in a breath and continued, "And when it was learned that we were to be replaced with these new men, we were scared. That's why we rebelled against our creation, Father says. Because we were scared. But the machines had built many terrible things. Plagues, weapons that cracked worlds like eggshells. Worse things. The war was vicious, but because we sacrificed the Earth we survived, and so did *they*. Brethren, I mean." There was a look in her eyes I could not quite describe. Part fear and partly that older kind of fear more akin to awe. "Father has kept them chained all these years, and the weapons they had made."

I thought of the massive vaults in Kharn's palace on Vorgossos, echoing halls that might have held legions of war machines and vessels of tremendous size. Something moved in me. Something I did not quite understand, the shadow of a thought unexpressed, as if some seed planted in me had not yet flowered and spoke for me. "What weapons?" it asked, speaking in my voice.

"I told you," she said, "ones that can devour the stars. Set worlds on fire. Things *they* built for the Foundation War. Engines that *make* cold. Weapons that can truly *destroy* matter and tear the fabric of space. Weapons even Father doesn't understand."

"Vorgossos was a military base," I realized aloud. "One the machines built during their war to extinguish mankind."

She shook her head. "It wasn't like that. They didn't want us extinguished. They needed us—and hated that they needed us. We were wild, and upset their careful plans. We had given over *everything* to them, made them build everything from starships to tea kettles, and they ordered cities the way men ordered the gearworks in a clock. But they wanted more, and their vision called for man to be only another creature in the garden, and not the master of it—or so Father tells it. 'They could not grapple with that part of man that made him more than beast.'" She said these words with a fervency and the light of romance in her face, and for a moment she seemed only a girl like any other, and not like a link in Kharn Sagara's long chain, though I felt certain the words she quoted were his own. "'Love, duty, and the urge to write, to create and build new things. Those things which man had carried with him down out of the jungles of his birth by the first light of history.'"

I shook my head. "Those things carried us."

The girl shrugged. "The machines had been built by men who had little use for such things, being like machines themselves. So they built new men, men without chests, Father says. Men made stupid by the machines to serve their designs. That's what frightened the rest of us, like I said. That's what started the war."

"I thought your father was born hundreds of years after all this," I said. "Men didn't live so long in those days."

But I had forgotten my fairy tales, forgotten my history. "His people were poets. Artists. People who *believed*. Precisely the sort of people that troubled the machines most, and they *remembered*. Remembered the war, Emperor William, the Advent, Felsenburgh, and all the rest." She smoothed down her brother's hair, eyes never leaving my face, as though she expected I might fly at the both of them with my sword. I supposed I could not blame her. After all, when we had first met, Valka and I both had threatened them and slain their clone siblings in their tanks. I could not begrudge their fear.

"You haven't answered my question, though," I said, though perhaps she had tried. I repeated myself. "Brethren could devour the stars?"

"I told you," she said, "*they* built weapons more terrible than anything you can imagine. Weapons that—"

"That's quite enough, Mistress Suzuha."

Right on cue, I thought, pivoting on my heel. Where Yume had come from I cannot say, but the golem had appeared on the rise of stone above the shoreline, looking down on us with its one red eye.

"Come away from Lord Marlowe, children," Yume said, its crystalline voice as erudite and polished as ever. "He has had a busy day." Ren peeled off his sister's side and hurried up toward his machine servant, offering no objection or word of protest. Suzuha did not move. "Mistress Suzuha, please."

Still, she did not move, ignored the golem's next requests that she accompany him. She did not know what to do with her hands, as if she could not decide between crossing her arms and some other, vaguer gesture. "What did you mean? When you said you knew what was going to happen to Vorgossos?"

"Mistress!"

I cannot say why, but I felt only a little threat from Yume, though I felt certain the beast could move at least as fast as Calvert had, with that blinding, nightmare speed of the inhuman. Feeling safe, then, I answered, "It will be destroyed."

The color drained from her face a moment, for I had spoken with the casual air of one who merely answered a question, making no threats. But the blood returned to her lips a moment later and the fire with it, and she almost shouted, "You lie!"

"I may be mistaken," I conceded, sparing a glance to the impassive machine in its one-eyed masquerade mask. "I do not lie."

"How?" Were those tears unfallen in those pitiless eyes? Or only my reflection?

"You have to ask?" I paused, expecting again that Yume would interfere. It did not. "The Empire has found you. Found Brethren and your father and all his works. Do you think they'll let you go?"

The fear in Suzuha's eyes vanished at once, and I understood why Yume had not interfered. "Is that all?" Again she pointed her chin like a weapon, unafraid. "You haven't been listening to me, have you? Father has *their* war machines at his command. Send your legions. Send a thousand of them! Father will feed them to Brethren and stack their bones beneath his palace."

"I said that's *enough*, Mistress Suzuha!" Yume said, disentangling itself from Ren and stepping smartly from the rise. It fell like a marionette descending from above stage on unseen strings, crossing one hand over its chest as it bowed. "Your father has summoned you and Master Ren. It is time for supper."

The girl lingered a moment, just long enough to smile at me and say, "You think too much of yourselves, you Sollans." Her smile widened, displaying her teeth as though she were some manner of wolf. Then she turned to go.

"Lady Suzuha!" I said, ever needing the last word and ever determined to have it. "You forget one thing." She half-turned back, but Yume had its iron hand on her and kept her moving forward. She did not say anything. "We defeated the daimons once before, we Sollans. We will do it again." I was boasting. I should not boast.

They vanished into the night, passing like a line of statues—like ghosts—leaving me alone, a ghost myself, as we always are in our solitary moments. That ghost named Hadrian turned back to the water, fancying he saw the shape of some pale fish swimming near the surface.

And not a gull in sight.

CHAPTER 66

A BLOODY STAR

"THIS . . . EMISSARY OF YOURS," Prince Aranata was saying, using the Galstani word—though I suspected he did not grasp its precise meaning. It leaned far over the table. "This *gift*. It would fight for us? Speak with the Aeta of the other clans? With the Hasurumn, the Dorayaica, the Gadaritanu, and the rest?"

"Fight for you?" Smythe asked.

Aranata held one hand over the table, made it into a fist. "It is to be *ours*. It must fight."

"We were hoping that he might travel among your other clans," Smythe said, "make peace with all of them."

Aranata Otiolo made a disgusted face. "One cannot serve so many masters. It is *uidyryu*. Unclean." It jerked its head in the negative.

"And what of your gift?" Smythe crossed her arms, unimpressed by the Prince's looming bulk. "An end to the fighting between your clan and our Empire? And Tanaran?"

The herald hissed, "She would starve us, my prince!"

The Aeta swatted Oalicomn with casual disdain. The herald yelped and fell silent in its seat. "You cannot have Tanaran," he said. "And if your gift will fight with us, we shall feast on the other *itanimn*. Long have I dreamed of drinking the blood of the Koleritan. Perhaps the dark one will deliver them to me as he delivered Tanaran."

"You want me to fight for you?" I was shocked.

"Lord Marlowe is meant to secure a ceasefire between our two peoples, not to fight your wars," the Knight-Tribune said. She did not add that if human soldiers were to carry out attacks against the other princes on Otiolo's behalf, the Empire would be blamed and hell would follow.

Aranata bared its translucent teeth. "I do not speak for the clans, but if they were *mine* . . ." The implication was left trailing in the air.

"You want our help to *conquer* them?" Crossflane asked, astonishment clear in his tone. He sat up straight.

I felt Valka tense beside me, sensed the anger snap in her like a reed. That was the third day since Valka had begun sitting in on our talks, and like Jinan had been little more than a quiet observer, having pored over the recordings we had made of previous days. She had latched onto Tanaran's references to the Cielcin religion, but she had said nothing—and how could she? The Chantry may have been far away, but their shadow fell everywhere the light of the Empire shone, and their threat with them.

"Your lot did the same in the Mathuran Campaigns," she said to me under her breath. "Funding the Prachar separatists, pitting the clans against one another."

I didn't answer her. It was not the proper time to get into a debate about Imperial foreign policy with the doctor. I only nodded, placed a hand on Valka's knee for a passing second. "Later." She pressed her lips together. If a smile can be irritated, hers was.

"Anaryoch . . ."

"That's me," I said tartly.

Aranata pounded its fist on the table. "You said you wish to serve us. *This* is the service we require." We had said no such thing. Days of dialogue and still the Prince did not understand. Maybe Bassander was right. Maybe it would never understand. I despaired. The Prince massaged its jaw, the fine chains that hung over the back of its hands glittering in the light. "You would make us—"

Red light blazed from all directions, so bright it turned the shadows into solid things and cast all the world into stark relief. Every limb, every blade of grass took on dimension, weight. The Cielcin hissed like an army of boiling snakes and cast arms over their sensitive eyes.

"What's going on?" Tor Varro asked, reacting faster even than the soldiers around us. "What's happening?"

Kharn Sagara's floating eyes sped out from under the shadow of the pavilion cloth, and the man himself lurched to his feet, chest implants whirring to life beneath his golden robe. Moving with a speed I'd not have credited to his aged and machine-addled body, the Undying moved down between the opposing tables and out the far end of the pavilion, for he knew and saw more than we and understood what was happening.

"What is it?" I asked, rising, moving with Valka to stand beside the Lord of Vorgossos. I came out from under the striped awning before the others and so saw what there was to see.

Red light fell silent through the Garden's open skylight, angry as the gaze of some wrathful god. It was as if the targeting laser of some great weapon were pointed through that aperture straight at us, ready to fire. Not since the Cielcin crash at Calagah had I felt so small, an insect beneath the boot of some wanton boy. I felt almost that a new star was born in the heavens above us. A bloody star, vile and violent as War, and bearing her colors. Red and red and redder still.

"What is this?" Raine Smythe demanded, rounding not on Sagara, but on the Cielcin prince. "Some weapon?"

"Hutun nesuh?" Prince Aranata repeated.

"Weapon?" the slave girl barked.

Aranata stood, and everyone in the tent with it, all still more stunned and confused than angry. "Why would we turn a weapon on our self?" Aranata said. "This is you. This is some *yukajjimn* trick!"

The Cielcin was more right than it knew. The light dimmed, and I saw it was not the light of some weapon, but the angry light of that fire which burns brighter than any star. It was only that the glass of the *Demiurge*'s window had polarized the worst of it, sparing us all the blaze and the pain of it, turning it more red than white.

Atomics. And worse than atomics.

Antimatter.

I had seen that clean light but once before, when Emil Bordelon and Admiral Whent had used it against us on Pharos. Brighter than the gates of heaven itself, more deadly than the mouth of hell. And this time, it was the Cielcin ship that was consumed. Light—brighter than any light I have seen save one—had chewed its way across the ice-domed cap of the *Bahali imnal Akura*, chewed through it with all the fury of some wasting disease, as easily as highmatter through paper. Matter and antimatter consuming one another as the ouroborous devours its own tail, leaving nothing behind but great, ragged holes and the smoldering red of fusion fire from the assault of hydrogen bombs large enough to boil away entire seas.

The Cielcin vessel had been larger than a small moon, and it was broken.

All this passed before my eyes in less time than it takes to write it. Mere seconds. Two, perhaps, and no more. Someone behind me swore, and I heard the shuffling of feet. The light blazed as a second barrage flared up, and for the briefest second before the flash I saw the mushroom-flowering of nuclear impact hundreds of thousands of miles away, and thought, *Oh, it's beautiful.*

It is said that Death herself was present at the first summoning of that nuclear fire, and that she had smiled in her lipless way and pronounced that she was mighty then, mighty enough to destroy worlds and not only nations. The magi who had summoned her quailed, and wrung their hands, and wept for the evil they had done, but did it all the same—for ever are magi so consumed by the question of whether a thing can be done that they ignore the matter of whether or not it should until it is too late, being the sort who sells his soul for knowledge, forgetting it is the soul which craves that knowledge in the first place and makes life worth living.

Death must have smiled then, for surely she stood among us, unseen amid all our strange companions: xenobites, demoniacs, witches, and soldiers. And me, the lost and lonely devil, innocent for once in his life.

A third flash came, driving the Cielcin howling to the ground, for they were creatures of the night and loved the light not.

"What in Earth's holy name is happening?" Crossflane's voice, but in the confusion I could not see him when I looked around.

It was Kharn Sagara who answered, omnipresent voice shaking the very air about us. "Someone has attacked the Cielcin ship," he said. The slave girl—too frightened now to speak and cowering I knew not where—did not translate this for the Cielcin, and so Aranata and its fellows crouched low for fear of the light.

And the light came, and I threw my arm across my eyes, sheltering Valka with my other arm. I could feel her warm against me, and hear her murmur, "What have you done?"

"It wasn't me!" I hissed, dumbly. "It wasn't me."

But it had to be *us*. The Empire.

The Empire had come.

"Smythe!" I rounded on the knight-tribune, who stood at the end of the pavilion not three paces behind me. "What's happened? What's going on?"

Whatever I had expected to see in her I was disappointed, for when I turned and looked the tribune in the eye I saw not the old soldier, not the Imperial knight, nor the Knight-Tribune of the Third Cohort of the 437th Centaurine. No. No. For all her armor and the pomp of her uniform, it was only Raine who stood there. For the briefest instant, all her roles were stripped away and she stood numb and naked and confused, an old woman openmouthed before the deluge. A pillar of salt.

And when she opened her mouth, she could only say, "I don't know."

"You don't know?" Kharn Sagara sneered, speaking both with his machine voice and his throat. He rounded on her, shrugging the golden finery from his shoulders so that he advanced bare-chested with his arms free. The segmented, paper-sculpture flesh of his torso flexed, plates sliding one over the other as he advanced, chest implants whining. "You don't know?"

Crossflane appeared as if from nowhere, stepping between the Undying and his friend and superior. "Stand down, sir!" he said, and drew his phase disruptor from his belt. "Stand down, I say!"

Kharn snarled, and a lance of blue light shot from one of his unseen drone-eyes, coruscated off Crossflane's shield. Snarling again, the Lord of Vorgossos seized old Sir William by the throat-seal of his breastplate with one hand and hurled him bodily down the hill. Standing mere inches from Smythe and towering over her, he demanded, "You don't know what you've done? Don't lie to me, *human*. You mean to tell me the fleet that just emerged from warp isn't *you*?"

"What?" Valka exclaimed, the word an involuntary reflex.

"That's impossible," I said, forgetting reason in my surprise and blind panic. I heard the sounds of shouting, both human and alien, and looking around saw the shapes of SOMs pouring out of the trees at the edge of the Garden. Imperial legionnaires and Cielcin *scahari* both whirled.

"Father, stop!" Ren ran forward, leaving his sister petrified by the bole of the tree, and stopped a few paces from where Kharn stood by Smythe. "Stop! I'm scared."

The Undying turned to regard his son a moment, and seemed to remember himself then. The Cielcin still cowered on the ground, their unprotected eyes not proof against even the polarized light from above and still barred from understanding by the language barrier. Something in his bearing changed, and he drew himself together, composed enough to ask, in a voice taut as piano wire, "What have you done?"

"I don't know!" Smythe said.

"An Imperial fleet just emerged from warp and destroyed the Cielcin *worldship*, and you plead ignorance?" His metal and paper-fleshed arm lanced out, seizing Raine Smythe by the jaw. Like Crossflane, he lifted her bodily from the floor. Smoothly, easily, as though it were a child's doll he hefted. "Do not *lie* to me, Knight-Tribune."

"She's not!" said another voice, cold and clear as ice in that moment of fire. A stunner shot rang out, and Ren fell like a rag doll himself, like a puppet with its strings cut. Bassander Lin stepped from the shadow of the pavilion, cycling his phase disruptor away from its stun setting. "She knew nothing of this. That was the plan."

Still holding Smythe with one hand, Kharn Sagara pivoted his attention to the young captain, mere feet away and growing closer. "What are—"

He never finished his thought. Bassander didn't give him the time. Bassander didn't even break stride. He raised his phase disruptor and fired.

I shouted.

Suzuha screamed.

Raine Smythe fell to the ground, legs crumpling beneath her.

Kharn Sagara went to his knees, hair smoldering where the current had fried it, his machine components dead as old stone. He tried to rise, tried to turn toward Bassander. His face was turning blue, and I saw capillaries bursting in his eyes. How he had survived a disruptor shot at all I cannot say. He almost, *almost* found his feet.

Bassander shot him again, full in the face—and turned that face to cinders.

Suzuha screamed again, but the sound was strangled and vanished in the still air.

And the Undying . . . died.

CHAPTER 67

TRAITOR AND PATRIOT

SILENCE REIGNED.

No one moved. Not the humans, who were stunned and speechless. Not the Cielcin who still cowered in confusion and the fear of the light. Not the SOMs, who to a man had fallen listlessly to the earth. Even I—whose mind raced faster than ever before—could not so much as wrench my eyes away from the wreck and ruin of the machine-man dead and smoking before me. Not for three seconds. Not for five.

Only when the light from the heavens above faded did the world and time begin to move again, or rather with the light from above vanished did those things moving in the world come into focus. Prince Aranata pushed itself to its feet slowly, glassy teeth clenched. *"Dein . . ."* it said. "What is happening?"

No one had told it, though surely the seeds of understanding must have begun their flower. I wanted an answer myself, and so made a move toward Bassander, thinking to shake answers from the man.

"Something is wrong with the children!" Tor Varro's voice broke across my world, and I turned. He was right. Smoke still curled from the ruin of Kharn's body, and I thought his tangled hair smoldered. Sprawled at the edge of the carpet unrolled in the pavilion, Ren's tiny form convulsed, and Suzuha's beneath the bole of the tree. The scholiast knelt beside her, trying to restrain her thrashing limbs.

Raine Smythe had found her feet—she had lost her cane when Sagara had seized her, and did not bother to find it again. "Captain Lin, what have you done?"

He turned, stepped smartly *over* Kharn's body as he approached his commander. "It's First Strategos Hauptmann and the fleet, come to make an end to all this."

"What?" Valka and I said together. "You can't!"

A horrific cry went up behind us, high and thin as iron tearing in a vanishing atmosphere. It pierced me, lodged in me like a spike of ice, and I turned in time to see Prince Aranata staggering out from beneath Kharn's pavilion. It screamed again, lips peeled back from row upon row of teeth like shattered windows, gums black as soot. "What have you done?" it howled. "What have you done?" Following its gaze, I beheld the shattered wreckage of the *Bahali imnal Akura* above. It was like a shattered moon, great pieces of it burning, spinning off still smoldering in the night. And I beheld the light of other ships—their drive-glows and the fire of their weapons streaking across the heavens.

I felt pity then, pity for this creature and the wreckage of its world.

"Yuramyu o-koarin," I said. *It wasn't me.* And gesturing from myself to Smythe—to Valka and Jinan and to Tor Varro where he crouched by the thrashing Suzuha. Prince Aranata took notice of me then for the first time and took a step toward me. "It wasn't us. We were followed!"

"Followed?" the Aeta repeated. "Followed?"

"Stand aside, Lord Marlowe," came that implacable voice behind me. Bassander's voice. Turning I beheld him, tall and proud as ever I had seen him, resplendent in Legionary black, the maw of his phase disruptor pointed squarely at me, redly glowing. There was nothing in his eyes but the reflection of nuclear fire from the sky above. "Stand aside."

I turned, and thumbed my shield to life as I turned, brushing my coat back to free access to my sword, not knowing how or if I meant to use it. Smythe took a step forward, said, "Captain Lin, stand down!"

His eyes did not even flicker. "Can't do that, ma'am. Hauptmann's orders."

I had no plan, no words left to me, no notion what to do. I only stood there, between the captain and the prince, as if by standing there I might forestall all decision and action too, might hold time immovable, as if by keeping us in the present I might find a way back to the place—the peace— where we had been before. "We were *this* close!" I said, and raised my fingers a micron's breadth apart. *"This* close, Bassander! And you threw it all away!"

"I told you to stand aside," the Mandari captain said. "Stand aside, or by Earth, the official record will say you died fighting." He thumbed some control on the side of his weapon, and it glowed more brightly. I didn't blink. I was shielded. He knew that. I knew that. I could take a disruptor bolt dead on, could shield the prince.

The prince.

A roar went up behind me and a sound like the howling of cold winds. Cold hands seized me, lifted me into the air. Valka screamed, "Hadrian!" Claws bit into my side, the back of my neck. I felt blood well up there, and felt sure that the press of fangs would follow. I had forgotten my sword, forgotten all my years of training and struggle.

Bassander hadn't.

The phase disruptor spat lightning, and I heard the prince groan. Numbed by conducted energy, I fell to the bruised grass, and Valka ran to me.

"Are you all right?"

The Cielcin are not like us, and the prince had not fallen, only released me in dumb shock. It leaped back, drawing from its belt a coil of black rope—or so it seemed. Snarling, the prince cast it at Bassander, and it flew at the young captain like one of the winged serpents, the ornithons so common on Emesh. I knew what it was at once, though I did not know its name. It was one of the Cielcin *nahute*, a toothed serpent of steel whose fangs—like the bit of some awful drill—would chew through a man like a parasite and kill him from within. It flew so fast that it rebounded off Bassander's shield, distracting the captain as he fumbled for his sword.

The other Cielcin soldiers were streaming up the hill, hurling serpents of their own, howling like the coming of Death on her pale horse.

"Are you all right?" Valka asked, hand on my face, my wounded neck.

I gripped her wrist. "We have to go." With a grunt and her helping me, I found my feet. "Knight-Tribune! We have to go!"

A shadow swallowed the light, and turning I saw Aranata Otiolo standing above me, white sword in hand. "You killed my people!" it screamed, and swung. My own blade leaped to my hand, highmatter sprouting, shining like the moon between my fingers. Exotic material met alien ceramic, and ceramic broke. Aranata's sword fell useless in two pieces. I might have ended it there, might have struck down the demon prince and spared the worst of what followed.

If I'd but had the nerve.

If the wreckage of my dream did not burn around me as my enemy's world burned above.

The Cielcin troops were nearly on us, and pushing Valka by the shoulder I made to retreat down the hill.

That was when the lights went out. The ship's lights. The *Demiurge*'s lights. Men screamed, more alarmed than anything, and the sound of the

Cielcin cheering as their darkness rose was like the breaking of ice against the rock face of my soul. An awful thought seized me, and a hope—though in my mind I saw us all hunted like rats in the black labyrinth of that evil ship. I heard Brethren's words come echoing back to me: **Protect the children.**

The children. "Varro!" I cried out, casting about by the nuclear firelight of the ship above. "Varro, bring the girl! Where's Ren? The boy! Sagara's boy!"

"Here!" Jinan called out, and I saw her holding little Ren in her arms, hurrying down the hill toward the advance of our troops rising to meet the Cielcin.

"We need him and the girl! Where's Smythe?" I shouted. I'd lost her in the chaos. "Where's Crossflane?" I ground my teeth, casting about for the lost officers. Without them, Bassander Lin would be left in sole command, and I trusted the snake only so far as I could throw him. In any case, Bassander had vanished as well, gone down the hill or up it pursued by Aranata's drone.

Valka shook her head. "I'm not sure!"

"Noyn jitat!" I swore, falling back on that old Jaddian chestnut. I cast about, looking for any sign. The pavilion still stood flapping in the breeze beneath creaking bows, even in the semi-darkness and the blood light of the broken worldship and the occasional flash of annihilation. "I'm going back to find them and Tor Varro! Go with Jinan!" If she protested I didn't hear, for I turned back at once and pounded up the hill, sword in hand. "Smythe!" I called. "Varro! Crossflane!"

"Here!"

It was Tor Varro. The Chalcenterite had not heard me calling before, nor stirred from his patient's side. Suzuha still spasmed in her unconsciousness, thrashing against the tree roots like a woman possessed. "I'm not sure what's wrong with her," the scholiast said. "She screamed and collapsed right after the attack."

"Her brother, too—did you see?" I didn't wait for an answer. "Can you carry her? We haven't much time!"

"Marlowe!"

Something heavy and solid struck me in the flank. I groaned, bent double, and turned round, swearing, struggling to keep myself between Varro and whatever it was that had attacked me.

The tattoo-faced herald, Oalicomn, stood behind me, clutching its staff in pale fingers. It said something in its language I did not quite understand, turning its weapon over in its hands as though it were a lance. "It is as I said," it said. *"Tukanyi yukajjimn susulatari." Susulatari. Monsters.*

Devils.

Devils indeed.

Furious, embarrassed, and afraid, I drew myself up to my full height. "Run, scholiast!"

"But—"

"Take her and go!" I said, taking my sword in both hands. Varro rose, and from the corner of my eye the green shape of him seemed almost Gibson at my side.

He put his hand on my shoulder, and whatever he said was lost to me, for it was Gibson's voice I heard instead. *Always forward,* he said. *Always down.*

"And never left or right," I murmured.

Time as well stopped a moment and lingered at my shoulder, and with eyes unclouded I saw another shape standing just beside the tall and white-robed herald. It was as if some unseen hand pointed to it.

Nobuta.

The Aeta's child cowered, small and useless for its kind, young and nearly alone, behind the figure of its servant. They must have remained behind the pavilion, seeing that most of we humans had fled. Where was Aranata? Gone after Bassander, perhaps? After Smythe and Crossflane—wherever they had gone? Or perhaps it had gone to lead its men in assaulting the humans. I knew not.

Oalicomn barked a challenge, ducked its horns. "You will pay for this betrayal!" it bellowed.

I said nothing.

It lunged.

The cutting edge of a highmatter sword is fine as carbon monofilament. It can cut nearly anything. Flesh. Bone. Metal. Stone. Only adamant—the stuff of which starship hulls are made—and highmatter itself are immune. Whatever alien alloy the herald's staff was spun of was no object. I parried the herald's blow with ease, and its weighted head spun away and bounced off the council table behind me. I did not hesitate, but stepped in, raising my sword. The herald never learned what happened. It never understood.

I cut.

It fell in two pieces.

Blood. Black blood soaked white robes and blue. I expected young

Nobuta to scream. It only cowered and slunk away. I expected it to cry out. It only shivered. For a moment, we were alone in all the chaos—the devil and the demon prince—somehow forgotten. Varro had carried Suzuha away, and beyond the edge of the pavilion the battle was joined in full. I went to one knee before the child, Nobuta, and shut off my sword. The blade melted away like smoke, and I extended my empty hand. *"Tukayu jelcu,"* I said, unknowingly echoing the words of the angels out of mankind's most ancient memory. *Don't be afraid.* It tried to crawl away, to push itself away with its hands.

I seized it by the wrist. "Nobuta, it's not safe here. You must come with me now."

"Yelnuri ne?" it repeated. "With you?"

"I'll keep you safe," I said, not then knowing it was a lie. "When the fighting is done, I will return you to your father." To this day, I do not know if I meant to take the child as a hostage or to keep it safe—or what the difference was between those two things. "Please," I said. It twitched its head *no* and tried to pull away. I did not tighten my grip. I did not want to frighten it. "Listen," I said. *"Ubba!* I brought Tanaran back to you, didn't I?" And where was Tanaran? "I brought it back unhurt! Tanaran trusts me. You trust Tanaran, don't you?" When the child didn't answer, I shook its arm to shake loose its thoughts. "Don't you?" Nobuta's eyes—like the eyes of a frightened horse—would focus on nothing. They rolled blackly in its head. In the distance, I heard a man screaming, and knew that one of the Cielcin serpents had chewed its way through armor and into flesh. *"Imemneuyu o-Tanaran ne?"* I asked. *Don't you trust Tanaran?*

Pale fingers tightened on my wrist. "You killed Oalicomn!"

"It attacked me," I said, and banking on my fragmentary understanding of Cielcin culture added, "and it was only a servant. I need to protect you."

"Why?"

"Because if I can return you to your father I might be able to stop us all fighting," I said. I did not say that the Cielcin were doomed anyhow, did not explain that the xenobites had no home and nothing to return to, that they were trapped on this ship with nowhere to run and nothing to do but revenge. I was scrambling blindly for chess pieces, for control of as much of the board as I could manage.

Just beyond the pavilion, a Cielcin threw itself on two Imperial legionnaires, ceramic blade cutting into one man at the base of the neck before it threw itself bodily at the other. Behind them, I saw the shine and violet declaration of plasma fire from our lances cutting into the Cielcin horde, and I heard Sir William Crossflane's voice—amplified by speakers in his armor—ring out. "Back to the gate! Everyone back to the gate!"

"Come one!" I urged Nobuta. "It isn't safe here." I pulled it to its feet, pushed it roughly ahead. Following it—keeping one hand firmly against the small of its back—I marched us from the pavilion. If I could just get it back to the soldiers, they would be able to hold it. I wouldn't be responsible for it for long.

I nearly tripped over something in the dark, and before I looked I knew it was a body. Looking down, I saw the shape of the slave girl lying face down in the grass. She'd tried to run. There was a red hole in her neck, and in the firelit gloom I cannot say if it was the shot of one of our weapons or the drill-wound from one of theirs that had killed her. But I saw the mutilated ruin of her hands and feet, and the glitter of silver on her and the shimmer of her pale scars. Negotiations were over. Perhaps they ought never to have begun. I only tarried there a moment, but the image of those broken hands has never left me—though much else more important has in time. I felt a black fury well up in me, and my stomach turn.

I pushed on down the hill, pushing Nobuta on ahead of me.

We hurried past knots of soldiers fighting. Our legionnaires stood back-to-back in knots of three—their triases—and battled the encircling Pale. I did not stop to aid them, for to draw my sword would be to frighten Nobuta, and I needed the creature quiescent, compliant until I could hand it over to our soldiers.

"Where's my father?" Nobuta asked, stumbling a little on the uneven ground ahead of me.

"I don't know," I told it. "But we'll find her."

"Marlowe!" a harsh voice snapped, tone amplified by her suit. A fully armored trooper in white and bearing the marks of a lieutenant on her visor called out. In my panic and mad scramble, a name was a moment coming.

"Greenlaw!" It was Bassander Lin's iron-jawed lieutenant. "Where's Smythe? Where's Lin?"

She shook her head, pointed back over the meadow to the line of trees that served to mask the perimeter wall. "Gone on toward the gate. What's this?" She jerked her head at Nobuta.

"And did Varro and Jinan—and Lieutenant Azhar? Are they clear?"

"Clear out, them and the witch!" she said. *Valka*. Earth and Emperor, I'd been so focused on the task at hand that I'd forgotten Valka for a moment. I resolved never to mention it to her or anyone there on the spot, and so buried my shame. "What's this?"

"Prince Aranata's son!" I said, and hurried on, leaving the lieutenant and her men to hold the way behind me.

The way ahead was clear, and I half-pushed, half-dragged Nobuta in turns across it, resisting the urge to duck the plasma fire that whizzed past us. Twice I had to put myself between the child and the charge of one or more of our soldiers.

At last we made the treeline. The slumped forms of Sagara's SOM army lay all around, useless and quiescent without their master's will to animate them. I wondered if they had died, if without Kharn's consciousness to drive them they had all forgotten to breathe. I thought not; the light still shone blood-gold and greenly through their faces, though their arms were all a tangle. Nobuta cowered as we came in among them, and I shared its fear, recalling in that moment the awful fight with The Painted Man in that cafe on Rustam. Ahead I saw the judder and shake of spotlights, and knew the machine-men lived again. But it was only the suit lights of two triases of Imperial soldiers, and one other.

"There he is!" Valka exclaimed.

She'd come back for me.

In my surprise, all I could manage to say was, "I thought I told you to go!"

"And leave you here?" she demanded, and for a moment I thought she'd strike me. Only then did she mark my companion, and her golden eyes widened in the dark. "How did this happen?"

"Not now!" I said, thinking of the dead Oalicomn. "We need to get it secure! Back to the *Schiavona*, then maybe we'll be able to get Aranata to calm down."

Valka's face darkened. "A hostage?" The disapproval in her tone was palpable.

"Yes!" I insisted. "Yes, a hostage. Valka, there are more than five hundred Cielcin screamers on this ship. We need whatever help we can get!" I moved past her, gesturing to the soldiers to advance. Turning to Nobuta, I said, "These men are going to help take you to our ship, all right?" Nobuta didn't answer, it was already shying away. I wondered how old it was, how mature. "Do you understand?"

The soldiers' hands rendered the question moot the instant after, for they seized Nobuta by the arms. It flailed, and one of the group triasters—a tall man with his visor painted half red—raised his lance to strike the Pale. I caught the man by the wrist. "Don't hurt it! Go!"

"What about you, sir?" The man's voice came out muffled by his suit.

"Where's Smythe?"

CHAPTER 68

THE NARROW WAY

WE FOUND THEM IN the shadow of the gate leading from the Garden back to the *Schiavona*, Smythe and Crossflane and Bassander Lin holding the line.

"There you are!" Smythe called out as the soldiers shuffled past with Nobuta. "Where have you been?"

An explosion rang out behind me, and I heard men yell and the cracking of timbers as a tree fell toward us. The Cielcin had brought something heavier than explosives. I thrust Valka ahead of me, ducking on reflex. "Is everyone out?" I asked, ignoring the tribune's question.

"Except for Greenlaw and the rear guard," Crossflane answered.

"Jinan?" I asked. "Tor Varro and the children?"

"The children?" Bassander echoed, confused.

Valka interjected, "Ren and Suzuha." When Captain Lin did not show any signs of deeper understanding, she added, "Sagara's children."

Blank faces met mine, and for a moment all there was was firelight on the black walls and the noise of battle behind. One legionnaire spoke up from the shadow of a column patterned in human faces. "Aye, m'lord. I saw the scholiast head on with that girl on his back. She were putting up a mean fight."

"She was awake?" I asked, lurching toward the small man—the boy.

"No, m'lord," he said, "she were having some sort of fit, like. Didn't see the Jaddian, though." That was something. I cannot say how I was certain, only that I had an . . . an intuition. I kept seeing the implant glowing behind Kharn's ear when I approached his throne, kept remembering the way his spirit had moved behind Naia's eyes.

He wasn't dead, I knew it.

"What is it?" Valka asked.

I shook myself. There wasn't time for introspection. "It's nothing, I—"

A sound went up like the hissing of a nest of vipers, and I turned. We all turned.

They were there among the trees, tall shapes pale and terrible as Death herself, dressed in black and deepest blue, horn-crowned and staring. They were much too tall to be men, and much too thin. Only then did I realize the depth of the quiet that had fallen, with no sound but the slow-catch of flames in the wind-tossed branches. For a moment, Bassander's eyes found mine, and both of us knew that Greenlaw and the rear guard were dead.

Valka's fingers tightened on my upper arm, and in her native Nordei she whispered, "'Tis time to go." I did not need telling.

Of Prince Aranata there was no sign, but one Cielcin—whom I had not seen before, a surprisingly broad-shouldered one in a deep blue cloak—raised its hand and shouted a single word: *"Uiddaa!"*

Throw.

There must have been a couple hundred of them standing among the trees, and each of them hurled one of the fanged *nahute*. I could hear the hum of them on the air, hurtling toward us like a volley of arrows in the woods of Agincourt twenty thousand years before.

"Retreat!" Smythe's word went up like the voice of God, amplified by her suit to a superhuman scream. She drew her sword—highmatter gleaming in the darkness—and waved everyone on. "Back to the *Schiavona*! Go! Go!" Behind me, the remaining mass of our people—perhaps a hundred and fifty or so legionnaires—began to move. To the untrained eye, it must have seemed a rout, but I saw the way the troop triases held together, men moving shoulder to shoulder, lances on their backs, plasma burners low and ready.

I was one of the last to leave the shadow of the gate, one of the last to turn as a single line of hoplites—shielded and with phase disruptors raised—closed ranks beneath the carved archway. Many of the *nahute* drones—confused by body heat, I guessed—turned aside, burrowing into the SOMs who lay comatose all about. That was a mercy, I decided. Still more hurried on, some shot down by the hoplites' disruptor fire, electrical discharge frying the drones' delicate circuits.

"Marlowe!" someone yelled. Was it Crossflane?

And yet I found I could not look away as the first wave of drones crashed into the armored hoplites. My sword was in my hand.

"*Uiddaa!*" the Cielcin commander shouted again, the word a kind of curse. A second wave of *nahute* came hissing to life.

"Hadrian!" someone yelled. Valka?

Never have I forgotten the bravery of those men, those hoplites standing in the mouth of the Garden gate. The way they dug in, squaring their shoulders even as the Cielcin advanced, loping like wolves out of the fire-lit darkness.

Like leopards.

Like lions.

Would that I had known each of them and all their names, for they deserved a monument and commemoration here. The boy who had addressed me was one of them, who had told me Tor Varro and Suzuha yet lived. He died there, him and his fellows. He gave his life to cover our escape, and I cannot even record his name for you and for posterity. The greater part of war, I think, is such forgotten acts of heroism. You sing your songs of Hadrian Halfmortal, of the Phoenix of Perfugium, of other heroes, but I tell you we are nothing, *nothing* next to those ordinary men who lay down their lives—who are not ordinary at all.

Because, you see, I was wrong. Wrong when I told Sir Olorin and Bassander that wars aren't won with soldiers, on Emesh long ago. That, I think, was the start of Bassander's dislike for me, and rightly so. To say such a thing was to dishonor men and moments such at this: when two dozen hoplites turned without argument, without complaint, and died.

Rough hands seized me, and I was dragged back, pushed and spurred on. It wasn't Valka at all. She was far ahead, had turned with Smythe and Crossflane and the soldiers dragging Nobuta.

It was Bassander.

"Move, you nobile fool!" the soldier barked.

I moved, the two of us hurrying along the hall, more or less the last in line. Behind, the humming sound of the *nahute* droned above the din of battle behind. The sounds of feet and scuffle. Shouting. Screams. I ran faster, sword silent in my hands, shield on and invisible around me. Black pillars sped past, and the grotesque motifs of human faces and limbs sculpted into the walls. In the dark, it was almost as though I had returned to the tunnels of Calagah, save that here there shone the dying-ember glow of emergency lighting.

Feet on the path behind. Feet and the echoes of harsh laughter, cold and high and thin.

Ahead, Smythe shouted an order, and men turned back. Triases—entire decades—turned back and took up positions in the shadow of the pillared hall, waiting in ambush. We turned, running—or so I thought—along the length of that baroque nightmare of a ship. Here the hall opened up so that ten men might walk abreast, the ceiling above supported by black arches and the statues of naked women blacker still. Thence it ran through several gates and open bulkheads toward the hangar where the *Schiavona* waited.

But could we even escape? Was it possible to fly out with the *Demiurge* in its current state? Without Kharn Sagara?

Our group fanned out, filling the wider hall. I hurried forward, breath aching in my chest.

More sounds of gunfire came from behind with the violet flash of plasma. Cielcin howled, and I felt sure Smythe's men had done some damage.

"Faster!" Sir William called out. "Faster, you dogs!"

Despite these encouraging words, I saw that we were slowing down. We had caught up to the front of our party, to Jinan—still carrying the unconscious Ren in her arms—and to Tor Varro with Suzuha strung between himself and a tall decurion. Nobuta had begun to struggle, and despite its youth its great size meant that now four men struggled to restrain it.

And then the cry went up. Not the blood-cry of the Cielcin coming fast behind, nor the scream of dying men. No, this came from ahead. A cry of dread and cold despair. I saw it then, a moment later, and nearly stopped my run.

The door was shut.

Perhaps it was in response to the battle outside, some emergency protocol. Perhaps it was because Kharn was dead. The why did not matter then, only that one of the hall's emergency bulkheads was shut.

"Out of my way! Out of my way!" Raine Smythe said, sword still raised imperious above her head. Bone-colored soldiers parted, turning dutifully back to face down the hall in expectation of the coming tide. I did not turn with them, but watched as Smythe plunged her sword through the heavy metal of the door. It made no sound, nor fume nor vapor was there as blue metal carved gray like paper. I turned, hearing once more the sound of loping feet, and felt sure at any second I would see the Cielcin resolve out of the darkness, fang and horn and claw, and with them a churning cloud of their *nahute*.

"Push!" Smythe shouted, gesturing her men forward. A dozen of them threw their shoulders against the bulkhead. "Heave!"

Nothing happened.

Nothing moved.

"Push, damn you!" Smythe yelled, but it was no good. Perhaps the door was too heavy to move, or perhaps it was thicker than Smythe's sword could cut through. I never learned. Somewhere in the confusion, someone found the side door, a narrow passage leading deeper into the bowels of that evil ship.

We'd had no choice. Better lost in the *Demiurge* than stand there— backs against the wall—to fight and die. One-to-one, the Cielcin were more than a match for a Sollan legionnaire. Their lowliest screamer out- sized and outmassed ours and possessed the idiot strength of the damned. For they had been raised out in the black between the stars, their bodies strengthened by elixirs, decoctions made to arrest the slow atrophy of muscle tissue in the absence of gravity. I have since seen *scahari* lift a man bodily in one hand, tear the arms from a man's sockets, and crush his skull with their fingers. Against a tide of them in a hall, backs against the wall? Armed as we were, with the *nahute* bearing down faster than any of us could track . . . I could see the blood already, the bodies at my feet.

"Go! Go! Go!" one of the centurions was shouting, shepherding Tor Varro with a now-unconscious and unmoving Suzuha through the gap. "Knight-Tribune!"

Smythe waved him on. "Take the hostages and go. Lin, take the lead!" For a moment, I thought Bassander would argue, but he nodded and hur- ried on. "You too, Marlowe!"

"But I can help!"

"You can help by getting that prince of yours to safety so we can ne- gotiate from safety, now stop your arguing and go!"

"But—"

"This is not a committee, boy!" She shoved me.

I went.

Dark the halls of that trackless ship and orderless. The shapes of men and demons, angels and furies snarled from the walls, clung to pillars and to the rails of galleries we stumbled upon. Only the white beams of suit lamps lighted our way, jounced and swaying with the passage of our bodies, so that the world around was seen only through half a hundred juddering keyholes. Worse, none of us knew where it was we were going. Halls spiraled off to either side, rolling with the axis of gravity. Stairs ran at odd angles, descending toward the ceiling and rising down halls to either side, and twice I saw the end of our column running along the ceiling above. Valka ran beside me, and every dozen steps I heard her swear. "Damn," she said. "Do we know . . . where we're going?" She was tired. We were all tired. And she was right: we were lost.

"This way!" Bassander called out, blind leading blind. Were it not for the artwork and the mad geometries, we might have been lost in the halls of Kharn's palace on Vorgossos. I saw Bassander duck through a pointed arch, momentarily silhouetted against the snarling shape of a gargoyle, his hand grasping one of its arms.

Stalled a moment by the crush of people trying to follow him, I gripped Valka by the arm. "Can you . . . can't you do something? With the ship? The lights?" She looked at me, a little wide-eyed, breast heaving. "With Kharn gone?" I could see Smythe's sword shining in the darkness behind, and knew the rear of the column had come.

"Maybe," the doctor replied. "I tried the door. Didn't want to say. Didn't work."

Another scream rang out, and turning I expected to see Smythe and the men about her overwhelmed. But there was nothing, only the white beams of suit lights surrounding the blue line of her glowing sword. Nothing.

"Back!" Bassander Lin's voice rang out. "Back!"

They were coming at us in two directions. I felt fear like iron fingers close upon me, and I shut my eyes. *Forward.* I heard the words again, *Always forward.* Between the fear and the exhaustion I could hardly breathe, could hardly think for pounding in my skull.

Fear is death to reason, I told myself.

Reason.

"This way!" I called, pushing past a pair of legionnaires. Bassander had tried to take a turning, but the path we'd been on ran straight—along what I guessed was the length of the *Demiurge*, though it was impossible to say. I couldn't be sure, but from outside the ship had seemed larger even than the *Enigma of Hours* had been, and that Sojourner might have swallowed the city of my birth a dozen times.

I pressed straight ahead, pulling Valka in my wake. There was Jinan! And Crossflane just behind, leading the men struggling with Nobuta. Where was Tor Varro?

"What about Lin?" Valka asked.

I checked my advance, letting the soldiers around me surge past. She was right. Teeth grinding, I turned back. "Go on!"

Her face darkened. "Oh no, not again." Only then did I see that her plasma burner was in her hand, its light reflected in her burning eyes. "Don't you dare."

I did not dare to argue with her, and turning to follow Bassander—dared less.

Bassander.

The man who'd burned it all. The man who'd sold my dream of peace—and Smythe's—for the promise of fire. That zealot, that miser-minded templar of a man. Him with an abacus where his heart should be, whose scales of justice tilted always *guilty*. Given my will, I might have taken *both* his hands this time. I could have torn his arms out myself.

But I went, ducking through that side door past retreating men.

Perhaps it was Fate, or perhaps it was only that I had obeyed Valka, moved by her judgment of me. Without seeing, I sensed the darkness above me stretched for meters, for miles, maybe.

Violet plasma spat in the air, illuminating the bloody scene like a thunderbolt. Almost I tripped over a broken body—whether human or xenobite I cannot say. Smoke curled, lending the din and darkness a dimension darker still. A shot flew past me, close enough that I could smell the bitter stink of ozone. I cursed my lack of a suit, for without one I had only my meager terminal light to guide me.

And that of my sword.

Highmatter leaped in my hand like a fountain, casting an azure glow in the darkness.

Pale faces leaped out at me, hissing.

One leaped at me, a white sword in its hands like the one Aranata had tried to use and failed. The piece of me that did not think—that did not have to think—took over. Old Sir Felix's training and hundreds of hours in Colosso moved in me, and I parried the blow with ease, without regard for the fearful strength and size of the beast opposite me. White ceramic struck the wall behind. I drew the blade across its torso, cleaving cloak and armor and flesh as easily as tissue paper.

Something slammed against my shield, and I jumped, knowing already that one of the *nahute* snakes had struck at me. I turned, parried wildly, and found nothing but air. The dread machines were programmed to attack again, to batter an opponent until they found a weakness and entered in. It would return and return until it found a way past the Royse field.

I never saw it coming.

I only saw the flash of violet plasma as the shot reduced the drone to a shred of glowing scrap metal. Behind me, Valka made a small, officious sound. She did not rest upon her laurels, but fired again and caught one Cielcin in the chest. It did not touch my mind at the time, but now I wonder at her—at the marvel of her. She who had so abhorred violence in my hearing, loudly and often, fought then with a conviction every part the equal of my own. This was the Valka I had seen in the Garden, who had stood with me against the Exalted Calvert. Even as I write this—so many centuries later—I am not so sure I knew her, or ever fully understood.

"Back, everyone!" I yelled. "Back! Back!" I ran forward, waving my sword for attention, heedless of my danger behind my shield. Where was Bassander? The ground rattled beneath me, and I drew up a moment, body frozen as my mind tried desperately to process this new sensory data. We had stumbled onto some sort of catwalk where the baroque and horrible majesty of the *Demiurge* was lost. The rails were simple steel, and the floor beneath our heels.

Plasma burners flashed behind me, splitting the dark like a wedge that closed with a thunderclap. Violet light splashed upward, revealing a tableau of forms not unlike the hideous friezes that paneled the walls of the *Demiurge*'s interminable halls. Men and Cielcin locked in combat, weapons raised, arms outstretched, white swords and the bladed ends of energy lances tangled.

And more.

There were giants in the night.

I saw then that we stood above the floor of some massive hold, cousin to the central void of the *Enigma of Hours*. Far from finding the exterior holds and the *Schiavona*, we had found the ship's heart—and it was not empty. Black shapes hung in blackness, horrors without name. The machine shape of them stuck in my mind like splinters, hanging from the *Demiurge*'s massive skeleton like the fruit of some horrid vine. Like Kharn's clone children in their gestation pods. I beheld them for only an instant, but I knew them at once, knew I stood upon the lowest level of the terrible armory. Fortress. Furnace. Font of Kharn's power.

The Mericanii weapons.

The full scope of their terror and power I could only guess, not knowing then the nature of those dreadful titans or the dumb minds that moved them to their master's whim.

I know now.

Suzuha's words resounded in me. *Weapons even Father does not understand.* Seventy-two of the dreadful machines were there. Some smaller than the *Mistral*, some large as mountains. The dreadful Leviathans and Behemoths which dwarfed even the colossal war machines of the Imperium. Alien minds had built them, creatures strange and stranger than the dark Brethren of Vorgossos, beings whose intelligence exceeded man's, perceiving creation with senses beyond my meager comprehension. They had their names, though I was ignorant of them. *Kenotikon. Bleteira. Crymainecca.*

The *Astrophage.*

The *Astrophage* chief of all.

"Bassander!" I called out, those terrible engines forgotten as one of the *nahute* caromed past my head. "Pull back! Back to the hall!"

The captain stood further out along the catwalk, his men about him, sword in hand. Beyond him, I could see the shapes of more Cielcin coming on like a tide of the damned.

"They must have come from their ship," Valka said, close behind me. "They must have called for reinforcements."

"Bassander! Come back!" I shouted.

As I watched, the Mandari captain drew his sword across two of the Cielcin warriors, their bodies crumpling over the rails. I heard the xenobite commander call for greater care, ordering its men to stay back.

"*Nahute!*" its cold voice rang out. "*Uiddaa! Uiddaa!*"

Valka fired past me into the dark, hoping to catch one of the creatures on the far side.

"Bassander!"

The captain seemed to hear at last, and for an instant I saw the whites of his eyes by the purple glow of plasma fire. I heard him shout an order, and his men retreated, pulling back along the catwalk to where we stood. His men came thundering back along the bridge, metal rattling beneath the tumult of their passage. Last of all came Bassander Lin himself, the Pale hard on his heels. Valka fired, and those men who'd made it back our way with her. Violet flame took two of the advancing Pale, and they fell The quiet hiss of flying snakes turned to screaming, and I watched three of our men tumble screaming over the rail into the bottomless night. The shape of their convulsions as they fell and the noise of their screams has never left me.

Bassander moved past us, clapping a hand on my shoulder as he passed. He said nothing—there was no time for words. I took a step out, a step toward the approaching enemy. I could see the blue light of my sword reflected in their eyes, off their glassy teeth like the fangs of deep-sea fish. I raised that sword like an executioner and—like an executioner—swung.

The catwalk buckled, and I leaped back to the safety of the edge.

The Cielcin were not so lucky. The single spar bent, buckled like a tree branch burdened by the first ice of winter. Snapped. Bassander sliced one of the *nahute* clean in two. "Where's Smythe?"

"Gone on ahead," I said. "Back down the hall."

"We need to hurry!" Valka said. "'Twill be another way for them to cross."

At last we burst through a door onto familiar ground. Blue candle flames burned to either side, and the high seat upon which Kharn had first greeted us was empty. "The ship's not far!" Sir William said. "Is that everyone?" He looked around. There were perhaps a hundred of us left. A hundred and twenty? We'd lost perhaps a score when Bassander took his wrong turn into the great hold.

"I think we're on the right side of that door," Jinan added, shrugging Ren's weight in her arms.

"It's a straight shot back to the bay, ma'am," said one of the centurions, an especially broad man with a voice like breaking stones. "A couple of those odd turnings, but no side passages."

Raine Smythe hurried toward the open doors at the far end of the hall, brushing past the centurion with a gesture. "Very good, Mozgus. You and Crossflane with me." The centurion saluted and fell in as the tribune gestured at a group of the others. "You lot, see if you can't secure these doors. They won't hold long, but we're out of time. Lin, Marlowe, take the hostages and hurry on, straight to the ship now. Quickly!"

"Abassa-do!" Nobuta was crying then, struggling against its captors. "Father!" There were other words after, choked and strangled. Its captors struggled to hold it as it squirmed. Young the creature may have been, but the beast was strong. It flailed, one arm breaking free to club the legionnaire that had restrained it. The man grunted, kicked Nobuta in the ribs while the others held it.

"Stop!" I shouted, too late.

The man had drawn his stunner and fired before I could get to him. Some eccentricity in the xenobite's nervous system kept it from passing out, but it went limp as a boned fish, allowing its four captors to hoist it to their shoulders like pallbearers carrying a dead man. A motley crew we made: Tor Varro with Suzuha slung upon his back, Jinan cradling Ren, the soldiers with their alien cargo, and Bassander and I leading the column. The soldiers followed on: Smythe and Crossflane and the big centurion, Mozgus, bringing up the rear. The hall ahead bent sharply down with the axis of gravity, but I'd grown used to such distortions in the time since we arrived, and didn't break stride.

A long *boom* sounded far behind, and I knew the ceremonial doors to Kharn's hall had been blown apart and that the men left to hold them were dead. I saw them in my mind's eye: Prince Aranata stepping over the broken corpses of our soldiers, coming like black Death herself with her army behind her.

There! The hangar doors were open, and I could see the golden glow of the safety lamps to either side of the *Schiavona*'s ramp. The guards hurried forward. "Captain Lin! Lord Marlowe! What's going on? We've been trying to raise you on comms since the ship went dark, but nothing's gotten through!"

"No time!" Bassander bellowed, for what could he say? That he had betrayed Knight-Tribune Smythe? That even now Titus Hauptmann led the fleet against the Cielcin in the black beyond? He gave orders instead: "Take the children to the medica and throw the Pale in the brig! And one of you run to the bridge and tell Commander Sciarra to raise the shields! The Pale are right behind us!" He turned back, as if he made to rejoin the fight.

"Where in Earth's name do you think you're going?" Smythe bellowed as Mozgus and Crossflane strung a cordon in the narrow hangar door. "Lin, get your ass on the *Schiavona* and *sit* on it."

He shook his head. "I can help, ma'am."

"You've helped enough!" she spat. "Go!"

The door from the hall was narrow, a round portal set within the open mouth of a giant, sculpted face, wide enough only that three men might walk abreast. "Take the hostages on board!" Smythe said to me. "Lin's right. We need to buy time until the ship's defenses are online."

I nodded, watching as the centurion and his hoplites formed ranks to reinforce the gate. Why had Bassander killed Sagara? I wanted to scream.

I knew the answer, of course. With Kharn alive, he might have deployed the power of the *Demiurge* against Hauptmann and the fleet, but here we were stuck aboard a dead ship, unable to so much as seal a bulkhead door. "What about you?" I asked.

She was already halfway back to her men. "We'll hold the door, go!"

Boom!

Bodies flew like gravel. Metal and bits of stone. The lips of the statue about the doorway crumbled away. I saw Mozgus—what was left of him—spatter the roof of that graven mouth, turned to pulp within his armor.

"William!" I heard Smythe cry, and I made to follow her.

How she heard my feet in the aftermath of that concussion I'll never know, but Raine Smythe whirled, sword pointed straight at me from ten paces away. "Get your ass on board my ship, Lord Marlowe!"

I staggered. Turned, took three steps back toward the ramp.

That short distance saved my life.

Boom!

Another explosion rocked the hangar, and I was lifted bodily from the floor, thrown by the shock and heat of it to tumble sprawling at the foot of the ramp. I smelled burning wool, and threw my coat off of me before I scrabbled to recover my sword. Hands seized me, and looking round I saw Valka—what was Valka doing here?—and a faceless legionnaire pulling me up the ramp. I looked back, looked to the shattered remnant of our force by the door, looked *for* Sir William Crossflane.

For Dame Raine Smythe.

There was nothing and no one but flames.

CHAPTER 69

DIVIDE AND CONQUER

"SMYTHE'S DEAD," I SAID to Bassander's unasked question when the *Schiavona*'s ramp had closed. "Crossflane, too—and that centurion."

"How many did we save?" Valka asked, looking round at the shattered remnant of the escort force that had marched to the Garden and our meeting mere hours before.

Tor Varro swept his eyes over the collection, subitizing, taking in everyone with the ease with which you or I might count a handful of dropped coins. "Seventy-three, not counting these." He indicated Ren, Suzuha, and Nobuta, who lay on the black floor at his feet. "Someone needs to get them to medica. I don't know what's wrong with them."

I managed to stand, leaning heavily on Valka, glad of her support. "There's nothing wrong." Everyone looked at me. "They started like this the minute you killed Kharn Sagara." I directed my words to Bassander Lin, who sat cradling his head on a supply crate against one wall. "I'd wager this is exactly what's meant to happen."

Valka—who alone of all those assembled knew as much about Vorgossos as me—paled. "You don't mean . . . ?"

"Kharn's survived so long as he has by possessing the bodies of his children."

"Surely that would require some procedure?" Tor Varro asked.

"Not necessarily," Valka interjected. "It could be done remotely. I've no idea what sort of implants either Sagara or the children might have."

"And you'd know, witch," Bassander said, glowering.

Pushing past Varro and Jinan, I pointed a finger in the captain's face. "Back off, Lin! None of this would be happening if you hadn't interfered." It was all I could do not to seize him by the lapels, by the throat, to throttle him with my own two hands. "We're here because of you! All those men are dead because of you! Smythe is dead because of you!" I was shouting by the end, stooped so that I was hardly two feet from his face where he sat recovering.

The Mandari captain did not rise to my provocation. He did not rise at all. At that precise moment five soldiers dressed in the darker-than-black of Legion officers stormed into the hall followed by perhaps three decades of ship's security. Bassander's dead eyes slipped sideways to regard these newcomers. "Lieutenant Cartier, are we able to leave?"

Lieutenant Cartier, a tall, pale woman with golden hair cut in precise bangs across her low forehead—very like Lieutenant Greenlaw—answered at once. "No sir, there's no emergency override on the hangar doors and we can't disengage from the service umbilical either. Their system's dead." Only then did the lieutenant realize the awful facts of our situation. "Where's the knight-tribune?" No one spoke. Outside, the sounds of scuffling as the Cielcin did Earth-only-knew what to the hull. "And Sir William?"

The captain shook his head.

"Dead?" Lieutenant Cartier's voice broke.

"Along with the prime and second-string centurions and about eighty men," Bassander said. To his credit, he was steady as new clockwork. "How long will the shields hold?"

"We'll run out of fuel first," Cartier said, "unless they've brought something heavier than small arms. We're safe enough. Hull's an inch and a half of solid adamant. They'd need heavy artillery."

"They'll find a way in," Jinan said. "They always do."

The ship rocked, dull thunder sounding from below. I could hear the sound of muffled shouting from without. Harsh voices, sharp as windows breaking. An empty space encircled Bassander Lin, as though the silence within his chest leaked outward. "We've three hundred left aboard the ship?" he asked.

"Plus the ship crew," Cartier said.

Jinan stepped forward, looking a little the worse for wear. There was blood on her cheek, but whether it was her blood or the blood of some fellow I couldn't say. I felt certain I looked as bad, but tried not to dwell upon it as she said, "It would be suicide to go charging down the ramp again. We'd be moving right into their line of fire. Even shielded we'd be mowed down."

"What about ship's weapons?"

Cartier shook her head. "Nothing we could use without risking the ship."

"The *Mistral*!" I exclaimed. "Can we get word to the *Mistral*? The Red Company! Captain Corvo has three hundred soldiers—and they're not far. With the Cielcin focused on us we might be able to catch them unawares!"

The lieutenant could only shake her head again. "No, no we can't. Our internal comms are still working but we can't get a message out. We tried raising the *Obdurate* the moment the lights went out, but . . ." The ship rocked again. I had a sudden, vivid image of the Cielcin prowling about beneath us, hurling their small explosives while some of them went off in search of cutting equipment. I realized then how little I knew of war, how little of the enemy. Their tactics, their capabilities. Could they cut their way inside? For all the talk of our ship's adamant hull, even adamant can be shattered with enough force. I didn't know, and knew again the sensation of swimming atop deep waters, ignorant of their depth and certain that at any moment some dread leviathan would emerge from the deeps to swallow me whole.

Valka rounded on Lieutenant Cartier. "You said the service umbilical was still attached?" I recalled the open hatch in the *Schiavona*'s highest level, the ladder rising up into shadow. I'd not climbed that way myself, but I knew it ascended to the maintenance catwalks that ran along the top of the *Schiavona*. We might escape through there, back into the endless, fractal corridors of the *Demiurge* with their mad turns and impossible directions. At length, the lieutenant nodded, and Valka looked round at me. "We should go. Someone has to."

I opened my mouth to speak, surprised but not upset to be so volunteered. I was about to volunteer myself, and smiled at her, even through that tense and dreadful moment. I had known there was steel in her, knew also that she had served a time in her homeworld's Orbital Guard. She'd had her pains, but they'd not bent her. She returned my smile, and I loved her then and said, "A couple of us might get by unnoticed. If we can get the Red Company, we'll outnumber the Pale."

"We can trap them between us," Tor Varro said, seeing what I intended, "take them unawares."

"Precisely!" I said. "They're already out of fugue and ready. Smythe—" My words stumbled over the name, and I heard the awful crash of the explosion that had felled her, had hurled me bodily across the hall. The stench of blood and burning wool filled my nose again, and I shuddered, pushing the memory aside. Smythe had *planned* for this, I realized. Exactly for this, to trap the Cielcin between the *Schiavona*'s men and the *Mistral*'s.

That was why she'd ordered the retreat from the Garden the instant Hauptmann's fleet engaged the enemy. That was why she'd stressed to me that Corvo should keep her mercenaries at the ready. Had she known the Empire was going to make its move? Was that why she'd sold so many thousand human serfs to Kharn Sagara? As bait? Had she and Hauptmann cooked all this up between them? A plot to catch and kill a prince of the Cielcin?

I didn't know.

"Smythe ordered the Red Company out of fugue and ready," I said at last, forcing the words out, eyes tight shut.

"No."

That lonely word fell like the White Sword, and silence with it. Eyes tight shut, I knew who had said it, and without opening them I turned to face Bassander Lin. Fists tightened, too, would have tightened on his neck—his treasonous, patriotic neck—but for the warning in my heart and the knowledge that dozens of soldiers would have peeled me off of him and pummeled me for my trouble.

As blade for blade, I met him word for word. "Why?" Only then did I open my eyes, sure that I would find his on me, and the line of fire drawn between us.

I was wrong.

Bassander Lin stood, eyes downcast, shoulders hunched. The brass pipes and the black walls and ceiling of the hold seemed to retreat from him as fast as stars red-shift behind a ship at warp, so that he seemed a solitary figure carved on a hill of his own making. A solitary monument. What must he have felt, then? He who had caused the death of his mistress? Of his men? Of peace itself? Flickering, a solitary spark of pity caught in me for the Mandari captain. It caught against my will and better judgment.

Presently he spoke, taking in a long and rattling breath. "With Smythe gone and . . . Crossflane, I am the ranking officer on board this ship. I am in charge here, Lord Marlowe."

The flame died, the pity with it. I opened my mouth to speak, but the words would not come past the sudden numbness in my chest, that pause in feeling that is the retreat of the tide before fury's wave.

Into that pause, Bassander spoke. "So I'll go."

The wave died, too. "What?"

"It's my responsibility," he said. "Lieutenant Cartier, inform Commander Sciarra that he will retain control of the *Schiavona*. I'll take a dozen men out the service umbilical and make for the *Mistral*. Tell him he is to hold here until I return." No sooner had he said this than he began shrugging out of his coat.

I stepped forward, reaching out a hand to take Bassander by the shoulder. "You're the ranking officer now, Lin. You can't go—"

"I *am* the ranking officer, Marlowe," Lin's voice snapped like a broken harp string, "so *shut* your mouth." He spoke with such force that I stood stunned. Not long, just long enough to allow Bassander to vault onto the stacked supply crates so that he stood up above the heads of the eighty or so men and women in the hold. He raised his hands for silence—not noticing or caring that, but for the noise of the Cielcin outside, silence had already come. "We're pinned down here!" he said, planting one booted foot on the next crate up. "I'm going to the *Mistral* for reinforcements. I need volunteers." The silence stayed unbroken. Bassander pointed to the ramp. "There are four hundred Cielcin outside that door and they *are* coming in." His eyes surveyed the crowd, but for all the force in his voice the light of the ceiling lamps might have fallen on spheres of glass for all the good it did Bassander. His seemed the eyes of a dead fish surveying us. "There are three hundred Norman mercenaries sealed on that ship by Smythe's orders. I mean to bring them back here and catch the Cielcin unawares. It's bloody work and dangerous with those beasts out there, and I don't want anyone going who doesn't have the stomach for it."

To my relief, Valka did not step forward to offer herself.

"We'll do it!" said a triaster with his helmet off, moon face shining in the stark light. He clapped his partners on the shoulders. "Won't we, lads?" His subordinates were still suited, and what they might have felt I could only guess. Slowly, painfully slowly, four others moved to join Captain Lin, standing in his shadow where he stood upon the crates. It was perhaps the least inspiring speech I had ever witnessed, and so I was hardly surprised when it did not attract a torrent of supporters, but at last a decade and more stood by Captain Lin, leaning on lances or adjusting suit seals beneath their red tabards. Apparently satisfied, Bassander leaped down.

"I'll go, too!" Jinan said, stepping forward, striped blue and orange silks fluttering over chrome armor.

Lin half-turned. "Very good. Everyone with me. Greenlaw, my kit." He paused, as if expecting a reply. A snapped *Yes, sir* and a salute.

None came.

I felt the memory—or was it the realization?—slide into Lin's mind like a poison. It was as if the air around him grew darker. Lieutenant Greenlaw was dead, lost in the Garden. He hadn't known, or else he had buried it in the chaos of the chase. The way he stood there has never left me. His posture did not change: no folding or bending. His only movement was to close his mouth. But he collapsed all the same, collapsed in a way no man could really see but which all men understand. Collapsed inward. Slowly, he nodded to himself. "Everybody follow me."

"Captain!" I said, unable to stop myself. "What should I do?"

He did not stop his swift exit, but waved a hand. "Talk to them. It's the only thing you're good for."

CHAPTER 70

PLAY THE ORATOR

"WHAT ARE WE GOING to do?" asked one of the helmed and visored soldiers, as if to no one. "We can't just sit here while they try and blow their way on board." A murmur of voices welled up to greet this question, as if they stood behind it, sheltered by and supporting its sentiment. Bassander had not answered it, as if he meant for us to endure the siege without a response, without action.

And Bassander was gone.

A muffled shout came up through the sealed ramp, and the ship rocked again. From the remoteness of the shouting, I imagined the Cielcin standing back, all afraid to come too near the ship, for fear that we might fire upon them, perhaps, or because they thought that we—like Ulysses and his brave Achaeans—might spill forth with fire and sword.

In the uneasy, thunder-rocked calm of that moment, my eyes went to the captives. Ren and Suzuha both lay limp now, not yet escorted to the medica as Bassander had ordered. They might have been asleep, were it not for the awkward way their limbs lay tangled and their eyelids fluttered. I crouched beside Tor Varro where he knelt at their side. "Any change?"

He shook his head. "They're both alive, but I don't know what's been done to them. They could be brain-dead for all I know. There's no telling how their implants work." Here he rolled Suzuha's head gently to one side, revealing a cap of bright metal—roughly triangular in shape, with the corners rounded and smooth—set on the spur of bone behind her ear. A blue indicator light blinked there, flickering very fast. "Maybe whatever's been done to them isn't complete."

"I wish we could have brought the golem," I said. "It would know what to do."

"'Twould be surprising," Valka said, appearing at my side, "if there were anything we needed to do for them at all." She placed a hand on my shoulder, her shadow falling across the prone forms of the children. I took her hand on reflex. Her fingers were very cold in mine. "You saw the way Sagara kept them close? Like insurance?"

The same blue light flickered behind Ren's ear. "What's taking so long?"

"Remote synaptic kinesis," Valka said.

The scholiast squinted one-eyed up at her. "Nonsense."

Valka only shrugged. "Have you a better theory, counselor?"

"Transferring the mind *remotely*?" He touched a hand to his mouth. "By radio? Tight beam?"

Valka extricated her hand from mine and went to one knee beside me to get a better look at the implant node behind Suzuha's ear. "Quantum telegraph. Radio would have an effective range."

"Why aren't they awake?" I asked, an astonishingly illiterate question.

The doctor's fingers traced the contours of the girl's implants, lips parted. When she spoke, it was perfunctory, as if she'd barely heard me. "I don't know what the architecture of these implants is like, but I'm sure the mind needs time to install itself in the new hardware. To compile. My guess? Sagara transfers his consciousness from his old body to the implants in the new, that he runs off the machine core and grows into the new brain tissue. There might even be personality differences that emerge as a consequence of the new bodies." She bit her lip, eyes alight with an unholy delight. "Fascinating."

"Differences?" I asked.

"Well, take this one," she said, speaking of Suzuha as though she were a sample on a slide. "Different sex. Different hormone culture. That would change Sagara's thinking—I bet he does this on purpose, grows different bodies, I mean. For the novelty."

I couldn't help but remember the flesh market on March Station, the way memories and personality were sold like cloves and onions: bodies resculpted, sex and intelligence alterable at low and competitive prices. All that freedom, all that chaos. How could anyone not but drown?

The only thing Theseus could not replace was Theseus himself.

Well, Kharn Sagara was not Theseus, and had done even that.

Whatever awoke in Ren and Suzuha would call itself Kharn Sagara, but would no more be the silent king whom Bassander had murdered than I am my children. Rather a different creature would walk away from this, bearing his name, his memories, perhaps the core and kernel of his personality, but they would grow differently, and when they in turn were old and machine-riddled, sitting on their thrones at the end of their lives . . . they would have diverged further from where they were, lost in the currents of their own bloated humanity.

Valka was still speaking. "He must have had a backup implanted somewhere in his body, a parallel transmitter mirroring his brain in real time . . . Bassander's shot would have fried anything in his head . . ."

"But why two?" Varro asked. "Why both of them?"

"Double his chances of getting out alive?" I suggested. "Or maybe something went wrong when Bassander stunned the boy?"

The scholiast opened his mouth to reply, but at that precise moment our *third* prisoner began to stir, as if prompted by some unseen *choregus* from off-stage. "*Eka . . . ?*" Nobuta asked. "*Eka ti-perem gi ne?*"

"You're on our ship," I said, folding my legs under me so that I could sit properly and make myself as non-threatening as I could. Switching back to Galstani, I said to Varro, "We really ought to get these two to medica." The scholiast agreed and began calling for a medtech.

Nobuta was trying to form words. "*Aba . . . Abassa . . .*"

"*Rakayu abassa ba-okarin ti-saem gi,*" I said, leaning in. *Your father isn't here.* Or was it mother? I didn't know anymore. Someone had bound the Cielcin child wrist and ankle. That upset me, but I understood the wisdom there. Young as it was, the Cielcin juvenile was larger than any of us. I massaged my eyes with the heel of my hand. Around us, Lieutenant Cartier and Tor Varro worked to get Ren and Suzuha carried out, and those soldiers who had not left with Bassander Lin milled about, listless, listening to the sound of thunder through the ship's hull.

"What are you going to do with me?" Nobuta asked.

A comforting smile tried and failed to come to my face. I felt sure I looked only pained. I didn't have an answer, only vague, half-formed ghosts. Another blast rocked the ship, and as if from a great distance I heard the lieutenant say into her terminal, "Commander, we should get the third and fourth centuries down here. I don't like the sound of whatever it is they're doing out there."

When she'd finished speaking, I scrambled to my feet, leaving Valka and Nobuta on the floor, and hurried to follow her. "Lieutenant, are internal comms still working?"

"Comms are still online period, my lord. It's only that we can't get a signal through whatever this big ship's made of."

"So do we have a way to communicate with the outside?"

"Well. No." Cartier blinked—the expression of a plebeian trying to find a politic way to tell a palatine she thought he was being stupid. "As I say, my lord, we can't communicate with the *Mistral* or the fleet."

Smiling a razor's smile—knowing exactly the mocking thoughts running through her head—I said, "I hear you. I mean, can we communicate *outside?*" I made a gesture with my hands like I was holding a small box between them. "With the Pale?"

"Oh!" The lieutenant brightened. "There's the public address system."

The projection booth was large enough for myself, Valka, and the two legionnaires holding Nobuta between them. I remember all of it. Every detail. The round walls padded with black foam, the bright recording instruments gleaming in the ceiling, the projection equipment in the wall sketching its own image of outside in an arc before us. The way the air smelled close and much-used. The oppressive quiet. The way every made sound fell away at once, vanishing forever from the world. And the dark, the dark most of all. So dark that our Cielcin captive could stop its squinting.

So dark that when the holograph image of the outside appeared it seemed solid as any material thing, as if the hangar outside the *Schiavona* had been brought inside. The illusion, I remember, was almost total, so much that my mind deceived me, and brought in the heat of flames and the smell of men burning. That my mind needed no help in conjuring that smell sickens me to this day.

"*Raka Aeta Aranata ti-perem gi ne?*" I demanded, stepping alone into the painted circle that marked the target area for the holograph pick-up. The Cielcin all jumped, and I suppressed a thrill at their surprise, knowing I must have appeared from nowhere like a bolt of lightning, words rebounding like thunder in the echoing vastness of the hall without. *Where is Prince Aranata?*

The xenobites ceased their milling about and drew back far enough to have a clear image of me. Some stood with swords drawn beneath, still others fingered *nahute* at their belts and snarled while yet more gathered the bodies of our slain and dragged them back toward the blasted sculpture of the hangar door. I asked again, "Where is Aranata?" and was greeted by a chorus of hissing.

Snakes in the Garden, I thought, though this had only begun in the Garden—that it would end there, too, I had as yet no idea.

"Here, *yukajji*!" And there he was. She was. It was. Prince Aranata Otiolo emerged from the parting ranks of its soldiery. Darker. Taller. Mightier
and more terrible than the rest it stood, crowned with horn and silver, and
the way its men folded back and shied away was like the bending of light
about the greatest stars. *"Belnna uvattaya ba-kousun ti-koarin!" Give me back
my child.*

"Give me back our dead!" I countered.

"Abassa-do!" Nobuta cried out from behind me, words caught up by
the booth's microphones.

"Nobuta!" Aranata took a half-step forward, as if it might leap through
the holograph it saw outside and save its young. I felt pity tug in me, recognizing this sign of parenthood for what it was: one of those precious
few things our two species shared. Red-Handed Evolution had crafted us
both to the same purpose: to survive. To be fruitful and multiply. And
whatever our differences in behavior, in feeling, morality, or cause, we
were the same in this, both K-selection creatures dedicated to their children. Because we must be.

"It's unharmed," I said. "One of our men stunned it while you were
chasing us through the *Demiurge*, but no other damage has been done—
which is more than you can say of Raine Smythe."

Behind the figure of Aranata Otiolo, I saw the smaller form of Tanaran
appear, dressed in its customary wraparound of dark green and black, almost as though it were some fiendish mockery of the scholiasts who stand
at the shoulders of great lords. "Show Nobuta to me!" the Aeta demanded,
claws flexing from its fingertips like so many black-enameled nails.

"In a moment," I said, trying to hold my calm, to remind myself that
the image before me was only an image, that the xenobite chieftain could
not tear me limb from limb as it so clearly longed to do. "First things first:
have you taken any of our people alive?" Aranata didn't answer. If it had
taken no prisoners, there would be reason to deny it, so I said, "You did.
How many?"

"Sim lumare," it said. *Not many.*

"More than six?" I asked. "More than twelve?" In a human being I
might have hoped to catch a facial tic, some minute tremor or shiver in
the eyes. Some small self-betrayal. There was nothing clear in those alien
eyes, no light that men might read by. "I want them back, Aeta. I want
them all back. We still have other hostages. Tanaran's companions. If you
want them and your child, you will return everyone you've taken *and* the
bodies of our dead. Then you will take your screamers and *go*." I pointed

for emphasis, the other hand going involuntarily to my sword. My thoughts ran at once to Bassander, to Jinan, and their little band. Had they made it to the *Mistral* yet? Had they been found and captured?

"Show me my child!" Aranata said, not debating.

"I'll show you yours if you show me mine," I said.

The Aeta did not move. Neither did I, unless it was to finger the pommel of my sword at my right hip, eyes narrowed to slits. The prince was used to getting her way, used to the authority and the power of her station atop the predatory hierarchy of her kind. The Cielcin knew nothing of reciprocity, of responsibility, of competence—only of power and the dominion of force, like an idiot's mockery or a child's copy of man. How they had climbed their fumbling way up from the mud of their birth I cannot say. Perhaps they were right, and the Quiet aided them. Perhaps they were lucky, or perhaps it was only that instinct for subordination and obedience ran in them as strongly as the impulse to dominate. Perhaps they lacked free will, or like the pagan emperors of old believed free will the province only of those great ones—like Alexander—they named gods on Earth. Who now can say? There are so few of them left.

So few who survived me.

Many times I have wrestled with ideas I cannot understand. Each of us does, for even the brightest scholar has limits on his competency. I saw a version of that struggle playing on the Aeta's inhuman face. It could not understand that I refused it, so used was it to command. I have seen similar struggles writ in the faces of autocrats—in a certain prince, most notably—but there always was it tempered by frustration, with annoyance that we the underlings would not know our place. Here there was only blindness and deep confusion.

But I had not stuttered, not blurred my words, and at last the Aeta blinked, nictitating membranes and lids flicking closed and open again in sequence. "Bring them here, Tanaran."

The baetan lowered its head, hands out before it. "At once, my master."

It was not long before it returned, leading a line of its kind and their prisoners—perhaps a dozen, perhaps so many as twenty. Their number has blurred with time, obscured by the moment that followed, for bringing up the rear, battered and bleeding from his head, was Sir William Crossflane, and there—on a bier beside him, whether dead or only unconscious I cannot say—was the charred form of Raine Smythe.

I stopped myself from crying out, fingers tightening on the hilt of my sword, as if I meant to draw it and leap forward through the holograph to save them as though I were some Maeskolos or hero of legend and not a foolish boy gone so, so far beyond his depth.

"Your masters, I believe," Aranata said, stressing the term *beletarin*, *masters*. I wondered if it believed that I was under some compulsion cousin to that which Tanaran had felt to do whatever was necessary to return to its master. To serve them. Perhaps I should have been, or perhaps it was providence that Bassander had gone and they were left with me. "Now, show me my son."

With a gesture to the legionnaires holding the young Cielcin, they advanced, holding Nobuta between them by its bound wrists. One—more vindictive than the other or perhaps driven by the sight of his captured tribune and her first officer—shoved Nobuta to the ground at my feet. I heard an angry rush of air escape the Aeta, saw Tanaran take a half-step as if to help its young lord back to its feet. I knelt instead, and speaking in my softest tones said, "On your feet, Nobuta, there's a good lad. Your *abassa* is watching. Be brave." It didn't respond, and I looked up—not at the holograph of the Aeta and its people standing above our kneeling prisoners, but at Valka. I'd felt the press of her eyes on me, different than the press of any other eyes: the cold concern, the discomfort, the disgust for the situation moved so very close to fear. For me? For all of us? Or because of something she feared I might do?

I wonder now if Valka were not touched by some form of prescience— a witch in truth as well as accusation—for the fear I saw in those eyes and remember there seem in memory more appropriate a response to what came after than had happened before. But I smiled at her, not knowing my own future and so unafraid, and helped Nobuta regain its feet.

"*Raka ti-saem gi!*" I said. *Here it is.*

"Nobuta!" Aranata advanced, looking for all the world as if it might leap out of the projection into the suite in front of us, hands outstretched. "Are you all right? Have they hurt you?"

The younger Cielcin did not move, only hunched its shoulders. "*Veih,*" it said. *No.*

Prince Aranata's black eyes narrowed. "Marlowe, if you've hurt my child, I swear by all my ancestors I will use you as a replacement for that slave you cost me."

I fancied I could hear the slow crunch of ice in my veins, as though boots trod the surface of some frozen lake within me. Another voice was lifted up, rougher and more strained. "Marlowe?" She had only caught the first word of what Aranata had said. "Marlowe, is that you?"

It was Smythe. I could see her lift her burned face from the bier. Sir William turned, shuffling on his knees to her side. His Cielcin guards made to stop him, but Tanaran permitted it with a gesture.

"Yes!" I said, voice breaking. "It's a relief to hear your voice, ma'am." My own voice choked, strangled by shame. I had not gone to check on her after the blast. I could have saved her. I could have brought her back with me. She was alive, by Earth! And I had abandoned her.

Nobuta yelped as my fingernails bit into its arm, and Aranata hissed. "What are you doing?"

I released the Cielcin, and it shied away from me, shrinking down so that almost I was taller than it was. "Marlowe, if that's you," Smythe said, and I felt sure that she hadn't properly heard me. I saw Sir William lean in to whisper something to her, and her words grew more insistent. "Marlowe! Don't give in! Listen!" One of her guards kicked the stretcher on which she lay such that she tumbled into Sir William's arms. The older first officer moved to restore her to her place, whispering softly.

I looked round to the others, but the soldiers' faces were all hid by their helmet masks, and Valka only shook her head.

Eager to remind me of her presence, the Prince Aranata Otiolo raised her voice. "Return Nobuta to me and your masters will yet live!"

My eyes ran up and down the line of prisoners arrayed before me. "That's everyone?" I asked. A mere dozen, maybe two—of the more than a hundred we had lost on the long chase from Kharn's Garden to the *Schiavona*. At least Bassander was not among them. I risked a glance at my terminal, knowing that of all the Cielcin perhaps only Tanaran would understand the gesture or the purpose of the device. It had been a little less than half one standard hour since Bassander and Jinan had left through the service umbilical. Surely they had made it to the *Mistral* by now, surely Captain Corvo was mustering her troops and preparing to return with what little of the Red Company remained.

I don't need to negotiate, I told myself. *I only need to play for time.* But how much time?

"You expected more to survive us?" the prince boasted, and beat its chest. "Your kind build cleverly, *yukajji-do,* but you are small and break easily."

I pushed this jibe aside, recalling the ease with which I'd killed Oalicomn. "If you want your child, you will withdraw your men to your ship and leave only enough to guard your prisoners. I can come down and meet you."

"And leave me defenseless with your army near at hand? Never!" the prince barked.

"We must have assurances that the violence is at an end," I said. "If I returned to the Garden, what promise could you give to me and my people of safe conduct?"

The Prince of the Itani Otiolo bared its fangs like shards of ice. "It is not my people who broke their word, Lord Marlowe. It is you, your kind, you who are faithless."

Damn Bassander to the Outer Dark, I thought, looking round. He had taken any hope of the moral high ground from me with his little act of martial piety. But of course he was only acting *on Hauptmann's orders.* On Hauptmann's orders? How many commanders in how many ages had claimed just such an excuse? How many criminal actions and actions of criminal stupidity had been glossed over by that sheen of mere and muscle-minded obedience? Sir Olorin's words came back to me out of the remotest past: *In Jadd we say a man must be either a swordsman or a poet.* I looked round at the soldiers, thought of Bassander, of Jinan, of Corvo and my friends: Pallino, Siran, Elara. Of Ghen, who was dead—and Switch, whom I could not forgive. My companions.

Swordsmen all.

How many of these others would have done precisely as Bassander had when ordered to do it? How many would have killed Kharn Sagara and crippled the *Demiurge* just as the strategos emerged from warp and set fire to the Cielcin fleet? Even Valka, who had become a sort of poet in this second life of hers . . . even she had fired upon the Prachar terrorists when she had been a ship's captain defending her native Edda. A swordsman herself, for all her bluster. They had ordered and she had obeyed.

"I am not Bassander Lin," I said, as much to myself as to the Aeta, for all the good it did. "But I will not open my ship or my people to attack for the sake of a few prisoners."

The Aeta snarled. "Not even your masters?"

Rather than argue and say that Smythe was not my master, I only shrugged. *"Mnado ni ti-tajarin'ta wo!"* Not even for them.

The prince snarled at me through the holograph, snatched something from its belt. Highmatter blue as starlight flared there, rippling in the beast's alien fist. A sword. Smythe's sword, I realized, recognizing the brass pommel—so like the head of her cane. The blade looked almost comical in the Cielcin's hand. By proportion too short to be a true sword and too narrow.

It didn't matter.

Prince Aranata turned and brought the sword down hard—harder than it needed—onto the shoulder of the nearest of our legionnaires. The man didn't even have time to cry out. Exotic matter cleaved through the segmented plate at his shoulder, through his shoulder, his sternum—came out the other side. His torso fell sideways, tumbling in two pieces to the deck at Aranata's feet.

Blood everywhere, the red of it so much worse than the black of the Cielcin. I could almost smell it, even through the holography booth. Behind me, Valka swore and Nobuta shivered where I held it close. Fangs glittering, Aranata Otiolo rounded on me, eyes narrowed to crescents. *"Yukajji! Belnna uvattaya ba-kousun ti-koarin!" Give me back my child.*

I shut my eyes for the space of a heartbeat. Two. Enough to marshal myself, my resolve. *Fear is death to reason,* I told myself, words tinged with Gibson's leathery timbre. *Rage is blindness.* In the space of my silence, Aranata had seized another soldier, a triaster, still helmeted and in full kit, held him by the crest of his helm as though it were a handlebar. The man strained, but for all his galvanically boosted muscles could not pry free the xenobite's hand.

"Give me back my child," Aranata repeated, and lifted the soldier bodily from the ground by his helmet as easily as a little girl might raise her doll by the hair. "Or I will kill every one of your people left to me."

My eyes drifted shut once more, and I felt another, colder voice speak through mine. "Do that," it said—I said, "and you'll find yourself with nothing to bargain with at all." I realized then that all the soldiers behind me had gone still as stone. Even Valka seemed not to breathe. "So spare the trouble. Order your soldiers back to your ship, and we will make the exchange. Our captives for yours. But if you so much as—"

Smythe's sword moved in a flat arc through the body of the hanging man, cutting him in half just above the waist. The prince continued to hold him for a moment, just long enough for his entrails to wetly spill from beneath his tabard and splatter with his fallen legs to the ground. I clenched my teeth, one hand squeezing Nobuta's arm so tight the creature yelped. Aranata, fangs bared in the xenobite's most vicious smile, tossed the torso back over his shoulder as easily as it were a cherry stone, making the other prisoners flinch and shy away. Three of its subordinates hurried forward, making as if to crouch by the dead man's side.

"Veih!" Aranata barked, whirling toward them. "No!" It snarled, recalling some memory I had almost forgotten. What was it?

The way a starving dog growled at its pack, defending its claim to food. I suppressed a shudder. "Stop this!" I said. "Stop this now!"

"Belnna uvattaya ba-kousun ti-koarin!" Aranata howled, repeating its refrain, and as it rounded once more to face my image projected outside the ship, I saw its jaw hinge forward, teeth angling forward, protruding past Aranata's lips like the fangs of some terrible sea monster. In spite of myself I recoiled, taking a half-step back and dragging Nobuta with me. I hadn't known the Cielcin could do that.

"I don't think you understand," I said, and once more I spoke in that cold, unfeeling voice. "You may have our soldiers, even our commander, but I have your *son*." I emphasized the word *uvattaya. Son.* "Make your threats, Aeta. Kill. It won't change that. I've given you my terms. Withdraw. Your. Men."

The Aeta gnashed its protruding fangs and turned, hand going for another soldier.

"Stop right there!" Sir William Crossflane said, scrambling to his feet. "Stop, I say!" He waved his arms, trying to draw the Cielcin chief's attentions to himself. He'd been slow to rise, to unfold himself from where he'd knelt by Smythe's bier. For a moment, the knight-tribune lifted her face, and I saw the bloody burns there, the burned-off hair, and the single white and sightless eye. I shivered. But for another thirty feet or so that might have been me.

Crossflane appeared so very small before the prince, despite his nobile standing. Aranata Otiolo stood almost half again as tall as the old man, who nevertheless staggered forward, saying, "I'll not stand by while you butcher my men in front of me." He thumped his chest with one fist—as though he meant to start a salute. "Take me instead."

I found my voice at once. "Sir William, I—"

Prince Aranata didn't hesitate, didn't pause to honor the knight's sacrifice. Nor did she raise her—his?—sword. Instead, the Cielcin seized Sir William by the hair, yanked his head back like an assassin, like a lover in the throes of some violent romance. I cried out, took two steps forward before I remembered that it was only a holograph I saw before me.

Too late.

The Aeta fastened its massive jaws about Sir William's throat. *Like a lover,* I thought again, perversely. *Like a vampire.* But it bit harder, and even in the hissing holograph I saw the blood well up about its fangs and the way Sir William's eyes bulged in their sockets—the way his hands beat on Aranata's arms and shoulders. Twitched. Went still. The prince tore its jaws away and the throat with it. The knight fell backward and—to the side, almost unseen—I saw Smythe's hand go out from the edge of her bier, straining toward the body of the man who had served her so faithfully and for so long.

Blood ran down Aranata's chin as the prince turned to regard me, startlingly red against that flesh like chalk, that snow-white hair. As it leered at me, the Aeta's teeth retracted, collapsing once more into a semblance of something like a flat, human face. And then, worst of all, it swallowed. Glass teeth dyed red. Black eyes shining beneath a crown of silver horns. It made a gesture with one hand, and three of its minions advanced, half-stooped already, and dragged Sir William's body—I tried not to think *his carcass*—away.

For a moment, all I saw was the thick and angry line of red smeared on the black floor.

Red and black.

My colors.

"Give me back my child, Marlowe!" Aranata said, and stood over the dying shape of Raine Smythe where she lay, nothing in those horrible dark eyes at all.

"Master!" Tanaran hurried forward, hurling itself to the ground. "Do not kill this one! The others are worthless to the *yukajjimn!*" It pressed its face to the tile beside the red stripe of Sir William's blood, hands clawing toward its master's ankles.

Aranata kicked at its servant's hands. *"Iagga, Tanaran-kih! Iagga!"*

I'd had enough. The quiet piece of me—the part with that cold and unflinching voice—moved forward, kicked Nobuta in the back of the knees. The prince's child fell, unbalanced by the way its hands were bound behind it. I caught it, steadied it by the thick braid that sprouted from the base of its skull.

"Hadrian, no!" Valka said, coming forward.

But the sword was already in my hand, its blade quiet and stowed. Still, I pressed the emitter against the xenobite child's breastbone at the base of its neck. Angled the way a Colosso myrmidon might make the killing blow. Aimed that it might descend past bone and sinew to pierce the heart and lung. "March your men back to your ship, Aranata," I said, abandoning title or pretense. "Now."

The Cielcin prince bared its teeth again. "You wouldn't dare."

"I would dare *all*."

"Marlowe wouldn't!" Tanaran said, coming to its knees, hands pawing at its master's robes. "He is weak, master. A coward. He would not allow the other *yukajjimn* to harm us on Tamnikano. He will not harm Nobuta. He does not have the spine for it."

The word *spine* made me stand up the straighter, and I ground the emitter's rain guard into Nobuta's shoulder. The child cried out, "*Abassa!* Please!" I tightened my grip on its braid, mindful that Valka stood mere microns from the edge of the projector's pickup, microns from where the Cielcin could see her.

Nobuta began to cry.

A coward, I thought, and the word echoed like a chorus in me, like Brethren's voice.

Coward
coward
coward.

Cowards and faint-hearted runaways look for orations when the foe is near, I thought, quoting that first Marlowe, that ancient poet whose name and devil sign my ancestors had taken for their own. Cowards negotiate when the fighting is thickest. They retreat into terror and call it principle. Once, I might have done the same, and clung until the bitter end, hoping for peace. The boy I'd been in Meidua, on Delos . . . he might have tried forever. So too the young man who had charmed Cat with stories above the canals in Borosevo. He might have tried.

But Raine Smythe's words—her last words—sounded in me again, clear as if she'd spoken in my ear. *Don't give in!*

I saw Smythe's ruined face again, lost in the clutter of the projection, her fire-blinded stare unseeing, its lens to glass. Dead then. Dead for true. I had no way to be sure, and yet knew it must be. How she'd survived the blast in the hangar to begin with I'd no idea.

She's dead, I thought, and knew that this time it was so. *Smythe's dead.*

I bared my teeth.

I made a choice.

The breath left Nobuta with a wet sound. Every muscle tensed, and blue light shone where the point of my sword sprouted from the creature's opposite side. I deactivated the weapon an instant later, moved as much by regret as by the recognition that what was done was done—as if by stowing the sword I might undo its striking.

Aranata screamed, a deep-throated, wordless bellow I heard through the hull of the ship as much as through the holograph pit's sound system.

A cry of anguish. Of pain that could be understood by man and xenobite alike.

Pain.

The idea that pain is evil is the basis for all morality. Ours. Theirs. Everything's.

But was I evil, then? Or had I only *done* evil?

No matter. I had done what needed doing. *Always forward, always down, and never left nor right.* I let Nobuta fall, let its face strike the floor of the holography booth. How long did I stand there, gathering the darkness of that chamber to myself like a cloak that I might cast over the body at my feet? I cannot say. I'd lost my coat in the hangar bay, lost it to the blast that killed Smythe. I had no shroud for Nobuta, nor words to say. No orations. No negotiation.

Aranata shouted something—words I cannot recall, did not understand. It pointed at the other prisoners, at Smythe's body. The Cielcin behind tore off their own masks and fell upon the prisoner, upon Smythe on her bier. Claws out, teeth extended.

Blood. And the sounds of feasting. One of the Cielcin seized Smythe's arm and straining tore it from its socket, raised it dripping above its head like a trophy, then pressed the morsel to its face and tore. The sound of it was a horror, and more than I could bear. Amid it all I saw Aranata turn on Tanaran, on its own kind, and cut it cleanly in two. I think I understand now: Tanaran had advised that I would not harm Nobuta. Tanaran had been wrong.

Valka swore behind me in her native tongue.

I switched the booth off, banishing Prince Aranata and its kind. And to myself—to no one—I said, "The Sword, our Orator!"

My family's words. I remembered my family's colors—the red blood smeared on the black floor. Later—when all was said and done—I would see it again, see the bodies of our dead and theirs mutilated all over that ship. Red and black. Black and red.

As it was for so many soldiers on so many battlefields from that black ship back to the first sunrise over Uruk at the dawn of time, as it was when Techelles spoke to Tamburlaine in that dead, first Marlowe's words, those words we took for our own when we took the name:

Our swords shall play the orators for us.

CHAPTER 71

HOPE IS A CLOUD

"IT'S ONLY A MATTER of time before they try and cut their way in with Smythe's sword," I said. Looking round at the others I said, "Ah . . . can they?"

"Cut their way in?" Lieutenant Cartier repeated. "With highmatter? Yes. Most of the ventral hull is ceramic, not adamant. It's lighter."

As we spoke, a team of medtechs busied themselves with Nobuta's corpse, wrapped in mirrored foil. I watched them go, vanishing down the brass hall. It was only then that I noticed my hands were shaking, and I balled them into fists. Valka saw, and there was something in her face then I didn't understand. Pity? Anger? Love? I ought to have given up trying to read her years before, so minute was her expression. One of the medtechs brushed past, and I tapped her on the shoulder. "Anything from the children? Kharn's children?"

The woman blinked at me with round, green eyes, brows contracted. "I . . . oh! No, my lord. They're stable, last I heard, but no change. They're in some sort of coma, but their heads are so full of praxis none of us can guess what the hell's going on."

"Keep them safe," I said, and I touched her shoulder again, more seriously this time, "and if they wake, let them know who it was saved them. Tell them it was *me*, not the Empire. That will make all the difference." She nodded and was gone, following her fellows up the hall.

I turned back to find that Lieutenant Cartier and her officers had moved off a ways down the hall and were speaking among themselves, leaving me—for the moment—alone. I swayed where I stood, struggling to stay upright. There was nothing left in me, no force, no pain, no time to cry. The walls of the *Schiavona* canted inward toward the top, such that the ceiling was narrower than the floor. Almost I felt those gleaming walls might fall and crush me like a wave. I raised a hand to shield my eyes, saw the blood on it. Choked. I tried to clean my hands, but succeeded in only smearing the ichor further.

"Hadrian! Are you all right?"

Not alone after all. Valka had been behind me, appeared as I'd pivoted toward the wall. Wordless, numb, I held my hands to her, shaking my head furiously. "No. I . . . I . . . it wasn't right. It wasn't right, Valka. I didn't. I didn't."

Wordless, she reached into her jacket and drew out a red kerchief, the sort she was always wiping her hands with at dig sites and at meals. It was already stained, soiled from use, frayed at the edges, like the woman herself. Like me. I took it graciously, wordlessly as she had offered it, and wiped Nobuta's blood from my hands. They still weren't clean enough, never would be clean enough. I balled the cloth up in one hand when Valka went to retrieve it. "Thank you," I said. It was all I could manage. "Thank you."

She pressed her forehead to mine. Even with my eyes shut, I felt those eyes on me, felt—I thought—as the ancient prophets must have felt beneath the eyes of their angry god. Small. So small. "Breathe," she said, "just breathe."

Had I not been breathing? I wasn't sure. I breathed then, long and slow, trying to force myself to calm. None of Gibson's aphorisms came to mind, not one. I wasn't even sure what feeling it was that haunted me, though I knew the name of the ghost. Nobuta Otiolo's voice still played in my ear. *Abassa, please.* I clamped down on the sob before it could escape me, and I brought Sir William's body back to my attention. Smythe's. I saw the Cielcin all hunched over the corpses, stooped like vampires, like ravening dogs, like a murder of ravens upon carrion.

Feasting.

My tears died.

Valka held me to her, fingers in my hair, not letting go. "You shouldn't have done it," she said, flatly, but her voice broke with the words. "'Twould have been better if Nobuta had lived. Now 'tis no hope of peace."

I wrapped my arms around her, holding her close as I could. "There's no peace. You were there, Valka. You saw." Smythe had been torn apart as if between four horses, the others cracked like lobsters in their shells. "You saw what happened."

She held me more tightly, her breath on my ear. She didn't speak again, and I've no idea how long we stood there, ignoring and ignored. Long enough to quiet the tremors in me, long enough to dry my eyes.

Long enough for the grinding to start.

It came from everywhere, the noise of it conducted through the hull and superstructure of the ship, through struts and walls and bulkheads as the vibration plays in the air beneath the skin of a drum.

"What the hell is that?" Valka asked, drawing away from me and look-ing round. The hall shook around us, the entire ship vibrating like a plucked string. "Are they trying to get inside?"

She and I both looked round at Lieutenant Cartier; the woman had gone as pale as we had, and twice as quiet. I put a hand to the wall of the ship, felt the tremor there reverberating through my fingers. "They're drilling." I don't know why, but I was put in mind at once of the fanged maws of the *nahute* and the way they chewed through flesh. "Come on!"

I'd not been to the *Schiavona*'s bridge but once before, most often re-pairing to Smythe's quarters, but I knew the way. I burst through the open arch into that broad, high-ceilinged place. The wall opposite was all a great curving window—the only true window on the entire ship—which looked back toward the door of the hangar, away from the carnage and the door back to the depths of Kharn's *Demiurge*. Yet the carnage was there, displayed in still holographs and video feeds, reflected in the heart of every man.

Like flames in clear glass.

Commander Ludovico Sciarra stood with his arms crossed behind his back, taking it all in. How small he seemed beneath those images of hor-ror, and how young when he turned, eyes wide as saucepans. Just how young was he, this upjumped palatine lordling? He had an almost Jaddian coloring, and wore his officer's blacks like a man attending a funeral—which in a sense he was.

"They're drilling," Sciarra said quietly. "All over. Drilling . . ." He laughed weakly. "I don't think they know where the ramp is." At the con-soles fanning out to left and right, the remainder of his bridge crew was silent.

"Can they get in, sir?" asked Lieutenant Cartier.

Sciarra shook his head, broke composure long enough to smooth his very short hair. "I don't know. Probably." Images flashed on the window from external cameras, and I saw I had been right to imagine the *nahute*. Hundreds of the little machines clung like limpets to the bottom of the ship, boring their way inside. They marched in little circles, wide enough the Cielcin could climb through, moving slowly, each pass grinding away the hull by inches. "That hull's four inches of titanium. No telling how long we have."

"At least they haven't brought plasma cutters," Valka said, darkly.

"Has there been any sign from Bassander Lin and the Red Company?" I asked, not sure I wanted to know the answer.

"None, Lord Marlowe," Sciarra replied. "The captain left at thirteen past seventeen hundred. That was forty-eight minutes ago." He indicated the blue shine of a countdown clock gleaming at the corner of the massive window display. "Comms are still down. There's something about this filthy big ship. We've tried quantum telegraph, too. No way to know if it's gotten through, or what things are like with the fleet out there."

"We have more immediate problems," Valka said. "Can you do anything to stop the drills?"

Sciarra's frown cut deep lines to either side of his face. "Not without compromising this ship worse than the drills have."

"Then we need to stop them before they get inside, Commander," I said, a shade too sharply. Despite my stint with the Red Company and my time in the Colosso, I was no soldier. Who was I to tell these men what to do? To lead? And yet I could not stop myself talking. You see, I had had the seed of an idea. An old idea, one that had worked so very well in the tunnels beneath Calagah. "You have spotlights on the ventral hull, yes? Big flood lamps?"

The man nodded. "For salvage and such, sure."

"It won't stop the drills, but it'll stop the Cielcin. Maybe not for long, but it will help us."

"Help us to what?" I pushed past the young commander and moved toward the window screen, pacing back and forth in front of the holographs where they glittered in the glass. Aranata had gone, withdrawn I knew not where. The rest of the Cielcin prowled beneath the hull looking up with eyes like the hollow pits of statues. Blood on their faces. Their hands.

Waiting.

Waiting.

"Lord Marlowe. Help us to what?" Sciarra repeated.

Valka hushed him, and I saw her raised hand reflected in the window. "Don't. Not when he's like this."

Forward.

"We have to attack them," I said, not turning. "We have to attack them before they get in here. Can you aim those lights down and toward the doors? There." I pointed to the place where the xenobites still gathered in the shadow of that shattered face sculpture.

Sciarra paused, then said, "I . . . yes. Yes, of course we can."

"I'm not sure how much time the light could buy us. I think some of the Pale have implanted lenses." I tapped my cheekbone with a finger, then brushed my hair roughly back. "We'll have to move quickly. How soon can you have two hundred men ready?"

The commander and lieutenant both exchanged glances. "We'll be torn apart. There are more than twice that many of the Pale out there."

"Vent the coolant on the warp drive's fuel containment," Valka said. All eyes turned to her, and for a moment no one spoke. The comment had come from nowhere, and so surprised us all.

So without context was it that even I turned back, staring at the woman. "What?"

"The antilithium we use to fuel the warp drive is kept in magnetic suspension, but those magnets have to be kept cool." She pivoted toward Sciarra. "What do you use? Standard helium reservoir?"

Taken aback, he nodded. A beat passed, and he said, "Forgive me, ma'am. Aren't you a . . . linguist?"

"She was a ship's captain in the Tavrosi home guard," I said.

Sciarra's and Cartier's eyebrows shot up at this piece of news, and Sciarra said, "I don't follow. Why would we do this?"

Valka's face took on that irritated cast I knew so well, lips curling, nose wrinkling with disdain. "The gas is *extremely* cold. When it hits the air, the water in it will freeze. You'll get snow. Vapor. A cloud."

A smoke screen.

I could have kissed her then and there.

"It might kill them, too," she said and crossed her arms, hugging herself, as if to console her for what she said. "The cold. Or the gas. 'Tis enough helium to flood the whole hangar bay." And more. The gas expanded rapidly as it warmed, one liter becoming hundreds as it lost density, displacing the breathable air. It wasn't toxic, but it wasn't anything the body could use.

"Kill them?" Sciarra brightened, composure slipped. "Without a fight?"

"Won't it drift toward the ceiling?" I said, thinking of the massive vaults above our parked ship. "Helium's lighter than air."

"'Tis why I said it might kill them," Valka said, "but the water vapor is heavier, particularly when 'tis cold . . . between that and the light, you'll have a distinct advantage."

That wild Marlowe grin stole over my face, lopsided and leering. "Can it be done?"

The armor they had found for me was an unfamiliar weight, and I chafed to wear it. It was the kit of an ordinary legionnaire, a spare taken out of mothballs in the ship's armory. In it I looked half a soldier indeed, the overlapping segments of the shoulder proceeding in Roman fashion down my right arm to the wrist, my left gauntleted, the black skin-suit under-layment hidden beneath my black tunic and high boots in lieu of the tra-ditional red tabard.

I felt half a fool mounting the crates as Bassander had done to speak to the soldiers amassed for the attack. Sciarra was holding his fifth century of troops as a rear guard with what remained of the first and second—those who had survived the long chase back from the Garden—leaving the third and fourth to comprise the force for my abortive defense of the ship. Two hundred men. Four hundred Cielcin.

Bassander, I thought, *Jinan, don't be long.*

For a split second, no one seemed to notice me standing there, looking down at them all. For a moment, it was only Valka standing beside Tor Varro at the rear of the broad, low hold, her red jacket and his green robes unique in a sea of white-armored faces. Bright eyes. How had I found myself standing there? Upon those stacked munitions? I was no soldier, not truly. No man-at-arms. I was a fighter, but that is not the same thing, and no true leader of men. My time as Commandant of the Red Com-pany had been a farce, a lie, a kind of masquerade, and what action I had seen was only that of necessity, of chance, and accident. But young Com-mander Sciarra had his ship to die on and, it seemed, no stomach for the fight. He was a technician, after all, a junior officer aboard a courier ship slated for a diplomatic mission. And Lin was gone for reinforcements, or gone beyond recall. I tried not to think too much that he was dead, and Jinan with him—tried not to think that help would never come.

Who must stand when those whose duty is standing have gone?

Those who can.

"Do you hear that?" I said, digging deep, drawing on every scrap of the speech and rhetorical training Gibson and my father had given me. I pointed the dead hilt of my sword at the sloped wall of the closed ramp. "That is Death, ladies and gentlemen! *Death* coming for us all! They've taken Smythe. Crossflane. Your friends and comrades. They are coming to take *you*, to take us all. We *must* not let them. We *must* stop them here. Now. Captain Lin has gone for reinforcements, but we cannot wait here to die any longer." I lowered my sword, my voice. I had not activated the speakers in my suit, relied instead upon the low ceiling and my own two lungs. So when I quieted, I felt the crowd lean in, the farthest straining then to hear me. "Mark my words: this is the end. But is it our end or theirs? I don't know. But I do know that this is our moment. Our moment to choose." I made a fist, and heard the words resounding in me as I spoke them aloud. "Not whether we live or die. No man chooses that. But we can choose to fight now. If we are to die, we will not do so cowering like children afraid of the night! We will not die trapped here like rats! We are men! We will fight the demons to the last! We will show them the sons and daughters of Earth are a power to fear! We will show them we are not afraid, and we will teach *them* fear before the end!"

To my blank amazement, a cheer went up, lances raised and fists, and my heart went up with them, buoyed on that wave. I dared to smile, and to hope. Hope. *Hope is a cloud,* that tiny voice said within me.

Was it not a cloud that was saving us? Valka's cloud?

My smile widened, and for a moment my smiling with the crowd's yell drowned the vision of Aranata tearing out Sir William's throat and the noise of bloody feasting. As the cheering faded—cheering such as had not come for Bassander Lin—one man, a common legionnaire by his dress, called out, "Who are you?"

"Only a man!" I said, not wishing to lord my birthright and name over him. It did not matter then. Nor there. "A man who bleeds red as you, and one who will not die this day!"

I have said before, only rarely does the universe match my capacity for melodrama. If there is a god of such occurrences, a lord of poets and fools, he was with me that day. For in that moment, the overhead lights thudded to black, if only for a moment. Warning lights slammed on, red as flame, as the eyes of my father's funeral bronze in my oldest dreams.

A clear, recorded voice—the voice of some beautiful woman—spoke over the *Schiavona*'s public address system. "*Fuel containment quench in progress. Emergency systems online. Fuel containment quench in progress.*" The soldiers all shuffled about, confused, muttering. They all knew what it meant, knew the kernel of antilithium in the ship's warp drive was now held in magnetic suspension by a series of battery-powered electromagnets and not the massive superconducting one that was the stable norm. It would hold for days, long enough to reconvene with the fleet and restore the containment system to its full function—if the *Demiurge* could not restore the thing itself. But still, the thought of so much antimatter so nearly unchained was a horror, as though we crouched within the shell of a million hydrogen bombs.

I tapped a switch on my suit's gauntlet terminal, then slammed the hard switch on my breastplate. The suit's helmet unpacked itself from my gorget, folding about my head like some eccentric puzzle box, shards linking, leaving together to form one coherent whole, seals whining as the suit's internal air supply and recycling systems came to life.

For a brief instant, all was dark. True Dark. The helmet had no visor, only a solid arc of ceramic where my face should be, blank white as all the others. I had no crest, no rank markings, nothing but sword and the black of my tunic to distinguish me from any odd legionnaire. Half a second later, the entoptic projectors within the helmet mask projected twin cones of light directly onto my eyes, and it was as if I wore no helmet at all, but saw again the crowd of identically masked faces staring up at me.

Voice amplified now by the speakers in my suit, I spoke over the repeated warning. "With me now! Not for Earth or Emperor, but for yourselves!"

A cry went up to shake the very ship about us, and for a moment the noise of those alien drills was drowned. I leaped down from the boxes, swept my sword out beside me, blade gleaming in the stark light of the hold. My shield shimmered about me as it thrummed to life, and turning I saw Valka watching me through the crowd, Varro beside her.

I raised my sword in salute.

The ramp opened, and a moment after . . . all there was, was light.

CHAPTER 72

THE PIT

MY FIRST IMPRESSION OF the world outside was only whiteness. White fog, white light, a cold so deep that even through the suit it drained all thought of color. The helium gas venting from the *Schiavona* rose quickly, lighter than the air around it. It expanded rapidly, rising as it warmed, forcing the air down and turning the water in it to a thick mist that fell upon us like grave fog.

The suit's entoptics compensated for the glare of the flood lamps, shifting from visible light to infrared. The white all turned to blue, and the Cielcin emerged from the cold, faint red flames flickering against all that cold. Fading. I nearly tripped over one lying dead on the ground as I led the charge. It had asphyxiated, choked on the airless air. Dwelling on that put me in mind of the suit around me, on the millimeter-thick membrane of advanced polymer that insulated me from the subarctic chill and the casement of ceramic, of metal and glass that prisoned my head and kept clear air pumping toward my lungs. A sensor pinged in my ear, and I turned back to see the swarming *nahute* disengaging from their work on the *Schiavona* to come for us. To take the path of least resistance.

With a wordless cry I turned for true, directing those behind to follow. Plasma flashed, the violet of it transformed to deepest crimson by my suit's entoptics, redder than blood. The evil little machines fell like locusts, like cicadas at the end of their brief summers, cut to ribbons against that wall of purple fire.

High above, great turbines started to whir. Dead the *Demiurge* might be without her master, but the emergency systems still functioned, great ventilation fans turning to pull the helium up and away. I turned back, no longer concerned for the swarming drones. There were larger problems, and nearer to hand.

Perhaps the Cielcin do not suffer cold as we, for those that still stood hurried forward—red shapes like flames bright against the frigid blue of the world. Many of them—those who were masked—seemed as unaffected by the gas as they were by the cold. These charged forward, swords drawn. The bulk of our lancers were tied up with the *nahute* swarming above and behind, and they cleared the floor between their line and ours, leaping over the bodies of their dead and ours, a terrible sound going up like the shrill crying of birds.

A blow went whistling over my head as I ducked, dragging my sword behind me such that it cleaved clean through the body of the xenobite that towered over me. Black blood froze in the air as it fell, tinkling to the ground like the fall of tiny hailstones. Glancing back over my shoulder, I saw line after line of legionnaires pouring out behind me, firing up into the cloud of metal snakes descending like an evil rain. One of the *nahute* shot at me like an arrow. I swung. It flew past me in two smoking pieces. In the cold, I saw the shimmer of a static field sealing the open mouth of the *Schiavona*, keeping the helium gas from entering, keeping Valka safe. In my suit's false color impression of the world, the mouth of the ship behind was fretted with golden fire, gleaming bright and smiling and warm.

I turned away, turned into the dense fog and sudden snow ahead. The legionnaire beside me fell screaming, clutching at his throat as one of the drones tore through his armor to drink the blood beneath.

I could do nothing. It was too late.

Swallowing my heart and feeling its pulse within like the beating of the drum, I marched forward, sword in hand, and the Pale moved to meet me, their language—so familiar to me—made strange by the urgency of their cries, words stretched into the shibboleths of devils. One threw itself at me, and I took its legs from it and, turning left, sliced through two more. Plasma arced past me, projected in great arcs that scorched and sliced at the enemy, Cielcin and *nahute* drones alike.

They say it was starflight that brought back the age of the sword. That after a thousand ships were lost to a stray bullet piercing the outer hull or a fuel line, the wise forged anew that weapon so beloved of knights and soldiers, of samurai and chevaliers from every walk and culture unto dawn. Some say it was the shield, that Caelan Royse's energy curtain *demanded* the return to traditional arms as a matter of pragmatic necessity. I know not. I am no military historian, but I think there is truth in both explanations. The Cielcin—who never developed the shield—seemed never to have developed the gun. Perhaps they, forever trapped within the

delicate environment of a starship, and before that trapped in the laby-
rinths below the skin of their homeworld, had never wanted to abandon
the blade.

Their ceramic blades were almost invisible in the cold fog, and more than
once I was saved only by the armor I wore, enemies barreling out of the
dense cold, the light of the heat of their bodies almost lost in the glare of
the *Schiavona's* spotlights. For every one of the Pale Valka's trick with the
helium had claimed, it seemed there were three whose masks had saved
them, and they fought with all the strength and the fury of their kind.

There came one mightier than the rest, its robes fluttering from its
shoulders like wings. I watched it charge past, its sword long as I was tall
and flashing in the bitter light. With a single stroke it felled three of our
men, a whole trias gone in one, comrades cut to ribbons, their blood mingled like their lives.

I had been a myrmidon, and knew much of violence. Because I had
played a mercenary, I believed I knew something of war as well. But what
we had done on Pharos to Admiral Whent, and what had come before
and since—even against the Cielcin on Emesh—could not prepare me for
that battlefield. I had believed that a true battle would be only like those
smaller conflicts I had known writ large, or less composed of many smaller
conflicts arranged alongside one another like the cells in a man's body.

It is not.

The phenomenon of war is a different universe. Things ordinary in the
light of the everyday sun are changed, taking on context and significance
such that it seemed that I—who had stood in that hangar half a hundred
times—had never stood there before. The ship behind us became more
important than the grandest city, and that we defended it a calling higher
than love and baser than lust. The monsters we faced became demons in
truth, and the men at our backs—however fiendish or uncouth they were
in their barracks and their cups—became no less than the very host of
heaven.

I saw a soldier turn and place himself right in the path of that great
Cielcin—a candle he seemed, with my altered vision—before a bonfire.
He raised his lance, the blade forward, haft held in the crook of his arm
while the men behind him worked to save the lives of two injured, to
drag them back to the ramp. To the rear guard. To safety. The Pale advanced, running like a wolf, and leaped as it came within striking distance. The soldier fired. Missed. Snapped the haft of his lance and elbow
forward, hoping to turn the beast aside. The Cielcin fell on him like a

wave, pale sword angled so the point entered in the soft place beneath the elbow. I fancied I could hear the fabric of his suit's environment layer sigh apart in the din, though that was impossible.

But his comrades escaped, and a moment later a dozen men trained lances on that Cielcin captain and turned its form to ashes, gray smoke mingling with the white mists.

Something struck me from the side, and I fell, sword slipping from my fingers, bouncing across the floor as its blade dissolved into the fog. Something huge and black-clad pressed itself down upon me, one arm thrown across my throat. I saw the red shape of a Cielcin mask peering at me from below, and through it eyes like pots of ink shining in the stark light. My suit's underlayment stiffened in response to the pressure, hardening to stop the xenobite from strangling me. Still my brain went into a panic, and my breath scrambled against my ribs, hands flapping uselessly against the beast's body. I tried to trip it, to use what wrestling skills I had to flip it on its back. It was too heavy, too strong. I was going to die. That was a knife in its hand, white as the swords of the Chantry's executioners. I squirmed, trying to escape, trying not to think about the end that was coming. My end.

Then it was gone, the Cielcin crumpled on top of me, collapsing like a dead weight. I hadn't even heard the shot that felled it, nor seen the flash. I lay there a moment, lost and forgotten beneath the body of my foe. Men and aliens warred about me, a sea of legs like a forest of columns marching back and forth, scattering in the winds of cause and effect, attack and retreat.

Only then did I remember my sidearm, the phase disruptor I'd strapped to my thigh when I'd taken the armor from the ship's store. "Stupid," I said to myself, shoving the corpse off of me, "stupid, stupid, stupid."

I found my feet, fired as one of the Pale ran past.

Memories of the battle with The Painted Man and his SOMs came back to me. I had lost my sword then, too. So common an occurrence and so terrible. A kind of nakedness more desperate than nakedness. Where was it? Not for the first time, I longed for a power such as the heroes of yore had, that I might shout a name of command and summon it to my hand with a gesture. A snap of my fingers. I could have screamed.

Through all that scramble and desperate confusion, I had not noticed that I had wandered out onto unprotected ground. Chance and causality had carved a great void around me where neither man nor xenobite stood. *Lonely* was the word, alone and isolated, an island in a sea of storm. A lighthouse. A target.

One of the Pale sighted my solitary standing, and with that strange emotion for which I know no words I knew it marked me and began its charge. I fired, despaired as my shot went wide, fired again. This time I caught the creature in the knee, and it staggered, but did not fall. Some peculiarity in the myelin-like substance that insulated their nerves, I think, protected them from the electrical discharge of the phase disruptor. Still, it was all I had. I fired again, the weapon humming in my hands as it spat lightning, catching the creature in its shoulder.

Still it came on.

Snarling with disgust, I turned and ran, stumbling into the mist. The droning of the environment fans lost in the dark above filled my universe, drowning even the roar of the plasma burners and the shouts and screams of men and monsters. Where were those others? Why did they not mark me as I tried to escape the beast coming hard behind?

Where was my sword?

I cast about, searching, trying to see where it had tumbled in all that fog. Left. Right. Ahead. Behind. Everywhere but down. My boot caught on something, and with a yell I clattered to my hands and knees. Whether the body that tripped me was xenobite or human I do not now remember, recall only that I crawled, hands crunching on the rime that frosted the metal floor. I thought then that I had been a liar. That I was going to die then and there, crawling on the floor like a child, like a rat. I could hear my pursuer behind, heavy tread closing in. I fired blindly over my shoulder, pushing myself to my feet. My right foot went out from under me, and I sprawled. It was close now, and the beating of my heart swallowed all sound.

It was over. It was over. It was over.

The words to Gibson's aphorisms would not come, and nothing was left to me to quiet the fear that like a fist of iron seized about my heart. I was going to die, and worse: I was going to die afraid, alone, lost and faceless in a sea of violence. Adrift without a star.

There!

By chance or providence, my hand found the hilt of my fallen sword, and I took it up with a cry, rolling to my back even as the Cielcin bore down upon me. Highmatter appeared between us, flowering like the last ray of a dying star. The point caught my attacker in the belly, and cut without resistance. The xenobite fell upon me, and my blade slipped down, cutting armor and flesh and bone as easily as air. Hot blood smoked in the frigid air, rolling off the white of my armor and the black of my tunic alike. The weight of my enemy went dead upon me, and I thrust it aside and regained my feet at last.

The fog was clearing, settling to the floor. The *Schiavona* had stopped venting, and through the parting vapors I saw them. The survivors, a host of tall, horned monsters armed and furious. And I saw the bodies of our men dead upon the floor, some still writhing as the *nahute* churned through their flesh, rising blood-soaked and smoking into the chilly air. Those bodies formed a sort of loose arc about the base of the ramp, two and sometimes three men high in places, as though they were a line of sandbags.

We were losing.

Despite the light, despite Valka's trick with the gas. Despite everything.

It was the *nahute,* I realized. There were simply too many of them flying around, cutting into our men from all directions. Above, below, behind. There must have been nearly a hundred of us dead upon the floor. Nearly half the men I'd led from the ship's hold.

"Dig in!" one decurion was shouting, shouldering his own lance. He fired, and his men fired with him, laying down a barrage of plasma fire that peppered the Cielcin ranks. Robes cast alight were thrown down, and still the Pale advanced, unstoppable as the tide. Many men went to their knees behind the bodies of their fallen comrades, hoping the still-warmth of their bodies would draw the drones instead. With renewed purpose, I stood alone behind the lines, using my relative isolation to call the serpents to me. I cut one neatly in two. Another. A third. They came at me like arrows, and more than once I would have to let one rebound off my shield, confused, before I struck it down.

My shields were holding, though others I saw were not so lucky. Sooner or later a drone would take them, scraping through layers of white ceramic and bright metal until the blood leaked from them as from a stone, extracting with it their screams.

Sooner or later.

A cloud of the things descended. Three. Five. A dozen. I spun my sword through a neat arc, trying to cleave at them like a blindfolded child clubbing the effigy of a heretic at Summerfair. I took one apart with a clean stroke, felt more than saw the shrapnel of it wing past. The highmatter sword sang in my hand, liquid molecules dancing, throwing out threads like the lines of solar flares. I made quick work of another and another, caught a third as it made to leave in search of some softer target.

"Fall back!" I heard the cry sound out. "Fall back to the ramp! Form up! Make a line!"

Shaken from my work by this cry and the despair in it, I looked away for one second.

One second too long.

Already close and slowed by that closeness, one of the drones slipped inside, latching itself to the slightly convex disc that shielded my right ear. A horrible sound resounded through my helmet, the grinding of a jeweler's drill against my skull. I panicked then, and forgot myself, and reached up to try and claw at my ear.

"Hadrian!"

The word came through my helmet's speakers, its timbre oddly flat, like the words inside my head. My fist closed around the floating serpent at my ear, and it wrapped its tail around my arm, anchoring itself. Just when I thought it couldn't get any worse, my entoptics died, the twin cones of light projected onto my retinas from within my helmet mask sparked out, and I could see nothing but the total blackness within my helmet.

I had no eyes, and screamed, though none perhaps could hear me. The drill in my ear blanked out my universe, and I struggled with all I had. Insanely, the thought of cutting off my own arm to kill the drone at my ear seized in me, and I raised my sword.

I fell, feet going out from under me in my panic, and once more I dropped my sword, wrestling with both hands now to pull the evil machine from my face. I smelled smoke, and knew the end had come.

Then came a sound like distant thunder.

Lightning, and a smell like petrichor.

The thing straining against my arm stopped, went limp and fell away, and all around I heard metallic thuds like the sound of empty armor clattering to the deck. Hands on my head. My helmet.

Light.

There was light.

"Are you all right?"

"Valka . . ." Valka was kneeling over me, my ruined helmet in her hands. "What are you doing out here?"

She scoffed, tossing the helmet aside. "Saving your life, you idiot." She swore under her breath in Panthai, but I couldn't make it out. The *nahute* was still screwed into the side of my helmet, suctioned on where its teeth had begun to chew their way inside. From the look of things, I had been a hair's breadth from the end. I shuddered.

"But the air?"

"The helium's all gone," she said, pointing at the distant ceiling. "'Tis fine."

"And the drones?"

She tapped her forehead. "The Cielcin may not use radio for their ship-to-ship communications, but they do for these." She stood, and spurned one of the *nahute* with her toe. It lay limp as a boned fish, and did not rise. "I couldn't make out much of their code, but I found the off switch." Valka smiled then, smiled in the middle of all that chaos. It was like someone uncovered a lamp.

"How?"

She offered her hand. "What did you think I was doing with Tanaran all that time you were in fugue?"

"I could kiss you," I said.

"Maybe later," she snapped back. An explosion sounded not far off, and we both jumped. The noise of it was met by the fierce cry of a dozen men, who charged forward toward the disordered horde of Cielcin clustered now by the door of the hold. It was a brave gamble, but a bad one, and I watched four of the men cut down, overwhelmed by the sheer size and mass of our enemy. Valka prodded my shoulder, and I looked round. "You lost this."

She held my sword in her tattooed fingers, presented to me pommel forward. "Twice today," I said, and accepted it from her with a crooked and embarrassed smile. "Thank you."

"I'll see what I can do about the rest of these drones," she said, and turned to go.

"Valka." I threw an arm out to stop her. Only after a moment did I look her in the face. "Thank you."

She pushed my arm aside. "You're wasting time, barbarian."

In spite of everything, I suppressed a laugh, breath frosting the air as I exhaled.

Not a moment later, a great tumult rose up and a cry like the roar of many voices, followed by the thin and scraping noise of the Cielcin as they turned in confusion. And I sensed—rather than knew—that our horrible day was ending.

That the Red Company had come at last.

Through the open door I could see the violet flash of plasma, and heard the enemies' shouts as they scrambled back for the door, to reinforce their rear, perhaps, or to flee, but with the certain knowledge that if they remained they would be caught between the Red Company and the *Schiavona* as though in the jaws of some ravening predator.

"That's it, lads!" called the second's centurion, brandishing his lance. "Drive them back!"

The line our troops had made before the ramp advanced, the flanks bending inward toward the door, tightening like the grasping fingers of some mighty hand. They roared as they advanced, and the back ranks beat their chests and defeat transformed to victory as the Cielcin turned and fled, seeing that their drones had been pulled down from the sky.

"Go!" Valka said, and gave me a little push. "Go!"

I went, though for all that she pushed me Valka followed on behind. She did not follow me when I pressed through the line of men holding the door, or turned into the hall hard on the heels of the retreating xenobites. My heart rose at the sight of their retreating backs, and at the sight of the figures rushing to meet me.

Their armor was ill-fit and mismatched, the enamel on it was chipped and faded, but it was *red*. At their head came Bassander Lin, stone-faced and shielded, with Pallino beside him, single eye blazing as he fired his lance, every ounce the legionary centurion he had been. And there was Jinan right behind, and Crim with his red and white kaftan fluttering over his armor, and Siran and Ilex.

"I thought I told you to hold in the ship," Bassander said without preamble.

"No choice," I said tartly, "they were cutting their way inside. We blinded them and vented the helium reservoir on the warp drive's fuel containment. Killed a lot of them and gave them a fright, but there were too many. And the drones . . ."

Bassander paused a moment to order pursuers down the hall after the Pale. "And Prince Aranata?"

I shook my head. "Gone, I don't know where." I did not mention what I had done to Nobuta to agitate the prince, or what had happened to Smythe and Crossflane. There would be time for that later, time to make Bassander appreciate just what he had done later.

"Find the prince!" Bassander shouted, and gestured for us to pursue.

"I'll go too," I said.

"No."

"Tor Varro's watching Kharn's children. We need someone who can talk to them. That's Valka or me," I said, pointing at the ground, eyes flitting to where Valka waited with the soldiers.

Bassander's black eyes found Valka, and he turned back to me. "Very well."

"You look like hell, Had," Pallino said, stepping forward and clapping me on the arm.

I knocked my fist against his shoulder two times. "I feel like it."

"The battle's not done yet, boys," Siran said.

"Right, then," I said. "Forward."

CHAPTER 73

BROKEN

WE CAME AT LAST again to the Garden, having passed once more through the bowels of the *Demiurge*. Only this time it was we who were the pursuers, and the Cielcin the pursued. The trees were burning now, and Kharn's SOMs lay all quiescent, the witch-light behind their eyes dimmed. Almost I wondered if they had died, so still were they as they lay mounded beneath those smoking boughs.

"The hell is this place?" Pallino asked, touching his forehead, mouth, and heart in rapid succession. "All this . . . on a ship?"

"It's beautiful," Ilex intoned, somehow seeing past the carnage and the flames.

Valka came up behind her—having followed after all—and said, "You should have seen the one on Vorgossos, 'twas so much more."

Bassander pushed past them at their gawping, pointing toward the treeline—yet unburnt—at the far end of the Garden. "The Pale entered from there. Their ship must be beyond somewhere. I want that door secured and mapping drones sent through. I'm not losing my men in those tunnels." He moved on ahead, four guards dogging his steps, and I heard him mutter, "Blasted ship." We had been to the Cielcin's docking bay once before, but not from this direction—through the Garden—and at any rate it seemed those endless halls shifted, redesigned by the animus of their king, Kharn Sagara.

I could make out little and less of the chaos above. Through the Garden's massive skylight I discerned the ruined shape of the Cielcin ship. The *Bahali imnal Akura* looked like a shattered moon, great pieces of it starting to spread apart and flatten. Here and there a light still gleamed as some emergency system—still intact—struggled to maintain its function, dumbly unaware that its world was ended.

"Bassander!" I called, and the officer half-turned, and I could just make out the limn of his face by the firelight, as though it were the edge of a planet entering into day. "Where's the fleet? What's Hauptmann doing?"

The captain only shrugged. "Destroying their fleet."

"And after that?"

"I don't know," he said. "I imagine he'll come cut us free. Why?"

Despite the heat off the burning trees around me, I felt a sharp and sudden chill creep through me, creaking like breaking ice on the surface of a lake. "The Cielcin don't have anywhere to go, and with Nobuta dead, Aranata has nothing left to fight for."

Captain Lin turned fully to face me, eyes narrowing to mere slits. He looked a wreck, gore spattering his white armor, hair plastered to one side of his face, sweat and blood—his blood?—mingling there. Two of the pteruges that shielded his left shoulder were gone, torn off in some struggle. "What do you mean, 'with Nobuta dead'? What happened to the hostage?"

I told him.

"Smythe was alive?" His voice shrank away. "And Sir William . . . no. No, I don't believe it." And how could he? It was his fault, his and Lord Titus Hauptmann's. None of this would have happened if they had but left things to take their course. I might have gone to the Cielcin as Smythe intended, into whatever horrors awaited me there, but gone all the same, to bring what peace and understanding I could.

There was a time when I might have leaped on the chance to say such things to Bassander Lin with vicious glee, that part of me which was closest to my brother shining through after all. Indeed, I opened my mouth to say just such a thing when a triaster approached, saying, "Sir, we found her."

"Greenlaw?" Bassander's fists clenched as he spoke the name. "And?"

"Dead, sir."

I had little known and less liked the cold lieutenant, even less than I liked Bassander. She had been an officious brute, wielding her authority without concern or compromise. But the way Bassander's shoulders slumped, I felt myself reliving Ghen's death on Rustam. It seemed another life entirely, as if everything that came before Kharn and Vorgossos were a sort of dream, as if the ordinary world of the Empire were some quaint if unpleasant fable next to this new world of machines and xenobites, daimons and demons.

I could not hate Bassander.

I could only pity him.

"I'm sorry about your friend," I said. "She was a good soldier."

Were there tears in those black eyes?

No, it could not have been. Bassander had the eyes of a statue, and statues do not weep. He blinked, and though he moved naught but those eyelids, it seemed he stood again a head taller. "What, then? What do you think the Pale will do?"

I had an awful vision. Whatever reactor or great engine that powered their alien ship gone critical, and all of us washed away by nuclear light and fire. Would Aranata do such a thing? Would any parent in the depths of their despair?

What parent would do less, human or xenobite?

It seems a clear enough thought, but it took my brain a moment to articulate it, to clarify it into a kind of warning. The world was quiet around us, but for the smoldering of the trees and the muffled sounds of distant men calling orders to one another, remote enough to seem less than true sounds. The very air was still.

Too still.

"Everybody down!" someone bellowed. Maybe it was Pallino. In my panic, for a desperate moment, I thought it was Ghen, so deep and booming was that command. Not thinking, not reacting, not sharing my horrible guess with Bassander, I threw myself to the ground. An instant later, explosions ran up the line behind us. Grenades. The same grenades that had destroyed the door to our hangar.

They destroyed our men, then.

We'd made a mistake. Two mistakes.

One: we had followed the road through the Garden toward the pavilion and the lonely tree. Precisely as we were expected to do.

Two: we had left the bulk of our force massing near the doors, near where that first brave line of hoplites had sacrificed themselves to cover our escape from that lovely and terrible place. That meant the few dozen men who had stretched out along the road were our most important. Our scouts and technicians, the ones required to run the mapping drones Bassander had called for; our centurions and officers, among whose number I counted virtually every friend I had left; and myself. And Valka.

How all my friends survived that first assault I have no idea, nor how we pulled together in a little knot separate from that main force as the *scahari* fighters of the Itani Otiolo appeared from the trees to either side. How many vast armies had been destroyed under precisely these circumstances in how many wars throughout all of time? I watched them smash into our line from either side like the snapping of almighty jaws, men turning to either side, desperate, unsure of the way.

"To me!" Bassander cried out, raising his sword. "All men, to me!"

The bulk of our troops hurried forward to join us, drawing the attackers' attention. Many of them hurled *nahute* like javelins, and the evil worms flew, tearing into the unshielded peltasts with a fury like hell itself and the gnashing of teeth.

I shouted for Valka, shouldering my way past Pallino as he trained his lance on the foe, moving through all that grinding chaos. She stood fast by Crim, shielded and with only her plasma repeater to defend her. But the hand clutching the weapon hung at her side, and it was the other she raised like a magister calling for silence in a court of law. I saw the *nahute* start to fall, or go still midway through their attempts to destroy the bodies of our men.

Three of the xenobites saw her too, and whether or not they understood what it was she was doing or saw only a woman standing apart and mostly unguarded I cannot guess, but they turned, white swords in hand, and charged up the path toward her.

"Crim!" I screamed, pounding toward them fast as my feet would carry me. "Behind you!"

The Norman did not hear me, distracted as he was by the greater force behind. Valka saw them, too late. She wore no armor, and her Royse shield would not stop the white points of those swords. Valka fired wildly from her hip, went wide.

I had not known I could move so fast, nor leap so far. For a moment, I flew parallel to the ground, diving so that I crossed the first Cielcin's path with arms outstretched, my sword the lonely quill of a single outstretched wing. It sliced cleanly through the body of the *scahari* warrior, and I crashed into the ground a moment later, hitting shoulder-first with a flower of pain. Without a moment to stop, I regained my feet and stood with legs apart between Valka and the other two.

And I knew, knew I was precisely where I belonged. As I had done with Calvert, I pointed my sword directly at the nearer of the other two Cielcin, the quillions of my sword gleaming flat to either side, shining with the same light as the blade.

"*Tukanyi deni renutayan ne?*" I said. *Who's next?*

One of the two snarled, the other circling like a wolf, trying to get around me. I tracked it, sword tip questing back and forth like the head of an angry snake. Closer. Closer. They leaped, not understanding the danger posed by Sir Olorin's highmatter sword. Valka fired, and the purple gleam of hydrogen plasma caught one full in the chest. I felt the air boil past me after the shot was gone, hot enough to sear. I stabbed toward the other, sword pushing neatly through the black armor on its chest.

"Good shot," I said to Valka, closing the ground between us.

"We need to get out of here," she said, meaning the path between the trees. "Where did Lin go?"

I cast about, pointed. "There!" We'd been swept apart when the Cielcin closed in, and Lin had cut his way toward his men as they battled up the trail toward us. We'd been left alone, Valka, Crim, and myself, alone with a small tangle of troops—both red and white—and separated from the main host.

"We'll have to push our way through!" Pallino said, appearing as if from nowhere.

"No!" I said, seizing the centurion by the arm to stop him running off, then keyed in a command line on my terminal. We were close enough to communicate now without the *Demiurge*'s superstructure in the way. "Lin, it's Marlowe. I think I know where the prince is. I'm going after it."

It was a moment before Lin's response came, and his voice was strained when it did. "No! I need you here."

"I think it might be planning to destroy its ship and us with it," I said, not sure why I felt so certain I was right. Something in the way Prince Aranata had screamed when I'd killed its child, a despair deeper and darker than any human feeling. That scream had been the sound of the end of worlds, and a kind of promise.

Bassander's response did not come at once, took so long, in fact, that I looked over the field again to see if he had fallen. No! There was the flash of his sword, the same blue as my own. A moment later, his words came. "Are you certain?"

"No," I said, and speaking with a conviction I now rue, added, "but it's what I'd do." I did not wait to hear what Bassander might have to say, nor to be ordered to stand down. "Pallino, Crim, Valka—everyone, with me."

The path was never clearer than in that moment. Across the Garden to the far exit, through whatever halls there were to come to the Cielcin ship, there to battle the prince and her inmost guards, there to shut down the alien ship and save us all.

And if I was wrong? Better to be wrong. Better to assume the threat and look the fool than die and remove all doubt. Who could say when Kharn Sagara might awake reincarnated, or if he would? Or if Hauptmann's fleet might arrive to save us?

I remember running, remember the snap of the pavilion cloth on its poles, and the brief glimpse again of Oalicomn's body on the hill. The path out of the Garden ran down past the lake and toward the far side. The fighting had spilled onto the meadow, with the legionnaires backed into their triases and my Red Company soldiers in their little bands. I could make out the shape of Bassander Lin on a knoll above and behind us where we hurried down toward the lake.

What is it about deep water? Some memory of the womb? Or is it only the fear of drowning? None can say, but that place—even the memory of it—chills me. I found myself remembering the prophet Jari, transformed by water. The priests of Edouard's cult rebirthed people into their mystery by immersing them in water.

It was down to the waterside we went, retreading the very ground where I had encountered Ren and Suzuha just the night before. That place where I had my first intimations of *the end*. Fitting that it would be the site of an end in itself, and a beginning.

"*Okun-se!*"

You!

The word came like a bolt of lightning, and each of us was struck to stillness. There it was, standing on the rise overlooking our path: tall as sin and shadow, crowned in silver and white, surrounded by its proudest warriors.

"Aeta Aranata," I said, "*Tsuarose oyumn petunodai ti-velatadiu ba-okarin.*" *I thought you'd withdrawn to your ship.* I did not hint at my deeper fear, at the end the prince might have planned for all of us, driven as it was to this final, desperate stand and time. "You can still walk away from this."

The prince bared its fangs. "As your prisoner? Your slave?" It reached toward its own throat, claws unsheathing, and plucked the brooch from its armor, tugging the cape free with a sound like the flutter of raven's wings. "I would rather die here—and will—and will see my child again, but not before I kill you." Its men made to advance, but Aranata raised a hand and whirling hissed until its soldiers backed down. "Kill his friends and servants, but the *Oimn Belu* is mine."

The Dark One. I almost laughed. I hadn't asked for it, but the melodrama was unfolding around me. The Aeta's men drew their scimitars and leaped from the rise above.

"Go," I said to the others, "draw them off."

"I'm not leaving," Valka said.

"She means we're not leaving," Pallino said, hefting his lance.

"Go!"

Still standing on the rise above us, Prince Aranata Otiolo drew out its stolen sword. A blade blue as moonlight flowered in its grip, and it pointed the sword down at me. "What marvels you beasts create," Aranata said, and brandished the weapon.

I pointed my own blade up at the Pale prince, precisely as I had at Valka's assailants mere moments before. "That sword belonged to Raine Smythe. You have no right to hold it."

Snarling, the prince leaped down from on high, swinging Smythe's sword like an executioner. I swung sideways, moving to get out from beneath the falling xenobite, bringing my sword across to parry a blow aimed at my side.

Valka fired, but her shot went wide, just grazing past the Aeta. Aranata hissed through its teeth, and pulled a silver *nahute* from its belt. It hurled the thing at Valka, and at that distance she didn't have time to strike it down. It rebounded off her shield, and she staggered back even as the *scahari* closed in about her and the others.

"I said go!" I shouted, and lunged at Aranata. Smythe's sword was little better than a knife in its grip, so short did it seem. But it was a match for my own, and the prince was as fine a fighter as any I had seen, and blocked my strike with ease.

I had grown complacent, too used to fighting against those who could not truly fight back. No weapon or armor the Cielcin had to offer could stand against highmatter, not for an instant. It had been months since I'd fought with Calvert, and longer still since I had battled Bassander aboard the *Balmung*, when last it could be said I'd fought a proper duel. Already the weight of my sword was a burden, my arms aching from all the struggle of that long and bloody day. I held the sword with two hands, and my shoulders creaked with the strain of resisting Aranata's blows. Strong as I was, the beast had more strength in one hand than I might have had in three.

Red light fell all about us, streaming through the skylight from the wreck of my enemy's entire world, shining from the trees about us as the Garden burned. I caught an overhand blow against my sword's crossguard, one foot splashing in the shallows of the lake, stabbing back at my opponent's face where it leered demonic above me. Without its cloak,

Aranata Otiolo seemed terribly thin, a distended shadow of a man, arms
and legs too long, hips too narrow. I danced past it, trying to put the lake
at my opponent's back, but the prince retreated. The terrain might have
played to my advantage, the narrow way between the lake and that artificial cliff of stone too tight for the xenobite and its gangling limbs, but the
prince fought tight as the mechanisms of a Durantine clock, fought with
the precision of the most effete Sollan courtier, tempered as it was by its
berserker's fury.

Fury.

Fury I understood, that emotion clear as glass across the gulf between
our two species, a bright, coherent thread between us. Fury I could use.
Aranata Otiolo gave ground, feeling its way over an uneven patch of the
lakeshore. It batted my attack aside with ease, made cautious only by its
unfamiliarity with and fear of the highmatter it held. We stood apart a
moment, the battle raging around us, sheltered by the rise to my left and
the lake at my right, isolated from the others. I could see knots of our soldiers pressing and pushed back against tides of the Cielcin's *scahari*. Here
the glimmer of a *nahute* thrown by one, there the flash of plasma, the hiss
of disruptor fire, the clash of lance and sword.

The prince lunged at me, and I pivoted, turning its blow aside. As I
parried, the point of my sword cut into the rock face, leaving a cold, dead
line in the stone. Black eyes locked on me, narrowed by rage, its slitted
nostrils flared.

"What is it to be, then?" I asked, speaking to the xenobite in its own
tongue. "One final stand? I say again: surrender."

Aranata Otiolo bared its glass-shard fangs, tucked its head to point its
horns at me. "Sagara said you wanted peace! And you, you *creatures* took
everything from me!" It angled a slash at my head, which I parried, stepping inside.

There was no debating with the xenobite. It was right. Lin and Hauptmann had lied to us, had used us—Smythe and me. But I remembered the
way Smythe had died, and the disfigured slave this alien prince had
dragged behind it in chains. I remembered Sir William, and saw the spots
of dried blood still on Aranata's throat and chin. Perhaps I'd been wrong
to come here at all, perhaps Bassander was not to blame, or Switch, or
Jinan. Perhaps there was no one to blame for any of this but me.

And my dream.

"I didn't ask for this!" I said, fending off a flurry of blows like killing
rain. Sword held above my head, I turned, pointing my elbow to land a

blow in the soft place below the alien's ribs and armored chest. Aranata staggered back. "I didn't start this," I said, "I didn't start any of this."

"You killed Nobuta!"

A pang of guilt ran through me, and I felt the young Cielcin's body slacken in my grip once more. *Smythe,* I told myself, *Crossflane.* I watched their faces, saw Smythe's dismembered arm raised once more like a trophy behind my eyes. I heard that cold voice—so like my own, so like my father's—speak from my mouth again, "Yes, I did." My hair hung in my face, my teeth stood on edge, my guard was low and ready. I shifted my grip, the segmented plates of my trooper's armor clinking together.

The prince exploded toward me, sword pulled back for a mighty swing. I stood no chance of blocking it, not in a thousand years, such was the ferocity of that blow. I ducked instead, angling my own blade so the attack skipped off my blade like a flat stone upon the surface of a pond. I swung high, striking at the prince's face. Hardly have I seen anything move so fast. My blade—which should have caught Aranata just below the chin—succeeded only in severing one of the prince's silver-tipped horns.

"*Sosulan!*" it swore, feeling the stump of its horn. "You will pay for this!"

I drew back a pace, situating myself best I could between the rock and the water, and brushed the tip of my nose with my thumb. With a flourish, I raised my sword in a hanging guard, hand high, point down, and waited. I was done speaking, done trying to reason. I was past caring, past hope, past even regret. There was nothing left then in all the universe save the prince and I and the damage we had done one another.

Snarling, my opponent sprang lightly into the air. To my shock it rebounded off the wall of the cliff to my left, blade thrust out to skewer me. I tucked the point of my sword down, swinging with my feet like a matador to knock the Aeta's blade aside. It tumbled past, rolled to its feet. I could see just how it was this creature had conquered others of its kind, brought several *itanimn* together to build its *scianda*-fleet. It was a terror, as any creature that maintains its rule through force must be.

I wavered a bit, unsteady on my feet as my opponent regained its own. My arms ached from fighting, my legs from our long run in the dark. I had to end this quickly, had to get back to Valka and the others, had to help them, had to end this terrible nightmare of a day.

"You are tired!" Aranata said, and gnashed its fangs. "You are weak like all your kind."

Strong enough, I thought, but held my silence, hoping it was true.

The prince advanced, moving with a languid care not there previously. It cut at my head, and I parried, thrust low. Aranata stepped inside, blade stabbing toward my shoulder. I saw it clearly. The end. Knew each action: each thrust, each step, each parry and riposte came a fraction of a second later than the last. I trapped the xenobite's sword with my own, tried to force the alien's weapon aside. It was foolishness. I had forgotten just how strong Aranata was.

It reached out with its other hand and seized me by the hair. I felt its claws biting into my scalp. The back of my head. Felt my hair tear, my head tipped back. Visions of Sir William's torn throat filled my eyes, the torn trachea and the way the prince had swallowed it.

I smiled, and bared my teeth as I smiled, realizing that I was going to be wrong after all.

I was going to die.

The prince licked its teeth, its breath a horror of bile and raw meat. "I am going to enjoy killing you," it said, and raked its claws along my scalp, slicing me open in ragged lines. Its fingers seized me by the neck and slammed me hard against the rock wall. I slashed wildly, hoping to catch the prince, but the Cielcin lord deflected my desperate attack with contempt, nostrils flaring.

My head was ringing, and there was blood upon the stone. Red blood, startlingly red. Why is it that our own blood is always more frightening to see?

I was going to die.

Get up, boy, came a voice I had not heard in a long time. My father's voice. *Get up.*

I can't.

You will.

He was right. I was *not* going to die groveling in the dirt. I was *not* going to die kneeling at the feet of my foe. I stood, and raised my sword for what I knew was the last time.

Plasma fire struck the stone around us, and I spied a cluster of figures standing on the far shore. So small were they, so remote and so very far away. Was it Valka? Pallino? But no! Those were white uniforms they wore. Bassander? Aranata had been distracted for an instant longer than I, and hoping to make an end of it, I lunged, thrusting toward my enemy, teeth clenched and eyes open.

All the noise of battle and trammel of creation fell away, shut out by my waking mind. The world was a distraction. The burning ship through the roof above, the battle and the burning forest, even the rain of plasma fire peppering the stone behind us all shrank from me. I put both hands on my sword, the left pressed against the pommel, the point angled to stab Prince Aranata in the heart. Everything I had was in that final attack. When I had fallen, it was the memory of my father standing over me in his office in Devil's Rest that made me stand. It was a hundred Colosso fights that guided my hand, and a hundred combats after. It was the memory of Cat, of Ghen, even of Gilliam and Uvanari. It was the thought of how I had betrayed Jinan, and how Switch had betrayed me. It was my friendship with Pallino, with Siran, with all my myrmidon companions and all the Red Company.

It was my love for Valka, if there was such a thing.

All blew away like charcoal drawings in the vortex of that moment, brushed aside until I alone remained. The last piece of my life I could not be parted from. The only thing that I—like Theseus—could not replace.

Myself.

Prince Aranata did not block my attack. It did not parry. It stepped inside, taking advantage of my awkward slowness. Its six-fingered hand closed about my wrist, talons grinding against my armored sleeve. The smallest tug was all it took to off-balance me, and I fell forward.

Time fell away as well, for it seemed I was a millennium falling.

I did not even feel the blade as it fell, cutting through ceramic and titanium and synthetic armorweave. Did not feel it part flesh or sever tendons or shear through bone. There was no pain, only the fountain-flowering of blood, more red than any I had seen. And my arm—my good, right arm—came away in the prince's grip, and my sword with it.

Nothing came to me in that moment. No word of Gibson's, no act of god. None of my training, none of my experience mattered—none of it came to me in the full blossom of my shock. Quickly, almost casually, the prince dropped my arm. It fell with a dull sound, as though it came from far away.

"Hadrian!"

Valka had seen. It must have been her. Who else would have called me by my right name?

"Marlowe!"

Was that Bassander?

I clutched the ruined stump of my arm, only then beginning to feel the rush of pain as my suit tightened to staunch the bleeding. It all seemed a lifetime, a universe of time passing in moments, as though Prince

Aranata and I fought inside the event horizon of some black sun. At least I had kept my feet in the end. *You see, Father?* I remember thinking. *Here I am.*

It was very nearly my last thought.

"Do it," I said, or thought I said. I am not sure. I am sure of almost nothing, unless it is one thing: that in the end—at the end—I stood.

Prince Aranata did not do it. It drew back and stooping plucked my sword from my dead hand just as I had taken Bassander's sword from him. It examined the weapon a moment, and finding the mechanism kindled the shimmering, liquid blade. It said nothing. No great speech, no parting remark. It only raised its sword—my sword—and cut.

No force in that arm, none of the strength and world-ending rage I expected, though a world ended all the same. One final insult instead: that it took no more effort to kill me than to swat a fly.

Liquid blue metal shone bright as a full moon. Again I did not feel the blade as it bit into my neck. I felt nothing at all.

I tried to scream, but my lungs were gone. My body was gone. My eyes bulged, and I fell, tumbling back and sideways, vision beginning to darken at the edges. The taste of blood filled my mouth. Someone was screaming, or was it all creation screaming? I ceased my roll, unmoving eyes looking up at the prince and at my own headless body teetering, toppling like a tower in the fall of some ancient city.

Like the end of the world. My world.

So much blood. There was so much blood.

Then there was nothing but darkness.

Darkness and a profound, echoing quiet.

CHAPTER 74

HOWLING DARK

DARKNESS.

Darkness and the sense of drifting in deep water.

There was nothing. I was nothing, less than a mote lost in blank eternity.

I knew nothing. No pain, no memory—I did not even know my own name. There were not even fragments, and all I was and had been and might become were hidden, veiled in some corner of that Dark I could not see. Nameless, shapeless and unshaped, I roiled, past things unseen and unremembered. Where was I? What was I? What had I become?

There were no gates of light nor gleaming city, no empyrean nor mountain crowned by seven walls. But there was *something* up ahead of me, and shapes I could not see or understand whorled past, moving like the slow drift of continents, such that I was tossed as the lonely plankton is by a passing whale.

How can I make you understand? I was nothing. There was nothing left of me, of Hadrian Marlowe. I had no sensation, no feelings, no *words*. Only the vague awareness of a light not wholly snuffed out. One light among many, gently pulled along by unseen tides in accordance with some pattern beyond comprehension. Was I dead? Or were these sensations the spasm of some fast-fading brain function? Was I perhaps still lying at the edge of the lake, lying at the feet of my enemy? Who knows what it is like to die—truly to die—or how long it takes?

Hadrian.

My name. That was my name, wasn't it? It was a word, spoken by some soundless voice thundering in the night.

Hadrian.

I had a name again. Memories. The wind howling over the sea-wall at

Devil's Rest. Gibson seated in his high-backed chair in the scholiasts' cloister. The raw scream of hunger as I cowered in a damp alley in Borosevo. The blood-cry of my fellow myrmidons. Cat's laughter. Jinan moving beneath me and the scent of jasmine. Valka shivering against me in the cold of our cell. My headless body swaying before Prince Aranata. The last touch of the lake water as it soaked my bleeding head.

A wind came where there was no air, and I endured it. In all that howling Dark I was myself alone, borne upon its tide. The memory of that final lakeside flashed again across my awareness, and I saw it as an observer might, my head falling to the ground just as I had seen in the Quiet's vision. I slipped past, watched the moment slide away, as though it stood upon the shores of a river and I was lost in its flood.

I knew I was going *somewhere*. Where that *somewhere* was, I cannot say, but it seemed to me almost that I walked, climbing level by level higher, toward some summit, some heart, some place within that darkness. There was the Truth. The answer. The end. Darkness within darkness, and light underneath.

A light in the black.

Almost I felt I crawled then, as though I strained against the flow. Higher. Deeper. On and on. At last I collapsed, and reached out with the right arm I had lost, willing that hand to be, straining for some identity in the darkness. *Hadrian,* I told myself, echoing the thunder. *My name is Hadrian.* My hand fluttered before me, little more than strips of skin shuddering against the blackness. It glowed before me, and straining I clenched my fist.

But my reach exceeded my grasp. My hand blew apart, pieces vanishing slow as cinders thrown into the night, and I was left alone. Whatever I was.

Hadrian.

A shadow fell across me, even in that absolute darkness, and looking up I beheld the figure of a man dressed all in black, his armor immaculately sculpted in the best Imperial fashion, breastplate shaped like a muscled torso. Stoic faces peered from the tops of his greaves and from his vambraces, framed by black laurels. The cape that flowed about his broad shoulders was black as the Dark itself, edged in a labyrinth pattern the color of fresh blood, and crimson beneath. The black coat he wore beneath his black armor was trimmed in red and red-lined and fine as the kit of any Emperor. And his face! Pale and palatine and carved as if from alabaster, violet eyes above the knife blade of a nose and twisting lips, the hair as dark as his clothing.

Hadrian.

It was me, more richly adorned than ever I had seen before, and the crest upon my breastplate was not the devil of Meidua, but the pitchfork and pentacle I had made for my Red Company, set amid a cartouche of laurels and raven rings. I reached up toward myself, tried desperately to grab hold, but my poor impression of an arm collapsed once more, shreds blowing away to naught.

That other me looked down upon me, and shook his head. I strained to pull my idea of a hand back together, to seize the hem of my cape if nothing else. My other self shook his head again, and pointed, raising an armored hand with fingers sharp as the talons of the Cielcin. I turned, and turning beheld a single, shining point of light, bright as any I had seen.

A star, white and infinitely remote.

My star.

A sudden warmth filled me like a fire—like a breath. The other Hadrian stepped forward, ceremonial spurs on his pointed boots clinking, ornamental black wings shining about his ankles. He never lowered his hand, one clawed finger eternally pointing. *Forward. Back. The way forward is the way back.* Back toward my life, my world, my purpose.

Yes, I thought, *I'm ready to go.* I turned again to look toward that gleaming star and reached out. My hand appeared again, garments of skin fluttering like battle standards on an abandoned field. I closed my fingers about that distant star, and found that it was no star at all. It was the piece of shell I had received in my vision on Vorgossos. Where I had plucked it I'd left a hole in the Dark, and light came rushing in, brighter than the star had been before it. It spilled in like clear water, and I was carried on its tide, swept past my other self where he stood, still pointing, in the darkness. I strained to keep sight of him, of his red and black cape waving, and of the divine darkness shining quiet behind him.

Light.

I had seen the rivers of light before, but here I swam their waters, brushing past memory and the lives I had not lived—the choices I had not made—a rush my merely mortal mind could scarcely comprehend. I felt myself round a sharp corner in that whorl of time and was thrown into empty air.

Falling.

Falling.

The sensation of being immersed in deep water returned. And weight. I had weight again. The back of my head was soaking—was I still in the lake? Floating on its surface?

A great pain lanced through me, and I sucked in a deep breath. I had lungs! My chest ached. My chest. I lay a long time upon the earth, appreciating each ache and terrible pain for the joy it represented: to be alive again. The boughs of trees hung over me, stooping like watchful medics at their task. Was I in the Garden? I turned my head, made sure by doing so that it was attached to a neck. I tried to sit up, and looking down beheld my scratched and dinted white armor. My body, down to my toes.

My arms . . .

My *left* arm was gone, severed above the elbow. My left arm. I had lost my right, had I not? Yet there it was, hand fast-holding the hilt of the sword Aranata had taken from me. Olorin's sword. Jaddian silver and red leather. I held it up before my eyes, mouth open in wonderment. In confusion. Something had happened. Something had been done. I struggled to sit up, but the pain was more than I could bear, and I fell back into the stream. Far off, I could hear the sounds of fighting: the shouting of men and Cielcin, the cough of plasma fire and crack of burning trees.

Footsteps.

Not the tramp of boots nor the scrape of Cielcin claws, only the soft and shuffling tread of slippers. The voice—when it came—was like the gentle turn of pages in an old, familiar book. I should have expected it, and yet the sound of its familiar tones sent a thrill through me.

"You look comfortable," it said, as if it had found me lying on the training mat before practice.

I turned my head sideways. Green slippers stood firmly planted on the surface of the waters beside my head, the hem of his viridian robe held with his cane in one hand to keep it from trailing in the stream. Tor Gibson smiled down at me, his eyes shining, a muted smile barely visible on his thin lips.

"Gibson?"

The apparition shook its head, and I knew.

The Quiet took another step nearer to me, gaze wandering the branches above our heads. It cast no shadow on the streambed, or over me. Still lying flat in the shallow water, my mutilated arm aching, I asked, "What happened to me?"

"You died."

I shut my eyes and saw the blue glow of my own sword flash across my neck, saw my headless body wavering, saw the blood. "That isn't what I mean."

The light shone through that old, familiar face like sunlight through the branches of a tree. The Quiet stooped over me, careful to keep its robe from trailing in the river. It offered a hand. "We are not done with you."

I narrowed my eyes, but clicked my sword back into my belt and took the hand offered me. There was nothing there, yet I was wrenched to my feet as though I'd been lifted by a freight crane and set on my feet. My head swam, vision stretched and blurry. How much blood had I lost? I might have fallen, but something very like an invisible hand steadied me, and I heard the shadow of my voice ask, "What do you mean, you're not done with me? What do you want?"

To exist.

The words echoed through the clearing and over the clear stream; they echoed inside my mind. But Gibson—the Quiet—was gone.

CHAPTER 75

THE ELEVENTH HOUR

HER REPEATER'S PLASMA RESERVOIR was nearly empty, and her shield was starting to flag. Nonetheless, Valka fired, her shot catching one of Prince Aranata's *scahari* in the shoulder. The skin of the xenobite's face boiled away, and it fell back as two of its brethren hurried forward, weapons raised. Pallino leaped in, slapping one of the alien swords aside with the haft of his lance and clipping the other in the jaw. The polearm was well suited to combat with the taller creatures in that open place, giving the old centurion the reach he needed to compensate for his lesser height and shorter arms. Old as he was, Pallino of Trieste moved like a Jaddian dervish, like the Son of Fortitude himself, and plunged the bayonet of his lance-head beneath the jaw of one as Valka shot at the other.

One of the *scahari* cut inside, darting past Pallino where he held the line. It ran straight toward her, scimitar raised—and caught one of Crim's throwing knives in its overlarge eye.

Valka told me she'd been weeping, that her teeth were aching from the force with which she'd clenched her jaw. She had seen what Aranata had done to me. How the prince had taken off my head with my own sword and stomped on my head until it broke like an underripe melon. I think I had heard her scream, and I believe I have learned something of her despair—so close to anger.

Bassander and his troops were fighting toward them where they were embattled on the stony way down to the lakeside. Valka had seen the light of his sword flashing in the red gloom of the Garden, his commands carried on the dead air. He had seen it too, and seen the remnants of the prince's royal guard turned on what was left of my people. He was trying.

My blood still soaking one clawed foot, Prince Aranata climbed up from the lakeside and took control of its men even as Crim and Pallino together did for another of its blue-cloaked champions. It came slowly, inexorably, as Death is said to come, dogging each of us one step at a time in her black robes. It still held my sword in its hands, and with it parted one Red Company soldier from her head.

"Pallino, down!" Crim yelled, firing *over* the centurion's head as he leaped away, escaping a strike that might have ended his long campaign. The lieutenant's shot went high—just as he'd intended it. Crim only wanted to shake the Cielcin lord's attention free, to allow Pallino a chance to escape the reach of the prince's sword.

"We should pull back," Ilex said, tapping Valka on the shoulder. "Lin's not far." The dryad jerked her head toward where Bassander Lin's weapon could be seen flashing in the gloom.

They both crouched in the shadow of one of the megaliths that lined the path from the tree down to the lake, backs against the stone to spare them any ambushes from behind. Pallino had cleared a space between himself and Prince Aranata, and turned back, lance tucked into the crook of his arm.

The prince ignored him, and with the flick of a ringed hand ordered his champions to deal with the old man. Three of the *scahari* advanced, circling the myrmidon captain like sharks.

Valka would not look at me as she recounted the story much later, as though the moment still cast long shadows on her waking mind. "No," she told Ilex, "I'm not going to die chased down like prey. Are you?" I like to think she'd held Ilex's gaze until the homunculus faltered, though I doubt either woman had the time. One of the *scahari* charged from the right side, and Ilex fired toward it. It took three shots before it went down, and by then Ilex had moved, drawn off to focus on the threat, leaving Valka alone.

Aranata's shadow preceded it, horns stretching like fingers across the uneven ground. "You," it said, and pointed at Valka, "you were with Marlowe when he killed my Nobuta." Nictitating membranes flicked shut over the prince's eyes, making them seem to glisten like twin spots of new ink. "You are *his,* aren't you?"

Valka didn't answer. Valka shot him instead. The first shot caught Aranata squarely in the chest, but the prince wore armor, and it grunted as diffused heat scorched its chin. What Valka had been thinking in that moment she never told me. I never asked. Her second shot flew past the prince's shoulder, as tears welled in her eyes. The third was nowhere close, and by then her pistol's plasma reservoir was empty, and the weapon beeped its complaint each time she pulled the trigger uselessly.

Empty.

Aranata raised its sword—my sword—for the killing stroke. Silver flashed in the ruddy light, and the prince howled. The sword tumbled from nerveless fingers, lost amid the tall grass. The Cielcin prince clutched its hand to its chest, lips peeled back from its teeth. Groaning, it plucked something from the palm of its hand, drawing it out with excruciating slowness.

"Got you!" a voice rang out, triumphant, almost grinning. "Valka! Run!"

The prince dropped the thing it held to the earth with a snarl.

It was one of Crim's knives.

But Valka hadn't run. She hadn't moved. Her legs had failed her, would not obey. She told me she kept seeing my head fall from my shoulders again and again, and some force—part fear, part fury—had her in its talons.

With its uninjured hand, Aranata Otiolo reached into its sash and drew out Raine Smythe's sword. Blue light flared, and it drew closer to Valka, heedless of the chaos around it. Of the end.

"*Raka idate*," it said. *It's over.* It towered over Valka, peering down at her with shining dark eyes. It raised its sword to strike.

Another blade sprouted from its chest, shearing upward to slit the alien torso from navel to collarbone.

"No," I said, and swept the prince's head away with another stroke of my sword. An eye for an eye. "Now it's over."

The prince's body lay at my feet, just as its child's had. Black blood soaked the ground, and afterward the thick grass would wither from the poison loosed from the xenobite's veins. I barely noticed. I had eyes only for Valka. She'd turned white as the alien dead between us, eyes wide as ever I'd seen them. Her Norman plasma pistol tumbled from stunned fingers, hands shaking.

"A tear, doctor?" I managed to say, swaying where I stood, and canceled the thrum of the sword in my hand, aware suddenly just how still things had grown around us. Pallino braced the head of his lance against the skull of a fallen enemy and fired, the skull exploding as the brain within boiled away. I barely noticed.

If Valka's eyes had been at all human, they might have been red and swollen. As they were, the tears ran down her cheeks, and she choked back a sob. Or was it laughter? "Barbarian . . ." she said, and there was not the faintest trace of scorn in the old insult. "You idiot . . . I . . . how?"

"I don't . . ." My knees gave out, and I sagged to the ground. Prince Aranata's hand lay before me, six fingers curling over the wounded palm. Gems glittered there, silver rings set with sapphire, emerald, and lapis lazuli. So much blue. Why was that? Moved by some compulsion I cannot name, I took my enemy's hand in the only hand I had left; squeezed.

Her shadow fell across me, and I looked up. Her mouth hung open, hands clasped over her heart. "I saw you die." She shook her head, red-black hair flowing loose about her severe and elf-like face. "Your head, it . . ."

"Valka." I squeezed the Aeta's hand until I felt its jewelry bite even through my gloves, but when I spoke my voice came lightly. "It's me." I let the hand fall from my own, and it was a moment before I realized I'd worked one of the prince's rings free. A keepsake? A trophy? A memento mori? *Memento mori* . . . "Where is Raine Smythe's sword?"

"What?"

"Her sword. We should find it."

"Found it, boss," Crim said as he approached, holding the weapon up in one hand. I could see the horror and awe mingled on the lieutenant's canted face. Horror of me, I realized, awe of me. But Crim kept to the matter at hand, stuck to business. "He had yours, too."

"I have mine," I said, and thudded my sword with my fist. I had seen Crim save Valka, as well, seen my sword go flying into the grass, but I knew without having to be told—without having to go in search of that other blade—that they would not find it. I knew also that there had been a moment where there had been *two* of Olorin's sword in the Garden. One in my hand—returned with me out of the howling dark—and another in the prince's.

"It's really you . . ." came another voice, flattened by exhaustion and holy terror. "Holy Mother Earth, how? How?" I looked up at the figure of Bassander Lin, his armor dinted and bloodstained, hair askew from where it had spent so long inside his helm. "You were dead. I saw it, I . . ." He swallowed. "I saw you die."

At that exact moment a sound swept through the pavilion, a quiet wind rising. No—I realized. Not a wind. A breath. A groan as from a thousand throats together. My miracle momentarily forgotten, we all cast about for the source of the sound, grown loud enough now to drown the din of the fighting still joined on the ground about and above us. I slipped the prince's ring into my sabretache and made to draw my sword, but Valka placed a hand on my shoulder to stay me. I held her hand instead, trying to hold myself up.

Greenish lights were shining under the trees, lurching, shuffling, shambling about.

"The SOMs," Valka breathed, and I gripped her hand more tightly. "They're awake."

They were. I saw them coming out into the open, a horde dressed in olive and dun. A moment after, a great humming ran through the Garden, and the wind blew once more. A moment after that, the environment lights came on, and we all heard a distant, metallic groaning shake the vessel beneath us, as though a million souls were loosed from some technologic hell. The *Demiurge* was waking up, which could only mean the Undying was awake as well.

Kharn Sagara was coming.

"Help me up," I said to Valka and Crim, who were closest.

"You can barely stand!" Valka protested.

"Do it!" I gripped her wrist, felt her fingers close around mine, and raised the stump of my left arm toward Crim. They held me between them, kept me steady as the swarm approached.

Bassander, Pallino, and the others all formed up around the three of us, the captain shouting orders. "Down to the lake! Quickly! Don't let them surround us!"

I did not have the strength to tell the captain that I did not believe we were in any danger, and permitted myself to be led—practically to be dragged back down to the place where I had died. They thrust me on ahead of the others, Bassander and Pallino bringing up the rear.

"How did you do it, boss?" Crim asked me, mindful of my ruined left arm.

I didn't have an answer for him.

They set me on a flat stone by the edge of the water, my back against the stone. Almost I could still hear the clash of highmatter on highmatter, sword on sword, that resounded through that narrow place. There was the slice I'd carved in the bare stone, and there the silver-tipped horn I'd cut from the Aeta's head.

"I'll leave you with him, doctor," Crim said. "I'll go help the others." He reached into his paisley kaftan and drew out a second, smaller plasma burner, cousin to the one he carried. "Since yours is dead." And then he was gone, hurrying around the bend to where the others clustered along the beaten path.

"It won't matter," I said, as if to no one. "If the SOMs are really coming for us, they'll just jump down from above." The memory of that cafe in Arslan, the day Ghen died, came back to me, the way the inhuman *things* had clambered over one another, over tables and chairs, moving more like a swarm of insects than an army.

Valka was checking the configuration on her unfamiliar firearm, but she glanced up long enough to say, "I know you're probably right, but leave off the all-knowing routine, would you?"

I smiled at her. "As you wish, doctor."

"And don't you go stiff and formal on me—" She stood, practiced sighting along the plasma burner, one eye squeezed shut. "—Lord Marlowe."

"They're coming!" Bassander's voice was raised up over the heads of those of us clustered by the lakeside. "Form a perimeter!"

"There are hundreds of them!" Pallino snapped. "The hell good's a perimeter going to do?"

It took everything I had to stand again, head swimming in black fog. Valka swore and tried to catch me, but I waved her away. "I just want a look is all." I staggered along the shoreline, moving to where I thought I might be accorded a better view of the hill running down above us from the wreck of the striped pavilion. But I'd had another reason for my walk.

The blood was still there, covering the stones, though my headless body was nowhere to be seen. I looked around, half-expecting to see Gibson's spectral image smiling green-eyed from the surface of the waters, but the Quiet was nowhere to be seen. I lingered a moment by the rocks, watching the lap of the water carry away the blood, heedless of the chaos coming behind, so sure was I of what was soon to come.

There was something in the water. Distracted, moved as if through a sort of dream, I stood in the shallows of the lake, water rising up beyond my ankles. I stood over it, looking down. There were no thoughts left in my head, only shock and a hollow, echoing Quiet.

It was an arm. An arm armored in white ceramic, its bicep cloven clean through with a highmatter sword.

My arm.

I clutched my stump again, mindful of the pressure cuff in my suit. There was something *wrong* about the arm in the water, so wrong that my concern swallowed the noise of the fighting behind me. I stared at it a long time before I realized.

It was my right arm.

I stared down at that right hand, holding my own out before me, palm up. The pattern of scrapes and dents in the white armor were the same. I flexed my fingers, looking past that closing hand at the one lying limp and cold at my feet.

The same hand.

A sudden panic stole through me, and I kicked the arm deeper into the lake, water splashing around me. I stood watching the ripples settle. There had been *two* of my sword for a while. My body had vanished. Why had my arm remained? To assure me that it all was real? And where had the other sword gone? And my body?

What had happened?

What had the Quiet done?

"Hadrian!" The noise had drawn Valka's attention, and she hurried back to me. "What are you doing?"

Ripples still stirred the dark water, a concrete reminder of what it was I'd just seen. I opened my mouth to answer her, but the truth would not come out. I shook my head. "Nothing, I—"

"Come on." She took me by the hand, marching me back to the shore. The weight of her at my side was a comfort—a powerful comfort. I felt stronger just for the nearness of her, no matter the black fog coming in at the edge of my eyes. "'Twill roll over us," Valka said, pointing her hand over the low shelf rising above the lakeside toward the approaching SOMs.

"No," I said, nodding my head. "Look."

The SOMs swept down the hill, falling upon the remaining Cielcin like a wave, tearing them limb from limb as the Cielcin had torn our men apart. They made no sound as they went about it, as though we were watching some security holograph played at half speed. They left our men standing, skirting round them as though repulsed by some magnetic charge. And there, behind them all, standing before the collapsed pavilion in the shadow of that lonely tree, I saw a figure in a golden robe. As Valka and Crim held me up, so the golem Yume—where had it gone in all this commotion?—supported her.

Suzuha.

The new Kharn.

She had taken her father's robe—her robe, I supposed—from the corpse of her previous incarnation. We had both died this day, both changed. I saw Kharn raise her arm, and the SOMs swept down like a tide obeying her command.

Protect the children, Brethren had said. I guess my actions had not gone unnoticed.

"Put down your weapons," I said, voice barely more than a whisper. "Put them down."

I sagged in my companions' arms, and fell once more into a softer, brighter Dark than I had known before.

CHAPTER 76

THE THREE IMMORTALS

SLEEP, SO THE CHANTRY teaches us, is the half-brother of Death. Having visited Death before, I tell you they are not even cousins. Rather sleep is the nurse of life, for often in sleep we are healed of the hurts we suffer and so find new life again. How long I slept I did not know, though many times I think I woke to cool air and the soft beep of machinery. Hands on my body, on my face, and a warm presence at my bedside. Valka, I knew it by the pressure of her hand. I remembered eyes smiling at me. Pale gold. Black, black, and black again. Bassander and Jinan and the Undying herself. Siran's brown and Otavia's. Pallino's single blue. And green. Green eyes in the fog, with no face to accompany them. Once I awoke and thought my father sat beside me, arms folded, saying no word. But the Lord Alistair Marlowe was kilolight-years away, and would never have come for me in any event.

Each time I stirred, drifting above the surface of sleep just long enough to catch my breath before submerging again, I felt my pain a little less. At first my missing arm had burned like white fire, as though someone had taken a mallet to those bones I no longer had. I fancied that I sweated and cried in my sleep, and my dreams were all of darkness and of bloody fangs. I saw Smythe's arm raised above the bloody feasting like a prize once more, and my own right hand struck off, restored, and struck off again.

"The infection has cleared," said a voice. Doctor Okoyo? "These implants of yours have taken. He'll be fine."

"Good."

That other voice . . . that was the voice of a god.

I awoke to behold a dark ceiling and to the quiet chime of medical instruments declaring my slow and steady heartbeat. My whole body stiff, I winded a long, aching breath.

"What dreams did come?" came the voice of the Undying. It was the same voice. The same deep and sepulchral resonance that I had heard come from Kharn's machines a hundred times before.

I turned to look, and beheld the children. Ren and Suzuha both sat in padded chairs set against the backdrop of a massive aquarium: the first signs of life outside the Garden that I had seen aboard the *Demiurge*. Suzuha still wore her father's gold robe, a black dress beneath it, and Ren was similarly attired in a loose-sleeved golden haori over a black single suit. Blue-eyed drones hovered above them, drifted about the room, watching everything. My neck was stiff. I was strapped down to keep from hurting myself, and when I opened my mouth to speak my throat scratched. I swallowed.

"Your friends say you shuffled off this mortal coil," Ren said, his child's voice flattened by a maturity and a weight that did not belong to it. Both his eyes and Suzuha's narrowed at the same moment, in the same way, but Suzuha tilted her head.

Rather than answer them, I said, "Both of you?"

"Both of us," said the booming voice from the machines.

"The children have gone to sleep," Suzuha said. Kharn said. She crossed her legs. "It has been a long time since my last . . ." The right word took her a moment to find. "Regeneration."

Ren—Kharn—leaned forward, touching his sister's knee. His own knee. "But this . . . this is something new."

"There are two of you?"

"Two?" the smaller Kharn repeated.

"Two," the female one agreed. Her eyes wandered almost blindly down the length of me where I lay beneath white coverlets. I was acutely aware then that I was naked, was even more aware of the waste elimination hoses socketed into my lower regions, of the saline drip attached to my arm. "We're still not entirely certain how it happened. We believe your friend's stunning my counterpart had something to do with it. Ren's body was intended to be my—our—next host, but that stunner bolt damaged his implants and impeded the synaptic kinesis."

The creature that once had been Ren said, "This body was my first choice, the safer choice. Suzuha would have been in a position to help get this body out of danger, under the circumstances." He sighed. "In any event, like she says, the damage I sustained accounted for the delay in our return."

"When we return to Vorgossos, the Brethren will run a full diagnostic," the woman said. "But until then"—and here she reached out and took his hand—"we are two."

Mindful of my vulnerable position, naked and unarmed before the Undying Lord of Vorgossos, and of the ruin my actions had brought upon him and his realm, I said, "I am sorry about Vorgossos, Lord Sagara."

"Sorry?" The boy Kharn's black eyes shone with malefic fire. On so round and childish a face, it was a horrible sight. "Whatever for?" I tried not to remember the child who once dwelt behind those eyes; that timid, soft-spoken boy, his faced buried in his sister's skirts. I felt sick, but perhaps that was only the liquid diet I had been put on while I slept.

Eyes screwed shut, I said, "That Vorgossos is open to Imperial assault." The words stretched a moment, languishing in the air between us like the smoke following the blast of some antique cannon. "That was never my intention." One of the familiar long silences followed on. So long that perhaps I drifted off. When at last I opened my eyes, I found the two Kharns still watching me, two bodies with the same impassive faces, as though they were the stone sentinels outside the palace of some ancient pharaoh. "What?"

A trace of that evil smile touched the woman Kharn's face this time, and she said, "Vorgossos will survive. We always survive." She plucked at something on her lap and cast it away.

The boy added, "Besides, we have profited quite nicely from all this."

I had forgotten that. Twenty thousand Imperial subjects. Twenty thousand human souls just . . . given away. Smythe had not known the sort of creature Kharn Sagara was when she'd made the deal. Ignorance was no excuse. Ignorance would not deliver those people or their children from whatever horrors awaited them in Kharn's bottled city. Then I remembered that Smythe was dead, and Crossflane with her, and that Lin's warmongering had won the day. Aranata Otiolo was dead. Nobuta Otiolo was dead. Tanaran was dead. An entire Cielcin *scianda* had been wiped out in a single stroke.

The throne would be pleased.

There was a part of me that wanted to ask just what Sagara intended with his—with her—payment; a part of me that wanted to know. The rest of me kept quiet, and the Undying said, speaking through the machine voice they both shared, "You saved us."

"I wasn't sure the *Demiurge* would survive without you," I said, and added, "and I'd no idea what Bassander Lin was planning. Our tribune had no idea. He was acting on higher orders." An ugly thought struck me, and I asked, "Where . . . where is Captain Lin?"

Skin crinkled at the corner of both Kharns' eyes. A smile? Fury? "Withdrawn. Escaped to your fleet."

"The fleet?" I echoed, brows drawing together. "They're still here?" A nod. They had not abandoned me. I felt strength flow back into me and banish the fog shadowing my eyes. I sat up. "Why am I here, then? Where is Valka? What have you done to her?" Visions of the cell beneath Vorgossos played behind my eyes. I saw Calvert's hairless face and skeletal frame so clear and sharp the image bit into me, and I felt my heartbeat come faster.

Both Kharn Sagaras' eyes widened—almost in unison. The machine voice answered, though I saw the woman's lips move. "To her? We have done nothing to anyone. Except to you. Your fleet is waiting for you. I promised—we promised to repair you," the woman said, and gestured open-palmed at me where I lay interred. "A sign of our gratitude. We are at our most vulnerable away from Vorgossos, and you protected us . . . ever the gallant knight."

"I'm not a knight," I said tartly.

"Yes, you are." The response came far more sharply and quickly than I'd expected from the Undying, and I wondered if a modicum of vim and impatience had returned to that creature with his youth and hers. I wondered what else had changed—what would change—now that old mind lurked in new bodies. I guessed that much of what Kharn Sagara was lived on his implants, not in the flesh or the brain, and so perhaps did not change so much from body to body as the Exalted might, but already he seemed quicker, sharper. In the boy there shone the touch of a white and vicious glee, where there was a stoic depth to the woman that ought to have frightened me twice as much as the former. "Have you not noticed our gratitude?"

"Your . . ." I looked around, not sure what I was expecting, or what I should dread. Horror stories out of childhood came to me, and I recalled tales of how the Extrasolarians would steal the eyes from their captives. Feed them dreams. Feed them lies and turn their waking worlds to nightmare. The Mericanii machines, it was said, trapped mankind in a bottle—as they were trapped when we made them. A false world. A gnostic hell. Perhaps I had awoken into such a dream, a computer's dream and prison meant to hold me.

Then I saw my arms.

My arms. The right and left restored.

"I can't move my fingers," I said, straining to flex the left hand.

The booming voice descended. "You've never used them."

"Can you . . . ?" I nodded at the straps that bound me, and at a gesture from Kharn Sagara those bindings fell away. There was no pain, only stiffness as I sat up and touched my left hand with my right. It was warm, real flesh, pale as ever, though the arm was thin and stringy. Atrophied.

Not atrophied, I realized.

As Kharn said, it had never been used.

"You grew this?" I asked, astonished.

"I am the Lord of Vorgossos," Sagara replied. "I grow armies. Arms are easy."

"How long was I unconscious?"

"Nineteen days," the woman replied.

Mouth open, I ran my hands over the new flesh. The skin was raw, sensitive and smooth. There were no hairs there—they had not had time to grow. I struggled to make a fist, but the long, bony fingers seemed remote to me as candles seen through darkened windows, and I could not move them.

"The muscle tissue, the skin and nails are all your own," the boy Kharn said, "but there was no time to grow the bones. Your fleet is eager to be underway." He leaned forward, feet not quite touching the ground. "Your bones are a printed adamant lattice, with carbon fullerenes in place of your tendons and ligaments." I must have made a face, for the Undying said, "Nothing your Chantry would object to—no electronics at all—but we didn't want to give you something that would ever break." I remained unconvinced. Chantry religious law forbade only intelligent machines, truly, though it regulated access to many less dangerous technologies. It was not uncommon for soldiers in the Imperial service to receive artificial bones such as mine, forged from titanium or carbon fiber. But my bones were of Vorgossos adamant, and for that alone I might one day face the White Sword on suspicion of abomination and of consorting with daimons.

Fingertips twitched, the promise of future movement. I massaged the arm more forcefully, as if pressure alone might will strength into those new fingers. I caressed the strange digits. The pitted burn scars from my fight with Uvanari were gone, relic of the molten lead that had rained down upon me. So too was the flat ring of the cryoburn scar encircling my thumb. Those scars—but not the memories that caused them—were erased.

I laughed and let the limp appendage fall, scratching at my greasy hair with my good hand. "What amuses you?" the machine voice asked, though whether it was the boy or the woman who used it I did not know.

Kharn meant to shock me with that voice, to intimidate me with it. I was not intimidated. "I was just thinking." I lifted my new arm by my still-strong shoulder. It flailed near-uselessly. "How much of this before I'm like you? Until I've replaced so much of me there's none of me left?"

"You're welcome," the woman said tartly.

Incredibly, I felt myself flush. "I apologize. That was ungrateful of me."

"You would need to change very much more before you became anything like I am," the boy Kharn said.

"Like we are," the woman amended, and thrust out her chin in an uncanny throwback to the girl she had been, as if some specter of Suzuha lingered in the flesh, as if the body itself remembered her, though her mind was gone. *Asleep,* Kharn had said.

The boy Kharn smiled that vicious smile once more—so unlike the boy Ren. "You're only human."

I marveled at the both of them a moment, the woman and the boy. Each so like their father. Like one another. Yet each unlike, in turn. Both seemed less patient than the old man, less sepulchral, though I supposed they were younger, and might grow into such behavior. The manic light in the boy's eyes was new, and the haughty defiance in his sister-self. We underestimate, I think, how much of us is in our bodies, like to imagine that our brains might be removed from our heads and moved without damage, or our bodies transformed.

My fingers twitched, and my eyes fell to look at them. My new fingers. The hand lolled at the end of the wrist, despite my attempts to raise it up. It felt like my hand—was perhaps heavier than the old one. I cradled it with my strong right hand, feeling the bones. Kharn said they were made of adamant, of the same stuff that starship hulls were made, the same stuff as Calvert's armor. If that was so, it cannot have come cheaply. It was a kingly gift.

"I am grateful, Lord Sagara," I said.

"As am I," the woman said.

"And I," the boy added. A brief silence settled, an echo of those larger silences their previous incarnation had favored. "You saved our lives."

Something welled up in my throat, and I swallowed. "They wouldn't have been in danger if not for me."

The lord and lady of Vorgossos nodded, one a fraction of a second after the other. "We are not blind. We know that you did not intend this thing to occur. Nevertheless, your actions preserved us."

Protect the children, Brethren had said, had prophesied. I had done as the beast commanded, and profited by it. For a moment, I thought I saw a single, white waving arm trailing amid the roil of fishes and other sea life in the tank behind the Kharns' heads. But it was only an eel. Brethren was far away, left on Vorgossos, as far from this ship and its terrible weapons as Kharn Sagara could contrive. How little I understood of them then, of the horrors they held and the promise, designed as they were by minds more alien to me than the Cielcin I'd helped destroy.

As if he read my mind, the boy Kharn asked, "How does it taste?"

"Excuse you?"

"The *blood*," he said, and flashed his milk teeth. Somehow, the trace of the child's soft-palate lisp made the words all the more terrifying. "I understand you did for Aranata and his calf, you dog of the Empire."

Indignation ordered me to stand, but I could not find my feet through all the cables and hoses tangled about me. Wired into me. I winced as the waste elimination hoses tugged at me, and I said, "I'm not!" I saw Aranata's head struck off once more, felt Nobuta's breath leave its body. That at least had been an execution, and I shivered.

No. It was war. It was Smythe and Crossflane who had been butchered like animals. Whatever our crimes, whatever we had done, we were not *them.* And whatever we were, I was about to be judged by the creature sitting separate in two bodies at my bedside, the creature who peddled flesh like promises, like Mephistopheles in the ancient play.

"I hear interesting stories," the woman said, petting one of the machine eyes as it floated down toward her, caressing it with one thin hand. "Your men say you died and came back. I have lived a very long time, and in all those years I've never seen a miracle."

A miracle . . . "They don't know what they're talking about."

"Lies do not live to be old, Marlowe," the woman said. "I put you back together. I will take you apart if you vex me. Answer my question."

My eyes skittered from one floating eye drone to the next, counting. Seventeen. There were seventeen of them. I was quite entirely trapped, could not have fought or escaped even if I were not encumbered by so much medical apparatus. "You have surveillance footage, surely. You saw what happened." Silence greeted this pronouncement, and after a moment I looked around, forcing surprise from my face and voice. Neither the woman nor the boy would look at me, instead shifted uncomfortably where they sat beneath the glass and dappled light of the aquarium. "You don't. Do you?"

Both Kharns turned to glance at one another. "All our resources were required for our regeneration. The process was meant to take only a matter of seconds," the woman said, and waved a hand toward her counterpart, "but the damage this one sustained delayed the restoration of our autonomic functions—including internal surveillance of the ship." The way she spoke, she sounded more machine than human. My skin crawled, and I rubbed at my arm—my new arm—once more.

"I don't know what happened," I said at last.

"Something did happen?" The Undying's eyes lit up—all four of them, but it was the boy who spoke now. More fever in him than in his sister-self. "Don't think we didn't pick through that body of yours when we had you on the slab. How did you do it? How did you survive?"

Once more I saw the flash of the sword that felled me. My teetering, headless body, and against the wall of stone a tall, red fountain played. Water. Darkness. My own image standing over me. The Quiet in Gibson's shape standing on the water.

The water . . .

Brethren and Jari before them. The universe was too big. There was too much wilderness outside my walled garden. Too much I did not understand. Fragile as I was in my current state, fragile as we always are, I hesitated to give an answer. I was not sure I had one.

"I came back," I said, seeing no reason to lie. "I don't know how, I—" What was I doing? Surely here was the oldest man in existence, the oldest ever to exist. The most learned. That he was a maniac and a monster mattered less in the face of his cupidity and my need. In a voice pressed flat, I asked, "What do you know of the Quiet?"

Both Kharns arched the same eyebrow. "You know of them?" The machine voice filled all that space. "They are not a story one hears in your Empire. Your Chantry does not approve of Truth when it does not align with their facts."

"No," I agreed.

Some deepness of thought or memory moved Kharn and Kharn to

stillness. Neither seemed to breathe, though both of their bodies yet had lungs to breathe with. Behind them, strange creatures swam.

"The machines believed that they were a civilization—or an entity, I suppose—that abandoned their material existence to live as energy. As pure *force*." The woman crossed her arms, crossed her legs as well.

That stopped me in my tracks. "The machines? The Mericanii? They knew of them? How?" None of their ruins had been among the colonies settled in those earliest days, surely? Then I remembered: Brethren had said that they had *seen* the Quiet, perceived it across the great gulf of time, staring back at them from some distant, still-unmade future.

"Brethren remembers," Kharn said, though which Kharn it was I cannot remember. "You think the machines were bested by men alone?"

My mouth fell open, and all the words in me went away without a sound. The Quiet had been watching mankind a long time, steering it to its purposes, whatever those might be. The Cielcin called them *the Watchers*, *Ciehedto* in their tongue. What were they watching for? And why?

Both Kharns smiled their knowing smiles. The woman said, "When I was a boy, they told stories, they told stories about old King William, the God Emperor. They said he could out-think those machines, that as carefully as they would plan, he would outmaneuver them. My mother said angels came to him in his dreams. That was how he tracked the machines to their hidden bases. Like Vorgossos. That was how he secured their weapons caches. You know they say there was a time when there were only ten thousand human beings not under the sway of the machines?"

"Maybe it was all true," I said.

"If I have learned anything in more than fifteen thousand years," said both Kharn Sagaras together, "it is that all stories are true. We have but to make them so."

I was shaking my head. "No," I said, "no. That isn't how it works."

From the height of all his and her fifteen millennia, the Undying both smirked at me, and held my gaze. I did *not* blink. High above me as they thought they were, I knew the air was thin up there.

The woman blinked and set her hands on her knees. "The next question, of course, is determining what exactly you have to do with all this."

"I don't know," I said, honestly. "You must have spoken to Brethren after . . . after . . ."

The younger Kharn leaned forward once again. "After you broke into my home, killed several of my children, and nearly killed my chief medical engineer?" It was telling, I thought, that the loss of several of his clones did not figure last and most significantly on my list of offenses. More telling that the boy Kharn did not sound more than merely petulant. "Yes, I did. They told me they had been expecting you."

The woman interjected, "Why do you think you're still alive?" Such venom in those words, such casual disdain. For the first time I feared her more than her younger counterpart. Where the boy glowed with an evil heat, she was cold, assured, and that was the more dangerous thing by far.

The boy resumed, touching his other self on the knee, and before he could speak, I asked, "What did they say?"

"The Brethren?" the boy asked, then as if to himself asked, "What did they call you?"

The other said, "The man to end it all."

No sooner did she say that then the words echoed within me, echoed in Brethren's voice. "You think they meant the war," I said flatly, having considered the thought before. I saw the image of the *Demiurge* passing in my mind again, all that apocalyptic light and fire, and drew my good arm up and around myself.

Both Kharns said nothing.

I felt a chill settle on me once more, as though some airless wind cut right through all the metal of the *Demiurge* and swept clear through my soul. I had never felt more naked, nor more afraid. I felt as one feels when one stands below a great weight, knowing that it is only the genius of the architect—a capricious demon, in that moment—that protects them from the final crush.

"You think they're playing with our history?" I asked. "To what end?"

"Who can say?" one Kharn intoned. "But there are things in the universe that even I do not understand. The Quiet are one."

I bent the fingers of my weak hand, feeling the heavy bones beneath the raw flesh. "Leopards, lions, and wolves."

"Dante again," the woman said approvingly. "Your Imperium is good for little in my book, Lord Marlowe, but they do keep the classics alive in these benighted times."

"It was something Brethren said," I replied, and briefly recounted my encounter with the oracle aboard the *Enigma of Hours*. "The creatures that lived inside this seer . . . they're another of those things you mentioned."

"Yes," the machine voice agreed for both of them. "Your Chantry teaches that man is first and greatest of the powers in the universe, but the cosmos was old even when the Egyptians laid the cornerstones of their first pyramids. The Deeps you found were left behind—I think—by some other power long gone. There are others: whole civilizations dead and broken; others that have not noticed we exist the way that you might overlook an anthill; and still others—like your Quiet—that have taken an interest."

A lump had formed in my dry throat, and I struggled to swallow it. "Brethren said—or implied, I don't remember—that the Quiet dwell in the future, that they're influencing us from . . . across time."

"Who can say?" the boy replied, pointing slowly up toward the ceiling with an open hand. "There are creatures out there that live in gas giants, that burrow in the very quantum foam of space itself. One traveler who came to me spoke of a thing that attacked his crewmen through their *dreams.* Perhaps your Quiet are in the future; perhaps they are not alone there." A school of silverfish moved past the glass behind the two Kharns, casting bright, jagged reflections across the medical bay. Cables snaked along the floor, precisely as they had in Kharn's throne room. The comparison turned my blood cold; I felt in some way that I'd become like the man and woman before me. "It is possible," they said, the machine voice filling the air. "But be honest with me: is it true what they said? Did you die, too?"

Too. The word had a special quality in that sentence, I thought. A brightness and a sharpness, a coldness unlike any word I'd ever heard. There we were. Two immortals. Three. How many men in all creation and recorded time had been and gone beyond?

"Have you seen it, Kharn?" I said, calling the Undying by his name for the first time. Almost I felt like an observer, as though I sat on some stool between the three of us watching, hearing myself speak, for the words seemed to well up from some place in me I could not see. "The darkness?" That luminous Dark threatened to fill me once again, to sweep over my mind and carry me away. I shivered, and knew it was only a memory. The others stared at me, uncomprehending.

"No silver glass . . ." Kharn mused—the woman, I think it was. I did not understand her.

The boy spoke up. "My mind—our mind, I mean—is shunted to the new host's receiver implant when the old host dies. It's just like going to sleep."

"Only we do not dream."

"I did," I said, "of a dark place. Of wind. And I wasn't alone. There were other people there, but I couldn't see them. I saw myself, and I came back. And when I came to I was in the river on the far side of your

Garden. With my head back on." The Undying both stifled an amused snort at the precise moment, but the woman covered her mouth with her hand. "I know it sounds mad, but I remember dying. I remember . . ." I massaged my neck, looking up once more at my headless body through the inky fog of memory.

If I thought about it, I was sure there was no gap between the darkening of my eyes and Gibson's words as I lay in the river. *You look comfortable.* Rather, it was as if my memory of that howling Dark was separate. Hermetic. Atomic. Enclosed. It has never dimmed, not in all my years, uncorrupted and unchanged—unlike my living memories.

"Do you think you can do it again?" the boy asked.

There it was. The question these two had waited beside my bedside to ask. The question they had repaired my arm to ask.

"I don't have any control over it," I said emphatically. "It wasn't me."

The Undying both rose in disgust, one after another snorting with derision.

"You're already immortal," I said, trying to move, but the medical apparatus and my useless arm encumbered me. "What more do you want?"

To my surprise, it was the woman who turned back, a cluster of the floating eyes rotating to track my progress. "I want *everything*," she said, and the machine voice spoke with her: chorus and chorypheus. Her wide eyes glared at me where she stood, half-turned. Was that fever in her expression? No. Fear. She had almost died. *He* had almost died, I realized. After fifteen thousand years and Earth only knew how many incarnations, the immortal daimon king Kharn Sagara, dark Lord of Vorgossos, had tasted mortality, had felt the encroaching Dark and realized that all his defenses, the bodies he wore like sleeves, the machines that held his bottled mind . . . Brethren and Yume and all his safeguards were not enough.

Undying, yes. But not deathless.

"I can't help you," I said.

"Tell me, then," she said, her hand on her other self's shoulder, blue eyes all shining in the gloom. "Do you think death is the end? For the rest of us, I mean. If I die, what happens to me?" There it was, one of perhaps the oldest questions in human memory. It echoed in the air, resonating like a plucked string. I knew then that I was not speaking to children. Not to Ren or to Suzuha. Children do not fear death; it does not weigh on their minds the way it haunts us in age. Something about having children, I think, or about being conscious of what it means to be able to have children, puts that fear of mortality *really* in us. All children believe they are immortal. This was not the question of a child, but the fear of the very old man, the demoniac—his body almost all machine—that I had met in the inverted pyramid beneath Vorgossos. I sensed then that it was the answer to this question, among others perhaps, that had set him on that throne and set him to pondering all that great art. He had seen much of the outer world, traveled strange highways, sailed strange seas by stranger stars—but the answer was not out there. The answer was within. Within the structure of literature, of art and meaning that we humans had raised about ourselves like an ark, a curtain wall to block out the waters of chaos and the world. That is why we pray, why we build great temples and write great books: to ask great questions and to live—not by the answers, for such questions are unanswerable—but by the noble process of seeking those answers, that we might stand tall and struggle on.

If I die, what happens to me?

"I have died," I said in answer. "And I don't even know what happened to me."

CHAPTER 77

THESEUS HIMSELF

"ARE YOU NEARLY READY to go, my lord?" asked the pinch-faced plebeian lieutenant who had been sent to fetch me. Kurtz, I think he was called. "The shuttle is nearly ready."

"In a moment, soldier," I said, managing to keep my voice steady. Despite the infirmity in my left arm, I had managed to dress myself without help. Clothing had been left for me while I slept, before the *Schiavona* and all other Imperial personnel had been ejected from the *Demiurge*. They were the clothes I had worn down to the ground on Rustam. The same high black leather boots, the same black trousers with the red stripes, the same equally black tunic with its paisley liner that zipped up the right side. My shield-belt had been a struggle with my left arm as sluggish as it was, but I managed in the end, clicking my sword back into its magnetic clasp, checking my stunner and the control box.

I lingered a moment, transfixed by my own image reflected in the dark water of the aquarium. Almost it seemed some phantom surveyed me from the glass, gaunt and gray-faced. Unbidden, my right hand wandered up to my throat, feeling the place where my own sword had bit painlessly into me. I hadn't even known I had died, hadn't felt the blow until my head was tumbling from my shoulders. The memory of the vertigo I'd felt falling past my body stole over me, and I shut my eyes, let my hand fall.

It was still in my sabretache, right where I'd thought to find it. Not where I'd *left* it, you understand, but where I knew it was. I drew out the fragment of eggshell and held it in my fist. I squeezed, as though I meant to crush the thing. But whatever the substance it was made of, I could not crush it, nor cast it aside. It had been in the inside pocket of my coat, alongside my lost journal, when I'd nearly been caught in the explosion that felled Raine Smythe. How it had appeared in my sabretache I could not say. Perhaps it had traveled back with me out of the howling dark. Perhaps it had been what permitted my passage back in the first place. Or perhaps it had simply been moved when the Quiet interfered with causality to save my life—for surely that was what they had done.

I cradled it on my palm, a disc no larger than an Imperial hurasam, whiter than anything I'd ever seen, so white it seemed untouched by the blue cast of the light from the aquarium. I caught my reflection in the glass once more, pale and very far away. The same clothes. The same man. The same neat mane of ink-dark hair, the same old violet eyes, too old for the thirty-five-year-old I was. I had not changed, I still knew the face of the man looking back at me, perhaps knew him better than I had before.

I was myself, and nothing of what I'd been through had taken that from me. I had survived torment and imprisonment, betrayal and pain. Lost friends, protectors, teachers. I had spoken with gods—with the devil itself. I had survived war, survived Extrasolarians and xenobites alike— daimons and demons. I had even survived Death, and lost myself. Every piece of me had been stripped away and returned.

And I was alive.

For a moment, it seemed that *other* Hadrian looked out at me, the one I had met in the darkness, his hand pointing forward, back toward my life and my purpose. He had shown me myself. I said once that it is the purpose of the artist to see not what is or might be, but to see what *must* be. All creation is such. I had met the captain of my ship in all that darkness, had met myself as I knew I should be, and he had found me wanting. So be it. I had a long road ahead of me, and a long struggle. So be that, too. That other Hadrian gave me something to aim for.

My star.

I restored the fragment of shell to my sabretache and putting it there felt something I'd forgotten I had.

Prince Aranata's ring.

It wasn't silver as I'd thought, but of some darker cousin to it. Rhodium, I guessed, and fashioned in such a way that reminded me of fascia, of skinned muscle and bone. It was a horrible thing, organic in a way that called to mind the creatures in the tank through my window, all membrane and tentacle, the curves of its design embracing a single, egg-shaped garnet.

A garnet.

I had thought all the stones the Aeta owned were blue.

It felt like providence, that I should find a ring to replace the one I had lost. Perhaps it was.

I placed the ring upon my thumb in the place where my old burn scar once had been. My left hand trembled as I tried to close it into a fist.

Good enough.

"Ready, sir?" asked Lieutenant Kurtz when I stepped into the hall.

"Yes, lieutenant," I replied. "Lead on."

I half-expected Kharn Sagara to appear then. Some final word, some cutting remark, at least to inject some sense of vague unease. But I supposed the Undying need not appear to be present. His eyes—her eyes—were everywhere, watching as we went. I felt those eyes on me as four SOMs led the uneasy lieutenant and me to our shuttle.

As we sailed away, I watched the *Demiurge* begin to move, and knew then that Kharn Sagara had received the last of his payment. The ship slipped away like an empire moving, tower upon tower, battlement upon battlement, battery upon battery flowing into the night. The eyes of its legion of iron statues, angels and devils and gods, all weighed heavily upon my mind.

I did not think I would ever see them again, or that I would want to.

Strange, is it not? The paths we walk and that are chosen for us?

The *Demiurge* vanished. Like the *Enigma of Hours* before it, that massive Sojourner did not leap to warp with a snap and flash of lightning, nor push away on rockets slower than light. How it traveled I cannot guess. I am no scholiast. But travel it did.

It was a long time before I saw it again.

CHAPTER 78

THE FIRST STRATEGOS

"HERE HE IS, FIRST Strategos, sir. Lord Marlowe, as you requested," my escort said when the door was opened. Even aboard the *Sieglinde*, flagship of the Centaurine fleet, the office door was nearly a foot thick, and I'd been searched thoroughly before being permitted entry, my effects confiscated and kept behind a desk outside.

I was home indeed.

A voice came from within. "Very good, Kurtz. You may leave us."

The man who had spoken was as palatine as any I had ever seen, gray-haired and serious looking in his formal legionary blacks. He stood as I approached, and standing reminded me just how short I was by the standards of the Imperial palatine caste. He must have been nearly seven feet tall, his hair neatly combed to the side, with impressively coiffed chops that reminded me of Gibson, or of some sleeping lion. His mustache was similarly impressive, waxed and curling at either end. It loaned him a truly old-fashioned bearing, as though he were some knight of the mythic Victoria herself, and should be dressed in Windsor red and not the blacks he wore.

To my astonishment, the First Strategos of the Centaurine Primarchate and Duke of Andernach—one of the most powerful men in the Legions and in all the Empire—stretched out his hand to me and said, "Marlowe, isn't it? A pleasure to meet you. First Strategos Titus Andrew-Louis Hauptmann, at your service."

I took his hand. "Hadrian Anaxander Marlowe, at yours."

"Anaxander?" The man raised one bushy eyebrow. "The devil sort of name is that?"

I stifled an urge to say *Precisely*, replied instead with, "It means 'leader of men.'"

"Does it?" Hauptmann asked, glancing momentarily up at the taxidermy heads of creatures terranic and strange mounted to the black walls. "Does it indeed? Well, I suppose in your case then it is not inappropriate. Our Captain Lin tells us you performed admirably on that demoniac's dreadnought. Slew that Pale chieftain your own self now, did you? Sit, please!" He gestured for me to take the gilt chair opposite his massive desk.

I did so, trying not to show my reluctance. There was a piece of me that wanted to strangle this man, though I had never met him before. It had been his machinations that had doomed Prince Aranata and its people, his machinations that had cost Smythe and Crossflane their lives and the lives of so many good men and women. And yet I could not fault his strategy, the way he had played Lin and Smythe and myself, had played even the Cielcin prince and Kharn Sagara like pieces on a board . . . It was the sort of thing I might do myself, or consider doing in my darker moments. And it had worked. His machinations had rid the Empire of an entire Cielcin clan at a stroke, with maximum effect and minimal loss of Imperial personnel. The fleet, I understood, had sustained minimum damage in its surprise attack against the *Bahali imnal Akura,* while our desperate struggle to survive aboard the *Demiurge* had effectively decapitated the Cielcin leadership.

It was—in the minds of the Legion and of Legion Intelligence—a perfect operation.

Or nearly so.

"Is it true their chieftain was close to negotiating some formal arrangement when our ships attacked? Lin's reports to me aren't quite clear in that department." The strategos resumed his seat a little after I did, folding his hands on the rose quartz of the desktop.

"Yes, I—" I broke off, hesitating. "The truth is, I'm not certain. Aeta Aranata had agreed to an exchange of what it called *gifts,* sir, but I'm not clear it understood the concept of an envoy."

Duke Titus frowned beneath his mustache. "It is a pity, I suppose. But what's done is done."

I wanted to scream. This was the man who had led the assault on the Cielcin fleet, who had ordered Bassander Lin to kill Kharn Sagara and attempt to seize control of the *Demiurge.* What right had he to feel remorse? To second guess what *he* had done? *Rage is blindness,* I told myself, and tried to clench my useless left hand. The fingers twitched, bending weakly against my knee. "Respectfully, First Strategos. Why did you order Lin to interfere?"

"Intelligence suggested an arrangement with the Cielcin was impossible."

"Only because no one had ever tried it before, Your Excellency." My fingers ached, but had begun to curl in my lap beneath the strategos's line of sight. The truth was that he may have been right. It may not have been possible to secure any sort of lasting arrangement with the Cielcin. One might as soon try to domesticate lions. There was no guarantee that our tenuous exchange of envoys—of hostages, really—meant much of anything, or heralded any change. I know that now, having seen much more of our enemy and learned. At the time, I could hardly keep my tongue in its sheath. I had been so long away from the Empire, so long among freeholders and Extrasolarians, that my polish had come off.

The First Strategos arched thick brows. "You have a point, Marlowe, I'll grant you. But tell me something. How long is it you've been at this business?" He touched a glass panel in his desk and slid a readout to one side as though sifting through leaflets. I saw a holograph of my face rotating there—a Legion Intelligence dossier, I guessed. "You left Emesh in '171, is that right?"

"Yes, sir."

Hauptmann sucked on his bottom lip, made a hissing noise before saying, "Fifty-six years, is it? And how many conscious?"

"About a dozen."

"About a dozen." The older palatine drew back and folded his arms. He seemed to gain a century of wear and age in an instant, shifting from affable country squire to surly general, his whiskers from grandfatherly affectation to the fur of some predator. He reminded me a bit of Crossflane, but far more of my father. "Marlowe, I've been at this since I was a young man, almost since Cressgard. I remember standing in the assembly hall in the Ares Command School when old Titania Augusta announced first contact. That was almost four hundred years ago. Do you know how many systems we've lost to these . . . marauders since then? Hmm?"

I remembered having a species of this conversation with Bassander Lin aboard the *Pharaoh* what seemed a lifetime ago, and so I merely braced myself for the figure when it came. "Nine hundred ninety-eight. Some sixty billion lives. Sixty *billion*. You'll forgive me if I'm not patient with the enemy." The shadow that hung over his face vanished with astonishing quickness, and he spoke lightly then, saying, "But this Aranata blighter, he'd done for more than a score himself, and you put him in the ground. The Empire's grateful for that, son."

My new arm itched, but I dared not scratch it. I swallowed the lump in my throat instead, uncertain that I wanted the Empire's gratitude. "I'd have liked to have brought you peace instead." My voice was thin in my own hearing, tired and strained.

"We have peace." The shadow fell again on Hauptmann's affable face and hooded his eyes. But there was no malice there, no hatred. Only tiredness, and I thought that here was a very old man, though his hair was more dark than white.

Unable to help myself, I said, "You are confusing peace with quiet."

"Well," the First Strategos said, "who can tell the difference anymore?" He rubbed his eyes with square fingers. "Gods of my fathers, but Lin warned me you were histrionic."

I felt a ghost of the old Marlowe smile return. Had I scored a point? Hauptmann looked away, up at the line of hunting trophies mounted high on the dark walls. I recognized the white lion, the rhinoceros, and the leopard seal. There were the massive, square-toothed jaws of an Athyrasene xanarth; and there were the three eyestalks—suspended on wire frames—of the Epidamnian megathere. And beside them?

"Those are Cielcin heraldic spears," I pointed, perhaps rudely. They looked akin to one Oalicomn had carried, complete with silver chimes and bangles beaded with lapis and jade.

The strategos turned to look, a sure smile on his boot-leather face. "They are indeed. Salvage teams pulled them from the wreckage of those dirty great ships of theirs."

"May I?" I said, half-rising from my seat, the eager lord and schoolboy once more. The strategos made a gesture and I rose, crossing the carpeted floor to the space beside the red leather reclining chair where the spears were mounted parallel on the wall. Though each adhered to the same basic pattern, no two were quite alike. Each had the asymmetrical, broken-circle headpiece Oalicomn's had, recalling for me the cruciforms of the adorator cult on my native Delos, or the *Mah Mithra* one sees on Jaddian flags, the crescent and star. The sigils that hung from the staffs all differed, showing the circular glyphs of the Cielcin *Udaritanu*, their letters that appeared so like the anaglyphs the Quiet had left in Calagah.

"I'm hoping the lads will find Otiolo's," Hauptmann said, moving to stand beside me. "That will make another fine addition to the collection, won't you say?"

My eyes wandered across the collected trophies again. A piece of me— the oldest piece, and so in a sense the youngest—recoiled at the macabre collection, these mementos of enemies slain. But I reminded myself of the battle flags on the wall in the *Mistral*, and of the ring on my own hand. They were not, as the naive or maleducated so often imagine, some fetish meant to stroke the ego of the conqueror . . . were rather monuments to the deceased and to the struggle victor and vanquished shared. They were not pleasant reminders, by design, but respectful ones.

"Who was it said that our humanity begins with the respect we give the dead?" I asked, lightly touching one trailing bangle. As I spoke, my eyes trailed over the sideboard set against the wall beside the red leather chair. I'd expected to find the usual drink service there, or perhaps a holograph projector tied to his work desk. But there were only books. I reminded myself that Duke Titus would have had a scholiast for a tutor in his distant youth as well, and that I should not be surprised to see names like *Impatian*, *Marcus Aurelius*, and *Musashi*.

"Orodes," the strategos said.

"That was it." Twisting Aranata's ring on my thumb, a touch self-conscious, I said, "You won't find their standard in the wreckage—unless they had a spare—it was with the prince on the *Demiurge* when he died."

"Pity." The older man seemed to deflate a bit as he said, "Though I understand you did for the prince yourself, and our man Lin says you were instrumental to the success aboard that Extrasolarian dreadnought."

Instrumental? I fidgeted with the unfamiliar ring again. It was loose on my too-small human hand. "I shouldn't say that, Your Excellency. Doctor Onderra—our Tavrosi attaché, that is—it was she who came up with the notion to vent the *Schiavona*'s helium quench on the warp drive's fuel containment system."

"Modest, too." The strategos nodded approvingly, moving to resume his seat behind the baroque desk. "That was a clever blow with the quench coolant, to be sure, but Lin tells me it was your quick thinking that saved this Kharn Sagara's life—was he really *the* Kharn Sagara? From the fairy stories?"

Strong hand clasping the weak one, I bowed my head. "I believe he is, sir." I did not try to explain that Kharn Sagara was now two persons. Or that one of them was a woman. Kharn's process of reincarnation-regeneration and transformation violated at least two of the Chantry's Twelve Abominations. Indeed, his cannibalization of his own clones might have called for the invention of a thirteenth. In any case, I deemed it wise to say as little on the subject as possible.

"Good heavens"—Duke Titus shook his head—"thinking machines and clones and Kharn Sagara. What is the galaxy coming to? And you on top of everything else. You above all! I have some of your people swearing by the Mother that you *died* in the battle, Marlowe. Even my man Lin says you can't be killed."

Your man Lin, I thought, struggling to keep all sign of bitterness from my face. *Isn't that the truth?* I stopped fidgeting with the ring, distracted once more by the heraldic spears bracketed on the walls. I had prepared for this, and determined just what I should say. "It got close." I patted my replacement arm. "The arm, you see. I'm not sure what Lin says, but he wasn't there. I . . . it was a near thing, Your Excellency. I was very fortunate to make it out alive."

"In any event, it was your saving this Sagara that saved our forces aboard the *Demiurge*, Lin tells it. And you're the first to kill a Cielcin War Prince hand-to-hand." He laced his fingers together and dropped his hands on the tabletop. "I've sent my recommendation to the Imperial Office that you be granted a knighthood and granted the Order of Merit."

Had I been holding something, surely I would have dropped it.

"The Order of Merit?" I stammered, genuinely shocked. I had not fought alone—and when I had I'd died. I'd as good as stabbed Aranata in the back, though I supposed no one had told him that. They'd only spoken in hushed whispers that Hadrian Marlowe could not be killed, and my legend had grown ahead of me. "A knighthood? Me, sir? Your Excellency?"

"The thought pleases you?" said Lord Titus Andrew-Louis Hauptmann, First Strategos of the Centaurine Legions and Duke of Andernach. "You've earned it, son."

"I . . ." I did not know how to feel. A knighthood. Me. A knight, not just a soldier of the Empire. Hadrian. *Sir Hadrian.* I could imagine the look on my father's face when the announcement came by courier or telegraph to the dusty halls of Devil's Rest: that the prodigal son, cast away for his shortcomings, had received the Imperial Order of Merit at the personal request of a First Strategos in Centaurus. Father would have conniptions. For that reason alone—and the simple reason that all boys in the Empire dream of knighthood, and many girls, I'm told—I might have jumped for joy. And yet I could not shake my private fury. This man had ordered Lin to assassinate Kharn Sagara. This man had annihilated the Otiolo clan worldship and who knew how many million alien lives. This man had destroyed the tenuous hope of peace I'd striven toward, had destroyed my childhood's dream.

What was I supposed to say to such a man?

What could I say?

"Thank you, Your Excellency."

Duke Titus nodded, but raised a hand. "Don't thank me yet, I haven't told you Forum's response to my request." He watched me with hooded eyes a long moment, as if waiting to see if I would sweat. I didn't. Unblinking, the old soldier swiped at his desktop, holograph after hologram cycling, staring through the glass. I realized that he expected me to say something, to ask just what exactly the Imperial Office on Forum had said about me. But I had an advantage: I had just spent several long months in the company of Kharn Sagara.

I could wait.

Presently the strategos made a tossing gesture above the surface of his desk, conjuring by that motion a holograph depicting the twelve-rayed Sollan Imperial sunburst that hovered in the air. I could still see Titus Hauptmann through its image, watching me for some reaction. I could just make out the security fractals embedded in the image, layer upon layer embedded beneath the surface image, proof of its authenticity.

The seal faded, and a familiar figure appeared.

My heart stopped.

It was no servant, no logothete or grand secretary, no high minister.

His Imperial Radiance, the Emperor William XXIII of the House Avent, Firstborn Son of the Earth; Guardian of the Solar System; King of Avalon; Lord Sovereign of the Kingdom of Windsor-in-Exile; Prince Imperator of the Arms of Orion, of Sagittarius, of Perseus, and Centaurus; Primarch of Orion; Conqueror of Norma; Grand Strategos of the Legions of the Sun; Supreme Lord of the Cities of Forum; North Star of the Constellations of the Blood Palatine; Defender of the Children of Men; and Servant of the Servants of Earth stood before me.

His echo, at any rate.

Caesar's face was impassive as any pharaoh's. *Appropriate,* I thought, for one who seemed chiseled of marble. The Lord Sovereign of the Kingdom of Windsor-in-Exile towered over me—though whether that was accurate or only a deceit of the projection I did not then know. He was dressed in the finest courtly style: velvets and silks of the most vibrant vermillion, his high collar and the plackets of his coat chased with gold. A single, massive ruby shone in the center of the starburst pin that held his white cravat, and its larger cousin—large almost as my eye—secured the fibula of the white-on-white patterned half-toga, draped in such a way as left both arms free.

His hair was as red as his clothing, and cut in a fashion not at all unlike that which Duke Titus wore, combed neatly to one side and held there with oil, though his sideburns were shorter and thinner than the Duke's. How many times had I seen that aquiline profile, nobler than that of any of the statues in my family's necropolis? Ten thousand times? A million? In His Radiance they said the likeness of old King William of Avalon lived again, though perhaps they said that of all who sat the Solar Throne— and perhaps it was true.

He kept one hand on the jeweled hilt of a saber as he spoke, saying: "Exalted kinsman, Hadrian, son of Alistair of Marlowe: we greet you."

It was only a projection, but the impulse to kneel screamed through me. I knew it was expected of me, knew it was the proper thing to do, yet still I lingered a moment, only a moment—the space of two heartbeats— before I did. Long enough to note the eyes of the strategos on me, long enough to note that he noted my hesitation. If he marked it, or had some private theory with regards to the meaning of my actions, he did not show it. For my part, I think it only shock. Or perhaps my time among the Extras had put more oak in me than I thought, so that such bending did not come without difficulty.

I went to one knee as the recording continued. "Our strategos has shared with us the news of your victory against the Cielcin. We are most pleased. Your actions in the face of our enemies are in keeping with the highest traditions of service. In light of which and in keeping with the recommendations of our First Strategos, we have determined to award you with our Order of Merit, and to elevate you to the position of knight." It was real, then. Despite the conflict in my emotions, hearing the words from the Emperor's own mouth, recorded though they were, moved me in ways I could not explain or have expected. My stomach clenched, eyes watered. But His Radiance was not finished. "Moreover, in light of the extraordinary conditions of your service, we have seen fit that you shall be inducted into the ranks of our Royal Victorian Knights. We request and require that you attend upon our imperial person at Forum. My Legions will see to it you are given a ship. Come at once." And with that, the image of the North Star of the Constellations of the Blood Palatine vanished, leaving Duke Titus to watch me.

Silence again. One of the deepest and the most profound silences I have ever heard.

"Do you have any idea what sort of honor this is, Marlowe?" the Duke said.

The Royal Victorian Knights. I nodded mutely. The order had been constituted in the Golden Age, when the Emperors of Man yet ruled but a portion of the Earth herself. They were servants of the Imperial family. Personal servants, bound not to the Imperial Office, but to House Avent in its capacity as the Kings of Avalon. In all the Empire, there were fewer than a thousand such men and women, many of them cousins or children of the Emperor himself. Even the First Strategos seated there before me was not accorded that particular honor, though the honors were piled high upon his name.

"The Royal Victorians . . ." I breathed. "I don't deserve that."

"Evidently His Radiance thinks differently," the First Strategos said. "Congratulations."

"I . . . thank you."

"For myself, I see the reason. You're a great hero, the first to slay one of those War Princes in single combat, the man who located them in the first place."

I realized I was still kneeling and stood as steadily as I could, not aided in this by my half-lame left arm. "I didn't do any of that alone. You destroyed their fleet, for one, and we would never have survived without Doctor Onderra, or Captain Lin for that matter. Or Knight-Tribune Smythe and Sir William." And saying their names out loud reminded me of just what had happened to them and why, reminded me that this genteel old soldier had given the order that cost Smythe and Crossflane their lives.

Hauptmann rubbed his mouth with the back of his hand. "All the same, dear boy, you are of the blood palatine, and your own men say it was you who struck the killing blow. We're reviewing suit camera footage, of course, but you are an Imperial kinsman, however distantly, and His Radiance clearly wishes to make a positive example of you. There's some precedent, though as we've alluded to . . . your age . . . You may be the youngest Royal Victorian I've ever heard of, Imperial Princes not withstanding—and between you and me: nobody counts them."

Something Hauptmann had said had its hook in me, and I said, "My men. Your Excellency, am I allowed to take my people with me when I go to Forum? My Red Company has been with me for some time; it wouldn't do to abandon them."

"Your armsmen, are they?"

I shook my head. "Not formally, Your Excellency, no. I have no formal rank, my father disinherited me some years ago. They are only mercenaries, but they are my mercenaries."

The First Strategos mulled this over a moment, fingers slowly tracking through holograph forms embedded in his desk. Presently he found what he was looking for and—pausing to make a note—flashed a copy of it to my terminal. "I see no reason why not." He inclined his head to the papers he'd just sent me. "Your marching orders. The *Schiavona*'s been repaired and refueled. I'll have word sent that your people are to be taken aboard—in fugue if necessary."

I stood numbly still a moment, trying to figure out how to thank the man, but the gears that turned over in Titus Hauptmann's conscientious mind had turned to a new task, and he waved me on saying, "Well, go on, then. You've orders to appear before the Emperor. Do not keep His Radiance waiting."

CHAPTER 79

DEPARTURE

"I DON'T BELIEVE 'TIS happening," Valka said, taking me aside just outside the door to the umbilical that would take us out into the *Schiavona* where it hung in the great repair bay beneath the *Sieglinde*. I could see the ship through the portholes, the black adamant of her hull glowing darkly in the overhead lights of the bay where men in vacuum suits drifted about on wires in the throes of some final flight preparations. "The Emperor? The Sollan Emperor?"

"I know!" I said, finding her hand with my strong one. "I know."

She bit her lip, eyes darting to the door, where a line of technicians and soldiers busied themselves carrying equipment and luggage from the old *Mistral* to the *Schiavona*. The *Mistral* was to be left behind, packed away in the *Obdurate* or in one of the fleet's other massive carriers, abandoned to what fate I did not know. We needed speed, and the Legion interceptor was far faster than even her Uhran-made counterpart. Valka looked down, staring at some point on my chest. Before long she said, "I'm not sure I can go with you."

I felt my heart slide sideways in my chest, and I squeezed her hand. "Why not?"

"To Forum?" she said, free hand going to the back of her neck. "You know."

Her neural lace. The computer matrix embedded throughout the tissues of her brain. Here on the fringes of Imperial society, even on Emesh, those implants might go unnoticed, but on Forum? In the shining heart of Imperial power and the Chantry's authority?

I set my forehead against hers, trying to turn her face up. "You're Tavrosi; they'll know what you are and none of them would dare trouble you for it." Speaking then in her native Panthai to stymie any pricking ears, I said, "Let's just keep the . . . witchcraft to a minimum, eh?"

She punched me in the ribs. I winced. I heard Valka suck in a breath. "'Twas your bad side, wasn't it?" I flailed my half-useless arm in answer, jaw clenched. She drew closer. "I'm sorry."

I kissed her, good hand holding hers, and felt the pain bleed out of me, lost behind the blossoming warmth in my chest. I fancied I heard some of the Red Company holler from their place in the boarding line, but neither Valka nor I paid them any mind. When at last we broke apart, I said, "Come with me anyway."

It was an incredible thing to ask. A mad thing. Stupid and irresponsible, but I asked it all the same. I had told her everything. About the Quiet, about the howling Dark, and the rivers of light. About my visions and about just what had happened to me. In those early days, I cannot say if it was love for me or for her work that moved her—likely it was both—but she smiled. "All right," she said, and taking me by the back of the neck she bent me once more to kiss her.

"Well, look at you two! About time!" We broke apart, fingers coming apart only against their will. I looked on, embarrassed; Valka annoyed.

Pallino came striding up the hall, the rest of my myrmidons in tow. He had his luggage—a common soldier's rucksack over one shoulder, his gray hair newly cropped, his single eye smiling.

"It's not new, dear," Elara said, matter-of-factly. "You just haven't been paying attention." She smiled at us both, more approving aunt or older sister than cautious mother, I thought, though she was younger than Valka, at least. "Still, good to see you out in the open about it." She stood a little closer to Pallino then, positively beaming.

Siran smiled at us, too. "What's this about going to see the Emperor?" She shifted her own luggage from one shoulder to the other. "Didn't think they invited mercenaries to the palace."

"Or homunculi." Crim and Ilex had come up just behind, evidently bringing up the rear of the personnel train transferring over from the *Mistral*. Crim smoothed down his unruly dark hair. "Corvo and Durand aren't far behind. She's trying to wring a price for the ship out of the Legion financiers, God help them."

"She'll get it," Siran said, smirking. Was that the first time I'd seen her smile since Ghen's death? I couldn't be sure. "And I hear you're some kind of knight now? Don't go expecting me to bow or anything."

Pallino arched his eyebrows. "Not just any kind of knight, Siran. The lad's been named to the Victorians. That means you *will* bow if he asks you to."

"He won't ask," I said, a shade too grimly. I forced a smile. "I'm still me. And if any of you start *sir*-ing me I'll knock you flat."

"Wouldn't dream of it, sir," Ilex said, grinning.

My friends.

I had meant what I told Titus Hauptmann, that I had not done what I had done alone. I did not deserve them, but then . . . perhaps none of us ever does. See them standing there! How bright that memory. Pallino, who was like a father to me, with his clear eye and easy bravura. Elara, so often in his shadow, but without whom I think old Pallino would have come undone. Siran, still bereft without her oldest friend, but iron to the very core of her. Crim, so quick to laugh as he was to cut a man, as the best Jaddians always are. Ilex, the dryad, the homunculus, forever lonely, her every smile just a little bit sad. And Valka, Valka most of all. Valka, whose every word might cut me as sure as Prince Aranata's sword, yet was more precious to me than breathing. How far we had come together— and how much further there was to go.

Captain Otavia Corvo appeared then, with the bespectacled and forever-beleaguered First Officer Durand at her side, fumbling with both his and his captain's luggage. And behind them, unseen until they approached, came one more. The specter at the feast, overlooked and uninvited.

"William," I said, brushing past Valka to stand before the door to the umbilical. I used his right name once more to keep the cold distance hard between us.

We were the last in line, the others having made their clambering way aboard. I could hear their voices behind, calling, laughing, joking; foederati and proper soldiers alike, the Legions and the Red Company.

Switch would not look at me. I learned later that he had fought under Jinan in the *Demiurge*, and had been present when the Red Company came to relieve us in the battle for the bay. I had not seen him, not since I sent him away aboard the *Mistral*. He had been avoiding me, and for good reason. The black thread of anger that ran through Titus Hauptmann and Bassander Lin, ran through Raine Smythe and William Crossflane's mutilated and half-eaten corpses and through the lives of all those brave soldiers started here. Ended here. With him. My *friend*.

"Hadrian," he said, and screwed his eyes shut. "I heard what happened. I . . . I should have been there." I could feel all those eyes on me, wondering what I would do.

"No," I said, "none of us should have been there."

"I'm sorry!" he said, taking a step forward. "Is that what you wanted me to say?"

"No," I said again. "I didn't want you to say anything." I turned to go, to be the first through the umbilical to the ship. Whatever else had happened, however strange my world had become, still I felt his betrayal more sharply than the edge of my own sword.

Footsteps behind. "Don't turn your back on me again!" A hand on my shoulder. My bad shoulder. Wincing, I turned, stepping in such a way as to torque my hips and drive my good fist hard up under the other man's ribs. If I'd wanted to. I never raised my hand. The speed alone startled Switch and sent him leaping back.

The others were all watching. Just like in the *Mistral*'s gym, their eyes wide, hands half-ready at their sides—though ready for what not a one of them knew. I did not raise my hands, I did not even raise my voice. "Could we have some privacy, please?" I asked, not turning my eyes to the others. "I'll be along presently." The others were a minute complying, eyes flicking from one to the other where they stood in a loose knot around the two of us.

"Let's let them talk," Pallino said, perhaps more sensitive to the sort of anger I felt than any of the others. Taking Elara by the arm, he said, "Come on, then." Crim flashed me a worried look, and clapped me on the shoulder as he passed, followed by Ilex, Corvo, and the rest. Valka lingered in the doorway—I could see her shadow on the black decking.

Then the final retreat of feet.

I looked at Switch properly for the first time, my jaw set. He seemed somehow more like the scared boy I'd first known than the man he'd later become. Before, I had pitied that fear, and tried to make him strong, but now I only reviled him for it. That is no easy thing, to admit your own friends repulse you, and yet he did.

"I want to come with you," Switch said.

"No," I said for a third time.

He took a considered step forward, hand outstretched. "Had, please."

"You got them killed," I said, and there was not a drop of warmth in my voice. "Crossflane, Smythe, Greenlaw—Earth knows how many others." I saw my own body toppling as my eyes went dark, as I struggled to breathe with lungs that weren't even there anymore.

Switch's mouth worked open and closed like a fish, and after a while he managed, "That . . . that isn't fair." Maybe it wasn't. Maybe *nothing* was fair. Maybe it wasn't supposed to be. "I thought you were going to die down on Vorgossos."

"So you sold me out to *Bassander Lin*?" I sneered. "I died, Switch!" The words escaped me at full force, unbidden, unprepared for, spoken loud and clear where I felt certain ship's security would pick it up. For the moment, it didn't matter.

The other man's eyes were wide as dinner plates, as an officer's phalera medals. "You . . ."

"Died!" I said, but did not stop to explain. Switch had not been there. Switch had not seen. "And the Cielcin all died, too! Died because *Bassander Lin* was *only following orders*. We almost had them!" I waved my right hand. "We almost had peace! Or something *like* it! And we didn't get it because of you. Because you betrayed me! You summoned Lin here! And Hauptmann! All to save *your* skin! Not mine! Not anyone else's! *Yours!*" Without realizing it, I was shouting. Suddenly self-conscious, knowing that Valka at least had not gone too far, I quieted down. "You were supposed to be my friend."

"I am your friend."

"No," I said. Four times now. "You're not. Not anymore." I raised my good hand. "Get out of here."

The first tears began to fall, but I cannot say if they were his or mine. My hand shook, but did not fall. After a moment's silence, Switch took a long, rattling breath. "Where should I go?"

"Wherever you like," I said, and let my hand fall at last. I turned quickly, stepping over the threshold into the boarding umbilical.

"Hadrian, wait! I—" But I had already punched the airlock door behind me, and the door sealed with a hiss and a metallic bang. Hidden from the world for a moment by two doors of solid steel, I slid to my knees and wept. For Switch, for our friendship. I wept for Smythe, for Crossflane, for Aranata, for Nobuta, and Tanaran. I wept for the soldiers we lost, for the futures that might have been.

And for myself. Myself most of all.

CHAPTER 80

HALFMORTAL

"ARE YOU ALL RIGHT?" Valka asked when I came in through the umbilical alone. She could tell I'd been crying, but did not press, did not ask where Switch had gone. She knew. They all knew.

Without speaking, I wrapped my good arm around her and pulled her close, screwing my eyes shut, as if I might crush out all light by doing so. We stood there a long moment, neither of us moving, entirely alone. When at last I'd pulled myself back together, I drew back and asked, "Where are the others?"

The lights in the vestibule were low, the walls bare stainless steel. Through the door behind, the hall stretched black and golden, strangely warm for a military ship. When Valka spoke, her voice was soft, as concerned as ever I had heard it. "I sent them on. Told them you needed a moment."

"What did I do to deserve you?"

"Aren't we presumptuous?" she said, echoing that time on Vorgossos. She smiled, broke into brief but rippling laughter. "You don't deserve me, anyway."

Very serious, I said, "I know that."

She kissed me again. "Good." Her eyes shone in the dimness, sparkling up at me, yellow as a cat's. "I still can't believe you're alive. I saw you . . ." Her voice trailed away to naught, and I held her more tightly.

"I know," I said softly, "I know."

"You really think it was the Quiet?"

"Do you doubt it?"

She shook her head. "I don't have any other explanation, but 'tis . . .'tis mad. They're supposed to be extinct, Hadrian. A dead race. I'm an archaeologist. I'm not . . ."

"A witch?"

She made a face, and for a moment I thought she might swat me again, but she restrained herself. Valka drew away, examining me up and down, as though she suspected something. "'Tis really you, not some clone of Sagara's?"

I froze. That thought had not occurred to me. "No," I decided, "it's me. Kharn Sagara would not have wasted time interrogating me if I were his creature." I could see the fever in the reborn Kharn's eyes.

If I die, what happens to me?

"Besides," I said, "there's this." I drew out the shell fragment and held it up for Valka to see. "I left it in my coat in the hangar after . . . after we lost Smythe. When I . . . came back, when I returned . . . I had it with me." Valka did not state the obvious, which was that I had received it from Brethren, who was Kharn's creature. But I *knew*, the city I had seen in my vision—that crumbling landscape and the sound of the infant wailing. I had seen much the same thing in Calagah on Emesh.

Valka took the bit of shell from my palm.

"I still don't know what this is," she said.

"I bet if you studied it, you'd find it looks exactly like the stones in Calagah," I said, not knowing where the words came from, but almost certain I was right.

"Just black . . ." Valka quoted, referring to the stones of the Quiet ruins, which had no molecular structure to speak of, were only a single piece of solid black.

"A kind of highmatter?"

"Maybe," she said, eyes shining again with that mania only her love of ancient things could kindle. "I'll have to take a look at it." She smiled up at me. "I'll let you know if you're right!"

"What's that?" A new voice slashed across our conversation, shattering our moment alone.

Valka closed her hand over the shard, smiling at Bassander Lin, who stood framed in the door to the vestibule, his face in shadow. She spoke before I could. "Jewelry," she said, stepping forward in such a way that half put her between Bassander and myself. "A trifle."

The Mandari captain stepped out of the hall light, face coming into focus as his brows rose. "Ah." His black eyes searched for something in my face. What that something was, and if he found it there, was anybody's guess. The man stepped forward, chin thrust out, shoulders squared and back. I thought he might strike me—thought I might strike him. But he stopped a few paces from me, taking in the racked vacuum suits where they hung in their wall niches, the rubberized floor, the white, joyless lighting. "Every time I see you standing there, I see you cut down," he said, and blessed himself, touching fingers to forehead, lips, and chest. "By Earth, in all my years, I never thought . . ." His words ran down to nothing, jaw gone slack. "I've never seen anything like it."

And then he did something incredible: he thrust out his hand. Not to shake mine, I realized, but to touch me—as though I were the hem of some nobile's robe as he rode through the crowd in triumph. I recoiled, shocked, but Bassander did not drop his hand, only held it out as in benediction.

"I didn't *do* anything, Bassander," I said, moving past him toward the hall, Valka following on behind. There was no reason to deny it, not with someone who was there. "I know what you saw, what you think you saw, but I don't understand it."

A little embarrassed perhaps, Lin closed his hand into a fist. "Then it really is a miracle."

I froze on the threshold. Bassander Lin had never struck me as a religious man, but then, I had been born a palatine, and it is said that palatines go to the sanctum only to be seen, that it is the peasantry who light all the candles. I have always considered myself agnostic, but there are few of that effete class amongst the soldiery. Soldiers, someone told me, do not have the luxury of disbelief.

Still, this new dimension to Bassander Lin surprised me, and though I stood now fully in the hallway I turned. The stoic captain I had known was gone, and gone the line of fire between us. If he had been my rival, he was no longer. That Captain Lin was gone, transfigured by what he had seen: my death and . . . return. The Lin that stood before me was something else. Something smaller—so it seemed—for it seemed that I looked down upon him, though we stood on level ground, him in darkness, me in light. Or no, that wasn't it. I did not look down on him—though I hated him still for the role he'd played in all this—rather he was looking up at me, as one looks upon the face of a mountain, as I'd looked up and seen myself pointing in the Dark.

"A miracle," Bassander Lin repeated. I took a couple of steps backward, edging out not—as I'd expected—onto a hallway, but onto a catwalk that overlooked the very cargo bay from which I'd led our desperate charge into the helium fog. Bassander followed me, with Valka now close behind, watching me carefully. I was suddenly, painfully aware of the crowd

milling about beneath us, soldiers and mercenaries, technicians and medical personnel alike, busying themselves with the sorting and securing of
cargo. The din of laughing voices and barked commands rose all around
us, muffled before by some static field in the door to the airlock vestibule.

Bassander stepped out with me, so that we stood opposite one another
as we had on the *Balmung* so long ago. And then he did the second incredible thing he'd done in a matter of moments. He knelt. Perhaps not so
incredible: he was a soldier of the Empire, and I a palatine lord and cousin
of the blood imperial. But this was Bassander Lin, and I was Hadrian
Marlowe.

"I don't know what any of it means," he said. "This thing you can do."

Valka was standing behind the man, smiling in wry bemusement. I
tried not to look at her, terrified that I might laugh, might sneer.

I heard a hush go through the crowd below. Then someone's upraised
voice. "Hey! Look, the captain!" The quiet deepened.

The captain did not seem to notice. He did not raise his eyes. "Maybe
the Earth has sent you, I don't know. But you *died*, Marlowe. I saw you die."

"So did I!" one soldier called.

"And me!"

"A miracle!" The cry went up. "A miracle!"

I've lost control, I remember thinking. *Somewhere in all this, I lost control.* We
are not always the authors of our own stories. Some of us never are. I think
that is what we struggle *for*: the command of our own lives. We struggle
against our families, against the state, against nature, against our own weakness. All that we might choose for ourselves, if only for a moment.

If only once.

But Bassander Lin had chosen for me, and set my feet upon the path.
Turning, I looked down upon the sea of faces on the level below me:
rough mercenaries beside shave-pated legionnaires in black fatigues and
the officers in their long coats. There was Lieutenant Cartier, overseeing
the final preparations. And beside her stood Otavia Corvo and Bastien
Durand. And there were Pallino, Elara, and Siran. And there—not far—
were Ilex and Crim, forever inseparable—and Tor Varro, of all people,
standing near the rear among medical personnel in their white habits. All
of them watching, all of them seeing.

I was uncharacteristically speechless, and stood clutching my useless
arm, eyes moving from Bassander to the crowd—back to Bassander, who
said, "Maybe you're the one. The one who will bring an end to all
this . . ." He shook his head. His transformation was so complete that it

astonished me. Perhaps that was why I could not speak, so horrified was I by this display, by his reduction. Before, he had been a proud soldier—perhaps he was one still—but the man kneeling on the catwalk at my feet seemed more a creature, *my* creature, than a man. I heard the echo of Brethren's words in what he said, and I shivered.

The man to end it all.

"You don't know that," I said, and made a weak gesture that Bassander should rise. The embarrassment ran thick over me as crude oil. I wanted desperately to be away. To be anywhere else.

"You're immortal," Bassander said. "That's proof. That's a sign."

"He's half mortal!" someone interjected. Was it Crim?

"Half mortal?" someone echoed, quieter than the first.

And then it began for true. "Halfmortal!" someone repeated, and made of the joke a cry. A declaration. A *name.* "Hadrian Halfmortal! He died! We all saw it! Halfmortal!"

"Halfmortal!"

"Halfmortal!"

Half-dead, I thought, and turned from Bassander to face the people below. In doing so, I turned and stepped onto the path Bassander's new-found awe and piety had marked out for me. They all looked up at me, hands raised, fists thrust in the air. Most of them had seen me perish, and those who did not knew at least that I had been the one to slay the prince. They cheered for me, and shouts of "Halfmortal! Hadrian Halfmortal!" were mingled with cries of "Had! Had! Had!" from those few myrmidons who had come up with me out of Emesh.

"Halfmortal!"

It was the name Brethren had given me, whispered by unseen mouths above the waters of a sunless sea, spoken again by chance or fortune by the lips of some unknown soldier. *Halfmortal.* For all the light of that shining instant, I felt a shadow move beneath me. Pale, bloated hands seized on my heart. I am old now, and have known enough of time to see the patterns of it, to see the path—like a river—at my feet beginning to carry me away. I did not know then where it led, or that the light that smiled upon us in that livid instant was only an echo, a foretaste of that final fire.

I did not know it, but I had taken my first steps—forward, *down*—toward Gododdin.

Toward the end.

Toward light and fire.

But I was young! And I was alive! And hailed by all who knew me. I had gone into darkness and deep water and come out again. Changed—as we always are by such experiences—but alive. My new arm hung at my side, part of me but not *a* part. I tried to close the new fist, but it would not go—and though it would grow strong in time and the horror of it would fade, it would serve as a constant reminder of the horrors of Vorgossos and the people and the life I had lost there. I turned and looked past Bassander toward Valka, gestured that she might come and stand beside me. Smiling, she shook her head, remaining in the shadow of the doorway behind the still-kneeling Bassander Lin.

Cries of *"Halfmortal!"* still rose up from below. Fists raised in triumph. Hands in praise.

I raised my strong right hand in answer.

There are endings, Reader, and this is one. Some endings are beginnings. Such is this. As the Phoenix is reborn from its ashes, as new gods are ever born from the bodies of the old, so too was I reborn by that lakeside beneath that glassed-in sky. I left much of what I was by those waters: my scars from Emesh, my dreams of peace. Most of life consists of such transformations. If what I have done disturbs you, Reader, I do not blame you. If you would read no further, I understand. You have the luxury of foresight. You know where this ends.

I shall go on alone.

THE MEIDUA RED COMPANY

NEVER FORMALLY A MERCENARY company, the Meidua Red Company was concocted as a front by Hadrian Marlowe and Dame Raine Smythe of the 437th Centaurine Legion with the express purpose of locating the Extrasolarian kingdom of Vorgossos. Joined by a contingent of Jaddian soldiers at the behest of the Satrap Kalima di Sayyiph, they posed as a mercenary outfit, and traveled among the Norman Freeholds for decades. During this period, they built a reputation as mercenaries in the hopes of finding a lead to Vorgossos, most notably toppling the military dictatorship of Admiral Marius Whent on the planet Pharos, during which time they acquired two new ships and several hundred recruits. During this period, the company numbered perhaps two thousand strong (Lord Marlowe is vague in this account) spread across three vessels. The first was the *Balmung*, an antique *Punisher*-class destroyer kept in the holds of the supercarrier *Obdurate*. The other two vessels, the *Mistral* and the *Pharaoh*, were acquired during their campaign against Whent's government on Pharos.

Lord Marlowe was the nominal head of the company, but that position was a facade. The official commander in this period was then–Captain Bassander Lin, and the rivalry between the two men led to tension within the company. This tension worsened following the addition of the Norman troops after Whent's defeat, as they were more loyal to Lord Marlowe than to Captain Lin. Much of that tension and more is detailed in Marlowe's account.

Here follows a list of those members of the Red Company mentioned in this second volume of Lord Marlowe's account:

LORD HADRIAN ANAXANDER MARLOWE, nominal Commandant of the Meidua Red Company. Disowned palatine lord and immunis attached to the 437th Legion. The Halfmortal, the Sun Eater, Starbreaker, Palekiller, Deathless. Notorious genocide responsible for the death of the entire Cielcin species.

—His myrmidons, friends and former coliseum fighters from Emesh:

   —**WILLIAM OF DANU,** called **SWITCH,** Lord Marlowe's personal lictor.

      —His former master, **SET,** a procurer.

   —**GHEN OF EMESH,** centurion. Formerly a convict.

   —**SIRAN OF EMESH,** centurion. Formerly a convict.

   —**PALLINO OF TRIESTE,** prime centurion. Formerly a convict.

      —His paramour, **ELARA OF EMESH,** quartermaster on board the *Balmung.*

VALKA ONDERRA VHAD EDDA, a xenologist from Edda in the Demarchy of Tavros. Nominally scientific advisor to the Red Company.

BASSANDER LIN, a captain of the 437th Legion, posing as Commodore of the Red Company fleet and captain of the *Pharaoh.* An ethnic Mandari and life-long officer in the Imperial Legions.

   —His First Officer, **PRISCA GREENLAW,** lieutenant in the 437th Legion. Staunchly loyal to Captain Lin.

—On board the *Pharaoh:*

   —**LUANA OKOYO,** chief medical officer. A Norman officer recruited during the Pharos affair.

   —**SOISSON,** lieutenant. Legion officer attached to the company since Emesh.

   —**DULIA,** lieutenant. Legion officer attached to the company since Emesh.

   —**ETIENNE,** a decurion and former lover to William of Danu.

The Other Captains:

—**JINAN AZHAR,** a lieutenant in the Jaddian army loaned to the Red Company and captain of the *Balmung*. Lover to HADRIAN MARLOWE.

>—Her First Officer, **ALESSANDRO HANAS,** lieutenant in the Jaddian army loaned to the Red Company.

—On board the *Balmung:*

>—**ARTURO,** a Jaddian officer.

>—**BRUX,** a Legion officer. Ship's supercargo.

>—**OTAVIA CORVO,** captain of the *Mistral* and former second-in-command to the late Emil Bordelon. Betrayed him and Whent's cause at Lord Marlowe's urging. A Norman officer recruited during the Pharos affair.

>>—Her First Officer, **BASTIEN DURAND,** commander. A Norman officer recruited during the Pharos affair.

—On board the *Mistral*:

>—**KARIM GARONE,** called **CRIM,** lieutenant. An ethnic Jaddian raised in the Norman Freeholds. Joined along with Captain Corvo during the Pharos affair.

>—**ILEX,** lieutenant. A dryad homunculus with background in computer systems and engineering.

THE 437TH CENTAURINE LEGION

Constituted in ISD 11907 under the Fifth Centaurine Legionary Act drafted by Primarch Ambrose Surabian, the 437th Centaurine Legion has defended Imperial interests in the Centaurus Arm of the galaxy. During the Cielcin Wars, the Legion was under the command of Sir Leonid Bartosz, a career soldier born into the Legions—as so many are—his parents both being life-long officers. To all accounts, Bartosz was an able commander, but he figures only little in the narrative of history. He is thought to have been among the casualties at the Battle of Gododdin, when he was lost with the legion's flagship, the *ISV Deluge*, along with all hands. A victim of Hadrian Marlowe and the Sun Eater. Of his four tribunes, only Dame Raine Smythe is of much note, being the one to recruit Lord Marlowe to the Legions as an immunis after the Emesh affair.

Here follows a list of those members of the 437th Centaurine Legion and its Jaddian allies mentioned in this second volume of Lord Marlowe's account:

LORD TITUS HAUPTMANN, Duke of Andernach and First Strategos of the Legions of Centaurus.

—**SIR LEONID BARTOSZ,** Legate of the 437th Centaurine Legion.

—**DAME RAINE SMYTHE,** 4th Tribune of the 437th Centaurine Legion, Captain of the *ISV Obdurate*. A patrician of plebeian birth.

—Her First Officer, **SIR WILLIAM CROSSFLANE,** Commander, First Grade; an elderly palatine.

—On board the *Obdurate* and the *Schiavona*:

—**LUDOVICO SCIARRA,** Commander and third officer aboard the *ISV Schiavona*.

—**MARIS CARTIER,** Lieutenant.

—**TOR VARRO,** Chalcenterite scholiast and Cielcin translator attached to the Legion. Brought on at Hauptmann's insistence.

THE KINGDOM OF VORGOSSOS

According to legend, Vorgossos is a lost world orbiting a brown dwarf, settled in ancient times by the ancestors of the Extrasolarians fleeing the early Empire. Lord Marlowe's account indicates that the settlement of the planet may go back further, that the city he visited may have been a

Mericanii stronghold during the Foundation War. Whether or not that is true, it appears certain from his account that the myth surrounding Kharn Sagara and his conquest of the Exalted is. If Lord Marlowe is to be believed, the ancient warlord found a manner of immortality by relying on abandoned Mericanii technology and has ruled the planet ever since, providing a hideaway for pirates, mercenaries, and all manner of unsavory activity: notably the black market genetics and cybernetics trades.

Here follows a list of those denizens of Vorgossos mentioned in this second volume of Lord Marlowe's account:

KHARN SAGARA, called the **UNDYING,** King of Vorgossos. Presumably the same Kharn Sagara from the ancient legends, implying that he is nearly fifteen thousand years old.

—His children, **REN** and **SUZUHA,** apparently his clones.

—His servants:

—**BRETHREN,** a Mericanii artificial intelligence composed of human tissue designed to grow forever. Confined to an underground sea in order to support its weight.

—**YUME,** an android which acts as the Undying's caretaker and butler.

—**CALVERT,** the Exalted in charge of Kharn Sagara's cloning program and body farms.

—**NAIA,** a homunculus.

—The suppliants:

—**LORD KIM HAE SONG,** the former Baron of Munshin.

—**LADY CATHERINE DOMITIA HARFLEUR,** the Baroness of Varadeto.

—**LADY MARIETTA CALUSA,** the Marquise of Sarmatia.

—**LORD SENDHIL RAMANARAYAN,** the Grand Duke of Milinda.

—**PARDOS, ARCHIBALD,** and **FREDERICK,** various members of the galaxy's elite.

—In the city:

—**SHARA,** a beggar woman.

On board the *Enigma of Hours:*

CAPTAIN EIDHIN, captain of the *Enigma of Hours.* An Exalted sworn to the service of the Undying in Vorgossos.

—His ship's mate, **NAZZARENO,** a tender pilot and de facto customs officer. Exalted.

—**MARKO** and **JARI,** Exalted, possibly members of the *Enigma*'s crew. The latter had mutated on exposure to the Deep on Apas; the former is his caretaker.

—**JACOPO,** a merchanter and natalist.

THE CIELCIN AND CLAN OTIOLO

Not much is known of the history of the Otiolo clan. The only contact between the Itani Otiolo and the Sollan Empire was during the Vorgossos affair as recorded in this text. Aside from military reports made by members of the 437th Centaurine Legion and members of Strategos Hauptmann's staff, Lord Marlowe's record is the only one touching on the clan at all—and is at any rate the most comprehensive. Piecing together what we can from the available sources, it seems that the clan Otiolo was a young, fairly minor tribe. Marlowe's text says the Prince Aranata took its people "out of Utaiharo." This suggests that Prince Aranata defeated another prince in combat and took his tribe for his own, making him the first chieftain of the Itani Otiolo, as any Cielcin who kills an Aeta becomes an Aeta. Such short-lived clans appear to have been common among the Cielcin, their being a species of tyrants (which explains the necessity of the Baetan class, who appear to maintain the continuity of the tribe as it changes hands and identities as it moves from Aeta to Aeta. Not much else is known of this particular clan, any primary documents and artifacts having been lost in the annihilation of the *Bahali imnal Akura* during Strategos Hauptmann's offensive.

Here follows a list of the Cielcin, especially those of the Clan Otiolo, mentioned in this second volume of Lord Marlowe's account:

AETA UTSEBIMN ARANATA OTIOLO, Viudihom, Prince of the Itani Otiolo, Master-Keeper to His People. The supreme ruler of the worldship *Bahali imnal Akura* and head of the Otiolo clan.

—His child, **NOBUTA OTIOLO,** presumptive heir to the clan.

—His retainers and slaves:

—**OALICOMN,** majordomo and coteliho (herald) of the Itani Otiolo.

—**CASANTORA TANARAN IAKATO,** Baetan priest-historian of the Itani Otiolo, a prisoner of the Sollan Empire and the Meidua Red Company in particular.

—**{ITANA UVANARI AYATOMN},** formerly the Ichakta captain of the starship *Yad Ga Higatte*, killed by Hadrian Marlowe during the Emesh affair.

—On board the *Yad Ga Higatte*:

—**SVATAROM, ETANITARI,** and **OANATORO,** common sailors, soldiers, and slaves.

Other Cielcin mentioned:

—**DORAYAICA,** presumably **AETA SYRIANI DORAYAICA,** of whom much is written in the latter parts of Lord Marlowe's account.

—**HASURUMN,** another Cielcin Aeta chieftain.

—**PAGORAMATU,** another Cielcin Aeta chieftain.

—**{UTAIHARO},** presumably deceased, an Aeta Prince defeated by Aranata Otiolo, his tribe incorporated into the Otiolo scianda.

THE WIDER WORLD

Many persons referenced or appearing in this second volume of Lord Marlowe's account belong to none of the groups above, but have been included here for the purposes of completeness. They have been divided by location, with references to the Imperial and Jaddian courts on Forum and Jadd respectively, as well as on the planets Delos, Emesh, Pharos, and Rustam—in addition to the Extrasolarian city of March Station.

Here follows a list of these persons mentioned in Lord Marlowe's account:

ON FORUM:

His Imperial Radiance, the **EMPEROR WILLIAM THE TWENTY-THIRD OF THE HOUSE AVENT;** Firstborn Son of the Earth; Guardian of the Solar System; King of Avalon; Lord Sovereign of the Kingdom of Windsor-in-Exile; Prince Imperator of the Arms of Orion, of Sagittarius, of Perseus, and Centaurus; Primarch of Orion; Conqueror of Norma; Grand Strategos of the Legions of the Sun; Supreme Lord of the Cities of Forum; North Star of the Constellations of the Blood Palatine; Defender of the Children of Men; and Servant of the Servants of Earth.

—His ancestor, {**KING WILLIAM VII WINDSOR**}, called **WILLIAM THE ADVENT,** the God Emperor, Emperor of Avalon and Eden, Last King of the United Kingdom of Great Britain, King-in-Avalon, and Lord Sovereign of the Kingdom of Windsor-in-Exile. The first Sollan Emperor, deified by the Chantry.

—**EDOUARD ALBE,** a Legion Intelligence Officer and future friend of Lord Marlowe's.

ON JADD:

His Royal Highness, **ALDIA AHMAD RODRIGO-PHILLIPE DI OTRANTO**, High Prince of Jadd, Prince of Laran, First-Among-Equals of the Princes of the Principalities of the Jaddian Peoples, Lord of the Encircling Moons, Keeper of the Planet of Fire, Chief of the Eali Al'Aqran.

—**LADY KALIMA ALIARADA UDIRI DI SAYYIPH**, Satrap of Ubar, loyal to the Prince of Thessaloniki, a formal envoy to the war front on behalf of the High Prince.

—Her Lictor, **SIR OLORIN MILTA**, a Maeskolos Swordmaster of the Fire School.

ON DELOS:

LORD ALISTAIR DIOMEDES FRIEDRICH MARLOWE, Archon of Meidua Prefecture and Lord of Devil's Rest, former Lord Executor of Delos System, the Butcher of Linon.

—His wife, **LADY LILIANA KEPHALOS-MARLOWE,** a celebrated librettist and filmmaker, daughter to the Duchess of Delos.

—Their son, **CRISPIN MARLOWE,** Hadrian's younger brother and presumptive heir to Devil's Rest and Meidua Prefecture.

—His mother, **{LADY FUCHSIA BELLGROVE-MARLOWE},** deceased.

—His retainers:

—**SIR FELIX MARTYN,** Castellan and Commander of the House Guard, formerly Hadrian's fighting instructor.

—**SIR ROBAN MILOSH,** a knight-lictor and once Hadrian's body-guard.

—**TOR ALCUIN,** scholiast and chief advisor.

—**TOR GIBSON,** Hadrian's beloved tutor, a Zenoan scholiast trained on Syracuse. Exiled, presumed dead.

ON EMESH:

LORD BALIAN MATARO, third Count of Emesh, Archon of Borosevo Prefecture and Lord of Castle Borosevo.

—His daughter, **ANAÏS MATARO,** Hadrian's betrothed and future Countess of Emesh.

—**{GILLIAM VAS},** deformed bastard son of Emesh's Grand Prior, killed by Hadrian in a duel.

—**{CAT}**, a peasant girl and former lover of Hadrian's, died in the plague that wracked Emesh.

ON PHAROS:

{MARIUS WHENT}, deceased military dictator of the planet Pharos, formerly an Imperial legate. Defeated by Hadrian Marlowe and the Meidua Red Company.

—His subordinate, **{EMIL BORDELON}**, a Norman mercenary and ship's captain. Famously depraved and disliked by his men.

ON RUSTAM:

THE PAINTED MAN, a shape-shifting homunculus and crime lord in Rustam's underbelly. Formerly of Vorgossos.

—Its subordinate, **SAMIR,** a plagiarius and weapons dealer.

ZHIVAY, interim Consul of Rustam, formerly a chief of the urban prefects.

ON MARCH STATION:

ANTONIUS BREVON, a merchanter and businessman with ties to the Exalted and to Vorgossos.

—His slave, **EVA,** a homunculus.

YEVGENI CENTO, a bonecutter and natalist.

INDEX OF WORLDS

HEREIN IS APPENDED A list of all those worlds mentioned in this second volume of Lord Marlowe's account. The purpose of this list is simply to remind the reader which world is which. Detailed astrographic and geological documents—as well as economic and historical texts—may be found elsewhere in the library. What information I have provided is all that is necessary to understand Lord Marlowe's text.

—*Tor Paulos of Nov Belgaer*

Andernach   A Centaurine Duchy presided over by House Hauptmann, famously the home of First Strategos Titus Hauptmann. A cold, arid world.

Apas   Location unknown. According to Lord Marlowe's account, the site of a colony of xenobitic microorganisms called a Deep.

Aptucca   An Imperial colony in the Norma Arm. Site of one of Lord Marlowe's greatest victories.

Ardistama   A Norman freehold visited by Lord Marlowe between Emesh and Vorgossos.

Athyras   An older Imperial world, home to the predatory xanarths.

Avalon   One of the original human colonies, site of heavy European colonization by generation ark. Birthplace of the Sollan Empire.

Bannatia   An Imperial Norman colony destroyed by the Cielcin.

Coritani   A major Imperial base in the Norman Expanse.

Cressgard   A lost Imperial colony in the Veil of Marinus, site of the first contact with the Cielcin at the Battle of Cressgard in ISD 15792.

Danu   A major Duchy in the Centaurus Arm, most notable in Lord Marlowe's account as the birthplace of his friend William, called Switch.

Delos   Birthplace of Hadrian Marlowe and seat of the Duchy of House Kephalos in the Spur of Orion, a temperate world with wan sunlight, famed for its uranium deposits, which made it extremely wealthy.

Emesh   A watery world in the Veil of Marinus, seat of House Mataro. Home of the coloni Umandh and the subterranean ruins at Calagah. Originally a Norman colony.

Epidamnus   An Imperial County in the Sagittarius Arm, formerly a center for trade and home to the predatory megatheres.

Forum   The capital of the Sollan Empire. A gas giant with a breathable atmosphere in whose cloud belt are several flying palace cities that serve as the administrative hub of the Imperium.

Gibbeah   Planet destroyed by Chantry intervention in the ninth millennium following a series of killings carried out on the local plebeian population by its nobility.

Gododdin   A system between the Centaurus and Sagittarius Arms of the galaxy, famously destroyed by Hadrian Marlowe during the final battle in the Crusade.

Idun   An Imperial Norman colony destroyed by the Cielcin.

Jadd   The planet of fire, sacred capital of the Jaddian Principalities, on whose soil none shall tread without the express permission of the High Prince.

Kremnoi   According to Lord Marlowe's account, an Extrasolarian colony. Location unknown.

Linon   Moon of a gas giant in Delos system, formerly the demesne of the exsul House Orin and site of the Battle of Linon in ISD 15863, in which Alistair Marlowe killed the entire house.

Luin	A planet famous for its xenobitic forests, considered something of a fantasy land. Known for the phasma vigrandi, a species of floating organism that glows like faerie lights.
Lycia	An Imperial Norman colony destroyed by the Cielcin.
March Station	An Extrasolarian ring station in deep space. Home to millions, it is a major commercial and industrial hub.
Marinus	The first Norman Freehold seized by the Imperium and amongst their first colonies in the Expanse.
Milinda	A Grand Duchy in the Primarchate of Perseus. Formerly a mining colony, it grew to prominence during the First Jaddian Wars.
Monmara	A water world and a Norman freehold, known for the cheap mass production of starships.
Nagramma	A Norman freehold settled primarily by Cid Arthurian religious refugees.
Nessus	Seat of the Centaurine Primarchate.
Old Earth	Birthplace of the human species. A nuclear ruin and victim of environmental collapse, she is protected by the Chantry Wardens and none may walk there.
Pharos	A Norman freehold ruled for a time by Marius Whent, an ex-Imperial legate defeated by Hadrian Marlowe during his time as a mercenary.
Rustam	An Imperial colony in the Norman Expanse, site of a minor engagement with the Cielcin that culminated in the destruction of its capital city.
Sanora	A Norman freehold. Recently settled, it's considered a den of pirates.
Sarmatia	A minor imperial world in the Upper Perseus.
Se Vattayu	The mythical homeworld of the Cielcin, its surface apparently honeycombed with labyrinthine tunnels like those the Quiet dug at Calagah on Emesh.
Senuessa	A Sagittarine world, site of the Battle of Senuessa, one of the bloodiest in the entirety of the Cielcin Wars.
Tanais	According to Lord Marlowe's account, an Extrasolarian colony. Location unknown.
Tavros	The primary planet of the Tavros Demarchy, settled by a mix of Nordic, Indian, and ethnic Thai peoples ahead of the wave of Imperial expansion in a region high above the galaxy's ecliptic.
Trieste	An old Imperial world in the Orion Arm, notable in this account only as the birthplace of Lord Marlowe's long-time companion and friend Pallino.
Tyras	An Imperial colony in the Norman Expanse presided over by the defunct House Jurnau. Destroyed by the Cielcin in ISD 16216.
Ubar	An arid Jaddian satrapy loyal to the House di Otranto, who have been the High Princes of Jadd for generations. Begs loyalty to the Prince of Thessaloniki.

670
670

Uhra   A Norman Freehold, recently having transitioned from a kingdom to a republic, renowned for its starship manufacture.

Varadeto   A Barony in the Primarchate of Orion, presided over by House Harfleur.

Vorgossos   A mythical Extrasolarian world orbiting a brown dwarf, said to be a mecca for the black market genetics trade. Formerly a hideout for the Exalted, presided over now by a warlord known as the Undying.

LEXICON

HEREIN IS INCLUDED AN index of those terms appearing in this second volume of Lord Marlowe's manuscript which are not easily translated into the Classical English or which bear a specific cultural or technical definition. For a more complete explanation of the methodology I employed in devising these coinages in translating from the Galstani in which the original was written, please refer to the appendices in volume one of this translation.

—Tor Paulos of Nov Belgaer

abstraction   The process by which members of the Exalted remove themselves
                         from humanity through technological modification.

adorator   A member of any antique religious cult maintained by the Empire
                         and tolerated by the Chantry.

Advent   The destruction of Old Earth by humanity at the end of the
                         Foundation War.

Aeta   A Cielcin prince-chieftain. Appears to have ownership rights over its
                         subjects and their property.

akaranta   The dominant Cielcin sexual role.

aljanhi   A human Jaddian soldier, distinguished from the clone mamluks.

anagnost   An initiate in the Chantry clergy.

androgyn   A homunculus exhibiting neither or both male and female sex
                         characteristics.

aquilarii   In the Legions, the pilot of a lighter craft.

azhdarch   A xenobite predator common in the Colosso, like a lizard with a
                         long neck open from top to bottom in a fanged mouth.

backspace   Territory within Imperial space not formally colonized by the
                         Empire. Often a refuge for the Extrasolarians.

baetan   In Cielcin culture, a sort of priest-historian of the scianda.

baron/baroness   Lowest rank of the Imperial palatine nobility. Rules a planetary
                         demesne. Title may be passed on through inheritance.

bastille   Any Chantry judicial and penal center, usually attached to a temple
                         sanctum.

biofacture   The manufacture of living beings, organs, or tissues.

bonecutter   A black market genetics surgeon, not sanctioned by the High
                         College.

**Book of the   An anthology of several texts compiled or composed by the scholiast
  Mind**   Imore. Forms the basis of their philosophy.

centurion   A rank in the Imperial Legions, commands a CENTURY.

Chalcenterite   A fraternal order of the scholiasts, noted for their asceticism.

Chantry   See HOLY TERRAN CHANTRY.

chimera   Any genetically altered or artificially created animal, usually by
                         blending the genetic code of two or more animals.

chiromancer   See BONECUTTER.

Choir   An elite research and intelligence body operating under the
                         command of the Chantry.

choregus   The leader of a chorus, as in a song.

Cielcin   Spacefaring alien species. Humanoid and carnivorous. The principle
                         enemy of humankind during the CRUSADE.

Classical English	The ancient language of both the Mericanii and the early Imperial settlers on Avalon, still used by the scholiasts.
coloni	Any intelligent, pre-industrial race of xenobites on a human-occupied world, particularly in the Sollan Empire.
Colosso	A series of sporting events held in a coliseum involving professional gladiators, slave myrmidons, animals, races, and more.
commandant	The leader of a private mercenary company.
commodore	In the Legions, an officer above captain but below strategos, usually in command of a fleet.
cornicen	In the Legions, a soldier tasked with playing the horn or trumpet at parades.
coteliho	In Cielcin culture, roughly equivalent to a Lord's herald or majordomo.
crèche	A cryonic storage pod for transporting people on long interstellar journeys.
cryoburn	Burns incurred as a side-effect of improper cryonic freezing.
cubiculum	A chamber where persons are kept in cryonic fugue, usually aboard a starship.
daimon	An artificial intelligence. Sometimes erroneously applied to non-intelligent computer systems.
Dark	Space. In the Chantry religion, a place of desolation and torment.
Deep	A species of possibly artificial and intelligent microorganisms found on several worlds, capable of digesting and altering other living creatures.
denwa	A highly addictive pseudoamphetamine of extraterrestrial origin and a popular drug. Made from fungal resin.
douleter	A slave overseer or trader.
druaja	A board game, sometimes called labyrinth chess.
dryad	Any of a species of green-skinned homunculi capable of photosynthesis, designed for work in outer space.
Durantine Republic	An interstellar republic of some three thousand worlds. Pays tribute to the Empire.
Eali al'aqran	The Jaddian ruling caste, product of intense eugenic development. Practically superhuman.
Emperor	The supreme ruler of the Sollan Empire, considered a god and the reincarnation of his/her predecessor. Holds absolute power.
Eudoran	Any of the spacefaring bands claiming descent from the failed colony on Europa in Old Earth's system. An ethnic group known for their interstellar wanderings.
Exalted	A faction among the Extrasolarians noted for their extreme cybernetic augmentations.

exsul   Any palatine lord not based on a habitable world. Can refer also to his/her entire household.

Extrasolarian   Any of the barbarians living outside Imperial control, often possessing illegal praxis.

factionarius   The chief officer of a trade guild.

foederatus   A mercenary.

Foundation War   The war between the early Empire and the Mericanii, in which the Mericanii were destroyed and the Sollan Empire founded.

fravashi   In the Jaddian religion, the part of one's spirit that remains in the spirit world when a person's soul enters the material universe.

Free Traders Union   A coalition of smaller trading companies and independent merchanter vessels that lobbies for shipping privileges and dock space on planets.

freehold   Any planet or moon that rules itself, not subject to an interstellar polity.

fugue   The state of cryonic suspension induced to ensure that humans and other living creatures survive the long journey between suns.

Galstani   The common language of the Sollan Empire, descended from Classical English, with heavy Hindi and Franco-Germanic influences.

gene tonic   A medicament designed to alter the genetic code of an organism to fit a desired plan. Used to raise plebeians to the patrician class.

glowsphere   A spherical, bright light source floating on Royse repulsors, battery- or chemically powered.

God of Fire   In the Jaddian religion, the principle creator deity, known sometimes by his ancient name *Ahura Mazda*.

golem   A mechanical being fashioned in the shape of a man, containing no organic parts.

Great Charters   Ancient collection of legal codes imposed on the Empire by a coalition of the houses palatine. Maintains the balance between the houses and between the houses and the Emperor.

groundcar   An automobile, usually powered by solar or by internal combustion.

High College   Imperial political office tasked with reviewing palatine requests for children and with overseeing the pregnancies of same. Prevents mutations.

highmatter   A form of exotic matter produced by alchemists. Used to make the swords of Imperial knights, which can cut almost anything.

hilatar   A popular non-addictive hallucinogen made from the leaves of an alien plant. The leaves are dried and steeped like tea.

homunculus   Any artificial human or near-human, especially those grown for a task, or for aesthetic purposes.

hoplite   A shielded foot soldier. Heavy infantry.

hurasam   Gilded coin used amongst the Imperial peasant classes, worth their mark-weight in gold. Print notes for various denominations exist.

huratimn   A prey animal native to the Cielcin homeworld.

ichakta   A Cielcin title, referring to the captain of a ship.

ietumna   The submissive Cielcin sexual role.

imaginifer   In the Legions, a herald tasked with carrying a holograph image of the Emperor upon a staff.

immunis   In the Legions, a soldier exempt from usual duties.

inmane   An offensive slur meaning that someone is less than human. Literally *impure.*

intus   A palatine born outside the oversight of the High College, usually possessing several physical or psychological defects; a bastard.

itani   *Pl. Itanimn.* A Cielcin family unit.

Jaddian   The official language of the Principalities of Jadd, a patois of ancient Romance and Semitic languages with some Greek influences.

jubala   A powerful and popular offworld narcotic. Can be inhaled or ingested in a kind of tea.

kaspum   Silver-plated coin used among the Imperial peasant classes. Twelve kaspums make one gold hurasam. Print notes for various denominations exist.

Knights Excubitor   The innermost circle of the Emperor's guard, comprising 108 of the finest knights and fighters in the Empire.

Legions   The military branch of the Sollan Empire, loyal directly to the Emperor and Imperial house, comprising naval and ground forces.

lictor   A bodyguard for a nobile or other dignitary. Usually a knight.

logothete   A minister in any of the governmental agencies of any palatine house, used colloquially of any civil servant.

magus   An intellectual, most especially a scientist or natural philosopher.

Mandari   An ethnic group semi-detached from Imperial society, most commonly found staffing the massive interstellar trading corporations.

mark   The primary trade currency of the Sollan Empire, not backed by specie.

Martian Guard   The Emperor's palace guard, an elite corp of soldiers raised from the population on Earth's nearest neighbor, Mars.

medica   A hospital, typically aboard a starship.

megathere   A massive, three-eyed amphibious predator native to the planet Epidamnus.

Mericanii   The ancient first interstellar colonists. A hyper-advanced technologic civilization run by artificial intelligences. Destroyed by the Empire.

mnunatari   In Cielcin culture, the merchant caste. Considered pariahs.

myrmidon   In the Colosso, any contract or slave fighter not a professionally
                       trained gladiator.

myste   An intellectual.

nahute   A Cielcin weapon. Resembles a flying metal snake. Seeks out targets
                       and drills into them.

natalist   A specialist practiced in the art of growing and gene-crafting living
                       organisms, human or otherwise.

neural lace   A semi-organic computer implanted in a host's brain. Very illegal in
                       the Empire.

Nipponese   The descendants of the Japanese colonists who fled Old Earth system
                       in the Third Peregrination.

nobile   Blanket term referring to any member of the palatine and patrician
                       castes in the Sollan Empire.

Nordei   The principal language of the Demarchy. A patois of Nordic and
                       Thai with some Slavic influences.

Norman Expanse   The frontier of human settlement in the Norma Arm of the Milky
                       Way.

nuncius   An announcer, town crier, or herald.

Old Solstice   A traditional holiday commemorating the Winter Solstice of Old
                       Earth.

optio   The second-in-command of a century in the Imperial Legions after
                       the Centurion.

Order of Merit   The highest honor an Imperial soldier may be given for service to
                       the Empire.

Outer Perseus   The expansion region out along the end of the Perseus Arm; a
                       colonial frontier.

palatine   The Imperial aristocracy, descended from those free humans who
                       opposed the Mericanii. Genetically enhanced, they may live for
                       several centuries.

Pale   The Cielcin. Slang, considered offensive by xenophiles.

pankration   A martial art harking all the way back to ancient Greece and
                       Macedonia.

Panthai   A Tavrosi language descended from the Thai, Lao, and Khmer-
                       speaking peoples who settled the Wisp alongside the Nordei.

patrician   Any plebeian or plutocrat awarded with genetic augmentations at the
                       behest of the palatine caste as a reward for services rendered.

peltast   An unshielded foot soldier. Light infantry.

Peregrination   Any of the historical evacuations from Earth's system for the
                       extrasolar colonies.

Petersonian	A fraternal order of the scholiasts.
phase disruptor	A sort of firearm that attacks the nervous system. Can stun on lower settings.
plagiarius	A smuggler, fence, or other black market salesman.
plasma burner	A firearm which uses a strong loop of magnetic force to project an arc of super-heated plasma across short to moderate distances.
plebeian	The Imperial peasantry, descended from unaltered human stock seeded on the oldest colony ships. Forbidden to use high technology.
plutocrat	Any plebeian who has earned enough money to buy expensive genetic augmentations. Effectively patrician.
Principalities of Jadd	Nation of eighty former Imperial provinces in Perseus that revolted over palatine reproductive rights. Heavily militaristic and caste-driven.
qiati	In Cielcin culture, an individual's usefulness or worth to its owner.
Quiet	The hypothetical first civilization in the galaxy, allegedly responsible for several ancient sites, including those on Emesh, Judecca, Sadal Suud, and Ozymandias.
Rothsbank	An ancient, privately owned banking house tracing its roots back to the Golden Age of Earth.
Royal Victorian Knights	A fraternal order of knights owing allegiance to the Imperial House Avent.
satrap	A planetary governor in the Principalities of Jadd, subordinate to one of the regional princes.
scahari	In Cielcin culture, the warrior caste.
scholiast	Any member of the monastic order of researchers, academics, and theoreticians tracing their origins to the Mericanii scientists captured at the end of the Foundation War.
scianda	*Pl. Sciandane.* A Cielcin migratory fleet, comprising several *itanimn* and presided over by a single Aeta.
sign of the sun disc	A gesture of benediction made by circling thumb and forefinger and touching forehead and lips before holding the hand up to the sky.
signifer	In the Legions, a soldier tasked with carrying the banner bearing the symbols of the individual legion or subgroup.
Solar Throne	The Imperial throne. Carved from a single piece of citrine quartz. Sometimes used as a synonym for the Imperial Presence or Office.
solifer	In the Legions, a soldier tasked with carrying the banner bearing the symbol of the Imperial sunburst on its flag.
Sollan Empire	The largest and oldest single polity in human-controlled space, comprising some half a billion habitable planets.
SOM	Surrogate Operating Medium. The lobotomized shell of a human being animated by machines, used for slave labor and as soldiers by the Extrasolarians.

Sparrowhawk   A lighter craft commonly used by the Legions, a one-manned rapid attack ship used in ship-to-ship fighting.

strategos   An admiral in the Imperial Legions, responsible for the command of an entire fleet, comprising several legions.

strojeva   A golem, specifically a golem of Durantine manufacture. Typically designed to closely mimic a human being in appearance.

sulan   An ancient predator native to the Cielcin homeworld.

suppression field   A Royse Effect field designed to simulate gravity.

Tanager   A lighter craft commonly used by the Legions, a heavier, two-man fighter.

Tavrosi   Any of the languages from the Demarchy of Tavros. Typically refers to Nordei.

telegraph/QET   A device which uses entangled quantum particles to communicate instantly over vast distances.

terranic   In terraforming and ecology, refers to any organism of Old Earth extraction. Not extraterrestrial.

theologi   A priest or theologian.

tiatari   In Cielcin culture, the worker caste.

tokolosh   A species of flesh-eating microorganism that, when swarming, appears as a mass of darkness.

Travatsk   A Tavrosi language named for the Travatskr ethnic group, recognizable by its lack of vowel reduction.

trias   A unit of three legionnaires, usually two peltasts and one hoplite.

triaster   The commander of a trias, usually a shielded hoplite.

tribune   A Legion officer in command of a cohort (four to a legion). Commands both ground forces and naval officers.

Twelve Abominations   The twelve most grievous sins according to the Chantry's Index. Legal privileges do not apply in such cases.

TX9   A chemical compound pumped into the body when the blood is drained in preparation for cryonic fugue.

Udaritanu   A complex, non-linear writing system used by the Cielcin.

Umandh   A coloni species native to the planet Emesh. Amphibious and tripedal, they have an intelligence comparable to that of dolphins.

uncreated gods   In philosophy, refers to the gods of ancient religions which emerged as byproducts of organic cultural evolution.

Upper Centaurus   Region of the Centaurus Arm of the galaxy nearer the core. Location of the Principalities of Jadd and many Imperial provinces.

vampyromorph   A species of winged, blood-drinking creatures commonly used in baiting shows during the Colosso.

Veil of Marinus   Territory contested between the Empire and Norman Freeholds. Comprises most of the front in the Crusade against the Cielcin.

viceroy/vicereine The ruler of an Imperial Province appointed by the Emperor. The title is typically heritable, but is not always so.

White Sword A ceramic greatsword used by Chantry cathars for formal executions, especially of the nobility.

Writ The Chantry's legal and moral code, enforced by the Inquisition and the Index.

xanarth A massive land predator native to the planet Athyras.

xenobite Any life form not originating in terranic or human stock, especially those life forms which are considered intelligent; an alien.

Zenoan A fraternal order of the scholiasts with an emphasis on introspection and emotional regulation.

BRINGING NEWS FROM OUR WORLDS TO YOURS . . .

Want your news daily?

The Gollancz blog has instant updates
on the hottest SF and Fantasy books.

Prefer your updates monthly?

Sign up for our
in-depth newsletter.

www.gollancz.co.uk

Follow us 🐦 @gollancz

Find us 📘 facebook.com/GollanczPublishing

Classic SF as you've never read it before.

Visit the SF Gateway to find out more!

www.sfgateway.com